THE MILLION-COPY

WILLOW ROSE

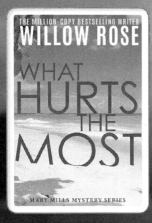

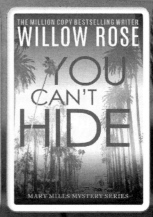

MARY MILLS

MYSTERY SERIES

BOOK 1-3

BOOKS BY THE AUTHOR

MYSTERY/THRILLER/HORROR NOVELS

- Sorry Can't Save You
- In One Fell Swoop
- Umbrella Man
- Blackbird Fly
- To Hell in a Handbasket
- Edwina

HARRY HUNTER MYSTERY SERIES

- All The Good Girls
- Run Girl Run
- No Other Way
- Never Walk Alone

MARY MILLS MYSTERY SERIES

- What Hurts the Most
- You Can Run
- You Can't Hide
- Careful Little Eyes

EVA RAE THOMAS MYSTERY SERIES

- Don't Lie to me
- What you did
- Never Ever
- Say You Love me
- Let Me Go
- It's Not Over
- Not Dead yet
- To Die For

EMMA FROST SERIES

- Itsy Bitsy Spider
- Miss Dolly had a Dolly
- Run, Run as Fast as You Can
- Cross Your Heart and Hope to Die
- Peek-a-Boo I See You
- Tweedledum and Tweedledee
- Easy as One, Two, Three
- There's No Place like Home
- Slenderman
- Where the Wild Roses Grow
- Waltzing Mathilda
- Drip Drop Dead
- Black Frost

JACK RYDER SERIES

- Hit the Road Jack
- Slip out the Back Jack
- The House that Jack Built
- Black Jack
- Girl Next Door
- Her Final Word
- Don't Tell

REBEKKA FRANCK SERIES

- One, Two...He is Coming for You
- Three, Four...Better Lock Your Door
- Five, Six...Grab your Crucifix
- Seven, Eight...Gonna Stay up Late
- Nine, Ten...Never Sleep Again
- Eleven, Twelve...Dig and Delve
- Thirteen, Fourteen...Little Boy Unseen
- Better Not Cry
- Ten Little Girls
- It Ends Here

HORROR SHORT-STORIES

- Mommy Dearest

- The Bird
- Better watch out
- Eenie, Meenie
- Rock-a-Bye Baby
- Nibble, Nibble, Crunch
- Humpty Dumpty
- Chain Letter

PARANORMAL SUSPENSE/ROMANCE NOVELS

- In Cold Blood
- The Surge
- Girl Divided

THE VAMPIRES OF SHADOW HILLS SERIES

- Flesh and Blood
- Blood and Fire
- Fire and Beauty
- Beauty and Beasts
- Beasts and Magic
- Magic and Witchcraft
- Witchcraft and War
- War and Order
- Order and Chaos
- Chaos and Courage

THE AFTERLIFE SERIES

- Beyond
- Serenity
- Endurance
- Courageous

THE WOLFBOY CHRONICLES

- A Gypsy Song
- I am WOLF

DAUGHTERS OF THE JAGUAR

- Savage
- Broken

CONTENTS

WHAT HURTS THE MOST

MARY MILLS MYSTERY BOOK 1

PROLOGUE
COCOA BEACH 1995

THEY'RE NOT GOING to let her go. She knows they won't. Holly is terrified as she runs through the park. The sound of the waves is behind her. A once so calming sound now brings utter terror to her. She is wet. Her shirt is dripping, her shoes making a slobbering sound as she runs across the parking lot towards the playground.

Run, run! Don't look back. Don't stop or they'll get you!

She can hear their voices behind her. It's hard to run when your feet are tied together. They're faster than she is, even though they are just walking.

"Oh, Holly," one of them yells. "Hoooollllyyy!"

Holly pants, trying to push herself forward. She wants desperately to move faster, but the rope tied around her feet blocks them and she falls flat on her face onto the asphalt. Holly screams loudly as her nose scratches across the ground.

Get up! Get up and run. You can't let them get you.

She can hear them laughing behind her.

You can make it, Holly. Just get to A1A right in front of you. Only about a hundred feet left. There are cars on the road. They'll see you. Someone will see you and help you.

She tries to scream, but she has no air in her lungs. She is exhausted from swimming with her legs tied together. Luckily, her arms got free when she jumped in the water. They have pulled off her pants. Cut them open with a knife and pulled them off. Before they stabbed her in the shoulder. It hurts when she runs. Blood has soaked her white shirt. She is naked from the stomach down, except for her shoes and socks. Holly is in so much pain and can hardly move. Yet, she fights to get closer to the road.

A car drives by. Then another one. She can see them in the distance, yet her vision is getting foggier. She can't lose consciousness now.

You've got to keep fighting. You've got to get out of here! Don't give up, Holly. Whatever you do, just don't give up.

Their footsteps are approaching from behind. Holly is groaning and fighting to get a few more steps in.

So close now. So close.

"Hurry up," she hears them yell. "She's getting away!"

Holly is so close now she can smell the cars' exhaust. All she needs to do is get onto the road, then stop a car. That's all she needs to do to get out of there alive. And she is so close now.

"Stop her, goddammit," a voice yells.

Holly fights to run. She moves her feet faster than she feels is humanly possible. She is getting there. She is getting there. She can hear them start to run now. They are yelling to each other.

"Shoot her, dammit."

Holly gasps, thinking about the spear gun. She's the one who taught them how to shoot it. She knows they won't hesitate to use it to stop her. She knows how they think. She knows this is what they do. She knows this is a kick for them, a drug.

She knows, because she is one of them.

"Stop the bitch!" someone yells, and she hears the sound of the gun going off. She knows this sound so well, having been spearfishing all her life and practiced using the gun on land with her father. He taught her everything about spearfishing, starting when she was no more than four years old. He even taught her to hold her breath underwater for a very long time.

"Scuba diving is for tourists. Real fishers free dive," she hears his voice say, the second the spear whistles through the air.

It hits Holly in the leg and she tumbles to the ground. Holly falls to the pavement next to A1A with a scream. She hears giggles and voices behind her. But she can also hear something else. While she drags herself across the pavement, she can hear the sound of sirens.

"Shit!" the voices behind her say.

"We gotta get out of here."

"RUN!"

1

SEPTEMBER 2015

BLAKE MILLS IS ENJOYING his coffee at Starbucks. He enjoys it especially today. He is sipping it while looking at his own painting that they
have just put up on display inside the shop. He has been trying to convince
the owner of the local Starbucks in Cocoa Beach for ages to put up some of
his art on display, and finally Ray agreed to let him hang up one of his turtle
paintings. Just for a short period, to see how it goes.

It is Blake's personal favorite painting and he hopes it will attract some
business his way. As a small artist in a small town, it is hard to make a
living, even though Blake offers paintings by order, so anyone can get one
any way they want it and can be sure it will fit their house or condo. It isn't
exactly the way the life of an artist is supposed to be, but it is the only way
to do it if he wants to eat.

Blake decides to make it a day of celebration and buys an extra coffee
and a piece of cake to eat as well. He takes a bite and enjoys the taste.

"Looking good," a voice says behind him. He turns in his chair and
looks into the eyes of Olivia.

Olivia Hartman. The love of his life.

Blake smiles to himself. "You came," he whispers and looks around.
Being married, Olivia has to be careful whom she is seen with in this town.

"Can I sit?" she asks, holding her own coffee in her hand.

Blake pulls out a chair for her and she sits next to him. Blake feels a big
thrill run through his body. He loves being with Olivia and has never had
the pleasure of doing so in public. They usually meet up at his studio and

have sex between his paintings on the floor or up against the wall. He has never been to her place on Patrick Air Force Base, where she lives with her husband, a general in the army. Blake is terrified of him and a little of her as well, but that is part of what makes it so wonderfully exciting. At the age of twenty-three, Blake isn't ready to settle down with anyone, and he isn't sure he is ever going to be. It isn't his style. He likes the carefree life, and being an artist he can't exactly provide for a family anyway. Having children will only force him to forget his dreams and get a *real job*. It would no doubt please his father, but Blake doesn't want a real job. He doesn't want the house on the water or the two to three children. He isn't cut out for it, and his many girlfriends in the past never understood that. All of them thought they could change him, that they were the one who could make him realize that he wanted it all. But he really didn't. And he still doesn't.

"It looks really great," Olivia says and sips her coffee. She is wearing multiple finger rings and bracelets, as always. She is delicate, yet strong. Used to be a fighter pilot in the army. Blake thought that was so cool. Today, she no longer works, not since she married the general.

She and Blake had met at the Officer's Club across the street from the base. He was there with a girl he had met at Grills in Cape Canaveral, who worked on base doing some contracting or something boring like that; she had invited him to a party. It was by far the most boring affair until he met Olivia on the porch standing with a beer in her hand overlooking the Atlantic Ocean. She was slightly tipsy and they exchanged pleasantries for a few minutes before she turned and looked at him with that mischievous smile of hers. Then she asked him if he wanted to have some fun.

"Always," he replied.

They walked to the beach and into the dunes, where they enjoyed the best sex of Blake's life.

Now it has become a drug to him. He needs his fix. He needs her.

"Congrats," she says.

"Thanks. Now I just hope someone will grab one of the business cards I've put on the counter and call me to order a painting. I could use the money. I only had one order last month."

"They will," she says, laughing. "Don't you worry about that." She leans over and whispers through those pouty lips of hers. "Now let's go back to your place and celebrate."

"Is that an order?" he asks, laughing.

"Is that an order, *ma'am*," she corrects him. "And, yes, it is."

2

SEPTEMBER 2015

BEING WITH OLIVIA IS EXHILARATING. It fills him with the most wonderful sensation in his body because Blake has never met anyone like her, who can make him crazy for her. Not like this. But at the same time, it is also absolutely petrifying because she is married to General Hartman, who will have Blake killed if he ever finds out. There is no doubt about it in Blake's mind.

Yet, he keeps sleeping with her. Even though he keeps telling himself it is a bad idea, that he has to stop, that it is only a matter of time before he will get himself in some deep shit trouble. Blake knows it is bad to be with her. He knows it will get him in trouble eventually, but still, he can't help himself. He has to have her. He has to taste her again and again. No matter the cost.

Their lips meet inside Blake's studio as soon as they walk in. Blake closes his eyes and drinks from her. He doesn't care that the door behind him is left open. Nothing else matters right now.

"I thought you couldn't get out today," he says, panting, when her lips leave his. "Isn't the general on base?"

"He is," she mumbles between more kisses.

It has been two weeks since they were together last. Two weeks of constantly dreaming and longing for her. They communicate via Snapchat. It is untraceable, as far as Blake knows. Blake wrote a message to her a few days ago, telling her about the painting being put up in Starbucks, knowing that she probably couldn't come and see it. He even sent a picture of the painting. It is also her favorite. She messaged him back a photo of her sad face telling him she didn't think she could get out, since her husband was home. Usually, she only dares to meet with Blake when her husband is travelling. Even then, they have to be extremely careful. General Hartman has many friends in Cocoa Beach and his soldiers are seen everywhere.

"I told him I was seeing a friend today. It's not like it's a lie. I don't care anymore if he finds out about us. I'm sick of being just the general's wife. I want a life of my own."

Blake takes off his T-shirt and her hands land on his chest. He rips off her shirt and several buttons fall to the floor. She closes her eyes and moans at his touches. His hands cup her breasts and soon her bra lands on the wooden floor. He grabs her hair and pulls her head back while kissing her neck. His heart is pumping in his chest just from the smell of her skin.

"You can't," he whispers between breaths. "You can't let him know about us. He'll kill the both of us."

Olivia lets out a gasp as Blake reaches up under her skirt and places a hand in her panties, and then rips them off. He pushes her up against a table, then lifts her up, leans over her naked torso and puts his mouth to her breasts. He closes his eyes and takes in her smell, drinking the juices of her body, then pulls his shorts down and gently slides inside of her with a deep moan. She puts her legs around his neck, partly strangling him when she comes in pulsing movements back and forth, her body arching.

"Oh, Blake...oh, Blake ..."

The sensation is burning inside of him and he is ready to explode. Olivia is moaning and moving rapidly. His movements are urgent now, the intensity building. He is about to burst, when suddenly she screams loudly and pushes him away. Blake falls to the floor with a thud.

"What the...?"

Blake soon realizes why Olivia is screaming and feels the blood rush from his face. A set of eyes is staring down at him.

The eyes of Detective Chris Fisher.

"Blake Mills, you're under arrest," the voice belonging to the eyes says.

3

SEPTEMBER 2015

"I'M SORRY, Mary, there's nothing I can do."

I stare at my boss, Chief Editor, Markus Fergusson. He is leaning back in his leather chair in his office on the twenty-eighth floor of the Times-Tower on the west side of mid-town. Behind him, the view is spectacular, but I hardly notice anymore. After five years working there, you simply stop being baffled. However, I am actually baffled at this moment. But not because of the view. Because of what is being said.

"So, you're firing me, is that it?" I ask, while my blood is boiling in my veins. What the hell is this?

"We're letting you go, yes."

"You can't do that, Markus, come on. Just because of this?"

He leans over his desk and gives me that look that I have come to know so well in my five years as a reporter for *The New York Times*.

"Yes."

"I don't get it," I say. "I'm being fired for writing the paper's most read article in the past five years?"

Markus sighs. "Don't put up a fight, will you? Just accept it. You violated the rules, sweetheart."

Don't you sweetheart me, you pig!

"I don't make the rules, Mary. The big guys upstairs make the decisions and it says here that we have to let you go for *violating the normal editing process.*"

I squint my eyes. I can't believe this. "I did what?"

"You printed the story without having a second set of eyes on it first. The article offended some people, and, well…"

He pauses. I scoff. He is such a sell-out. Just because my article didn't sit well with some people, some influential people, he is letting me go? They want to fire me for some rule bullshit?

"Brian saw it," I say. "He read it and approved it."

"The rules say *two* editors," he says. "On a story like this, this controversial, you need two editors to approve it, not just one."

"That's BS and you know it, goddammit, Markus. I never even heard about this rule. What about Brian?"

"We're letting him go as well."

"You can't do that! The man just had another kid."

Markus shrugs. "That's not really my problem, is it? Brian knew better. He's been with us for fifteen years."

"It was late, Markus. We had less than five minutes to deadline. There was no time to get another approval. If we'd waited for another editor, the story wouldn't have run, and you wouldn't have sold a record number of newspapers that day. The article went viral online. All over the world. Everyone was talking about it. And this is how you thank me?"

I rise from the chair and grab my leather jacket. "Well, suit yourself. It's your loss. I don't need you or this paper."

I leave, slamming the door, but it doesn't make me feel as good as I thought it would. I pack my things in that little brown box that they always do in the movies and grab it under my arm before I leave in the elevator. On the bottom floor, I hand in my ID card to the guard in the lobby and Johnson looks at me with his mouth turned downwards.

"We'll miss you, Miss Mary," he says.

"I'll miss you too, Johnson," I say, and walk out the glass doors, into the streets of New York without a clue as to what I am going to do. Living in Manhattan isn't cheap. Living in Manhattan with a nine-year old son, as a single mom isn't cheap at all. The cost for a private school alone is over the roof.

I whistle for a cab, and before I finally get one, it starts to rain, and I get soaked. I have him drive me back to my apartment and I let myself inside. Snowflake, my white Goldendoodle is waiting on the other side of the door, jumping me when I enter. He licks me in my face and whimpers from having missed me since I left just this morning. I sit down on my knees and pet him till he calms down. I can't help smiling when I am with him. I can't feel sad for long when he's around. It's simply not possible. He looks at me with those deep brown eyes.

"We'll be alright, won't we, Snowflake? I'm sure we will. We don't need them, no we don't."

4

SEPTEMBER 2015

"DO YOU COME HERE OFTEN?"

Liz Hester stares at the man who has approached her in the bar at Lou's Blues in Indialantic. It is Friday night and she was bored at the base, so she and her friends decided to go out and get a beer.

"You're kidding me, right?"

The guy smiles. He is a surfer-type with long greasy hair under his cap, a nice tan, and not too much between the ears. The kind of guy who opens each sentence with *dude,* even when speaking to a girl.

"It was the best I could come up with."

"You do realize that I am thirty-eight and you're at least fifteen years younger, right?"

Kim comes up behind her. She is wearing her blue ASU—army service uniform—like Liz. They are both decorated with several medals. Liz's includes the Purple Heart, given to her when she was shot during her service in Afghanistan. Took a bullet straight to her shoulder. The best part was, she took it for one of her friends. She took it for Britney, who is also with them this night, hanging out with some guy further down the bar. They are friends through thick and thin. Will lay down their lives for one another.

Liz's eyes meet those of Jamie's across the bar. She smiles and nods in the direction of the guy that Liz is talking to. Liz smiles and nods too. There is no need for them to speak; they know what she is saying.

He's the one.

"So, tell me, what's your name?" Liz asks the guy. She is all of a sudden flirtatious, smiling and touching his arm gently. Kim giggles behind her, but the guy doesn't notice.

"I'm Billy. My friends call me Billy the Kid."

"Well, you are just a kid, aren't you?" she says, purring like a cat, leaning in over the bar.

The guy lifts his cap a little, then puts it back on. "You sure are a lot of woman."

Liz knows his type. He is one of those who gets aroused just by looking at a woman in uniform. She has met her share of those types. They are a lot of fun to play with.

"Well, maybe I can make a man of you," she whispers, leaning very close to his face.

The guy laughs goofily. "You sure can," he says and gives her an elevator look. "I sure wouldn't mind that. I got an anaconda in my pants you can ride if you like."

Liz laughs lightly, and then looks at Jamie again, letting her know he has taken the bait.

"Well, why don't you—Billy the Kid—meet me outside in the parking lot in say—five minutes?"

Billy laughs again. "Dude! Whoa, sure!"

Billy taps the bar counter twice, not knowing exactly what to do with himself, then lifts his cap once again and wipes sweat off his forehead. He has nice eyes, Liz thinks, and he is quite handsome.

As stupid as they get, though.

He leaves her, shooting a finger-gun at her and winking at the same time. The girls approach Liz, moving like cats sliding across the floor. Liz finishes her drink while the four of them stick their heads together.

"Ready for some fun?" she asks.

They don't say anything. They don't have to.

5

SEPTEMBER 2015

SHE WAITS for him by the car. Smoking a cigarette, she leans against it, blowing out smoke when she spots him come out of the bar and walk towards her. Seeing the goofy grin on his face makes her smile even wider.

"Hey there, baby," Billy says and walks up to her. "I have to say, I wasn't sure you would even be here. A nice lady like you with a guy like me? You're a wild cat, aren't you?"

Liz chuckles and blows smoke in his face. "I sure am."

Billy the Kid moves his body in anticipation. His crotch can't keep still. He is already hard.

What a sucker.

He looks around with a sniffle. "So, where do you want to go? To the beach? Or do you...wanna do it right here...?" he places a hand next to her on the car. "Up against this baby, huh?"

Liz laughs again, then leans closer to him till her mouth is on his ear. "You're just full of yourself, aren't you?"

"What?" he asks with another goofy grin.

"Did you really think you were going to get lucky with me? With this?" She says and points up and down her body.

The grin is wiped off his face. Finally.

"What is this?" he asks, his face in a frown. "Were you just leading me on? What a cunt!" He spits out the last word. He probably means it as an insult, but Liz just smiles from ear to ear as her friends slowly approach from all sides, surrounding Billy. When he realizes, he tries to back out, but walks into Jamie and steps on her black shoes.

"Hey, those are brand new! Dammit!"

Jamie pushes him in the back forcefully and he is now in the hands of Britney. Britney is smaller than the others, but by far the strongest. She clenches her fist and slams it into his face. The blow breaks his nose on the spot and he falls backwards to the asphalt, blood running from it.

"What the...what...who are you?" Billy asks, disoriented, looking from woman to woman.

"We like to call ourselves the Fast and the Furious," Liz says.

"Yeah, cause I'm fast," Kim says and kicks Billy in the crotch. He lets out a loud moan in pain.

The sound is almost arousing to Liz.

"And I'm furious," she says, grabbing him by the hair and pulling his head back. She looks him in the eyes. She loves watching them squirm, the little suckers. Just like she loved it back in Afghan when she interrogated the *Haji*.

Haji is the name they call anyone of Arab decent, or even of a brownish skin tone. She remembers vividly the first time they brought one in. It was the day after she had lost a good friend to an IED, a roadside bomb that detonated and killed everyone in the truck in front of her. They searched for those suckers all night, and finally, the next morning they brought in three. Boy, she kicked that sucker till he could no longer move. Hell, they all did it. All of them let out their frustrations. Losing three good soldiers like that made them furious. Liz was still furious. Well, to be frank, she has been furious all of her life.

Everybody around her knows that.

Liz laughs when she hears Billy's whimper, then uses two fingers to poke his eyes forcefully. Billy screams.

"My eyes, my eyes!"

Liz lets go of his hair and looks at her girls. They are all about to burst in anticipation. She opens the door to the car, where Jamie has placed a couple of bottles of vodka to keep them going all night. She lets out a loud howl like a wolf, the girls chiming in, then lifts Billy the Kid up and throws him in the back of the Jeep.

6

FEBRUARY 1977

WHEN PENELOPE and Peter get married, she is already showing. It is no longer a secret to the people at the wedding, even though her mother does all she can to disguise it by buying a big dress. By the time of the wedding, Penelope has grown into it and her stomach fills it out completely. Peter's mother tells her she looks radiant and gorgeous, but Penelope's mother hates that people will talk about marriage as a necessity or *the right thing to do,* and their daughter is only getting married because she is pregnant. Because she has to.

But that is just the way it is, and no one cares less about what people think than Penelope and Peter. They are happy and looking forward to becoming parents more than anything.

Soon after the wedding, the bank approves a loan for them and they buy their dream house in Cocoa Beach. As a young lawyer who has just been made partner, Peter is doing well, and even though it is one of the most expensive locations in Cocoa Beach, Penelope doesn't have to work anymore. She quits her job as a secretary and wants to focus on her family and later charity work. It is the kind of life they have both dreamed of, and no one is more thrilled to see it come true than Penelope.

"I can't wait to become a family," she says, when Peter is done fixing up the nursery and shows it to her.

Seeing how beautiful he has decorated it makes her cry, and she holds a hand to her ready-to-burst stomach. Only two more weeks till she will hold her baby. Only two more weeks.

She can hardly wait.

Peter is going to be a wonderful father; she just knows he will. He has such a kind and gentle personality. She has done right in choosing him. She knows she has. This is going to be a perfect little family. Penelope already knows she wants lots of children. At least two, maximum four. She herself comes from a family of four children. Four girls, to be exact. There was a brother, but he died at an early age after a long illness. Being the oldest, Penelope took care of him, and it was devastating for her when he passed away. It is a sorrow she can never get rid of, and often she blames herself for not being able to cure him. Later in life, she played with the idea of becoming a doctor, but she never had the grades for it.

Peter, on the other hand, is an only child. His mother has spoiled his socks off all of his life. She still does every now and then. And she still treats him like a child sometimes. It makes Penelope laugh out loud when she spit-washes him or corrects his tie. But she is nice, Peter's mom. She has always loved Penelope, and there is nothing bad to be said about her.

It was always the plan that Peter would follow in his father's footsteps and go to law school, and so he did. He met Penelope right after he passed the bar and started working at the small law firm in Rockledge where she was a secretary. Soon he moved on to a bigger firm and now he had made partner.

Peter's career exploded within a few years, and now he is talking about going into real estate as well. He has so many plans for their future, and she knows he will always take care of them. She is never going to want for anything.

Two weeks later, her water breaks. Penelope is standing in the kitchen admiring the new tiles they have put in, with a coffee cup in her hand. The water soaks her dress and the floor beneath her. Penelope gasps and reaches for the phone. She calls Peter at the office.

"This is it," she says, with a mixture of excitement and fright in her voice. "Our baby is coming, Peter. Our baby is coming!"

"I...I'll be right there."

Peter stumbles over himself on his way out of the office and the secretary has to yell at him to come back because he has forgotten his car keys.

Peter rushes her to the hospital, where the contractions soon take over and after a tough struggle and fourteen hours of labor, she is finally holding her baby girl in her arms.

"Look at her, Peter," she says through tears. "I...I simply can't stop looking at her. I am so happy, Peter. You made me so happy, thank you. Thank you so much."

7

SEPTEMBER 2015

I SPEND the evening feeling sorry for myself. I cook chicken in green curry, my favorite dish these days, and sulk in front of the TV watching back-to-back episodes of *Friends* with Snowflake and my son Salter next to me.

"They can't fire you!" Salter exclaimed, when I told him as soon as he got home from school. He knew something was wrong as soon as he saw that I'd made hot cocoa for the both of us and put marshmallows in it.

That is kind of my thing. Whenever I have bad news, I prepare hot cocoa with marshmallows. I have also baked cookies. That is another diversion of mine. Nothing keeps me as distracted as baking or cooking.

"You're the best damn reporter they have!"

"I am, but there's no need to curse," I say.

I enjoy spending the rest of the evening with the loves of my life, both of them, and decide to not wonder about my future until the next day. Salter is so loving and caring towards me and keeps asking me if there is anything he can do for me, to make me feel better.

"Just stay here in my arms," I say and pull him closer.

He has reached the age where he still enjoys my affectionate hugs and holding him close, but lately he has begun to find them annoying from time to time, especially when it is in front of his friends.

I named him Salter because I have been a surfer all of my life, growing up in Cocoa Beach, and so is his dad. Salter means *derived from salt*. We believed he was born of our love for the ocean. How foolish and young we were back then.

It feels like a lifetime ago.

"So, what do we do now?" Salter finally asks when the episode where Phoebe fights with a fire alarm is over.

I take in a deep breath. I know he has to wonder. I do too, but I try not to think about it. Mostly to make sure he isn't affected by it.

"I mean, now that you don't have a job?" he continues. "Can we still live in this apartment?"

"I have to be honest with you, kiddo," I say. "I don't know. I don't know what is going to happen. I am not sure any newspaper will have me after this. I pissed off some pretty influential people."

"That's stupid," he says. "They're all stupid. Your article had more views than anyone's."

"I know, but that isn't always enough, buddy."

I sigh, hoping I don't have to go into details, when suddenly my phone rings. I let go of Salter and lean over to pick it up from the coffee table. My heart drops when I see the name on the display.

It's my dad.

"It's Mary," I say, my heart throbbing in my throat. I haven't spoken to my dad in at least a year. He never calls me.

"Mary." His voice is heavy. Something is definitely going on.

"What's wrong, Dad? Are you sick?"

"No. It's not me. It's your brother."

I swallow hard. My brother is the only family member I still have regular contact with. I love the little bastard, even if he is fifteen years younger than me.

"Blake? What's wrong with him?"

"It's bad, Mary. He's been arrested."

Arrested?!?

"What? Why...for what...what's going on, Dad?"

My father sighs from the other end of the line. "For murder. He's been arrested for murder."

8

SEPTEMBER 2015

THEY TAKE HIM FOR A RIDE. Billy the Kid is crying in the back when the girls take him first to the Super Wal-Mart in Merritt Island that is open 24/7. Placing a knife to his back, they walk through the store and pull bottles of wine, gin, and tequila from the shelves. They even find a fishing pole that they think could be fun to buy. Along with some chips Jamie wants, and sugarcoated donuts. Kim has a craving for cheesecake while Britney wants chocolate. And loads of it. Liz holds the knife in Billy's back and asks them to throw in some Choco-mint ice cream for her. Then she grabs a bottle of drain cleaner. They tell Billy to take out his wallet and pay for everything.

"If you as much as whimper, I will split you open," Liz whispers, as they come closer to the cashier. "I'll make it look like you attacked me. Who do you think they'll believe, huh? A surfer dude or a decorated war-veteran? A female one on top of it."

After he pays, they open a bottle of gin and take turns drinking from it while they drive, screaming and cheering, back to Cocoa Beach where they park in front of Ron Jon's surf-shop, which is also open 24/7. Yelling and visibly intoxicated, they storm inside with Billy and take the elevator to the second floor. They run through the aisles of bikinis and pull down one after another.

"I always wanted a yellow one," Kim yells.

"I'm going red this time," Britney says. "Wouldn't this look cute on me?"

"Grab me one of the striped ones over there," Liz says. "Size medium."

Kim giggles cheerfully then grabs one. They don't bother to try them on. There is no time for that. Kim also grabs a couple of nice shirts from Billabong, and then some shorts from Roxy for Liz.

"Oh," Britney says and points at the surfboards on the other side of the store. She looks to the others. "I always wanted a surfboard!"

"Me too," Jamie exclaims. "Let's find one!"

"I...I can't afford that," Billy whimpers. "Aren't they like four hundred dollars?"

"This one is five hundred dollars," Jamie says, and looks at a seven-foot fun-shape. "Doesn't it look GREAT on me?"

"Adorable," Liz says and laughs.

"I can't afford this," Billy whimpers over and over when they pull the boards out.

"Grab one for me too," Liz says, ignoring his complaints. She presses the knife into his back, puts her arm around his neck, then kisses his cheek, making it look like they are a couple.

"You'll have to," she whispers. "I'll make a scene. Make it look like you tried to rape me."

"Okay, okay," he says with a moan. "Just don't hurt me, okay? Just let me go after this, alright?"

She doesn't make any promises. That's not how Liz rolls.

They charge everything to one of Billy's credit cards, then run out of the store carrying surfboards and plastic bags with bikinis, hollering and laughing. They throw everything in the car and strap the boards onto the roof before driving to the International Palms Resort a few blocks further down A1A, where they book a suite for all of them, charging it on his credit card again.

"Please don't make me pay for any more," he says in the elevator.

They ignore his complaints, and then storm into the room. It is huge and has great views of the ocean. Liz lets go of Billy, then throws him on the white couch. Jamie grabs one of the bottles of Vodka and places it to her lips. She drinks it like it is water. Liz laughs and pulls the bottle from Jamie's hand. She places it to her lips and closes her eyes while it burns its way down her throat.

"Hey, leave some for the rest of us," Kim yells, and grabs the bottle out of Liz's hand.

The vodka spills on Liz's white shirt. Liz looks angrily at Kim. "What the hell...?"

Kim laughs, then drinks from the bottle. Liz clenches her fist before she slams it into Kim's face as soon as she lets go of the bottle again. Kim falls backwards, then stares, confused, at Liz.

"What...what happened?" she asks.

Liz grabs the bottle out of her hand forcefully. Jamie and Britney remain quiet. They dare not make a sound. The feeling of power intoxicates Liz. Liz looks at Billy the Kid, who is squirming on the couch while staring at them with terror in his eyes.

Liz approaches him. He squirms again. Liz leans over and kisses him forcefully. He tries to push her away, but two of the other girls grab his arms and hold him down while Liz has her way with him. She pulls off his pants and then she laughs.

"Is that all? Is that the anaconda you wanted me to ride?"

"Please, just let me go," Billy says, crying in humiliation "I've done everything you wanted me to. I've paid for everything. Please, just let me go."

"Now he wants to leave. You finally have the chance to get laid and now you want to leave? No no, Billy, tsk tsk. That's not what a woman wants to hear, is it, girls?"

The three others shake their heads.

Liz puts her hand on his penis and starts to rub. Soon, his anaconda grows sizably and he starts moaning.

"Please...please..."

She puts her lips on it and makes him hard, then sits on top of him and rides him. The other girls are screaming with joy. Liz rides him forcefully, and soon they both come with deep moans.

Liz smiles when Billy arches in spasms and she feels his semen inside of her, then leans over and kisses his forehead.

"If you tell the police what we did tonight, I'll tell them you raped me," she whispers. "That you were holding a gun to my head and you raped me. Boy, I do believe I even have three witnesses. Three VERY reliable witnesses."

Liz finishes with a laugh, then climbs off Billy. "Come on girls," she says. "Let's get *really* drunk."

She grabs a bottle and drinks from it. It is strange how it feels like she can't get drunk anymore. Not like *really* drunk. Not like in the old days. Liz likes being really drunk. It makes her forget. It is the only thing that can make her forget.

The girls throw themselves at the chips and candy they bought at Wal-Mart. Liz looks at them with contempt. They have no self-control, these girls. Kim buries her hands in the cheesecake and eats it, licking her fingers. Jamie stuffs her face with donuts and has sugar all over her mouth.

Liz sighs.

"You want some ice cream?" Jamie asks.

"I don't want some stupid ice cream," Liz says, mocking Jamie. "I'm bored." She looks at Billy, who doesn't dare to move on the couch. "He bores me."

"What do you want to do?" Kim asks.

"Yeah, do you want to have another go?" Jamie asks.

Liz throws the bottle in her hand against the wall. It breaks and leaves a huge mark that Billy is probably going to pay for. Liz growls and kicks the ice cream bucket.

"I'm sick of the prick. He's no fun to play with."

Liz grabs the drain cleaner and walks towards Billy with firm steps. The girls all look at her. Serious eyes follow her every step. The atmosphere in the room immediately changes. No one is laughing anymore. No one is eating.

"What are you doing with that, babe?" Jamie asks.

"Don't do it," Kim yells.

But Liz doesn't listen. She opens the lid and grabs Billy's jaw. She forces it open. Billy is squirming too much and she can't do it on her own.

"Help me, dammit," she yells.

The girls hesitate, but don't dare not to do as they're told. Who knows what Liz might do next? Who will be next? They have seen too much to be able to say no.

Britney is first to grab Billy's right arm and hold it down. Jamie then grabs the left one. Kim holds his head still, while Liz pours the liquid drain cleaner into his mouth and down his throat. The three girls stare at her while she empties the bottle completely. They dare not even to speak. Billy's screams pierce through their bones. No one dares to move.

Liz throws the empty bottle on the ground, then looks at her friends. "Let's get out of here," she yells.

Her words are almost drowned out by Billy's scream.

9

SEPTEMBER 2015

I LAND at Orlando airport around noon the next day. Salter and Snowflake are both with me. We have packed two big suitcases, not knowing how long we are going to stay. My dad tried to convince me there is no need for me to come down, but I didn't listen. I need to be there. I need to help my brother.

"What about my school?" Salter says, as we walk to the rental car.

"I called them and told them it's a family emergency," I say. "They told me you have to be back in ten days or your spot goes to someone else. They mean business, that school."

It is one of the best schools in New York and one of the most expensive ones too. I haven't decided if I like it or not. The uniforms I can do without, but that kind of comes with the territory. It is mostly the way they shape them into small soldiers there, always running all these tests, making them stand straight, and never having time to play. It is all Salter knows, so to him, it is fine. But there is something about the school that I don't like. I find it hard to enjoy that my child is going to a school like this. Joey and I are both surfers and free spirits. This school is not us at all. Yet, we signed Salter up for it as soon as we moved to New York.

We moved because of my job, but unfortunately it turned out to be the end of our little family. Joey had nothing to do up there, since no one would hire him, and soon we grew apart. Staying at home and not having anything to do wore on him. He never felt like he accomplished anything or that he was supporting his family, and that is important to him. He started to feel lonely and sought comfort in the arms of a young girl who worked at a small coffee house on our street. He would go there every day to drink his coffee and write. He wants to be an author and has written several books, but no publisher will touch them. I think they are beautiful and inspiring, but I guess I am biased. I love Joey. I still do. But when he told me he had slept with the girl at the coffee house several times a week for at least a year, I threw him out. Well, not right away. First, I gave him a second chance and we tried to make it work for a couple of weeks, for Salter's sake, but I couldn't stand thinking about it all day, whether he'd been with her again. It tore me apart. I have never been a jealous person, but this I couldn't handle. I tried hard to, but realized I wasn't as forgiving as I thought I could be. I didn't have it in me and I felt like I could never trust him again. So, I finally asked him to move out.

"Where do you want me to go?" he asked.

I shrugged. "Go live with that coffee house girl. I don't know."

He decided to go back to Cocoa Beach where we grew up together. That was four months ago now. I miss him every day. But I can't forget what he did. What hurts the most is the betrayal, the deceit. I don't know how to move past it. I don't know if I ever can.

He calls as often as he can and talks to Salter. It's been hard on our son. He loves his dad and needs him in his life, needs a male role model. Salter went to visit him during summer break, and it is the plan that he will be going down for Thanksgiving as well.

"You think I can call Dad now?" Salter asks, as soon as we are in the car and hit the beach line.

I sigh. It is such a big blow to Salter that his dad moved this far away. I know he is excited to see him again. I hate to see that look in his eyes. He doesn't know his dad cheated on me. He only knows that he left, and that is enough. I know he feels guilt and questions if he had something to do with it. I try to tell him it wasn't because of him, that sometimes grown-ups grow apart, that they can't make it work anymore. I am not sure he is convinced.

"Sure," I say.

Salter smiles and grabs my phone and finds his dad's number. While driving towards the beach and listening to him talk to his father, I feel a chill go through my body. I watch the big signs for Ron Jon's surf shop go by and realize my hands are shivering. Everything about this place gives me the creeps. I haven't been back in almost twenty years. Not since I left for college.

Blake was three years old back then. Joey and I have lived all over since. He worked with whatever he could get his hands on, mostly as a carpenter.

I spent five years working for CNN in Atlanta, which became my biggest career jump. Before that I held a position with *USA Today* in Virginia. I started my career as a journalist at *Miami Herald* and we lived for a while in Ft. Lauderdale before my job took us out of the state, something I had dreamed of as long as I could remember. To get away.

Salter puts the phone down.

"So, what did he have to say?" I ask, as we approach the bridges that will take us to the Barrier Islands. In the distance, I can see the cruise ships. A sign tells me I can go on a casino cruise for free. Gosh, how I hate this place...with all its tourists and tiki bars.

"He can't wait to see me," Salter says.

I turn onto A1A, where all the condominiums and hotels are lined up like pearls on a string.

"At least you'll have fun seeing your dad," I say, while wondering what is waiting for me once I arrive at my childhood home. What is it going to be like to see my dad again? What about Blake? I haven't seen him in several years. He visited me in New York five years ago, but other than that, we have mainly spoken over the phone or on Facebook. We aren't very close, but he is still the only one in my family I like. He is all the family I have, and I will do anything to help him out.

Anything.

10

APRIL 1977

PENELOPE AND PETER take the baby home to their new house a few days after the birth. In the months to follow, they try everything they can to become a family. But the sleep deprivation is hard on them. Especially on Penelope. She gets up four or sometimes five times a night to breastfeed, and all day long she feels sick from the lack of sleep.

Only a few weeks after the baby arrived Peter gets a new case. It is a big deal, he explains to Penelope, one of those cases that can make or break a career. And Peter is determined to make it.

But that means long days at the office, and Penelope is soon alone for many hours at the house. Sometimes, he even stays away the entire night just to work, and when he finally comes home, he is too worn out to even speak to his wife.

Penelope, on the other hand, longs to speak with an adult and can hardly stop talking to him and asking him questions.

"How was your day? What's the latest on the case? Do you think you'll be done in time?"

Peter answers with a growl and tries to avoid her. As soon as he comes home, he storms to the restroom and stays in there for at least an hour, reading a magazine or the newspaper just to get a little peace and quiet.

The first weeks, Penelope waits outside the door and attacks him with more questions or demands as soon as he pokes his head out again.

"The garage door is acting up again. Could you fix it or call someone who could? We need to start thinking about preschool. I've looked over a few of them, but I need your help to choose the right one. What do you think? I was thinking about painting the living room another color. A light blue, maybe?"

One day he comes home at nine in the evening after a very stressful day and all he dreams of is throwing himself on the couch, putting his feet up, and reading the newspaper, enjoying a nice quiet evening. When he enters the house, Penelope comes down from upstairs holding the baby in her arms with a deep sigh. The look in her eyes is of complete desperation.

"Where have you been?"

He sighs and closes the front door behind him. He doesn't have the energy to explain to her what's been going on at the office.

"A long story," he says, and puts his briefcase down.

The baby wails. Penelope looks at her with concern. "No. No. Not again. Please don't start again." She looks at Peter. "She's been like this all day, Peter. I don't know what to do. I don't know anymore. I just really, really need time...just an hour of sleep. I'm so tired."

Peter looks at her. Is she kidding him?

"We're both tired," he says.

"No. No. It's more than that, Peter. She's driving me nuts. It's like torture. I can't eat. I can't think. I can't..."

"Could you shut up for just one second?"

Penelope stares at her husband. "Excuse me?"

"Do you have ANY idea what kind of day I've had? Do you have ANY idea what I am going through these days? I think you can manage a little crying baby, all right? I would give anything to be in your shoes and not have to deal with this case."

Peter snorts, then walks past her into the living room, where he closes the door. Penelope has a lump in her throat. She feels so helpless. So alone and so so incredibly tired. She looks at the baby, who is still crying.

"Why are you crying little baby, huh? Why are you crying so much?"

She puts her lips on the baby's forehead to kiss her, but the kiss makes her realize something. Something she should have noticed a long time ago. The baby isn't just fussing.

She is burning up with a fever.

11

SEPTEMBER 2015

I DRIVE into the driveway at 701 S Atlantic Avenue and park in front of the garage. I turn off the engine with a deep sigh. Everything looks the same from the outside. Same brown garage doors, even though the painting needs to be redone, same lawn in front and same old palm tree, even though it is a lot taller. The bushes to the right have been removed and new flowers have been planted. I know nothing about plants or flowers, but these are orange and look stunning.

"How come we have never visited granddad before?" my son asks.

I look at him. I knew the question had to come at some point. But I am not ready to provide the answer.

"Let's go in," I say.

We grab our suitcases and drag them across the bricks towards the entrance to my dad's beach house, my childhood home. I can smell the ocean from behind the house. I close my eyes and breathe it in. So many memories, good and bad, are combined with this smell. I love the ocean. I still do. Joey and I both love it and spent so many hours surfing together while growing up.

But there is also all the bad stuff. The stuff I haven't talked about since I left town for college at age eighteen. The stuff I had hoped I never would have to talk about again. Ever.

Just before we reach the front door, I turn my head and look down at 7th Street behind me, on the other side of Atlantic Avenue or A1A as we call it. 7th street continues all the way down to the Intracoastal Waters, or Banana

River, and in most of those houses had lived kids. I had known all of them. We used to be a tight bunch of seven children. All of us went to Roosevelt Elementary and later Cocoa Beach High School. We used to bicycle to school together and after school we would rush back to check out the surf from the crosswalk on 7th, then grab our boards if the waves were good and surf for hours. We used to call ourselves *The 7th Street Crew*. I was the rich kid among them, with the biggest house on the ocean with a pool and guest-house. But I was never the happiest.

"Mary!"

The face in the doorway belongs to my dad's girlfriend, Laura. We don't like her. She came into our lives two years before I left home, so I had the privilege of living with her for two very long years before I could finally leave.

"Hi, Laura," I say, forcing a smile.

"Oh...and you brought a dog. How wonderful," she says, staring at Snowflake like he is a vicious monster. Snowflake is anything but that. He is the gentlest dog in the universe, and the fluffiest. He loves children and will run up to anyone simply because he loves people so much. He is white as snow, but has the brownest, deepest puppy-eyes in the world. He is also my best friend in the whole world. He is no guard dog, though. That he cannot do.

"Don't worry," I say. "He doesn't shed. He has poodle in him and they don't shed. He doesn't drool either or bark. He won't be any trouble."

"Well isn't that...nice." Laura speaks through tightened lips. I know she is going to hate having him here, but I couldn't just leave him in the apartment back home. She will have to live with it.

"And this must be Salter," she says with a gasp. "My gosh, how much you look like your granddad."

"Speaking of...where is the old man?" I ask, feeling uncomfortable already.

"He's in his study. Come in. Come in." Laura makes room for us to enter. Salter goes first.

"Whoa!" he exclaims. "This house is huge." He looks at me like he expects me to have told him about this sooner.

"I put you two in one of the rooms upstairs," Laura says.

"I think we could fit our entire apartment just in this hallway," Salter continues. "Don't you think, Mom?"

"Probably. Now let's get our suitcases to our room, Salter, and then find your granddad."

"I'll let him know you're here," she says. "He hasn't really been himself since...well since Blake...you know."

"He got arrested, Laura. You can say the words. It's not like it's a secret."

"I just didn't want to...in front of the b-o-y."

"He's nine, Laura. He knows how to spell boy. Besides, he knows everything. He can take it."

Laura looks at me like I have no idea how to be a parent. She herself has two daughters of her own that had already moved out when she met my dad. They are a little older than me. I met them once at a Thanksgiving dinner right after Laura moved into our house, and that was no success. Since then, I have passed on all invitations to Thanksgiving and Christmas. After a few years, I think they got the message and stopped asking if we would join them.

"Let me show you to your room." Laura goes ahead of me up the stairs. I am surprised that she hasn't placed me in the guesthouse in the back to keep me out of the house as much as possible, like she did when I was a teenager. As soon as she moved in, I was asked to move to the guesthouse in the back. She wanted to turn my old room into a gym. Back then, I didn't understand why she didn't just chose one of the six other bedrooms in the house, but today I do. She wanted me out and maybe my dad did too. I wasn't exactly an easy teenager. I had a lot of anger built up and was constantly taking it out on him. I blamed him for everything that happened with my mother.

I still do.

12

SEPTEMBER 2015

"MARY IS HOME!"

Sandra slams the door as she runs inside with Lucky, her brown Chihuahua. Her husband Ryan is sitting by the computer. Usually, they will go out surfing on a day like today where they are both off for once at the same time, but the waves simply aren't good enough. At least not for her.

"I just saw her when I passed her dad's house on my run with Lucky," she says, and takes the leash off the dog. "She parked the car in the driveway."

"And, who is Mary again?" Ryan asks, without looking up from the computer.

A boat passes on the river outside their windows. Ryan wants to go boating later today, but Sandra isn't really in the mood for it. It is so rare she has a Saturday off like this and is home to enjoy it. Usually, she is in California, New York, or Milan. For the first time in years, she has the entire week off and doesn't have to be anywhere until next Monday, when she is going to Germany for a shoot. If they go on the boat, Ryan will take his friend Phillip with them, and then she will feel all left out once they start talking fishing stuff. Still, she wants to be with her husband on this beautiful day.

"Mary is the girl who used to live in the big house at the end of 7th Street. The one on the ocean. She must have come home because of what happened to Blake. I don't think I have seen her in...what is it? Twenty years? Oh, my gosh I'm getting old."

Ryan's eyes leave the screen and he grabs Sandra around the waist and kisses her stomach. "You still look fine to me, babe."

"Are you ever sad that we never had any children?" she asks.

Ryan pauses. "Not really. I never thought much about it. I mean, you're busy with all your modeling and I have my construction business. You travel way too much to have children, and I could never ask you to stop your career. Not as long as you're doing so well for yourself."

"Yeah, but still. My career won't last forever, you know. I might still look great now at thirty-eight, but in a few years, the calls are going to stop coming. I can already feel them slowing down."

"Doesn't Heidi Klum still work? And she's older than you, right?"

"Well, I'm hardly a Heidi Klum."

"Well then, Claudia Schiffer and what's the name of that other one? The one with the mole..."

"Cindy Crawford."

"That's right. I see her everywhere on TV."

"She has this whole furniture business going. It's different with her."

"No, it's not. You could do that. Or something else just as cool. The world is your oyster, baby."

Sandra kisses her husband gently, even though she is sweaty and nasty from her run in the heat.

"Plus, you still make more money in a month than most do in a year," Ryan continues. "I say, you work as long as it's still fun, and then we see what happens. If you want children, we'll have children."

Sandra laughs. "Except I might be too old to have them. The clock is ticking. I can't have children forever."

"Then we'll adopt." He grabs her waist again and pulls her onto his lap. "As long as my baby is happy."

"You're sweet," she says and kisses him again.

"Now, go grab a shower. You're sweating on me," he says with a grin. "And you're hurting me. You're heavy."

Sandra pushes him lovingly, then jumps down. She has gained a little weight lately, which is a big no-go for a woman in her position. She has already got a few lines around her eyes that the magazines Photoshop out, if she is getting chubby as well, it will be the end of it.

"You should go talk to her," Ryan yells after her as she enters the bathroom.

Sandra peeks out. "Who?"

"That Mary person. Catch up on old times."

Sandra's heart drops. "I don't know about that," she says. "I don't think she would want to see me."

13

SEPTEMBER 2015

I HAVE my heart in my throat as I walk the long walk through the hallway downstairs to my dad's study. Laura has told my dad I have arrived and tells me I can just walk in. I don't feel good being in the house again. The walls seem to be closing in on me. I can hear my mother's voice calling for me and imagine myself running down the stairs, my mother telling me not to run on the stairs, afraid I will slip and fall.

Once again, I feel a shiver run through my body at the thought of her. *Why mom. Why?*

I knock on the door to my dad's study and wait for his response.

There he is. My old man. Sitting in one of the leather chairs in the room that I as a child was only allowed into when I had to be scolded. He looks tired and old.

My dad looks up at me. If he is happy to see me, he hides it well.

"Mary," he says.

"This is Salter," I say, and urge my son forward. I feel bad using my son as an icebreaker, but what can you do?

Finally, my dad smiles. "So, this is Salter, huh? Come here boy and give your granddad a hug."

Salter looks up at me, as if he is asking for my permission. I nod him along. "Go ahead."

Salter hugs my dad a little reluctantly. My dad closes his eyes and holds him for a little while, then grabs him by his shoulders.

"Let me look at you, boy. Hm. You have your mother's eyes and your father's nose."

"I've been told that I look a lot like you," Salter says.

My dad bursts into laughter that soon turns into a cough. My dad has been a smoker all of his adult life. It is a miracle he is still alive at the age of seventy-five. I know Laura doesn't let him smoke inside, but I also know that won't stop him.

"Well, they're right," he says. "And that's not such a bad thing."

Salter laughs. My dad coughs badly again and lets go of Salter's shoulders. The boy comes back to me and grabs my hand in his. He looks up at me with worried eyes.

"Is he sick?" he asks.

"I'm just old, boy," my dad says between coughs.

Salter chuckles. My dad catches his breath then looks at me seriously. "You didn't have to come. There really was no need for it."

"Salter," I say, addressed to my son. "Why don't you go upstairs and find your iPad. Granddad and I need to talk for a little while. Grownup stuff."

"He doesn't need an iPad," my dad intervenes. "He's a kid. Let him run down to the beach or go in the pool. He needs some fresh air. And some sun. Look at those pale cheeks."

"Can I, Mom? Can I go in the pool?"

"He's not a very strong swimmer," I say. "Someone needs to watch him."

"A boy of his age? That's ridiculous," my dad says. "Kids around here swim like fish in the ocean by the time they're two. You used to live your life more under the water than above it."

"This is Florida, Dad. It's different. There's water everywhere. Plus, it's warm all year around. Where we come from, kids don't go swimming every day like we did."

"No, they go on iPads," my dad says.

I sigh deeply. I am already regretting coming here.

14

SEPTEMBER 2015

WE COMPROMISE. Salter is allowed to take the iPad to the beach and sit in one of my dad's chairs and play a game until I am done. I promise I will take him swimming in the ocean when I am done talking to my dad. I am dying to get out in the waves myself anyway. That is the one thing I have missed about this town. The one thing I am sad that Salter doesn't have in his life growing up.

"So, what's the deal, Dad?" I ask, when Salter has left. "What's going on with Blake?"

"They arrested him at his place yesterday," my dad says. "They're charging him with murder."

"Murder? Blake?" I laugh mockingly at the idea. It's ridiculous. "Blake is many things. He is lazy, he is...well, he's never done a day's work in his life..."

"He's a spoiled brat," my dad interrupts me. "You can say it the way it is."

"But, a murderer? That he is not."

I look at my dad. It is scary how much we look alike. I see it every time I look in my mirror. Every day, I am reminded of where I have come from, even though I try so hard to forget.

"I'm guessing you have put your army of lawyers on the case?" I ask. "Has bail been set?"

"No," he says, shaking his head. "There's a hearing today. But there is no way a judge will give him bail for murder."

"But...but we've got to get him out of there," I say.

"I got him a good lawyer; that's all I can do. But the charges are severe. He risks prison for life. They have an eye witness that claims to have seen Blake kill the woman."

"What?"

My dad draws in a deep sigh. This entire affair is wearing on him. Blake has always been his favorite; there is no doubt about it. He is sort of his second chance to make things better, but it hurts him that he has turned out to be the way he is.

"They claim he met the two girls in a bar and brought them back to his studio, where he had some kind of weird sex game with them and stabbed the one to death while the other managed to escape. They found a bloody stone-carving chisel in his studio when searching it after his arrest."

"A chisel? Stone carving? But Blake is a painter. He doesn't use chisels," I say, confused.

"Well, he's been experimenting a lot lately with his work. He's been doing everything from coffee tables to decorative water-fountains to cutting tiki bars for people's yards. He had to expand a little if he wanted to make money, you know. I couldn't keep supporting him. Laura wouldn't have it."

Of course she wouldn't. Just like she never wanted me in their life either.

"Well, we have to help him the best we can," I say. "I mean, you do believe in his innocence, right?"

My dad hesitates just long enough for me to know. He doesn't. It makes me furious. I try to hold it back.

"You're kidding me. This is your son. It's Blake. He's a good kid, Dad. Confused, yes. Spoiled, yes. Lazy, heck yes. But no killer, and you know it. Deep down, you know it. Don't tell me you believe he could have done this."

"I still have a hope that he didn't do it, but Laura feels differently. She believes he got himself into the mess and that he doesn't deserve our help. She's got a point, you know. I can't keep cleaning up his messes."

I freeze. "You're not going to pay for his lawyer, are you? You're going to let him take care of it himself, even though he has no money? Just because of *her*?"

"It's his mess, Mary."

I stare at my old man sitting in his chair. He is even more pathetic than I remember him. I can't believe a man like him, with the esteem he has in this community, with all the power he has, that he can be such a wimp. My dad is among the most influential people in Brevard County. If he says jump, they all do, simultaneously. But when it comes to making decisions concerning his own family, he is such a coward. It is one of the things that make me loathe being his daughter.

"All right," I say and walk to the door. "I'll take care of it. Like always, I'll take care of everything."

"You're wasting your time." My dad stops me as I am about to leave. "Oh, and about that dog of yours. Try to keep it in your room, would you? Laura isn't much of a dog person."

15

SEPTEMBER 2015

BLAKE FEELS sick to his stomach when they come for him. The hearing ended less than an hour ago and he has been put back in his cell. He is shaken. Constantly on the verge of crying. But he tries to hold it back, tries to be tough. A guy like him has no place in jail. He isn't going to last a week.

Blake looked for Olivia during the hearing, but didn't see her. He saw his older sister Mary and their eyes met briefly while his lawyer pleaded with the judge for bail. As expected, he didn't get it.

It made him feel a little comforted to see his sister's face in the crowd. He doesn't know her very well, but they write messages on Facebook and sometimes talk on the phone. She never comes to visit. But, still, he knows she will always be there for him when he needs it.

Mary is the closest he will ever come to having a mother. Growing up with Laura was no party.

They sent him away to a boarding school in Jacksonville for a few years once he reached school age, but he was caught smoking weed on the school grounds in seventh grade and sent home. After that, he lived at the house with them, but tried hard to stay out of Laura's way. He believes his dad feels sorry for him, and because he knows that Laura doesn't like him, he spoils him with a new car every year, his own boat, and basically gives him everything he wants. Either that or he just gives him everything to get him to leave him alone.

"You have a visitor," the prison guard tells him.

Blake feels a sting in his heart. He hopes it is Olivia. He doesn't know what they did to her afterwards, after they dragged him away. He just hopes that he didn't get her in trouble with the general.

He is taken to a small room where his sister is waiting. Blake tears up when he sees her again. He is disappointed that it isn't Olivia, but at the same time happy that she is here.

"Blake," she says and stands up when he enters.

He can tell the sight of his orange uniform and chained feet and hands horrifies her. He sits down.

"It's good to see you, Mary," he says with a sniffle. "What has it been since I was up to visit you? Three years?"

"Five, Blake," she says with tears in her eyes. "It's been five years. How are you?"

He scoffs and answers with sarcasm. "Great!"

"Blake, be serious. How are you holding up in here?"

He looks into her eyes and feels tears pile up. He has tried to act so tough ever since the arrest, but the reality is that he is devastated. Completely. It is a nightmare. He doesn't know what to do. He has been questioned for hours and hours, and still they keep asking him the exact same questions. No, he didn't kill that woman. No, he doesn't know who she is. How could he have stabbed her in his studio if he has never seen her before in his life?

"I'm trying my best," he says.

"It's awful," she says. "I can't believe anyone would think you could have killed that woman."

Blake smiles through his tears. Finally, someone believes in him. Finally. "Where is Dad?" he asks. "I didn't see him at the hearing."

Mary hesitates before she gives him her answer. "It's just me for now."

"He's not coming, huh?" Blake bites his lip. It is dry and sore.

"Maybe later," Mary says, but he knows she is lying. "You know how he is, Blake. Let's not focus on him. Let's focus on you. You have to tell me everything. From the beginning."

16

SEPTEMBER 2015

"THERE REALLY ISN'T MUCH I can tell you," Blake says.

I am trying hard to keep myself collected in the small room with the guards listening in on our every word. I know if Blake says anything about the case that he hasn't mentioned before they can use it against him. But I have to know more. I have to hear it from his own lips. I just have to make sure he doesn't say anything to make it worse on himself.

I can't stand watching my younger brother in distress like this. He is so pale and the look in his eyes so terrified it makes my stomach turn. I feel so bad for him. Especially since I can tell he is trying to play the tough guy. Blake isn't a tough guy. He is a sweet little boy, an artist. He drinks too much, he parties way too much, and thinks the world revolves around him, but he could never hurt a fly. I just know he couldn't. Prison is going to kill him. He is way too soft and sensitive. That was his problem at the boarding school my dad sent him to. My dad wanted to toughen the boy up, but he came back an even bigger mess than he left. He isn't cut out for this world and all it's harshness.

"I've never seen the girl in my life," he says. "I swear I haven't."

"What about her friend? The one that testified against you? Do you know who she is?"

Blake shakes his head. "I have no idea."

"Could you have met them while drunk in a bar or something? It's no secret you like to go out and drink every now and then."

Blake shrugs. "I...I mean, it is possible, but I don't remember it. She's not even my type. I don't like blondes."

"Hardly an argument that will stand in court."

I look into the eyes of my baby brother. He still has the innocence of youth in them. I always thought he would be one of those people that simply never grew up, the ones that hustle through life, but always seem to make it even if they don't take life as seriously as the rest of us.

But now I see something else in those eyes of his. Something I have never seen in them before. He is afraid. He is shaken to his core.

"I spoke to your lawyer earlier today, and he told me the witness was capable of describing your body in detail, and could even remember the mole on the lower part of your back. How could she know this stuff if you've never met her before?"

"I...I...I don't know, Mary. You have to believe me. I really don't know. I didn't kill this woman. I didn't."

"They found the bloody chisel in your kitchen, under the sink," I say, quoting the lawyer's information. "It was thrown into a bucket like someone had to hide it fast, and then a dishtowel had been thrown on top of it to cover it. Now, they haven't matched the blood on the chisel with hers yet, so that part is still open. Besides, there was no bloodstain evidence found in your studio, which speaks well for your case. The state attorney will argue that you could have cleaned the place up, whereas the defense will try and make the case that blood always leaves some kind of evidence behind. Even when the scene has been wiped clean, there are still ways for forensic investigators to detect washed away blood, like using a reagent called Luminol, which reacts with iron found in hemoglobin. And, as far as we know, the forensics haven't been able to locate anything, but they're still working your apartment for evidence, so we'll have to see about that."

"I'm not getting out, am I?" he asks.

"Don't say that, Blake. We don't know anything yet."

Blake is suddenly short of breath. He starts hyperventilating.

"Calm down, Blake. You've got to calm down."

"I'm going to be one of those cases, one of those that are convicted of a crime they didn't commit. Oh, my God, like those you hear about that are put away for life even though they're innocent."

"Not if I have any say in this," I say.

I have a lump in my throat from watching my baby brother lose it like this. He is panicking. It is the worst thing he can do in this situation.

"But, you don't, do you?" Blake pauses and leans back in his chair. "It doesn't matter what we do. It doesn't matter that I didn't do it. They told me I could get a shorter sentence if I pleaded guilty..."

"Don't you even think about that!"

Blake's eyes widen. He tries to speak, but is choked up.

"He's not going to help me, is he?"

"Who?"

"Dad. He's not coming because he thinks I'm guilty. He's not going to pay for that lawyer he sent me, is he?"

I sigh. I have to be honest. "No. He has paid the bills so far, to make sure you have a chance. But he is not going to pay anymore."

Blake lets out a sound of despair. "How am I going to pay for it then? Boy, am I screwed."

"You will have an attorney appointed to you by the court," I say, knowing very well that it is far from the same. Right now, all Blake needs is the best lawyer money can buy. The same kind that got O.J. Simpson acquitted.

17

APRIL 1977

PETER TURNS pale when he feels how warm the baby is.

"We have to get her to the doctor immediately," he says. "Oh, the poor thing. No wonder she's been crying all day."

He helps Penelope get into the car with the baby and they drive fast to the emergency room, where a doctor attends to them immediately. Penelope feels a huge sensation of relief when the baby is finally in the hands of the doctors and nurses. It is like the responsibility is no longer hers and she isn't alone anymore.

Peter has a complete change of attitude towards her and puts his arm around her. He holds her tight while the doctor takes care of the baby. Penelope closes her eyes and enjoys his embrace once again. How badly she has missed it, has missed being close to him, has missed being his one and only. A tear escapes the corner of her eye and rolls down her cheek. Peter sees it and wipes it away.

"Shhh, she'll be alright. Don't worry. Our baby is in good hands now. She's safe here."

Penelope opens her eyes and looks at him. Yes, her baby is in good hands now, and so is she. Standing in the waiting room with her husband's arms around her again, Penelope feels something she hasn't felt since the baby came into their world. She feels safe. She feels loved.

"Your baby is going to be just fine." The doctor approaches them carrying the good news.

"See, I told you, Penelope," Peter says joyfully. "So, what is wrong with her, Doctor?"

"An ear infection. It's very common at her age. But it can give a nasty fever if not treated. It's amazing what that small size can cope with, right? I mean, a fever this high would kill most adults, but babies, they have them from time to time and still they're fine. Nevertheless, I have prescribed some eardrops for her and something for her rash as well. She has a little diaper rash, which is very normal. You can take her home right away if you like."

"Home?" Penelope asks, concerned. "Wouldn't it be better if she stayed the night? For observation? She might get worse."

"If you treat her with the eardrops, she'll be fine very soon," the doctor says. "Like I said, it's very common and highly treatable."

"But, I'm no doctor," Penelope says.

Peter chuckles. "I think you might be able to handle a few eardrops, right?"

"It's not that hard. Just hold her head still, then let the drops land inside the ear. Three times a day. The infection should be gone in a few days."

"But, what if it doesn't go away?" she asks, feeling very uncomfortable with having to take the baby home right now when she is still sick. She doesn't feel safe alone with her at the house when she isn't well. This time, she hadn't even known that she was sick. Will she know the next time? Will she be able to make the right decision? She doesn't want to be alone with her again.

"Tsk, of course it will go away if the doctor says so," Peter says. "It's nothing serious. Why are you so worried all of a sudden?"

"I...I just don't feel like...I mean what if I don't...what if..."

The doctor places a hand on her shoulder. He looks into her eyes. There is something about him that makes her feel safe.

"It's only natural to feel insecure as a young mother. It's a big responsibility. How about you go home now, and then I'll call you in the morning and make sure everything is all right. Let me know if there is anything, and I do mean *anything*, that is wrong, and I'll have you come in and we'll look at it. I believe you can do this."

Peter puts his arm around her waist. Penelope relaxes.

"I'll be there too, remember? You're not alone."

18

SEPTEMBER 2015

I CRY in the car on my way back to the beach. I can't believe what a mess my little brother has gotten himself into. I feel so terrible for him and want to do everything I can to help him. I decide I am going to use whatever little money I have saved to pay for his lawyer. He needs the best there is. But I don't have much to offer, and it won't last long. Still, it is a start. I call the lawyer, James Holland, and tell him to continue his work.

"I'll go as far as I can for you, Mary," he says. "Me and your dad go back many years, but I still can't work without getting paid. I hope you realize that."

"I'll pay you. I'll find the money; don't worry."

"That's good to hear, Mary. I'll get to work, then."

I draw in a sigh of relief and turn the car in front of the driveway to my dad's house. I am about to drive in when I spot a face from my past. She is standing on the pavement in front of the fence, with a dog on a leash. I roll down the window. She doesn't seem surprised to see me.

"Sandra?" I ask. "Is that really you?"

She smiles and nods. "I heard you were home. I wanted to stop by and say hello."

Sandra. Sandra was probably my best friend growing up. The best surfer on the block, and by far the most gorgeous one of us. She used to be so good she was invited to join the pro-tour for women once, back when she was eighteen and everyone wanted a piece of her. She was so beautiful and cool that all the brands and magazines wanted her as a model, and soon after the modeling took over more and more. Since she is also tall, she soon became a fashion model who travelled all over the world and did fashion shows for the big names and became friends with Naomi Campbell and Helena Christensen. For years, we all envied her the life she had.

She still looks great. Unbearably great.

Looking at her now at the age of thirty-eight, she still takes the prize for best looking. She is stunning. And slim. Looking at her makes me feel fat. Ever since we hit the teenage years, I became the chubby one between us, and the years have not been kind to me in that direction. I guess I just like food a little too much. Apparently, she doesn't.

"How have you been?" I ask.

"Good. I'm good. Married," she says, and shows me her ring finger.

"That's right. To Ryan, right? He was a senior when we started high school, as far as I remember. Who would have known it was going to be you two?"

Sandra chuckles. "Not me."

"So, you're back here?" I ask. "Last thing I heard you were living in Italy?"

"I was. For many years I lived in Milan. But then my mother got sick and I came back and ran into Ryan. He had just started his own construction company. A year later, we got married and when my dad died two years after my mom, I inherited their old house right down there by the end of 7th Street. We rebuilt it, so you can probably hardly recognize it."

"So, you're still in that old house? That's amazing," I say. "You still work?"

"A little here and there," she says.

I can tell she is being modest.

"I bet you've made enough to last you a lifetime, huh?"

She shrugs. "I guess. It's not all it's cracked up to be, though. I mean it was fun when I was younger, but the pressure...I'm feeling it now that I'm getting older. I try to say yes to anything they give me. I still travel a lot."

"Any kids?"

She looks at me, then shakes her head. "There just hasn't been time, you know?"

I do know what she is talking about. In my career, I have met so many women that believed they were too busy to have a child. I have the impression many of them simply let time pass, thinking there would come a perfect time to have children. But the thing is, it will never come. There is no such thing as the perfect time to have children. My son came to me when I least expected or wanted it. I was at the highlight of my career, rocking it at CNN in Atlanta, so I blamed God for having bad timing. Of course, today, I wouldn't change him for any career in the world. Not even Sandra's.

"So, any of the others from the old crew still live around here?" I ask.

Her face lights up. "Yeah. As a matter of fact, they all do. You know how it is. You go away, but you come back because it's the best place on earth, right?"

To hear Sandra call Cocoa Beach the best place on earth is very strange. Can this really be the same girl I grew up with? She used to go on and on about how she couldn't wait to get out of here and how she dreamt of touring the world as a pro surfer.

"Well, I guess you already know that Joey recently came back," she says.

"I know that, thank you very much," I say with a sigh.

I can tell Sandra wants to go deeper into the subject, but she holds back.

"Well, Marcia has been here since she divorced her husband four years ago. She bought a condo on the beach close to 8th Street. You'll see her around. She had her license revoked because of a DUI, so she rides her bike everywhere. Alex works at the school. He's a teacher at Roosevelt now. Danny has been promoted to captain at the fire department. They just recently got a new big building down by Minutemen, and Chloe...well, you know Chloe...she is who she is. She still lives in her mom's house down the street."

I chuckle. "She still lives there?"

"Yeah. We don't see her much. She is nocturnal. Only up when the sun goes down."

"What does she do? Is she still hacking?" I ask, thinking about how Chloe back then had engaged in a world none of us had any clue about. I always believed she was an overlooked genius.

"Actually, she works in cyber-security now for some of the biggest companies around here, one of her clients being NASA. But she works from home. Takes care of her mother that way. I think she makes a decent amount of money doing that."

I picture Chloe sitting in her old room, surrounded by chips and sodas, her eyes fixated on a screen and her fingers dancing across the keyboard. She was never among the best surfers around here, but she used to go out with us anyway. I wonder if she still surfs.

"So, I take it you're back because of what happened to Blake?" Sandra asks after a long pause, where I sense she was working up the courage to ask me.

"Yes. To be frank, I really don't know how to deal with it right now."

"And your old man?"

"Washing his hands, as always," I say. "He believes Blake needs to get himself out of it. He doesn't really care."

"He still called you, didn't he?" Sandra asks.

"What do you mean?"

"Well, he called to tell you, so he has to care to some extent, right?"

"I guess you're right," I say and look at my old childhood friend. I realize I have missed her. We used to be able to talk for hours and hours. Now it feels awkward.

"Maybe we should get the old crew together while you're here," she says. "Just for old time's sake."

I freeze completely.

"Unless you don't want to?"

I shake my head. "No. No. I mean, I do. I think I do. There is just so much...I mean we haven't seen each other in a very long time; we haven't hung out since..." I pause and look at her, not knowing what to say. We both know what I am talking about. We have avoided bringing up the subject and we both know everyone will try to avoid it if we are brought together again. It will only be awkward. So extremely awkward.

"You know what?" Sandra says. "Maybe it was a bad idea. It was good to see you again, Mary."

She touches my shoulder briefly and walks past me, nudging her little Chihuahua along as she walks across A1A towards her own house by the end of 7th Street. I watch her walk away, her perfect little behind moving beautifully in her tight shorts, then curse Blake for getting himself—and thereby me—into this awful mess. I was doing so well up there in New York, minding my own business, slowly forgetting my past. Now it has all come back to laugh in my face.

19

SEPTEMBER 2015

JEAN SCHMIDT CLOSES the window of her small house. She feels a chill of happiness rush through her body while looking out on the canal where the sun is about to set in the distance. She can't believe they have finally moved into the house of their dreams. She has dreamt of living canal-front ever since she was just a young child growing up in Cocoa Beach. She remembers sitting on the school bus, driving around town picking up kids, her nose pressed against the window, dreaming about living in one of the houses that has a view of the water and a dock and maybe a boat in the back. And for years, she worked to save enough to buy it. Neither she nor her husband, Danny, make much money, so for years they lived in a small townhouse by Fifth Street. But three months ago, Danny was made captain at the fire station, and with his raise, the bank finally agreed to give them the loan for the house of their dreams. They had saved just enough for the down payment.

They bought a beautiful two-story house with a dock big enough for them to have a table and six chairs and a tiki bar on it, and it even has a boat ramp. That is their next goal, Danny says. To get a boat. Jean doesn't care about sailing. She just wants to have it so the neighbors can see it docked by her house.

"I'm going to my room to watch TV," Daniel Junior says, as he enters the kitchen where Jean is standing admiring the view and the sunset over the Thousand Islands. It is gorgeous. There is nothing like a Florida sunset.

Jean turns her head and nods. "Sure."

Junior grabs a soda from the fridge. Jean gives him a look. "Soda right before bed? Is that a good choice, do you think?"

Junior growls. At the age of eighteen, she can rarely still tell him what to do and what not to. Junior puts the soda can back and grabs a water bottle instead.

"Is Dad at the station?" he asks.

Jean nods. "Last night of his 48-hour shift. He'll be home in the morning. He talked about taking you fishing if you like?"

Junior nods. "Sure. I mean whatever. If he wants."

"Great. I'll tell him. Once he has slept, he'll take you out on Alex's boat."

Junior shrugs, pretending like he doesn't care, but Jean knows he loves to go fishing with his dad. It just isn't cool to show it.

"Okay. Goodnight."

Junior leaves and Jean returns to look at the sunset. She takes a picture of it with her phone and posts it on Facebook. Not that her friends haven't seen it before. She has posted those pictures every day since they moved in, but she just can't help herself. It is truly spectacular.

Jean pours herself a glass of wine and walks outside to catch a glimpse of the orange sun. She sits in one of her lounge chairs and sips her wine. She has the entire weekend off from the DMV office, but she is tired from having worked all week. Gosh, how she loathes her job. Sitting all day taking care of people that need to renew their driver's licenses, or who have lost them somehow, is so tedious, so mind numbing she sometimes has to swim away in strange fantasies about her piercing their eyes with a pen or using the stapler to make art out of their faces. What would it feel like to put someone's finger inside a stapler, then accidentally press it down? Would she hear the bones crush if she pressed hard enough? Would it bleed? Would the idiot scream? It's those small fantasies that keep her going. Otherwise, she would simply go insane. These people are so stupid, so idiotic, it is mind-blowing. But it pays the bills, and now it had helped Jean get the house of her dreams. Well, that and Danny's promotion.

The sun disappears behind the islands and darkness surrounds her fast. There is no wind and soon the mosquitoes have a feast. Especially the *No See Ums* are terrible at this time of day. Those small bastards will eat you up in seconds and leave small red bumps, but you can never see them, hence the name. They are even small enough to go through your screen. It is so annoying.

Jean tries to ignore the itching and burning sensation that soon covers her legs, but soon it is too overwhelming and she has to go back inside. She didn't know the No See Ums were this bad by the canals, but apparently this is where they live and multiply. They love the murky fresh water in the canals. And when there is no wind to keep them away, like this evening, there is no way to fight them. Jean has tried everything. Candles, different sprays. Nothing works.

Jean takes her wine and sits in the living room and turns on the TV. She watches an episode of *CSI Miami*, but halfway through she has emptied her glass of wine and needs a refill. Junior is quiet upstairs and she figures he has fallen asleep. Jean likes having the house to herself. Danny is a sweet man, but he is incredibly boring. The way he eats is the worst part. She simply loathes eating with him. She always looks forward to when his shift starts. That gives her forty-eight hours on her own to enjoy her life.

Jean sighs and pours more wine into the glass, then throws away the bottle. It has become a habit for her to open a bottle of Cupcake white wine every afternoon and finish it at night. It is the only way she can really get through the day...knowing that a bottle of wine is waiting for her at home.

Jean closes her eyes and sips her wine, standing in the kitchen, when suddenly the wind chime on her back porch starts making an awful lot of noise. Jean opens her eyes. There is nothing but darkness outside of her windows.

That's strange, she thinks to herself. *Has the wind suddenly picked up? Are we expecting a storm tonight? There wasn't a cloud in the sky at sunset. Has it come from the ocean side?*

The wind chime plays again. The music is haunting. Jean opens the door to the porch and peeks out, but there is nothing there. The wind chime is completely still now. It isn't even moving. Jean looks at the flagpole with the flag they have put up and put a spotlight on. The flag is hanging flat down.

That's odd. There is no wind at all.

Thinking that she is probably just imagining things, Jean decides to go back into the house. Just as she closes the sliding door, the music starts over again. Jean gasps and looks out through the window. She can't see anything.

Maybe it's an animal? Could a bird have flown into it?

Jean shakes her head. She is probably just tired. All those hours of listening to people and all their crap is making her hear things.

She decides it's time for bed and turns off the TV, then the light in the living room. As she walks through the kitchen, she hears the noise again. This time, the wind chime is louder than any of the other times.

What is this?

"That's it," Jean says. "I'm taking that thing down. I won't be able to sleep if it is going to make this loud noise all night."

With determined steps, she walks to the sliding door and opens it out to the porch, where the wind chime is so noisy it drowns out every other sound, even the crickets that are usually very busy at this time of night.

The chime is hanging from a hook under the roof of the porch. Jean turns on the light to better see. She looks in the direction of the chime, then stops.

A woman wearing a surgical mask is standing underneath it. Jean stares at her. She is short, wearing a black coat hiding most of her body.

"Who are you? What are you doing in my yard?" Jean asks.

The woman tilts her head. "Am I pretty?" she asks.

Jean stares at her. "I can't see your face because of the mask, but I am sure you're very pretty. Now get out of my yard before I call the police."

The woman tilts her head to the side a few times, then asks again. "Am I pretty?"

"What does that have to do with anything?" Jean asks. "I really have to..."

"Am I PRETTY??"

The yelling startles Jean. She feels all of a sudden very uncomfortable in the presence of this strange woman.

"You do know we are pro-gun in this house, right? There's a sign by the driveway."

The woman doesn't seem to react. Something about her eyes seems familiar to Jean. Is she one of the weirdoes that she has met at the DMV office? Jean sees so many faces every day. It is hard to tell them apart.

"Am...I...Pretty?" she asks again. This time much calmer.

Jean sighs. The woman is probably drunk or stoned. She rolls her eyes at her. "Well, if you have to know, then yes, you're very pretty."

That seems to help. The woman's face lights up. She grabs the surgical mask and pulls it off. The sight that meets her makes Jean gasp, horrified, and clasp her mouth.

"How about now?" the woman asks.

20

FEBRUARY 1992

ALLY MEYER STARTS at Cocoa Beach High in the middle of ninth grade. She has just moved to town because her mother is starting a new job at Kennedy Space Center. Ally is angry with her mother for pulling her away from her comfortable surroundings once again, and even before she has given it a chance, she hates the new place more than all the others she has moved to over the years.

On her first day, she keeps to herself. Or at least she tries to. Decisive that she doesn't want to make friends, she doesn't want to be happy here, she avoids talking to anyone or sitting with anyone at lunch.

Still, she can't be left alone. Two of the girls from her class come up to her during lunch break and sit with her. Mary and Sandra are their names. They both live on 7th Street, they tell her.

"We all surf. Do you surf?" Mary asks.

She is the chubby one. The other, Sandra, is so beautiful Ally feels intimidated by her. And on top of it, she is also sweet. It is too much. Almost nauseating.

"N-no. I don't," she says, shaking her head.

Ally isn't very athletic. Never has been. When all the other kids on the street ride their bikes or jump rope, Ally stays inside listening to music on her Walkman. Sports just aren't her thing.

"Maybe we can teach you," Sandra says.

"Yeah," Mary says. "Sandra here is the best. You should see her turn off the lip. Slam! She's like Kelly, dude."

"Who's Kelly?" Ally asks.

"Kelly Slater!" Mary exclaims. "Only like the best surfer ever."

"Well, Mary thinks he is," Sandra says.

"Oh, he's gonna be. Just you wait and see. Used to go to this high school, you know. He's only like five years older than us. He won Rookie of the Year last year on the pro tour and he is in the lead to win the world title this year. Isn't it crazy? I even heard rumors that he is going to appear on an episode of *Baywatch* this year."

"You're kidding me, right?" Sandra says.

Ally stares at the two girls, not knowing what to say to them. She has no clue who this Kelly-character is, and she certainly doesn't like to watch *Baywatch*. She has a pretty good idea that surfing probably isn't her thing either. She has no desire to show herself in a bikini.

"I-I have to go," she says and grabs her things, then leaves the table. Ally feels a huge relief as she walks away. There is no way she is going to make friends here at this school. None of them are like her.

At least she doesn't think they are, until another girl approaches her as she reaches her locker. Ally is fighting with the lock on it. Ally doesn't notice the girl until after she slams her fist into the locker in anger because it won't open.

"Nice punch," the girl says.

She is flanked by two other girls. They are all wearing black makeup around their eyes and the girl in front even has a green Mohawk. Ally thinks she looks so cool. She has at least four or five earrings in each ear and one in her nose as well. She is like a rock star.

"Thanks," Ally says, feeling even more intimidated than earlier.

"Say, I saw you with the surfers earlier," the girl says. "Are you one of them?"

"I-I-I don't know them. They just came up to me and started talking about surfing and some guy..."

The girl chuckles. "Yeah, they're all about that. Always talking about Kelly Slater and surfing and the waves and crap like that. There are a lot of those in this school. Surfers are all over. The question is, will you be one of them or are you with us?"

She is very upfront. Ally likes that. She stares at the girl, who now slams her fist into the lock and smashes it, then pulls the door to Ally's locker open. "You might need a new lock for that," she says.

"Thanks. I'm Ally." Ally holds out her hand.

The girl looks at the hand, then laughs. "Welcome to our school, Ally," she says, and walks away.

"Hey, how will I know your name?"

The girl turns and smiles.

"People around here call me AK," she yells back. "Like the rifle."

21

SEPTEMBER 2015

I FINALLY HAVE some time to spend at the beach with Salter. The next morning, we grab two of my old surfboards and paddle out together. Salter has surfed a bit this past summer when visiting his dad, so he is eager to show me how good he has become. I feel nervous because he is not a very strong swimmer.

It is a gorgeous day out. Not a cloud in the sky and the ocean is glassy. The waves are really good. There is a storm in the Atlantic. Hurricane Joaquin is roaring somewhere far out and creates some good and decent ground swell for us, and soon we both ride one wave after the other. I am impressed with how good my son has become. He seems to have no trouble anymore, not even with the swimming. I realize I was mistaken about him.

I am a little rusty, but surfing is kind of like riding a bike. You never forget completely. In the beginning, when we moved to Manhattan, Joey and I would go up to Montauk and surf, but as the years passed we did it less and less. Just like all the other things we never did anymore. It wasn't something that happened all of a sudden. It kind of snuck up on us.

While waiting for a wave, I wonder if things would be different today if I had been better at taking care of my marriage, if I had prioritized it more. As soon as Salter came into our lives, Joey moved down to like number three on my list of priorities. I kept Salter and my career ahead of him. That can never be a great cocktail. Looking back, it is pretty obvious. It just isn't when you are in the middle of it. I somehow kept telling myself things were going to change soon, as soon as I was done with this assignment or that project, as soon as Salter grew a little older, or as soon as Joey got a job. But things never improved. Not when I didn't do anything about them. I let this happen. I was as much at fault as he was.

And now there is no going back.

After about half an hour in the water, the line-up is beginning to get crowded. It is Sunday and the waves are good, a very rare combination. They are usually always perfect Monday morning when everyone has to work or go to school. I must have skipped the first two hours of school a hundred times because the waves were good on a Monday morning.

"Hi there. I thought I might find you here."

"Daaad!"

Salter almost falls off his board while trying to greet his father. Joey paddles up and stays close to him so they can hug. Seeing them together makes me happy and sad at the same time. Why did I ruin this? Why did he?

"Hi," he says when our eyes meet. "I hope it's all right with you that I join you?"

I smile. "Of course. Just don't drop in on me."

Joey laughs. It seems a little forced. "What happened to *sharing is caring?*"

Sharing is caring is something we used to say when the 7th Street Crew surfed together. We made it a deal to never get angry if someone dropped in on your wave. Between us, we knew how to share a good wave and sometimes it made it even more fun.

I feel a pinch in my heart, remembering all the Sundays we used to spend out here on the ocean, cheering each other on when someone had a good wave, laughing at Marcia when she wiped out, which she always did. Or cheering on Danny when he finally made it to the nose of his humongous long board.

As I sit on my board remembering all this, I spot Sandra paddling out on her short board. Alex, who has the same big smile on his face as he always used to when paddling out, follows her.

"Yeah! The 7th Street Crew breaks rules," he exclaims with a loud cheer.

I can't help smiling. Even if it is not all of us, it suddenly feels a little like the old days. It fills me with both joy and sadness as well. I say hello to Alex as he comes out and sits on his board. He hasn't changed much. Still small and chubby like me. Well, he has gotten a little chubbier, but he still has great hair and the sweetest smile. I have always loved hanging out with Alex. He is such a happy guy. Easy to please.

I look at Joey, who instructs Salter to start paddling for a wave.

"It's your wave, go get it, go, go. Now get up. Get up fast!"

And there he goes. I have never been more proud of my son than in this moment when he catches the wave and I see the smile on his face as he rides it in.

"That's it, Salter. Take it all the way to the beach."

Joey laughs. Meanwhile, Sandra catches a wave and shreds it completely.

"Almost like the good old times, huh?" Alex says. "I should bring my kid out here next time. He's about your kid's age. We could all hang out together."

"We're only staying a few days," I say.

I like the thought of the kids hanging out together like we used to, but it also reminds me of something I was trying to forget. I can't have Salter making friends here. He can't get attached to the town. We won't stay here.

"There is someone on the beach who wants to talk to you," Salter says, addressed to Joey when he comes back out. "She told me to tell you."

We all look to the beach and spot another of our old friends, Marcia. She is standing with her arms over her head, waving at us to come back in. She is using the old sign with her arms that we used to for letting someone know to come back in.

I shrug. "I guess it's time for lunch anyway," I say, addressed to Salter.

"Let's all go in and see what she wants," Alex says. "Here's a wave. Wanna share it?"

22

SEPTEMBER 2015

WE ALL GRAB the same wave and ride it into the beach. It is the party-wave of a lifetime for me. I can't believe I am riding it with my son. I feel so happy when we hit the beach and I run to give him a high-five. Sandra is, of course, shredding the wave to pieces ending on a floater, while Alex nose-dives and Joey rides it old school and cool on his long board.

"That was a good one," he yells at me once we get up on the beach. He looks so handsome coming out of the water with his well-built torso and long curly hair. I always picture him being played by Chris Hemsworth if they ever make a movie about our lives. Okay, so Joey isn't quite as hand-some as the Thor-actor, but he is up there. At least in my opinion.

"What's going on, Marcia?" Sandra asks when we approach her.

Marcia looks very upset. She has gotten old, I am surprised to see. She used to have a very pretty face with deep brown eyes, but age hasn't been good to her. She has gained a lot of weight, but we all have, except for Sandra, of course. Marcia's skin is damaged. Lots of age-spots from too much sun, and visible veins on her nose bear witness of too much alcohol.

"I-i-it's Danny. I-I-I can't believe it..."

"What happened, Marcia?" Joey asks.

We are all beginning to feel uncomfortable. The look in Marcia's eyes tells us something is terribly wrong.

"It's Jean...Danny...he came home...police...Junior..."

She is making no sense at all.

"What happened to Danny, Marcia?" Sandra asks, putting her hand on Marcia's shoulder to calm her down.

"It's Jean. He came home around ten-thirty. Danny came home from his shift this morning. He found her on the porch. Stabbed in the throat. The scissors were still there. Sitting in her throat. She was in a huge pool of blood. The police are there."

"Oh, my God," Sandra gasps, cupping her mouth.

None of us can believe what we hear. A million thoughts run through my mind. I have known Jean since we were in Kindergarten. She is one of the local girls. I know her pretty well, even though I have never been particularly close to her.

"Is she dead?" Alex asks.

"Yes. I saw the body be moved on the stretcher in a closed bag. I've seen enough *CSI* to know what that means."

Sandra lets out a moan of terror. Alex hugs her. She cries. I feel like crying too, but hold it back.

"Poor Danny," Sandra says.

"How did this happen?" Joey asks. "Who?"

Marcia shrugs. "I just spoke shortly with one of the neighbors, then thought I would bike down here and tell you guys. Danny needs us now."

"Maybe we should go there and see if there is anything we can do," I say.

The entire flock turns and looks at me. Marcia hasn't noticed me until now.

"Mary? You're home?" she says very loudly, then throws herself in my arms. She reeks of alcohol.

"Yes, I'm home. Just for a few days, though," I say, and give her a quick hug. "Got a few things to take care of."

"Ah, don't pretend like we don't know about your brother," Marcia says with a sniffle. "Everyone here knows what happened, and everyone here believes he is innocent. Don't you ever doubt that. We're behind Blake in all of this. Right guys?"

They all nod, to my surprise.

"Yeah, we know Blake," Alex says. "He is many things, but not a killer."

"Thank you," I exclaim, maybe a little too loud. I am just so happy to hear it from someone else. "That's what I keep telling people."

We leave our boards on the beach and walk up to the crosswalk and down 7th Street. The sun is baking from the clear sky, the moisture in the air making it feel hotter than it really is. I know the others don't feel it as much as I do, since they are used to it. But it has been a long time since I was last in Florida's humid climate, and even though I am wearing nothing but a bikini bottom and a rash guard, I am sweating heavily by the time we arrive at Danny's house in Snug Harbor after a fifteen-minute walk.

A crowd has gathered in front of the police tape. Some are crying, others just staring at the scenery, shaking their heads in disbelief. I know what they are thinking. This is a quiet neighborhood. Nothing like this happens around here.

The ambulance is still at the scene, and we spot Danny, who is speaking to an officer. He is sitting on the bumper of the ambulance, shaking his head, his son sitting next to him, crying his eyes out, the poor thing. Danny is shaking his head, then pointing at the house like he is explaining. The officer takes notes. Danny looks devastated. The officer leaves him and he is just sitting there, staring at his house and the people coming in and out of it, wearing gloves and body suits.

"Danny!"

Joey yells. That is so typically Joey. The entire crowd turns their heads and lets him go through. Joey walks up to the police tape. Danny spots him, then gets up and walks closer. An officer stops Joey from going under the tape. We are all right behind him. Danny approaches us, his eyes bloodshot and disoriented.

"Oh, man," Joey says. His voice is breaking.

Danny was probably his best friend growing up. Joey reaches in over the tape and hugs his buddy. Danny hides his face in Joey's shoulder and sobs, his upper body jerking back and forth.

"I'm so sorry, man," Joey says, then repeats it over and over again. "I'm so sorry."

"She's gone, Joey. She's really gone. I can't believe it," Danny says. "How am I going to do this? How am I going to get through this?"

"One step at a time, man," Joey says.

"Yeah, one step at a time," Marcia says, and puts her arms around him as well.

"We're all here for you," Sandra says, and joins in.

Alex nods and wipes away a tear, then he leans in on me, and not knowing what else to do, I try to comfort him. That is when I spot someone in the crowd. She is kind of hiding behind a bigger guy, but I can always spot Chloe from a distance.

"Chloe," I say and wave. "Chloe!"

She approaches me with her arms crossed in front of her chest. "What the heck is going on?" she asks and gives me a quick hug.

I can't believe how much she has changed. It is quite a surprise to me.

She looks nothing like the old Chloe from twenty years earlier. Gone are the many piercings. Gone are the military boots and the black hair. Now she is wearing sporty shorts and a T-shirt and a baseball cap, making her look like any of the other soccer moms around here. But in her eyes, behind the glasses, I still spot the defiance I always loved so much about her.

"Something happened to Danny?" she asks.

I shake my head. "Jean is dead," I say. "She was found killed this morning."

Chloe looks at me. "Jean is dead?" she whispers back. "Killed here in this neighborhood?"

I nod.

"I bet he did it," she says, looking in Danny's direction.

"Chloe!"

"I know. I know. Danny could never have done it. But I wouldn't blame him if he had," she says. "That woman treated Danny like he was garbage. Nothing was ever good enough for her."

"That's hardly a reason to kill her," I say.

I know she is right about one thing, though. Jean has made a lot of enemies over the years. She wasn't a very nice person, at least not back in high school, and I never understood what Danny saw in her. But, still, I can't imagine why anyone would want to kill her.

"He loved her," I say. "Danny loved her."

23

MAY 1977

THE EAR INFECTION is gone quickly, and soon everything goes back to normal. Penelope stays at home with the baby while Peter goes to the office and spends long hours working on his case. Long afternoons turn into evenings, and soon he doesn't even come home at night.

At the house, Penelope tries to make everything work. The baby doesn't cry as much as when she was sick, but it is still enough to drive Penelope crazy. She feels so claustrophobic in the house. It is like the walls are closing in on her, like the house is getting ready to suffocate her.

Penelope tries to make the best of it. She takes long walks on the beach with the stroller or drives to Lori Wilson Park and sits at the playground while the baby sleeps. She looks at all the small children playing, running, screaming, and thinks that this is soon going to be her life. Worried mothers are chasing the youngest among them around, making sure they don't fall and hurt themselves or put dirt in their mouths.

Is she looking forward to this? She isn't sure. She loves her little girl and is looking forward to seeing her grow up, but she is just so insecure of her own abilities as a mother. Is she good enough? There is so much that can go wrong, especially when they start walking and running around. Penelope doesn't feel certain she will be able to be there constantly, watching over the baby every minute of her life. What if something happens?

One day, when Penelope is watching the kids on the playground, one of them picks up a small piece of metal and puts it in his mouth. The mother doesn't see anything and soon it is stuck in his throat. The kid starts to cough and turns blue before the mother discovers it and completely panics. Minutes later, the kid is taken to the hospital.

Penelope watches the scene with terror, thinking anything could happen at any moment if you aren't careful.

That same night, she prepares dinner for her husband at six, as usual, and sits down and waits for him to come home. At seven, when the lamb has turned cold and grey, she decides to clean it all up again. Peter isn't coming home for dinner tonight either. While cleaning up, she wonders where he is and what he is doing. She knows he is done with the case he worked on before, but apparently he has a new one now that takes up all of his time. She doesn't understand how he has to work this much constantly. Isn't there any time for a break? Any time for his family?

She grabs the phone and calls the office to hear how he is doing. It isn't something she has ever done before, because Peter told her not to unless it is an emergency, but today she is tired of waiting. She is sick and tired of sitting alone in this big, empty house talking to a baby all day. She wants to be with the man she loves; she wants him to be with her, to notice her, to love her like he used to. In the days after the ear infection, he was like in the old days. He stayed at home when they came home from the hospital. He was with her and the baby and looked at her like he used to back in the days when their love for one another was still new and warm. But as soon as the ear infection was healed, he stopped paying attention to her again. He went back to his old self, his old overworking, and serious self, telling her she can handle the home and the baby perfectly fine and that she doesn't need him around now that the baby is well.

"Hello, Penelope? What's wrong?" he says when he answers. "Is the baby sick again?"

Penelope looks at the sleeping baby in the crib. Then she starts to cry.

"Penelope. Is everything all right? Why are you crying?"

"The baby is sick again, Peter. You'd better come home."

24

SEPTEMBER 2015

I TAKE Salter back to my dad's house and take a shower while Salter walks Snowflake. Dogs aren't allowed on the beach, so he has to walk him on the street. Meanwhile, I get all the salt and sand washed off of me while wondering about Jean. I remember her vividly from my high school days.

She belonged to a flock of girls that I hadn't socialized a lot with. They were sort of the outsiders at the school. When the rest of us went surfing or skateboarding, they liked to just hang out and drink at the beach. Often they would stay there after dark. They would steal chairs from people's yards or old wood, or even break down part of people's fences to have wood for their bonfires. Then they would get drunk and be very loud all night. Our neighbors often called the police on them, especially when they had fires on the beach during turtle season. When the police came, they would confiscate the girls' beers and send them home. But the next weekend, they would be down there again. They always chose 7th Street as their location, and always right in front of our house. Sometimes, they would have boys down there with them and could be very loud. My dad never called the cops on them, yet they still had it in for us. One morning, when I came down to the beach to clean up after them as usual on Saturday mornings, they had written something, a message using the empty beer cans. It said:

BURN IN HELL MILLS

I felt extremely uneasy reading the message. Coming back to the house, I told my father about it, but he told me to leave it alone. They were just *drunk and fooling around.* Meanwhile, I was terrified of these girls and avoided them the best I could in school. But their dirty looks were always on me when I walked the hallways or in class.

I shiver thinking about them again and turn off the shower. I grab a towel and get out. I can't help but wonder if Jean had changed since those days. We were, after all, very young...just teenagers. I can't believe that our sweet Danny would marry her if she hadn't changed.

I get dressed and brush my hair. I am about to put on make-up, but decide not to. I am not going to impress anyone anyway. It is a very liberating feeling to not wear make-up for once. I leave the room feeling ten pounds lighter. Today, I am just going to wear a light summer dress and no makeup.

This is me. Nothing but just me.

Salter has apparently decided to take a longer walk, so I have nothing much to do while I wait. I decide to go down to the kitchen and prepare some lunch for the entire family. I know Laura won't make anything; she probably doesn't even eat lunch while on her paleo-gluten-free non-fat, no-sugar diet. Does she eat at all? I wonder. She doesn't look like it.

I walk down the stairs and into the hallway. When I am supposed to turn right to go to the kitchen, I stop instead and look down the hallway to the left. I don't know what comes over me at that moment, but my heart suddenly starts racing. I have a hard time breathing, and I feel an enormous pressure on my chest. I gasp for air as I look down the hallway to the rooms at this part of the house that no one ever uses except for Laura. I hear a voice in my head, a small childlike voice.

Please! No, no, please, please don't.

I grasp the railing of the stairwell so I won't fall. I am panting for air as the many pictures run through my mind. Usually, I can block them out, but these won't go away. I see my mother, my beautiful, stoic mother on the stairs. She is smiling, smiling at me.

Please don't! Please stop!

The screams get louder, then are replaced by a child crying. I see myself. I am not a child, though. I am a young teenager. I am crying. I can't stop. I feel so helpless. Then the screams are back. Squeals of pain. I close my eyes and try to focus on my breathing.

Think about something good. Think about Salter. Salter and Snowflake. The two things in your life that are good, that make it all worth it.

My heart is finally calmed down and I can open my eyes again. At the top of the stairs, I spot my dad. He is looking down at me. I can tell he has been there for a long time. He watches me for a few seconds, then turns and walks away.

I want to yell after him, tell him to come back, to face me and my pain, but I don't.

25

SEPTEMBER 2015

LIZ CAN'T FIND REST. She goes for a run at the track on base. The sweat is springing from her forehead. She is alone on the track. No one in their right mind would run in the middle of the day in the baking sun in Florida.

Liz doesn't care. She wants it to be hard. She wants to sweat and exhaust herself, she wants to get some of all that anger inside of her out.

So far, there has been nothing in the local media about Billy the Kid or anyone talking about what happened to him at the resort. Liz smiles to herself when thinking about how much pain she inflicted on the guy. It fills her with so much pleasure, she has goose bumps in eighty-six degrees.

The sucker. Thought that he could get lucky, huh? I guess I showed him. Oh, I showed him good.

The other girls were scared when they were driving back to base.

"What if he tells the police?" Kim asked.

"What if he is found by a cleaning lady or something?" Jamie asked. "And she calls the police?"

But they were wrong for worrying. Liz always knows what she is doing. She knows a guy like Billy will never admit to anyone that a bunch of girls humiliated and degraded him like that. It is just like back in the schoolyard. Boys never tell if a girl beats them up. They know they will never hear the end of it from the other kids if they do.

"Take it easy, guys," Liz had told them. "It's me, remember? I've got this. Anyone who wants out can simply say so."

That quieted them down. They all knew what happened to the last girl who had tried to leave the group.

Liz has no idea what happened to Billy the Kid after they left him. Maybe he died? Nah, then she would have heard about it. It would have been on TV, and there was nothing the next morning or today. Part of her wants the media to tell about what she did. She likes it when they shiver in fear of what she can do. It isn't like they would ever know it was her. She is very good at covering her tracks. It is easy for her. Almost too easy.

She likes being in control. She likes having all the power. It almost went wrong once, but she always lands on top. She is that good at what she does. It is almost a sport for her.

In this moment, while running the track in the burning heat, Liz is feeling a great thrill go through her body. She saw the girl. Early in the morning, Liz took a drive up the coast, burning some rubber, speeding across A1A like she loves to do when she is not on duty, and right there, she saw her. She saw her walking across the street along with all the other idiots from back then.

Mary. Mary Mills.

Seeing her, Liz sped up with the intention of killing her right there on the spot, simply run her car into her floppy body. Oh how much she desired to do it, to finally finish her off, but in the last moment she had decided not to.

Not like this. Not yet. When she goes, it has to be spectacular. Your best work to date.

She isn't surprised that Mary Mills is back. Of course she came. Liz was waiting for it. Of course she came down to help that stupid brother of hers. Of course she is here.

Miss Mary Mack, Mack, Mack,
All dressed in black, black, black,

Liz laughs out loud while running and pretending to be punching someone.

I'll grab you hard, hard, hard
And give you smack, smack, smack

Liz speeds up and storms towards the finish line, pressing herself to the utmost, her heart pounding in her chest, threatening to burst. She throws herself on the grass, panting for her breath, then looks at her watch. She has beaten her personal best. She is in even better shape than when she was in her twenties and travelled all over the world as a soldier. She feels invincible, unbeatable. She is a freaking goddess. *The goddess of revenge.*

And she is ready to settle the score.

26

SEPTEMBER 2015

"COULD you please keep the dog in your room?"

My dad is standing in the entrance to the kitchen. Salter and I are sitting at the kitchen table, eating the salad I have created from what little I could find in the kitchen. I am not much of a salad eater, so I have poured a lot of cheese on it and found some pieces of chicken that I prepared and put in. I am planning on going grocery shopping afterwards to get us some real food.

I look down at Snowflake, who is sleeping under my feet. Salter walked him for a long time, so he is exhausted.

"He's not really bothering anyone, Dad."

"Laura doesn't like him being in here," he says.

Of course. Laura. She came in here briefly and gave us one short look, then ran to tell. Tattletale.

"I know, but he needed to get some water and food as well, and I thought it was better to keep his bowls down here instead of on the white carpet upstairs, where he will only spill and stain."

My dad sighs and rubs his forehead. "Alright. Just take him to your room when he has eaten and you're done. I'll take care of Laura. Could you please remove the surfboards from the yard as well?"

"Oh, those. Well, I kind of told Joey he could keep his board here, since he wants to go surfing with Salter tomorrow morning, and then Alex and Sandra asked if they could leave theirs as well. It's just till tomorrow."

"Well, we can't have them all over the yard, Mary," my dad says. Again,

I can hear this isn't coming from him. He never used to care when people left their boards in our yard, so they didn't have to carry them so far. But, of course, Laura has changed that as well.

"It looks terrible. All the neighbors can see them."

"Come on, Dad! One of our friends just lost his wife this morning in a terrible tragedy. We're all pretty shaken up here. Can't it wait till tomorrow? They plan on stopping by and surfing early anyway before work, and I'll tell them to take their boards home afterwards, all right? I think we have more important things on our minds right now. Like your son. Remember Blake?"

My dad stares at me, then turns on his heel and leaves with an angry grunt. Salter looks at me.

"Eat your food," I say. "After this, we're going to Publix to buy some real food for this house. I can't survive on salad alone. I am a woman in my growing age. I need calories and so do you."

Salter laughs, then finishes his salad. I drink my carrot juice, holding my nose so I won't taste it.

"Maybe I could spend the day with Dad instead?" Salter asks cautiously.

"You mean to tell me you'd rather be with your father, whom you never see, than spend the next couple of hours with your mother whom you *always* see, buying groceries?" I ask with a smile.

I mess up his hair. He hates when I do that. I think it's a little early for him to be vain, so that's why I keep doing it. He has just recently gotten a new haircut and a lock of hair keeps falling into his face, making him look cool. I like it, but I don't like that he is getting so teenage-like. It is too early. I, for one, am not ready.

"All right, kid. I'll call your father and drop you off on the way there. You'll miss out on the samples, though. They have some good ones down here. And you won't be able to pick what we eat for dinner either."

"I think I'll live," he says.

I chuckle, yet feel a pinch of sadness. Grocery shopping is our thing to do usually on Saturdays. We love it. Eating all the samples that the nice ladies hand us, buying a delicious dinner and ice cream for dessert, then killing a bag of chips while chasing the aisles for the things that are actually on our list.

I enjoy having him as my life companion, and I'm not ready to let him go. At least, not yet. It is my greatest fear that he will ask me if he can move in with Joey. It would simply kill me.

"Mom, call him," he says, and pushes my phone closer to me.

"All right, all right. Hold your horses, cowboy."

27

MAY 1977

WHEN PETER COMES HOME, Penelope is holding the baby in her arms while she throws up violently. Peter is startled to learn that their baby is sick once again.

"What happened?" he asks.

Penelope looks at him. "I don't know. She just started to throw up all of a sudden. And I think she has a fever."

"We better take her to the emergency room again," Peter says. "She looks all pale."

Penelope nods and shows him she has packed a bag with diapers and extra clothes, in case they have to stay the night.

"We're not going to need that, Penelope," he says. "It's probably nothing. I think it needs to be really bad for them to want to keep her overnight."

But Penelope insists on bringing the bag, and soon they rush out to the car, and just as they get in, the baby vomits once again, all over the car seat.

Penelope immediately tries to wipe it off, but Peter stops her. "It doesn't matter. We need to go. Nothing is more important than our baby right now."

Penelope looks into the eyes of her beloved husband and nods. "Of course not."

When they arrive at the hospital, a doctor and a nurse take care of the baby after only a short waiting period, during which the baby throws up once again. Penelope feels such a relief when they examine her. Peter puts his arm around her while the nurses take her temperature.

"She'll be fine," he whispers. "Don't worry."

"What about your case?" Penelope says.

"Well, the hearing is tomorrow," he says. "I put Greg and Mark on it. They can gather the things we need."

"Don't you want to go and call the office and hear how they're doing?" she asks, hoping he won't. "There was a payphone down the hall. I can stay here and hear what they say."

"No. They'll be fine. This is more important."

Penelope sighs deeply. Yes, the baby was the most important thing now. She is so relieved he also feels that way.

"I can't seem to find anything wrong with your baby," the doctor says, when he is done listening to her heart, checking her ears and throat. "She has a little fever and she is a little dehydrated. I would like to, however, keep her for the night. Just for observation and to make sure she keeps hydrated."

Penelope looks at Peter, who seems baffled. "Keep her overnight?"

"I assure you, it's nothing but a precaution," the doctor says. "If she continues to throw up all night, she will need lots of hydration. She is, after all, still only a very young baby. We can't be too careful."

"Of course not, Doctor," Penelope says. "See, I told you we were going to need that bag. I even packed some clothes for you as well."

Both parents sleep in chairs in the baby's room at the hospital. The baby vomits another time violently before she finally finds rest. Penelope and Peter stay by her side and hardly sleep all night. Every time the baby makes the smallest sound, Penelope calls the nurses and asks for the doctor to come and see her. Peter tells her she is just too worried and the doctors assure her the baby is in good hands. Penelope listens to everything they tell her, and even writes little notes in her notebook afterwards. She is determined to know everything there is to know about this to make sure she is prepared.

The next morning, the baby wakes up feeling fine. She is cooing and smiling in her bed. Peter wants to pick her up and hold her in his arms, but Penelope stops him.

"No. Not until the doctor says it's alright," she says.

Peter looks at her like she has lost it. Still, he decides to wait.

A nurse enters the room and looks at the baby. "Aw, she is such a cutie. How is she doing this morning?"

"She still seems very pale," Penelope says. "I hope she's not going to vomit again."

"The poor thing. Does your tummy hurt, little baby? I feel bad for her," the nurse says, taking her temperature with a thermometer. "I hate it when they're this young. Being in a hospital bed when you're this young is no fun, is it? No, it isn't. You should be at home in your own comfortable bed with your mommy and not all these tubes and machines everywhere that go beep-beep-beep." The nurse tickled the baby on her tummy. The baby responds with a huge grin.

"I know," Penelope says. "It's tough. But it's for the best. She was really sick yesterday. I'm not sure she'll be better today. I fear the worst. She threw up a lot. It was bad, right Peter?"

Peter nods. "It was pretty bad."

The nurse looks at Penelope. "How are you holding up?"

"Me? Ah. I'm fine. Don't worry about me." Penelope let out a light laugh. "This is not about me."

"I bet neither of you got much sleep last night, huh?"

Penelope shakes her head. "No, you're right. It's hard when your little one is sick."

"It's the worst. I tell you that," the nurse says. "My oldest has leukemia. He is home now, but you never know when you're going to spend a night like this holding his hand, you know? And all the medicine he has to take constantly. Argh. I tell you. It's tough on a mother. I feel for you. I really do. Sometimes I think we mothers feel the pain as much as the child."

The nurse put her hand on Penelope's shoulder and she feels suddenly a lot more relaxed, like the anxiety that is constantly eating at her suddenly is drowned out for a little while. It feels good. Penelope feels calm. She can't remember feeling like this ever since the baby came into her life.

"It hasn't been easy," she says.

"Oh. I know," the nurse says. "No one ever notices the mother when the child is sick, but she is suffering as well, you know."

"So true."

"Anyway. I sure hope your baby will be better," the nurse says and waves at the girl who gives her a big toothless grin. "She seems to be doing very well this morning." The nurse looks at the thermometer in her hand. "There is no fever. That's a good sign. The doctor will be with you shortly on his rounds. I'm sure she is ready to go home."

Home? Now? But...but what if she gets sick again?

Penelope looks at the baby in the bed, feeling all of a sudden terrified once again. The thought of having all the responsibility on her shoulders, alone, is weighing her down. She doesn't know how to do it. She really doesn't.

Peter comes up behind her. "Did you hear that? She said the baby seems better. That's great news, huh honey?"

Penelope swallows hard. "Yes, dear. That is wonderful news. Wonderful indeed."

28

SEPTEMBER 2015

I DRIVE up in front of the complex where Joey has rented a small town-house. I kill the engine, then look at Salter. His cheeks and nose are red from the exposure to the sun this morning. Surfing does that to you. Even if we slap on a lot of sunscreen before we go out. Our skin hasn't been in this much direct sunlight for a very long time. I wonder how I all of a sudden have become this indoor person when I have always been the opposite. But the past many months, after Joey left us, I didn't want to go outside. I wanted to hide from the world. I wanted to stay in with Salter and Snowflake and eat chips on the couch and feel sorry for myself. I still want that. Being fired hasn't helped.

"Aren't you coming in to say hello?" Salter asks.

Joey has heard us drive up and is in the doorway waiting for us. He is wearing a T-shirt and he is still in his board shorts. That is Sundays for you in Florida. I remember wearing nothing but my swimsuit all weekend. You might as well. It is so extremely hot, and either you are in the ocean or you are in the pool. There isn't much time you spend dry on land in this place.

Joey looks devilishly handsome.

I bite my lip while staring at him from inside the car. I really don't want to come in. I have so much to do.

"I just saw him earlier," I say. "I don't think..."

I have barely finished the sentence before Joey opens the door to my rented car and peeks in. "Are you coming, or what?" he asks Salter.

Salter jumps out. Joey looks at me. "Do you want to come in for a beer or something?"

I shake my head. "No. I was just..."

And there it is. The look in Joey's eyes that I simply can't resist. I miss him. I miss talking to him.

You can't have a beer with him! He was a bastard, remember? He cheated on you!

"I- I-I have to go buy some groceries..."

Joey looks disappointed. "Oh. Okay. See you later then."

I stare at him. Stare at those deep-set blue eyes. He doesn't leave. It's like he knows I am fighting within.

"Ah, what the heck. Just one beer can't hurt anything. Lord knows I could use something after the morning we had," I finally say and get out.

You have the spine of a worm!

It is true. I have no backbone. Not when it comes to Joey.

"Let me give you a tour of the palace," he says, when I walk inside. The townhouse is a lot bigger than it appears from the outside. It has two nice bedrooms upstairs and a living room downstairs with a nice new kitchen. It is astonishing to me how much you can get for your money down here, compared to The Big Apple.

When he opens the door to the bedroom, a big black lab comes jumping out. It jumps up at me and I squeal in surprise. Behind it tags a small brown pig. I stare at Joey.

"Really?"

"They kind of came together," he says.

"Like a package deal?"

"Yeah. Kind of. They grew up together at a farm in Fellsmere. A friend of mine had them, actually he used to live right next door, but he had to move to California. He was a drummer in a band and they had a break-through so he had to leave. He couldn't take Bonnie and Clyde, so I said I would take them till he came back. If he ever comes back. Who knows."

"Bonnie and Clyde?"

"Yes. One can't live without the other. They need to stay together. What can I say? They keep me company when I get lonely down here. Besides, Salter loves them."

I look at my son, who pets the pig on her head and kisses her. Bonnie returns the gesture with a series of grunts. Salter laughs. I don't know what to think of this entire set-up. It is very far from the life we lived in Manhattan. But I can tell Joey enjoys it. He likes being back. It is like he is suddenly that same old Joey that I have known most of my life, the same Joey I fell in love with in high school.

He smiles. His white teeth light up his tanned face. He is in a lot better shape than before he left me. Probably all that surfing.

"So, how about that beer?" he says. "We can bring Bonnie and Clyde out with us in the backyard. They need some fresh air."

29

SEPTEMBER 2015

SALTER PLAYS WITH THE ANIMALS, throwing a ball around in the grass, and for the most part it is Bonnie who picks it up. I wonder if it is like in the movie *Ice Age* where the mammoth thinks she's a possum and acts like one. Maybe Bonnie thinks she is a dog like Clyde. She sure acts like one.

"So, some day, huh?" Joey asks. "I can't believe what happened to Jean. I keep thinking about it."

I sip my beer. I grabbed a light one since I am driving after this. It feels good to be with Joey again, back in our old *hood*. Even though I still hate this place, it is kind of beginning to grow on me a little. If only it wasn't combined with so much pain for me.

"I know. It's crazy."

"It's all over the local news. They say she was stabbed in the throat with a pair of scissors, then bled to death. Can you imagine coming home and finding your wife like that? I would be devastated. I don't know how I would be able to keep on living."

Being still his wife, even if we are separated, it makes me feel flattered.

"He seemed pretty shaken. Have you heard from any of the others?"

"Alex called just before you got here. Danny is still at the police station for questioning. I can't believe they can't let a man grieve in peace. I mean, he just lost his wife. Give him a break."

"But, they know Danny, right? He is, after all, captain at the fire station next door to them."

"I know. They work pretty close together. They won't give him a hard time, but still it must be so hard for him to have to go through the interrogation right away."

"I'm guessing they need to. Because of the investigation," I say, drawing on my experience from writing crime stories as a reporter. "It all needs to be fresh in his memory. Any little detail might help in finding whoever did this."

Joey shrugs. "I guess. I still think it's inhuman."

"I'm guessing there isn't much we can do right now, is there?" I ask.

"Just be there for him," he says. "Alex told me he had picked up Junior and that the boy was at Alex's house now. He is going to pick up Danny as soon as he's done at the station. Then I figure we all should go there."

"Sounds like a good idea. I thought I might cook for them. I can throw something together for all of us and fill Alex's freezer, so they have food for some days while Junior and Danny stay with him. It will be a few days, maybe more, before Danny and Junior can go back to their house again. Forensic work takes a long time."

Joey looks at me. "You cook now?"

I put a hand to my side. "And why do you sound so surprised?"

"Maybe because in the fifteen years we were married, you never cooked."

"That's not true!"

"All right, you did cook a few times. A *few* times in fifteen years."

"That was because I was always tired when I came home from work."

Joey's face turns serious. "Oh, yeah. That's right. Your precious work. I remember that." His eyes avoid mine all of a sudden.

My heart drops. I know I took him for granted back then. Since he didn't work much, he had done most of the cooking or we had ordered in. I am not very good with compliments. Growing up in a house where compliments were something you had to work hard to get, it doesn't come natural to me. I want to say something nice to him at this moment, but simply can't get myself to it. I can't get it through my lips. I am still so angry at him for sleeping with that girl, for leaving us. I am not sure he deserves a compliment.

"Well, I brought home the money, didn't I?" I say instead. "I never heard you complain about that. Or maybe you did when you went to the coffee house?"

I immediately regret having said it when the words leave my lips. I sense how Joey almost jumps when I say it.

"Are you saying I didn't work? You were gone all day long, every freaking day. Who picked up Salter? Who changed his diapers when he was a baby? Who took him to the park? Who was there when he took his first step? Who grocery shopped? Who washed and ironed all your little skirts so you could wear them at your fancy office? Huh? Who did all that?"

And there it is. We are right back where we started.

I put the beer bottle down on the patio table. "This was a mistake," I say and get up. "Salter, give Mommy a kiss. I'll be back to pick you up at four."

30

MARCH 1992

ALLY IS ALREADY HAPPIER in Cocoa Beach than in any of the seven other places she had lived in. She never shows her parents, though. To them, she is still angry, slamming doors and yelling at them, but she has immediately fallen in. She has found her place hanging out with the girls from school. None of these girls are like any of the others at Cocoa Beach High, Ally soon learns. They aren't the pretty ones; they aren't cheerleaders or surfers or soccer players like the rest. They don't care about good grades or pleasing the teachers. Instead, they skip school together, a lot, and go downtown to hang out on the streets. Their favorite thing to do is to yell mocking words at tourists. That is a lot of fun. If they see a tourist waiting for the light to turn green at a crosswalk, one of them will approach him while the others watch. The dare is to steal his wallet without him noticing it.

They have tried to get Ally to do it too, but so far she has refused. One of the girls, AK, soon starts to nag her about it, telling her that *you can't just be a bystander*. You can't just let all the others do the hard work while you have the fun laughing at it. Not in this group. They all contribute.

"Besides, it's fun," she says, while touching her Mohawk. "It's like a drug. Once you've stolen your first wallet, there is no going back. You'll want to do it again and again to feel the kick."

A few days later, Ally volunteers herself, even though she really doesn't want to. She isn't sure she has it in her, and she is terrified of getting caught.

She walks up to a couple that are clearly tourists (fanny packs, T-shirts that say Ron Jon's, that look in their eyes that tells you they have no idea where they are going). They are standing at the intersection at Minutemen, looking clueless, when the girls nudge Ally along.

Ally smiles kindly. "Are you looking for something?"

The man looks at Ally. "Yes. Yes we are. We want to find a nice place to eat. Do you know any around here?"

"Heidi's just opened on the corner over there. I don't know if it has good food, though," she says, sounding nice and polite.

Meanwhile, the other girls giggle behind her as her hands creep into the woman's purse and pull out a wallet. Ally's hands are sweaty. Her heart is racing. She has never done anything like this before. Her hands are shaking heavily as she pulls it out and places it inside the pocket of her neon windbreaker that she wears backwards like *Kris Kross*. Her forehead is itching underneath her bandana.

"Thank you, dearie," the woman says.

"You're welcome. By the way..."

"Yes?"

"Did anyone ever tell you you're fat?"

The woman looks at the man like she expects him to clarify what she just heard. "Excuse me?"

The girls are giggling loudly behind her now. It makes her feel strong and more self-confident to know they are with her. She wants to show them. She wants to earn their respect and her worth in the group.

"Did you just tell my wife that she is fat?" the man says.

Ally smiles like he has heard her wrong. "No, no, no. That's not what I meant. I meant you're *both* very overweight. You really should consider exercising or maybe lay off the donuts a little, huh?"

Ally pokes the woman's belly, then laughs. "See. It's not supposed to move like that."

The man steps up. He gets threatening. Ally stays in position. It is all about not showing fear now. The man's face turns red.

"Why. You little..."

He swings out his hand with the intention of slapping her face, but Ally ducks and he misses. Instead, she throws a punch as hard as she can and knocks the air out of him. He gasps and bends forward, then falls to his knees. The woman lifts her hands in the air and screams.

"Help! Police! Help!"

Ally stares nervously at the man and realizes what she has done. Then she looks at her girls for approval. They all laugh. Especially AK seems captivated by the situation. She walks up to the man, who is still on all fours, and kicks him in the stomach. The man screams in pain. Ally looks at him, terrified.

What have I done?

"We gotta go now," one of the girls yells. "We're attracting too much attention."

The girls take turns to throw one last punch each into the man's stomach before they flee the place.

While running, Ally is happy to realize she now has the approval of the group. No one will ever question her again. Not only has she convinced the girls that she is capable of almost anything and getting away with it, she has also discovered a new side to herself.

31

SEPTEMBER 2015

I COOK ALL AFTERNOON, much to my stepmother's irritation. I am making a mess of the place, and when she peeks in now and then, she does nothing but send an annoyed sigh my way before she leaves, and soon after my dad comes into the kitchen and tells me to remember to clean up after myself.

That little spectacle goes on for a few hours, while I create so many dishes I could open a restaurant. Cooking helps me relax; it makes me forget all the bad emotions, all the frustrations from arguing with Joey again. Even all the sadness from knowing my brother might end up in prison, along with the sorrow from knowing Danny lost his wife in such a brutal manner last night, and the worry that Salter will never want to live with me again. I try not to think about it, but I am certain that he will choose his dad over me, and then what do I do?

There is a lot going on inside of me, to put it mildly. And the cooking takes all that away for a few hours. It makes me clear my mind. It is my yoga, my meditation, if you will.

Around four o'clock, I take the car to pick up Salter. I take both him and Joey with me to Alex's place. We don't speak to one another the entire drive there, only Salter babbles on about how he and his dad went fishing in the river and he almost caught a rainbow trout, but it got away from him, and how he wishes he could do that every day.

"That's great, honey," I say, not really listening. My mind is elsewhere. I am thinking about the argument and the emotions that have once again been ripped up between Joey and me. I am beginning to long for Manhattan and my quiet life up there. Except I don't look forward to facing unemployment with no money in the bank. I am spending the last of my savings on Blake's lawyer, and I don't like to think about what is going to happen after that.

"Could you help me with the food?" I ask both of them, as we park the car in front of Alex's beach house on 7th Street. He can peek over to my dad's house on the other side of A1A. It was a little overkill to drive there, but there is no way I could have carried all this food.

It is amusing that Alex now actually lives on 7th Street. Growing up, we always made fun of Alex because he lived on 6th, whereas the rest of us lived on 7th. We would always tease him—lovingly of course—and call him an outsider, a loser, since he wasn't a real 7th *Streeter*. Living on this street now means he is almost a neighbor to Sandra, which to me is a little odd. He and Sandra used to have a thing for each other back in the day. I wonder if they ever think of each other in the same way they used to. I never understood what went wrong with them, why they didn't end up together. They were so perfect for each other, and we all thought they would become a couple, but it never happened.

I am about to ring the doorbell, my hands full of lasagna and burritos, when Joey walks in front of me, grabs the handle, and opens the door.

"Around here, we just walk in," he says. "But I guess you've forgotten about that. Or maybe you're too tired or too busy to care?"

Ouch!

I think long and hard for a comeback, but unfortunately I have never been fast at those things. I can always come up with something a few days later, something real clever and witty, but never in the moment. I often wonder if people will think it weird if I call them a few weeks later and give them the line.

Joey walks inside. Salter and I follow. Everyone is there. Alex, Sandra and her husband Ryan, Marcia and four kids I assume are hers, since they look just like her. Danny and Junior are there too, and even Chloe.

"Mary!" Alex says. "I want you to meet my wife, Maria."

"Nice to meet you," I say and smile at the woman in front of me. She is short and has long black hair that she obviously dyes. She has pretty blue eyes. She seems nice. I guess I could approve of her for Alex, even though I always wanted him to be with Sandra. Alex is a sweet guy. He needs a sweet woman.

"I would shake your hand, but...well, they're both pretty full, as you can see."

"Where are my manners?" Alex says and grabs the food out of my hands.

"I made some for tonight," I say, "and then a lot for the freezer. You know, for Danny and Junior and all of you. To help you out."

"That is very nice of you," Maria says with a smile. "Here, let me take the rest." Maria grabs the dishes Salter is carrying.

I look at all the familiar faces and feel slightly emotional. It has been a long time since the crew was back together. I miss every one of them, but at the same time seeing them again, together like this, overwhelms me with a deep sadness as well. I am not sure I can cope with it. I am suddenly not sure I am ready. The thing is, I am not sure I will ever be.

I spot Danny and walk up to him, drawing in a deep breath. I have to get over myself. This night isn't about me or how I feel. It is about him and his son and being there for them, no matter what. That's the deal with friends, right? They are there for you no matter what.

32

SEPTEMBER 2015

"I KNOW you've probably gotten this question a lot," I say as I approach Danny.

He is sitting in a barstool at the breakfast bar, scratching the label on his beer. Meanwhile, it seems that everyone else is somehow moving around him and not talking directly to him. He looks up.

"How are you holding up?" I ask and sit down on a barstool next to him. The expression on his face is rough to take in. Those eyes and the deep sadness in them almost make me cry.

Oh, you're such a crybaby, Mary. Pull yourself together.

"Actually, you're the first one to ask me that since I got here," he answers. "The rest are only asking me if I want something to eat or drink. Apparently, people think food can make pain go away or something."

I blush. "Yeah, well...some people can be so insensitive. Pah. Food. As if that ever made you happier."

"Exactly," he says. "The last thing I want right now is to eat."

Wow. Right to my face, huh? That's okay. I can take it. I'm a big girl.

"Yeah, well. You still didn't answer my question."

He scoffs. "How am I holding up? Right now I'm just trying to stay on this stool, sit still, and hold onto this beer. I want to drink it. I want to drink all of the beers in Alex's fridge. I want to get so drunk I can't feel anything, but I can't get myself to do it. It feels wrong. I feel like I need to grieve and feel the grief, if you know what I mean? I keep thinking I deserve to feel pain."

He pauses and looks first down at his beer, then back up at me. "You know what it's like," he says. "Like back when…"

Danny pauses. I stare at him, hoping, praying that he won't finish the sentence. Luckily, he doesn't.

"I'm sorry," he says and drinks from his beer.

"That's okay," I say. "I still don't like to talk about it. Maybe I will one day. I don't know."

Awkward silence between us. I sip my beer and throw a glance around the room. Junior is sitting in the corner on a couch while the other kids are storming around. Salter is playing with Marcia's many kids, having a blast, it seems.

"You just wonder, you know?" Danny says.

I look back at him. He is ripping off parts of the label on his beer. "Who would do this to her? You wouldn't believe how much blood there was on the porch. A pair of scissors? I mean, come on. That's brutal!"

"It sure is," I say, trying not to picture Jean lying on the porch in a pool of blood with a pair of scissors in her throat. It is hard not to. "What do the police say?"

"Not much so far. But they don't believe she was a random victim. It wasn't a burglary gone wrong."

"Wow. So brutal murder, huh? Do you have any idea who might have had it in for her? I mean, did she have any enemies or anything? Someone she pissed off? A neighbor or something?"

Danny scoffs. "You knew Jean. Probably half the town had it in for her. People hated her."

I nod and drink again. I am glad he said it so I don't have to. "May I ask what you liked about her?"

He looks at me. I regret the question. Have I gone too far?

Me and my big mouth!

Then he laughs. Waves of relief go through my body.

"She had a great body," he says. "Yes, you heard me. I was that superficial. I took her because she was gorgeous back then. I wanted to have sex with her so bad, and then she got pregnant. It wasn't like I had much of a choice. It was the right thing to marry her."

I throw a glance back at Junior on the couch. It makes sense. The boy is about eighteen now, ready to graduate high school.

"So, do they have any clues?" I ask.

He shrugs. "They say they believe the person can't have been very tall. Something about the angle of the scissors or something. I have to admit, I can't remember. It's all a blur. I just really hope they find whoever did this. Mostly for Junior. To give him closure, you know?"

33

FEBRUARY 1978

BY THE TIME she turns one year old, Penelope has had her baby to a myriad of doctors, but they still don't know what is wrong with her. The baby can hardly hold any food down and she hasn't grown much in her entire year of being alive, much to her parents' and the doctors' concern.

Finally, after a year of running from doctor to doctor, one of them concludes it has to be her heart, or *it could be her heart* are his exact words.

The diagnosis, even if it is vague, makes Penelope at ease finally. She is weary and tired of telling all the doctors that she believes something is wrong with the baby's heart, but no one believes her. They keep telling her the baby's heart is fine, but the heart palpitations and weight loss tell her a different story.

"So, what do we do next?" she asks the doctor. "Will surgery be necessary?"

The doctor lets out a deep sigh. "She is still so very young." He looks at the baby in her mother's arms. She is able to sit on her own, but no crawling or even standing up like other children her age. Her legs simply aren't strong enough yet. And she is way too sick to be moving around, let alone be with other children. It is too risky.

"We usually don't operate on children this young, if we can help it," he says. "But based on the tests we have so far, I'm thinking it might be necessary to do a heart catheterization procedure in time. In a child who has a congenital heart defect, a heart catheterization shows how the blood is flowing through the heart. The exact heart problem can be seen, and sometimes treated during the same procedure or a later one. If your child has a complex heart defect, he or she might need a combination of surgery and catheterization to treat it. But, as I said, it is very unusual to perform this procedure on such a young child. It has never been done before, as far as I have been informed. You might need to wait a few years till she is older."

"But, Doctor, we don't have a few years. If something is wrong with her heart, she needs the surgery now," Penelope argues.

She glances at the empty chair next to her where Peter is supposed to sit. He wasn't able to come with them this morning to get the results. He has lost too many hours at work running to doctors constantly. Penelope can't wait to tell him that, finally, she has found a doctor who believes her. Their baby is sick and she isn't just a hysterical mother.

The doctor looks at the baby again. "It's too risky," he says.

Penelope scoffs. "How can you say that? She might die if she doesn't get the surgery now! Look at her. She is very sick."

The doctor sighs again. He touches the bridge of his nose.

"I think we should wait and see, maybe give it six months, then run more tests. She needs to be at least three years old before I would dare to do a procedure like this on her."

Penelope stares at the doctor. How can he say that? Three years old? That is two years from now.

"But...but, Doctor...just this morning she threw up again. She can hardly hold anything down. She is so weak. I can't stand it. Please. Could you just perform the surgery? I'm willing to take the risk. Any risk. Anything to help my baby get better. Please, Doctor. I'm desperate here."

"I'm sorry. I can't. I won't risk her life. Come back in six months and we'll have a look at her and see how she's doing. We'll monitor her closely for the next couple of years. If she's not better by the age of three, we'll do the procedure."

"You can't risk her life?" Penelope says and stands up. "That is exactly what you're doing. If my baby dies, it's your fault."

The doctor gesticulates, resigned. "I'm sorry, but..."

Penelope snorts angrily as she opens the door. "Well, if you won't do it, then I'll find a doctor who will," she says and walks out.

34

SEPTEMBER 2015

WE END UP GETTING DRUNK. Danny and I sneak outside on the porch to get away from the others and all their pity-looks. They mean well. We know they do, but it's just not what Danny needs right now.

Danny decides it is all right to get wasted, and he is in charge tonight. I find a bottle of whiskey in Alex's kitchen and start spicing our drinks up a little. I figure we both need it.

The more drunk Danny gets, the more he opens up to me about his marriage and how awful it was. It is a relief for me to hear and I can tell it helps him to talk about it.

"I wanted to leave her, Mary," he says. "I did. I thought about it so many times. But I was a wimp. I should have left her years ago. You want to know the funny part?"

"Sure," I say and pour each of us another whiskey. We both drink and he looks at me with his bloodshot eyes.

"I was afraid of her. Can you believe that? I was such a wimp, I didn't dare to leave her. I was terrified of what she would do. I was so scared she would keep Junior from me, you know? I would never be able to handle that."

"You probably shouldn't tell this to the police," I say, laughing. "It kind of gives you a motive."

Danny stares at me, then bursts into laughter. We laugh for a little while, then stop and sit in silence. Each lost in our own train of thought.

"So, how's Blake?" he finally asks.

In the distance, I can hear the waves crashing. I think about my dad and Laura. They are going to be pissed that we'll be getting back so late.

Screw them. I'm not a child anymore.

"Awful," I say. "He's in that terrible prison halfway to Orlando, and I don't think he will survive it. I've got to get him out somehow. The thing is, they have a murder weapon and a witness. Pretty solid case, if you ask me. I'm spending all my savings, the last of my money, on his lawyer."

"What do you mean the last of your money?" he asks. "I thought you were a big time reporter at *The New York Times*?"

I scoff. "Not anymore. I just got sacked a few days ago."

"What? You got fired?"

"Keep it down," I say, and look through the sliding glass-doors behind me. The others are sitting around the table. Alex's daughter, Ava, who I met earlier, is playing on an iPad. Three of Marcia's kids are sleeping on the couch, the last playing with a truck on the floor. Junior and Salter are watching TV.

"I haven't told anyone. Not even my dad and Laura."

I sip my whiskey and enjoy the burning sensation in my throat. I close my eyes, hoping it will make it all go away. My brother in jail, my separation from Joey, me fearing the future since I got fired, the terrible memories being brought back to life ever since I stepped into that house again. All of it. I just want it to be gone.

"There you both are. Hey, guys, they're out here!"

Marcia has opened the door and peeks out. "We were all wondering where you two were." She is holding a plastic cup in her hand. By the look of how she is swaying from side to side, it isn't soda she has inside of it.

Well, who am I to talk? I suddenly feel nausea overwhelm me. Danny doesn't look too well either.

"Maybe we should go inside," he says, and gets up from the small couch where we have been sitting.

When I rise to my feet, I feel dizzy and have to hold on to the wall behind me. "I think I've had enough," I say with a giggle. I am way more drunk than I had thought.

We follow Marcia inside, where the rest of the crew is sitting around all the food and chips. They're talking. Sandra smiles when she sees me. We used to be inseparable in high school.

"Come, join us," she says.

I shake my head. "I think I've had enough. We need to go home."

Danny stumbles towards me and gives me a heavy bear hug. I close my eyes and enjoy it. Danny has always been one of my favorites. Always so kind to others, so loving. It isn't fair that he has had such a lousy life as a grown-up.

"Let us know if there is anything we can do to help you with Blake," he says when he lets go. "Have you spoken to Olivia yet?"

I frown. "Olivia?"

Danny look surprised. "Blake didn't tell you about her?"

"No."

"He was seeing her. You remember Olivia, don't you? I think she is married now, right, Alex?"

Alex nods. "Yeah. To some general in the army. What's his name?"

"Hartman," Joey says.

"That's it." Alex snaps his fingers. "Olivia Hartman is her name now. It started out being all about the sex, but I think Blake was in over his head a little here."

"What do you mean?"

"He committed the only sin you cannot commit when being with a married woman," Danny says. "He fell in love with her."

35

MARCH 1992

"WOW! Did you see the face on that woman?"

The four girls run down to the beach and hide in the dunes while they hear wailing sirens throughout the city. Ally's hands are shaking. She can't believe what just happened. What she has just done.

"Help. Help. Police," the girl with the Mohawk who calls herself AK says, imitating the woman. Then she laughs again.

AK is the leader of the group and impressing her means a great deal for Ally. Seeing the look in her eyes now makes Ally feel better about herself, about what she has just done.

"You're badass," she says to Ally. "I like you. From now on, we'll call you AL. Like in the song, right? *You can call me AL?*"

AK laughs. So do Double O and JJ. It is AK who has given them their street names, as she calls them, and apparently, Ally is now AL. Ally has been waiting for AK to give her a new name. She wonders if this means she is now officially part of the group. If it is enough.

The next day, the police arrive at the school and start asking questions about the students' whereabouts on the day of the attack on the tourists. Ally is worried that someone might rat her out, but to her surprise, the girls all stand up for each other and give each other alibis. The police suspect them, the girls all know they do, but they can't prove anything. AK even pays a teacher to tell the police that they were in class all day. AK always has a way of getting away with things. No matter how bad they are. Ally admires her for that. She admires her for many things. Her strength, her courage, her looks, the way she doesn't care what people think about her. She can terrorize the kids in the school without anyone daring to tell on her. Just by walking down the school hallway with her, Ally can hear the student's teeth clattering in fear. No one even dares to look at her directly. Kids flee from her presence. Even teachers fear her.

AK is one of those kids who has nothing to lose. She has no parents and lives in a home with other children that have no parents. She never thinks about the future or growing up or getting good grades. She knows she will never make it to college, since no one can pay for it, so there is no use in trying. No one believes in her, so why should she? She has a fire in her eyes that makes people tremble in her presence. Even the grown-ups.

AK is untouchable. And by being her friend, Ally becomes superior as well. Together, they kick the garbage cans in the school cafeteria and tip them over and throw garbage at the other kids. They terrorize students and tourists in the streets, they knock bicyclists off their bikes on A1A and make them fall, and then threaten to kill them if they ever tell anyone. They smoke cigarettes and place the burning butt on the arm of a woman if she tells them they can't smoke somewhere, then chase her off by threatening to burn down her house with her family inside of it.

That's who they have become now.

A few weeks after the incident with the tourists, AK approaches Ally in the schoolyard and tells her to walk with her during their lunch break.

"It was awesome what you did that day," she says, referring to the day when they beat the tourist. "I believe you're probably the strongest member we've had in our group. I believe in you a lot, but I need you to prove yourself to us. Your loyalty to our group," she says. She turns and looks Ally in the eyes. Ally sees the flame inside of them.

"I need to know that you're with us. With me. All the way."

"Of course I am. You know that I am, AK." How can she not know by now? With all they had done?

"Good. I need your complete loyalty. I have something I want you to do. With me. Just the two of us, alone."

AK then asks her to meet her at an address that coming Friday evening at midnight. She isn't allowed to ask any questions or to even speak to the other girls about it. Ally feels special sharing this secret, this upcoming event with AK.

Ally goes home that day, wondering what AK wants her to do. Will it be like some kind of initiation ritual? What will she have to do? Get drunk and run around town naked? She can do that. As a matter of fact, she is willing to do anything right now to be accepted by AK, to prove her loyalty. Moving around as much as she has while growing up, this is the first time she has actually made some friends, the first time she feels like she fits in. She will do anything to stay with these girls. To finally feel accepted.

36

SEPTEMBER 2015

BLAKE WAS SEEING A WOMAN? Why didn't he tell me? Why has no one told me about this?

I am lying awake in my bed, staring at the ceiling of my father's house, wondering about my younger brother. I can't believe he hasn't told me anything about this. Maybe he thinks it isn't important, and maybe it isn't, but still.

I sit up and grab my laptop. I Google her name and find various articles about her husband and a lot of pictures of the two of them together. Apparently, they are sort of a celebrity couple within the military.

I grab the phone and call James Holland to hear how he is doing on the case. It is almost noon Monday and my head is throbbing heavily as I wait for his reply. I badly want to go down for a meeting, but he tells me there is no need to. Not yet.

"There is nothing new to tell, Miss Mills, I'm sorry."

"So, what do we do now?"

"We wait for the State Attorney to charge Blake. Once we know the charges, we can start to build our defense."

"So, let me rephrase. What can I do?"

"There isn't much you can do at this moment," he says. "We have to wait. I'm sorry, but that's all we can do right now."

Is that what I am paying you those big bucks for?

"Did you know anything about a woman he was seeing?" I ask.

James Holland scoffs. "No."

"I need help getting the details straight," I say. "Why doesn't he have an alibi for the night of the murder? It happened on a Thursday night, right? Thursday the week before he was arrested?"

"Yes. According to the eyewitness, Blake picked the two girls up at Grills Riverside in Melbourne and took them back to his studio, where they arrived at eleven o'clock at night. According to the eyewitness, they were all three of them engaged in some sex game and that suddenly Blake stabbed Jamilla Jenkins using the chisel. The eyewitness screamed and ran out of the studio and into the street, where she grabbed a taxi. Afraid that Blake might kill her as well, she kept quiet until it was all over the news that the body of her friend had been found. Then she came forward. She is still terrified of Blake and her name has been kept a secret so far."

"Could she be lying?" I ask.

He sighs. "It doesn't matter if she is. She's army, a decorated war hero from both Iraq and Afghanistan. No one will believe us if we claim she is lying."

"Alright. What else do we have? What has Blake told the police?"

"In his statement given to the police, Blake has declared that he *was* at the bar, the same bar where the girl claims he picked them both up, at Squid Lips in Melbourne on the evening of the murder. He was drinking heavily and was seen by a lot of people. People that have testified to seeing him drinking and dancing and being very loud, making quite the spectacle of himself. Apparently, the establishment was used to that from him. He is known around here as quite the party monkey. Anyway, the last thing he says he remembers is the band going on at seven o'clock. Some one-man-band named Johnny Danger took the stage. Your brother remembers it specifically because he loves Johnny Danger. The strange part is that after that he doesn't remember anything anymore. Not a single detail of what happened the rest of the night. It's all black, he says, which makes this case even harder. The problem is that is not unusual for your brother...to drink till he blacks out. He claims he woke up the next morning in his own bed. A week later, he goes to Starbucks to see his painting get hung up on the wall there. When he gets back to his own place, the police are waiting for him there. They found the bloody chisel under his sink. That and the eyewitness, who states she saw him stab Miss Jamilla Jenkins during a sex game the night before, is probably what they're basing their charges on."

"And the body? Where was it found? If I remember it right, there was no blood in the studio?"

"That's one thing I don't understand," he says. "The body was found in a hotel room at a Motel 6. How was Blake supposed to take her there, rent a room, and carry her inside after he stabbed her?"

"And, why would he do that?" I ask. "It's not like it's a great place to hide a dead body."

"Exactly. I have found no one at the motel that remembers him or her, neither is his name found anywhere. His credit card wasn't even used to pay for the room. It was paid with cash. There is no evidence in the car, no trace of blood, or even any of the girl's hair. That's the angle I'm working on right now. That's where the police's investigation is inconsistent. And that's all I can do with what I have."

I write everything down on my notepad, then tell James Holland I will be in touch before I hang up. I grumble while going through the details once again. I have been over it so many times and can't make it work. The part about the motel room is new to me. So is the girlfriend I never knew he had.

I circle the name Olivia Hartman a couple of times, wondering about her and Blake. I get that he has kept her a secret because she is married and all...to not get her in trouble. That makes a lot of sense. Especially if he really likes her. But he told Alex, Danny, and Joey about her, apparently. Why only them and not me? I can't help feeling a little offended. He and I aren't close, but we talk over the phone every now and then. Is he more comfortable talking to the boys? Is that what this is all about? Or is he bragging maybe? Maybe it's a boy thing that I wouldn't understand. Well, I can't blame him if he is bragging, I think to myself, looking at her picture on my computer screen. She is quite the beauty. But she is old. Much too old for him. I remember her vividly from when we were teenagers.

I decide to get moving, despite the headache and nausea. I, for one, am not going to sit here and wait for my brother to rot in that jail. I want to figure out what the heck is going on. I only have around eight days till Salter has to be back in school, and besides helping my brother get out of this mess, I have to find a new job. With the reputation I have by now, it could prove to be just as hard as getting my brother acquitted.

Salter has already walked Snowflake and comes back with a big smile on his face. I am just getting out of the shower. Snowflake jumps me and licks the water off my legs. His fur is filled with sand. I give Salter a look.

"Did you walk him on the beach?"

"Well...he..."

"You know you're not supposed to do that. Grandpa and Laura would kill you if they knew. And look at all that sand that he dragged inside the house. Oh, my God, Laura is going to kill me."

Salter is still smiling.

"What are you so happy about?" I ask.

"Dad called while you were sleeping. His job today on that roof has been pushed because of the high possibility of rain later today. So, he told me he would take me fishing again."

"That's great, honey," I say, longing for a cup of coffee to kill this hangover. "I'll drop you off on my way to Starbucks."

37

SEPTEMBER 2015

I DROP Salter off outside his dad's place and don't bother to say hello to Joey. I don't want him to see me like this. He'd be able to tell right away that I am hung over. He knows me too well, and I would never hear the end of it. Besides, I am not in the mood for a new confrontation with him. I have no energy, nor the will to argue.

I park in front of the new Starbucks on State Road 520 and walk inside, still wearing my sunglasses. The girl behind the counter smiles at me and I order a pumpkin spice latte and a chocolate donut. I spot my brother's big painting on the wall and walk to it. *It is actually quite good,* I think to myself, while sipping my coffee and taking the first bite of the donut.

I grab a chair and sit down in front of the painting, admiring my brother's creativity. I have never been able to create anything but words on a piece of paper, and I have always found it astonishing what Blake can create. I never understood why he doesn't have more success. I know he has tried everything. At one point, he even painted cell phone cases for people, but he didn't make much on that either. My guess is that he still borrows money from my dad to get by, and I can't blame my father for being fed up with it. Especially with the lifestyle my brother has led the past years, ever since he got his art degree from college.

"You like the painting?"

It is the girl from behind the counter. She has come over to clean the table next to me. "It's for sale."

I chuckle. "Oh, I'm not looking to buy."

She picks up an empty cup, then stops in front of the painting. "It's really good, though," she says. "Too bad he won't be able to make more."

I almost choke on my donut. I swallow the bite that almost got stuck and look at her. "What do you mean?"

"Haven't you heard? He's going to jail. Apparently, he killed someone. Kind of hard to imagine him doing that, though. But that just shows...you never really know people, right? He seemed so nice."

"You know him?" I ask.

"Sure. He used to come here every day for his coffee. Then he would ask to talk to Ray, our manager. Every day for almost a year he asked him to let him put up one of his paintings for display. Finally, Ray got tired of saying no. He's pulling it down later today. Says he doesn't want some killer's painting in his shop. I'll miss it, though. I kind of like it."

"Say, did he ever come in here with anyone?" I ask. "Or was he always alone?"

"He was always alone," she says. "Until the day when we put up the painting. Someone was with him that day."

"Who? Was it a woman?"

"As a matter of fact, it was. I remember we talked about it, since we had never seen him with a woman before and some of us wondered if he was gay. I never thought he was, though. Just doesn't seem the type. He always flirted with me."

She makes a shy movement then returns to cleaning up. She throws out the cup. I pull out my phone and find a picture of Olivia Hartman, which I show to her. "Was this the woman who was with him that morning?"

The girl looks at it, then nods with surprise. "Yes. Yes. That was her. How did you know?"

I sigh and put my phone back. "Just a hunch. Say, did you notice if they left together?"

"They did. Drove in separate cars, though. Why?"

I finish my donut and grab my cup. "Tell your boss to not throw away the painting. I'll buy it and come for it later."

38

SEPTEMBER 2015

THE DOOR to my brother's studio is decorated with black-and-yellow tape that says CRIME SCENE DO NOT CROSS.

I slide under it and through the door without breaking the seal. I enter his small studio. The place is a mess. Old beer bottles, cigarette stubs on dirty plates, food with mold on it. The studio is just one big room under the ceiling of the building. His bed is in one corner. Nothing but a mattress on the floor.

Who lives like this?

I pick up a sock from the floor, then realize there is nowhere I can put it, and let it fall to the wooden floor again. There is dust in the corners and on all his lamps; the floor needs to be washed. Shoes that have stepped in paint have left marks all over the wooden planks.

"Probably wouldn't count on getting that deposit back once you leave, dear brother," I mumble and walk into the kitchen. A chair is knocked over and I pick it up. I sit down on it and try to take in the room, wondering why I am even here.

"What happened, Blake?"

According to Holland, Blake was arrested right here on that morning he came back from Starbucks.

I want to go visit him again today or tomorrow, but the lawyer has told me not to talk about the case with him. They're still in a phase where they will be listening in and use anything he says against him. I know we have to be very careful now.

The crime scene investigators have swept the place. I see marks on the walls where they have dusted for fingerprints and same marks on the floors where they have taken footprints. The place doesn't look much like a crime scene. It's dirty and messy, yes, but there is no blood anywhere. The kitchen table is in an odd position, though...pushed up against the wall while the chairs are in the middle of the floor. I walk to it and look at the footprints on the floor. Someone stepped in blue paint. The prints are all over the floor underneath the table. What strikes me is the shape of the print. The print from the heel is very small, almost nonexistent. It can only have been made by a pair of high-heeled stilettos. The paint is fresh. I get some on my finger when I touch it.

Who wears stilettos to a crime scene?

I have been at my share of crime scene investigations, covering them as a reporter, and seen many female investigators and detectives, even sometimes the district attorney is female, but none of them ever wore high-heeled shoes, let alone stilettos.

I stare at the print and wonder, then take a picture of it with my phone.

I turn around and look at my brother's paintings. They are beautiful. I am surprised at how good he has become. I can actually say that I can see myself hanging one of them in my living room without lying anymore. Maybe I am not giving my dear brother enough credit. Maybe he isn't just some lazy parasite, sucking money out of our dad.

I sigh and walk around in this strange place he calls home. I am about to leave when I realize I need to pee. I walk to his bathroom and hope and pray there is toilet paper in there. Luckily, there is, and I do my business. I wash my hands and look at myself in the mirror, then get curious and open the cabinet. In it, I find Blake's toothbrush, mouthwash, toothpicks, and deodorant. I find his razor and inside of the case, next to the razor, I spot a ring. A silver ring with a beautiful green stone in it. I know nothing about jewelry, but I know enough to know that this is expensive. Completely out of Blake's price range. I grab it and put it in my pocket, even though I know it's a crime.

Just when I am about to leave the bathroom, I hear a voice. I pause and wait. The voice is coming closer. I peek out through the crack in the door and spot Detective Chris Fisher. He is one of the Cocoa Beach kids as well. I remember him. I saw him in the newspaper article in *Florida Today* where I read about my brother's arrest. I know he is the guy who took him in.

He has a phone to his ear and is speaking loudly while walking into my brother's studio.

"Yes, yes, of course I've got it under control," he says.

I hold my breath as Chris Fisher walks closer to the door leading to the bathroom, but then changes his mind and walks into the small kitchen instead.

"I know. I know," he says, while kneeling by the kitchen table. He is looking for something. I stand completely still and hold my breath. Me being there is an offense in itself. I stare at the front door and wonder if I can make a run for it. No. There is no way I can make it out without him seeing me. My heart is pounding in my chest.

I can't get caught here. He can't find me here!

"No, I'll find it. Don't worry," he says. "It must be here somewhere."

I feel the ring burning in my pocket. The detective is looking for something. Can it...Could it be...?

I don't want to take any chances. I pull the ring out of my pocket and place it on the sink when I see the handle on the door turn.

39

SEPTEMBER 2015

THE HANDLE IS MOVING and I manage to jump into the shower and hide behind the curtain. I hold my breath as detective Chris Fisher enters the bathroom and starts to look around. When he spots the ring on the sink, he lets out a small breath.

"There you are, little fella," he says and picks it up. "You had us all scared there for a second."

I watch him put it in his pocket, then rush out of the bathroom. I wait and listen as his footsteps walk across the wooden floors. I wait till they disappear. I don't dare to breathe until minutes later. Or, at least that's how it feels. I sit down in the tub until my heart is beating normally again. Then I get up and walk cautiously back into the studio.

As soon as I feel sure that the detective has left, I run across the floor and slide under the tape to get out into the hallway again. I take the stairs down and walk to the street, feeling like a criminal, like everyone's eyes are on me, that they have all seen what I just did. I jump into my car and drive off.

I can't believe what I just saw. Who was Detective Fisher talking to on the phone? His superior? Why was he looking for the ring? Why hadn't they found it and brought it in when they searched the place after the arrest, if it was that important?

I don't understand it. That and the high-heeled prints have me wondering. Was Olivia there with Blake when he was arrested?

I think about going back to my father's house, but I don't want to. There is something I need to do first. An itch I need to scratch.

I park the car in front of Chloe's house and walk up the small driveway and ring the doorbell. It takes a while before she opens. She looks at me.

"Mary?"

"Do you have a minute? I need your help," I say.

She doesn't even think about it for a second before she steps aside and lets me in. "I was just making coffee," she says. "You look like you could use a cup."

"Thanks," I say, and follow her into her kitchen. I see many bottles of pills on the counter. And a tray with food half eaten.

"How's she doing?" I ask, thinking about how much I had always loved Chloe's mother. She was the cool mom around. The one who always listened when you spoke, like *really* listened to what you said and wanted to know how you were feeling. I spent many hours talking to her, while going through the hardest time of my life. She took care of me when I needed it the most.

"So-so," she says. "You know how it is. Some days are good, others are bad. You never know when it will be her last day, so we try to cherish every moment."

"That's nice," I say, and take the cup she hands me. The smell alone makes me feel better already. I could use something to eat as well, but don't say anything. I don't want to impose.

"She's asleep right now. She sleeps most of the day. So, what can I do for you?" Chloe finally asks.

We sit down in her kitchen. The smell of sickness is everywhere. The air in the house is stuffy. In the corner, I spot her old surfboard. It doesn't look like it has been in the water recently.

"You know about my brother, right?" I ask.

"Sure," she says, and sips her coffee. "He was arrested this Friday, right? I was shocked when I heard."

"Me too," I say. "But the thing is, I am beginning to think something is very wrong with this case."

"Like what?"

"Okay, first of all, they found the body in a motel room a week before they decided to arrest my brother. Why did it take so long? Second, there is nothing that indicates he was ever in that motel room; he never paid for it with any of his credit cards, nor did anyone see him there. Third, the eye-witness says she was with him and Jamilla Jenkins at his studio when he stabbed her, but there was no blood found in his studio or in his car."

Chloe nods and looks at me pensively. "Good points, but still...they might have needed a week to figure out it was him; it takes time to gather all the evidence and find the witness. He could have worn a disguise and paid cash, and he could have cleaned his place and the car afterwards. After all, he had an entire week to hide it."

I stare at her.

"Just playing the devil's advocate here," she says, gesticulating with her hands in the air.

"I know it's not much, but it's still enough for me to wonder. Why would he move the body to a hotel room? Why not throw it in the river or the ocean?" I ask.

"Maybe he figured someone else could take the blame. Maybe he thought they would react exactly the way you did. If the eyewitness hadn't stepped out, no one would have thought of him, the way I see it. Listen. I know he's your brother and we all love him and care for him, but you've got to admit he looks pretty guilty. They found the bloody chisel in his place, for Christ sake."

"I know," I say and drink my coffee, suddenly wishing it were something stronger. "I still think he's been framed. I just don't know how to prove it. I also believe he wasn't alone when he was arrested. Someone was with him. A woman. I need to know if she was there."

"And how do you plan on doing that?" Chloe asks.

I look at her while a smile spreads across my face.

40

SEPTEMBER 2015

CASSIE MORGAN IS WAITING. Standing outside the door to the nursery, her ear pressed against it, she waits for the baby to start crying again. When it doesn't happen, she closes her eyes and lets out a deep sigh.

"I'm too old for this," she mumbles to herself.

She walks downstairs, cursing her husband, Ben. It was all his idea. *Let's have another baby. It'll be fun!*

Cassie thought she was done with all that, since the two others were teenagers now, but Ben kept asking her, begging her to have another one, one last baby. Cassie said no, but somehow he got his way anyway. Accidentally, she became pregnant and now they have started all over again.

"It'll be fun," she mumbles to herself, mocking her husband's voice. No wonder he thinks it is fun. He gets to do all the good stuff with the baby. It's not like he's the one who has to give up his job and his entire life for this.

Cassie places the receiver to the baby monitor on the counter in the kitchen and starts to empty the dishwasher. Just like every other morning. Cassie sighs and puts the dishes away, then the glasses and the silverware. With every fork she puts back in its place, she grumbles and curses her husband.

Cassie hates being a housewife. She loathes having to stay home and take care of the baby while everyone else gets to go out in the wide world and be with grownups and have grown up conversations. She misses her job like crazy, and with the age she is, there is no guarantee that she will get it back once she is ready for it. Ben wants her to take at least three years off, like she did with the others. But she doesn't want to spend three years like this, doing house chores and walking the baby in the stroller. She hates it. And, worst of all, there is no one her age with babies around here. All the other moms are in their early twenties. She has nothing in common with them. Nothing at all.

Cassie sighs again and closes the dishwasher. No. Life hasn't been any fun for many years. It's always about them and what they need and what activity she has to drive them to.

Cassie looks at the baby monitor and is filled with peace. It looks like the baby is finally really heavily asleep.

He sure needs the sleep, she thinks to herself. *After the night we had with him waking up every other hour. He must be exhausted.*

Cassie grabs her phone and smiles when she sees the picture of little Jared. She never admits it publicly, but of course, she is glad she had him. Even if it is a lot of trouble and a lot of work all over again, she loves him dearly. He's the only boy she ever had, and she is fonder of him than either of the others. There is no doubt about it. She would do anything for that little munchkin. It's the lack of sleep and the overload of work that gets to her.

But it'll pass. Just like it did with the others. It'll get better.

Cassie finds her friend in her contacts and calls her. Her friend is a stay at home mom as well, even though her children are all grown up. She never made it back to work. Now she is doing charity work and is in charge of the girl scouts.

"Hey, it's me. How's it going?" she asks.

"Great. Getting ready for the spook-tacular event next month. We're raising money for the orphanage in Titusville."

"Sounds exciting," Cassie says without meaning it. The friend throws these events every year to raise money for a charity of her choice, but it is really all about them getting together and getting drunk, just for a good cause.

"I've been thinking about getting some of Blake Mills' paintings for the auction," she says. "I think they will have great value this year."

"Oh, what an excellent idea," Cassie says. "The works of a local murderer. How very spook-tacular, indeed."

"I thought it might attract some attention."

Cassie agrees, then pauses and takes the phone away from her ear. She looks at the baby monitor.

"What's wrong?" her friend asks.

"Nothing. I just thought I heard Jared, but there is nothing on the monitor. You were saying?"

"I was just saying I wanted to find out who to ask to buy the paintings. I bet he has a lot."

"Maybe talk to his dad. I believe the old Mills still live on 7th Street right on the water. Maybe you could just drive down there and ask. I heard Mary is home too."

"I just don't want to impose, you know. I don't want to come out like a vulture."

"Wait a minute," Cassie says and looks at the monitor again. "I thought I heard something again, but it was nothing."

"Don't you have one of those with a camera?" her friend asks.

"Nah. I just have the old type with a light display." She looks at it again and sees the light moving.

"You should get one with a camera. That way, you always know if he is just turning over in bed."

"Well, there is definitely sound. I gotta go," she says and hangs up. The monitor is quiet now again, and Cassie stares at it. She feels like screaming at it for controlling every minute of her life. She really wants Jared to sleep longer.

He gets so cranky if he doesn't get enough sleep. It's going to ruin the rest of my day!

The monitor remains quiet and Cassie breathes a sigh of relief. Jared was probably just turning over in bed. She puts the monitor down, then walks to the kitchen to grab a soda from the fridge. She opens the door and peeks inside. Her hand is on the can of Coke when she hears something that makes her entire body start to tremble. It's the voice of someone singing, singing quietly, hauntingly.

Listening to the lyrics of her once favorite song *Cat's in the Cradle* being sung over the baby monitor immediately brings her back to her past, a past she has tried so hard to forget. A past with so many bad memories it makes her hands shake. She can no longer hold on to the can of Coke and drops it on the tiles. It explodes and sprays the floor and the cabinets. Normally, Cassie would be all over it to clean it up, but not in this moment. This time, she doesn't even notice. Not the stains it leaves on the cabinet doors, nor the pool of Coke on the tiles, not even how it soaks her socks. All she is thinking about is the baby.

Jared!

She grabs a knife, then storms up the stairs and stumbles on the last step; the fall buries her nose deep in the carpet. She gets up again and runs for the door to the nursery and opens it. Someone is in there. Someone is standing by the crib, her back turned toward Cassie while singing.

"Don't touch him!" Cassie groans. "Get away from the crib."

Cassie holds the knife out in front of her. It's shaking heavily. She can't make it stay still. The baby wakes up. He is crying.

"Get away from my baby!" she says.

The woman turns to look at her. She is wearing a surgical mask. She tilts her head slowly. She is still singing.

"*The Cat's in the Cradle...*"

"Stop!" Cassie yells. "Stop it! Stop singing that song!"

The woman stops singing. Jared is crying helplessly. Cassie takes in a deep breath. She wants to go to him, but doesn't dare to. She is still holding the knife out in front of her. "What do you want?" she asks. "Why have you come here?"

The woman takes a step closer.

"Don't!" Cassie yells. "Don't move!"

The woman pauses. She tilts her head once again.

"What do you want? Answer me!"

"Am I pretty?" she asks.

Cassie stares at her. Her mind is only on Jared, who is demanding her attention now. "What?"

"I asked: Am I pretty?" the woman repeats.

"What the heck...why? Get out of my house!"

The woman giggles, then suddenly changes expression and yells: "AM I PRETTY!"

"Yes!" Cassie yells back. "Yes, for crying out loud. Now get the hell out of my house!"

Jared screams loudly now, and Cassie runs to him. She looks at him and smiles, then caresses his head. "Shhh," she says.

When she glances back at the woman, she has taken off the mask. The sight makes Cassie gasp for air. She drops the knife in her hand and it makes a loud noise as it lands on the tiles.

"How about now?" the woman asks.

41

SEPTEMBER 2015

"OH, NO! NO. NO. NO!"

Chloe is raising her hand in the air like she is waving away an annoying fly. She is shaking her head at the same time. "I don't do that kind of stuff anymore," she says. "It's over. Caput. Finito. Done!"

"Come on, Chloe. It's me, Mary. Please, do it for me."

"No."

"Please?"

"I can't, Mary."

"Yes, you can. You can help me. You're the world famous Dr. Claw, remember? I helped you find the name?"

"Inspector Gadget's nemesis, yes," she says. "I still think the name is lame. That was your favorite cartoon. Not mine."

I chuckle. "I remember I thought it was so cool. Dr. Claw! Remember when they wrote about you in all the papers nationwide? You were world famous for that hack that gave you access to the White House, remember? You were so scared they'd find you. But they couldn't even track you to Florida. They even, at one point, believed you might be someone from Russia. You were that good."

Chloe laughs at the memory. So do I. What an innocent time it was. I can't believe how much has happened since then.

"Come on, Chloe. It's just a small peek into a police file, that's all," I say. "I know it'll be a walk in the park for you. No one will ever find out."

Chloe sighs. "But I'm done with that stuff. It's different now," she says. "This is what I do now." She points at her computer screen.

"Cyber-security for businesses?" I ask.

"Not that. That's just what I get paid to do. No, this is where my heart belongs," she says and taps on her laptop. She turns the screen so I can see better.

"Nochildporn.org?" I say.

"Yes. I founded it. It's an anti-child porn organization. We use a software that I created. Software that automatically gleans information from tens of thousands of suspected URLs and tracks those that are sending and receiving data with those websites. I share my information with the authorities once I have it, and they make sure to find and prosecute the bastards."

I stare at my old friend, not knowing what to say. I am impressed. More than that. I just don't know how to express it.

"Wow," I simply say.

She nods her head. "So, now you can understand why I can't help you hack into the Brevard County Sheriff's Office."

I grab her arm. "But you have to help me, Chloe. Please. It's important. You know my brother. He'll never survive jail."

Chloe hesitates when I mention Blake. He was only three when I moved away, but she has been here ever since. She has seen him grow up.

"Alright," she says. "For Blake, I'll do it. He's a good kid."

I wonder about her change of heart. Had Blake made such a deep impression on Chloe while growing up? I shake my head. It doesn't matter. As long as she does this for me.

Chloe gets up from her chair and finishes her coffee. I follow her. She looks at me.

"Remember the time when I changed your grades for you?" she asks with a mischievous smile.

"I will never forget that," I say. "I would never have gotten an A in Geometry if it wasn't for you."

Chloe laughs. "Especially not since you were always skipping classes to surf," she says.

42

MARCH 1979

"PLEASE, help us. Someone please help me."

Penelope storms into the ER with her baby girl in her arms. The child is throwing up. A nurse runs to Penelope.

"What's wrong?"

"She's been throwing up all morning," Penelope says anxiously. "It won't stop. And, suddenly, she seemed to have had a seizure of some sort, like a staring spell. I had no eye contact with her for at least three minutes. She was just gone." Penelope talks while panting from running. She has driven there on her own. Didn't want to wait for an ambulance.

"She does have problems with her heart," she says. "We're waiting for an operation."

The nurse takes the baby out of Penelope's hands. "I'll get her to a doctor immediately. Walk with me."

Penelope follows the nurse down the corridor, while all the eyes in the waiting room are on her. Penelope knows what they think.

Poor woman. It's always the worst when it's the little ones. So tough on the mother.

"How old is the girl?" the nurse asks while they walk.

"Two years old. She just turned two. We've known something was wrong since she was just a baby."

"Doctor," the nurse calls. "This child needs immediate attention," she says, as they approach a doctor.

"What seems to be the problem?" he asks.

The nurse opens her mouth to speak, but is drowned out by Penelope.

"Vomiting. Heavily all morning. And seizures. Staring spells. She was absent for at least three minutes. She has a heart problem. Might need a heart catheterization procedure."

The doctor stares at Penelope, then at the child. "Alright," he says. "Let me take a look at her."

Penelope breathes a sigh of relief. She follows the doctor into an examination room, where her child is put on a big bed. Penelope stands next to her and holds her hand.

"It's going to be fine, baby," she says with a smile. "The nice doctor will take good care of you. Don't worry." The girl, who is still very small for her age, chews on her binky.

"Doctor?" the child says and points at the man in the white coat, who is now looking into her eyes with a flashlight.

"Yes, doctor," Penelope repeats.

The nurse smiles. "That's a big word for such a small girl."

"I know. She has seen her share of doctors in her short life. It's her heart that is the issue."

"That is tough," the nurse says, and puts her hand on Penelope's shoulder.

Penelope nods with a sigh. "It is. It really is."

"You can tell she is used to it," the doctor says, and tries her reflexes. The girl's leg reacts like it's supposed to. "Usually, I need the mother to hold a two-year old still for examination. But not this girl. She sits nice and quiet through it all."

After the initial examination, the doctor pulls Penelope aside and speaks with a low voice. "We'll be running a series of tests, and I will try and get a hold of Dr. Mussels, our pediatric neurologist, and have her take a look at her. It's the part about the seizure that makes me nervous. You say she was out for at least three minutes? That's a very long time. And she has a history of heart problems?"

"Yes. We're waiting for an operation, but no one has wanted to perform it because she is so young. I have been to every heart-specialist in Central Florida. But they all believe I am mad for wanting to perform heart surgery on this young a child. I just want to do what is best for her, Doctor. I just want her to be well."

The doctor places his hand on her arm and Penelope relaxes finally.

"We'll get to the bottom of this. Whatever is causing the vomiting and the seizures, we'll find it and make her well. Don't you worry about it. You're not alone with this."

43

SEPTEMBER 2015

THEY MAKE it look so easy in the movies, but it really isn't. I realize that as I wait for Chloe to hack into the server at the sheriff's office. It takes hours.

Meanwhile, I go and say hello to Chloe's mom, Mrs. Edwards. She is awake for just long enough to hear my story. I hold her hand in mine and tell her how Joey and I grew apart, how I was fired, and how I am trying to get my brother acquitted. Even this sick, she still listens to everything I say.

"It'll all work out," she finally says, right before she dozes off again. "Eventually it will. It always does. Just don't worry too much."

Hearing her comforting words makes me feel a lot better. When she is heavily asleep, I walk to Chloe's kitchen and find some Oreos in the cabinet. I eat them while waiting. When the box is empty, I make us some more coffee. I call Joey and ask if Salter can stay with him for the night. They both make a thrilled cheering sound, and I am certain I hear them doing fist bumps. They're getting close. That's good. Why do I feel so awful about it? Because I am left out? Am I that selfish?

Apparently.

I sigh and look at Chloe, who is sitting in front of her many screens, working the numbers and running her fingers across her keyboards. I have no clue what she is doing, but I am fascinated, and very impressed.

"There you go," she suddenly says.

I jump up. "You're in?"

"Almost. I found a hole. They all have one if they don't have someone like me to secure their systems. Now, I'll be able to use this hole..."

She taps eagerly, the tip of her tongue sticking out between her lips. I smile to myself because I remember she always used to do that when she was younger too. Some things never change. I know she doesn't notice it, so I say nothing.

"...and I am in."

Chloe leans back in her chair with her hands behind her head with a victorious smile. "Here you go."

I pull up a chair and sit next to her, while she opens the file containing the police report of Blake's arrest. I pull my chair close to better see, and together we read through it. Most of it is a lot of technicalities written in police lingo that I don't think is important. I ask her to go further down to the description of the arrest, and then read through it. I shake my head and read it again.

"There is nothing there," I say. "Not a word about any woman being with him. I was so sure..."

"Why did you think someone was with him when he was arrested?" Chloe asks.

"I found footprints in the studio, high-heeled footprints. And he was seen with this woman at Starbucks right before he was arrested," I say, and pull out my picture of Olivia Hartman.

Chloe whistles when she sees her. "Blake was involved with Olivia?"

"That's what the boys have told me. Apparently, he told Joey, Danny and Alex, but not me."

Chloe goes quiet. I look at her. "Did he tell you?"

"What? No. No. We never spoke about his personal life."

"But you spoke of other things?" I ask surprised.

"Well...no...I mean, yes...sometimes."

"I need the full story, please," I say.

Chloe avoids looking me directly in the eyes. "Okay. Okay. I helped him set up his webpage for his paintings and the other stuff he creates, to make it easier for him to sell them. You know he did coffee tables too and sculptures, and wanted a page where people could order exactly what they wanted, like ordering a pizza. We talked a lot. One thing led to another... He hung out here several days during the week. It only lasted for about a month. It was nothing, really."

"You're kidding me, right? You do realize you're fifteen years older than him, right?"

Chloe blushes. "Of course. But, so is she," she says, and points at Olivia Hartman. "What was it they called her back then?"

"Double O," I say.

Chloe nods. "Because her last name was Owens, that's right. I guess your brother has a thing for us older ladies, huh?"

44

MARCH 1992

THEY MEET on 7th Street at midnight. Ally has butterflies in her stomach. Her mother is travelling again, so she doesn't even know she is out. Not that she would notice if she was home anyway. She is always wrapped up in her work. Always on the phone, always occupied, even when Ally walks into her study and asks her something.

"I'm swamped here. I had a rough day. Can't you solve this yourself? You're a big girl, right?" is her standard answer. Even on the day when Ally wanted to tell her she got an A on her math test. Even on the day when Ally was seven and had been bitten on her arm by the neighbor's dog and she came in to tell her. Even then, she had no time.

"You're late," AK says. She hands her something. "Put this on."

AK pulls her ski mask over her head and covers her face. Ally does the same. AK told her to wear black from top to toe. To make sure she isn't seen in the night. Ally wonders what they are going to do. She still hopes she is just supposed to get drunk and do something stupid, but she has a feeling that is not it. AK points at the house next to them, the one they usually do the campfire in front of. AK has something against the family living there, but she has never told Ally what it is. She always talks about how much she hates them. She once wrote a message for them using their empty beer cans after a long night of drinking.

AK stares at the house. Ally can sense her anger, her hatred. It frightens her slightly.

"Follow me closely," AK whispers. "Don't make a sound. If we get caught, it'll be your fault, and I'll tell the police you put me up to this, that it was all your idea, all right? So you better do it right."

Ally swallows hard, then nods. She doesn't dare to do anything else. She knows AK will do it. A big part of her wants to run away, to get the hell out of there, but she doesn't dare to. She would lose everything. She would lose all of her new friends...all the trust she had worked so hard to gain. She would never have a friend in this town again.

"All right. Let's go AL," AK says. She lights up her face with her flashlight like she was telling a scary story, and Ally can tell by her eyes that she is excited. Her eyes look a little mad. Ally wonders if she is.

AK shuts off the flashlight, then signals for Ally to follow her. They sneak up towards the gate and crawl over the fence. Ally wonders if they have cameras or alarms on the house. But she can't hear anything.

She follows AK up the driveway towards the main entrance, but AK walks past it. She stops at a small window on the side of the house.

"It's broken," she whispers. "It can't lock."

Then she pulls it hard and it opens without making a sound. She looks at Ally triumphantly. "Told you so."

Soundlessly, AK slides through. From the inside, she signals Ally to follow her. Ally sticks her legs through and slides in as well. She lands on the floor with a thud. AK gives her a look. She wants to say she is sorry, but decides it's better to not speak.

AK seems to know her way around the house. She sneaks through the hallways, opening drawers, pulling out jewelry and cash that she apparently knows exactly where is stashed away. She fills her pockets with the valuables, then glides on to the next room. In the kitchen, she finds a checkbook that she steals and a wallet, where she takes a credit card and some more cash. She has a bag that she fills with CDs from the living room. Ally watches her, but doesn't want to take anything. She grabs a photo from above the fireplace and looks at it, then lets out a small gasp. She recognizes the girl in the photo, standing between what can only be her parents. AK sneaks up behind her and looks at it too. Then she pulls it out from between Ally's hands and throws it at the floor. She steps on it with the heel of her black boot, and the glass breaks. It makes a loud sound and the light upstairs is turned on.

"Is someone down there?" a voice asks.

45

SEPTEMBER 2015

I DON'T LEAVE Chloe's house completely empty-handed. Before I go, I find out everything there is in the report about the deceased, Jamilla Jenkins, and I get the name of the witness who claims she saw my brother stab her to death. I know it's illegal, but I don't care. I want to know who she is.

I tell Chloe thank you and run up 7th Street towards my dad's house. The sun has set and it is dark now. I can't stop thinking about poor Snowflake, who has been alone in that room all day. I have completely forgotten about him and the fact that Salter isn't there to walk him.

I open the front door and run upstairs. Snowflake attacks me when I open the door to our room. He is wagging his tail and licking my ears. I giggle and sit on the floor until he stops whimpering.

Then, I spot it.

Right there on the middle of the white, thick, very expensive carpet is a big round yellow spot the size of a paperback. I sigh and look at Snowflake.

"Now what do we do?" I ask him.

He looks at me and wags his tail intently, then creeps up between my legs and hides his head. I can't stop laughing.

"Is that you, Mary?" I hear a voice in the hallway outside the room.

It's Laura! Think fast!

I turn and grab my son's T-shirt from the bed, then let it fall to the carpet. It lands in the second she enters and covers the spot. I smile. I know it must look phony, but she is used to that from me.

"Hi," she says, showing her fake teeth in just as fake of a smile. "I haven't seen you all day. I was beginning to think you wouldn't come home to spend the night. But then I thought, well she can't stay out all night because she has a dog to take care of," she says with a light laugh. "Silly me. Where is Salter?"

"He's staying with his dad tonight. A little bonding time. They need it. He never sees his dad. You know how it is. " It's way more information than I usually give her about anything. It sounds suspicious, even to my own ears.

"How nice," she says, and looks at the T-shirt on the floor next to me. "Maybe you could use the time off from your motherly duties to clean up a little." She sniffs the air and makes me think of a poodle I once knew. Even her hair looks like it. "It's getting a little stuffy in here."

Can she smell the pee?

I can tell that the T-shirt on the floor bothers her. She wants to pick it up herself, but holds herself back. She lets out a sigh.

"I guess you should take the dog out first. It hasn't been out since this morning. It probably needs to...take care of its business."

"Yes. Yes. Come on, Snowflake," I say, and find his leash. "Let me take you out for a little walk. We don't want any accidents to happen, now do we?"

I put the leash on, then walk towards Laura, who is still staring at the T-shirt on the floor. I know she wants me to pick it up, but I don't.

"Excuse me," I say. "I kind of need you to move in order to get out."

"Yes. Of course," she says and moves to the side. "I'll just grab this..."

Before I can stop her, she moves past me, reaches down, and picks up the T-shirt from the floor.

Uh-oh.

I close my eyes, and when I open them, she is staring at the big spot on her nice carpet.

"That's funny," she says, her lips tightened. "I don't recall having a spot on the carpet right there." She looks to me for an answer, then down at the dog. She turns pale, as the realization sinks in. There isn't anything I can say or do anymore. It's over.

Laura doesn't speak another word. She holds a hand to her chest, then storms right past me. She disappears into another room, her own bedroom that she shares with my father, for the most part, when he is not sleeping in one of the other rooms. I hear her yell. Then my dad talks quietly.

Seconds later, my dad comes out. "I'm sorry," he says. "I need you to find somewhere else to stay while you're here. We can't have that dog here."

Even the way he says *that dog*, makes me want to scream.

46

SEPTEMBER 2015

SANDRA IS LOOKING through her book. She stops at a picture of her on the cover of *Elle*. It is one of her favorites if not *the* favorite. It is hard to determine. Every one of these pictures has their story to tell, and right now they are telling the story of Sandra's life. In the beginning, it was mostly surfing brands that wanted to use her. Swimsuits, clothing, surfboards. She had posed with it all. Oh, my, how incredibly young she was back then.

How I miss those days. How I miss looking that young.

Sandra sighs deeply, then puts the book down. Now what? She has never wondered about the future before. Things simply just happened to her when she was younger. She never had the time to wonder what to do when it was all over. Is she getting closer to *that* point now?

Of course she is. She gets older every day, and lately there has been less demand for her. But, can she live without it? She loves the work, loves the way she is pampered and looked at. It is hard work; it's no walk in the park. A photo shoot is many hours spent getting it just right, so it's not something that anyone can just do, you have to be cut out for it. But it has its benefits. It certainly does. Sandra loves the travelling. She loves going places she would never go otherwise. She loves how everything is taken care of when she arrives, the hotel is booked, the people are already there waiting just for her. She is the star. And she does love seeing the end results once the magazine or the commercial comes out. She likes to look at herself and how beautiful they can make her look. Sometimes, she hardly recognizes herself.

Sandra looks at her face in the mirror. She places a hand on each side of her face and pulls the skin back to smoothen out the fine lines. Every day now, it seems they're getting bigger and more plentiful. There is no way of reversing it or even stopping it from happening. Every day, she gets closer to being done in the business. And then what? Is she just going to hang out here in Cocoa Beach with Ryan? He has his business. He is gone all day. There really isn't anything here for her.

"You'll get bored after a week," she tells her own reflection.

She could always go back to surfing full time. But the waves aren't always good, and it would get boring too eventually.

As she is looking at herself, thinking it is all over, her cell phone rings. Sandra picks it up.

"I've got a great job for you, girl," her agent from the agency in New York chirps from the other end.

Yes! I am not done yet!

"It's not until two weeks from now, but it's *Vogue*, so it's worth the wait."

"*Vogue?*" she asks smiling from ear to ear.

If Vogue *wants me I am definitely not done yet.*

"Yes, baby. They want both the cover and three pages inside."

"The cover? You're kidding me?" Sandra asks. It was ages since she last did one of the big magazines...and then the cover on top of it?

"Nope. They love you. They asked for you specifically. I didn't even have to pitch you to them. You're getting hot up here. Once the word is out that you're doing *Vogue* next month they'll be calling from all over for the rest of the year. You're back, baby."

"Really? I'm hot right now?"

"Sure. Retro is in right now. They're bringing in all the faces from the nineties these days. It's hot."

Sandra hangs up, feeling like her life has been turned upside down. She can't stop smiling. Just as she thought it was over, she gets a new life in the business. She had not expected that.

Sandra sits down, staring at her phone. *Florida Today* is on the table underneath. She barely notices the small note on the front page when she puts the phone down on top of the paper. Her eyes pass it, hardly taking it in.

MAN HOSPITALIZED AFTER DRINKING DRAIN CLEANER

At first, her mind is on how stupid people can be. How do you accidentally drink drain cleaner—could he not see the label—or see that the bottle doesn't look like anything else you would drink from? But then, as though a fist suddenly bursts from the page and hits her in the face, she looks again. The picture, the man's name, is it...? Well, yes, it is.

47

SEPTEMBER 2015

I MOVE in with Joey the next morning. I called him after my little chat with my father the night before and he told me he could take me in. Salter is still there and his eyes sparkle when he opens the door for me. I know he loves having all of us together again. Of course he does.

"You can sleep in here," Joey says, and shows me into the bedroom. "I put new sheets on and everything."

"B-but that's your bedroom," I say, slightly confused.

"That's alright," he says. "I'll sleep on the couch downstairs."

"I can't throw you out of your own bed," I say. "I can sleep on the floor in Salter's room."

Joey smiles. "Just take it, okay?"

I nod. "Okay. That is very nice of you."

"You can thank me later," he says with a mischievous smile.

I throw a pillow at him. Meanwhile, I hope he doesn't think this means anything more than me needing a place to crash. I am beginning to long for Manhattan more and more. I don't know why I stay. Well, yes I do. I stay for my brother, because if I don't try and help him, no one else will and he'll get himself killed in jail. But still. I can't wait for this to be over.

Snowflake is already loving the place and running around in the small yard like crazy, playing wildly with Salter and Bonnie and Clyde. Salter is in heaven. So is Snowflake, it seems. He and the other animals seem to take an immediate liking to one another.

I let them play, then pull out my laptop and sit in Joey's kitchen. He places a cup of coffee in front of me. I look up and smile. Our eyes meet.

"You looked like you could use it," he says with that boyish smile of his. Even though he has just woken up, he is still cruelly handsome. I wonder if he is seeing anyone since we split up. I know the girls must be all over him.

"That is very kind of you. Thanks."

"What's all this?" he asks.

I draw in a deep breath. "My brother's case. I'm trying to piece all of it together. The lawyer says it's all about finding holes in the investigation now. If we can sow any doubts about the police doing their job properly, then we might have a chance. Something like that. I'm not a lawyer, obviously."

"Obviously."

Joey grabs a chair and sits on it the wrong way. *He is such a cowboy*, I think to myself.

"Tell me what you've got," he says. "Who was the girl?"

"Her name was Jamilla Jenkins," I say, and open the file on my desktop. I had written down everything the night before, while snorting and heavily cursing my dad.

"She was a military girl, lived on base. She was thirty-three when she died. Her parents were both in the military as well, and she grew up on bases all over the world. I guess it was the world she knew, and therefore it was only natural for her to stay in it once she grew up. She served three times in Iraq and once in Afghanistan. She is a decorated war hero."

"Ouch, that makes it even harder on Blake."

"Tell me about it. The woman testifying against him, claiming she saw him kill Jenkins is also military. Who's going to believe Blake's word over hers?"

"Him, a local artist who never held a real job in his life and who never served his country or risked his life for our freedom or them. That's going to be difficult."

I nod and look at the screen with my notes. I try to picture the two girls standing at the bar in Squid Lips, listening to the band, maybe even dancing and drinking some beers. Witnesses in the bar stated in the file that they saw all of them. They saw the two girls and they saw my brother. They were all hanging out at the bar. Even Blake admits to having been there, sitting at the bar, but he doesn't remember the girls. There were a lot of girls that night, he is quoted saying. He was drunk. He doesn't remember. That isn't new for my brother.

I groan and lean back in my chair. I lift my cup to drink more coffee, but it is empty. I put it down a little too hard. I feel so frustrated.

"Who am I kidding?" I ask. "I'm no investigator. There is no way I can figure out what really happened."

"Have you asked this one?" he says and points at the picture on the table.

"Olivia Hartman?" I ask. "She wasn't there that night. They were just screwing around."

"No, but she is also military. She must know these other two. Maybe Blake told her something. Maybe she knows something. It's worth a try."

"Yeah, but the thing is, she lives on base as well, and there is no way I can get in there," I say.

Joey looks pensively at me. "I might know a guy."

48

MARCH 1979

THEY KEEP the child at the hospital for two days. Penelope never leaves her side. When she needs water, she brings it to her, when she is sad, Penelope strokes her head gently and sings to her. She does everything a good mother is supposed to do. When she has a break, she walks to the payphone and calls Peter, who is still swamped by his work.

On the morning of the second day, the doctor asks Penelope to step outside with him.

Penelope feels anxious as she follows him out into the hallway, where nurses walk by with quick and urgent steps.

"Any news, Doctor?" she asks.

"We have now performed a variety of tests," he says.

She can tell from his face that he is tired.

"And?"

"We tested her blood sugar and blood calcium, we did a urine culture, a lumbar puncture, X-rays, and an intravenous pyleogram, but the tests revealed no abnormalities whatsoever. Neither does the cardiovascular exam that we performed. I did have Dr. Neuhart, our ear, nose and throat specialist, examine her, and he found evidence of a low-grade infection, and because of her previous ear infection, I will recommend an operation called a myringotomy, which entails removal of fluid from the ear drums."

"An ear infection?" Penelope asks. "But...but her heart? What about her heart? What about the vomiting, the staring spells, the seizures?"

"It could all have been caused by the infection she is battling," the doctor says.

Penelope shakes her head. "No. No. Something is wrong with her heart. I had a specialist tell me so. He told me she needs surgery. Her physician told us her heart is sick..."

The doctor places a hand on Penelope's shoulder. "Her heart is fine," he says. "We've run all these tests, and all she has is an ear infection. That's it."

But Penelope is not convinced. She shakes her head again and again, desperately, on the verge of breaking into tears. Her pointer finger is waving in the air.

"No. No. No. You promised me you'd get to the bottom of this. You promised me. It's her heart. I just know it is. Why won't anyone listen to me? I can't believe I can never reach you people."

The doctor looks at her, then at his watch. "I have to go. I will schedule the myringotomy for later today. After the operation is done, I will discharge your child within forty-eight hours."

The doctor turns on his heels and leaves Penelope standing in the hallway. She watches him as he leaves. She doesn't understand. Why won't they listen? How is she supposed to take the child home now? She'll only get sick again. She'll have more seizures, and then they'll have to start all over again. Why can't they figure out what is wrong with her?

Penelope walks back to her child, who is now smiling and seems much better. She strokes her hair gently, then leans over and kisses her. The child is visibly happy to see her mother. The nurse soon brings her breakfast.

"Someone seems to be feeling better," she says, as she places the tray in front of the child.

Penelope smiles and nods. "Yes, she is better. The doctor told us they will remove the fluids in her ears later today, and then we'll be discharged."

"That is excellent news," the nurse says, then leaves.

Penelope waits for her footprints to disappear in the hallway, then reaches into her bag, and pulls out the jar of salt. She pours three handfuls into the child's milk and uses the spoon to mix it. Then she smiles and hands the child the cup.

"Now, finish up, baby girl. Just like last time. You have to drink it all."

49

SEPTEMBER 2015

OF COURSE JOEY knows a guy who can help us get on the base. Joey knows everyone. And, somehow, they all always owe him a favor. It turns out this guy is actually in security and that he can help us get one day passes to the base, even though we can't say we actually have business there.

Admittedly, I am impressed.

Joey drives the car; Salter sits in the back as we approach the gate. A guy in a uniform comes out. I break a sweat. I always do that when people in uniform approach me, especially the police. I can pass a police car in the street, not having done anything at all wrong, and I still find myself shaking, my heart racing, and my hands get clammy. I don't know why. That's just how I am. I hate authorities and I assume they always have it in for me as well. It's not like we're about to do anything illegal. We're just going to talk to someone.

"That's Tim," Joey says, and rolls down the window.

"Hello," he says, then hands us the passes through the window. He looks inside the car, like he is probably supposed to. He looks tough and serious. "We're even now," he says, addressed to Joey. "If anyone asks, you didn't get these passes from me, alright?"

All three of us nod. Tim pulls his head out from the car and signals someone that we are cleared. With my heart in my throat, we drive through the security gate with the many guards following our every move. At least that's what I feel they're doing...watching us closely.

We drive past a big sign welcoming us. We are in. We're inside the base they call *the control center for Cape Canaveral Air Station, America's gateway to space.*

We find the road taking us to the South housing areas. We drive along the big runway for the airplanes, and I watch as a big one takes off into the air. There is water on both sides of the base, since it is located on a thin area of the barrier island. Many of the houses have views over the Intracoastal waters.

Before we left, I called Chloe and had her find the general's address for me. I am holding the piece of paper in front of me where the address is written. I feel nervous, but also determined. I want to find Olivia Hartman and ask her about my brother, about her relationship to him, and if she knows anything that might help us. I pray and hope this pays off somehow.

"It's here," Joey says. "Number 1145, right?"

"Right," I say, and fold the paper with the address on it. I put it in my pocket, then take in a deep breath as Joey parks the car in front of the house.

"Do you want me to go with you?" he asks.

I think about it for a second, and then tell him I can do this on my own. I get out of the car and walk up to the front door and ring the doorbell. It doesn't take long for it to open. There she is. The famous Olivia Hartman. The woman whose picture I have been staring at ever since I found out she was seeing my brother. She is just as beautiful as her picture, and a lot more so than back in high school. Some people age better than others.

"Mary?" she says.

I nod. "We need to talk."

She looks behind me and around us to make sure nobody is looking, then tells me to come inside. I follow her into the house. It's big. Two stories with great views of the Intracoastal. It's nicely decorated as well. Double O has good taste. Expensive as well.

We sit down in her living room. The couch is soft and delicate. The fabric is white. It is obvious they have no children. She looks at me with a sigh.

"I guess I know why you're here."

50

SEPTEMBER 2015

LIZ CAN'T BELIEVE her eyes. Did she just see Mary Mills on the base? Did she just see her drive up to the general's house and walk up to the entrance? Yes, she did. She watched it all when she got back from her run at the track. She saw her ring the doorbell and Olivia Hartman open the door. She can't believe the general's wife actually let her inside.

Liz feels a pinch of worry. What is the bitch doing here, and why is Olivia letting her inside her home?

Liz is doing jumping jacks in front of her own driveway. She is panting and groaning, mostly with anger, and a little with worry. She waits and watches. Waits and watches patiently. When Mary doesn't come back out, Liz decides to go inside her house. She searches through her things frantically and pulls out her gun. She looks at the clock on the wall. She is off until 1300 hours. There is still time. She feels the cold gun between her hands when she loads it. She grumbles in anger.

How the hell is she supposed to do this? She's on base, for crying out loud. If she fires a gun, she'll get caught. She can't escape. Not from the base. Can she pull it off somehow anyway?

Liz growls and looks out the window. The car is still there, parked in the general's driveway. There is no way she can go into the general's house and fire a gun and get away with it. No way. But she can't let her go either, can she? No, she has to do something. Anything.

You should have hit her with your car when you had the chance, you idiot. Now she is here, who knows what she is up to, how she will destroy everything for you again.

Just thinking about Mary makes everything turn inside of Liz. The anger hasn't decreased over the years. On the contrary. She feels it much stronger now than back then. Back when...Argh, just thinking about it makes her want to just go over there and shoot her in the head, not caring one bit about what will happen afterwards. Heck, she could shoot them all if she wants to. She can get away with it, can't she? She has gotten away with so many things so far.

No, it's too dangerous.

Liz looks at the car. It looks like someone is sitting inside of it. Who is it? It looks like a child in the back seat. Is that Mary's child? It looks like it. Could she use him, maybe? But wait. There is someone else in the car. It looks like a man.

Damn it!

Liz sighs, frustrated. She isn't good with spontaneous decisions. She likes to be in control. She likes to plan ahead and then act. Like the day with Billy the Kid. She had planned what she wanted to do and bought the drain cleaner. The past few days she has thought long and hard about what to do about Mary, now that she is back, and she believes she has come up with an idea that will be her best to date. But now this happens? Liz doesn't know what to do. She lifts the gun and walks to the window, pointing it at the car. Liz is an excellent shot. Always hits her target. Never misses a single shot when in the field. She always gets her man.

Or woman.

Liz knows she can shoot the boy from where she is standing. They're less than a mile away. Her 9mm can make the shot. But then what? She needs to think about her escape as well. Maybe she can think about that later. Her desire to hurt Mary drowns out all other thoughts. Right now, she is blinded by it. By her rage.

God, how I hate her. How I loathe everything about her.

But she wants her to suffer. To feel pain, to be hurt. That is when it hits her. That is when the idea comes to her mind like lightning from a clear blue sky.

What hurts the most?

Liz laughs at her own cleverness. She looks at the car across the street and is filled by a triumphant sensation.

51

SEPTEMBER 2015

"I NEED you to tell me everything you know about my brother," I say.

Olivia, or Double O, looks at me. I know she doesn't want me there; in fact, I am probably the last person she wants in her house right now. But I am not leaving. Not until I get some answers.

"And don't tell me you don't know him, 'cause I know you two were seeing each other."

Olivia's green eyes stare at me. To my surprise, she seems frightened. Maybe she is just acting.

"I...I don't know what to tell you." She sighs and looks away. "Yes, we met at a party at the Officer's Club, and we have had some fun, that's all."

"Fun?" I ask feeling, anger rise inside of me. Was that all my brother was to her? A toy?

She shakes her head; her eyes search the floor. "I don't know what to say."

"Start by telling me what happened. Why is he in jail right now?" I ask.

Olivia looks up again and our eyes meet. Hers are full of regret. "You should go...if my husband finds out...he has eyes and ears everywhere here. It was very dangerous of you to come here."

"I don't care about your husband or who he is. I demand to know what happened to my brother. You were with him, weren't you? You were with him when he was arrested, weren't you?"

Olivia shakes her head. I can tell she is lying. She is not a very good liar.

"Come on!" I say. "You were seen at Starbucks together. You were seen leaving together. Did you go back to his place to have sex, huh? To have some of your *fun*, huh?"

Olivia's eyes are growing wider.

"You can't lie to me, Olivia. I know you were there. I saw your shoeprint in his studio. You stepped in some blue paint. I just can't seem to figure out why that part was left out of the police report. Are they working together? Is the detective in the general's pocket?"

I can tell by the look in her eyes that I am right. "So, they framed him, huh? They framed my brother because he was sleeping with you." I look down at her hand and spot the ring with the green stone from my brother's bathroom. "Nice ring, by the way."

Olivia reaches out and grabs my arm with a gasp. "You've got to be careful, Mary. These people are capable of anything. Yes, they framed Blake. They even forced me to place the bloody chisel under the sink so the police would find it. The general found out about us weeks ago and has been planning this all along. He'll do anything. He'll get rid of you as well if he knows that you know."

"I am not scared of him," I snort.

"You should be. And now you must leave. The word about you being here must have reached my husband by now."

I stare at the woman whom I used to go to school with and wonder what happened to her. Back then, she had been so strong. So tough. Now she was reduced to this shadow of her former self.

That's when I notice the bruises on her arm. She sees it in my eyes and rolls down her sleeve. Even though Olivia has never been and will never be my favorite person, I feel bad for her all of a sudden.

"You should get out of here," I say. "Why don't you leave him?"

Her eyes turn moist. I can tell she is terrified just by the thought.

"Don't you think I've tried? I love your brother. I wanted to leave the general for him. It was more than just a fling to me. Blake was...well...it doesn't matter anymore. There is no way out for me. Now you must go before they get here."

I rise to my feet. I walk towards the door when I turn and look at her again. "If you planted the evidence that framed my brother, then who killed Jamilla Jenkins?"

Olivia shakes her head. "I don't know. Now, please. Leave."

52

SEPTEMBER 2015

I WALK BACK to the car and get in. Everything inside of me is pumping like crazy. I feel so angry, yet so frustrated at the same time.

"What happened?" Joey asks. He puts down the phone. I can tell he has been playing Candy Crush. Salter is on his iPad. My pulse is throbbing in my throat. I feel like crying. Or screaming. Maybe both.

"He was framed," I say. "Olivia told me they framed him. She was in on it. Because of the affair. The general has it in for my brother and he has got the police working for him."

"Wow. That was a lot of information you got from that brief meeting," Joey says.

I sigh. "Yes, but what can I use it for? If the police have decided that Blake is guilty, they'll make sure to prove it. They have all the evidence in the world. And there is no way I am ever going to get Olivia to tell the truth in a courtroom. The woman was terrified just to talk to me. Yet, she is the only one who knows the real story." I hit my hand a few times hard on the dashboard. "Damn you, Blake!"

Joey puts a hand on my shoulder like he always used to when I was upset.

"I don't want to calm down," I say to him. "I am entitled to be angry. He messed with the wrong people, Joey. And now he is paying the price. But it's a price that is much too high. It'll end up killing him. And there is nothing I can do to help him."

"So, if they planted the evidence, then who killed the girl?" Joey asks all of a sudden.

"That's what I asked," I say. "Olivia said she doesn't know. I believe her. She's a bad liar."

"So, let me get this straight. They had Olivia plant the chisel, but what about the witness? They had her lie too?"

I shrug. "Yeah, sure. She's an army girl too. They're all in on it."

"Do you have a name?"

"Sure. Jamie Barley, why?"

"Why not pay her a visit while we're here? There's a guy walking over there. I bet he knows where she lives."

Before I can protest, Joey jumps out of the car and runs to a man in uniform. I think about what Olivia said about the general having people everywhere. If that is true, then this guy is probably one of them. Joey talks to him and I watch as they chitchat. I can tell by Joey's body language that he is getting what he wants. He smiles when he returns to the car.

"She lives further down the road and to the right. I got the address," he says, and gets in.

We drive down the road and find the address. I walk up to the door and ring the doorbell. I can't help but look around me constantly. I feel like there are eyes on me everywhere.

The door is opened immediately. But it is not Jamie Barley that is in the doorway. It's a man. A uniformed man.

"Hi. I'm looking for Jamie Barley," I say, trying to sound like I'm not terrified, but my eyes give me away. I smile awkwardly. The guy is quite intimidating. He looks at me and doesn't smile back. He grabs my arm and leans over and speaks with a very low voice, almost a whisper, in my ear.

"If you know what's best for you, you get the hell out of here. You are not welcome here. Go back to your son, your dog, and husband and take them with you back to New York before it's too late."

He lets go of my arm and I gasp because it hurts so badly. Now he smiles. Widely.

"A message from the general," he adds.

53

SEPTEMBER 2015

"LET'S GET OUT OF HERE."

I get in the car and avoid looking at Joey.

"What happened? You're all pale," he says.

I shake my head. "I...I think I was just threatened by someone working for the general."

Joey turns the engine over and starts driving. I can't figure out what I am feeling. I am angry. I am so angry I could explode, but I am also terrified. I have never been threatened like that before. If it was only me, it would be different, but I have responsibilities. I have to think about my child. Still, I have to help Blake, right? I can't leave him like this.

I have no idea what to do. Where to go from here.

"So, I take it you didn't get to talk to Jamie Barley?" Joey says, as we leave the housing quarters. I am sweating heavily. I feel so paranoid, thinking they are watching us, watching our every move.

"No," I say. "Only the guy that said he had a message from the general. He basically told us to leave town because we weren't safe or welcome here. It scared the crap out of me. He even knew we lived in New York. And that we had a dog. Look, I still have goose bumps and I'm not cold. On the contrary, I'm sweating."

Joey hits his hand onto the dashboard in anger. "I shouldn't have let you go in there alone. I knew it. I just knew it. They can't do this to you. They can't threaten you like that. I just wanna...I wanna go back and...Scaring you like that. Who do these people think they are?"

"Well, in here, they're the people in charge. But they're not getting to me. I might be leaving the base, but I am not going anywhere. I am not stopping. I will find out what happened to Jamilla Jenkins and have my brother acquitted. I feel more determined than ever. After what Olivia told me, there is no doubt in my heart that my brother is innocent, and I will do whatever it takes to prove it," I say, as we approach the exit of the base.

We have to wait in a line to get out. Soldiers are picking out random cars for a more thorough check. Making sure people don't take out anything they're not supposed to.

Joey looks at me while we wait for it to be our turn. I can tell he is scared. "You're not doing this alone," he says. "I'll be with you, and I am sure the rest of the crew will as well."

"Me too, Mom," I hear Salter say, just as the soldier at the gate points at our car and pulls us aside. They ask us to get out because they are doing a random search and our car has been chosen.

Yeah right! Random!

We wait while they split the car to pieces. They even take out the seats. I have to really focus to keep calm. I want to tell them how I feel about all this, but Joey's arm around my shoulder keeps me from doing it. I look at him and he smiles from ear to ear and thanks the soldiers for doing their duty. I want to pull his hair out, but know that he is right. That it is the only way to go about this, even though I hate it. This is their territory, and they have the power to make us wait all day if they like.

It takes forty-five minutes before they are done and we can finally leave the base. I feel a huge relief as we drive out into A1A, where it no longer feels like a thousand eyes are constantly examining us.

I still have this feeling of extreme unease as we drive back into Cocoa Beach. We stop at the gas station and buy some candy for Salter and me. I am in desperate need of something sweet to make me feel better. I buy a bag of chips as well, and some sodas for later. Joey fills up the car while Salter and I fill up on goodies. I open a chocolate bar right away while we walk back to the car. Sirens are wailing and a huge fire truck drives past us on A1A. Joey points.

"Looks like there's a big fire somewhere," he says.

I see the smoke in the distance, but take no further notice of it. Neither does Salter or Joey. We get in the car and drive off. As we get further up A1A, we realize the fire is getting closer. As we reach 10th Street, my heart drops and I stop breathing.

"Oh, my God," Joey exclaims. "The fire. It's at your dad's house! The fire is in your father's house!"

54

MARCH 1992

ALLY LOOKS to AK for a signal, a sign, anything to tell her what to do. Mary Mills is standing at the top of the stairs looking down at them. She has seen them, but still she is not saying anything. It's like she and AK are staring at each other, sizing each other up.

Ally is waiting for Mary to scream and for AK to run, but nothing happens. They are just staring at each other. Does Mary know it is AK? Does she recognize her behind the mask?

"What do you want?" Mary finally asks.

AK doesn't answer. She is staring at Mary, her body trembling. It's like she is paralyzed. Ally has never seen her like this before.

"Why have you come here?" Mary asks.

There are more steps coming from upstairs and a door is opened. A man comes out and stands behind Mary. Ally guesses it's her father. It's the same man from the picture that AK just smashed. The one that is scattered all over the floor.

"What's going on?" he asks. "Who is this? What are you doing in my house?" he yells.

Mary turns to look at him. "It's her," she says. "It's Anne-Katelyn."

The man calms down. His shoulders fall back into place. "Oh."

Ally is surprised. She had never heard AK's real name before. She is stunned that Mary knows it. Mary's dad reaches out his arms.

"Katie," he says.

"Don't," AK suddenly yells. "Don't call me that. You have no right to call me that. And don't come any closer!"

Then she says something that makes Ally's blood freeze.

"I have a gun!"

"Katie," Mary says. "I know you don't want to hurt anyone."

"Yes! Yes, I do," AK yells, then pulls out the gun and points it at them. "I want to hurt all of you."

Ally gasps and pulls back. She has never seen a real gun before. She can tell by AK's voice that she is desperate. It scares her. It terrifies her to her core. She doesn't know what AK is capable of. Could she kill someone?

This is not going to end well.

"AK...maybe we should..." She tries to speak to her, but AK doesn't listen. It's like she is in this trance of anger that she can't escape. Ally can't reach her.

The gun is shaking in AK's hand. She is sniffling behind her mask.

"We never meant to hurt you, Katie," the dad says.

"We only did what was best," Mary says.

Ally tries hard to figure out what the heck is going on. She has no idea what they're talking about, how they know each other. She feels like crying. She wants to get out of there so badly. She looks towards the entrance door and wonders if AK would shoot her if she tried to escape.

Probably.

Ally doesn't dare to try. She stands completely still and hopes AK will calm down and come to her senses.

"Katie. We..." The dad tries to say something, but he doesn't get any further before AK interrupts him.

"You know what hurts the most?" she yells with bitterness to her voice. "That I was so close. I was so damn close."

"What is going on out here?"

A woman Ally recognizes from the picture as the mother comes out of the door and approaches the others.

"Who is yelling? You're waking the baby."

When the gun goes off, the bullet moves so fast that Ally only sees the mother freeze in the air before the blood spurts out of her stomach. While Mary screams, the woman tumbles down the stairs, one step at a time.

55

SEPTEMBER 2015

"MY FATHER'S house is on fire!"

I storm out of the car. A fire truck has just pulled up and they're trying to get the fire under control. I spot Danny among them and run up to him. He grabs my shoulders and looks into my eyes.

"Is there anyone in there, Mary?"

"I...I don't know," I say. They're usually home at this time. I think. Can't you send anyone inside to check?"

He shakes his head. "It's way too dangerous right now. The fire has gotten to the roof, and it's going to crash in a matter of seconds."

I am desperate now. As we speak, a car drives up, and a woman jumps out. She screams. I turn and look at her. It's Laura. She is cupping her mouth and screaming. I run to her.

"Laura, where is my dad? Laura!"

She doesn't even look at me. She points at the fire and simply screams in shock.

"Laura!" I yell. "Is my dad in there?"

She looks at me and nods. My heart stops.

"H-h-he was taking a n-n-nap," she stutters. "I went to Publix for just half an hour."

I turn to look at Danny, then I scream at the top of my lungs while running to him.

"My dad is in there! My dad is in the house!"

As I yell, I am drowned out by a loud crash when the roof collapses. I fall to my knees and scream.

"NOOOOO!"

Joey grabs me in his arms and tries to pull me away from the fire. The firefighters are yelling at each other and at people to stay back. They're yelling at me and Joey to get out of there. I can hardly hear them anymore. It's all a blur. The smoke, the people, the screams. I can't take it anymore. Joey is pulling me, but I can't let him. I can't just go away. I refuse to give up.

I pull myself free of him, then storm towards a window on the side of the house that hasn't popped yet. I see nothing but smoke on the other side, but I also know this is my father's study, his favorite room to work in and nap in his chair.

"No! Mary, no!" Joey yells.

"It's too late!" Danny yells.

While everyone is screaming behind me, I jump. Like Superman, I jump through the glass window. Glass is everywhere. I cut myself on my hands and face before I land on the floor inside. Fire is licking up the walls in the room and I stay low to not inhale too much smoke.

"Daaaad?" I scream, while beams are falling on all sides of me. I realize I can't breathe and start to cough heavily, when suddenly I hear something. The adrenalin is rushing through my veins as I spot my dad. He's on the floor, so close to the window, lying flat on his stomach, his arm stretched out like he is reaching for the window, for the outside.

You almost made it, didn't you?

He is stuck underneath a fallen beam. It's still on fire, so I can't touch it. Instead, I kick it with all I have, while pieces of the roof are still falling around my ears. I get him free, then grab his arm and pull him up on my back. As I approach the window, I scream.

"Heeeelp!"

I see something. Through the smoke, I see movement. I carry my dad closer, hoping and praying we won't be hit by anything falling, when I spot Danny jumping through the window, wearing all his gear. He spots us when he lands, then runs to us. He's got a couple of big wet blankets that he throws on top of us, then he grabs my dad and lifts him up, while I run forward, my arms covering my head, holding the blanket over my back. I manage to get myself back out the window, cutting my leg and ripping my dress. When I am outside, I throw myself on the ground. Exhausted, out of breath, coughing, and scared to death.

Joey runs up to me and helps me get to my feet. I watch as the firefighters help Danny carry my father out of the window and towards the paramedics. They're all over him. I try to get close.

"Is he alive?" I ask.

No one answers. I try hard not to cry.

Please, dear God. Please, don't take him too.

"We've got a pulse," I hear someone say, then fall to my knees and let it all go.

56

SEPTEMBER 2015

I GO with the ambulance to the hospital in Cape Canaveral. Joey drives Salter there and they meet me in the waiting room. Salter runs into my arms and holds me tight.

"That was really dangerous, Mommy," he says.

"You gave us quite a scare," Joey says and hugs me as well. We hold each other like we used to, back when we were still a family. "I thought I was going to lose you."

"I am sorry," I say, crying and holding my loved ones close. Gone is all the hurt; gone is all the pain. It doesn't matter anymore. These are the people I love and I am so grateful to still be alive and to have them in my life. So happy I can still hold them in my arms.

"I am so sorry," I say through tears. "I just couldn't leave him in there to die. I just couldn't."

We let go of each other and sit down to wait. Salter keeps ahold of my hand. Joey has a hard time holding back his tears.

"Have they checked you?" he asks, biting his lip. "You could have suffered from smoke inhalation injury or something. They need to check you."

I nod. "I know," I say and cough.

"Is Grandpa going to be alright?" Salter asks with concern.

I pull him closer and kiss the top of his head. "We don't know yet, sweetheart. We don't know. But I do have hope."

A doctor enters the room and I get up. "Any news about my father?" I ask, but he shakes his head.

"We're doing all we can to save him, but we need to take a look at you as well. Right now. Smoke inhalation is a serious thing."

I follow the doctor and they put me in a bed. They do a chest X-ray to determine if there is lung injury. They attach a probe to my finger to determine the degree of oxygen in my blood. They run a series of blood tests and finally they hook me up with an oxygen tank. I am hoarse and I do find it hard to breathe on my own, so I am happy to be in good hands. But several hours later, I still don't know how my dad is doing. I am terrified of losing him.

Finally, a doctor comes to my bedside. He tells me I have suffered a minor smoke inhalation injury and that there may still be shortness of breath with minimal exertion in the coming days.

"It may take time for your lungs to fully heal, and some people may have scarring and shortness of breath for the rest of their lives. It's important to avoid triggering factors, such as cigarette smoke. You'll need to have follow up visits with your own doctor, but other than that, I'll recommend you'll be discharged tomorrow morning. Seek medical help if your symptoms worsen," he says.

I pull off the oxygen mask to speak. I still have shortness of breath, and speaking makes me tired.

"How is he?" I ask, not caring one bit about what he is telling me about myself. "Is he alive?"

"Your father is alive, yes. He is still in critical condition. It's too early to say."

"But he's still alive?" I say.

"Yes."

The doctor leaves and I lean back in my bed. Minutes later, Salter and Joey peek in.

"How's the patient?" Joey asks.

I can tell that Salter is scared.

"I'm fine," I say, sounding more cheerful than I feel. I didn't like the look on the doctor's face when he told me about my father. It wasn't hopeful.

I ask Salter to come closer, then have him sit on the edge of my bed. I look into his eyes. "Mommy will be fine, alright? The doctor just told me so."

"Why do you have all that, then?" he asks and points at the oxygen mask that I have pulled down to be able to speak.

"Ah, this old thing? It's just to help me breathe better, they say. I don't really need it. They're just being very overprotective around here."

I end the sentence with a deep cough and have to pull the mask back on to breathe. I take in a few deep breaths, then pull it off again. Salter looks at me, worried. I try to smile.

"There's someone else here to see you," Joey says, and opens the door.

In comes first Danny carrying a fistful of balloons. Then Alex, Sandra, Marcia, and Chloe follow him.

It melts my heart to see all of them here, and now I start to really cry.

"Aw, you guys."

57

JANUARY 1984

"HERE'S YOUR DAUGHTER. She is a little shy."

The lady from the adoption agency kneels next to the young girl. "There's no need to be scared," she says to her. "These are your new parents."

The young girl looks up at Penelope and Peter. She is seven years of age, the agency has told them. Just like their own daughter.

"Oh, Peter, she is perfect," Penelope says, smiling. She is happy. They both are. After years of trying to have a second child, it was the right decision to adopt.

"We've wanted another child for so long," Penelope says to the lady from the adoption agency.

The lady smiles. "I'm sure you'll all be very happy together. I understand there is another child in the family?"

"Yes, we have another daughter. She is actually the exact same age. I hope they'll have so much fun together. It's going to be almost like having twins."

"Where is your daughter now?" the lady asks.

Peter's smile stiffens.

"She is not well," Penelope says. "She had an emergency last night and had to be taken to the hospital. We'll go there now and see her with her new sister."

The lady from the adoption agency looks at Penelope. "Oh, I am so sorry," she says. "Will she be alright?"

"We hope so. The doctors simply can't figure out what is wrong. It is frustrating."

"That must be very hard on you both."

Peter doesn't say anything. Penelope nods her head. "It is. It's always tough when it's the little ones, you know? You want so badly to make them feel better, but there isn't anything we can do. That reminds me. We should get going. They're running more tests this afternoon."

Penelope looks at the little girl and reaches out her hand. "Hi there, sweetheart. What beautiful eyes you have. How do you feel about going to the hospital to meet your sister?"

The girl looks at Penelope, terrified. Penelope knows her story and knows she has to be careful with her. She has to gain her trust.

"I understand she has moved around a lot?" Peter asks.

"Yes. As you know from the file we sent you, she lost her parents when she was three, and since then she has been moving around to different foster homes and families, and it has just been a mess for her. I do hope it'll work out with you. She needs a stable family now."

"Oh, we can provide that for her," Penelope chirps. "Come with us."

The girl is still staring at Penelope's hand with skeptical eyes.

"And you do know about the last family she was with, don't you?" the lady asks.

Penelope nods. "Yes. Awful story. To think that they would have those orgies at their house with the child there; it's painful."

"And you must know that she was abused by several of the members of their satanic cult. That was why we had to remove her."

"Well, you won't see any of that stuff around here," Penelope says. "We're good old God-loving church-going folks."

Then she laughs. Peter chuckles along. The little girl stares at them still, while she makes her decision.

"Come on," Penelope says, and moves her hand closer. Finally, the girl decides to grab it.

Penelope smiles. "We'll take good care of you. Don't you worry."

58

SEPTEMBER 2015

"WE'RE STILL WORKING on the site, but I wanted to tell you in person that we're ruling it arson."

Danny is standing at my bedside, looking seriously at me. "The electrical wiring, the appliances, and all other potential accidental causes of a fire have been ruled out. The burn patterns show the fire was set in a back room of the house with the use of an accelerant—gasoline. I have seen it enough times in my professional life to be sure."

"So, you're telling me someone broke into my father's house and set it on fire?" I ask.

"Yes. That's what we believe."

"With him inside of it!" I exclaim, feeling the anger build.

Joey grabs my hand in his. I pull away. I am angry right now. I am entitled to be. I don't want comfort or pity. I want whoever did this to pay, to go to jail.

"Have you informed the police?" I ask.

"We will. As soon as the investigation is done."

"Good."

Sandra approaches me, her head slightly tilted, pity in her eyes. "I am so sorry," she says. "It's terrible what has happened to you and your father."

"Do you have any idea who might have wanted to hurt your father?" Danny asks.

I look to Joey. Our eyes meet. He knows what I think.

"No," I say. "But I do have an idea who wants to hurt me."

Joey tells them about our visit to the base and the threat from the man in Jamie Barley's house.

"You really think they would go this far?" Marcia asks. She seems more present than usual. She doesn't smell like alcohol, but her eyes tell me she is on something else.

I shrug and look to Joey again. "I didn't hear the threat," he says. "I was in the car, but you were pretty shaken up when you came back. These people are dangerous."

"They're the ones who framed Blake," I say.

All eyes turn to look at me.

"What?" Sandra asks.

"What are you saying?" Chloe asks, stepping closer to me.

I take a deep breath of oxygen through the mask to better be able to speak. The sound reminds me of the time when I went scuba diving in the Keys. "I spoke to Olivia Hartman earlier today. You all remember her, right? Double O?"

They all nod. Alex and Danny look at each other while nodding, and I can tell they still find her hot. "Well, she was seeing Blake. Some of you already know this, but they had an affair. I have a feeling it has been going on for quite some time. She is married to General Hartman, and he apparently found out about them, then decided to get rid of Blake once and for all. Olivia told me that he forced her to put the bloody chisel under the sink and informed the police about it. Somehow, I believe Detective Chris Fisher is in his pocket, because when I went to Blake's studio, Chris Fisher came in and was looking for a ring. Olivia's ring. And when I visited her today, she was wearing it. I think Detective Fisher is in the general's pocket. He helped him frame Blake, told him where to find the body and the chisel, and provided a witness for him. Jamie Barley. It was at her house that I was threatened."

I stop to breathe in the mask again. I feel tired, but the anger still keeps me going. I can't believe the general would try to kill my dad just to scare me.

"So, Blake is innocent," Chloe says. "We know that for sure now. He just slept with the wrong woman."

"Yes," I say. "And I am determined to prove that."

"But how?" Sandra asks.

"I don't know yet. It's not like Olivia will testify. She's way too afraid of her husband. If only I could get to Jamie Barley, the witness, and talk to her. Or if I could somehow figure out who really killed Jamilla Jenkins."

I sigh and put on the mask again. My throat is sore and I am hoarse. I can feel the aftermath of the smoke inhalation injury now. The doctor told me it would happen, that I would feel tired and short of breath. I look at Danny and grab his hand.

"How are you doing?" I ask. "Any news about the investigation?"

He shakes his head, then looks down.

"There was another one," Alex says.

"What?"

Danny nods in agreement. "It's true. Someone else was killed yesterday in her home here in Cocoa Beach by the same killer as Jean."

"How do you know it was the same killer?" I ask, baffled.

"She was found in her home with a pair of scissors in her throat," Alex says. "Just like Jean."

"The strange part is that it is another person we know from high school," Danny says.

"Who?"

59

SEPTEMBER 2015

CASSIE MORGAN? Cassie is dead? I can't believe what they are telling me. I am breathing hard in my mask now, sucking all the oxygen I can out of it, while trying to calm myself down. What the heck is going on here? Another woman from my high school who has been murdered? Is someone targeting people from my high school? Just going randomly through the yearbook or what? And why?

"They used to be friends," I say, once I remove the mask again. "Do you remember? Jean and Cassie?"

"Sure," Sandra says. "They always hung out together. Knew each other since preschool at FUMC."

Most of us actually went to the same preschool together, those of us that were born and raised in Cocoa Beach. I mostly remembered Joey from back then, since he had already decided that we were going to get married once we grew up, and told me once when his grandfather brought him into school one day.

He pointed at me and said: "This is the girl I want to marry."

All the grown-ups laughed, naturally. But Joey and I both took it very seriously. We remained friends all the way through elementary and surfed together constantly through high school. We even went away to college together, and that was when we started dating. We had always been together, always enjoyed hanging out so much. How could we have gone so wrong?

"Anyone else freaking out about this?" Marcia asks. "I mean, it is kind of creepy that two girls, two best friends that we grew up with have been killed. It doesn't sound like some burglary gone wrong or some psycho walking in randomly from the street. These girls have been murdered. Targeted and murdered. So, the question is...who is next? I, for one, am locking my doors tonight."

I nod pensively, thinking it is amazing that Cocoa Beach is still this small community where people don't lock their doors. After living in New York for a few years, I can't imagine not locking everything safely. But I get what she is saying. Something is off here.

"What do we know about Jamilla Jenkins?" Joey suddenly asks. "I mean, the only way we can help Blake is to figure out who killed her, or at least get the jury to doubt he could have done it. Like the lawyer told Mary, we need to show that the investigation wasn't done properly or thoroughly enough. Now that we know he was framed, there must be evidence out there that the police have overlooked."

I shrug. "Not much. She was a soldier. Was found in a motel room, Motel 6 on A1A, stabbed in her chest."

"Don't they have surveillance cameras on these places?" Chloe asks.

I shrug again. "Sounds like they should have."

"They do," Danny says. "At the front desk. There was a fire a few years ago in one of the rooms. It turned out to be an arsonist traveling through town, and they found his picture from the surveillance cameras when he checked in."

I look to Chloe. She nods. She knows what I am thinking. "I can give it a try. I might also be able to find a little on the girl from the army's database. It might not be usable for anything, but they have her files there. I can check them out."

"The army database?" Danny says. "That sounds like something you could go to jail for, for a long time."

Chloe shrugs. "They'll never know it's me. Patrick Air Force Base is one of my clients. I work on securing their systems. I already have access."

"All right," I say. "I'll call the lawyer and tell him what I know so far."

"Do any of you remember Joanne?" Sandra suddenly says.

We all nod. Joanne is a girl who went to our school as well. She became pregnant at only sixteen and had to drop out of school. Most of us haven't seen her since. Except for Sandra, that is. They used to be good friends.

"I kept in touch with her over the years and helped her out with the baby. Her life changed completely and we drifted apart, but every now and then, when I came back from my trips I would go visit. Her son is now twenty-two. His name is Billy."

"Yeah. And?" Marcia asks impatiently.

"Well, yesterday I saw his picture in the paper. Apparently, he was hospitalized for drinking drain cleaner. I couldn't believe it was him and went to visit. He has suffered severe damage to his mouth and trachea, the windpipe. They don't know if he will be able to breathe on his own again."

"That's terrible," I say.

"The thing is, the doctor told Joanne that it looks like it was forced into his mouth. The way he was bruised around his mouth and the fact that it went into his windpipe and not the gullet shows that he was in distress, and therefore he hyperventilated and pulled the liquid into his lungs. Like he was panicking. Unfortunately, he is unable to speak to tell what happened. The police say they believed he drank it himself, that he tried to kill himself, but Joanne doesn't believe he would do that."

"That's odd," Joey says. "Who would be so cruel as to force him to drink that stuff?"

"That's what I was wondering," Sandra says. "I found it very strange. But the reason I mention it is that he was also found in a hotel room, at the International Palms Resort. The police say they don't want to spend resources on investigating it, but I thought, what if he wasn't alone? Maybe Chloe could find out who he went there with. Just to help out Joanne? For old time's sake."

60

SEPTEMBER 2015

THE NEXT MORNING, I am being discharged. Joey has taken the morning off from work to come and pick me up. Salter is with him. They're smiling and have even brought me a box of chocolates. I open the box right away. Hospital food hasn't done much for me, and I'm craving something sweet.

We all go to see my dad. He is lying in his bed when we enter. Tubes and everything. His eyes are closed. It's just like the movies. Instruments are beeping, telling me he is in fact still alive, even if he seems more like he is dead.

I take in a deep breath. My throat is still sore. I walk to him and take his hand. Salter and Joey stay behind while I approach him. A nurse walks in and stands on the other side of him.

"He doesn't seem to react to anything," she says. "Maybe he will when he hears his daughter's voice."

My dad is still in a coma. He is severely burned on two thirds of his body. They had to transplant skin from other places of his body. He looks terrible. I start to cry and lean in over him.

"Oh, Dad. I am so so sorry. This is all my fault. I am so sorry. Please, don't give up. Please, come back to me. I need you. We never talked. We never made amends. We just let time pass. Why did we do that, Daddy? Why didn't we ever talk about what happened?"

Joey comes closer. I feel his hand on my back. He pulls me closer and hugs me. "Don't be so hard on yourself," he whispers.

I sob heavily. "I blamed him, Joey. I blamed him for everything. I always wanted to talk to him about what happened, but I never dared. Instead, I became angry with him. Bitter and angry. I can't blame him for running into the arms of Laura. I was a terrible teenager. When Mom died, I went completely mad and blamed it all on him. I never thought about how it affected him. He lost her too. So did Blake. I only thought about how bad I felt. And he was the only one I could take it out on."

"I know," Joey says. "I was there, remember?"

I look at him and chuckle. "True. You were always there. You have always been here by my side. What happened to us?"

Joey shrugs. "We grew up. We believed life would be a dance on roses once we got married and had a child. But it wasn't. It's not easy being a grown-up."

I chuckle again while Joey wipes away a couple of my tears. Our eyes meet and lock for just a second. I want him to kiss me, and then I don't. I am vulnerable right now and don't want to do anything I'll regret. I love him, yes. But do I trust him? Do I want to open that door again? I don't think so.

"We should go," Joey says. "I gotta get to work."

I nod and sob again. I grab my dad's hand in mine again and squeeze it. When I let go of it, it falls flat back on the bed. I touch his cheek. It feels cold. I wonder if he can hear anything in there behind those closed eyelids. The instruments keep telling me that he is alive, with their little beeps and dings, but I feel like I have lost him. Maybe I already did many years ago?

I lean over him and kiss him on the forehead. The nurse smiles at me when I draw back.

"We'll let you know immediately if anything happens," she says. "Hopefully, we'll have good news soon."

I nod. "Thank you. I appreciate it."

When we walk out of the room, I feel Joey's hand in mine. I let him take it because I need his care right now. I only hope that Salter doesn't believe that we're back together again.

When we're in the car, I find my phone and call James Holland, Blake's lawyer. Joey drives out on 520 and I have a lump in my throat, thinking about my dad, who is still back at the hospital all alone.

"We need to talk," I say, when the lawyer comes to the phone. "I have reason to believe Blake was framed. As a matter of fact, I spoke to someone who admitted to having placed the chisel in his studio to make sure he was arrested for it. Now, I can't convince her to testify. So what do you suggest we do?"

James Holland lets out a deep sigh from the other end. I don't understand why he doesn't sound happy.

"I wish you would have brought this to me a little sooner," he says.

"Why?"

"Yesterday, your brother declared himself guilty."

61

MARCH 1992

THE GUN DROPS to the floor. AK is staring at the woman, who is no longer falling. She is lying at the bottom of the stairs, head first into the plush carpet, blood gushing out of her and coloring the carpet around her.

Ally's heart has stopped. She can't breathe. The sight of the woman lying lifeless on the stairs makes her sick to her stomach. She bends over and throws up. Meanwhile, Mary and her father rush down the stairs. There's a lot of screaming and crying and yelling. AK looks at Ally. Her eyes are terrified.

"Run," she yells through the chaos.

Ally shakes her head. "Where can we go?"

AK grabs Ally's arm and pulls. "I don't know. Just out of here."

Not knowing what else to do, Ally decides to follow AK out the front door and into the street. They throw their ski masks in a bush and run. When they hear sirens in the distance, they decide to go down to the beach and run instead. To not be seen. It's dark down there. Ally doesn't care. She's in shock. She doesn't know what else to do. So she just follows AK, tears rolling down her cheeks, wondering where they can go. There is nowhere to hide, nowhere for them to stay.

I just watched someone die. My God, what have I done?

They reach the lifeguard tower on 16th Street and Ally knows they're now leaving downtown Cocoa Beach. They can still hear sirens and they spot a police car drive past on the road. By now, everyone is looking for them. There is no way they can get away.

"What do we do?" Ally whispers with a pounding heart.

"We keep going," AK says.

They run across the sand. Ally is sweating and panting heavily. They pass Taco City and continue till they reach the last house on Cocoa Beach, where Ally knows the Air Force Base starts. She is tired now and can barely even walk anymore. AK is worn out too. But they have to. They have to keep moving.

That's when they spot the three houses. Three small houses on the beach that are owned by the Air Force, that they know are used to house military personnel.

"Come," AK says and pulls Ally's arm. "They look empty."

They choose the first one and walk up to it and look in the windows before AK breaks one of them with her elbow. She cries in pain and then crawls through. Ally feels sick again and throws up once more. She suddenly misses her mother more than ever.

What have I done? How will I ever get out of this?

AK opens the front door and grabs Ally's arm. She pulls her inside and closes the door. They both fall to the floor, panting heavily. Ally starts to cry. She pulls her knees up underneath her chin and cries while rocking back and forth. AK growls angrily at her.

"Stop it," she says.

"What have we done?" Ally asks. "What have you done? You shot that woman. You shot her and she...she fell."

"Shut up! Shut the fuck up!" AK says.

But Ally can't stop. Now that everything is quiet, her mind is spinning with all the scenarios.

"They're going to come for us, aren't they? They'll find us and bring us in. Oh, my God, we're going to be put away for life, aren't we? We're going to spend the rest of our lives in prison?"

"SHUT UP!"

AK is standing up now. She slaps a hand across Ally's face. "Shut up so I can think!"

"Who's in here?"

The voice is coming from one of the rooms. Ally gasps and looks. She sees a man come out of the darkness. She can't see his face because there is no light other than what comes from the streetlamp outside. But as he walks closer, she spots a gun between his hands.

62

SEPTEMBER 2015

THE POLICE CALL me later in the day and ask me to come down. I take Salter with me and enter the small building next to City Hall. I glance at the new fire station that has just been built and wonder if Danny is at work.

Detective Chris Fisher greets me at the entrance and shows me into a small room. Salter is left to sit on a chair outside. I feel very uncomfortable as the detective sits down in front of me. He is a few years younger than me, and I remember him as a little punk.

"You want coffee or anything?" he asks.

I shake my head.

"We have donuts," he says with a smile. He is annoyingly nice to me. It pisses me off greatly.

"I'm good, but thanks," I say, even though every fiber of my body craves something sweet right now.

"First of all, I would like to tell you how deeply sorry I am for what happened to your father. I hope he'll get better. We're all praying for him. He is a big contributor to our small town. A very respected member of our community."

I always loathed the way they talk about Cocoa Beach like it was a sect or something. Now even more than ever, since the words are coming from his mouth.

The hypocrite.

Did you do it, huh? Did you set the house on fire for the general, did you?

"The reason I have called you down here is that I am in charge of the investigation of the fire. As you know, we believe it was arson. Since your dad was inside of the house, it has suddenly become an attempted murder investigation. I want to assure you we take this matter very seriously, and I intend to find whoever did this and make sure they are brought to justice."

All the right words.

"I appreciate it," I say, trying to stay calm.

"Do you know of anyone who might wish to harm your father or your family?" he asks.

"I was threatened yesterday," I say.

Chris Fisher looks surprised. "By whom?"

Like you don't know.

"By a soldier at the base. He told me he was giving me a message from General Hartman, told me to leave town if I knew what was best for me. Those were his exact words. An hour later, my dad's house was set on fire and he was almost killed."

I can feel how my voice is cracking as I speak the last words. I feel so much anger at this instant I can't hold it back. It's bigger than me.

Detective Chris Fisher stares at me, biting the end of his pen. "You mean to tell me the general actually threatened you? And that you believe he is responsible for the fire?"

He sounds like he is trying hard not to laugh. I want to slap him across his face and wipe the smirk off like I remember doing once when he was still in middle school and groped Sandra's boob at his sister's pool party.

"Yes. I don't believe he set the house on fire himself, but I do believe he had someone do it for him."

Detective Fisher is still staring at me. A smile is emerging slowly. He doesn't know what to say. I can tell he is looking for the words.

"You're kidding me, right?"

"I'm deadly serious. The general has it in for my brother and doesn't want me to help him. He is trying to keep me from finding out what really happened to Jamilla Jenkins. My brother had an affair with his wife. That's why."

Chris Fisher blows out air and whistles. "Wow. I don't know what to say to that, Mary. That's a lot of conspiracy right there. I never took you for being one of those. The general is a very well respected man."

I slam my palm on the table. "He threatened me, Chris."

He is still just staring at me and shaking his head. I can tell he is laughing on the inside.

"What did he do to you?" I ask. "Why do you work for him? Does he have something on you? Did you cheat on the wifey and did he threaten to tell her?"

I know I'm on thin ice now, but I can't help myself.

"I saw you, you know," I say. "In my brother's studio. You were looking for the ring. The ring that I later saw on Olivia Hartman's finger."

Chris Fisher stops smiling. "What?"

"I was in the studio when you got there, when you looked for the ring. I saw you grab it and take it. That's tampering with evidence, my friend."

Chris Fisher leans forward with a sigh. "I don't believe the ring was of importance. The general wanted it back; there is nothing wrong with that," he says. "It's a very expensive ring."

"Did you write Olivia out of the police-report as well? Did he tell you to?" I ask.

Chris Fisher's face turns red all of a sudden. He leans in and snorts at me. "I did him a favor. The general feared that it would come out in the open that his wife had an affair. He thought it was embarrassing to them. I can't blame him. His wife was sleeping around right under his nose. Humiliating the man. Yes, I helped him out when he asked me to. You'll never hear me admit it outside of this room, but yes, I did. I left Olivia out of the report, and when the general realized the ring was missing and Olivia told him where it might be, that your brother might have it in the apartment, then yes. I helped the guy out. He's an old friend of mine. We served together. I didn't destroy any evidence, nor did I ruin the investigation. Olivia had nothing to do with the murder of Jamilla Jenkins."

"And my brother did? Olivia placed the chisel in his studio. The general told her to."

Chris Fisher leans back in the chair. "What?"

"You heard me. She admitted it to me yesterday. That's why the general wanted me to leave town."

Chris Fisher runs a hand through his hair. "That is a serious accusation. You do realize that, right?"

"I can't prove it and she'll probably never admit it if you ask her again, but yes. She told me she did it. She placed the bloody chisel in the bucket under the sink because she had no other choice."

"But...but your brother just admitted his guilt?"

I let out a deep sigh. I feel so confused right now. Chris Fisher doesn't seem to be as bad as I expected him to be. I don't hate him. I feel like he is being honest with me. A lot more honest than I had ever expected. It confuses me deeply. He sounds sincere. He looks sincere. But I suspect he is only acting. Quite the actor he could have been.

"I know," I say with defeat in my voice.

"Why would he declare himself guilty now?"

"I don't know. That's what I intend to find out." I get up from my chair. "If you'll excuse me."

Detective Chris Fisher gets up as well. He looks at me intensely. He is handsome and it annoys me that I like him. I suspect he is still playing a little game with me, trying to be the nice guy and make me believe in him. I am not falling for it.

"Let me know if there is anything I can do," he says.

Ah! Come on!

63

SEPTEMBER 2015

I AM STRUMMING my fingers on the table while I wait. I feel so frustrated, so confused and lost at the same time. I have left Salter at Sandra's house. I don't think he should be with me when I visit my brother in prison.

The door opens and my brother comes into the barren room. He looks pale and tired. He has lost weight. His cheeks are hollow, his eyes dark and sad. I feel like crying when I look into them, but hold it back by forcing a smile.

"Mary!" he exclaims.

"Blake. How are you?" I ask when he sits down. "Are you okay?"

Blake nods, but I can tell he is lying. "I'm good. I'll be alright."

"What's going on Blake?" I ask.

"What do you mean?"

"You plead guilty all of a sudden?"

Blake sighs. His eyes are avoiding mine. "Yeah, well..."

"Well what Blake? Explain it to me. I'm out there trying like crazy to get you acquitted, trying to help your lawyer make your case, and you go out and destroy everything?"

"Well, it's the truth. I did it."

I slam the palm of my hand onto the table. The guard watching us looks at me. I pull it back.

"Goddammit, Blake, why are you saying that?"

"Because it's the truth. I couldn't remember before, but now I do. I got my memory back the other day. I killed her, Mary. I should be punished for it. I belong in jail for what I have done. I am sick. When I get drunk, I do things I wouldn't ordinarily."

"Yes, like sleeping with a married woman or getting in a bar fight with someone, but you don't kill people, Blake. That's not who you are," I say, trying to keep my voice down. It is hard, though. I am so mad at him right now.

"What do you even know about who I am?" he says. "I was three years old when you left. A lot of years have passed since then. People change, Mary. I've changed. And I need to be responsible for my actions."

I stare into his eyes. I try to look for something, anything that tells me he is lying to me.

"I don't believe you," I say.

"Suit yourself. I can't help you with that."

"They got to you, didn't they?" I ask.

"Who?"

"The general, Detective Fisher. They got to you somehow. What did they do? Threaten you? Oh, I know. They threatened to kill Olivia, didn't they?"

I look deep into his eyes to see his reaction. I know he won't give it to me verbally because then the guard will hear it. I detect a flinch in his eyes when I mention Olivia's name. That's enough for me.

"That's it, isn't it? They came here and told you they would hurt Olivia if you didn't plead guilty. Am I right?"

He doesn't say more. He bites his lips. His eyes are flickering. He is right. I haven't known him much through his life, but he is still my brother.

"The bastards," I say and slam my hand onto the table again. The guard gives me a glare and I excuse myself. I lean back in the chair instead. "I can't believe them."

Blake leans in over the table. His chains rattle when he moves. "Mary. You need to leave it alone. I appreciate all you have done for me. But, for my sake. If you love me, you'll leave it alone."

64

SEPTEMBER 2015

LEAVE IT ALONE? Leave it alone? What the hell is he thinking? That I should just leave him to rot in jail?

I am angry as I drive back to Cocoa Beach. No, that's too mild. I am more than angry. I am furious. I don't have the words to describe it. I have come all the way down here to a place I'd rather never see again in my life, with so many bad memories that I have been busy trying to forget, just for him, just to help him out, and then this? Then he goes ahead and does this? He declares himself guilty and has the nerve to tell me to leave it alone.

"If you love me, you'll leave it alone," I say out loud, mocking him. I drive over the bridge leading to the islands. I take no notice of how fast I am going and once I reach the island and the entrance to Cocoa Beach, I get pulled over.

Crap.

The officer gives me a ticket and I drive on, growling and cursing even more than before. I drive to Joey's house and park in the driveway. Joey is back from work and is standing in the yard when I drive up. He is wearing nothing but shorts. He is dirty and sweaty and way too hot for me to handle right now. He waves as I approach him. He looks me in the eyes.

"Hey. What's wrong?"

Not knowing what to say or do, I stare at my gorgeous ex, who I could never quite live up to.

"I...I just had a real bad day," I say.

"Did you visit Blake?" he asks.

"Yeah. He pled guilty and he wants us to leave it alone. So, there you have it."

"We can't do that. He'll get life in prison. He'll never survive it," Joey says and wipes sweat off his forehead.

"That's what I said, but he won't listen. He ended up getting mad at me and that was it."

"You think someone threatened him?" Joey asks.

I nod. "They must have. Why else would he all of a sudden change his statement like that? When I visited him last time he told me he didn't remember anything and that he had never seen the girl before. I don't buy his crap about all of a sudden remembering everything. It's just too weird. But it changes everything, the lawyer says." I can feel the tears are pressing from behind my eyes. I can hardly speak for the lump in my throat. I sit down in one of his chairs on the porch. Joey disappears for a second, then returns with two beers. He hands me one. I open it and drink. It doesn't help much. I still feel like breaking down.

"What am I supposed to do?" I say.

Joey shrugs. "If he wants you to leave it alone, then maybe that's what you ought to do. Go back to New York with Salter. You probably have to be back soon anyway, right? I mean they can't live without you for long at the paper, can they?"

I scoff and lean back on his patio chair. I can hear the waves in the distance. I love that sound.

"I was sacked," I say.

"Excuse me?"

"Fired. They fired me."

Joey almost chokes on his beer. "You're kidding me?"

I shake my head. "Nope."

"You? Their star reporter? They fired you? How? Why?"

I sigh and drink my beer with my eyes closed. I am not sure I can cope with all this right now. Talking about it makes it all so real all of a sudden. I don't want it to be real. I want it to be a bad dream that I can forget about. Just like everything else in my life, I just want to close my eyes and make it all go away. But it never does, does it? It always comes back somehow to haunt you. The past never leaves you alone.

"It's a long story," I say.

He leans back in his chair. "I don't have to be anywhere."

I exhale deeply. I really don't want to talk about it. "Alright," I say. "To make a long story short, I wrote the wrong story. I pissed off some big shot people from a big medical company, Mirah, by revealing how they lied to the public about their results with a specific medicine that people are taking all over the U.S., but yet got it approved by the FDA. The FDA approved the medicine, a non-steroidal anti-inflammatory drug and a prescription painkiller, for use three years ago. I wrote the story of how the company was accused of misleading doctors and patients about the drug's safety, fabricating study results to suit the company's needs, continually thwarting an FDA scientist from revealing the drug's problems and skirting federal drug regulations. Last week, Mirah withdrew the drug from the market after a study revealed the drug more than doubled the risk of heart attacks and death. They had tried to keep this study a secret from the public, but I got my hands on it and published it. By that point, more than 8,000 deaths were already related to the use of the drug, and up to fifteen million Americans had taken the drug. The story went viral. People loved it, and hopefully we saved some lives because they were forced to withdraw the drug, but apparently both my editor and I had to pay a price. I don't know who is in the pocket of whom, but that's what happened."

"That's crazy," Joey says and finishes his beer. "They should give you an award instead."

I scoff. "Well, that is not how the world works, unfortunately."

"You should write about that," he says.

"About what?"

"About how you were fired. How they're all in bed with each other. You could do it, you know. Now that you're famous for the article. People would listen to you. You have a voice."

I shake my head and finish my beer. "Nah. I'm in bad standing everywhere in the publishing world. The company says I violated the regulations for printing an article. Nobody will touch me after this. Who would publish it?"

"You could."

"Me?"

"Yes. Do it online. Create a blog and write about it. Have Chloe help you create it. She could probably give it a real cool design and everything. She knows what it takes."

"True, but still...come on," I say. "Why would I?"

"So they won't get away with it. Don't let them do that. Those bastards should pay for what they did to you. They deserve to pay big time. If you keep quiet, they've won. Do you want them to win? To keep you down? Do you want them to silence you?"

I look into Joey's blue eyes. *This is nice*, I think to myself. To sit with him like this again, just talking. Just the two of us. I can't remember the last time we did this. I miss him, I realize. I miss him so terribly. We were invincible when we were younger. Together, we could conquer the world. I am sick of feeling like I am defeated.

"That's not a bad idea, actually," I say with a smile. "Not bad at all."

65

SEPTEMBER 2015

I WALK to Chloe's house with Joey. We have brought a twelve-pack of beer to smooth the way a little. Chloe likes beer. I knock on the door and she opens it.

"Good," she says. "I was about to call you. I have news. Come."

We walk to her room in the back. I feel like I am sent back to twenty-five years ago when I would visit her in that same house in that same room where she would be all cooped up behind her computer screens. The computers had changed, they had changed a lot, but Chloe was still the same. It amazed me how all of us were still pretty much the same. We quickly fell into the same roles as back then.

Chloe sat down in her chair behind the big screens. The room was dark and the curtains pulled, as always.

"First of all, I've been going through old cases," she says. "I went through criminal complaints and missing persons reports over the past fifteen years to see if I could find any similarities to what happened to Jean and Cassie."

I grab a chair and sit next to her. Joey does the same. The room is small and stuffy, but I like it there. I like hanging out with Chloe again. I have always been so impressed with her and her talent. I have never met anyone like her. And she is, by far, the most trustworthy person I know. Loyal to the bone.

"And?"

"And this is what I found," she says. She pulls up a document on the screen and opens it. "You remember CC?"

"Coraline, sure," I say and look at Joey. He shakes his head. He never remembers any names. He never forgets a face, but names he can't remember if his life depends on it.

"Coraline was found killed in 2004."

I gasp. "What?"

"She was found killed in a hotel room," she says. "A pair of scissors in her throat."

"Why haven't we heard about that?" I ask.

"It was in Orlando. Coraline Cane, married name Densley, moved to Winter Park in 1999. She was married to a senior pastor at some church there. According to the case file, she was supposed to meet someone at the hotel room, a man she had been seeing for years on the side. He was the one who found her lying on the bed with the scissors in her throat, blood everywhere. The killer was never found."

I swallow hard. I can't believe what I am hearing here. This is getting very strange. "Coraline was friends with Cassie and Jean," I say.

"Exactly," Chloe says. "They always hung out together."

"I don't remember that," Joey says.

"You don't remember them?" I ask. "They were this group of girls who were always causing trouble everywhere they went. It didn't last long, but for like a year, they were *the* troublemakers of Cocoa Beach High. Right before..."

"And that's what I'm getting at," Chloe says. "I think there might be a connection of some sort to what happened to Joanne's son, Billy, recently. I've read up on the story, and from the outside, from what they write in the papers, he tried to commit suicide, but I managed to pull the surveillance camera from the International Palms Resort," she says and touches the mouse. "From the night when Billy checked in. They have, like, the worst security in town, for your information. I could have pulled any credit-card information if that was what I wanted, but that's beside the point. I found these pictures," she says and clicks the mouse.

In the surveillance video, we watch as someone enters the lobby. There are five people. Four women and one man. I am guessing the man is Billy. The three women stay behind as the fourth woman grabs Billy's arm and puts it around her neck. They laugh and walk up to the woman behind the counter. They speak to her. I can tell Billy is not happy; he is not enjoying the situation. They check in and get the keycard to the room. As they're about to turn, Chloe pauses the movie. She looks at me. Her face is dead serious. It makes me uneasy.

"What is it?" I ask.

"I hope you're ready for this," she says with a deep exhale.

"Ready for what?"

"This," she says and zooms in the picture.

With my heart pounding in my throat, I watch as the picture of the woman next to Billy gets closer and clearer. Seconds later, I have a clear picture of her face.

My heart freezes to ice.

"You're kidding me, right?"

Chloe shakes her head. "Nope. It's her," she says. "She's back."

66

MARCH 1992

"WHO ARE YOU!"

AK looks at the man with the gun pointing at them. Ally is shivering in fear. She wants to cry. She wants to go home so badly.

"No. You first," the voice says. "Who are you and what are you doing here?"

"I...We..." Ally tries to speak, but AK stops her with just one look.

"I'm sorry if we have intruded," AK says. "We didn't mean to. We just needed a place for the night, that's all."

The man steps closer. He finds a light switch and turns it on. He lowers the gun when he sees their faces. He is wearing a white T-shirt and jeans. Around his neck, Ally spots a military tag.

"What are you running from?" He looks out the window as more sirens howl by.

"Please, sir," AK pleads. "Please don't turn us in."

Ally is surprised to hear the soft tone in AK's voice.

"Why? What have you done?" the soldier asks.

"I...It...It was an accident," AK says. "Right, Ally?"

Ally nods with a whimper. The soldier suddenly smiles from ear to ear. "So, let me get this straight. You two did something tonight, something really bad, since the entire police force is looking for you, and now you want my help?"

AK nods cautiously. Ally doesn't say anything.

The soldier laughs loudly. "Ha! That's the best news I've heard in a long time."

Ally is confused. Why is this such good news? She doesn't understand. But she doesn't like the look in the man's eyes either. He is looking at them in a way that makes her feel uneasy.

He walks closer to AK with the gun in his hand. He lifts the gun and lets it slide slowly across her cheek.

"So, no one knows you're here, huh? I can have my way with you two. Any way I like. Sure sounds like a great deal for me."

He leans over and kisses AK on the neck. She gasps a little at first, but soon decides to roll with it. Ally stares at them, paralyzed, while the soldier puts his hand up under AK's shirt. He grabs her jeans and pulls them down, then opens his belt, bends her over the table, and has his way with her while Ally watches with terror. She wants to scream. She wants to stop him, to wake up from this terrible, terrible nightmare, but she can't. She can't move. The soldier stares at her while he grunts and growls and forces himself on AK, who is crying heavily underneath him. Ally feels desperate. She doesn't know what to do; still, she doesn't dare to move. Not even an inch. Yet she is desperate. She is crying, because she knows she is next.

"Two young girls running right into my arms, now there's a dream I never thought would come true."

When he is done with AK, he lets her go. AK sinks to the floor, crying and sobbing. The soldier looks at Ally. He walks to her and places the gun under her chin. Ally gasps. The gun feels cold against her skin. She is shivering all over.

"It might turn out to be your nightmare, though," he whispers.

Ally whimpers as he grasps her around the throat and applies pressure. She can hardly breathe and gasps for air.

"Please," she whispers.

The man laughs. "Please, what?" he says, while smelling the skin on her neck. Ally is scared. She has never been with a man. She doesn't know what it feels like. She is scared he will hurt her.

She can hardly speak. "Please, sir."

The soldier shakes the gun in front of her face. "No. No. That's not good enough, my little girl. You have to do better than that. It's please...*General*."

67

SEPTEMBER 2015

THE SIGHT of Anne-Katelyn on the screen in front of me makes the blood leave my head. I stand up, feeling sick to my stomach. So many emotions are awakened all of a sudden, so many memories. I feel dizzy and close my eyes. Voices in my head are screaming, crying. I see the stairs at my dad's house. I see my mom. I see her fall from the top of the stairs. I can still hear the sound of her body thumping down every step. Every time she hits a new step, it's like a knife to my heart. I am running, but I can't help her. There is blood smeared everywhere. I run to her and she is lifeless. She is dead. I look up, and there I see *her*. Those same eyes that I am staring at right now...looking into the camera at the International Palms Resort.

Anne-Katelyn, or AK as she liked to call herself, since it sounded more dangerous. I haven't seen those eyes since that night. That fatal night when she shot and killed my mother. The police never found her. She was never punished for what she did. And there she was. Once again, mocking me. Once again, causing trouble and doing what she does best, ruining people's lives.

"Are you alright?" Joey asks. He grabs my hand in his. They all know the story. They were there. They were a part of me back then. A part of my life. When my mother died, it all ended. They all tried so hard to be there for me, but I simply couldn't stand this town anymore. I finished school, then left. But until I left, Joey was the only one who was allowed into my life. He was my strongest supporter. The rest of the crew, I couldn't deal with. They reminded me of what had happened, and I didn't want that. It wasn't their fault. It's just what happened. How I reacted. I pushed everyone away. Even my own father, whom I blamed for everything, for letting it happen. Shortly after, he threw himself into the arms of Laura, and after that, everything changed. Blake was just a baby, and he never really knew our mother, only Laura, who hardly wanted to know of him.

"I...I can't believe it's really her," I say, my voice cracking. "I mean it's... it has been so long and I...I never thought I'd see her again."

"But, here she is," Chloe says. "Alive and well. As soon as I saw her face, I ran a face recognition program, and here's what came up. See how she's dressed in an army uniform? Well, apparently, she has had quite the career in the army. Decorated and everything. Has served time in both Iraq and Afghanistan. But the interesting part is her profile. Apparently, her name is now Liz Hester."

I sink back into my chair with a heavy thud. "She changed her name?"

"She changed her entire identity. Liz Hester, with this social security number, didn't exist until April 1992. She enlisted two years later, in 1994, when she turned seventeen."

"I thought you were supposed to be eighteen to enlist?" I ask.

"Yes, usually, but you can do it earlier with parental consent," she says.

"Parental consent?" I ask. "But AK lived in a home? She had no parents," I say.

"According to this," Chloe says and pulls up another document on her screen. "Her enlistment papers were signed by a guardian, under the name of Henry Hartman."

Chloe looks up at me.

"*General* Henry Hartman," I say.

I stare at the screen, wondering what the heck this is supposed to mean. A thousand thoughts are running through my mind. I can't connect the dots. I can't figure out how this is related. If AK is responsible for what happened to Billy, is she then also responsible for what happened to Jamilla Jenkins, who was also found in a hotel room? And what about Coraline? And Jean and Cassie? They were all friends back then. Was she targeting her old friends? Killing them one by one? The thought made a chill run down my spine. If AK was responsible for any of this, there was one thing I could be sure of. At some point, she would be coming after me. Just like that night at my father's house. She had aimed that gun at me, but accidentally killed my mother. I had always been sure of that. She came for me that night, and she was going to come for me again.

68

SEPTEMBER 2015

OLIVIA HARTMAN CAN'T FIND rest. She is walking back and forth in her living room, nervously rubbing her hands together. It's getting dark outside and she is watching as the sun sets over the mainland. It's a beautiful sight, but Olivia doesn't notice.

She is way too afraid.

Ever since her old school friend, Blake's sister Mary had been to her house at the base, the general had been giving Olivia a hard time.

Now, it is getting late, and he will return within an hour, maybe less. She is terrified of what he might do to her. She is petrified of his anger.

She has thought about leaving, about simply running away all day, but where can she go?

Olivia sits down on the couch. She sits on the edge like she is ready to jump up and run if necessary. After a few seconds, she realizes she is biting her nails again. She has just been able to grow them long and nice, but now they're almost gone.

She still remembers with terror the night she came home after having spent the evening with Blake and he was sitting in the living room, on that same couch, waiting for her, fire in his eyes. She still remembers how she froze, how every cell in her body froze to ice. He had come home early from his trip, he told her. And what had he found? That she wasn't here. She wasn't at the house or even on the base.

"I was out with an old friend," she lied.

But he didn't buy it. He had her followed, he told her. Had been doing it for about two weeks now. And, guess what he learned? She didn't need to answer. She knew from the look on his face she was in deep trouble. Just like she knows it now. The general is always one step ahead of her. She is never going to get out of this mess. She is never going to be able to get the divorce she has been wanting for so long.

He'll have to die before you can be free.

Olivia lets out a deep sigh. She looks anxiously at the clock on top of the fireplace. It will not be long now.

She gets up from the couch and walks to the big window facing the Intracoastal waters. The sun is completely gone now. Bugs are swarming outside the windows, drawn by the light from her living room. Olivia wonders what will happen if she takes the neighbor's small boat and simply rows into the darkness. Will he find her? Of course he will. In minutes, he will have hundreds of men in helicopters and boats searching the area.

Of course he will.

She'll just have to stay here and take it like the big girl she is. She'll have to face his wrath like she did the day before.

"You have humiliated me! Do you understand? And now, they come running here on the base asking questions in front of everybody, and what do you do? You invite them into our home?"

Olivia exhales to calm herself down. She closes her eyes and tries to think of something nice. Her stomach is in knots. She hasn't eaten all day. She has been too nervous. And sad. She is sad because Blake is still in that awful prison. She misses him terribly. She wonders if she will ever see him again. She doubts it. The thought makes her want to cry.

A sound startles her. The sound continues, and she turns to look. It sounds like a tapping on the big dark window. A continuing rhythmical tapping.

Tap-tap-tap

Tap-tap-tap

She chuckles lightly when she realizes it's just a big bug that keeps hitting the glass, probably thinking it can get through and swarm towards the desirable light. Olivia shakes her head thinking what a fool she is, to be scared of such a small bug. She, who used to be a fighter pilot, who used to beat all the boys in most of their training. How had she become this shaky shadow of herself?

You're being ridiculous. So what if the general is angry? What can he do to you?

Olivia takes in another deep breath and looks at the clock once again. Only a few minutes till he is usually home on a day like this.

Tap-tap-tap

Tap-tap-tap

The sound behind her is back. Olivia chuckles again and decides it's just the bug again. The sound is louder now and more persistent.

Tap-tap-tap

Tap-tap-tap

Tap-tap-tap

Thinking it has to be a really big bug this time, Olivia turns to look, then gasps. On the other side of the glass, her eyes meet those of her past. A set of eyes she thought and hoped she was never going to see again.

69

MARCH 1984

"HELP ME!

Penelope runs into the emergency room holding her adopted daughter in her arms. A nurse approaches her. Penelope doesn't know this woman. She usually knows everyone, but this one is new.

"What's wrong?"

"She's been vomiting all morning; it won't stop. She has severe diarrhea and can't hold anything down," Penelope says, then adds. "It's the third time this week. I think it's her heart. Something is very wrong with her. She had seizures on our way here in the car that lasted about three minutes, and her eyes rolled back in her head. She is not responsive to any contact. You might want to do surgery right away on her heart."

The nurse nods, then takes the child out of Penelope's hands. "I'll get a doctor to take a look at her."

Penelope smiles vaguely, then nods. "Thank you."

A doctor is called and soon arrives. He knows Penelope and looks immediately at the unresponsive child.

"Doctor, you have to help her. She is in a very bad condition," Penelope says.

"This is not the same child," he says and starts examining her. He lifts her eyelids and looks into her eyes with a small light. Penelope knows the procedure and knows what he will do next.

"She is adopted," Penelope says. "We brought her home only two months ago. Unfortunately, we don't know her family medical history, if there are heart problems among her close relatives," she says, sounding more like a doctor herself. "I am afraid surgery might be necessary."

The doctor finishes his initial examination, then admits the child to intensive care. Penelope waits all day in the hospital and lives on nothing but coffee and snacks from a vending machine. She calls home to Peter, who is with their other daughter. He was supposed to go to the office this morning, but decided to stay home and take care of their other daughter, who is still very sick and needs observation. Penelope only hopes he doesn't have to go to the office tomorrow, in case their daughter needs to stay for several days or even go through surgery. They'll have to understand at the office, won't they? Yes, of course. After all, they are only doing what they can for their children. It's not their fault they are very sick...both of them. It's just what happens. They'll understand. Of course they will. There really isn't anything else they can do. They're all doing the best they can.

A few hours later, the doctor comes out to Penelope. She stands up from her chair. He rubs the bridge of his nose and closes his eyes. Penelope has been with enough doctors to know their every little sign. The rubbing of the bridge of their nose is always bad news.

"Is it bad, Doctor? Tell it to me straight. I need to know. It's her heart, isn't it? She needs surgery, doesn't she?"

The doctor clears his throat and then looks at Penelope. "She is stable now. I have run several tests on your child and found nothing wrong with her heart."

"But...but, I was so sure...There were palpitations. Definitely. Maybe if you take another look."

The doctor interrupts. "But I did find her sodium levels to be highly elevated, beyond what is healthy in such a young child. Sodium in this amount in such a small body can be fatal."

"Sodium...but...I don't understand..."

The doctor sighs. "Penelope. I can't help but notice a lot of similarities with the symptoms your other daughter is suffering from. I hate to ask you this...but do they somehow have access to salt? Or have you maybe given her salt?"

Penelope stares at the doctor. She holds a hand to her chest. "What... what are you implying, Doctor? Are you saying I somehow did this to my child?" Her voice is breaking as she speaks. "Here I am, in the worst place a mother can be in, while her child is fighting for her life in there. I can't eat, I can't sleep, I can hardly breathe until she is better. Do you have any idea how hard this is on a mother? And...then you...then this? How can you be so heartless, Doctor?"

"There is a condition...I have been thinking about it as objectively as possible, I mean, these two girls are not related in any way and...it just seems incredible that they could even possibly have the same type of problem. I was recently at a pediatric staff conference where I heard about this condition. They call it Munchausen Syndrome by Proxy..."

"A condition?" Penelope asks, baffled. "You mean to say that something is wrong with me? How dare you...?

"As a doctor, I have to consider the possibility that your children are being poisoned. If that is the case, then it needs to stop immediately before one of the children dies. This is very serious."

Penelope snorts. She can't believe the doctor would talk to her like that. She turns on her heel, then walks right into the room where her child is lying in the bed, pulls out all tubes, and lifts her up in her arms. A nurse comes running in.

"What are you doing?"

"I'm taking her home," Penelope says.

70

SEPTEMBER 2015

"WE NEED TO WARN HER."

I look at Joey. We're still sitting in Chloe's old bedroom. Chloe is upstairs feeding her mother. I feel so bad for Mrs. Edwards. She is eaten up by cancer. The doctors gave up on her years ago, and yet she is still alive.

"Who are you talking about?" he asks.

"Olivia Hartman. She was one of them back then. She was in the same group of friends as Coraline, Jean, and Cassie. Olivia might be in danger."

"So, you want to go back to the base?" Joey asks. "After the general threatened you? They're never going to let us in again. Besides, it looks like AK is in there somewhere as well. It's hardly safe for you."

I shrug. "You got another suggestion? If AK is in there, she can get to Olivia any time she wants."

"Call her?"

"Great. Do you have her number?" I ask.

He shakes his head. "Maybe Chloe can get it for us."

"Maybe Chloe can get what?" Chloe asks, as she walks into the room.

"We're thinking about calling Olivia Hartman," Joey says, "to let her know that most of her old friends have been killed and that she might be next. But we don't have her number. She lives on base, maybe you could find it somehow on your computer?"

"Sure," she says and sits down. Ten minutes later, she hands me the number. I am relieved that I don't have to go all the way back to the base for this, but still it feels really awkward to have to call her and give her a message like this. How do you begin?

I dial the number, but of course she doesn't pick up.

"Come on," I say, and try again. "Pick up, pick up, pick up."

The answering machine starts and I hang up again. "It's not working," I say. I look to Joey. "What do we do? I don't like it."

"I have a boat," Chloe says.

"A boat?" Joey says.

"It might work. Olivia's house is on the shores of the Intracoastal," I say. "It had a great view, and it also had a big flagpole in the back yard that I would be able to recognize from the waterside. The moon is pretty bright out there tonight. We might be able to see it even in the darkness. Banana River goes right past it."

Joey is shaking his head. "You're not serious, are you? You'll get arrested. Or shot. This is an army base. They're not going to let a boat come anywhere close to the shore."

Chloe looks at me. "We'll tell them we're tourists who took a wrong turn."

I nod. I think it's a brilliant idea. Joey, not so much. We don't care. Chloe and I have decided to do it. I have to warn Olivia, no matter how much I dislike her and always have. She deserves to know that her old friend has it in for her. I won't be able to live with myself if I haven't at least tried to warn her. It is worth getting arrested for. Maybe not shot, but I don't believe they'll try and shoot us; we could, after all, really be tourists or just some drunk people on their way back from a trip down the Intracoastal highway.

"We'll be fine," I say, and call Salter at Sandra's. I explain to her what we're up to and ask her if Salter can stay till we get back.

"Sure," she says. "It's no problem at all. He's a sweet kid. Be careful, though."

I hang up, wondering why Sandra never had any children of her own. She would be such a wonderful mother. Maybe if she had married Alex instead, then everything would have been different for her. Who knows?

"Are you ready?" Chloe asks and looks at the both of us.

"As ready as we'll ever be," I say.

Joey doesn't say anything. He only grunts, but still follows us out the door.

71

MARCH 1992

ALLY IS PANTING. She is running across the dunes. She falls and the air is punched out of her lungs. She is crying. She can hear the general yelling behind her.

"Come back here, you little whore. I'll call the police if you don't get back here immediately. I'll tell them everything!"

But Ally is not going back. There is no way. She gets up from the dunes and continues to run. As fast as her legs can carry her through the heavy sand, she runs towards the city, towards the lights, leaving the three cabins on the beach behind her. She has a hard time breathing. Her cheek is hurting from the fist the general planted in her face before she managed to get out of his grip. Her nose is bleeding, but she doesn't care. She wipes it off and continues. All she can think of is getting the hell out of there. Anywhere is better than that cabin of hell and the rough hands of the general. AK is still back there. There is no way Ally can help her, but she can save herself. Anything is better than him. Even the police. Even prison.

She had kicked him. As hard as she had ever kicked anything or anyone. He was holding her down and had put the gun on the table, because he needed his hands to hold her down. She was screaming and squirming when he tried to pull off her pants. That was when she got the opening. Just as he was about to mount her, she had planted the kick right in his balls. She had managed to do it hard enough for him to fly through the air and land on the floor. It had given her enough time to storm to the door and run out. He had grabbed her leg as she did and started to pull her back into the cabin, but she had screamed and kicked, and finally hit him in the face. Then she had run for her life.

"I'll get you," he is yelling behind her.

She is getting tired now. So completely worn out of strength, she slows down unintentionally.

No, you can't. You have to keep going. He'll get you if you slow down. Keep running. Just keep running!

"Ha! I see you," he yells behind her. "Getting tired, are you? You will. But I won't. See, I'm a soldier. I can keep running like this for hours. You can't. Then I'll get you. And then I will kill you. See, no one knows you're here. They all think you're on the run from the police. They think you're hiding somewhere and they'll never think to look for your dead body buried under a house belonging to the Air Force Base, will they? No, they won't. Months will pass by and they'll give up searching for you. After a year, your parents won't even wonder anymore. They'll forget about you, thinking you just ran off with your little friend and maybe you're living on the streets somewhere or hiding in South America. And the best part is, they won't care. Why? Because you killed someone tonight. You did the inexcusable and robbed someone of her life. People don't look for murderers because they feel sorry for them or because they want to help them. They look for them because they want to see them hang or go to prison for life. When you kill someone, people stop caring about you."

Ally is gasping for air. Her lungs are hurting. That damn moist air makes it impossible to breathe properly and to get rid of the heat. Her face is boiling. She is crying and tears are streaming down her cheeks. She senses he is close now and wonders if she should simply give up. She can't run anymore. Her legs are so heavy they can hardly move. The general is whistling behind her. He is so close now; she can almost feel his breath.

There is no way out of this, she thinks to herself, seconds before she feels his hand on her neck. *This is it. This is the end.*

When her head hits the dunes, her mouth fills with sand. She is gasping for air, but getting nothing but sand. She can't breathe. Pressure on her neck makes it impossible for her to lift her head.

Oh, my God, he's holding you down. He's going to kill you right here.

Ally struggles all she can, but the hand doesn't move from the back of her head. Her nose and throat are filled with sand; she is gasping, but the little air she gets in her lungs is not enough. She is almost unconscious when she hears a voice in the distance.

"What's going on here?"

Finally, the pressure on her neck is lifted and she can raise her head into the air. A bright light hits her face.

"I am so glad you came, Officer," the general says. "I captured this girl and stopped her. I believe she is one of the two girls you are looking for. I saw it on the news earlier, and then spotted her down here on my evening walk."

"Thank you, General," the officer says, and grabs Ally by the arm. He helps her to her feet. She coughs and spits out sand.

"Well, little lady. Guess you're done running."

72

SEPTEMBER 2015

"GO AWAY."

Olivia waves violently at the woman on the other side of the window. "Get out of here."

But the woman doesn't move. The way she stares at Olivia makes her break a sweat. What is she doing here? She tilts her head still while staring at Olivia, and still tapping her fingernail rhythmically on the window.

Tap-tap-tap

Tap-tap-tap

It's driving Olivia insane. She opens the sliding door leading to the backyard and walks out. The woman keeps tapping while she turns to look at her.

"Enough with the tapping, would you?" Olivia says angrily. "It's driving me nuts."

The woman stops. Olivia forces a smile. "Now, get out of here," she says. "My husband is coming home soon. He won't be happy to find you here."

"Am I pretty?"

"What?" Olivia stares at the woman wearing the surgical mask covering the bottom part of her face. Does she really think no one will recognize her because she is wearing that thing?

"Am I pretty?" she repeats.

Olivia frowns.

What the heck is all this?

"What are you talking about? Go away. Go back to wherever you came from and leave me alone. I have enough to deal with as it is."

"AM I PRETTY?"

The woman yells so loud a dog starts to bark from one of the neighboring houses.

Oh, great. Now they'll start talking, and soon the general will know.

Olivia sighs. "What do you want? Can't you just tell me what it is so we can move on?" she asks.

"Am I pretty?" the woman repeats with a lower voice.

"What? Why do you keep asking me that? Sure, you're very pretty."

The woman grabs the surgical mask and pulls it off. Olivia can feel how her blood freezes when she sees what is underneath.

"How about now?" she asks.

Olivia can't speak. She stares at the woman like she is paralyzed. "I...I...I..."

She doesn't even notice the scissors in her hand until they're in the air and the woman is leaping towards her, moving almost unnaturally fast. But then, something else happens. Olivia is about to scream when she hears voices cutting through the darkness.

"Olivia!"

The woman is about to plunge the scissors into Olivia's throat, but the intruding voices coming from the river disturb her and she hits her arm instead. Olivia screams in pain as the scissors pierce through her right arm. The voices are coming closer as she falls to the ground, blood gushing out of her wound. Meanwhile, the woman runs around the corner of the house, dragging her long black coat after her. Olivia tries to speak as she watches Mary Mills' face come closer. She is flanked by two other faces that Olivia remembers well from school.

"Olivia, are you okay?" Mary yells. She leans down and sees the scissors in her upper arm. "We need an ambulance."

Olivia looks down, and, to her terror, watches as the blood colors the grass and she feels dizzy. She closes her eyes and tries to calm herself, but the dizziness soon takes over. She has no feeling of what is up and what is down, what is real and what is not. She can hear many voices and steps; she is certain she hears someone yell and others scream. She is even sure she can hear guns being pulled, and is that a helicopter? She doesn't know what is going on, and she hardly cares anymore. When she loses consciousness, she is certain she even hears the voice of the general.

She can't stop smiling, thinking at least he can't touch her now.

73

SEPTEMBER 2015

"EVERYBODY STAY STILL."

I am lying in the grass. I have someone's boot in my back. He says he is from the Military Police. I believe him. After all, I have just entered the military base from the waterside without permission. I know I am in trouble. There are weapons pointed at us from all sides. Even a helicopter swirling above us. But I am happy because I believe I saved Olivia Hartman's life. She was about to be killed, but my screaming as we approached shore in Chloe's boat disturbed her just enough to have AK miss her target and hit Olivia's arm instead. Olivia is passed out, but I have heard them call for an ambulance, and soon she will be in the hospital getting the treatment she needs. I, on the other hand, am in deep...over my head.

"I'll take this one from here," a voice says.

The knee is removed from my back and a pair of boots appears in front of my nose. I am pulled up by my hair and I look into the face of the man I know as the general.

"General Hartman, I presume," I say, and sit up on my knees.

The general stares at me. He is skinnier than in the articles I have read about him. I am guessing he keeps himself in great shape, the suntan tells me he might be one of those who constantly runs on the beach. He is maybe twenty years older than me. Just the sight of him fills me with disgust.

"And you must be Mary Mills," he says with a stiff upper lip. "Sister of the infamous Blake Mills."

"Can't say it's a pleasure to meet you," I say, and rise to my feet.

"What the hell are you doing here, breaking into a military base after nightfall? Do you realize I could have you shot and no one would lift an eyebrow?"

I wipe away some blood from my nose. I have hurt myself falling to the ground with that MP on my back.

"I'm saving your wife's life," I say. "Those scissors were about to land in her throat. Had we come a few seconds later, she would be gone by now."

I turn and look at Joey and Chloe, who are still face-down in the grass. Chloe's small speedboat is parked halfway on the lawn. We took that baby as fast as we could onto the ground, then jumped out. I feel a little like James Bond. Or Tom Cruise. Definitely Tom Cruise.

The general is looking at me, completely baffled. "You saved her...why?"

I am surprised he believes me. Something in his eyes, a look, tells me he loves her. It doesn't fit well with the picture I have of him.

"We went to school together. Three of her other friends from back then have been killed—with a pair of scissors stabbed in their throats. I believed Olivia might be next. Guess I was right. You're very welcome."

I can see the vein in the general's forehead grow. The porch light lights his face. I wonder if I should tell him whom I believe is behind this or if it would be a stupid idea. He is, after all, her guardian, or was when she was younger. I don't know what kind of relationship he has with AK, but I can't help wondering if he is in on it all as well. He looks like he could kill someone just by snapping his fingers. But again, he is a soldier, a general in the U.S. army, so of course he could. And he probably wouldn't even blink. I have to remember, he framed my brother.

The general growls and runs a hand through his hair. A soldier approaches him. "Sir. What shall we do with the prisoners, sir?"

The general sighs. I can feel my heart rate go up. I know the general wants me wiped off the surface of the earth along with my brother. I believe he is the one who set my dad's house on fire, or at least had someone do it for him. I hate his guts and I want to spit in his face, but I also know he is the one in control right now. He has the power to put me in jail for treason. My life is completely in his hands right now.

What will he do?

"Let them go," he says.

What??

"Let them go, soldier," he repeats. "They pose no threat to us. It was all just a mistake. A mistake that saved my wife." He turns and looks at me. I fight my urge to rethink my opinion of him.

He almost killed your father. He put Blake in jail.

"Now we're even," he says. "Remember that."

74

SEPTEMBER 2015

I SLEEP in Joey's bed again while he takes the couch. I don't close an eye all night. I stare at the ceiling while going through everything in my mind. I feel so confused, so frustrated.

Why did he let me go? Why didn't he arrest us?

I don't understand. I thought the general had it out for me. Maybe he is really just angry at my brother for sleeping with his wife. I can't blame him. I wanted that coffee house girl gone from the planet once I found out about her and Joey. I couldn't even stand driving by the coffee house. It was like torture. I wanted her to get fired; I wanted her entire family to be fired and never work again. I wanted all the world's misery to come upon her and her descendants for all eternity. But, in reality, I knew it wasn't her fault. It was ours. We hadn't taken care of our marriage. We had lost touch with one another.

I think about us back then. Me and Sandra hanging out in the school cafeteria, Joey coming up to us with his tray between his hands and sitting next to me. Us talking about waves being good, talking about skipping a few hours of school this afternoon when the tide is going out. I think about AK and how she would always send me hateful looks when we passed each other in the hallways. How she and her little gang would whisper as we walked by. She scared me back then. But I also felt sorry for her. Until she shot my mother.

Mommy, no! Mommy, no!

I see her in my inner eye as she falls down the stairs again and again. It makes me feel the sorrow that I felt back then, the emotions I had tried so hard to forget for so many years. I hate that I can't stop it, that I can't hold it back like I used to. A tear rolls from the corner of my eye onto my pillow. Another follows, and soon I am crying heavily, sobbing, pulling my legs up under my chin. So much sadness, so much anger. All these years.

Burn in Hell Mills!

I close my eyes and turn to the side while crying. I don't even notice when the door to my room opens and someone enters. A body creeps into bed with me. I feel his warmth, his arms around my waist, as he spoons me and caresses my hair. I can't stop crying. Not now that I have opened the faucets.

Joey is kissing my neck and holding me tight. I let him. I have missed him and his touch. I can't hold it back anymore. I can't pretend like I don't love him, like I don't want to be close to him.

I want this. I want to be with him again. What's the use in fighting it?

Joey moves his mouth to my ear. "Don't give up on us," he whispers.

I turn my head and look into his eyes. I see such deep intensity in them. It moves me. I touch his face, the rough edges, and the unshaved chin.

God, I love him! Why does it have to be so hard?

His eyes drop to my lips. I can tell he wants to kiss me. This is it; this is the moment when I make my decision. I want him to kiss me; I want it desperately. But everything inside of me screams that I can't. That I shouldn't. That it would be wrong of me.

He was the one who cheated on you, remember? You'll only get hurt again. Don't fall for it. Don't.

Yet, I close my eyes and pull him closer. He hesitates, then kisses me. Gently at first, then demanding, insisting. His hands are on me, on my body and soon my T-shirt is pulled over my head.

I'll explode if I don't let him.

It's like a surge of electricity that goes through my body when he enters me. I realize I have wanted this for so long, ever since I threw him out, ever since I found out about him and that coffee house girl. This is what I have craved...him, being close to him, feeling him inside of me again. I don't think of consequences, I simply give in to this urge of mine.

I surrender.

MAY 1986

"SIT STILL, sweetheart. It's going to be a long drive."

Penelope drives onto the highway leading to Miami. It's a four-hour drive, but it's going to be worth it. Next to her sits her daughter. Peter is at home with their adopted girl, who is still throwing up a lot. Penelope has told Peter to keep a close eye on the girl. If the vomiting continues, he has to take her to the hospital, she instructed him before she left. Once again, he had to stay home from the office. It's never popular when he does that, but Penelope has told him it's vital that he helps her out when they have two very sick children like they do.

"Will we be there soon?" her daughter asks. She is looking at the landscape passing by her window. She is skinny, and still way too small for her age.

"Just three more hours," Penelope says cheerfully. Today is a good day. "I am so happy we finally found a doctor to do your surgery," she says. "The nice doctor will make your heart much better, and then you'll be well. Doesn't that sound good? I think it does. I am excited."

"But...but, Mom..."

"No buts here, little missy. Once you have the surgery, you'll feel much better. I promise you. You'll be strong and healthy like your classmates."

Penelope turns on the radio and whistles along to *What's Love Got to Do With It* by Tina Turner. Her daughter keeps looking out the window.

"Are you alright?" Penelope asks when the song is over.

"I'm fine, Mom. I feel just fine. I keep telling you."

Penelope looks at her daughter's face briefly, then back at the road. She doesn't seem pale anymore. Come to think of it, she hardly seems like she is sick. It's been weeks since she last threw up. She has some color in her cheeks now, her eyes are sparkling, and she seems happy.

Almost like a normal nine-year-old.

"Mom, can I get ice cream when we get to Miami?" she asks.

"Ice cream? No, you most certainly cannot have ice cream," Penelope exclaims. "You're way too sick to have sweets."

"Mom. I feel fine. I don't feel sick at all."

"Don't let that fool you," Penelope says with a lifted finger. "Your heart isn't working properly; that's why you need surgery. Don't let one day of feeling better make you believe you're well now. It's just tricking you into believing that. You're still sick, even though you feel better right now. It's only temporarily. Make no mistake. It won't last."

"But...but..."

"Now, don't forget to tell the doctor how bad you feel when he asks, alright? Tell him how many years you have been sick, how much you throw up, and by all means, don't forget to tell him about the seizures you have all the time. Those are important. You have to really rub it on thick. Otherwise, he might not want to do the surgery, and that would be really bad. I've looked for a doctor who would do this for many, many years. Don't blow it, okay?"

The child lets out a deep sigh. "Okay."

When they arrive at the parking lot in front of the hospital in Miami, hours later, Penelope parks the car, then turns to look at her girl.

"Now, the paleness we can't get back. It's too late for that. But it is important that you look sick. And right now, you're smiling way too much; your eyes are way too bright. What can we do about that? Let me see...you haven't eaten in two days; I made sure of that. You should feel lightheaded and have heart palpitations. You do feel those things, don't you?"

The girl nods.

"Alright, that's good."

Penelope looks at her daughter, then leans over, grabs her head, and bangs it against the car window.

"Now, act sick, okay?" she hisses. "No smiling, no eating, and no laughing. You hear me?"

76

SEPTEMBER 2015

WHEN I WAKE UP, I'm alone in the bed. I can hear Joey and Salter talking in the kitchen. I get up and walk out to them.

"Hey. Look who's finally awake," Joey exclaims.

"Mom!" Salter runs to me and hugs me. I feel overwhelmed. Salter has reached the age where mommy is mostly a source of constant embarrassment, and physical contact is kept to an absolute minimum. Suddenly, he is kissing me and hugging me like I have been gone for months.

"Dad made pancakes!"

Joey turns around with a smile. He knows how much I love to start my day with pancakes.

"I also made eggs," he says, and shows me the pan. "Cooked just the way you like them."

Someone is on the charm offensive. Or maybe he is just happy. I can't help feeling it a little too. It feels good to be a family again. But, is it enough? Do I dare to let him in again?

I am still not sure.

I sit down at the table and let him serve breakfast for me. Salter sits between us. He is smiling from ear to ear, looking at Joey, then back at me again. He's like a child at Christmas. I can't stand it. I mean, nothing thrills me more than seeing him like this, but I am not sure it's a good thing. I am afraid he might get disappointed again. And that is the last thing I would want for him.

"Let's eat," I say, and we all dig in simultaneously.

Joey has placed a jar of Nutella next to my plate, knowing how much I like to smear my pancakes with the chocolate. I chuckle when I see it.

"Seriously?"

He shrugs. "I think it is beyond disgusting, but hey, if you like it, you should have it."

I don't know what to say. Back in New York, when things were going bad between us, Joey had been on my case about my weight. He had criticized me for letting myself go. Where is that now? Has he simply parked it outside until later? I don't believe you can do that.

I smear my pancakes with Nutella and enjoy the food immensely. I don't have to make any decisions yet. Right now, I want to enjoy whatever it is we have. I want to enjoy Salter's happy face. I want to enjoy the feeling I have inside, the feeling of being where I belong.

After breakfast, I go and visit my dad. Joey doesn't have to go to work until ten, so I ask if Salter can stay with him. I have an hour. Laura is there by his side, and I give her an awkward hug. She seems smaller and very skinny, and I wonder if she has eaten at all since the fire.

"How are you holding up?" I ask.

She shrugs with a sob. "I'm doing my best."

"Where are you staying?"

"At the Hilton."

The Hilton. Of course.

"So, what are they saying?" I ask. "About his condition? What are the doctors telling you?"

"They say he is stable, but they're not sure he'll ever wake up again," she says with a loud sob. "I'm terrified that he won't, Mary. What if they ask me to make the decision to pull the plug on him? I don't think I can do that. On the other hand...this is no life for him, is it? He would have hated seeing himself like this. He would want me to do it."

I swallow hard and look at my stepmom. I know she is right. My dad would never want to be a vegetable. Better to end it. But the thing is, Laura and he never married. So, if it comes to that, the decision will have to be mine.

The thought gives me nausea. I feel like crying again. I can't lose him too. I simply can't. And it is all my fault he's lying there. If I hadn't pissed off the general.

I need to find proof that it was him. He might have gone easy on me last night, but I still loathe him. I want to nail him for what he has done. There must be a way of doing that. And AK. I have to get her too. She killed my mother in 1992. She is wanted for that murder, but how do I prove that she is who I believe she is? She has another identity now. Who will believe me? If I could somehow get her for the killing of Coraline, Jean, or Cassie... If only. If only I could somehow prove that she killed Jamilla Jenkins. In that way, I would get my brother back, as well as get AK. But who will believe me?

"Listen, I have to get back to Salter; Joey has work to do, so I need to go. But let me know if there is any news, all right? I'll try and be back later today or maybe tomorrow."

I speak fast. It's obvious I am trying to get out of there. I don't feel well all of a sudden. Watching my dad lie there fills me with such tremendous guilt. I can't breathe. The walls are closing in on me and I just need to get out of there. I don't wait for her answer. I storm out of the hospital, and don't stop running till I reach my car.

I need to fix this somehow. I have to fix it.

77

SEPTEMBER 2015

I TAKE Salter with me to Chloe's house. I bring his iPad so he won't be too bored. His eyes grow wider than wide when he sees all her computers.

"Wow! It's just like the movies. Are you a famous YouTuber or something?" he asks.

Chloe laughs. I do too. In the world of a nine-year-old, the biggest stardom you can reach is to be a video game tester for a living and make videos about them on YouTube.

"No, but I do have Minecraft on the computer over there," she says, and points at an iMac in the corner.

"Oh, my God," I say. "You have no idea what a lifesaver that is. Salter has been so mad that he can't play his precious Minecraft down here, since all I brought was his iPad and my laptop, which he is not allowed to play on."

"Well, knock yourself out," Chloe says. "I think it is already turned on."

Salter exclaims happily, then rushes to the computer. Chloe hands him a set of headphones, and soon he is occupied in his own little world of bricks and stones. I never understood that game much, but I know it is Salter's entire world. He meets all of his friends on there, and they play for hours every day, talking on Skype while they play. It is a whole new generation of super nerds growing up. I don't mind him being a computer nerd and the fact that he speaks an entire language I don't understand at times, but I do worry that he doesn't get enough fresh air and real life human contact. Maybe I am just being a mother.

I decide to take him surfing this afternoon to make up for this morning. I know I probably won't do it, but it makes me feel better.

"I have something for you," Chloe says, as we sit down in front of her many computer screens. "I've been up all night going through old cases in the database, and look what I came up with. You might remember this."

I look at the screen. "Holly?"

"Holly Leslie. Born in 1977 like the rest of us. Moved to Cocoa Beach in 1990 with her family. Went to Cocoa Beach High School, friends with Jean, Olivia, Cassie, Coraline, and Anne-Katelyn."

"Has she also been killed?" I ask, agitated.

"No, but something else happened to her. In 1995. According to the police report, she was found on the side of the road at Lori Wilson Park. She had been cut several places on her body with a fishing knife and shot in the leg with a spear gun. According to this, her family never pressed charges. Holly refused to tell who was behind it. No one was ever arrested in the case."

"I remember her," I say. "She disappeared all of a sudden in the middle of the school year. I had several classes with her. There were a lot of rumors about her and what happened to her. Some people said they had met her at the mall months later, but that she didn't want to talk to them."

"It looks like she moved to Rockledge and she continued school there," Chloe said. "She graduated from Rockledge High School a year later."

"So they moved her because of the attack?" I ask.

"It sure looks like it."

"I need to talk to her," I say. "If for nothing else than to warn her about AK, and tell her that the others have been killed, in case she doesn't know."

Chloe glances at Salter. "I'll look after him while you're away. Seems like he's not going to cause much trouble."

I laugh and look at my son, who is completely in his own world, building castles and mining for diamonds.

"He won't," I say.

78

SEPTEMBER 2015

I DRIVE up to the house in Rockledge and park in front of the garage. I haven't called first. I am afraid she will tell me to not come. I don't know if she is home. The house is a small one-story house with a porch in front. I walk up, open the screen door, and knock.

It takes a while before someone opens. I recognize her eyes right away. The face is older, the eyes filled with a sadness they didn't have then, but other than that she looks like herself. Except for the long scar on her cheek that I don't remember having seen before.

She looks at me for a long time. It's like she recognizes me, but isn't sure. Seeing me here seems to bring back memories.

"Mary Mills?"

I raise my hand in an awkward wave. "Hi, Holly."

"What are you doing here? Last thing I heard you were a big time reporter at CNN in Atlanta."

"I was...what feels like a lifetime ago," I say. "Can I come in?"

She looks surprised. "Sure."

She steps aside and lets me in. She limps when she walks. "If I had known you were coming, I would have cleaned up a little," she says, and picks up a toy from the floor. It looks like a dog toy. A pit-bull in a crate in the living room tells me it is his toy. It snarls at me when I enter.

"Don't mind him," she says. "He helps me to feel safe. He guards the house. I keep him in the crate when I'm home. Sit down."

I sit on the couch. It is small, but very soft. It goes well with the small living room. I am guessing Holly hasn't had much success in her life.

"Do you want coffee? Or maybe a beer?" she asks.

"No, thank you. I'm good," I say. I don't want her to go through the trouble of making me coffee. "I already had two cups this morning."

She sits down with her hands in her lap. "So...what brings you here?" she asks and corrects her hair.

"1995," I say. I go directly to the point. I don't have time to beat around the bush. When I say the year, her face freezes completely. "I know it must be hard for you to talk about, but I need you to."

Holly's eyes drop to the ground. She touches her thigh on her bad leg. "It's such a long time ago," she says.

"I know. And I know it must be terrible for you to think back about, but things have started happening around Cocoa Beach, and I think you might be able to help me figure out why, or at least who is behind it. Three of your former friends from back then have died. Last night, the killer tried to kill Olivia as well, but was interrupted. I think someone is targeting your old group." I pause and wait for her reaction. It doesn't seem to surprise her. Then, I go in for the kill. "I think AK might be behind it."

Her eyes meet mine. She shakes her head. "AK? But how is that possible? No one has seen her since 1992. Since that night when...when she shot your mother."

I chuckle. "You're a terrible liar, Holly."

She sighs. "It's such a long time ago. Why do we have to start digging up these old stories again? I really don't want to..."

"Because they're not old stories. They're still here. They don't just go away because we stop thinking about them. They're real. We can't keep running from them. You have to tell me, Holly. Was AK among those who attacked you back then? Was she behind it?"

Holly clasps her mouth. I can tell that I am ripping up stuff she hasn't allowed herself to think about for years. I know how she feels. I know exactly how that feels, but sometimes it's necessary to dig up the past in order to not get stuck in it. It's like quicksand. The more you wriggle and try to get away from it, the more it pulls you back. Running from it will do you no good.

I slam the palm of my hand onto her coffee table. "Goddammit, Holly. Answer me! Was AK one of those that attacked you in 1995?!"

79

SEPTEMBER 2015

"YES! YES, SHE WAS!"

Holly closes her eyes when she yells it at me. The words hit me like a punch in the face. It's what I wanted to hear, but it's also shocking. Back then, I believed AK was long gone, and now I realize that she was still here? Still right here? The police could have found her; they could have put her in jail for killing my mother and we could have moved on with our lives, feeling justice had been served. Instead, we walked around in this haze, this daze of anger and frustration. I lost my mother, my dad lost his wife, and since justice never came, we began blaming each other. We began loathing each other instead. Meanwhile, Blake had to grow up without a mother and with a father so distant he might as well not be there either. This thing destroyed us.

As I stare at Holly with my mouth wide open, I wonder if things could have been different, had AK gotten what she deserved back then. I had always believed it would.

"She was there," Holly says. "She was the one who started it."

"Tell me what happened," I say, suddenly wishing I had said yes to that coffee, or even the beer. I could use something strong right now.

Holly draws in a deep breath. She rubs her hands together. At the collar of her shirt, I spot another scar.

"I was so young," she says. "When I came to the school, I became friends with them. I hung out with them on the weekends doing all kinds of stuff, getting in trouble. I am not very proud of it today, but what can you do? What's done is done. I was just so incredibly naïve. Anyway, we were friends, and AK persuaded me to do all kinds of things that I didn't want to. But she can be very persuasive, you know? Suddenly, I was shoplifting and stealing bikes from the beach entrances. I did it to win their respect. I wanted AK to like me. If she liked you, then you were popular. You know how high school is. Anyway, I did a lot of stuff I wasn't very proud of. When AK went missing after that night...when she...well, you know, the police came to my door the next day. They took me to the station and asked me all kinds of questions about AK. I told them everything. My parents told me to. I told them everything we had done, how AK had led our group, and how we had bothered tourists downtown, and even sometimes attacked some of them, kicked them and stolen their belongings. I cried a lot when I told this. I hated that my parents had to hear this about me. I was never charged with anything, since I cooperated so willingly, they said. And I felt good about having told. It felt good to get it out and I pulled away from the rest of the group afterwards. When AK disappeared, the group kind of dissolved anyway. Without her, we were nothing. I think most of them were happy that she was gone."

Holly stops and takes in a deep breath before she continues. "I had a few very good years after that. But three years later, my doorbell rang one night when my parents were out of town. I went to open the door, and there she was."

"AK?"

"Her hair was different. It had been colored blonde and had grown long. She looked completely different. Her clothing was very different. But her eyes were the same. There was maybe even more anger in them."

"Was she alone?" I ask.

Holly shakes her head. "No. They were all there. All the girls from back then. They were right there next to her. I think they didn't really want to be there, but who says no to AK, right? They were terrified of her. She was out of control. If you said no, she would beat you up or cut you with the razorblade she often kept between her teeth. You just didn't say no."

"So, what did they want?" I ask.

"They were all giggling and laughing, and I think they were on something. They told me AK had come back to hang out with them tonight and that she would be gone in the morning. She told me she'd changed her name to Liz, I believe it was. That she lived far away now, but tonight she was back. *Let's go have some fun while I'm here*, I remember she said. While she spoke, she flashed her razorblade between her teeth, and I knew there was no saying no. It was too dangerous. They persuaded me to take them out on my dad's boat. They brought a lot of booze with them, and for a few hours we sailed the canals, drinking, listening to music, and fishing. For the first couple of hours, I thought I was going to be all right. That as long as I played along during this night, then AK would be gone in the morning, and I wouldn't have to see her again. But, of course, I was wrong. Suddenly, AK told me to take the boat to the ocean. I told her I had no clue how to do it, that you had to go through the lock system, and I wasn't sure you could do that at night. Nonsense, AK said. The lock is open till 9:30. Naturally, I had to give in to them, and we made it through right before the lock closed. We sailed into the ocean, and I was terrified, since I knew there was no way we could get back that same night. We would have to wait till it opened again at six in the morning. Were we going to be sailing the ocean until then, or what was their plan? I didn't dare to ask. I just went with what they told me to. I wasn't even sure there was enough gas in the boat to keep us going till the morning. The onshore winds were strong, and as soon as we sailed out of the canals, we hit rough seas. The boat was thrown back and forth in the waves. AK thought it was hilarious and wanted to start spearfishing. I told her she had to be in the ocean to do it, but she pulled one out from one of the compartments and aimed it at me for fun. They all laughed. AK drank heavily from a bottle of vodka and shot the gun out in the ocean. She didn't hit anything, but they all laughed, and she pulled back the spear. I tried to steer the boat and stay as close to shore as possible, so we could get in in case anything happened. I prayed and hoped the Coast Guard would find us. Maybe they would stop us. I was so afraid. When we had sailed down the coast in darkness for a little while, they suddenly surrounded me. AK was holding the spear gun and aiming it at me. *What are you doing?* I asked. *Getting rid of an unwanted smell around here*, she said. *And I am not talking about the stench of fish. No, it's the smell of betrayal!* I don't remember much of what happened after that, but I do remember someone coming up from behind me with a fishing knife, slicing my clothes into pieces, and cutting my back. Then I remember them pushing me to the floor of the boat and AK holding the knife, then stabbing me in the shoulder, and cutting me here on the throat and on the arm. They tied my legs and arms and cut off my pants. I remember screaming and the boat tipping back and forth. I remember somehow getting to my feet and jumping overboard, thinking I could swim to the shore. I was right. Luckily, the rope they tied around my hands came off in the water, so I could use my arms to swim. I thought I had lost them, that I had gotten away, but the girls followed me. They all abandoned the boat and jumped in the water. They came after me with the spear gun. I crawled on shore at Lori Wilson Park and ran across the parking lot, blood running from all my wounds. I almost made it to A1A when they shot the gun and it went straight through my leg. That's the last thing I remember. I woke up in the hospital and was told that a police officer had found me. I never dared to tell anyone what had really happened. Except my parents, who made sure we moved immediately afterwards. They too were scared that they might come back for me. Luckily, they never did."

I stare at Holly while she tells her story. I feel appalled. I am so angry with AK I can barely contain it.

"So, why do you think they did it? Why do you believe they turned on you like that? Because you spoke to the police?" I ask.

"Sure. I wasn't the only one who did, nor was I the only one who got punished for it," she says.

"What?"

"I have a feeling you remember Ally?"

80

SEPTEMBER 2015

"WE NEED TO FIND ALLY. Ally Meyer."

I am back at Chloe's house. Salter is still at the computer. I decide now is not the time to feel guilty for letting him play on the computer all day. There is no time for all that. It has to wait till later.

Chloe doesn't even look up at me. She stares at her screen and lets her fingers dance across the keyboard. "Ally Meyer?" she asks, surprised.

Chloe finally looks up at me. Her eyes are loaded with pity. I hate when people look at me like that. I used to see it all the time back then. That was one of the reasons I pulled away from my friends, from the crew.

"There's a name from our past I thought I'd never hear again," she says. "Are you sure you want to find her?"

"Yes," I say. "I have to."

"But..."

"I know. She was the one who was with AK when she shot my mother," I say. "They broke into our house. She was the only one who was captured. She told the police everything that happened. My dad decided to not press charges against her, since she wasn't the one who had fired the gun. She was just a kid, and she had, after all, cooperated with the police. He didn't want to ruin the rest of her life. All I know is that she and her mother moved after that. I don't know where to."

"And you're absolutely sure you want to find her, right?" Chloe asks.

"Yes. I need to talk to her. Holly told me she was attacked by AK and her gang in '95 like she was. As a punishment for having talked to the police. I've convinced Holly to testify against her and tell what happened. I want to do the same with Ally. I believe she owes me. I need to get to her before AK does. I believe she is killing off all witnesses from back then. Anyone who has something on her, anyone who might be able to testify against her...who knows her real identity. She is cleaning up."

"So that's why she killed Coraline, Jean, and Cassie as well?" Chloe asks.

"That's my theory, yes. I believe Jamilla Jenkins might have had something on her as well, maybe threatened to tell about what she's doing now. Like what she did to Joanne's son, Billy. She hasn't changed. Still leaves a trail of death and destruction behind her. I need to stop her. I believe she is coming for me as well. She's wanted me dead ever since...well, for as long as I can remember."

Chloe draws in a deep breath. She knows my story. I don't have to explain to her. She knows what I am up against.

"I got what I believe is her mother's address," she says. "They didn't move very far. Melbourne Beach. She bought a house there in 1992. It's worth a shot. Her mother's name is Janice Meyer."

I grab my purse and look at Chloe. "Could he stay here again?"

"Sure. But is it wise to go alone?" Chloe asks.

I hesitate. Is she right?

"I mean, you haven't seen her since back then, have you?" she says.

In the flash of a second, I see her again. Standing in my living room next to AK, who is holding the gun. I feel the anger; I feel the frustration all over again. "No, but that doesn't mean that I..."

"You're not going alone," Chloe says, and hands me her phone. "Call Sandra. I believe she's not doing anything today. She can go with you and make sure you behave. It's okay to admit that you need someone, you know. No man is an island. Or woman."

I nod and grab the phone. Chloe is right. I hate to admit it, but she is. I call Sandra and she tells me she just needs to run to Publix first, then she'll be ready to go.

I pick her up half an hour later at her house. She has a bag in her hand. "I brought some supplies for our little road trip," she says with a smile. She opens the bag and shows its contents to me. I laugh.

"You remember how we used to munch on this when we went on surf trips to Sebastian Inlet, or when we went to all my competitions in Melbourne Beach? My God, it's a long time ago. You know what I remember? You were there every time. The others came now and then to cheer me on, but you, you were there every weekend to cheer for me. I'll never forget that."

"What can I say? I loved to watch you surf. Even more, I loved to see you kick those other kids' butts."

Sandra smiles and I start the car.

"Are you even allowed to have chips and root beer? Don't you have to keep to your strict model diet to keep you looking like a stick?" I ask teasingly. "Don't you have that big shoot coming up...who is it again, *Elle* magazine?"

Sandra shrugs. "It's *Vogue,* and yes, but what can I do? A girl's gotta live a little, right?"

81

SEPTEMBER 2015

LIZ RUSHES BACK to her house after her day is over. She feels so empowered, so strong after a day at the shooting range. Nothing beats a good day of shooting targets. And Liz is the best at it. The best on the entire base, as a matter of fact. That's what has given her this great career with the army for the past twenty years. She has been living on bases all over the world since she enlisted, or since the general enlisted her.

As she walks into her house, she thinks about the time she met him at that cabin on the beach. He saw something in her back then. He saw a potential that nobody else could, not even herself. When Ally escaped and he ran after her, Liz thought about running too. She was terrified of him, afraid he would hurt her, but something made her stay. Today, she still doesn't know if it was simply the fact that she had nowhere else to go, that the cabin was the best hiding place, or if it was because she liked the general even though he terrified her. But once he came back and told her Ally had been arrested, she was glad she had made the decision to stay.

"Now it's just you and me," the general said. "You can choose to leave like your friend, run into the arms of the police, or you can stay here with me. I think I can make something of you. But only if you want to."

Liz stayed at the cabin for a week. The general knew so many people, and soon he came back and provided an entire new identity for her.

"Your name is now Liz Hester. Here's your passport and your social security number. When you're seventeen, I'll enlist you in the army and you'll work for me. I'll make a soldier of you. I'll make an excellent soldier of you."

She never dared to ask where he got the new papers for her, and to this day, she didn't know.

Liz sits down in a chair in her living room. She doesn't have much furniture. She doesn't need it. There isn't much in life she needs. Still, she never feels satisfied, she never feels complete.

Liz walks to the kitchen and grabs a glass of water. She drinks it while looking out on the street. A neighbor walks her dog. She is one of the stay-at-home moms that Liz loathes so much. She wants to pick up her gun and use the woman as a target. Start with the dog. Liz shapes a gun with her fingers and pretends to shoot her.

Liz is sick of feeling this way, of trying to find satisfaction in what will never fulfill her. She knows what she needs to do. She knows there is only one way for her if she wants to feel complete. She has been thirsting for this for so long. Thirsting for her revenge. She knows all the things she does, the things she has done throughout her life have only been substitutes for what she really wanted to do, who she really wanted to hurt.

Her phone rings. She picks it up. It's the general. He is coming over, he says. Half an hour later, he is at her house. As usual, he grabs her by the throat and pushes her up against the wall as soon as she opens the door. Then he pulls down her pants and has sex with her up against the wall. Liz doesn't enjoy it. She never has. But she has to do it. It's part of the deal they made back then. It's why he protects her. She thought that it would stop when he married her old school friend Olivia, but it never did. Olivia is for show. She is there for him to bring to parties and official gatherings. She's his trophy. It's Liz he comes for when he has other needs. Liz doesn't protest, even though it has been going on for twenty-something years. This way, no one can ever touch her. Having the general on her side makes her invincible. If she gets herself in trouble, he fixes it. He makes sure it goes away. It's their deal, their understanding. Just like he made everything go away back when they first met at the cabin. He even beat his own wife when she said she knew who Liz really was and threatened to tell the police one day when they had an argument. The general can take care of anything. Nothing is too big. At least it hasn't been so far.

While he finishes himself, Liz wonders if he will be able to clean up after her this time. When she is done with her little plan.

Maybe it doesn't matter.

82

SEPTEMBER 2015

IT FEELS SO good to be hanging out with Mary again. Sandra looks at her and smiles. It's been way too long. She misses her old friend. She has missed her terribly.

"Oh, my God, I absolutely love this song," Mary says, and turns up the radio really loud.

Nirvana and *Smells Like Teen Spirit* bursts out of the loudspeaker in the rental car. Immediately, they're both taken back in time. Mary starts to sing and Sandra chants along.

"*Hello, how low...Hello, how low...*"

Soon, they're both belting out loudly while memories flash in over them both. Sandra thinks about them driving in Danny's old beat up pick-up truck, all their surfboards in the back, the guys head banging with the long hair they had back then when everyone talked about grunge and wore flannel, even though it was way too hot in Florida. They would just cut off the sleeves and the guys wouldn't button their shirts.

Sandra chuckles at the memory. Then she remembers how in love she was with Alex. She wonders for a second why it never happened between them. Well, she knows. It's very simple, really. She chose her career over him. Fame and fortune. He would only hold her back, her parents said. The whole world was asking for her at that point. When she finally came back, he had married someone else. Maria. How Sandra loathes her. Not that she is entitled to. She made her choice.

She lets the thought go as Mary pulls up in front of a house and stops the engine.

"This should be it."

Sandra looks at the yellow two-story house across from the beach. On the porch, there is an old swing. Sandra always wanted that. She always dreamt about having a porch with a swing that she could sit on with all of her children and one day grandchildren. Suddenly, she can't remember why she never had children. It was her dream. It was what she wanted. But, it doesn't combine well with her career. Besides, Ryan isn't that interested in children.

"Let's go talk to them," Mary says, and gets out of the car.

Sandra follows her. She envies Mary so much for having both a career and a child. She even envies her for not having to care about her weight or how she looks. Sandra is sick of having to be on a constant diet. Right now, she eats nothing but raw food. It helps with her complexion and she needs to because of the shoot, but indulging herself in a bag of chips like she allowed herself to on the way here, felt so good. She misses it. She misses feeling alive. Misses enjoying her life.

Mary rings the doorbell, but no one answers. She rings it again, then opens the screen door and knocks on the door. Sandra can sense how it annoys her that no one answers.

"I don't think they're home," Sandra says.

They walk back to the car, Mary visibly annoyed, when someone walks towards them on the street with a dog on a leash. Sandra stops and pets the dog.

"Is it an Australian Shepherd?" she asks.

"Why, yes. As a matter of fact it is," the woman answers. "Not many people guess that."

"I love dogs. Have a Chihuahua at home."

"That's nice."

"Say, do you live around here?" Sandra asks.

"Yes, I do. I live right over there in the green house."

"We're looking for Janice Meyer. Do you know if she still lives in this house?" Sandra asks and points at the house behind her. Mary approaches them now, suddenly interested.

"Oh, she died five years back, I believe it was. Cancer. It spread. You know how it is."

Sandra nods in sympathy.

"Do you know what happened to her daughter?" Mary asks.

The woman smiles and nods. "Sure. She lives there now. Took over the house when her mother died. Keeps mostly to herself."

"Do you have any idea where we can find her?" Sandra asks.

"Oh, she's probably at work now. She drives one of those grooming vans. You know the ones that come to your house and groom your dog. It's very popular around here. *Groomers on Wheels*, I believe the company is called."

83

SEPTEMBER 2015

I GOOGLE the name of the company while sitting in the car, still parked in Ally Meyer's driveway.

"Grooming on wheels," a singing voice says at the other end.

"Hello, I'm looking for Ally Meyer," I say.

"My. She is a popular woman today," the voice says. "Well, she is one of our best, so it's actually no surprise. What do you need to have done?"

"Eh, I need my Goldendoodle groomed. Does she have time today?" I ask, looking at Sandra, who shrugs.

I am not lying. Snowflake could really do with a trim.

"How long since his last grooming?"

"Three months."

"Three months on a Goldendoodle? That's a long time. It'll probably be a big job then. I don't know if Ally can make it today."

"It's not that big of a job. I've kept his fur brushed every day. He has hardly any mats," I lie. Snowflake seriously needs a grooming, and I haven't been brushing him every day as I should, like you have to do with a long-haired doodle. I lie because I feel like the woman is judging me, making me feel guilty. I wonder why I care.

"It will still be a big job," she says. "Let me see. Right now she is in Cocoa Beach. After that she is going to the base around four, but if you can wait till around six this evening, she might be able to make it. I know it's late, but it's all I got with this short notice. Where are you at?"

"I'm in Cocoa Beach. Did you say she has a job at the base, as in Patrick Air Force Base?" I ask.

Sandra's eyes meet mine.

"Yes. We have a lot of clients there," the woman says.

"Thank you," I say, and hang up.

"She has a job on the base at four o'clock," I say to Sandra.

"You think it's AK?"

"That's what I'm afraid of," I say, and start the car. "Last night, she tried to kill Olivia, and now she's going for Ally."

"So what do we do now?" Sandra asks.

I drive onto A1A and accelerate. "We get the crew together," I say. "Start calling them."

Half an hour later, we all meet at Joey's house. Snowflake is enjoying all the company, not to mention the attention and visits from person to person to get petted. Bonnie and Clyde follow in his trail. They seem to go wherever he goes.

Joey gets there last.

"So, what's going on?" Danny asks.

"We believe we know who killed Jean," Chloe says.

"We think someone is targeting a group of girls from our high school. Coraline Cane is dead, Cassie Morgan is dead, and so is Jean Schmidt. I spoke earlier today with Holly Leslie. I don't know if any of you remember her, but she was part of their little gang as well. She told me how she was attacked in 1995 by AK and the other girls and shot with a spear gun. She was lucky to get out of it alive. We believe AK is trying to kill all of them. Last night, there was an attempt to kill Olivia as well; someone tried to stab her in the throat with a pair of scissors, but we managed to stop her. It happened on base, and as we, or as Chloe has found out, AK lives on base where she is now called Liz Hester. We need your help to find AK's next target. I have reason to believe it is Ally Meyer. Sandra and I tried to locate her earlier today, but were told she was here in Cocoa Beach."

"Ally Meyer...?" Alex looks at me, then at the others.

Joey gives me a concerned look as well. "But...isn't that?"

I nod. "Yes. She is the one who was with AK when they broke into my house that night when AK shot my mother." I take in a deep breath, pushing back the memories and emotions. "I know what you're all thinking, and yes, I am pissed and I can't forgive her for what she did, but she still doesn't deserve to die. We need to stop AK or Liz or whatever her name is now, before she kills more people. For all we know, she might come after any one of us next. I know she has it in for me. We need to find Ally before she gets to her."

"How?" Danny asks. He is always the practical one. If there is a problem, he wants to find out how to solve it right away, instead of spending time discussing the issue. He has always been like that. I love that about him.

"She drives a grooming van for Groomers on Wheels. She has a client here in Cocoa Beach now, and then at four o'clock, she is going to the base. We have to get to her before she gets there."

Danny nods and finds his phone. "I'll tell the boys to look for her van. We can easily search the area if we bring out all the trucks."

"How about alerting the police?" Alex asks, while Danny leaves the room with the phone to his ear.

I look at him and wonder if he is right. I am just not certain I trust them. Especially not Chris Fisher. Besides, I am not sure they'll believe me.

"No police," Marcia says. "We don't need them. I'll take my bike and drive down to Minutemen. I know everyone that hangs out around there. I know every drunk, every homeless person in town. They usually have eyes on every corner. They'll know if she's here."

"I can get us access to the police's surveillance cameras on all the stoplights," Chloe says.

Sandra looks at me while everyone is scattered. "What do we do?"

I look at Joey, then back at Sandra. "The only thing we can do."

84

SEPTEMBER 2015

"HOW SHORT DO YOU WANT IT?"

Ally looks at the woman holding the poodle. The woman has been a client for two years. Ally can't stand her. Not her fancy home across from the country club, nor her spoiled poodle, and especially not her stiff upper lip that she always presents when Ally shows up in her van.

"Just like last time. Not too short, though," the woman says.

"And you want the nails clipped and the ears cleaned, right?"

"Yes."

"And the private parts."

"Yes. By all means. How much is it again that you charge for all that?"

As if you don't know.

"Seventy-five."

"That's a little much, don't you think?"

Here we go again!

"It's the standard price. I don't make them."

"I'll give you sixty-five," the woman says with a snort.

It's not like you can't afford it, lady!

Ally sighs. The first time she came to the woman's house, she agreed to the sixty-five, since she was new and afraid that the woman would take her business elsewhere. But the company made her pay the last ten out of her own paycheck, so she hasn't made that mistake again. And she isn't going to today either.

"It's the price. As I said, I don't make the prices."

The woman snorts again. "Okay then."

The woman hands Ally the leash and the dog walks to her reluctantly.

"I should have her back in less than an hour," Ally says.

She takes the poodle to the van and helps her get inside. The poodle tries to fight her, but Ally is a lot stronger, and soon she has the dog inside and can close the door behind them.

Ally sighs and sits down. She is tired. Sick and tired of dogs, and especially their owners. Driving a grooming van got you in contact with some of the worst of them. The rich upper class ones who just wanted everything done for basically no money at all. Why are the richest always the cheapest? Grooming dogs is hard work. Ally should be paid for it. She should be making a lot more than she does.

The poodle is not comfortable in the van. It knows what's going to happen. Ally turns on the water in the bathtub and puts in the soap. The dog squirms and tries to escape. Ally fights with it for a little while, hurts her hand in the process, then pulls out a syringe and injects a sedative in the dog. She waits a few seconds till the dog calms down before she finally manages to put it in the bathtub. The owners don't know that she sedates the dogs to make the grooming go smoother. Neither does the company. It was one of the other groomers that taught her the trick when Ally asked her how on earth she managed those troubled dogs. She even sells her the drug. It makes things a lot easier. The sedative is out of the dog's body within an hour, just in time to hand her back to the owner. She might be a little groggy afterwards, but not enough to make the owners suspect anything.

Ally bathes the now heavily sleeping dog, then grabs the shaver and cuts the hair. She cuts her around the eyes, then clips the nails, trims the ears and the private parts. She blow-dries the hair and looks at her work. It all takes about twenty minutes, then she waits till the dog wakes up again. The dog is big, and therefore wakes up before planned. Ally is happy to get out of there early.

She hands back the dog. The woman writes her a check for seventy-five dollars.

"See you in two months," Ally says, then leaves.

She gets into the van and looks at her list of today's clients. Only one more left. She starts the van and drives up Minutemen Causeway and soon finds herself on A1A, where she turns right. On her way, she passes three fire trucks, which strikes her as odd, but she doesn't take any more notice. On the passenger seat besides her lies her phone. It lights up, but is silenced, so she doesn't hear that it is ringing. Ally is whistling in the car when she continues on A1A towards the base and her last client of the day.

85

SEPTEMBER 2015

"SHE'S BEEN SPOTTED on Minutemen two minutes ago."

Marcia sounds agitated on the phone. "Johnny, who hangs out on the corner by City Hall, saw her drive onto A1A in the intersection."

"Two minutes ago?" I ask and look at my watch. "That means she is probably already down by 15th Street, maybe even further."

I hang up and look at Sandra. Joey is sitting in the back. We have been driving around our neighborhood and Snug Harbor to see if we could spot her somewhere around here. Meanwhile, I am debating with the woman at the groomer's main office on the phone. I want her to tell me where Ally is; I even tell her it's a matter of life and death, but she keeps telling me she is not allowed to give me the address. Instead, I tell her to call Ally on her cellphone and tell her to call me. I keep looking at my phone, hoping she will.

I hit A1A and speed up, when Danny calls. "She's been spotted at 16th a minute ago.

"16th! That means she is halfway to the base," I say, and hang up. I press the gas pedal down and exceed the thirty-five mile limit by...well, by a lot.

I pass 10th, then 11th, and when I reach 16th, I receive a text from Chloe. Sandra reads it to me.

"Her truck just stopped for a red light at the Officer's Club," she says.

The break in front of the Officer's Club is one of our old favorite surf spots. It is the first red light you meet after you leave Cocoa Beach, driving south towards the base. She is going faster than I expected. I have to accelerate, hoping the red light will hold her for a long enough time for me to catch up with her. If she makes it onto the base, then I can't get to her anymore; I can't help her.

"Hurry up," Sandra says.

"I'm trying to. But these cars won't get out of my way. I'm stuck." I honk the horn at the pickup truck blocking my way going twenty-five miles an hour. Next to him, a Toyota has parked on the inner lane. I can't get past them.

"If she's at the O Club, then there is only maybe thirty seconds till she reaches the base," Joey says.

I look at my clock. "She's early. By half an hour. She isn't supposed to be there until four. I had planned to go there just before four and stop her if we hadn't found her before," I say. "How was I supposed to know she would get there half an hour early?"

I growl and honk again. Finally, the car on the inside moves out of my way and I can go around the truck. I race past Summer Street, past Taco City and my favorite surf shop, Oceansports World.

I reach the O Club and realize the light has turned green. I speed up and think that I can spot the van in the distance.

"Is that her?" I ask Sandra. She has better eyes than me. "Is that the grooming van?"

"I...I don't know," Sandra says. She leans forward to better see, but still shakes her head. "It might be."

"We've got to get to her," I grunt. "We've got to stop her."

"Yes," Sandra suddenly exclaims. "I see it now. It's her. It's the van. It says *Grooming on Wheels* on the back. Hurry up. We're almost there. You can make it, Mary."

I literally stand on the pedal in order to press it to the bottom. I can see the van getting closer now.

"Almost there," Joey says.

"Almost," Sandra repeats.

I can see her now. I can see the van getting closer and closer. I realize she has stopped for another red light, at the intersection leading to the base. I have to reach her before the light turns green and she turns onto the base. I have to.

"Hurry, hurry," Sandra says.

"I'll make it. Once I get up to the side of her van, you roll down the window. Both of you. Then you yell at her, all right? Tell her to pull to the curb. All right? I need both of you to do it."

"Got it," they say in unison.

We can make it. I think we can. I know we can. Come on!

I manage to convince myself that we'll actually make it, when I hear the siren behind me.

86

SEPTEMBER 2015

"IT'S THE POLICE! You've got to stop, Mary!"

Sandra is screaming now.

"No! You can't stop now," Joey yells. "We're so close."

The siren is wailing behind us. He is flashing his lights at me, trying to get me to stop. Meanwhile, the light turns green, and the van with Ally Meyer in it starts to go; it blinks to signal that it is turning, but holds back for oncoming traffic.

"You've got to stop," Sandra repeats. "I don't want to get shot. He will shoot. You know what they're like. Or he will hit our car with his to try and stop us. I don't want to die."

"You watch too many movies, Sandra," I say.

I keep going. I don't stop. The police car is getting closer to us. It has a stronger engine than my rental car. In a few seconds, it will be next to us.

"Stop! Mary, stop!" Sandra yells, and hides her face between her hands, just as I reach the van.

"Now!" I yell and turn the car to get up onto the side of it.

Joey is the only one who reacts. He rolls down the window. He yells and waves. "Stop! Stop the van! Don't go! STOP!!"

I have to keep looking at the road, so I can't see if she notices him. "Did she see you?" I ask.

"She saw me! She turned her head and looked at me," Joey says. "But..."

But she doesn't stop.

Our car screeches across the asphalt and lands in the grass, while her van continues through the gates of the base. She stops to talk to the guard shortly, but is let in within seconds. They know her.

I curse and growl. The police car has stopped behind us. The officer gets out of his car and walks to ours, pointing his gun at us, yelling for me to keep my hands on the wheel.

It takes maybe ten minutes, maybe fifteen, but finally I manage to convince him that I am not dangerous, that I am not drunk or intoxicated. I go through all the tests and don't fail even one. Not even the walking straight on a line, even though I am so agitated it is hard for me to focus.

He gives me a ticket for reckless driving, then tells Joey to take the wheel going back.

"Thank you, Officer," I say, trying to keep my cool. As soon as he is gone, I look at my friends, holding the ticket in my hand.

"Now what?" Joey says.

"I might have an idea," I say.

I grab my phone and call Danny. Meanwhile, Joey drives us to the nearest parking lot in front of the O Club. Danny arrives a few minutes later in his fire truck. It shines brightly in the sun.

"What's going on?" he asks and gets out. "Did you stop her?"

"No. She went in. I need you to get me onto the base," I say.

"No. No. No," he says and waves his finger at me.

"Yes. Yes. Yes," I say. "I know you can. In that thing. They'll never question a firefighter, a fellow hero. There's a fire station on base, right? Tell them you're here to visit your colleagues."

Danny looks at me.

"Please?" I say. "You're the hero here. You would want to save a life if you could, right? I should be the one hating Ally and not caring about her, but come on. She doesn't deserve to be killed. And we can't let AK get away with it. She has gotten away with way too much in her life. If we can get to Ally and get her to testify against AK, then maybe we could get her locked up. But we can't if she is dead."

"She's got a point, bro," Joey says.

Danny stares at me, then nods. "Alright then. I'll see what I can do. You can hide in the back. I can't promise you anything, though. Just pray that we don't get picked for a random search."

"Let me do it," Joey says. "It might be dangerous."

"No," I say. "I am the only one Ally will listen to. I am the one she wronged, remember? She owes me and she knows it."

I jump in and lay flat on the floor of the fire truck. Danny puts a blanket over me to cover me up. Sandra and Joey stay behind. Joey's and my eyes meet just before Danny closes the door. I can tell he is concerned.

Frankly, so am I.

87

SEPTEMBER 2015

WE'RE IN LUCK. The guard at the gate buys Danny's story about paying his buddies a surprise visit. The guard calls the fire station and they're thrilled that Danny is stopping by.

We're let in. Once again, I have tricked my way onto the base.

As soon as we drive past the big signs and huge buildings, Danny tells me I can get up from the floor. I rise to my knees, and watch out the window as the base passes by.

"So, where are we going?" Danny asks, and I realize I have no clue. "We don't have long," he says. "The guys at the fire station will start to wonder where I am. Then they'll start looking for us."

"I know," I say. "I am trying to figure it out." I grab my phone and text Chloe. I ask her if she can find Liz Hester's address. It's my theory that AK has called the groomer and asked specifically for Ally to come to her home to take care of a dog that she probably doesn't even have.

Seconds later, she texts me back with an address.

What would I do without her?

I spot the van in front of the house as we approach the address and swallow hard.

"I hope we're not too late," I say.

Danny parks the truck in front of the house, then turns to look at me. "There's a box in the back, could you give it to me?"

I find the box and hand it to him. He opens it and reveals two guns. I know nothing about guns and have never even fired one. The mere sight of them makes me jump. Danny picks up one of them, then checks the holster, and then hands it to me. He grabs the other one himself.

"We have these for protection," he says. "Sometimes, we have to go into very dangerous neighborhoods. We need to protect ourselves."

"Of course," I say, and hold the gun in my hand. It looks so wrong. It feels so wrong. I am more terrified of accidentally shooting myself, but still I take it...just in case.

Danny tucks his into the back of his pants like in the movies, and I do the same. It feels strange and I try to walk carefully, afraid it might accidentally shoot me in the leg or worse.

We walk up to the house and stop at the front door. I ring the doorbell, then hear a loud crash coming from inside. I look at Danny, who takes out his gun. I do the same and watch while Danny walks back, then kicks the door in, like he is probably used to from his line of work.

The door slams to the ground and we enter. I steel myself. I tell myself I can do it. Of course I can.

Then we walk in.

I point the gun and walk after Danny inside the living room, my heart pounding in my chest. I can feel my pulse against my temples. I hold my breath.

"Hello?" Danny yells. "Is everyone okay in here?"

No answer. A noise comes from the kitchen. We hurry in there. Then we stop. On the kitchen floor is Ally; her face is smashed into the tiles. On top of her sits AK or Liz, whatever she goes by these days. She is holding a gun to her face, pressing it angrily against her temple.

I gasp.

"AK," Danny says.

AK looks up, and her eyes meet mine.

"Don't do it," I say. "Don't kill her."

AK grunts, then laughs while still staring at me. Her eyes are like needles on my body. She raises the gun and points it at me.

"Maybe I'll just kill you instead? How about that, huh?"

88

MAY 1986

PENELOPE TAKES her daughter into the lobby of the hospital. After fifteen minutes of waiting, a nurse tells them to come in for preparation. They put the girl in a bed and insert tubes and a drip.

"Now, this operation will take a few hours," the nurse tells Penelope. "She will need to have general anesthesia. Has she had that before?"

Penelope nods. "Yes. Once."

"So, she has no problem with it. That's great. It will take a few hours for her to wake up, and then we will need to monitor the heart for the next several months. Will you be able to come down here for check-ups, or do you want to have them done up in your own area? We can recommend a doctor if necessary. It is an awfully long drive. I couldn't blame you if you wanted to find someone closer to you."

"No. It's fine," Penelope says. "We've tried all the doctors up there, and they have proven to be quite incompetent. We will come here for her check-ups. It's no big deal; it really isn't."

The nurse stares at Penelope, then smiles. "Well, okay then. I'll make sure to set it up." She looks at the child, then smiles compassionately. "I'll take you to preparation now."

"I'll come too," Penelope says.

"I'm sorry," the nurse says. "Only the patient is allowed."

Penelope looks disappointed. "Really?"

"Sorry. Those are the rules here. We have a nice waiting area out in the back. There's a cafeteria where you can get something to eat and some couches with a TV and some newspapers to keep you busy. I know it's hard having to wait for this, but it's how the doctors want it. There is nothing I can do."

"Alright then," she says with a sigh.

She watches as the child is rolled away. The nurse takes her to an elevator, then takes her to the third floor, where she is rolled into her own room.

"Here. This will be where you wake up once you get out of the anesthesia. It's no hotel room, but I think it's pretty nice. Look at all the drawings on the walls from other children who have stayed here. They all had the same procedure that you're about to have. Now, you shouldn't worry. I can tell you're afraid. I've seen that look many times, but I tell you, the doctors here are the best. They'll take really good care of you and make that heart of yours work normally again."

The nurse taps the girl on her chest as she speaks. As she does, tears start to roll down the child's cheeks. The nurse sees it.

"No. Don't cry, little girl. It's all going to be just fine. Don't you worry. These doctors have done it so many times. You'll be just fine."

"But..." the girl says, then stops herself. She looks nervously at the nurse. "What are you going to do to me?"

"You mean you don't know?"

The girl shakes her head. More tears stream down her face. The nurse sits next to her on the bed, then caresses her hair. The girl's legs are dangling from the side of the bed.

"Well, the doctor will cut you open right here," she says and points at the girl's chest. "Then he will do a heart catheterization procedure."

The girl gasps and looks up at the nurse with terror in her eyes.

"Aw, don't worry," the nurse says. "You won't feel a thing. You'll be sleeping the entire time."

"She's making it up," the girl suddenly says with a small quiet voice.

"What's that, sweetie?"

"My mom. She's making it up," she says louder now.

The nurse laughs. "Now, don't go around saying stuff like that. I know it's an uncomfortable situation, but I'm sure your mom is nothing but a concerned mother."

The girl looks into the eyes of the nurse. The nurse suddenly senses the urgency. It scares her.

"No. I mean she is making it up. Really. She is," the girl says.

89

SEPTEMBER 2015

I CAN'T BREATHE. The sight of the gun pointing at me makes me panic. I drop my own gun and raise my hands. I feel like an idiot. So stupid. Not so much Tom Cruise anymore. Danny puts down his gun as well.

"Don't do anything stupid," he says.

"It's quite the little reunion we have going here," AK says. "Are there any more of you people coming? I'm sorry I didn't put on a pot of coffee. I've been quite busy with this little monster here."

"AK," I say and walk closer. "It's me you're angry at. Why not let the others go? You know as well as I do that it's me you want. Am I right?"

AK stares at me like she is making up her mind. Then she shakes her head. "Sorry. No can do."

"Come on, AK," I say. "What has Ally done to you that is so bad?"

"Well, first of all, she's a snitch. She told everything to the police. If I hadn't run into the general that night, I would be in jail by now. She would have made sure I was put away for the rest of my life."

"But, AK. This is really about you and me," I say. "Come on, let's get it out in the open."

AK is still pointing the gun at me. Ally is growling underneath her. "Get off me," she yells. But AK doesn't move.

"So, you're mad at me," I say. "You've been mad for, what? Almost thirty years now? I am sorry. I am sorry for what I did."

"No, you're not," she says. "You're not the least bit sorry. I know you're not. I can tell. I know you better than you think, Mary."

"Alright. You got me. You're absolutely right. I am not the least bit sorry that I spoke up. I am not the least bit sorry that I stopped them from cutting my heart open when there was absolutely nothing wrong with me. I did it to save myself. And to save you, AK. My mother, *our* mother was killing the both of us. She wouldn't have stopped there if I hadn't spoken up. She would have continued. When I told the nurse that day at the hospital, she called the doctors and they immediately called the authorities. Why no one did that before, I don't know. I have wondered so many times, blamed so many people for closing their eyes. Munchausen Syndrome wasn't a well-known disease back then. But the thing is that once the authorities were informed, our mother finally received help. She was admitted. She received the help she needed to get better, and when she had Blake, she never did anything bad to him. So, no, I am not sorry for what I did. I saved you, AK. I saved your freaking life."

I can feel the tears rolling down my cheeks now. All the memories. All those days spent in bed, when I wasn't sick. All the doctors and nurses and emergency trips to the ER. The worry in my mother's eyes, the doctors constantly running tests, not knowing what to do. All that salt my mother shoved down my throat to make me throw up, all the crying for her to stop. I had thought it was normal...that this was how mothers were. That was just the way life was. I never questioned it until that day when she took me to the hospital in Miami and a nurse told me they would do surgery on my heart. That was when I couldn't take it anymore. That's when I finally spoke up, even though it killed me to defy my mother like that, to go against what she had told me to do.

"I am sorry, though," I continue, "about what happened to you. I am sorry that the adoption agency took you back and placed you in that home. I am so sorry about that."

"You...you destroyed my life," AK says. She too has tears rolling down her cheeks now. The gun is shaking in her hands. "You have no idea what they did to me at that home. How my life was ruined. I had a family, Mary. When your parents adopted me, I finally had a family. I had a father and a sister. But most of all, I finally had a mother. A mother who cared about me. I had never had that before. Penelope cared so much for me. I have never had that, Mary. Never." AK wipes her face on her sleeve. "You don't know how much it hurt to get that close. And then to have it taken away from me? You haven't even a clue. You got your life back afterwards. You continued to live in that big house on the beach, having a mother and a father and even a brother later on. I had to watch you every day at school, see your happy face while my life was in ruins. You are so spoiled, Mary, and you don't even know it. That's why I wanted you to feel what it was like to not have any parents, to lose everything. So I killed your mother and set your father's house on fire. With him in it. How does it feel, huh? Seeing him in that bed at the hospital? I'm sure he won't survive. I bet you'll have to turn off his life-support soon, right? I can't think of a better way to take you down than this. You'll have to kill him yourself. Now, how do you like that?"

90

SEPTEMBER 2015

"NO!!"

I am staring at AK, my nostrils flaring. I scream the word, right before I leap through the air. I don't care if she shoots me. I don't care if I get hurt anymore. Or even if I die. I am so angry now, I can't hold it back.

I hate her for what she has done.

My move takes her by surprise, and she doesn't shoot until it's too late. The shot hits the ceiling and ricochets back towards her. It hits her in the leg. Danny throws himself to the ground. I land on top of AK and pull her off of Ally's back. I manage to throw in a few punches while AK screams in pain.

"This is for my mother!" I scream, and throw in a punch in her face. "And this is for my father!"

I run my fist into her face again and again. AK is screaming and yelling. Blood is gushing out of her leg from where the bullet hit her. Meanwhile, Ally gets to her feet and stands next to me. I don't pay much attention to what else is going on in the room. I hardly even hear Danny screaming, *NO!*

I don't notice what's around me. Not until I hear another shot being fired and blood spurts into my face. AK's body goes limp beneath me. Her head has a hole in it and her blood is creating a pool around her.

I gasp and let go of her. Her blood is all over my hands.

I look up and into the eyes of Ally, who is standing with the smoking gun. She is still pointing it at me. On the floor behind her, I see a pair of scissors. That's when it hits me. That's when I finally realize what I should have a long time ago.

"You?" I say.

Ally nods. It's not until now I realize she's wearing a surgical mask covering half of her face.

"You killed Coraline, Jean, and Cassie? You tried to kill Olivia and now you've killed AK."

Ally nods again, still pointing the gun at me. Danny stays completely still in the corner.

"Why?" I ask.

"Because of what they did to me," she says.

Ally then grabs her surgical mask and pulls it off, revealing a mouth slit from ear to ear.

I gasp and clasp my mouth.

"They did that to you?"

"They came to my door in 1995," she says. "We had moved away. My mother and I lived in Melbourne. I thought AK was long gone. I thought she was out of my life for good. It had been three years since the night we... when we broke into your house. I had told the police everything. I had moved on with my life. Started a new school, made new friends, stayed out of trouble. I was a straight A student and doing so well for myself. I was back on track and determined to stay there. Until they rang my doorbell on that night in March. They attacked me at my house when I refused to go with them. They cut me with a knife. Do you have any idea how hard it is to get a job when you look like this? I had nothing for so many years. When my mother died, I had to find some way to make money. So I came up with the idea of grooming dogs. No one cares that I wear a mask. But I can never have a normal life. Never!"

"So, you killed them?"

I look at Danny, thinking it must be hard for him to hear all this. Jean was his wife through almost twenty years and the mother of his son.

"Yes, I did. And now I have to kill you as well. Both of you."

Everything happens so fast. I believe I am the first to hear it. Footsteps outside closing in. And then...the piercing smash. Glass is shattered every-where. Flying through the air is something, or maybe someone, crashing through the window.

I am thrown to the floor. All three of us fall down. Someone jumps over me. I scream while glass surrounds me. Someone is on top of Ally, holding her down. Chaos and shouting. Danny is pushed down. The person on top of Ally is struggling to hold her down. I blink my eyes. The man is in uniform. I recognize his face.

It's the general.

Ally is screaming. She reaches for the gun and grabs ahold of it. I don't think the general has seen it.

"She's still got the gun!" I yell.

Ally lifts the gun up in the air and I lunge forward to try and grab her, but I am not fast enough. She places the gun on her temple.

"NO!"

And then she pulls the trigger.

91

OCTOBER 2015

TWO WEEKS LATER, I am standing in front of the prison as my brother is let out. I see him and wave when he approaches the gate. The door makes a buzzing sound and he can finally step out.

As a free man.

"Yay!" I yell and run to him. I throw myself in his arms and hug him tightly. A tear leaves my eyes and ends its days on my lip before I wipe it away.

"Hey, sis," he says, and kisses my forehead. "Boy, it feels good to be out." He takes a deep breath of the intoxicating fresh air. He closes his eyes quickly, then looks at me again. "Thank you for never giving up."

"Let's get out of here," I say, and point at the car where Salter and Joey are waiting. Behind them is Sandra, parked in her Escalade. Inside sits Marcia, Chloe, Alex, and Danny. They poke their heads out of the windows.

"Hi, Blake! Welcome home!" Marcia yells. She holds a bottle of gin in her hand, which she gives to him. "Here. I bet you've missed this." Then she laughs with her hoarse voice.

"Everyone came?" Blake asks, looking at me.

"Well, we're almost family, right? Not one of us believed you were guilty."

"I'm moved, guys," Blake says.

"What are you waiting for?" Marcia says. "Let's get out of this dump. I have a beer with my name on it at the Beach Shack."

Blake gets in the car with me, Salter, and Joey. We all drive back to the beach. I, for one, am feeling grateful. I am so glad I finally managed to get my brother out. It wasn't easy. Ally was gone and couldn't admit to having killed Jamilla Jenkins. But once I got the general on my side, Chris Fisher finally listened to my story. The general told me he had received a phone call from the firefighters at the base telling him about Danny, who had announced his arrival, but never showed up. He immediately knew something had to be wrong and started a search. They found the truck parked outside of Liz's house. Worried about Liz, he looked through the window, where he saw Ally pointing a gun at us, and immediately took action. It was the general who made sure Chris Fisher would listen to what I had to say. I told him what Ally had told me and all the details about AK, alias Liz Hester. I told him how she admitted to having killed all the girls, but it bothered me that I had never asked about Jamilla Jenkins. I told him I had a feeling the four killings had to be connected, since they had many similarities, and asked him to look into it. Ten days later, he told me they had searched Ally's house and found Jamilla Jenkins' purse in her closet. They had also found out that Ally groomed Jamilla Jenkins' dog about a year ago, but they got into a fight over the price. The fight that was heard by many neighbors turned bad, and Ally Meyer ended up threatening Jamilla Jenkins. That was enough to drop the charges against my brother, and now he is finally free.

"Free as a bird. Boy, it feels good," he says, and stretches in his seat.

Blake rolls down the window while we drive across the bridges and sticks his head out like a dog. The rest of us laugh. It's such a relief for me. I can't believe I actually pulled it off, that I actually got him out.

We drive back to Joey's house, where Blake gets the bedroom and I sleep with Joey on the couch. It can be pulled out, so it's big enough for the both of us.

"Are you guys...?" Blake asks the next morning when we eat our pancakes that Joey so generously made for all of us. I am smearing mine with Nutella when the question is asked.

I stop moving. I can feel Joey's eyes on me. I don't know what to answer. I have made no decisions yet. I don't want to. Right now, I just want to enjoy whatever it is we have. I don't want to think about the future. I really don't.

I avoid looking up. I don't want to look at anyone. I want them to stop staring at me. It makes me uncomfortable. I can't help it. I can't help myself. It starts as a giggle. Soon it turns into a loud laugh. I can't stop it. It overwhelms me.

Seconds later, the others laugh along with me.

92

OCTOBER 2015

BLAKE IS PACKING HIS SUITCASE. It's been three days since he left
the prison. He has been to his studio once to grab his clothes and the few
belongings he can't live without. His paintings, he has placed in Joey's
garage. He'll ask Mary to try and sell them for him. She has put the one
from Starbucks up in Joey's living room. He likes to look at it and sense how
proud she is of him. He has no idea when he'll paint again, though. He's not
going back to the studio. Too many bad memories. He needs to move on
with his life. Jail was a bad experience. A real bad experience.

Mary steps in.

"So, Joey took Salter to work with him today. Guess it's just going to be
you and me here." She pauses and looks at the suitcase. "What are you
doing?"

He detects disappointment in her voice.

"I'm leaving, sis. Gotta get out of here, you know?"

She looks surprised. "You're leaving? But why? To go where?"

Blake shrugs. "Anywhere but here. I need to get away. I'm kind of tired
of Cocoa Beach, if you know what I mean."

"But...but what about Dad?" she asks. "He might wake up soon."

Blake sighs. "Sis. Come on. The only reason he is alive is because of the
machines breathing for him. You know it. I know it. He is not going to wake
up. You have to let it go. The doctor even told you to shut off the life-
support. I've already given my consent. Even Laura agrees. He's gone.
You've gotta realize that."

Mary shakes her head. "I'm never going to shut him off. He'll wake up soon and then...then what?"

"You're hopeless," he says with a sigh. "I'm sure you'll take very good care of him. If it ever happens. "

Mary grunts and slams her hand onto the suitcase. "You can't just leave. Goddammit, Blake. You're the only family I have."

"You have Joey. You have Salter and Snowflake. Besides, you'll be going back to New York soon, and then what? I don't want to be left down here alone. I'm running off. Getting out while I can."

"I'm not sure we're going back," Mary says.

"What? What about your career?"

"I was fired. I didn't tell you because of all you were going through, but they sacked me. I have nothing to go back to. Salter doesn't even have a school anymore. He stayed down here for too long. They gave his spot to someone else. I can't pay for it anyway. I used all my money on a lawyer for you."

Blake sits down on the bed next to Mary. "Wow," he says.

"I know. It's bad. You can't leave too. You just can't. You're the only one I have here."

"What about Joey? What about the crew?"

"Alright, I have them as well. And I love them, but I don't know what to do about Joey. I love him, but I still don't know if I want to be with him or not. You know what I mean?"

"Sure."

"See. That's why I need you. You understand me."

Blake puts his arm around Mary's neck. He kisses her forehead. "I'll come visit."

She sniffles. "Do you even have any money?"

"Well, I don't. But Olivia does."

Mary stares at him, startled. "Olivia?"

"Yeah. She's leaving with me. The general agreed to a divorce."

"So, you're still together?" Mary asks.

"I guess so."

Mary smiles and looks at him. "As long as you're happy."

"Well, I am," Blake says, and gets to his feet again. He walks to the suitcase and grabs it with the intention of closing it.

Mary watches him. She gets up and walks to the door. On her way, she passes his phone on the dresser. It lights up. Before he can stop her, she picks it up.

"Olivia sent you a message," she says teasingly.

Blake opens his eyes wide. "Give it to me," he says. "It's private."

But she doesn't. She opens the message. "I'm your sister. You can't have any secrets from me. Not anymore. Let's see what she wrote..."

Blake lunges towards her, but it's too late. Mary stares at the phone, her mouth open. It looks like she is trying to scream, but no sound comes across her lips.

Shit!

93

OCTOBER 2015

"WHAT'S THIS BLAKE?"

I stare at my brother. I can't believe my eyes. "What IS this?"

I yell in frustration. I am shaking all over while I stare at the picture of Jamilla Jenkins on the bed at the motel. Olivia is sitting next to her dead body with the chisel deep in her chest. Olivia is smiling and making a gesture like she is standing in front of the Statue of Liberty or another tourist attraction. I have never seen anything this appalling in my life.

"Why did she send you this picture? Can you tell me that? Blake?" I try to control my voice as I speak. "Why?"

Just like that, my brother's expression changes completely. He laughs, then walks to the door and shuts it. "Well, dear *Sis*, if you must know. *That*...is Jamilla Jenkins."

I drop the phone. I clasp my mouth with both my hands. I can't believe it. "You killed her? You killed her with...with Olivia?"

"Yes. Jamie Barley was there too. Just as she told the police she was. We picked them up at Squid Lips, then drove to the motel. To have some fun. They were very drunk. Apparently, Jamie was so drunk she believed we had gone back to my studio and not the motel. That was my luck, since it made it all so unbelievable, didn't it? Once you came down, you couldn't believe I would have moved the body, right?"

"But...but...Blake...why?"

"Let's just say Olivia and I like to play games. It went a little further than expected. When Olivia handed me the chisel, I didn't think I could do it, but she cheered me on, aroused me enough to do it. We cleaned the room, took the bloody sheet with us and burned it. Left nothing but the body. We knew we couldn't move it without someone seeing us. But we left no trace, no fingerprints, no DNA. I even used a condom and we took the chisel with us."

"So, the general didn't frame you? He didn't plant the chisel, nor did he pay off Jamie Barley to testify against you? He didn't do those things to get rid of you because you were screwing his wife?"

Blake laughs. "He certainly didn't. He only told Jamie to never talk about Olivia, but that wasn't hard, because they knew each other well. But it makes a good story, doesn't it? It is very believable that the big bad husband, a general in the army on top of it, would go to these lengths to get rid of me, doesn't it? I can see why you would believe that. So I played along."

"And...what about the confession?"

"All part of it. I had a feeling you could get me out somehow. And I was right. I knew you wouldn't let it go. Especially not if you believed the general was getting to me. I knew it would make you speed up the process. I had nothing to lose, did I?"

I can hardly breathe when I speak. I can't wrap my mind around this. It's too much. It's simply too much to cope with.

"And the purse at Ally's house?"

"Planted by Olivia. We had the purse all the time. Or Olivia did. It was easy for her to drive down there and plant it in the closet behind some clothes. It was our luck that it turned out that Jamilla Jenkins had also been Ally Meyer's client. That made things a little easier on us. So, I guess what I am saying here, Sis, is thank you. I owe you one."

"What?"

I stare at my brother, who is approaching me slowly. I don't like the look in his eyes. "But that's not you, Blake. This is not who you are!"

He tilts his head while walking closer. "And, just how do you know that, Sister dearest? You left when I was three years old. You have hardly seen me since. How do you even know who I am? How do you expect to know that when you were so far away and you left me all alone with that dad of ours and a stepmom who would rather see me fall off a cliff than have to deal with me. HOW do you expect to know ANYTHING about me?"

He is getting too close to me now, and I back up. What is he going to do?

"Blake...I..."

"Shhh. No more talk," he says, reaches out his hands, and grabs me around the throat.

94

OCTOBER 2015

SANDRA IS WHISTLING as she crosses the street with Lucky on his leash. She has just gotten back from three days in Germany doing a big runway show in Berlin with Heidi Klum. Tomorrow, she is off to New York for the shoot for *Vogue*. This morning, she just received a call saying that they want her in Milan next week.

It ain't over till it's over, she thinks to herself. *And I am definitely not over yet.*

She is beginning to think she might be able to keep doing this for years to come. The thought makes her happy. This is what she is good at; this is what she knows. So what if she never has any children? You never know how life will turn out for you, and hers turned out differently than others. Sandra likes to be different and not just go the same way everybody else does. She even went out surfing yesterday and people on the beach gathered to watch her, clapping when she did a 360 in the air. She still has it. Indeed she does. Even at the age of thirty-eight.

Children aren't for everyone.

Her whistling turns into humming. It's that old song again, the one by Nirvana. Sandra can't get it out of her mind again. Not after that day in the car with Mary. Sandra enjoys having her old friend back so much. She doesn't know how long Mary will stay in Cocoa Beach, so she is going to swing by Joey's townhouse and have a coffee with her, enjoy her while she is still here. Maybe it'll be their last for a long time.

You never know.

Sandra walks with quick steps, thinking she might burn a few extra calories before the shoot. She is terrified that they'll think she is too fat or too old. The last part, she can't do much about. She refuses to do Botox, even though it has been suggested a few times by her agency. That, she is never going to do. Ever. But losing a few pounds, she can do. That, she is actually very good at.

A young pool guy is working at the community pool at Joey's place. Sandra greets him as she walks past. She enjoys feeling his eyes examining her body as she walks by.

Yup! Still got it!

Maybe she will be able to work for another five years? It's certainly not impossible the way things are turning out for her right now. She's at the top of her game, her agency says. The demand for her is growing. They can hardly believe it. It never happens, they say. And the names asking are big. Versace wants her for the spring fashion show in Paris. Versace.

Sandra walks up to Joey's front door. She can hear voices coming from inside. Loud voices. She wonders if Mary and Joey are fighting again. Her heart drops at the thought. She sure hopes that is not the case. She loves Mary and Joey together. It has always been them. Sandra is rooting for them. They are the ones who did things right. They chose right. Sandra loves Ryan, she really does, but she often wonders what her life would have been like if she had married Alex instead.

It's all water under the bridge, Sandra. No use crying over spilt milk. You might never have gotten the career you have if he had been your boyfriend at the time. He would have held you back. He would have kept you in chains.

The voices calm down inside the house. Sandra stays outside, not knowing what to do. Mary is the one who called her this morning and asked her to stop by for coffee. She must be expecting her.

Sandra knocks on the door, but no one answers. The door is ajar, and when she touches it, it pushes open.

"Hello?"

95

OCTOBER 2015

"HELLO?"

Sandra's voice cuts through the air. I want to yell back, I want to tell her where I am, tell her to help me. I want to scream, but I can't. I can hardly breathe. Blake has me pinned up against the wall. He is holding my throat tightly between his hands. He is pressing hard, his face strained with the effort, his eyes flaming with anger and hatred. It hurts. It hurts really badly. I can't get free.

"Please," I manage to whisper. "Please...stop...you're..."

I can't anymore. I can't hold on. I am getting tired, the lack of oxygen is making me dizzy. My vision is blurry. I am only making gasping, spurting sounds. I am feeling a distinct tingling sensation in my legs and fingertips, my head is hurting badly; it feels like it's about to explode.

"Hello, Mary?"

I can still hear Sandra. She is entering the living room now.

Help! Sandra I'm in here! Help me!

"Are you home, Mary?"

Help me! Please help me!

It feels like I am about to slip. I can't hold on anymore. My vision is so blurry, I can hardly see Blake anymore. I can hear him. I can hear him grunting with effort as he puts further pressure on my throat.

As I am drifting in and out of consciousness, I suddenly remember something. A thing my mother always taught me as a child. What was it again?

Sandra's steps are on the stairs. She is coming closer. I can't determine where they're coming from anymore, nor can I sense what is up and what is down. It's all so fuzzy.

"Are you in here?" I hear her say. Her voice seems close now.

That's when I feel the grip on my throat loosen for just one second as Blake turns around. Just enough for me to get back to reality.

I hear Sandra gasp loudly.

"What are you doing, Blake? What are you DOING?!"

Go for the eyes. If someone ever attacks you, poke them in the eyes!

My mother's voice is loud and clear in my head. She taught this to both me and AK back then, when we had been a family. *A kick in the crotch followed by a poke in the eye, then run,* were her words.

"Stay out of this, Sandra!" he yells.

As Blake turns his face to look at me again, I have managed to lift my arm and poke two fingers forcefully into his eyes.

"My eyes!"

He screams in pain and lets go of me. I fall to the ground. I am gasping and coughing, making sounds I didn't know were even possible. Blake is yelling and screaming in pain. Sandra runs to me and helps me get up. I try to speak, but I can't. I get up and we start to run. My body is aching and hurting, but there is no other way if I want to survive. I gotta run. Get out of here as fast as I can.

We storm down the stairs. When we reach the door, Blake is yelling at us.

"Oh, no you don't!"

He is behind us quickly. Sandra lets out a scream. I open the door, and we rush out of the house, Blake right behind us. My vision is still blurry, my head dizzy, and it is hard for me to run. Sandra is in front of me as we enter the pool area. I slam the door to the fence after me, right when Blake reaches it, and he gets his hand stuck in it. Blake yells in pain and stops. I run across the pool area. The pool guy is standing with all his chemicals in big bottles, carefully measuring the acid in a small cup.

"Run, Sandra!" I yell.

But Blake is already over the fence. He is running the other way around the pool and cuts us off. The pool guy stops what he is doing and stares at us. Sandra and I both stop. Blake is standing in front of us, panting. His face is strained with anger. The pool guy remains clueless.

"Let us go, Blake," I say.

"You're not going anywhere! You'll only ruin this for me."

"If you mean that I am not letting you get away with murder, then you're damn right," I say. I know it's not tactically prudent, but I want him to know I would never let him get away with this. I can't believe how stupid I have been to let him trick me like this.

"Stop it, Blake," Sandra says. "You're never going to get away with this."

"Shut up!" he yells at her. "Just shut up!"

I look at the fence. It's not very tall. We can jump over it easily. I just want to get out of there, then call the police. I am ready to make a run for it. I grab Sandra's hand and start running. She follows me. I climb the fence and jump over it. Sandra is right behind me. As she is in the air, Blake grabs her foot and pulls her down. I watch as her face is slammed into the railing on the fence when he pulls her down.

"Sandra!" I yell.

Blake falls backwards and lands on his back. Sandra falls to the ground, face first. Next to her are the pool guy's containers. Blake is fast to get to his feet, then he grabs one of the containers, rips the lid off, and pours the liquid acid over Sandra.

After that, there is nothing but screams. Sandra's tormented screams.

Blake stares at her. He looks startled, then drops the container. I jump back over the fence and try to get her up.

"Water," the pool guy yells. "Get lots of water on her."

I manage to get her to the pool shower and hose her down. The pool guy pulls a hose and starts squirting her as well. Sandra doesn't stop screaming.

"My face! My face!"

While the pool guy fumbles with his phone and calls 911, I watch as Blake heads down the road, stops a car, pulls the driver out of the front seat, gets in, and drives off.

EPILOGUE
OCTOBER 2015

I AM ALREADY in the hospital when they call me. I am visiting Sandra. She is lying in her bed, her face all gauzed up. I am sitting in a chair next to her.

"I am so glad you're going home today," I say.

I look at what little of her face I can actually see. Her skin doesn't look good. I fear the worst for what it looks like underneath the gauze. A doctor comes in, along with a nurse, and gives the order to remove it.

Sandra tries to smile at me. Ryan is standing on the other side of her. I can tell by his face he is appalled by what he sees. I try to not let it show.

"Is it that bad?" she asks.

I shake my head. But it's a lie. The doctors have tried their best, but she still looks terrible.

"We had to transplant new skin from your back and thigh," the doctor says. "You're lucky it didn't get in your eyes," he continues. "At least it is all only cosmetic."

Only cosmetic? But that's her entire life! Her looks are her life!

"Is it really that bad?" she asks, looking at her husband. He is crying through his forced smile.

"We're just glad we didn't lose you," I say, and grab her hand.

"Can I see?"

"Are you sure you're ready for it?" Ryan asks.

"I have to at some point, right?" Sandra says. I can tell by her voice she is about to cry. She can't hold it together for much longer.

The doctor helps her get out of bed and walk to the bathroom, where she can look at herself in the mirror. I close my eyes as I hear her shriek.

"I'm...I'm hideous," she says.

I hold back the tears and walk up to her. "I am so sorry, Sandra," I say. "I am so, so sorry."

That's when my phone starts to ring. I pick it up. It's my dad's doctor.

"I have wonderful news," he says. "Your father just opened his eyes."

I look at Sandra as I hang up. "My dad's awake," I say through tears. "He's alive."

She tries to smile. "Go. Go see him."

"Are you sure you'll be alright?"

"Of course. Now go!"

I run down the hallway and find his room. I run inside, then stop. There he is. Still hooked up to all the instruments and tubes, but he is looking at me.

My dad is looking at me!

I walk to him and he follows me with his eyes. A tear escapes the corner and rolls down his cheek.

"Oh, Dad," I say, grabbing his hand. It feels limp.

"It doesn't appear that he can move it," the nurse says. "So far, there are no reactions in any parts of his body, except his eyes. He hasn't spoken yet."

I stare into his eyes, mine filling with tears. Right now, all that doesn't matter. All that I am thankful for is to be able to look into his eyes once again.

"I am so sorry, Daddy," I say. "I am so sorry for all this. It's all my fault. You were right. About Blake, I mean. He was guilty, and I wasted so much time trying to prove that he wasn't. You were right all along. Oh, Dad for so many years I blamed you for not doing anything when Mom was doing all those awful things to me while growing up. For so many years, I resented you for letting it happen to me. Only, the other day, I realized something." I hold his hand tight in mine and place the palm on my chest. "You didn't know, did you? You didn't realize what she was doing until it was too late."

I sniffle and wipe tears away from my cheeks. "I can't believe how badly I messed up. I came down here to straighten things out, to fix things, and look at what has happened. Look at everything that happened. You, Sandra..."

"It wasn't all bad," a voice says behind me. I turn and look at Joey and Salter. They're holding flowers and balloons. My dad's eyes light up when he sees them. Behind Joey, I spot Sandra and Ryan.

"I called them," Sandra says. "I hope it's okay. Oh, yeah, and I called a few others as well."

She walks in, and after her come Danny, Marcia, Alex, and Chloe. They all surround us.

"Thank you, Mary," Danny says. "For finding Jean's killer. For stopping Ally and for stopping AK."

"See. I told you. It wasn't all in vain," Joey says. "You stopped a serial killer."

I chuckle with tears in my eyes as the crew approaches me. We all hug for a little while. I am crying. I can't hold it back.

"You guys..." I say, and wipe my eyes.

"So, now what?" Alex asks. "Are you going back to new York?"

I look at Joey, who doesn't look at me. His eyes hit the floor. Salter looks at me in anticipation. I know what he wants me to say. I know what they all want me to say. And that is when I finally make the decision, because that is what I want too.

"Nah," I say. "I think we'll stay here for a little while. My dad has great insurance and the company agreed to build him a new house. He's going to need someone to take care of him. I have a feeling Laura isn't the nursing type. Besides, I have a blog I want to start writing, right Chloe?"

Chloe throws me a thumbs-up. "I already have the perfect design for it. Watch out, world!"

Joey's face lights up, along with Salter's. "So, we're staying, Mom? We're really staying?" my son yells, not even trying to hide his excitement.

"I guess so," I say. I look at Sandra. "We have work to do here. I intend to catch my little brother and have him pay for what he did to my best friend. And I am going to need all of your help to do it."

"Guess the 7th Street Crew is back together again, then?" Danny says.

I smile through tears.

"I guess so."

The End

WANT TO KNOW WHAT HAPPENS NEXT?

YOU CAN RUN

MARY MILLS MYSTERY BOOK 2

There is only one difference between a madman and me. The madman thinks he is sane. I know I am mad.

~ Salvador Dali

PROLOGUE
MERRITT ISLAND, DECEMBER 2010

THE KIDS ARE SITTING in the living room. The youngest boy, Jack Jr., is on the floor. He is watching TV, the same movie he always watches on Saturday mornings. Kimmie, his older sister by three years is on the couch, a blanket wrapped around her legs, even though it is not cold.

"Could we watch something else?" she complains. "We always watch *How to Train your Dragon*. It's so boring!"

"You don't have to watch it if you don't want to," Jack Jr. says. "I love this movie."

His older sister rolls her eyes with a deep groan. "Come on. You've seen it seventeen times. Don't you get tired of watching everything over and over again? You're such a baby. Stupid little baby."

Her ten-year-old brother looks up at her, then bursts into a loud wailing sound. Seconds later, their mother, Lisa, is in the room with them.

"Quit shouting!" she yells. "Dad is trying to sleep in. He had a late meeting last night."

"She called me stupid!" Jack Jr. cries.

"Kimmie!"

"But, Mooom," Kimmie complains.

"Kimmie! You be good to your brother now. You're the oldest."

"But I didn't do anything."

"You called me stupid!"

"Did not!"

"Did too. Moom she's lying."

Lisa sighs and closes her eyes. She is tense. Jack's many late evening meetings are tearing on her and on their marriage. Mostly because of how they make her feel. Not knowing what he is up to, after...after that time with the secretary, when Lisa walked in on them, bringing him lunch as a surprise. Jack insists it's over, that it ended when he fired her, but how can Lisa be sure? She knows her husband and worries every day what he is up to. She hasn't been to his office since that day. She knows she won't be able to stand the pitiful looks from his colleagues. Not anymore.

"We always watch that same stupid movie, Mom. I want to watch *Harry Potter!*"

"That is not for your brother," Lisa says. "I don't want him to watch those movies yet. We have so many TVs in this house. Why don't you go watch *Harry Potter* somewhere else? You have your own TV in your room. How about going up there instead of arguing with your brother down here?"

"Why do I have to be the one to leave?" Kimmie shouts angrily. Her voice sounds like it's about to crack. Tears are in her eyes. "You always pick Jack Jr. over me, Mom. It's not fair."

Lisa clears her throat in a deep exhale while Jack Jr. throws his sister a triumphant glance. "Just do it, will you, Kimmie? Be the big sister for once? I can't really deal with this today."

Kimmie lets out an annoyed gasp. She is thirteen and getting worse every day, Lisa thinks to herself, right before she feels that overwhelming sensation of anger well up in her stomach and yells, "Just do as I say. NOW!"

Lisa points towards the hallway and the stairs. Kimmie lets out another annoyed sound, gets up, and walks, dragging her feet ostentatiously. Lisa decides she will deal with her later. Right now, she is looking forward to getting her coffee.

As silence falls upon the big house once again, she walks to the kitchen, and pours herself a cup, knowing she'll probably need more than one to get through the day. Maybe she'll even need something stronger later. But not before noon.

Never before noon.

She drinks her coffee, while glancing out at the lake with the water fountain, through the window that extends from the floor to the twenty-foot ceiling.

Upstairs, she hears Kimmie slam a door. Lisa puts down the cup and turns to walk up the stairs and have a word with her.

She doesn't even notice the figure staring at her from the window in the kitchen door, the same door Lisa left unlocked after taking out the trash earlier. Nor does she hear it when the door is opened and the person enters.

It's just not the kind of thing you'd expect to happen on an ordinary Saturday morning.

MERRITT ISLAND
DECEMBER 2010

"Sh. Don't make a sound or everybody dies."

The cold gun is pressed against Lisa's cheek and a hand is placed to cover her mouth. The fingers on her lips leave her with a taste of cigarettes.

Lisa gasps while fear grabs her heart. She is struggling to breathe through her nose. The panic is spreading like cancer through her body. The intruder is speaking close to her ear.

"Where is your husband? Show me to him. Nice and slowly. No sudden movements. No screaming. Do you think you can do that?"

Lisa nods carefully, while focusing on her breathing.

"Alright. Show me to him."

With the intruder still holding her mouth, Lisa starts walking towards the stairs. All she can think about is the children. She is hoping, praying, that the intruder won't know about them. She is hoping that the intruder has come for her husband or for valuables. They can give those away easily. They won't miss any of the things they have in the house.

As long as no one is hurt.

They walk into the master bedroom, where Jack is still sleeping. He grunts and turns in bed when they approach. Lisa is crying, whimpering behind the hand.

"Rise and shine," the intruder says. "You have company, Jack."

Jack opens his eyes and terror slams through his body as he sees his wife. He jumps to his feet fast. Something in the way he acts tells Lisa this intruder isn't a complete stranger to Jack.

"What the hell...?"

The intruder shows him the gun and places it on his wife's temple. "You can try and run...but I don't recommend it. Now, get dressed."

Jack wants to speak. Lisa can tell he wants to object to this treatment, and she throws him a pleading look not to.

Just do as you're told, Jack.

"Who...what...who the hell do you think you are? You can't just come here and...this is my house."

"Are you done?" the intruder says. The intruder is agitated. Lisa can tell by the shivering hand holding the gun.

Please, just do as you're told, Jack. Don't put up a fight. Don't puff yourself up like you always do, telling them who you are and how important you are. Just don't be your usual self. Think about the children, Jack.

"I will not put up with this," Jack continues. "I...you can't just...come in here and..."

"You do realize I could kill your wife—and don't get me wrong, I will do it—if you don't get dressed and come downstairs with me right away," the intruder says, then turns the gun and releases a shot at a painting of Jack's mother on the wall. The gun makes hardly any sound when it goes off, and Lisa realizes it has a silencer on it. It makes it even scarier.

"Okay. Okay," Jack says, finally realizing the seriousness of the situation. "Just give me a second. Just don't hurt her, alright?"

Jack picks up his pants from the chair behind him. Lisa is crying heavily now behind the hand. The taste of the intruder's fingers in her mouth makes her nauseated. The fingers are hurting her jaw. She wants to scream. She wants to scream and yell for help, but she can't, and she doesn't dare to.

Please, God. Please don't let the children be involved in this. Please keep them out of it.

When Jack is finally dressed, he looks at the intruder. "Now what? What do you want?"

"Take me to the children."

MERRITT ISLAND
DECEMBER 2010, FOUR HOURS LATER

The neighbors will hear us. They must have heard Kimmie scream when the intruder came into her room, right? Didn't they? They heard Jack Jr. when he screamed for his mommy, didn't they? They'll come to our rescue, won't they? Of course they will.

They have to.

Lisa is trying to convince herself that the neighbors have already called for the police to come. She tries to calm herself down by thinking about it, by imagining the police cars arriving outside the house.

But she still can't hear them.

They have been lying on the floor of the living room for what feels like forever. She still can't really grasp what happened after she heard the voice behind her in the kitchen, after she felt the gun being pressed against her back and the voice spoke into her ear, talking with a low, almost whispering, snakelike voice.

Maybe if the neighbors were paying attention—just for this once in their busy lives—to what is going on right down the street from them in their quiet neighborhood, then maybe they'd hear me if I screamed.

"Please!"

Still, nothing happens. No wailing sirens in the distance. No officers yelling outside or even footsteps approaching. The neighbors haven't heard anything.

Maybe someone else will hear me. A passerby will call the cops. Maybe they'll hear our cries for help, maybe they'll hear us, if only...Please, God...Please.

Lisa is praying silently while lying on the floor. She looks at her son, Jack Jr., who is lying face-down, a gun pressed to the back of his head, the intruder sitting on top of him. His entire body is shivering in terror.

Please, not my son. Please, don't take him from me. He's all I have.

"Fifty-thousand dollars or the son gets it," the voice says. "Get it here within the next hour. And no police, or the boy dies."

The pressure on Jack Jr.'s back is loosened and Lisa watches as her husband gets to his feet and—hands shivering—picks up the phone.

"Richard? It's me. Could you bring fifty-thousand dollars to me within the hour? Yes. Discreetly, please. Thank you."

Jack Jr. looks at his mother lying on the floor next to him. She tries to smile and hide her fear. She can almost touch him, but she doesn't dare to, afraid she might anger the intruder. Jack Jr. is crying, sobbing heavily. She wants to protect her son, she wants to hold his hand or hug him, tell him it's going to be okay, tell him that once Richard brings the money, it'll all be over.

Richard.

Richard will do something, won't he? Of course he will. He's Jack's accountant and best friend for ten years. He'll know something is wrong. He'll hear it in his voice or maybe they even have a word, something he is supposed to say in case something like this happens. Of course they do.

Reassured that Jack will somehow handle this, Lisa throws a glance at her daughter. Their eyes meet and she sees nothing but utter terror in hers. It frightens her. Nothing is worse than seeing fear in your kid's eyes and not being able to do anything about it. Nothing.

"It's done," Jack says, looking at the intruder.

"Good. Now call for pizza. I'm hungry."

"Pizza? But..."

The gun is pointed at Jack's face. "Just do it."

"Just do as you're told, Jack!" Lisa screams.

The eyes of the intruder are filled with madness as the gun shifts to point at her instead.

"Shut up, bitch! Shut the fuck up! Don't speak unless I tell you to, okay? Just...just don't!"

"Alright. All right. I'll call for pizza. Just...just don't hurt anyone, okay? We'll do anything you tell us, just don't hurt us." Jack hurries to the phone and dials a number.

"Pepperoni," the intruder says.

"One pepperoni pizza," Jack repeats, his voice shivering, his eyes fixated on the gun in the intruder's hand. The hands don't seem stable enough to carry such a mortal weapon.

"What? Nothing for the rest of the family?" the intruder asks.

"Make that two pizzas. Yes, both pepperoni. Thank you."

The intruder shakes their head, holding a finger in the air. "No. No. No. Not pepperoni. Ham. I want ham! I told you I wanted ham! I can't stand pepperoni. Can't stand it. Simply can't!"

Jack stares at the intruder, not knowing what to say. The gun is placed on Lisa's temple. She whimpers. The intruder growls and puts a hand over her mouth while whispering, "Shut up! Or I'll kill your kids. I swear, I'll kill them."

"Sorry. Could you make that ham instead? I must have heard wrong," Jack says. "Thank you."

"Now, lay back down!" the intruder yells, as soon as the phone is hung up. The yelling is loud, inconsistent, angry and mad.

Lisa studies the intruder's pale face. There is something about the eyes that tells her this person isn't well. The manic eyes, the constant rubbing of the hair, the hands that won't stay still.

It strikes Lisa that the intruder hasn't covered their face. They'll be able to identify the intruder for the police when it is all over. What does this mean? Could it be that the intruder simply forgot? That the intruder didn't think everything through? Or...? Or does it mean...could it mean that this person doesn't intend to release them when the money or the pizza arrives? That it was never the intention?

What if it isn't what the intruder came for?

PART I

WITH A LITTLE HELP FROM MY FRIENDS

1

JANUARY 2016

"LET'S GRAB A TABLE OUTSIDE."

I follow Sandra through the doors of our favorite breakfast place, Café Surfinista. We have both ordered the Acai Bowl, which is amazing. The weather is nice and chilly, the winds blowing in from the north making it dryer and the air cooler. I like it. I like January in Florida.

Sandra receives a glance from a passerby. She tries to hide her face underneath her cap. I feel a pinch in my heart. She has been used to people staring at her all of her life, but for a different reason. I'm wondering if she will ever get used to the stares she gets now. I fight the urge to yell something after the passerby.

People can be so rude.

Sandra's skin has healed, but she is still disfigured from the acid my brother threw in her face three months ago. On the day he got away with murder. I still hate myself for not being able to stop him. I was so close, and then it happened. He did this to my best friend and ruined her life completely. Having a great career as a model, her looks were everything. They were her entire life. Her recovery afterwards was long and filled with many more trips to the hospital. At home, she was forced to wear a plastic mask twenty-three hours a day to help her wounds heal. For weeks, she had no reason to get out of bed. The crew and I took turns visiting her and getting her up. Still, she hardly ever leaves the house alone anymore. She cries a lot, even though she tries to hide it. She still isn't herself at all, and I wonder if she will ever be.

"So, how are you doing?" I ask her, as we sit down and the passerby is gone. I can tell from her eyes that the stares hurt her.

Today is a victory. It took a long time of convincing her it would be good for her to go out for breakfast with me. She had all kinds of excuses. I can't blame her. Every time she walks outside, she is reminded of what happened. There is no way she can escape it.

She answers with a scoff. "I'm okay, I guess." She pauses and finally looks me in the eyes. "I removed all the mirrors in my house yesterday."

"Good for you." I say, almost choking on some granola. I cough and try to shake the feeling of guilt, but it's eating me up. I can't believe my brother got away with this.

I haven't given up on catching him and Olivia. None of us have. We want him to pay for what he has done. But finding him is proving to be a lot harder than expected.

So far, we don't know much. We know they ran away together. I've followed the police investigation closely, but so far, there has been no sign of life from either of them in two months. Not since a surveillance camera at a gas station in Ft. Lauderdale spotted my brother in November. The police, with Detective Chris Fisher in charge, lost track of him after that. Meanwhile, Chloe is using all her skills to try and track them online, tracking his and Olivia's credit cards, but so far without any luck. I fear they could be anywhere by now. The police found the car that Blake escaped in, in Melbourne, abandoned. It's my theory that he was picked up by Olivia there; her phone records show she received a phone call from a phone booth in the same area that day, and no one has seen her since. Both of their phones were found in a trash can near the Melbourne Mall. Chloe thinks Olivia might own a credit card or a bank account under a different name, and right now she is working on that angle. Meanwhile, the rest of the 7th Street Crew are doing all we can to keep our eyes and ears open. The two months of silence is eating me alive. Seeing Sandra suffer the way she does is tearing me up.

"But you have no idea how many things you have in your house where you can see your own reflection," Sandra says, sucking in her breath. "Just using my silverware or putting a pot of water under the faucet in my kitchen won't let me forget. Every freaking second of my life, I have to face it."

"What about surgery? What do they say?" I ask, knowing she has been through a marathon of reconstructive surgeries already.

A couple walks past us on the street. The woman stares at Sandra. The disgust is oozing from her eyes. Yet, she can't stop looking.

Sandra turns her head away and closes her eyes.

"You ain't exactly a looker yourself, lady," I say. I sound like an idiot, but I am so frustrated, I can't help myself.

Sandra places a calm hand on my arm. "You don't have to defend me," she says. "It's okay. It's not their fault."

She sighs and removes her hand before she continues.

"They can't do anymore. The damage is too severe. This is it for me. This is what I am going to look like for the rest of my life. I just have to learn to live with it. The worst part is Ryan. I can tell he is trying hard, but just looking at me still makes his eyes water. He has that look of disgust that I see in everyone who looks at me. And he definitely doesn't want to touch me. He used to be all over me, but now he tries to avoid even looking at me. He works constantly, and I think he might be avoiding being home because it makes him feel uncomfortable. I can't blame him. I would run away too. But I can't. I'm right here. All the time. I can't run away from myself."

"I am sorry, Sandra." I say. I am at loss for words and try with a joke instead. "I can beat him up for you, if you want me to?"

Sandra chuckles, but she isn't smiling.

2

JANUARY 2016

MARCIA LITTLE WALKS across the street at Minutemen Causeway. She hurries up and a car misses her as it rushes by, honking its horn.

"Ah, come on," she yells after it.

The driver throws a finger out the window. Marcia blows raspberries and laughs. In her hand, she is carrying a bottle of gin. It is wrapped in a brown paper bag. She has just bought it at ABC Wine, and now she is heading for the beach by Coconuts. The air is chilly today. The scarf she always wears doesn't keep her neck warm enough. Too much wind. She knows the others won't be in the usual spots.

Billy is the first one she sees. He is sitting in front of the Beach Shack, in the dunes, a guitar in his lap. He smiles and yells her name. Where he is sitting, you can't feel the wind when it is in the north.

With the sun in a clear blue sky, it will be nice to sit on the sand, she thinks to herself and joins him. He is finishing up a beer. Neither the Beach Shack nor Coconuts on the beach have opened yet. It's nice and quiet right now. Just the way Marcia likes to start her day. Especially since she lost her job at CVS on 520, the third job in just as many months.

Billy is playing a tune, and after a couple of sips from her bottle, Marcia is humming along. She used to be a great singer, back in high school, and everyone thought she would pursue a career in music, but...well it never happened. She played bars and venues all over Brevard County for nothing but free beer and food for years. That's how she met Carl, the father of her four children. He owns a bar in Orlando, where she would play regularly.

He liked her and kept asking her to come back. Soon, they hooked up, and she never got any further with her career. As soon as their firstborn came along, she was done singing anything but nursery rhymes.

Marcia had always been fond of drinking. Ever since her teenage years, when she had her first beer, she had known she liked it. But it was also what killed her marriage. Carl liked to drink too, and over the years, he turned violent. Finally, one day, it became too much for Marcia. That was when she caught Carl beating their youngest, who was only two-years-old till he was bruised on his entire back. That was when she knew she'd had enough. Carl could beat her all he wanted to. That she could handle. But not when he took it out on the children. That was it for her. So she left and came back to her hometown with the heavy load of having to raise four children on her own. She often wondered where the years went, how come her breakthrough never came, why she never got the career she had thought she would. Where did it all go wrong?

Well, you can't have it all. At least she has a place to live. She doesn't have to sleep on the beach or the streets like Billy and most of the other guys she hangs out with. At least she has a roof over her head and a bottle in her hand. Who needs a career?

It's all overrated anyway.

Marcia sips her bottle and lets the alcohol settle the uneasiness she always wakes up with in the morning. The mornings are the worst. Until she is able to send the kids off to school on the bus, she strives just to stay upright. Her entire body is usually shaking in withdrawal. That's why she normally starts the day with a couple of painkillers to keep her going until she can make it to the gas station, where she has her first beer of the day. After that, she is up and running again.

Today is a special day. Today, she is celebrating the fact that the court has told Carl to pay her a thousand dollars a month in alimony. Not that he will feel it. His bar is doing really well.

About time he pays up. After all, they're his kids too.

But the extra money means Marcia doesn't have to hurry up finding another job. She lost the condo two months ago when the bank took it and they moved into a small townhouse across the street from the beach instead that was much cheaper. The money from Carl is enough to pay her rent and groceries, so it's only the extra stuff she needs to make herself. With the money she borrowed from her sister last week, she'll get by for a couple of months, even if she doesn't find a job. It suits Marcia, since she hasn't been doing so well lately. She needs a little time to get better.

3

OCTOBER 2005

"I KNOW he's in there somewhere, Mom. I'm certain. Why won't you listen to me?"

Daniel looks intensely at his mother. Her eyes are tired, exhausted even. "I am telling you, Daniel. We've tried everything."

"I refuse to believe that my brother is going to have to live like this. I am the one who knows him best. I am the one who has been the closest to him all of his life. I know he understands what we tell him. He might not be able to speak, he might not be able to communicate, but he is in there. Behind those eyes is an adult who needs to be heard, Mom. There's got to be some sort of treatment."

His mother, Michelle, sighs deeply, then closes her eyes while shaking her head. "You've got to stop this, Daniel. Peter has Cerebral Palsy. He hasn't spoken a word in the twenty-five years he has been on this planet. He is and will always be impaired. You've seen how he is getting worse every day. You've seen the muscle spasms in his face, his neck, his torso and his arms and hands. You know it's hard for him to stay in one position, that muscle contractions sometimes twist his spine and clench his fingers in a useless ball. He can hardly make eye contact and keep objects fixed in view. He wears a diaper, for crying out loud. He can't even dress himself. He can walk only if someone steadies him; otherwise, he gets around by scooting on the floor. All we have ever been able to communicate with him is by his screams when he's unhappy and the chirps when he's excited, but he can't control his vocal cords. His last assessment shows he has a very low IQ.

That guy, the clinical psychologist, that Wills fellow, assessed Peter and found that his comprehension seemed to be *quite limited*. Those were his words, Daniel. Quite limited. Remember that? He also said that Peter's attention span was very short and he lacks the *cognitive capacity to understand and participate in decisions*. Peter can't even carry out basic, preschool-level tasks."

Daniel's mother grabs his hand in hers and smiles. "I know you love your brother. I know you want what's best for him. We all do. But we have fought this fight since he was a small child, trying to find treatment for him. Back when your father was still alive, we had him tested constantly; we refused to face the fact that Peter is severely handicapped and he will never be able to communicate with us."

"But..." Daniel tries, but his older sister sitting at the end of the dining table stops him.

"Leave it, Daniel. You heard Mother. We have tried everything. Peter is our brother, but he will never be able to communicate with us."

"Just leave it alone," his older brother chimes in. It annoys Daniel how they always stick together.

His four siblings sitting around the table in their parent's old estate seem to all agree.

"Am I the only one who hasn't given up?" Daniel asks.

"He is twenty-five now, son," his mother says. "I'm getting old. We have help here day in and day out, and he can stay here till I die, but as I said earlier, I want us to take a look at his other possibilities for when I'm not here anymore. All of you have jobs and families. You can't take care of him as well."

Daniel grunts. He wants to say something, but he knows it won't help. They've all made up their minds. Their mother has made all of them legal guardians of Peter when she dies. He will be their responsibility when their mother passes away. Daniel has feared the day for years. He is the one who has been closest to their youngest brother. Being only five years old when he was born, Daniel always felt responsible for him. Unlike the others, who were a lot older when Peter was born. Their oldest brother was nineteen and their sister sixteen. None of them have the same relationship with him that Daniel does. Not even the two other brothers who were seven and nine when Peter was born. They just don't get him like Daniel does. Still, he knows he can't take Peter in either once their mother dies. His wife would kill him for it.

Daniel looks to Peter, who is sitting in his wheelchair in the corner, his chin touching his chest. He wishes deeply that Peter could speak for himself. That he would speak up right now. Tell them they are wrong, that he can still have a life. That it is wrong of them to simply hide him away in a home somewhere after the death of their mother.

What if he hears everything? What if he understands everything? What if he just can't tell us?

The very thought terrifies Daniel. He hates the fact that his brother is trapped in his body like this. He has seen it in his eyes. Peter isn't stupid. He is smart, he is intelligent. The doctors have told them it is impossible. Over and over again, they have told them that Peter is out of reach. Yet Daniel stays convinced that all it will take is someone else besides him who believes it to be possible. Someone who knows of another way to reach into Peter's deeper inner self, inside where his thoughts are trapped.

4

JANUARY 2016

"MARK YOU KNOW you're not allowed to wear a hat indoors. Please, take it off."

Mark tries to avoid looking at his teacher, Miss Abbey. She is standing in front of his desk. He stares at her jeans while holding onto his cap.

"Mark. I told you to take off the hat."

Mark bows his head even further down. The entire class is staring at him. Some are whispering. He feels his face blushing.

"Mark!"

Mark doesn't react. He is holding onto the cap like his life depends on it. It sort of does. For an eighth-grader, this type of thing can ruin your life.

"Mark. I am not going to tell you again. You're being very disrespectful towards me right now. I am going to count to three and then you'll take off the hat or I see no other choice than to send you to the principal's office...again."

Mark closes his eyes and wishes it would all go away. His mom used to tell him it was possible.

"If only you want it enough, then you can change everything with your mind. Isn't it amazing?"

Mark opens his eyes, but she is still there. He doesn't understand why he can't make the teacher go away or even just this awful situation. Maybe he doesn't want it enough, like his mother said?

"One...two..."

Mark draws in a deep sigh and looks down at his desk.

"Don't make me say three, Mark."

Carefully, he lifts his cap and finally looks up at his teacher. When she sees what is underneath, her expression changes completely. A loud wave of laughter bursts through the classroom.

"Mark, what have you done to your hair?" Miss Abbey exclaims.

Mark's eyes hit the floor in embarrassment. "I...I...cut it."

He's lying. It wasn't him. It was his mother who did it that very morning, right before school. She came running into his room with the shaver in her hand, held him down on the bed, and shaved his hair off in big clumps, yelling weird things about some angel visiting her at night and telling her that Mark's hair was infested with flesh-eating bugs and that she needed to cut it off before he infested anyone else. Mark screamed and tried to fight her. He ended up running out of the house, grabbing his backpack and a cap on the way out. At school, he had looked at himself in the mirror in the bathroom and realized it was all uneven, that here and there big clumps of hair were still sticking out, while it was completely shaved off in other areas. That was why he didn't want to take off the cap.

"Mark...I...I...why would you cut it like this?" Miss Abbey says, baffled, while the laughter and giggling continues mercilessly. "And, come to think of it, what...are you still wearing your pajamas?"

Another wave of laughter rushes through the class. Mark blushes again. "I...I...guess I forgot to get dressed."

"Why...I never..." Miss Abbey's upper lip is getting tighter. She lifts both of her hands in the air. "I simply don't know what to do with you anymore. Last week it was that awful smell from that bug-spray you had used as deodorant all over your body. The other day your math book was completely destroyed, and now this. What is going on with you, Mark? Are you trying to get out of school or just annoy me? 'Cause I don't know what to do about you anymore."

Mark nods and keeps looking down. He knows what it sounds like, but he wants to avoid the truth at all costs. He doesn't want the school to know his mother was so afraid of bugs one morning she sprayed him all over his body with bug-spray, or that she was the one that had used his math book for killing imaginary bugs at the house, slamming it against the walls for hours and hours while screaming at the government that they'll never get her.

There is no way he is ever going to tell them that. No way.

Instead, he takes a deep breath, and once again bends his head in shame.

"I know, Miss Abbey. I'll try and get better. I promise."

5

JANUARY 2016

BLAKE WATCHES the blonde as she walks out of Walgreen's. He is sitting in his car, hands tight on the wheel, his knuckles turning white when he sees her, his jaw clenched. The blonde doesn't notice him. She has a bag in her hand. She walks to her car and gets in. Blake starts the engine and follows her closely, like he did on the way there from her house. He has watched her all day. On the display of his new phone, it says that Olivia has called him five times. He was supposed to go pick up some beers this morning, but then he saw her, the blonde, and couldn't take his eyes of her since. He doesn't know what it is about her. She reminds him of someone, someone he wants to hurt.

For the past three months, while they have been on the run, Blake has been able to keep his urges down. But the last couple of days or so it has been bugging him. That nagging feeling that keeps him awake at night, that makes him wake up bathed in sweat if he finally dozes off.

He has managed to keep it a secret from Olivia, how he really feels, but he is not sure he can keep it that way. All she thinks about is keeping a low profile, to not draw any attention their way. Blake knows she is right. He knows it is dangerous, but that only makes it even more tempting and the feeling even more overpowering.

As he parks outside the woman's house, his phone rings again. It doesn't say her name on the display, but he knows it's her. She is the only one who has his number. They bought the phones from a guy they met at the motel where they are staying. No one will ever know they have them. Just like no one will ever find them where they're hiding. Blake is certain of it. They're being too smart. They pay for everything in cash. It's his luck that Olivia saved up for years for her escape from the general. Month after month, she would stash away cash to make sure the general would never track her when she left. She even has a credit card that no one knows about. She had it all planned and figured out so many years ago; she created a fake identity for herself using her dead aunt's name. When her aunt died, Olivia stole her passport from the house when they cleaned it out, thinking it would be useful one day. And it sure has been. Especially for Blake.

The phone is still ringing insistently, and he finally picks it up.

"Where are you?" Olivia growls from the other end. "You've been gone for five hours!"

"I know. I know," he says, while watching the blonde get out of her car and walk up to the small house, if you can call it that. Looked more like a bungalow to him. "Just needed to check on something. I'll be right back."

"You better. What is it with you lately? You make a beer run at nine in the morning and then don't come back? What if someone sees you?"

"Baby, no one sees me. I can assure you of that."

Her voice calms down and she sighs. "Okay then. I guess I was just afraid since I didn't hear from you. I feel like there are police everywhere these days."

"We talked about this. You're just being paranoid. The plan is working. For all I know, they've already stopped looking for us. I mean, have you seen anything on the news about us lately? Anything?"

"No."

"Trust me, Olivia. They have no idea where we are, and as soon as someone else does something bad, they'll forget about us."

"What if that manager at the motel rats us out? I don't trust him much," Olivia says.

"Randy? Pah. He's harmless. He's had his own share of run-ins with the cops in his life. Besides, after we gave him that envelope of money from selling the watch my dad gave me, I think he is pretty satisfied. He won't talk."

Olivia exhaled. "I know. I know. You're right."

"Now crawl up on that bed and get naked because daddy's coming home soon and he's in the mood for a little action. Alright?"

Olivia giggles, then hangs up.

Real smooth Blake. That's how they like it.

Blake puts the phone back on the passenger seat as he pulls out the binoculars that he bought at Walgreen's while the blonde shopped. They work perfectly, and soon he is able to see her up close. The blonde is unpacking her groceries and putting them away one by one. Blake likes the parts when she is bending to reach the lower cabinets. He feels himself getting aroused and jerks off while watching her every move.

6

JANUARY 2016

JOEY IS home when I get back from breakfast. Salter has started at Roosevelt Elementary and loves it. It was the same school that both Joey and I went to, and I love it there still. It feels like I have come home.

"Home already?" I say with a smile, lean over and kiss him on the lips. Bonnie and Clyde are running after Snowflake, chasing him out the door into the backyard. They come back a few seconds later. Bonnie in the front, holding the ball in her mouth. The pig grunts victoriously. Clyde is barking, and I have a feeling that he and Snowflake are ganging up on the pig.

"Have you finished the fence job so soon?" I ask, leaving the animals to their little game.

"Yeah. I did as much as I could today. The rest of the wood won't arrive until tomorrow, so there isn't much I can do for now."

I nod, feeling a little sorry for him. There hasn't been much for him to do lately. I keep telling him it's because it was Christmas and people have been spending their money on presents and not on rebuilding their houses. Joey doesn't seem to think it'll pick up any time soon.

"I'll go work on the beach house after lunch," he says. "Help out Ryan's people a little."

My dad and I have hired Sandra's husband's company to rebuild my childhood home after a fire destroyed it three months ago. The same fire that hurt my dad and left him paralyzed from the neck down. Joey likes to go over there and see if they need his help. I have offered to pay him for his hours, but he won't hear of it.

"Is he still sleeping?" I ask, and nod in the direction of the room that we have made into my dad's room, since he was released from the hospital. Joey's place is only two bedrooms, so that means we all sleep together in the other bedroom. Salter, Joey, all the animals, and me.

"No. He asked for water a little while ago, so I gave him some and read the newspaper to him," Joey says.

"That was sweet of you. Thank you."

"No problem. I feel bad for him. Must be terrible to not be able to move a muscle in your body. I can't imagine what it must be like."

I nod. I feel bad for him too. Only his face is fully functional. He has regained the ability to speak, smile and blink, but not effortlessly yet. That is all. At least, so far. I refuse to give up on believing he will one day be able to walk again. I have hired a physical therapist who stops by three times a week and tries to work with him. But he still doesn't feel anything.

"I'll go check on him," I say, and walk to the door and knock. "Dad?"

"Come in," he says.

I walk in. My dad seems even smaller than he did the day before. Lying in bed like that makes him lose all his muscles, the doctor explained to me. And he is not eating much.

"How are you today?" I ask and sit on the edge of the bed. I take his hand in mine and lift it up. He has a nurse that comes in every day and washes him and turns his body so he won't get bedsores. His hand feels limp. I squeeze it, hoping he will feel something.

"Nothing new," he says, fighting to get the words out. He speaks three words at a time, then stops to catch his breath. It is good for him to keep talking, training his facial muscles to obey, the therapist explained to me. The more he speaks, the better it gets. It's always worst in the mornings.

"But you brought...a nice breath...of fresh air...with you when...you came in...I enjoy that."

I smile and touch his cheek gently. It is strange to watch your once-so-strong father like this. Devastating. But at least I can talk to him and he can answer me. I feel very grateful for that.

"It's nice and cool out today," I say. "Just under seventy degrees and sunny. Do you want me to open your window and let some of the air in?"

"That would be...nice. Thank you." He takes a break, and when he speaks next the words come easier. "So we're having a cold spell...these days, huh?"

"Yes."

"I miss those days...when the air cools off and everything is so...so..."

"So crisp," I say. I bite my tongue. I know I am supposed to let him find the words himself.

"The beach is usually the best place to be...I used to love walking...on the beach on days like this. It was fun to watch...all the tourists jumping...in the water when you felt like it was freezing."

"That's winter for you in Florida," I say. "Socks and flip-flops and all that."

My dad chuckles. "You hated it...as a child. Blake loved it...You were so different, the two of you."

He stops himself and looks down. We haven't talked much about Blake the past few months, but I know it is troubling him. I wonder if he is blaming himself for things turning bad like they did.

"I thought it would be enough...to give him what he wanted...what I believed he needed," he suddenly says. "Guess I gave him all...all the wrong things. I guess I...just didn't know how to handle him...you know...after your mother died."

I open the window and a breath of fresh air hits my face. I close my eyes and swallow the lump that seems to be stuck in my throat these days. I turn to look at him. "So, is Laura coming today?" I ask.

7

JANUARY 2016

"HI. I'm here about the room. I called earlier?"

Marcia stares at the man in front of her. In his hand, he is holding a suitcase. Everything is blurry and has been since she finished her bottle and left Billy and the beach. She can't remember much from the past few hours and has no idea what time it is. She stares at the man, trying hard to focus.

"My name is Harry Hanson. You told me to just drop by and take a look at the room."

"Ah. Harry," Marcia says, pretending like she remembers talking to him. She is gesticulating wildly while speaking. "Yes. Yes. Come on in. Take a look."

Marcia finds the key to her small townhouse in her pocket and opens the door. As she walks inside, she remembers placing the ad on Craigslist for a renter for one of the rooms. It's a three-bedroom house, so the kids will have to bunk up in just one room.

"It's right in here," she says, and shows him to the room. "It has its own back entrance, so you can come and go as you want." She stops at the end of the stairs. "It's right up here. On the second floor."

Marcia grabs the railing and walks up the stairs, almost loses her balance, but regains it and looks back at the man with a goofy grin before she continues. "There's a bathroom right across from it that's all yours. Me and the kids stay in the rooms downstairs and use the bathroom down there. You'll have the entire floor to yourself," she says with a smile, trying hard to seal the deal. Getting a renter in would mean she wouldn't have to work at all anymore. With the money she's getting from Carl on top of it, she could make it work if they keep their expenses low, which they are very good at. The kids all qualify for the food-program and eat at the school for both breakfast and lunch. Her sister offers them hand-me-downs of clothes and toys.

"It's right in here."

Marcia opens the door to the room and walks in first. She hurries to the window and opens it to make sure it doesn't smell. The man follows her with his suitcase in hand. He throws a glance around the small room and takes in the twin bed up against the wall.

"There's a nice-sized closet and a desk too," she says proudly, wondering if the man has a computer in his suitcase. "No pets and no smoking," she adds.

He puts it down and looks at her.

"Three-hundred a month, you say?"

Marcia nods excitedly. "Yes. I know it's a lot, but it's beachside. Right across the street. When you open the window like this, you can hear the waves. Doesn't get any closer to the ocean for this price."

"I went down to the beach when I got here. It looks very nice."

"You're not from around here, are you?"

The man turns away from her and doesn't answer.

"Do you have a car? I didn't see one in the driveway," she says.

"I didn't bring one."

"You don't have a car? All right. Neither do I," she says with a rough laugh. "You don't need it much around here. You can bike everywhere. The path outside of this window leads right to downtown Cocoa Beach. If you continue, it will lead you all the way to Cape Canaveral. Where do you work? At least tell me you have a job. You're not one of those losers who moves in and never pays the rent, right? The types I can't get rid of? Is that why you don't have a car, because you don't have any money?"

Harry turns to her with a smile. Even through her daze, she can see that he is different. He is not dressed like the typical no-good surfer type. He is wearing nice pants and shoes and his white T-shirt is tucked neatly in his pants. His hair is cut short and he is freshly shaved. He is quite the looker.

"I work from home. I don't need a car."

"Ah. I see."

"And the price includes everything?"

"Water, electricity and feel free to use the kitchen downstairs as often as you need to. And don't mind the kids. They're a wild bunch, but they mean well," she says with a nervous laugh. She knows four noisy kids can be a bit much for a neat guy like Harry. Especially if he needs quiet time for working. Well, that's not her problem. As long as he pays the rent on time.

"I'll take it," he says.

Yes!

8

OCTOBER 2005

THE AUDITORIUM at UCF is packed. Daniel manages to squeeze himself into the back row just as the doors are closed. He stands behind a man taller than him, so he can barely see the woman whom he has wanted desperately to hear for months, ever since he watched her Oscar-nominated documentary. The film describes a non-verbal girl with disabilities and an IQ of only thirty-two, who learns how to type and use facilitated communication, and somehow manages to put herself through college. The documentary has taken Daniel completely by storm, and the girl in the movie reminds him so much of his brother Peter, he can hardly believe it. Since he watched it, Daniel has read everything he can find that Kristin Martin has written, and he is stunned to realize that there actually is someone else who believes there can be more to his brother's world.

After the lecture is done, the crowd starts to move for the doors, but Daniel is not moving with them. He has a mission. He has to speak to her, to Kristin Martin. He manages to elbow his way against the moving crowd, and soon he finds himself standing in front of her. She is younger than he expected. And more beautiful. She is speaking to another man before him who wants her to sign his book. She does so, then looks up at Daniel with a smile.

"Hello."

Daniel swallows hard, his throat is suddenly dry, and he can't get the words to leave his lips. She continues to stare at him.

"Do you have a book for me to sign...or?" she asks.

Daniel shakes his head in embarrassment and clears his throat. Finally, he manages to speak. "No. No. I...I'm here on behalf of my brother."

"Your brother?"

"Yes. He has Cerebral Palsy. Never spoke a word in his life. I think he can. I think he desperately wants to. I think he is trapped in his body and that he could speak if only given the right tools. Do you think he could be able to use a keyboard like Maggie in your movie?"

Kristin Martin's smile widens. It makes Daniel feel comfortable. She has kind eyes and doesn't seem to want to reject him.

"Cerebral Palsy, you say?"

"Severe. Developed in early childhood and is getting worse still. His spasms prevent him from walking or even holding utensils. He can't do anything on his own. And he has never spoken a word. But I think...I mean with this...like that girl in the movie. I believe...if only someone gave him a chance. Somehow...I have seen it in his eyes, Miss Martin...I...I don't know much of how this works, but I do know I'll do anything for my brother. When I look into those eyes...I...I am sure I have seen him react. There's a want in there, a longing. He wants to speak."

Daniel stops himself to catch his breath. He is too agitated now; talking about Peter will do that to him. He wants Kristin Martin to believe in Peter like he does; he wants it more than anything in this world.

"Do you think using this keyboard could help him?" he finally asks.

She nods. A sigh of relief goes through his body.

"I don't see why not," she says. "Give it a try."

The woman reaches into her pocket and pulls out a business card. "Here. Give me a call next week. I think I might like to take a look at him. I have never had a patient with Cerebral Palsy before. Could be interesting."

She hands him the card and their eyes lock for a few seconds before someone from the university pulls her away from him and she is engaged in a new conversation. Daniel stares at the card in his hand and can't seem to hold it still.

As he leaves the university, he is filled with a hope and belief in the future for his brother, unlike anything he has ever had before.

I'm gonna hear what you have to say, baby brother. Don't you worry. You'll finally get your voice.

9

JANUARY 2016

MY THINGS ARE in boxes everywhere in Joey's house and it is all a mess. I can't find anything. I don't want to unpack either. We haven't really talked about our situation and if we are ready to move back in together or not. And, to be frank, I am not that thrilled about living here in this small townhouse that he has rented. There isn't enough room for all of us. I don't really know what he wants yet, and so far I am planning on moving back in with my dad once the house is done. He needs my help. I don't know how much my stepmom Laura is going to be there for him. So far, she is still staying at the Hilton using my dad's money and only stops by a few times a week to visit him. My dad keeps making excuses for her and tells me she has to get over the shock first, that she'll come around soon, just wait and see.

It's been three months.

Joey has given me a corner of the living room where I have put up my desk and I call it my office. I have started writing the blog and Chloe is doing the design and all the practical stuff that I know nothing about.

I started out three months ago writing the story about how I was fired from the *New York Times* because I wrote the wrong story, and to my huge surprise, the thing went viral. The next day, I had twenty thousand followers on the blog and even more on Twitter and Facebook. A few weeks later, I had a million. Now I am closer to four million. It has grown faster than I could have ever imagined, and I have to admit, I feel a little intimidated. My next story about the serial killer roaming the streets of Cocoa Beach killing off old high school friends after they mutilated her went crazy viral. Newspapers and magazines all over the world picked it up, and I was quoted everywhere. Later, I wrote about how a general from the air force base had taken in a fugitive, wanted for murder, and changed her name, her identity, and hidden her when she was supposed to face justice for killing a woman, my mother. That was an article people liked. I wrote it with a personal touch and it received more comments and shares that any of the others. Next thing, Chloe tells me some companies want to sponsor my site, and it is suddenly crawling with ads, and I am making money. I can hardly believe it myself, but that's what happened. Now, Chloe wants me to start making video clips with interviews or me trying to get a comment from some of the bad guys I write about, and small video blogs for my fans where I tell them what I am working on. It's kind of taking over my life, and I'm trying hard to keep it down. Chloe, on the other hand, is all over it. I am so lucky to have her helping me. She has given me a few stories about online child porn-sites and how bigger companies fund them, especially the gun-industry, that I have published as well, causing the companies to pull back their funding in fear of bad publicity. In that sense, we try to help out each other, trying to make the world a better place, one story at a time. That's actually our motto.

Today, I start working on the story of my brother and how he fooled all of us and is still on the run, wanted for murder. I have wanted to write the story from a personal perspective for a long time, but every time I sit down to write it, I just can't get the words onto the paper. It hurts so badly. I can't stand the thought that it was my fault. That I was so naïve, that I believed him. I was the one who got him out of jail, and then when I realized what I had done and tried to stop him, he poured acid over my best friend and mutilated her for life.

Just thinking about it again makes me want to throw up. I stare at the blank page in front of me and suddenly get the urge for chocolate. I find a Snickers in my drawer and pull off the wrapping. Eating it makes me calmer, but I still feel awful. I keep seeing Sandra's face when I dropped her off at her house after our breakfast, and I feel terrible. I open the drawer and look for more chocolate. The dogs and the pig are being noisy, running around the house again. I go through the drawer, but find nothing more. I get up and walk to Joey's kitchen and start to open all the cabinets. I feel like a drug addict looking for her next fix. Finally, I find some of Salter's Oreos and start to gulp them down one after another, while the dogs bark at

Bonnie, who once again has outsmarted them, and runs into the yard with the ball in her mouth. I look at myself in the mirror while eating another cookie.

How am I supposed to write this story without gaining fifty pounds?

10

JANUARY 2016

AFTER FINISHING the pack of Oreos, I turn on the TV, while the white computer screen with the blank page is staring at me, almost mocking me. I try to ignore it, thinking a little distraction might help my inspiration. I fall into an old episode of *Friends* and watch that till it ends. I am in the mood for popcorn all of a sudden, so I walk back to the kitchen and microwave a bag while a new show rolls over the screen. It's one of those crime shows with unsolved crimes from real life.

I love those, so I hurry back to the couch as soon as the popcorn is done. My dad is sleeping, but he is usually a heavy sleeper, so I turn up the volume to better indulge in the story they're unfolding. I tell myself it's okay to take a little break. After a few minutes, I realize I know the story. I watched the video clip they're showing a thousand times, over and over again, several years ago when it was all over the news back in 2010.

It's the story of the Elingston family. The footage taken by a neighbor's surveillance camera outside their mansion on South Merritt Island shows a person in a dark hooded sweatshirt leaving the house seconds before it bursts into flames. The last part always makes me jump. Knowing the family, and especially the children, are still in there, bound together, after what the police believe to be almost twenty-four hours of being held captive by the suspect, maybe by several of them. They still don't know much about the circumstances, the reporter says. All they have is the footage of the person in the hoodie and a missing Porsche owned by the family. It is believed the intruder escaped in that car, which was later found in the Indian River.

An old picture of the couple at a banquet comes up on the screen, while the reporter tells of the couple in their mid-fifties and their two children that were found dead in their two-million-dollar home. It is believed that gasoline was poured over their bodies before the fire was set. All four were found in the remains of the living room, all close together. Investigators found no signs of forced entry and believe the suspect or suspects were able to gain access to the Elingston home and stayed overnight. It is believed that they must have known the family, as they seemed to know how they lived their day-to-day-lives.

The next pictures are of the children. I forget all about the popcorn as I watch the old photos and listen to the reporter talk about how young Jack Jr. Elingston loved to play baseball and had a game on the Saturday they were held captive that he never showed up to and that had the teammates and the trainer concerned. A small clip follows from one of his Little League games, then a quote from the trainer, stating it was odd that he didn't come, since Jack Jr. was always there at the games.

Next, we see a school photo of Kimmie Elingston, the oldest child. We hear about her success on the school's debate team, how she was a straight A-student and wanted to be a vet. Police records show that friends and relatives tried to reach the family on the Sunday morning when they didn't show up at church, just hours before the house was set on fire and the bodies were discovered. It also shows that Mr. Elingston called their housekeeper around noon on Saturday and left a voicemail where he told her not to come in today, since they were all sick and didn't want to infect her.

"He sounded tense and very strange," the housekeeper says in a small statement. She also says she tried to call back to confirm, but no one answered.

The police believe the intruder entered the house on Saturday morning. By late afternoon, Mr. Elingston called the local Papa Johns and ordered two large pizzas first with pepperoni, then changed the order to ham. The pizzas were delivered to the property forty-five minutes later. The delivery boy spoke shortly to Mr. Elingston as he paid him in cash, but didn't notice anything strange going on at the house.

On the same afternoon, Mr. Elingston also called his accountant and friend of many years and had him withdraw fifty-thousand dollars in cash. The money was later delivered to the house, where Mr. Elingston greeted the accountant at the door and took the money.

"It wasn't unusual," the accountant now says in a new interview. The first one he ever agreed to give. "I worked for the man and knew to do as I was told and never ask questions."

"So, what do you believe he needed fifty-thousand dollars for on a Saturday afternoon?" the reporter asks.

"I...I don't know. As I said. I never asked questions."

"So, you didn't think that something could be wrong?"

The accountant sighs and shakes his head. "I know I should have. But how was I supposed to know? Jack sounded completely normal on the phone."

"So, you didn't think he looked or sounded tense?"

"Jack was always tense. If you ask me if he was more tense than usual, then no. I don't believe he was."

11

JANUARY 2016

"SURF'S BUILDING. Do you want to go?"

Joey rushes into the house and I turn off the TV in the middle of the accountant's sentence.

"I've watched it over the last hour from your dad's lot while working and I can't stay out anymore. It's getting better by the minute."

I jump up from the couch. "Let me get suited up."

"I'll wax our boards."

I walk to the bedroom and look at all my boxes that are stacked in there with a deep sigh. I know my wetsuit is in there somewhere, but how do I find it? It hasn't been cold enough yet this winter to need it, but today the temperature has dropped below seventy, and that is my limit.

I open a box and start looking, then another, and go through that as well. I look at the clock. I still have two hours before Salter comes home by bus, just enough for a good surf session. If only I could find...

"Found it!" Joey yells from the garage. "It was in one of the boxes out here."

He walks into the house and throws it at me.

"Hurry up. The others are already down there."

We meet them at the crossover at 7th Street. Alex and Danny have both left work early, using some dumb excuse that their bosses know perfectly well is not true. That's how it works in Cocoa Beach. When swell is good, people call in sick or leave early. Everyone does it and it is accepted in most workplaces. That's just the way it is in a community where everyone surfs.

"How's the article coming?" Chloe asks me, as we put on our leashes. In front of us, the waves are crashing in two feet overhead high sets. I close my eyes and enjoy the sound.

"It's alright," I say.

"Mary," she says, and grabs my arm.

"What?"

"If it's too hard for you, then let me write it for you. It's an important story. Who knows? Maybe someone will read it and help find them."

"Their pictures have been all over the news," I say and look at her.

"The way the world works today, you're more likely to have them listen to you than what is shown in the news. You have a big voice and it's not just in this area. It's all over the country. For all we know, they could be hiding in a different state where they will never see their pictures on the news."

I hadn't thought about it that way. That my article could actually make a difference in finding them, but Chloe is right. It fills me with motivation.

"I'll get at it," I say, and look back out at the waves. A gorgeous one rolls towards us. A surfer catches it. "Later."

Chloe laughs. Danny grabs his board under his arm. "Shall we?"

Joey, Chloe, and Danny run towards the ocean, while Alex and I walk. Alex turns to look at me before we hit the water.

"Where is Marcia?" he asks.

I shrug. "Joey tried, but couldn't get ahold of her."

Our eyes meet. We don't have to say anything. We both know it. Marcia isn't doing well.

"Has anyone seen her this week?" I ask, concerned.

He shakes his head. "I met her last week in Publix."

"Was she...?"

"Wasted? Oh, yeah. I don't think I've seen her not wasted in the past three or four months."

"It's that bad, huh?"

"I think it's getting worse. She's hanging out with all the homeless people down by Coconuts or at the Sportsbar."

"I thought she was in AA?" I ask.

"She was. She had to. It was court-ordered after her DUI, but I don't think she's actually following the program. Well, I know she isn't because every time I see her she's drunk."

We walk in silence and our feet hit the water.

"Have you heard from Sandra today?" Alex asks.

"I took her to breakfast."

"Wow. You actually got her to go outside? That's great. I've tried for days to just get her to take a walk on the beach with me."

"I know," I say.

"How was she?"

"So-so."

"I went to see her yesterday," Alex says. "I feel bad that she can't surf. Missing out on this swell must be killing her. They're just her type of waves; look at them."

"I know. It must be killing her. But she'll be able to surf once the doctor says it's okay."

"Maybe I'll stop by after we've surfed, and ask her again if she'll walk with me on the beach," he says, jumps up on his board, and starts paddling.

I follow in his tail. The others are already out in the back. I regret having eaten so much today. It makes me feel heavy. I promise myself to cut back.

Tomorrow.

12

JANUARY 2016

MARCIA WAKES UP WITH A GASP. She looks around. Where is she? She is outside somewhere. She sits up and realizes she's on a bench at the bus stop outside of Publix. How did she get here? She never takes the bus.

Where is my bike?

Marcia has a bad headache and she is shaking all over. Is it because of the alcohol or maybe because she is sobering up? Or is it the dream that is still lingering with her? She can still hear the screams as she sits up on the bench. Those screams that she keeps hearing again and again. It doesn't matter if she is awake or asleep anymore. She doesn't know if she is losing it or what is going on, but she is afraid she might be.

Those images. Those awful images of screaming faces, people in pain. They haunt her still as she gets up and starts walking in the hope she might find her bike somewhere.

But you know they're real, don't you? You know they are.

"No!" she says out loud, to silence that annoying voice in her mind always nagging at her, lying to her. "You're not real."

Marcia starts walking faster when she realizes it is late in the afternoon. The kids have to be home by now. She'll have to look for her bike later. Marcia starts running down A1A. Soon, she is wheezing to catch her breath and has to stop. She really should stop smoking. And drinking. But how can she? It's all she has. It's all that keeps those awful images and voices away.

She can't run anymore and has to walk the rest of the way. She sticks her hand out and tries to catch a ride, but no one stops. They never do anymore. They used to. In Cocoa Beach everyone used to hitchhike. But now people don't dare to pick up anyone anymore.

Fear has destroyed everything. Even our little paradise.

Marcia's head is aching badly now. And so is her arm. She pulls up her sleeve and realizes she is hurt. Badly. A long wound stretches from her shoulder to her elbow. Like she has been cut with a knife. It's not deep, though.

It's probably nothing. You probably just fell while drunk like usual. Ripped your arm.

Marcia is used to waking up with strange bruises on her body and not knowing how they happened. The blackouts are getting more and more frequent, though, and it concerns her. It's not a comfortable feeling to not know where you've been or what you've done.

She reaches the townhouse just before sunset and enters the front door.

"Mom!" one of the kids exclaims. "What happened to your arm?"

"Where have you been?" another one asks.

Too many questions, Marcia thinks and avoids looking at them.

She storms past them into the bedroom, where she takes off her bloody shirt. The wound is still bleeding and she tries to wipe it off. She doesn't care if it leaves a scar. As long as she doesn't have to go to a clinic and have to pay for that. Not now that she is finally on top.

What have you done? You don't even know, do you? You have no idea where you've been. Aren't you ashamed of yourself? You should be.

Marcia throws a glance at herself in the mirror. It's been a long time since she recognized her own reflection. She gave up on herself a long time ago. Now all she can think of is when and how to get drunk again so she won't feel the pain or hear the screams.

There's a knock on the door and her daughter Rose sticks her head in. Her beautiful, strong daughter. Is she really twelve already?

"Mom?" she asks carefully.

Embarrassed that she should see her like this, Marcia growls at her, "Give me some privacy!"

The girl's eyes water. "But...but I just..."

"I know! You want food, right? I can never get a moment alone. I'll be out and feed you birds in a minute, all right?"

"I...I just wanted to tell you we already called for pizza, that's all. We had a coupon for a free pizza," she says, then slams the door behind her.

Marcia looks at the closed door, tears welling up in her eyes. She wipes them off, telling herself that she's an idiot before she bends over and opens the bottom drawer in her dresser. She pulls out an emergency bottle of gin and places it to her lips. She doesn't remove it until it is empty.

13

JANUARY 2016

MY ARMS ARE SO sore I can hardly lift my fork to eat dinner. After we had surfed for two hours, Joey went to get Salter at the bus. He then brought him out to us, and we continued for two more hours before we finally had to cave in to the hunger and pain in our bodies. There is nothing like dinner after an afternoon of surfing. I have the biggest appetite in the world and we're all shoveling in our take-out from Cocoa Beach Thai and Sushi, while discussing who had the greatest ride.

"Did you see my turn off the lip on that last wave, Mom?" Salter asks. "Did you?"

"Of course I saw it," I lie. I saw most of his waves, but that one I missed.

Salter takes his plate out and takes the dogs for a walk. Bonnie stares disappointed at the door as he leaves with the dogs on their leashes. She is not allowed to be walked in the streets, the police have informed Joey. So, she stays at the house. I pour her some milk in her bowl. She doesn't even notice. She stands by the door and stares at it, like she is waiting for it to open and the dogs to come back. It's like she is completely lost.

"That's cute," I say with a chuckle.

Joey looks up at me. "What is?"

"The pig. I love how she can't live without the dogs."

"Yeah. It used to be only Clyde that she couldn't do without, but lately it seems that Snowflake has taken an even bigger place in her life. We might even be looking at real love here. Just sayin'."

I laugh and Joey springs for the refrigerator, where he grabs two beers.

He hands me one and takes the other himself. He walks up to me and kisses me. I close my eyes and enjoy it. He pulls his chair up next to mine and we sit close for a little while without saying anything.

"I was thinking I would put up a TV in your dad's room. Give him something to do when he's in there all day. I kind of feel bad for him."

"That would be awesome. Thank you. That's very thoughtful of you," I say. "Say, have you seen Marcia lately?"

He drinks from his beer, then shakes his head. "Nope. Not for several weeks I believe. Why?"

"I don't know. I have a feeling she's not doing so well. I'm just worried, that's all."

"Well she has been hitting the bottle pretty hard the last couple of months."

"I just wonder if there's anything we can do for her. I mean, can't we help her? What about the children? Is she even capable of taking care of them? I really don't like it."

Joey nods pensively. "I know. Maybe we should check in on them tomorrow? Maybe stop by in the afternoon when they're home from school and make sure they're alright?"

"I think that would be a very good idea."

My dad calls for me and I walk into his room. He looks at me and asks me to close the window, since it's getting too cold now. I lift him up and fluff his pillow to make it more comfortable for him. He smells nice, since the nurse was here earlier and gave him a bath. She was worried about some pressure sores he was getting on the lower part of his back. They looked like they might be getting infected, she told me just before she left.

"Are you ready for your dinner?" I ask.

"Not really," he says with a sniffle. "I'm not...hungry."

"You've got to eat, Dad. You haven't eaten anything all day. You've got to get some energy or you'll never get better."

His facial expression tells me I said something wrong. "What's wrong, Dad?"

He shakes his head. "Don't you realize...I am never going to get...better? I can't...feel anything. I am a...vegetable. I hate being such...a burden to you all."

"Don't say that, Dad. You know you can get better. The doctor said it's possible. A lot can happen with physical therapy. You can't give up hope, Dad. You can't."

He shakes his head in disbelief. "I don't want...to be chained to...a bed for the rest of my...life. I don't want to lie here and watch as my body...deteriorates in front of me and not...be able to do anything about it. I would rather...be dead."

I bite my lip in frustration. I want so badly to do something to help him, but I can't. Just like Sandra, I can't heal him; I can't make all of this go away, no matter how much I desperately want to.

"I'll make you some soup," I say, my voice breaking. "All right, Daddy? Dad?"

"Laura was here earlier," he suddenly says. "She...stopped by."

"That's nice. Weren't you happy to see her?"

He exhales. It isn't a good sound. "She's...leaving."

My heart stops. Literally.

She is what?

"Excuse me?"

"She's leaving. Tomorrow...she'll be driving back to Orlando...where she grew up. She is moving in...with her brother." My dad pauses and catches his breath. I can tell he is struggling to find the words. "Says she can't handle...seeing me like this, that she too needs a life and...and...and that it can't stop here. I...I can't blame her. I can't...offer her anything anymore. I don't...want her to...waste her life here...here with me."

I stare at my dad, not knowing what to say. I feel all kinds of anger flushing through my body. There is so much I want to say, but I don't. I can tell my dad is hiding how broken he really is over this.

"I'll make you that soup," I say, and walk out the door.

In the kitchen, I cover my face and cry. Joey is watching TV when Salter comes back home with the dogs, much to Bonnie's joy. The animals reconnect like they haven't seen each other for years, and soon they're back to playing with the ball again, the dogs chasing after Bonnie.

"What's wrong, Mom?" Salter asks, as he hangs the leashes up and takes off his shoes.

I wipe my eyes and force a smile. "Nothing, sweetie. I was just making soup for Grandpa."

"He's eating? That's great."

"I know. It's good."

Salter walks to his dad and sits on the couch with him. The news is talking about how the police still have no clue who killed a fifty-seven year-old woman whose body was pulled out of Indian River two weeks ago, just two days before Christmas Eve. I sit with my family while the microwave is heating the soup that I ordered for my dad from the Thai-place. I am not listening to the TV. I am thinking about Laura. I can't believe anyone could act like this. How you can pretend you love someone and then just leave them in their biggest hour of need? So what if my dad can't offer her anything. Maybe it is her turn to offer something. Maybe it is her turn to take care of him; maybe he needs her and not the other way around. Isn't that what love is all about? Isn't it all about sacrifice?

I look at Salter and Joey, while thinking how happy I am that I made the decision to stay here and to give Joey a second chance. My dad's house is supposed to be done in a month, if everything goes according to schedule —which it probably won't—but I still have to decide at some point what to do next. Should Salter and I move with my dad so we can help him, or should we stay here with Joey and be a family?

I know in my heart what I want the most, but I also know my dad needs me more than ever now. I can't just think about myself.

14

JANUARY 2016

"MOM. I HEARD A LOUD BANG."

Kelly blinks her eyes in the darkness. She can only see the outline of her daughter as she is standing by the foot of their bed. Kelly sighs, still half a sleep. Next to her, her husband, Andrew grumbles sleepily.

"What's wrong, honey? What are you doing out of bed?"

"I heard a loud noise. It woke me up and now I'm scared."

As she is speaking, their Beagle, Max, jumps into their bed. Max usually sleeps with their daughter. He runs to Kelly and starts licking her face. Kelly groans. She is so tired. It's still pitch dark outside.

"Just go back to bed, Lindsey. It's probably nothing."

"It was really loud, Mommy. I'm afraid that someone came into our house. I'm scared."

Andrew groans. He looks at his phone. "We still have three hours till we have to get up. Please just let us sleep a little longer."

"Go back to bed, sweetie," Kelly says. "I'm sure it was just a dream."

"But there was a loud noise, Mommy," the girl insists. "And now the light is on in the living room."

Kelly opens her eyes now. She sits up straight and looks at her daughter. She can barely see her in the darkness. "The light is on in the living room?"

"We probably just forgot to shut it off last night," Andrew says. "Lights don't just turn on and off on their own."

"Maybe we should check it," Kelly says.

YOU CAN RUN   319

Andrew groans ostentatiously. He knows where this is going.

"Would it make you feel better if Daddy checked it out, sweetie?" Kelly says.

"Yes," the girl says with a slight whimper.

"Okay. Come up here on the bed and lie down while Daddy checks it out."

"Seriously?" Andrew says.

"Just do it for her sake," Kelly says. "To give her peace of mind."

Andrew exhales deeply, then sits up. "You do realize I have an important breakfast meeting, right?"

"Yes. I know perfectly well about your meeting, but this is the only way we can get some sleep. So, if you would please...?"

"All right," he grumbles and pulls off the covers. He plants his feet on the carpet. The bed moves when he lifts himself off it. Andrew is no lightweight. Not like he was when Kelly met him. In a brief second, she misses those years.

Andrew leaves, and Kelly pulls her daughter closer. She kisses her forehead and holds her tight. "Shh. It's probably nothing, sweetie. You can sleep here. Just close your eyes. Daddy will take care of it."

Their daughter finally relaxes and closes her eyes. Kelly caresses her hair, while wondering if she will be able to fall asleep again. Their daughter has been known to sleepwalk from time to time, and Kelly now wonders if Lindsey dreamt she heard a bang, then walked into the living room and turned on the lights. Kelly chuckles to herself. That is probably what happened. Lindsey did and said the strangest things when sleepwalking. One morning they had found her in the living room, sitting on the couch, with all the lights turned on, sleeping with her eyes open. It had scared Kelly like crazy, until she realized the girl was just asleep. This was probably just another one of her stunts.

Lindsey is sleeping now and Kelly puts her head on the pillow next to her daughter. She likes to listen to her heavy breathing. Such peace.

Must be nice, she thinks to herself. *To be able to just let go of all your worries like that and enter that deep of a sleep.*

Kelly can't remember when she had last had a good and worry-free night of sleep. Not since she had her child probably. She wonders if she will ever stop feeling that anxiety deep in her heart, that deep worry that soon all of her happiness will be ripped out of her embrace, that it was all just a joke life played on her, a vicious game to make her allow herself to be happy, and then in an instant when she is not worrying or being aware it'll all be ripped from her. After all, she has everything. Finally, after many years of trying and waiting for a child, she has one. She has a beautiful family, a big house, four cars in the garage, money enough to last her a lifetime. Is she really allowed to have all this? Is anyone?

"I've checked the entire house. There's nothing."

Andrew closes the bedroom door behind him and turns off the flashlight. "Now, maybe we can finally get some sleep?"

15

OCTOBER 2005

KRISTIN MARTIN'S office is a mess. The room has high wooden ceilings, and books cover the walls from top to bottom. There are piles of newspapers and magazines. Clipped out articles cover her desk. It is just as Daniel has imagined it. The absent-minded professor in her right element.

"Ah, Daniel, come on in," she says, looking up from behind her desk. She takes off her glasses and gets up.

Daniel pushes Peter in his wheelchair in front of him. Kristin walks towards him with a big smile on her face. She looks at Peter and bends down.

"And this...I take it, must be...Peter. It's a pleasure to meet you Peter," she says, and touches his hand. Peter doesn't react.

It's rare that people talk directly to his brother, and it warms Daniel's heart. Kristin looks directly into his eyes while talking to him.

"I am so glad you are here, Peter."

Daniel feels a tug at his heart. For so many years, he has dreamt of finding someone like Kristin. His family doesn't know he has brought him there to see her, since they would only tell him it is a waste of time. He wants to give Kristin a chance; he wants it to work before he presents it to the rest of the family.

"Let's get started, shall we?" Kristin says, still addressing Peter. It's like she actually believes he understands what she is saying. Daniel is usually the only one who talks to Peter this way.

"If you will bring him over here. I have prepared a little game for us.

Just to get to know each other a little bit, alright?"

Daniel nods, but she isn't looking for his approval. She is looking into Peter's eyes, waiting to see his reaction.

"Alright," she says again, after Daniel has placed Peter where she wants him. On the table in front of him, she places a series of pictures and index cards.

"Let's do this. Are you ready? In what room would you find the refrigerator?" she asks, laying out a card showing a bedroom, a bathroom, and a kitchen. "Please, don't be offended by this," she adds. "I am sure these questions are very easy for you."

Kristin looks at Peter like she is waiting for his response, waiting for him to talk or point at one of the pictures.

"He can't..." Daniel interrupts, thinking Kristin doesn't understand how bad Peter's condition really is. "He can't do that."

Kristin pays no attention to Daniel. She puts a hand in the air to stop him from talking. Daniel is afraid that he might have made a mistake. This woman knows nothing about treating patients with Cerebral Palsy. He should have known better. Daniel feels his heart drop as the last hope threatens to leave him.

"Wait," Kristin says with a slow voice. "Did you see that?"

"See what?" Daniel asks.

"He is trying to communicate."

Daniel shakes his head. "He's not doing anything."

"Yes. Yes, he is. You're just not seeing it."

"Those are just spasms," he says, disappointed. "He has those constantly."

"In my eyes, it looks like he is trying to move his arm. His eyes are focused on the picture over here, the one of the kitchen, but when he tries to move his arm, it's like it...it locks, like it shuts up like...like a rabbit trap. It snaps back against his face."

A rabbit trap? This was a mistake.

"So, you think he's trying to answer?" Daniel asks skeptically.

"Yes. I've read about this. They helped a girl in Australia using this new technique. Here, let me."

Kristin places her hand beneath Peter's elbow. "This is to stabilize his arm," she explains to Daniel. "This is what they did to the girl in Australia and had great success with it. I think this might help. This way, I help to keep his arm balanced. I need to be acting as a responsive item of furniture, not moving his arm, but simply facilitating his own movement. Now, Peter, if you would point to the picture of the kitchen, please."

Daniel is holding his breath while watching his brother suddenly move his arm towards the picture. Kristin now uses her other hand to tuck Peter's pinkie, ring and middle finger lightly under hers, spooning their hands, with just his index finger sticking out.

"Great, Peter. Now point to the picture of the ocean, please."

Slowly, but steadily, the arm moves while Kristin is assisting it towards the photograph of an ocean. Daniel doesn't know what to say.

"And now for the hard one," Kristin says, and puts out three pictures. "Please point to the picture of the President of the United States."

"He doesn't have any chance of knowing who is..." Daniel starts, but stops himself when Peter's arm starts to move. It stops and points to the picture of George W. Bush.

Daniel is still speechless when Kristin smiles and looks up at him. Her eyes are sparkling with joy. Daniel thinks it makes her look stunning. He feels such a close connection to her in this instant. So many years he has been alone with this, thinking there was a way for Peter to express himself. Could it be? Could it really be true? Daniel is watching it happen and he is overwhelmed with the belief that it is in fact true. He wants to believe it, he has to.

"See! You did see it, didn't you?"

Daniel nods while biting his lips. He doesn't know whether to cry or laugh. Does his baby brother really know who the president is? What else does he know?

Excitedly, Kristin is now pulling out index cards with letters on them, and one after another, Peter identifies the letters.

"He even knows the alphabet!" Kristin exclaims, as they go through all the letters, and seconds later she asks him to put together words, and he does. Daniel holds his breath while Peter spells his first word, by pointing at the letters and Kristin writing them down. Soon an entire sentence emerges.

"I...am...hungry," Kristin reads out loud. She looks up at Daniel. "He just spelled *I am hungry*. Daniel, your brother's first sentence, the first thing he ever told you is that he is hungry. Isn't that wonderful? He *is* smart. Peter is smart! He does communicate. We just have to learn how to listen."

She looks back into Peter's eyes while Daniel's eyes fill with tears. He can't wait to tell his mother and siblings. Now they have to believe him.

"I believe I can teach you to speak, Peter," Kristin says. "Not with your mouth, but with your hands. It's about time your family hears what you have to say."

16

JANUARY 2016

I WORK on the article for the next several days and manage to write something that I end up trashing by the weekend. On Friday night, we decide to put on a movie for all of us to see. We even roll my dad's bed into the living room, so he can join us. We rent the new *Mission Impossible* and I make the popcorn and find the candy. I feed my dad while we watch it. Salter is allowed to stay up late. It's not something I let him do often, since he doesn't do well with not getting his sleep. Halfway through the movie, I look at Joey, and realize he is not watching. He's on his phone.

"Tom Cruise just died and you missed it because you were texting," I say and poke him with my elbow.

"Sorry," he says, and puts the phone away.

A few minutes pass, but I'm not watching the movie anymore. Something in his expression worries me. I know it is silly, but I have to ask. So, I do it as casually as I know how to.

"So, who was it?" I ask without looking at him. I pretend to watch the movie.

"Nobody," he says.

Not the answer I am looking for.

"You mean it's nobody that I know?" I ask, still looking at the screen.

Salter is hushing me now. I feed my dad a cookie. He enjoys it. One of the few joys he has these days. I can feel my heart is beating faster and it annoys me immensely. I recognize this feeling from back when we lived in

New York. Back when I found out about him and that girl from the coffee-house. It's the awful feeling that your beloved is hiding something from you. After this many years together, you just know something is off. And then comes the feeling of guilt for thinking like this. Because, what if you're wrong? What if it really was nobody?

But it is somebody. You saw the look in his eyes. He is hiding something. He doesn't want you to know who it was.

Oh, my. I can sense how the paranoia is running away with me now and I don't like it. I am not paying any attention to the movie anymore, especially not when Joey's phone vibrates again and he picks it up. I pretend not to notice he is reading something, and soon after, answering it. It makes my blood boil. I have no idea what to do. Should I ask again? I don't want to be this obsessive woman who wants to know and control everything he does, but I can't stop thinking about it. No matter what I do, I am screwed. If I don't say anything, I'll be wondering about this all night, and Joey will sense it and think I'm mad. I'll tell him I am not angry, and he'll just be annoyed with me because he can feel that I am. If I do say something, he'll get angry and think I am possessive and that I don't trust him. Which, I don't. To be perfectly honest, I don't. He did it before and, yes, I know the circumstances were different; he was in a terrible place, he was bored and feeling left out of my life. I know it was different, but still. What if? Why does there always have to be a *what if*?

Out of the corner of my eye, I watch as Joey finishes the text and puts the phone away. I try not to think about it anymore and feed my dad another cookie, while eating one myself. Soon, I can't stop. I have eaten four, five cookies. I had promised myself no sweets tonight, but now I can't stop. It's like I am trying to stuff my emotions back into my body by putting food on top of them. Like I am pressing my tears back with cookies. It makes me feel slightly better, but only for a few minutes.

"That is so cool!" Salter exclaims. "Did you see that, Mom?" he looks at me and I blush because I have no idea what happened in the movie. I nod.

"Pretty cool, huh?"

"You know that Tom Cruise does all of his stunts himself, right?" Salter says. "I think that is awesome."

"That is awesome," I say, and look at Joey. I swallow the lump in my throat. Joey smiles at me.

"Come here," he says, and pulls me closer. He starts to kiss me on the neck and nibble my ear.

I sigh and try to enjoy it, while Tom Cruise jumps on a motorcycle.

"I was wondering when he would do that," Joey says.

"Do what?" I ask absent-mindedly. I keep thinking about his phone and wondering if I can somehow get to look at it without him noticing it. I feel so silly for thinking like this, but if it is just an old friend he is texting, if it is just nobody, then it would certainly comfort me knowing so.

"The bike. I was wondering when he would ride one. He always does at some point."

"Ah, I see. Well, I don't think he rode one in *Edge of Tomorrow*," I say.

"Yes, he totally did," Joey says.

"I don't think he did," I repeat.

"Well, he did."

"Wanna bet?" I ask.

"Sure. You do the dishes the next two days if I'm right," he says. "And you give me a massage before bedtime."

"That's a lot," I say. "If I win, you do the same for me."

We shake hands on it, and as we let go, I put out my hand. "Give me your phone. I'll check it."

"Why don't you use your own?" Joey complains.

"My phone is in the kitchen, charging. I'll miss out on the movie."

"We can stop the movie."

"Come on. I don't want to have to get up," I say. "Just give me yours and I'll check it."

Joey looks at me like he doesn't want to. It makes it even harder on me. "What? Are you afraid I'll win?"

He chuckles and shakes his head. "I'll do it," he says, and takes out the phone.

Damn it. He didn't fall for it. And here I thought I was being so clever.

"We'll do it together," I say and crawl up next to him, so I can look at what he is doing.

He opens the Internet and starts the search. It doesn't take him long to find something about Tom Cruise and the movies he rides a bike in. As he opens the link, he receives a text again. I see it on the top of his phone. I can't see what it says, but I do manage to see that the name of the sender is Jack.

"You got a text," I say. "Don't you want to read it?"

"Nah. It's not important. Just some work I might get."

"That is important. Are you kidding me? That's great."

He shrugs. "You know how it is. I'm not celebrating till I'm sure I have it. Too many times I've been disappointed."

"I understand," I say, but feel like celebrating myself. I was just a fool for being suspicious. Never have I felt so relieved. For once, I did the right thing in not making an issue out of it. Jack is just some guy Joey knows, and it is probably just about work. Joey was right. It is just a nobody.

17

JANUARY 2016

"WHO ARE YOU? What are you doing in my house?"

Marcia is staring at the man in front of her. Her nostrils are flaring. Her blood is rushing through her veins. In her hand, she is holding a kitchen knife. The kids are all out, except the youngest, Tim, who is sitting on the couch coloring in a book. She's wondering if she will be able to protect him if this intruder tries to grab him.

"Get out!"

The man in her kitchen shakes his head. "But..."

Marcia is swinging the knife in front of her. "I swear, I'll hurt you. Don't come any closer!"

The man looks startled, almost desperate. "Don't you recognize me? I'm your renter. Harry Hanson? I moved in almost a week ago?"

Marcia stares at the man. She is baffled. What is this? A joke? "Renter?" she says.

"Yes. I live in the room upstairs. You told me I could stay there and use the kitchen when I needed to."

Marcia's pulse lowers.

A renter? I have a renter? How is this possible?

"But...I just put the ad in yesterday," she says. She lowers the knife a little, then pulls it back up with a grunt. "Is this a trick? You're not fooling me."

"No! It's not a trick! I paid you three hundred dollars. All my stuff is upstairs. I'm beginning to think you're the one trying to trick me."

"Don't turn this around on me," Marcia says. "You're just trying to confuse me and trick me. What do you want from me? I don't have any money, if that's what you think."

"I don't want your money. I just came down to make myself a cup of coffee," the man says, and shows her a jar of Nescafé in his hand. "I brought my own coffee, if you're afraid I'll take yours."

"It's true, Mom," Tim yells from the couch. "Don't you recognize Harry? He made us lasagna yesterday when you didn't come home for dinner."

Marcia looks at the boy, then back at the man. "But yesterday we went to Beef O' Brady's. Kids eat free on Tuesdays. You had chicken wings, remember? You spilled on your white shirt?" she says.

"It's Saturday today," Harry says.

"Yeah. That was last week, Mom," Tim says.

Marcia feels dizzy and stumbles backward. She sits on a chair and puts the knife down. "It was last week? But...but..."

"It's okay, Mom. You're just forgetful." He looks at Harry. "I told you she's forgetful. Sometimes she even forgets to come home."

Marcia looks at her boy. She understands nothing. It's a horrible feeling. What happened? Where has she been? What has she done? She remembers nothing. Not even Harry.

What the hell is happening to me?

She bursts into a loud fit of laughter and points her finger at Harry. "Gotcha. I was just kidding. Of course I remember Harry *Handsome*," she says, and winks at the boy. The boy shrugs.

"It's true," he says, addressed to Harry. "You are kind of handsome." The boy then turns around and returns to his coloring book.

Marcia avoids looking at Harry. She really doesn't remember him at all, and wonders how this could have happened. She turns her back on him and puts on a kettle of water.

"It should be done soon," she says. "I have to..."

Harry steps aside and Marcia hurries to her bedroom and closes the door behind her. Breathing heavily, she goes through her drawers, but finds no bottles. She curses and throws her clothes on the floor angrily. She is so sure she hid a bottle in the bottom drawer. She always has an extra, an emergency bottle. Who took it? Could it be this Harry-figure? There is something about him she doesn't like.

Instead of the bottle, she finds a bottle of pills, and she swallows some quickly and washes them down with an old glass of water from her bedside. She looks at her bed. It doesn't look like anyone slept in it last night. She doesn't remember making it this morning. Did she even sleep here last night?

18

JANUARY 2016

I GO to Sandra's and ring the doorbell around noon. I have Snowflake and Clyde with me on leashes, and they are both jumping up and down with excitement. I think they can smell Sandra's dog, Lucky the Chihuahua. She opens with a smile and I am surprised to see her this happy.

"Hey. I was wondering if you would take a walk with me on the beach today? I know Ryan is working at my dad's lot, so I thought you might have some time. We could bring all the dogs and hope the cops don't catch us? What do you say? Let's be daredevils for once."

Lucky is barking on the other side of the door. Snowflake can hear him and gets overly excited. I can hardly hold him. Clyde is barking back.

"I would love to, but I have someone here."

"Oh. Well, that's good. I'm glad you're not alone."

"Sorry to disappoint you, though."

"Nah. Don't worry about it. So who is it? Who's here?"

"Alex. Alex is here." She sounds funny when she says his name.

"Alex? Well I won't disturb, then," I say.

"Oh, you're not disturbing. We were just talking about you, as a matter of fact."

"About me?"

"Well. No. Not really. I don't know why I said that. We were talking about back in the days when you and I were best friends and...and Alex and I were...well, you know," she says with a nervous laugh.

I get a feeling I don't like. "Listen, Sandra," I say with a whisper. "I know that things haven't been easy lately, but this is not the answer. You're both married."

The look in her eyes changes drastically. "What are you implying? Why would you say such a thing?"

"I just don't want to see you make a mistake you'll later regret."

"I...I really don't appreciate this, Mary," she says, and comes out and pulls the door closed behind her. "Alex and I are friends, nothing more. Besides, do you really think he would be interested in me, that anyone would be interested in me now that I look...like this...like this...monster. Do you?"

I feel embarrassed. "I'm sorry, Sandra. I just worry about you, that's all. I don't know what it is about me lately. I seem to think everyone is having an affair. Last night I was certain Joey was texting with some girl, and it turned out to be this guy named Jack. I am sorry...I see ghosts. I guess I'm damaged after what happened to us in New York."

Sandra's eyes calm down as well. "Well, no one could blame you for being suspicious. It must be difficult to trust him again."

"I try, but it really is," I say. "Say, do you want me to take Lucky with me to the beach? He sounds like he would enjoy a good walk and playtime with the others."

"Would you? That would be awesome," Sandra says. "I haven't been out with him much lately, and he really loves the beach. Just don't get him arrested, though," she says with a small laugh.

"I won't," I say. "I'll take his place if needed."

She finds the leash and hands me Lucky. Minutes later, I have crossed the street and am standing with my toes in the sand watching the waves. It's pretty flat today, so no surfing, but that's okay. I am still very sore. As I walk, I wonder once again about Joey and me. I really hate that feeling I had the night before, and I don't want to live a life constantly being afraid of what he is up to. I want to trust him, I really do. But am I able to?

I put my feet in the water and walk the three dogs all the way to Sixteenth Street and back. I enjoy the fresh air and the dogs running playfully around my feet.

When I get back to Sandra's house and walk past the kitchen window, I see them. I stop with a small gasp as I watch Sandra and Alex engaged in a long, deep kiss.

19

JANUARY 2016

KELLY IS STANDING in her kitchen. She is looking at the ocean outside her windows. This fall has caused a lot of beach erosion, and the water is coming up closer to the house than usual.

Melbourne Beach. She never did like it much down here. Being from upstate New York, she thinks it's too hot and humid down here in Florida. But her husband loves it, and when they married this was where he wanted to live. This is where he grew up. For his sake, she pretends to enjoy it.

Andrew loves to fish on his boat, and today he has taken their daughter Lindsey with him. Kelly hates it when they go together. She always worries that something will happen to their fragile daughter.

"She's not a strong swimmer," she constantly tells him. She doesn't feel like he understands how delicate their daughter is. She's afraid that Andrew wants her to be the boy he never had, and she can't be. The girl suffers from severe asthma that has destroyed many nights of sleep for them, especially when she was younger.

Kelly feels a chill go through her bones. Not because it's cold, but because she can't stop imagining Lindsey hurting herself on a hook or a spear. She looks out at the raging ocean, while peeling an apple with a small knife in her hand. She is making a fruit salad for herself for lunch. She looks at the phone next to her on the counter, waiting, anticipating it ringing and a voice telling her that something has gone wrong, that her daughter is in the hospital. She goes through all the scenarios in her mind, thinking of all the things that could go wrong. Maybe they didn't even make it to the boat. They could have been in a car accident. What if there's a thunderstorm while they're on the ocean? Even though thunderstorms are rare in January, they do appear sometimes.

Kelly doesn't understand this sudden worry. She's not usually the worrying type. She just can't escape this unease. She has been feeling it ever since that night when Lindsey came to their room and told them she heard a loud noise and that there was a light on in the living room. She knows it's silly, but Kelly can't escape the thought that something bad is about to happen.

Evil forebodings, the Bible calls it. Do not let your heart get worried or troubled. You know it's all in your head, Kelly. Gotta shake it.

The morning after the incident at night, Kelly had realized that their telescope in the back of the living room, by the window, was tipped over. Naturally, Kelly couldn't help wondering if that had caused the loud bang that Lindsey talked about. But who had tipped it over? Lindsey while sleep-walking? That was the logical explanation, but Kelly didn't feel so sure. Why didn't it wake her up? Was she also the one who had turned on the light? And then what? Gone back to bed again? It was possible, but didn't satisfy her.

"What if someone was in our house?" she asked her husband, but he didn't want to hear about it.

"You're seeing ghosts," he simply said, then left for his important meeting with another client whose land he is going to develop into yet another massive area of houses and lucrative condos.

Maybe she was. But, then again, maybe she wasn't. She decided to let it go till two days later when she came home with her groceries, and as she put the key in the lock, she heard a loud noise in the back. She walked inside and realized the door to the porch was wide open. There was sand on the floor in her bedroom, and one of the drawers was open. Nothing was stolen.

"There's always sand on the floor of our house," Andrew argued. "That's what you get from living on the beach. And maybe you just forgot to close the back door; maybe the wind blew it open."

Kelly listened to her husband, but didn't agree. She knows she remembered to close that door. She always does when leaving. And it is no longer just those two incidents that make her uneasy. It's the feeling of being watched. When she goes to the library or the grocery store, she sees the same car. It was even parked outside of the gym this morning when she came out after her spinning-class. It appears to be everywhere she goes.

She noticed it the first time a couple of weeks ago, and since then, she seems to see it everywhere. In the beginning, she thought she was being paranoid. After all, there are a lot of brown trucks, but soon she noticed it had a dent on the right side of it, and now she recognizes it everywhere. She doesn't dare to approach it, at least not yet, but it scares her like crazy.

Kelly shakes the thought and cuts up the apple. She puts it in the bowl with the rest of the fruit, and then starts to eat while her stomach is still in a knot. She closes her eyes and takes in a deep breath to calm herself down.

You have to relax. You can't live like this. Expect good things to happen to you. Life is good.

She looks down at Max, the beagle who is sleeping on the floor. "You're not much of a watchdog, are you? You're more likely to lick any burglar to death should he enter, am I right?"

The dog doesn't even react. That's when the phone on the counter starts to ring, and Kelly looks at it with a loud gasp. The display says it's Andrew.

Please tell me she's all right. Please let nothing have happened to her!

"Hello?" she says, picking it up. She tries hard to sound normal, but her voice is shrill.

"Something happened," Andrew says.

Oh, my God! Please don't. Please don't take my baby from me!

Kelly gasps and clasps her mouth. "What happened, Andrew? Is it Lindsey?"

"Yes," he says. "She...she caught the biggest redfish I have ever seen in my entire life! It's bigger than her!"

Kelly stumbles backwards as Andrew yells the last part and follows up with some loud cheering.

"I am so proud of her!" he continues. "She wanted to tell you, so here she is."

"Mom? Did you hear?"

Kelly slides slowly to the floor, her back against the cabinets, while her heart is pounding in her chest.

"Mom?"

"That's...that's wonderful news, sweetie," she finally says, while relief goes through every muscle in her body. "That's awesome. I am so proud of you."

"Thanks, Mom."

They hang up and Kelly starts to laugh. She sits on the floor, holding the phone in her hand, and simply laughs at her own stupidity. To think that she let herself get carried away with fear like that. It is ridiculous.

You're ridiculous, Kelly. As always, it is nothing. Everything is fine.

Kelly shakes her head while finishing her fruit salad. She puts the bowl in the sink and looks down at the beach, when she spots someone down there. Someone with a set of binoculars pointed straight at her. As she sees them, the person puts the binoculars down and moves on.

20

JANUARY 2016

HE IS IN HER HOUSE. Blake is going through the blonde's drawers, looking through her underwear, and decides to keep a pair. He puts it in his pocket before closing the drawer. He looks at the closet and opens it. Rows of her neatly hung dresses appear in front of him. Blake smiles to himself. The blonde sure is a nice dresser. She likes to show off her legs, he has noticed. She does have nice legs, and she makes sure to stay fit. Blake has been watching her as she goes for her run every morning. Usually, he watches her as she runs through the park, but today he decided to go into her house instead. He wants to get close to her, to get to know her, every little detail about her. Why? He doesn't know. All he knows is that he can't stop thinking about her. When lying in bed at night with Olivia by his side at the motel, all he can think of is her, the blonde with the long legs. What it is about her, he can't explain. He just knows he wants her; he wants to be so close to her he can smell her skin. He keeps obsessing about her skin and how it tastes.

Blake is not popular with Olivia these days. She annoys him. All her constant nagging. He had no idea that's what it would be like to be on the run with her. He would never have brought her with him if he had known. She is constantly on his case, telling him he goes out too much, that they'll get caught if he doesn't stay in the motel room. Blake doesn't care. He can't stand it in there anymore. He needs to get out. He needs to see the blonde girl.

Blake smells her dresses one by one, and goes through an old shoebox of her private stuff. Mostly old pictures of the blonde and her friends. Blake laughs when he sees a picture of her from when she was a teenager with braces and big hair.

"Even then you were special, dear. I bet the boys were all over you," he whispers to the photograph, then puts it back in the box.

Blake picks up a postcard from the Philippines. It's from the guy she's dating. He's some army-guy and is away a lot. Reading the words on the card makes Blake's blood boil. He loses his temper and rips it to pieces.

As the pieces fall to the carpet, he hears the front door slam. Blake gasps. He picks up the pieces of the broken postcard, puts the lid back on the shoebox, and puts it back on the shelf, then turns off the light in the closet and closes the door. He hears her steps in the hallway as she gets closer to the bedroom, and seconds later, he watches her through the door as she enters. She is still wearing earplugs and humming to some song. She is sweating and panting from the run and wiping her face on a towel. Blake enjoys watching her. He especially likes those short shorts. She sits on her bed and pulls out her phone. Blake can still hear the music playing in her ears. She is looking at the display on her phone while Blake studies her. His breath comes in ragged bursts. His body is trembling. He has never been this close to her before. He can almost touch her, almost smell her, almost taste the salty sweat on her skin.

The blonde turns off the music and starts to undress. Right there, in front of him, she gets completely naked. Blake can't believe it. He can hardly breathe as he watches her move around the bedroom. She walks to the bathroom and he can hear the shower being turned on before she comes back, grabs her phone and writes something, sitting on the bed all naked.

Blake is holding his breath to not make a sound. He doesn't want to ruin this special moment. This moment that he will cherish for the rest of his life when thinking back on this day.

The girl leaves the phone on the bed, then gets up and walks into the shower. Blake waits for a minute before he makes his move.

Enjoy your shower, gorgeous, he thinks to himself, while watching her silhouette through her shower curtain. *You can run all you want to, but you can never ever hide from me.*

21

JANUARY 2016

I KNOCK ON THE WINDOW. Startled, they let go of each other and look at me.

"What the hell are you doing?" I yell.

They stare at each other, then back at me. Embarrassed, Sandra looks down, and then goes for the front door. I walk up to her and hand her the leash.

"Here's your dog. He pooped twice. Now, would you please tell me what the heck is going on? And don't try to make me feel all guilty and embarrassed again. I know what I saw."

"Mary, please. You don't know what it's like..."

"Well, I know what it is like to be on the other side of that. And that isn't funny, I can tell you that much. I really never thought you would be... how...how Sandra, how are you able to do that and live with yourself? How long has this been going on?"

Her eyes are avoiding mine. "Only a few days."

I sigh deeply. "I can't believe you."

"You don't know what it's like to have your husband look at you like you're some monster, Mary. To have him shiver in disgust every time he tries to touch you. You don't know what that is like."

"Alright, I don't. Then, leave him. Divorce him, and then you two can fool around or whatever it is you're doing. But not while you're still married. That's just wrong. No matter what you look like. I feel for you, you know I do, Sandra. But it's still wrong. It's not fair to Ryan."

Sandra looks at me. I can tell she is embarrassed. I grab her shoulder and pull her close in a warm embrace. "I won't tell Ryan. Don't worry," I say. "My loyalty is with you. But you have to sort out your mess."

Sandra promises me she will and I leave her house. I walk back with the dogs to Joey's place. Salter and Joey are engaged in a game on the Xbox and barely notice me. Bonnie grunts delightedly as she sees the dogs again. Snowflake and Clyde are equally happy to see her and get all tangled up in each other's leashes as they run around excitedly wagging their tails and sniffing Bonnie. As I let them all go, they storm towards the couches and jump up on them. Bonnie can't get up there, so she stays on the floor while Clyde and Snowflake play tug-of-war with a brown teddy bear. Joey yells at them, and I decide he can deal with it while I take a shower after the long walk.

When I get back out, the boys are still on the Xbox. I decide to work a little and sit by the computer, going through my notes. The trashed article is still in the trash can next to me and I pull it out and read it. I shake my head. No. Still won't do. Chloe is going to get mad at me. I have never been this long writing anything. She wants me to post on my blog every day, just anything to keep the site active.

"You can't lose momentum," she keeps saying. "Gotta strike while the iron is hot."

So, I decide to make a small video instead. Just to have something. I walk to our bedroom to find a quiet corner, and then turn on the camera on my laptop.

"Ah. This is hard," I say with a deep sigh. "But I am going to try anyway. As some of you might know, my brother is wanted for murder. As far as we know, he has killed one woman here in Cocoa Beach about three months ago. He was arrested for it, but tricked us into believing in his innocence. He fooled me into believing him, and not just me. The whole system. And now he is free again. He is on the run. The police are looking for him and his girlfriend, who was also present when he killed the woman. Now, I am trying to write an article about it. Trying hard to get the words onto paper, but I can't. I don't know what it is. It just hurts so badly to even think about it," I say.

"It's hard to put words to it. You see, my best friend was badly injured and almost lost her life while we tried to catch him. My best friend's life has been destroyed ever since, and I don't know how I can live with myself knowing this. She was a model. A gorgeous woman with a great career. My brother poured acid on her face, and now..." I stop and press back my tears. I try to keep my tone in check. "Now she can't work anymore. Her career is destroyed. All I know is I want to see him punished for what he did, and I'll do anything, give *anything* to find him. He is out there somewhere. What is he up to? Is he killing again? I don't know. It is up to us to catch him, hopefully before he hurts anyone else."

I turn it off and decide that it will have to do for now. I put the video on YouTube and then post it on my blog, along with a picture of my brother and Olivia, the same two pictures that have been shown on TV here in Florida.

At least I posted something, I think to myself, as I leave the computer and join the boys in the living room.

"What have you been up to?" Joey asks, as I lean over and kiss him.

"Just striking some iron while it was hot," I say.

22

JANUARY 2016

LATER IN THE DAY, I take my bike to Marcia's place. I have wanted to check in on her for days. I park my bike outside her townhouse and walk up to the door. I knock, and seconds later, the door is opened.

By a man I have never seen before?

"I...I'm looking for Marcia?" I say, worried. Who is this guy and what is he doing here?

The man smiles. He is annoyingly handsome. "You're probably wondering who I am," he says.

Well...just a little bit!

"Hi. My name is Harry. I've rented the room upstairs for a couple of days. Are you one of Marcia's friends?"

"Yes."

"Alright. Come on in."

"I didn't know Marcia rented out a room," I say, and shake his hand before I follow him inside. The place looks better than I had expected. Cleaner and tidier than usual. Two of the kids are sitting in the living room, reading books, I am surprised to see.

"She's not here right now," Harry says. "But I thought maybe we could talk for a little while. Do you have a minute?"

"I have many minutes," I say awkwardly. What is it about this guy? He makes me all goofy.

"Coffee?"

"Yes! I love coffee. Drink it all the time. Can't live without my coffee."

What's the matter with you? Why are you rambling?

"Milk?"

I shake my head. "Black. I prefer black. I mean I like white too...it's not a racist thing or anything..."

Will you stop talking? What are you? Twelve?

"Here," he says with a chuckle. I can see his muscles through his tight white T-shirt. I blush and look away, but not without thinking that Joey never had a chest like that.

"Thank you. You're very nice...I mean, it's very nice of you. You're very...handsome."

Did you just call him handsome? What's wrong with you!

Harry chuckles. Even his chuckles are sexy. We sit in the kitchen. The coffee is hot and steaming. So is Harry.

Will you stop it now?

"So, have you known Marcia for long?" he asks.

"You could say that. We've known each other since preschool," I say.

He nods seriously. "Good. Then it won't be too much to talk to you about this. I won't be overstepping my boundaries here."

I feel my heart drop. "It sounds serious. What's going on?"

"I have only lived here for about a week, but I have to say...your friend... Marcia is in need of help. She is hardly ever home, and when she is, she is... well, not really there."

I sigh and sip my coffee. "Is it that bad, huh? I know she has been drinking a lot since the divorce, but I thought she was getting by."

"Some nights she doesn't come home at all; other times, she comes home and then leaves again not long after. The kids pretty much have to take care of themselves," he says. "I have been cooking for them the past couple of days and taking care of the home, since she is in no condition to do so."

It feels like a punch to my stomach. All kinds of emotions go through me right now. Guilt being the biggest one of them. How had I not seen this?

"I had no idea it was that bad."

Harry nods. I can tell he is concerned. Genuinely. "Yesterday, she attacked me in the kitchen with a kitchen knife. She said she had no idea who I was. It appeared she thought I was here to rob her or something."

"And you've been living here all week?"

"Yes. It had me quite concerned."

"I can imagine," I say pensively.

"And then, there is this," he says, and places a letter in front of me. "I know I had no business opening it, but seeing who it was from, I had a feeling it was important."

"Oh, my," I say, when reading it.

"Apparently, she was court ordered to go to AA meetings when she had her DUI, but hasn't been showing up the last three months. "She risks going to jail if she doesn't do it."

I look at the children. "She's going to lose her kids, then."

"I am afraid so."

23

JANUARY 2016

"WE NEED TO FIND MARCIA. She needs help."

I look at the others. I've called everyone and asked them to meet me at Joey's house. Sandra and Alex still look guilty, but keep a distance between them. I can tell by their stolen looks that they're in deep trouble. I really hope for them that they figure things out before it gets messy.

"What's going on?" Danny asks.

"I spoke to the guy who is renting a room at her house earlier in the afternoon," I say.

"Wait. Wait. She has a renter?" Alex asks.

"I nod. I know. It was a surprise to me as well. But, yes, she rented out the room upstairs. Nothing wrong with that. Great that she'll get a little extra income. That's not why we're here. Harry, her renter..."

"His name is Harry?" Chloe asks.

"Yes. Harry Hanson," I say.

"What? His name is Harry Hanson?" Joey asks. "That sounds like the name of a cartoon character."

"It does sound like it's made up," Chloe adds.

"Whatever," I say. "It's his name. Anyway, he told me that Marcia hardly ever comes home anymore, and that he has been taking care of the children for the past several days, since Marcia is not there. I think she might be on a heavy bender."

The room grows silent. The seriousness is printed on the faces of my friends. They all know it is bad. We have all known for a while.

"But, that's not the worst part," I say. "She hasn't been to her court ordered AA meetings, and now she risks going to jail. She might lose the kids. It's bad, people."

"That is bad," Danny says.

"What do you suggest we do?" Joey asks.

"It's Saturday night, so my guess is she'll be in some bar around here. I say we spread out and hit all of them till we find her."

Everyone in the room nods.

"I can take Cape Canaveral," Danny says. "I'll hit Grills, Rusty's and Milliken's. They're like pearls on a string."

"Don't forget Fishlips," I say. "The deck upstairs."

"I'll take Sandbar and the Irish pub by 520," Joey says.

"What about Salter?" I ask and nod in his direction.

"Your dad is with him?"

"My dad can't move. He won't be of any help if anything happens."

"He's turning ten next month, Mary," Joey says. "He can stay here for the hour that it takes."

"Yes, Mom. I can be alone for an hour," Salter says with a deep sigh.

"I can stay with him," Chloe says. "I'll try and track her phone from your computer."

"Thank you, Chloe," I say. I know Joey is right. Salter is big and a very responsible boy. I am just not comfortable leaving him home alone yet.

"I'll take Slow & Low," I say. "Then hit the Sportsbar."

"Alex and I can take Coconuts and the Beach Shack," Sandra says.

I stare at them, wondering if I should say anything. I decide they're not children and don't make an issue of it. This is not the time. Right now, all that matters is finding Marcia and getting her sober.

24

JANUARY 2006

THE NEW TECHNIQUE works brilliantly for Peter. A few days after Kristin starts working with him, he is able to pick out word-blocks and form sentences, asking for a newspaper or something to eat. Just three weeks into his training, Kristin introduces him to a keyboard, and soon he is spelling things on his own, supported by Kristin's hand under his arm.

To Daniel, it is a miracle. Every time he drops Peter off at Kristin's office, he waits excitedly outside, wondering what new things his brother has told her, what wonders have been revealed about the world he lives in.

It took some convincing, but eventually the rest of their family has understood the miracle that is taking place in their youngest brother's life. Only their old mother doesn't seem to trust this new technique fully yet. It doesn't matter, Daniel tells himself. Peter has been given a voice, language. He has freed himself, and that is what is most important. Their mother will learn to see it with time.

Now, three months later, Daniel is waiting excitedly outside Kristin Martin's office, as always on Saturdays, as the door opens and she comes out smiling. For the first time, their mother has agreed to come and see it for herself.

"I believe we reached a milestone today," Kristin says. "Come and see for yourselves."

"Come on, Mother," Daniel says to his mother, and grabs her hand to help her get up from the chair. "Now you'll get to see it. Then you'll understand why we are all so excited for him."

Holding his mother's arm, Daniel walks into the office, where Peter is sitting in his chair. It's hard to tell that he is actually five feet tall the way he sits, with his skinny arms and legs and his drooping head. He is rocking from side to side and bangs his face against his hands again and again. Seeing Daniel and his mother makes him agitated, and, as always when excited or upset, he puts his hands in his mouth and bites them, leaving open sores.

"Peter seems to have a lot to say to us," Kristin says, as they approach him in his wheelchair.

Kristin helps their mother to sit on the leather couch, while explaining to her how the training works.

"At first, when we began this, his messages were simple and often misspelled, but his skills have improved as has his fluency. By a lot. You should be very proud of him. Now he hits a letter every second. It's truly amazing. I have given him books to read. He reads very fast. We're going through the books very quickly. And they're not just easy books. He's reading about everything from politics to fiction, and gobbling it all up, I might add. I should know because I turn all the pages for him. And then we talk about the books afterwards, and he tells me what he thinks of them. His knowledge of politics is quite extensive. And his math skills are amazing. We worked on fractions today."

Daniel sits next to his mother and holds her hand. Her hand feels stiff in his. She looks skeptically at the professor.

"We had no idea," Daniel says. "Did we, Mother?"

Their mother doesn't answer; she looks at her son in the wheelchair and Daniel can sense her hostility towards the professor. It makes him uncomfortable, irritated as well. All he wants is for her to see what he sees.

"Isn't it wonderful, Mother? Aren't you happy that he finally is able to communicate with us? To think that he is that smart, but never has been able to express it. I can hardly believe it."

"I understand if it takes a little while for you to get used to the fact that your son is communicating after all these years. I can't blame you for being skeptical. It is very remarkable," Kristin Martin says. "But it is vital that he learns to develop his skills and not just treat his illness. That's what I believe, and what I want to tell the world. In fact, our results here are so stunning, I want the world to know about it. I was wondering if I could borrow Peter for a couple of weeks. I want him to write an article about his progress. I want him to go with me to a conference next month, and together, we'll present this article to a room of professors and scientists like me. What do you say? Will you let me borrow him?"

"Under no circumstances," the mother replies. "My son is not a guinea pig."

"Now, wait a minute, Mother," Daniel says. "Peter's progress has made a huge difference in his life. For the first time in twenty-five years, he can actually talk to us, tell us that he is in there; he has opinions, and he is a lot smarter than we thought. What if him attending this conference could help others like him? Don't you want that?"

His mother stares into Daniel's eyes. "I know my son," she says. "I gave birth to him. I have been taking care of him for twenty-five years, every day. Peter likes to play with PlayDoh and mash it between his fingers. Peter likes to eat, he loves to be taken to the ocean, he likes the fresh air, and the highlight of his day is staring out of the big window and watching for the mailman to come driving in his small truck up the road. Peter doesn't know about politics. He doesn't do fractions or read books."

Daniel watches as his mother gets to her feet. She walks up behind the wheelchair and starts to push it. "Now, if you'll excuse us. Peter and I are going to our favorite place for ice cream."

25

JANUARY 2016

"HEEY, MARY! WHAT'S UP?"

I look at Marcia. Her eyes are hazy and blood-shot, her speech slurred. Even more than usual. I find her sitting in the bar at the Sportsbar on A1A. She is smoking a cigarette and kills it in the ashtray.

"You want a beer?" she asks. "Com' on have a beer with me. Hey, my friend here is a famous writer," she yells to the people in the bar. Everyone turns to look at me. Marcia is loud and clumsy. "It's true. A reporter in New York, and now she writes this awesome blog that has like millions of followers. She's really awesome. Isn't she awesome? I think she is...awesome."

"We have to go, Marcia," I say.

"Where are we going?"

I try to speak in a low voice, but the music and the people are being very noisy. "You need to go home."

"Home? But we just got here. Now, have a beer with me."

Her behavior angers me. I try to stay calm. I can't believe she sits here all drunk while some stranger takes care of her children. Who does that?

"Say, why don't we go outside?" I say. "It's easier to talk. Too much noise in here."

Marcia laughs and a beer lands in front of me. I grab it and signal for her to follow me outside. Finally, she does. She almost knocks over the barstool as she jumps down.

"Be right back," she says to the other drunks in the bar. They don't seem to care. I wonder what makes her want their company instead of that of her children or us. Why has she chosen this life?

We sit at a table outside. The air is nice and warm. Today has been a warm day for January. The cold spell has come and gone, and now we're back to temperatures in the eighties. It feels good outside. And less noisy.

"So, how have you been, Mary?" she says as we sit down. "I can't believe we haven't seen you in twenty years. How time flies, huh?"

Suddenly, she seems less drunk. Maybe the fresh air sobered her up a little.

"I'm good," I say. "But I am worried about you, and so are the others."

"Ah, I'm fine. Never been better, as a matter of fact. Say, what are you doing back anyway? Are you here on vacation?"

I look at her. "What do you mean? I moved back, Marcia. Three months ago. Don't you remember?"

Marcia shakes her head with laughter. "Of course I remember. Duh. Guess I've had enough to drink, huh? It just slipped my mind."

She doesn't seem convincing. For a split-second I am certain I see great fear in her eyes, but it is soon replaced with something else.

"So what did you want to talk to me about?" she asks.

I show her the letter. She grabs it and reads it. She looks up at me, surprised. "What is this?"

"Marcia. You haven't been going to your meetings. They're going to put you away if you don't go."

"Yes, I have."

"Marcia. Stop lying. It says here you haven't, and by the looks of how drunk you are, I don't believe you have been to any meetings."

She looks like she doesn't understand. She puts a hand on her forehead and shakes her head slowly. "I don't know what is going on, Mary. I swear, I remember going to the meetings. I can't seem to...it's like the days...they are so blurry."

I grab the beer in her hand and take it from her. "Because of this," I say. "The drinking is destroying you. You haven't been to a meeting in months. You risk losing your kids if this continues. You have to act now. We're all here for you, but you have to do your part."

Marcia looks at me seriously. Her speech is less slurred, but her eyes still give her away. She puts her hand on my arm.

"I want to get better. Tell me what to do."

"We need to get you sober," I say. "You have to quit drinking."

26

JANUARY 2016

"I SWEAR, there was someone with binoculars watching the house."

Kelly looks at Andrew. It angers her that he refuses to take this seriously. But that is so him. He never worries about anything.

"Worry is like a rocking chair," he always says. "It gives you something to do, but never gets you anywhere."

"You've got to relax," he says this time. "You're winding yourself up. It's not healthy. How do you even know he was watching our house? It was probably just some guy who likes to watch birds, or maybe a tourist. It's not illegal to look at our house, you know."

Andrew sits on the couch. Lindsey is asleep upstairs after a long day of fishing with her dad. Kelly grunts, irritated.

"And what about the truck I always see, huh? And the phone calls when I pick up there's no one there, huh? Is that also a coincidence? Or the tipped over telescope on the night Lindsey heard a loud bang?"

"Come on, Kelly," he says, and puts his feet up on the coffee table. He knows she hates when he does that. He leans back in the couch with a smile. "I am exhausted after a long day. I just want to relax with a beer and watch some TV. Can we talk about this later, please?"

Kelly groans, annoyed, and walks back to the kitchen, where she starts to clean up after their dinner. She washes a pot and slams it on the table so it makes a loud noise. She slams the doors to the cabinets when she shuts them and grunts in anger. Andrew doesn't seem to even hear her. He is watching a game. Either that or he is simply ignoring her outbursts. It makes her even angrier.

How can he not take this seriously? How can he keep telling her she is being paranoid? How can he ignore her like this?

What if he is right? What if it is all just in your head? You know how you get carried away sometimes.

There was the time when Lindsey had an allergic reaction to the new piercings in her ears. The doctor said she was just allergic to nickel, but Kelly was certain she was going to die from a blood infection and refused to let her out of her sight for three days. Kelly even slept with her, waking up every hour to check if she was breathing.

Kelly draws in a deep breath and tries to calm herself down. Maybe he is right. Maybe she is just imagining things. Who would want to stalk her anyway?

Kelly chuckles and puts the last pan into the cabinet and closes it normally. She looks at the kitchen with satisfaction. It looks clean. She then turns off the light, and as she does, she notices the full moon right outside of her window. It is hanging beautifully over the water, lighting up the ocean. It is so bright she almost wants to go outside. She walks to the window and looks down at the beach, when she notices a figure down there again. She stumbles backwards, then calls out.

"Andrew!"

Her husband runs to her in the kitchen. "What's going on?"

"He's down there again," she says, her voice shaking. She points to the window. Andrew moves closer and looks down.

"He's standing right down there, wearing a hoodie, looking up at us with his binoculars."

"I can't see anyone," Andrew says.

Kelly walks closer and looks down as well. But the figure is gone.

"No one is there," Andrew says.

"But there was. Someone was there a second ago. I promise you. I am telling the truth. I saw it!"

Andrew looks at her, just as the phone starts to ring. Andrew picks it up. "Hello?"

He looks at Kelly with troubled eyes. "Hello?" he repeats.

He hangs up.

"Alright now," he says and grabs her trembling shoulders. "Take it easy. Tomorrow, we'll talk to the police, okay?"

27

JANUARY 2016

SUNDAY MORNING, I go to pick up Marcia. I knock on the door and Harry opens it, wearing nothing but shorts and sneakers. He is sweating.

"She's almost ready," he says with that handsome smile of his. "Just got back from my run; sorry if I am sweaty and smelly."

"Great," I say with a smile, and walk inside trying to avoid looking at him. This guy is unbelievable.

Marcia comes out of her bedroom. She looks terrible. I can tell she has been crying. I am glad to see that she gets the seriousness of her situation now. She seems sober, but with her, I am never sure.

"Are you ready?" I ask.

She nods with a sniffle.

"Are you here in case the kids need anything?" I ask, addressed to Harry.

He nods on his way up the stairs. I watch him from behind as he disappears. I feel like I am cheating on Joey and turn to face Marcia again.

"Shall we?"

Marcia grunts something, then follows me to my car. I drive us there, and we walk in together. A small flock of eight people are already there, speaking amongst each other. As we enter, a woman around fifty, or maybe older, it's hard to tell, approaches us.

"Marcia!"

The woman opens her arms and hugs Marcia warmly.

"This is my sponsor," Marcia says. "She's also the therapist here."

"Hi. I'm Jess," she says.

We shake hands.

"I'm Mary. I'm a friend of Marcia's."

"That's wonderful. I'm glad you have such good friends, Marcia. We haven't seen you here for a while."

"Well, I haven't been doing so well," Marcia says.

Jess puts her hand on Marcia's shoulder. "I know how it is. But I am glad you're here now."

"I'm going to get some coffee," Marcia says, and walks away.

"She needs help," I say, addressed to Jess when Marcia can't hear us anymore. "She's in deep trouble."

"I know," Jess says. "She'll get what she needs here. But we can't force anyone to get better if they don't want to. She has to want it. I did try to help Marcia when she first came here, but I can only do so if she'll let me. I hoped she would come back. We haven't seen her in three months, I believe. She has to come to the meetings."

I nod and look at her as Marcia fumbles with her cup. I can tell she is not well. It breaks my heart. "It's just...it's been really bad lately. She hasn't been able to take care of the kids and it's like...yesterday, she didn't even remember that I moved back here three months ago."

Jess sighs. "That is not that uncommon, unfortunately. Alcohol is a slow killer, but it will destroy your body from the inside. The brain is no exception."

"So, you'll help her?" I ask.

Jess smiles warmly at me. "Of course. I am glad she has such a good friend in you. Many of us barely have any friends left. Now, if you'll excuse me, I have to begin the meeting, and I have to ask you to wait outside unless you yourself are struggling with an addiction?"

"Me? No. I eat too much, but hey, who doesn't, right?"

"Food can be an addiction too, you know," she says with a smile and a wink. Then she leaves me and starts the meeting.

28

JANUARY 2016

THE SCREAMING WON'T STOP. Marcia's head is about to explode as Mary takes her home. The only thing that usually makes it stop is the alcohol or the pills, but she hasn't had any all morning and it is killing her.

The meeting went great. Marcia told about how she had fallen in and how she wanted to get back on track again. She managed to not say anything about the blackouts or the screaming. The images and the voices in her head, she keeps to herself. They'll only think she is insane, that she has lost it.

"So, how did it go?" Mary asks with a smile.

Marcia looks out the window as Minutemen Causeway drifts by. She spots Billy walking next to City Hall towards the beach, guitar in one hand and a brown bag in the other. It is warmer today, so he'll be hanging out on the beach in front of Coconuts instead of in the dunes. She wonders who else will join him today. Marcia likes to hang out with them. Most of all, she likes who she is when she is with them, when the world is all fuzzy and warm and she doesn't have to worry about the screams or images in her mind.

"It went okay," she says.

"Good. So I'll take you again tomorrow, then?" Mary asks.

Marcia freezes. The thought of having to stay sober for even longer kills her. Can she do this?

You have to. Or you'll lose the kids.

The kids. Marcia feels awful that the kids have been suffering under this. She thought they were doing fine. Every time she saw them, they seemed fine.

You knew they weren't. You just chose to ignore it, you coward.

"I think I'd like that," she says, looking down at her shoes. There's a hole in the right one and one toe is sticking out. Her clothes are dirty and smell weird.

How did it come to this? How did I become this bum?

"Great," Mary says, and drives up in front of her townhouse.

Marcia stares at the front door. Does she really dare to walk in there sober? To face all the misery, her guilt, her own disaster?

Mary places a hand on her arm. "Listen. I can't say I know how hard it is to be you right now, because, let's be frank, I have no idea what you're going through. But I can tell you that I will be here. No matter what. You call me in the middle of the night. Anything. I'll take care of the kids for a few days if you need to get away. Anything, as long as you don't start drinking again."

You don't deserve her as a friend. You don't deserve to be loved like that. You're not worth it.

"Shut up," Marcia says.

"What?" Mary says.

Marcia hides her face in her hands. "I'm sorry," she says. "I am so sorry. I'm such an awful person. I don't deserve you."

"Hey!" Mary says. "Don't you say that about my friend. Besides I think I am the one who will decide whether or not you deserve me. Now, come here."

Mary grabs her around the shoulders and pulls her close. She holds her in a warm embrace for a long time, while Marcia tries to pull herself together. In her head, the voices are all screaming at the same time. When she closes her eyes, she sees these awful images of people in pain, in excruciating pain, people pleading for their lives. Where do those images come from? She doesn't dare to think about it. She is terrified of learning the truth.

"What do I say to them, Mary? How do I face them?" she asks, and looks at the house.

"You just do it, I guess," Mary says after a little while. "They'll be happy to see you sober. Maybe do something fun with them today. Play a game. Talk with them. Especially Rose. She needs you."

Marcia nods. She is not so certain that anyone needs her.

"So, same time tomorrow?" Mary asks.

Marcia nods and opens the door. While Mary drives away, Marcia walks up towards the front door. She grabs the handle, but hesitates before finally opening the door.

They'll never forgive you. No one will ever love you. Not when they learn who you really are.

Two young faces look up as she enters the room. Their eyes are wide, scrutinizing, wondering who it is that they're greeting through the door. Will it be drunk Mommy? Will it be yelling Mommy? Will it be sweet and funny Mommy or angry mean Mommy?

A third set, belonging to her daughter Rose doesn't even dare to meet her eyes as she closes the door behind her.

Marcia forces a smile. It feels terrifying to stand like this in front of them. It's like being naked; she feels like they can see straight through her, see her for who she really is.

You can't do it. You can't. You're not strong enough. Not without drinking. You won't make it. You're too weak.

"Anyone up for a game of charades?"

29

JANUARY 2016

MY STOMACH IS in knots when driving home from Marcia's. I can't bear seeing her like this. I feel guilty for not having reacted sooner. Those poor kids.

"How'd it go?" Joey asks from the couch when I enter the house. The dogs attack me and Snowflake licks me incessantly.

"All right, I guess," I say and sit next to him.

"Where's Salter?"

"A buddy from his school stopped by and asked him to go to the skate park with him."

I smile. "That's great. He's making friends," I say and lean back. I feel exhausted. Mostly emotionally.

"So, you think she'll get better now?" Joey asks.

I shrug. "I think we have taken the first small step, but there is still a long way for her. It's tough. Makes me appreciate what I have more, though."

Joey sits up straight, then leans over me and kisses me. I close my eyes and enjoy his kisses. Soon, his hand is inside my shirt. He is touching my breasts.

"Are we in a hurry?" I ask.

"You do realize we're childless, right?" he says. "It's been awhile."

I chuckle and look into his eyes. "I know. There has just been so much. With my brother and all that. It's getting to me."

Joey keeps kissing my neck and chest, and now he pulls off my shirt. He is not listening anymore, and soon I am not talking either. We make love on the couch and I feel so close to him, closer than I have in a long time. I am so blessed. So happy I made the decision to take him back. Especially for Salter's sake.

"By the way, Chloe has been trying to reach you. She came over earlier and said she needed to talk to you. Apparently, you don't answer your phone," he says, panting, when we're done.

"I had it on silent when I went with Marcia to the meeting," I say, and kiss his nose. I get dressed and find my phone.

Fourteen calls from Chloe. I call her back.

"What's up?" I ask.

"What's up? What's up?" she says on the other end. "Are you kidding me? Don't you know by now?"

"I am sorry. No, I really don't..."

"You're exploding; that's what's going on."

"Exploding?"

"Your numbers are. The little video you made went viral. It's a world-wide trending topic on Twitter!"

"What? Why?"

"I don't know why. Who knows why anything goes viral these days. But my guess is that people want to help find that brother of yours, so they share the video. It got picked up by one of the really big names on twitter, *RCThomas* and he wrote that we should all help her find this bastard, *so please share.*

"RCThomas? I have no idea who that is."

"I figured you didn't. But he's this famous YouTuber and tweeter. He's like Bono. Just on the Internet. People listen to him. If he says people should share this video, then they do it."

"Bono?"

"Okay, bad example, Lady Gaga then, argh you know what I am saying, right? The important part is everyone is tweeting your brother's picture now, and soon the entire world will know he is wanted. It's the best thing that could ever happen to us. We've already received a bunch of emails from people claiming they have seen him and Olivia. I am telling you. We're going to get him. He can run but..."

"We'll track him down no matter where he runs to," I say. "I'll be right over."

30

JANUARY 2016

MARK IS SITTING on the pavement next to his skateboard. He is waiting for his friend, David, who is eating dinner with his parents. They asked him if he wanted some and he really did, but he didn't want them to think he didn't get fed at home, so he said no and told David he would go home and eat as well, and then they'd meet back in front of his house. Not knowing what else to do, Mark stayed outside the house, his stomach growling with deep groans.

He doesn't want to go home. He doesn't like to be at the house in case his mother is there. The older he gets, the more Mark tries to stay out as much as he can. Sleeping over at friend's houses or even sometimes staying on the beach all night if it's warm enough. Anything to not have to go home.

He stares at a fire-ant crawling on his shoe when he hears the door to his friend's house open and David comes storming out.

"Let's go to the park," he yells, his mouth half full. "I have to be home at ten. Parents! They're so annoying."

"I know!" Mark says, but he doesn't mean it. The truth is, he would give anything to have someone give him a curfew. He would love to have someone want him home for once. But no one does. No one worries about him staying out all night.

They stay at the skate park for three hours, until David has to go home.

"Yeah, me too," Mark says. "Don't want to get in trouble with the old lady, right?"

He follows David home and then skates to the river and sits by the bank till midnight and he figures his mother is in bed.

Finally, he decides to head back. He enters the house as silently as possible and closes the door behind him. He takes two steps before he realizes someone is in the living room. His mother is sitting in the recliner, a is gun pointed at him. The streetlamp from outside lights parts of her face and the gun.

"Mom?"

"Shhh. They're listening, aren't they?"

"Mom. It's me. It's Mark."

Still, she is not lowering the gun.

"I am not giving in to them," she says.

"To who? What are you talking about, Mom?"

"You know damn well who!" she yells.

It startles Mark and he whimpers. "Mom? Please?"

"The government thinks they can get to me, but they won't. You can go back and tell them that."

"Go back? What?" he says, his heart throbbing.

"I know you're one of them. They got to you, didn't they? They had you place cameras everywhere, right? Don't you think I know they're watching me? Tonight they even spoke to me through the television. The guy on the news told me they would come for me tonight when I am asleep. But I am not going to sleep. Oh, no. I am not falling for that. And you better tell them that. I know you're with them."

"But, Mom. It's me. It's Mark," he repeats again and again with a shivering voice.

"It's not you. I know how these things work," she says. The gun remains steady between her hands. Mark has no idea what to do.

If I run, will she shoot? Will she shoot me if I stay?

Mark is crying now. "Mom. Please, you got to know it's me. I am your son. There is no one after you. No one is out to get you. Please, just lower the gun ..."

He doesn't get to finish the sentence before the gun goes off.

PART II

TWINKLE, TWINKLE LITTLE STAR

31

FEBRUARY 2006

"WHAT HAVE YOU DONE?"

Daniel's mother looks at him, her eyes icily cold. On the couch by the fireplace sits his older sister and one of his brothers.

"I sent him to the conference with professor Martin." His voice is shaking as he speaks, but he stays determined. He knew this would happen, he knew their mother would confront him about this, and he had the entire speech prepared. Only now, his tongue betrays him and the words don't come out the way he wants them to. He no longer feels so certain of his arguments.

"How? How could you have done this when I told you I wouldn't have it?" his mother says.

"It's the right thing to do," he says. "Think of all the other people out there living like him, trapped in their bodies like him. They need him, Mother."

"And what about what Peter needs, huh? Did you think about that? He doesn't need a flock of nosy professors and scientists observing him like he is some...some monkey in a laboratory. Peter needs stability. He needs surroundings that he knows, he needs to follow his schedule. I am supposed to be protecting him."

"I am his guardian too, Mother. You made all of us guardians, remember? We have a say in his future as well."

"No!" his mother yells.

It startles Daniel. Their mother has been weak for years and spoken only with an almost whispering voice. Her yelling feels overpowering, and Daniel becomes a little boy again. At least that's how it feels to him. He looks at his shoes. All his siblings are present in the room, but they aren't saying anything. They avoid even looking at him.

Cowards, Daniel thinks to himself. *We agreed to do this together. We took a vote and now they won't stand by it.*

"As long as I am still alive, I make the decisions of what is best for my son. Not you. Not any of you," she says and points at the others.

She walks to her chair and sits down. Daniel can tell she is in pain. He knows her leg has been bothering her. Her heart is not very strong, the doctor says. He suddenly feels overwhelmed by guilt and sadness from making her this upset.

"I just don't understand why you would do this to him, to your brother?" she asks as she regains her strength.

"Because it is good for him, Mother. Don't you see it?" Daniel says.

"No. I really don't. The boy is sick, Daniel. He needs his family. He needs his mother."

Daniel sighs. "But, Mother. That's the thing. He's not. He's not a child anymore. He's a grown man. And he knows stuff. He is smart and he wants to share that with the world. He wants a life, Mother, and that's what we're trying to give him. If you keep treating him like a child, he'll never be anything else. He has skills. He can communicate. Besides, he wanted this. He wanted desperately to go, am I right?" Daniel asks, addressed to his siblings. They're annoyingly quiet. Finally, his sister nods.

"It's true, Mother. He really wanted to go. He told us."

"He told you? He told you?" their mother says. "How?"

"He wrote it on the keyboard," Daniel says.

Their mother shakes her head heavily. "The boy has never been able to speak, and all of a sudden, this professor, this woman, comes along and holds his elbow and suddenly you believe he speaks? That he knows politics and math? It's ridiculous. Can't you see it?"

Finally, their oldest brother rises to his feet. "We took a vote, Mother. We believe in giving Kristin Martin a chance. It's the only shot he'll ever get at a normal life. We made a decision, and now it's done. Peter is in California, and he'll be back in three days. You just have to trust us."

32

JANUARY 2016

I WORK with Chloe until around midnight, going through all the emails and tweets arriving from people who believe they have seen my brother and or Olivia. Most of them are bogus and easily thrown away, but some, a good handful, sound plausible, and slowly we narrow them down to four possible places they may have been seen.

Chloe puts up a big map on the wall and pins down the four places.

"Tucson, Arizona; Savannah, Georgia; Charlotte, North Carolina; or St. Petersburg, Florida," she says.

"Sure would make the most sense if he's still in Florida," I say.

"I'm not so sure," Chloe says.

"He was last seen in Ft. Lauderdale?"

"Right, but he's not dumb. Neither is Olivia. They know people are looking for them all over the state. It would make more sense to get as far away as possible."

"So, you think he's in Arizona?" I ask.

She shrugs. "It's a guess. Maybe they're planning on going across the border. Maybe they already have."

"Mexico?"

"Yeah, I know," she says. "Sounds like a bad movie, but still. They can hide there easily."

"They have to live too," I say. "How do they still have money? It's been three months, and neither of them has used a credit card."

"I don't know," Chloe says. "But there are ways."

I look at the clock on the wall. "It's getting late. I should be getting back home."

"I want to take a closer look at the tip that came from Arizona. I think I'll continue all night and sleep tomorrow," Chloe says. "This is the time I usually think the best. No distractions, you know?"

I smile. I do know. Chloe has always been like that. I wonder how she still manages to live a life like this. Taking care of her mother and staying awake all night. I, for one, get completely out of balance if I lose just a few hours of sleep.

"Salter has school in the morning, so I have to get up at six thirty to get him on the bus. I need some shut-eye. I'll see you tomorrow."

I ride my bike back to Joey's house. I park it outside and walk in. Joey is sleeping on the couch, a half empty beer on the table. I check on Salter in his bed. He is sound asleep. The dogs and the pig are in there with him, all sleeping in his bed. He looks so happy, so safe, it makes me feel good. I walk back to Joey, and as I do he receives a text on his phone. It's from that Jack guy again. I decide it's none of my business and go to the kitchen and grab myself a donut that they have left out. It's a little dry, but I'm starving, so I eat it anyway. Joey is grunting in his sleep and sounds exactly like Bonnie. It makes me laugh. As I finish eating, there is suddenly a knock on the door.

It startles me, while Joey doesn't react. I walk to the window to look outside. I spot a girl, a young woman in a light dress, a small jacket over her shoulders. She has long blonde curls that bounce off her shoulders when she moves. She is stunning.

Thinking she probably came to the wrong house, I open the door. Her smile freezes as she sees me.

"Hello?" I ask.

"Hi. Is Joey home?"

As the realization sinks in, my heart goes cold. I have a lump in my throat. "He's sleeping. Who are you?"

"I'm Jackie."

Jackie as in Jack?

"Sorry. I've never heard of you...Jackie. What did you want with my husband?" I ask. It's technically not a lie, since Joey and I are only separated.

She looks baffled. "Husband? I...I didn't know...he told me he was separated." She takes a few steps backwards. "I'm...I am so sorry."

"Yeah, well, you should be." I say, and slam the door behind me. The noise wakes up Joey. He blinks his eyes and looks at me.

"Hey. You're back. I missed you."

33

JANUARY 2016

"WHAT'S THE MATTER?"

Joey looks at me. I realize I am shaking. I can't speak. I can't shape the words or push them across my lips. Yet there is so much I want to say. So much I need to get out of me. So many emotions, so much anger.

I can't believe he did this to me again. I can't believe I let him!

"What's going on, Mary? Why...what's..." Joey jumps up from the couch while I sink to the floor, slowly sliding my back against the door. I am staring at him, my mouth open, my heart pounding.

"Did something happen at Chloe's?" he asks, and kneels in front of me. "Talk to me, Mary."

I stare into his eyes. I want to cry, but I can't. I want to scream. I want to yell at him, but nothing happens. I feel so lost. So betrayed.

"Mary! You're scaring me," he says. "What happened?"

Do I even bother talking to him? Do I even want to hear him explain himself? I am fed up with excuses. I am fed up with trying to understand. Yet I do it. Yet I ask him, "Who's Jackie?"

As her name leave my lips, Joey's face changes. The corner of his mouth droops. The air is still for several seconds before he finally speaks again. Rage is swelling inside my chest. Joey pulls away. His hand touches his face.

He's trying to come up with an excuse. Wondering how to tell me, to say this gently and not make me mad. To not lose me. Doesn't he realize it's too late?

"I ..." he says.

"You know what? I really don't want to know," I say, and get up on my feet. I feel slain, conquered, but I haven't lost everything. I still have my dignity. And my son. I don't have to keep living like this.

"But ..."

"I don't need any more excuses, Joey. I don't need explanations. I needed to be able to trust you again, but clearly, that was a mistake."

He grabs my arm and forces me to look at him. "She is no one, Mary. I promise you."

"*No one* doesn't come knocking on your door at midnight, Joey," I say.

He exhales. I can tell he is struggling to find the right words. He's afraid of pushing me further away, of losing me. He's right. At this point, there pretty much isn't anything he can say.

"You have to believe me, Mary. I only saw her for a little while, when you were still in New York. You threw me out. We were separated, Mary."

"Oh, my God," I say and pull my arm out of his grip. Finally, I lose it. "Do you even listen to yourself? You know who you sound like? Do you? You sound like Ross! *We were on a break?* Is that the excuse you're going to come up with?"

"What's wrong with that? You threw me out. I found comfort with Jackie. She was nice."

"Nice? You destroy your family over nice?"

Joey points his finger at me. "Hey. You were in New York. We were separated. You said you wanted a divorce. Yes, I saw another girl for a few weeks, but it ended as soon as you and Salter came down here."

"You ended it? What about all the texts, then?"

Joey sighs. He is panting in agitation. "She wouldn't stop. I couldn't get her to stop texting me, all right? She wanted to see me and I told her not to come. I don't know why she would be so stupid as to come here in the middle of the night."

"I don't believe you. You even lied about it when I asked. I just don't understand why you would do this to me again. After all we have been through, Joey."

He grabs both my shoulders and turns me to look at him. His eyes are filled with tears. "Believe me. I want this. I want us, Mary. I am not losing you again. I can't lose you and Salter once again."

"Well, maybe you should have thought of that before you crawled into bed with the first hooker that came along," I say, and pull away from him. I walk to the bedroom and open the door. I don't look back at Joey before I walk in. I don't want to see his face.

"That's not fair and you know it," he yells, just as I close the door with a loud bang.

34

JANUARY 2016

I CARRY Salter into my bed and snuggle with him and all the animals all night, but don't get any sleep at all. When the alarm goes off, Salter opens his eyes and looks into mine. I can't think of anything more beautiful to wake up to.

"What's wrong, Mommy?"

I kiss his forehead. "I'm just a little sad, sweetie. It'll be okay. Don't worry about it. Now let's get you to school, alright?"

"Is it Dad?"

I sigh. "We had a fight."

Salter's eyes turn hard. I don't like to see that in him. I know he feels protective of me ever since we lived alone for four months. I know I have to be careful. I want him to love his dad, no matter what happens.

"Don't worry about it, okay?" I say. "We're grown-ups. We'll do the worrying and the problem solving. You focus on getting to school on time."

He nods, but I can tell he doesn't agree. He wants to solve everything. I know he does, but he can't. He can't fix this, no matter how bad he wants to.

We get out of bed and get dressed. I prepare his breakfast, while wondering where Joey is. I thought he would be sleeping on the couch in the living room, but he is not there. I am glad I don't have to face him, but still I wonder if he went to her place instead. The thought makes me miserable.

Am I that easily replaced?

I make Salter's lunch and hand him his lunchbox when he is ready to leave. I kiss his forehead and wave at him as he walks to the bus. My stomach hurts from worry that he'll be sad all day. He is so happy that his mom and dad are back together again. To have to take that away from him again is just simply devastating.

When he is gone, I make myself some coffee and make a tray for my dad with coffee and breakfast. I walk into his room. He's already awake.

I put the tray down and force a smile. "Ah, don't give me that," he says.

"What?"

"I heard you...last night."

"Oh."

"What's going on...with you two?" he asks, while I feed him scrambled eggs. He spits some of it out when he talks, and I wipe it off his bed.

"I don't know, Dad."

"You're not splitting up again...are you?"

"I said I don't know."

"You're being...way too hard on him. Always have, Mary." My dad is agitated and has to take a break before he can continue. His breath is ragged. "You...expect too much...He tries...I have seen him. He tries...his best. Nobody is perfect."

"He slept with someone else, Dad. Not just once," I say.

My dad falls silent for a few seconds. I can tell he is wondering what to say. "Well, maybe there's an...explanation."

"Really, Dad?"

"I like...the kid. Look at...look what he did. He took all of us in and took...care of me. He put up that...TV and...finally I have...something to do while lying around here. He cares, Mary. Not many...men do."

I know he is right. Joey is a sweet guy and a great father. I truly love him. I think I have loved him since we went to preschool together. I can't remember not loving him. But is it enough? I need more than that. I refuse to be one of those women that simply close their eyes to their husband's constant cheating because they don't have the strength to deal with it. Or to make the unpopular decision. I have to be able to trust him, and so far, he hasn't earned my trust.

"All I am asking...is that you give him...a chance, Mary. Don't...throw away what you have...because of one...or two...little mistakes. You have no idea...how lucky you are to have a man...love you like that." My dad looks at me intensely while catching his breath again. "I miss...Laura...every hour of the day...but she never loved me...not in the same way. There is no doubt... Joey...loves you."

"I won't, Dad. I promise," I say and kiss his forehead. I don't want to talk more about it with him. I turn on the TV and find something he wants to watch before I walk to the door. "You have physical therapy at three today," I say before I leave.

In the kitchen, I put down the tray when my phone starts to vibrate on the counter. I am certain it is Joey and pick it up. It's a text. It's not from Joey. It's from Marcia.

MEET ME BY OUR OLD SECRET SURFSPOT ASAP. COME ALONE.

35

JANUARY 2016

I TEXT Marcia back and ask her what's going on. What about the AA meeting? She doesn't answer back, so I try to call her, but her phone is shut off and I leave a voicemail. I can't help but get angry with her. This is not the time for her to go surfing. She's supposed to be working on herself and going to the meetings. Does she think I'll just forget about it? This is odd, even for Marcia. I wonder if she has fallen off the wagon already or if this is just her way of trying to get out of going to the meeting. I won't let her. I am determined to help her, even if I myself am a mess. I am not giving up.

I decide to go to our old spot and convince her to go to the meeting with me instead of surfing. When I open the door to go to the car, I spot someone coming up the driveway. I recognize him immediately. The long legs, the brown waving hair, the gorgeous blue eyes. But there is something different about him today. Something desperate and bleak that I haven't seen in him before.

"Harry?" I say. "What are you doing here?"

"Mary. Finally," he says with a deep sigh. "I've tried to get ahold of you all morning. But I don't have your number, and all the kids knew was where you lived. I had to get them out of the house before I could get down here..."

"I don't understand. What's wrong, Harry? Has something happened?" I ask, the feeling of dread quickly spreading throughout my body.

What is going on here?

"It's Marcia," he says.

Uh-oh!

"Marcia? What happened?"

A series of images run through my mind. Marcia driving drunk on her bike to our secret surf spot with her board under her arm. Marcia being hit by a car and lying on the asphalt. Is she dead? Is she unconscious? Is she alive?

Harry looks at me and shakes his head. It's bad. I can tell by the look in his eyes that he has no idea how to tell me.

"Last night...I have no idea how it could have happened. I was upstairs in my bed, sleeping, when I heard the shot."

The shot? Oh, my God, it's even worse than I thought.

"Marcia was shot?"

Harry shakes his head. "No. Not her."

"Then who? Who?"

"Mark. Mark was shot. He came home late, as he often does, if he comes home at all. As far as I know, she must have thought he was an intruder or something. When I came down, she was gone; Mark was lying on the floor of the living room, bleeding heavily."

I stop breathing. Everything inside of me is standing still. The words coming out of Harry's mouth are so unreal, so distant, so strange I can't take it.

"Marcia shot her son?" I ask.

"Yes. And then she just took off."

"How is he? Is he...?"

"He's alive. The bullet went into his shoulder. I called for an ambulance and he was taken to Holmes Regional. I stayed with the other children and sat with them till they fell asleep again. I called this morning, and he's still in intensive, but they expect him to make it. His dad came out here from Orlando and is with him now."

I stare at Harry, slowly shaking my head. Suddenly, I feel dizzy. It's overpowering me and I have no control of my body anymore. Harry grabs me just as I am about to fall and helps me get inside where I sit on a chair.

"Let me get you some water," he says.

I still feel like the world is spinning and I can't breathe. It's just too much right now. The whole thing.

"Here, drink this," he says, and hands me the glass. "It'll make you feel better."

I drink and close my eyes. It does make me feel better, but now I feel like I have to throw up. I bend down, but it doesn't happen. I raise my head again and look into Harry's eyes.

"Feeling better?"

"A little," I say. I finish the water.

"I'm glad that you were home," Harry says. "I had no idea who else to come to. I have only been in the house for a short while."

"The police," I say.

"They're looking for her. Mark told them she did it in self-defense. That he startled her and that she thought he was an intruder. I don't know what they'll do, but the kids were picked up by social services, and they're going to stay with their father in Orlando. It's bad, Mary. I am afraid you're all Marcia has right now."

36

JANUARY 2016

TEARS ARE STREAMING across my face as I drive towards Sebastian Inlet. I chose not to tell Harry about the text from Marcia. I want to meet with her myself and hear what she has to say. He doesn't have to be involved.

Our old secret surf spot where we used to meet and surf is reached by a small trail through the bushes that leads to a desolated beach known among surfers as The Spanish House. We used to go there when waves were small at Cocoa Beach, especially in the summertime. Down here, they would always be breaking beautifully, and the water is so clear you could often see turtles and dolphins underneath you as you surfed.

It used to be my favorite place to go, but not today. Today, I walk across the trail feeling awful, feeling sick to my stomach.

What do I say to her? How do I deal with this? Do I tell her to turn herself in? Do I tell her to run away? God, please give me the strength and wisdom to say the right things, to do what is right.

When I reach the beach, I am all alone. I spot someone sitting in a chair about half a mile away, but that's not her, I think.

She's not here.

I growl, annoyed, and turn to walk back through the bushes, when I hear a small voice calling my name. I look to the side and spot Marcia. She is sitting underneath a bush, crumpled up, her legs under her chin. She is shaking. Her eyes are flickering from side to side.

"Marcia."

I walk closer and kneel in front of her. I try to make eye contact, but without success. "Marcia. Look at me."

But she doesn't. Her eyes are constantly moving, her head shaking. "They're coming, Mary. I know they are. I'm not going with them. I won't let them get me. I'd rather die."

"Who? The police?" I ask.

Finally, she looks at me. I don't recognize the Marcia I know in those eyes.

"All of them. They are all in on it, Mary. Especially that man."

"What man? Harry?"

"Yes. Yes. Him. I don't trust him. He keeps me awake when he walks around up there all night. I think…Mary, I think he killed that woman."

"What woman?"

"The one they pulled out of the river."

"Why do you think Harry had anything to do with that?" I ask.

"Because of the pictures, Mary. He has her picture and all the articles in his room. He thinks I didn't see it, but I did. I think he's a killer, and now he's coming after me. He's going to kill all of us."

I remove a lock of hair from Marcia's face. I don't smell alcohol on her breath. When I look into her eyes, she doesn't seem intoxicated. Just…just like she is very far away. Too far away for me to reach her. It frightens me.

"What's going on with you, Marcia?" I ask. "Do you even know what happened last night?"

"Last night, we went to Beef O' Brady's. Kids eat free on Tuesdays. I had a steak burrito."

I cup my mouth and press back tears. I have no idea what to say to her. "You need help," I whisper under my breath.

Marcia holds both her hands to her head and closes her eyes like she is in pain. "Stop it," she says. "Stop screaming!" Then she grabs my arm and pulls me closer. "Do you hear it too? Do you hear them screaming, Mary?"

"Who is screaming, Marcia? You're scaring me."

"The kids. They're crying. They're scared."

"What kids?"

"The kids!"

I get a terrifying thought. I don't want to think it, but I do. "Why are they scared, Marcia? Who is hurting them?" I ask, petrified of the answer.

And then it comes.

"I think…I think it is me."

37

JANUARY 2016

"WHO IS IT? WHO ARE THEY?" I ask. I don't want to hear this, I really don't, but I feel I have to ask. I have to know what is going on with her.

"Are they your children, Marcia?"

She shakes her head.

"There's a girl and a boy. They're on the floor. The boy had glasses on, now they are on the floor next to him. Broken. He's chubby. Has a birth-mark on his cheek."

"And the girl?"

Marcia thinks about it for a little while before speaking. "She has long black hair. She's pretty. I think she is dead, but I'm not sure. She's wearing her PJs. They both are. *Twinkle, Twinkle Little Star*...there are stars on them. On hers. They're black. His say *Star Wars* on the front."

"And the grown-ups?" I ask, my voice shivering. "Where are the grown-ups?"

"They're right next to the children. On the floor too. The mother's eyes aren't closed. They don't blink. They don't move. The mother has a white shirt, but something is wrong with it. It's red in the front. There's a hole in it. There's a hole in her."

Marcia stops and looks up at me. "Did I do that? Did I, Mary?"

"I...I...don't know." I answer as honestly as I can. "But I think we need to find out."

She grabs my hand in hers and strokes it gently. "I love you, Mary."

I look into her eyes, and for one split second, I see her; I see the Marcia

I used to know. I smile and touch her cheek. "I love you too, Marcia. We'll get to the bottom of this. I promise you we will. Now, you need to come with me."

I help her get out of the bush. "Where are we going, Mary?"

"You need to turn yourself in to the police."

Marcia stops. I turn and look at her. She is shaking her head. "No, Mary. They'll kill me. They'll take away my kids!"

"They already have, sweetie."

She looks at me like she doesn't understand. I grab her by the shoulders. I force her to look into my eyes. I want to make sure she understands what I am about to tell her.

"Honey. You shot Mark last night. Now, I know you didn't mean to, that it was an accident, but he is in the hospital and the rest of your children are with their father."

Marcia's eyes widen. I see great fear in them. "I...I did what?"

I nod. "I'm afraid you shot Mark. He's going to be fine, though. Come."

Marcia shakes her head and pulls away from me. "No. No. I would never...not my son! It's not true. They're making this up. Someone is making all this up."

"You're not well, Marcia. I don't know what is going on with you, but you're not well. Come. We need to get you some help."

"No. They'll lock me away for the rest of my life. I bet it was Harry. He set me up, didn't he? You see, they're all linked with computers, Mary. And the phones. They have everything on us on the phones and computers. They spy on us and they know...everything. Harry is one of them. He did it."

"No!" I yell angrily. Where does she get these ideas? "You did this, Marcia. He took care of your kids. He's a good guy. He has tried to help you the best he could. Now, come with me."

"No. Something is wrong. I can feel it."

"You're not well, Marcia. That's what is wrong. You can't trust your own judgment. You're sick. Now come with me before someone else gets hurt."

She doesn't move. She stands still, looking at me, while shaking her head. I can feel I am losing her and it breaks my heart.

"Marcia, please. Just come. I'll do everything I can to help you, but you have to come with me. Now."

Marcia exhales deeply. She pulls out the gun that I am guessing is the same one she used when she shot Mark. I back off, knowing she might be capable of anything.

"I'm sorry. I can't," she says.

Marcia takes one last glance at me, then turns around and starts to run. I yell after her, but she disappears into the bushes, and in a few seconds, she is gone.

"Goddammit, Marcia," I moan. "How am I supposed to help you now?"

38

MARCH 2006

A MONTH after the conference in California, Peter starts taking classes at UCF. Daniel takes him there and picks him up, while Kristin helps him write his papers. Meanwhile, their mother has become ill and is in bed most of the time, so Daniel has taken over Peter's care, much to his own family's regret. His wife complains that he is never home and his children tell him they miss him terribly. Daniel feels guilty, but he is also on a mission to give his brother a better life. Peter starting at the university is one huge step in that direction. With Kristin's help, it is possible.

"Your brother is truly amazing," the teacher tells him one Wednesday when Daniel drops Peter off for class. "You should see the last paper he wrote. Best in his class."

Daniel is amazed. He can't believe that the man they all thought had the mental capacity of a toddler could now dazzle the world with his knowledge.

Daniel decides to stay with Peter for the philosophy class, curious to know more about what his brother is interested in. Kristin sits next to him, helping Peter when he needs it. Daniel looks at her while she works, and can't help but find her spectacular.

To engage yourself so much in another human being is truly remarkable, he thinks to himself.

In his eyes, that makes her the most beautiful creature he has known. But he also can't help feeling a little jealous of her as well. She is now the person who is closest to his brother, and the only one who he'll write with.

She has tried to teach Daniel the technique, but so far he has only failed. So have his siblings, and even his mother, that one time she gave in and tried. When anyone other than Kristin tries, Peter pulls his arm away and often scratches them.

After class is done, four of Peter's classmates walk up to him, books in their hands, backpacks on their backs. They ask him if he would like to go to lunch with them. He accepts by typing. Daniel goes with them. He goes in the line of the cafeteria to buy food for Peter. Kristin is right behind him, while Peter stays at the table.

"You know he usually buys his own food, right?" she says.

"Really?" Daniel asks.

"Yes."

Daniel grabs a pizza slice with pepperoni.

"Peter can't stand pepperoni," Kristin says. "He usually gets the ham."

Daniel wrinkles his forehead. "That's odd. He loves pepperoni pizza. It used to be the only thing we could get him to eat."

She shrugs. "Well, not anymore. Things change. People change, Daniel. Don't baby him. He's a grown man now with his own opinions, likes, and dislikes. And now he can express them as well."

With a feeling of defeat, Daniel puts back the slice and grabs one with ham instead. They walk to the table, where Peter's classmates have already sat down, and soon they're questioning Peter.

"How was it for you as a child when no one thought you could communicate?" a girl asks.

"Lonely," he types with the assistance of Kristin.

"So, how is it now?" another classmate asks.

"I am happy to be able to speak. I feel like I have finally come alive."

"What do you dream of? What do you want to accomplish in life?" the girl asks.

"I want to tell the world about us. I want to tell them people like me are more than just disabled. We can do more than just sit in a corner somewhere. We can do so many things."

The girl nods with a smile. Daniel is pleased to see how well they have taken Peter in. They seem curious, but not judgmental. It makes him feel good about his decision to let Peter take classes here. The girl especially seems genuinely interested in his story and who he is beyond what she can see. But then she asks a question Daniel had never thought would come, that he would never have thought of asking himself.

"Can you also fall in love?"

Daniel awaits Peter's answer with great curiosity. He has never thought of Peter in that way. That he could have feelings for anyone.

Peter types. Kristin reads his words out loud while assisting his arm.

"I can. I would love to be in a relationship more than anything in the world. But I don't know if someone like me can ever do that. I don't know if anyone would ever love me back."

39

JANUARY 2016

"I NEED YOUR HELP."

"Well come on in, then." Chloe steps aside and lets me into her house. She looks exhausted. Her hair is a mess and she is pale. "I was just napping," she says. "Stayed up all night working on that tip from Arizona. "It looks promising so far. What's up with you?"

"Marcia."

"What's with her?" I follow Chloe into the kitchen, where she pours each of us a cup of coffee. I go through her cabinets and find an old bottle of whiskey and pour a sip into my coffee.

"Uh-oh," she says. "You're making it Irish? Something is definitely up."

We sit down and I drink my coffee. I wait and let the alcohol do its job inside my body.

"So, what's with Marcia?"

"I don't know how to explain it," I say. "She is not well."

"Well she has been drinking a lot for a long time."

"That's not it. There is more. Did you hear what happened last night?" I ask.

"No."

"She shot Mark."

"That's awful! Is he okay?"

"Yes. He came home late, and according to Harry, she thought he was an intruder and shot him, but I have a feeling there is more to the story."

"How so?" Chloe asks.

"Don't tell anyone, but I saw her earlier today. She kept ranting on about how they were after her, out to get her, and how Harry was one of them, how he was a killer and she thought he had killed that woman who was found in the river recently. Then she had these flashbacks or visions or dreams; I don't know what to call them, but she saw things. She described something for me that was so terrifying I had goosebumps."

"What things?"

"Children that she believed she had hurt. And two adults. She kept asking me if she was the one who had hurt them. It was really creepy. I tell you I have never seen her like this before. And I am certain she wasn't drunk."

"What?" Chloe wrinkles her nose. "Well, maybe she took some pills."

"I couldn't smell any booze on her breath and she didn't seem intoxicated when I looked her in the eyes. She was all there, and yet she was so... far away."

"So, what happened to her? Where is she now? And what about Mark?" Chloe asks.

"Mark is going to be fine, they say. He was only hit in the shoulder. All the children are with their father. I tried to get Marcia to come with me, to turn herself in and get the help she needs, but she pulled a gun on me."

Chloe almost chokes on her coffee. "She did what?"

"She pointed it at me, then told me she couldn't come with me before she ran."

"Wow."

"I know." I sip my coffee. My hands are still shaking, and telling the story makes me feel terrible.

"Marcia? I can't believe it. She wouldn't hurt a fly."

"I know. But then I began to think. What if she has done awful things? She did shoot Mark. What if she is not well and has no idea what she is doing?"

"Hm. I'm guessing you want me to help you with that."

"Yes. I thought maybe you could help me look something up. Something she said. It requires that we get access to some old police files."

"I had a feeling that was where we were heading. All right. Anything for old Marcia."

40

JANUARY 2016

I STAY at Chloe's for a few hours, while she works on getting access to the police files. I walk up to her mom's room and sit down by her bedside. She is awake, but doesn't say anything. She reaches out her hand towards me and I grab it in mine. It feels so feeble, the skin paper-thin.

"How are you?" I ask.

"It hurts," she says with a whisper.

It makes me feel bad for her. I always loved Chloe's mom, Carolyn. She has been so good to me over the years when things were bad at home. I curse cancer while tears spring to my eyes.

"Is there anything I can get you?" I ask. "Water?"

"Yes, please."

I grab the glass on her side table and help her drink. The smell of death hits my nostrils. Carolyn grabs my hand again and holds it in hers. Then she looks me in the eyes. The way she looks at me frightens me slightly.

"Be careful, Mary. Things are not as they seem. Mark my words. The boy carries all the answers."

Carolyn stares at me intensely while I wonder what she is talking about. Her hands are both holding on to my arm. They are so cold on my skin. Chloe enters the room and Carolyn lets go of me, then slides back under the covers and closes her eyes.

"What's going on?" Chloe asks.

"I...I was just saying hello."

Chloe looks at the old woman in her bed. "She's still asleep."

"She wasn't a second ago. She looked at me and told me something about a boy carrying all the answers."

Chloe chuckles. We leave her mother and walk downstairs. "She's been saying a lot of weird things lately. I have a feeling she might have a hard time distinguishing between dreams and reality. She is sleeping most of the day away. I'm afraid she doesn't have long. The doctors stopped the treatments six months ago. She's not supposed to be alive at all. They gave her four to six weeks."

"Wow. Guess she beat those odds, huh?"

"I know. I just try and make the most of the time I have left with her, you know? I try to cherish every waking moment with her."

I think about my own father as we walk back to Chloe's computers in the back of the house. I have no idea how he's going to get by. Will he ever get better? Will he be able to do anything on his own, and is it a life worth living if he won't?

"So, how's your dad doing?" Chloe asks, as if she has read my mind.

I sigh and sit in the chair next to hers. "He's not doing any better, but not worse either. But the house will be done soon, and then we'll all move in with him, I think."

"You will? That's wonderful, Mary," Chloe says. "I am so glad you and Joey are together. It was always you two. The world isn't right if you two are not together."

I shake my head. "No. I meant me, Salter, and Snowflake are moving in with him. Joey and me are a completely different story."

Chloe looks at me skeptically. "What's going on, Mary? I thought you were getting better. Trying to mend the broken pieces."

"Yeah. Well, so did I. But then he went out and slept with someone else."

"He did not!"

"She came to his house last night at midnight asking for him. She had no idea I was living with him."

"How embarrassing."

"Mostly for her," I say with a light chuckle. "Can you imagine?"

41

JANUARY 2016

"I HAVE THE FILE FOR YOU." Chloe clicks the mouse and opens a file. I pull my chair closer to better see.

"The Elingston case is a huge file," she says. "Contains hundreds of pages. Might take a while to find what we're looking for. By the way, what are we looking for?"

"Pictures," I say. "Descriptions of the victims and what they were wearing. Marcia described the children's clothing in detail. The way she described the kids reminded me of the pictures I have seen of them while still alive."

"That's going to be hard," Chloe says. "The house was on fire and the bodies severely burnt when they were recovered. The only reason they know it was murder was the footage from the neighbor's surveillance cameras and the fact that the body of the wife had been stabbed first, before the fire was started. That's what it says here. I can't believe they never found this guy."

"I know. I remember hearing about the case often. Back then, I was still working in Atlanta, and the story was all over. I was so afraid my editor would send me back, since it was so close to my old hometown, but luckily he didn't.

"It was huge. The town was crawling with journalists. Everyone was terrified. Can you imagine someone entering your house on a Saturday morning and holding you hostage only to get fifty-thousand dollars, and then, as you think it's all over because all they want is the money, they kill you and burn the house down with you inside of it. For what? Fifty-thousand dollars? It's so strange. Everything about this case puzzled us. People started locking their doors at night and even during the day. Not something we did a lot around here. Everyone became suspicious of each other, because the police believed the guy knew the family well enough to know their routines and know that they were capable of getting fifty-thousand dollars within a few hours without anyone thinking it was suspicious. Either they knew them or they had been observing them for a long time. People became suspicious of their lawn or pest guys or anyone that had access to their houses and lives."

"What's that?" I say, and point to a paragraph in the forensic report. "It looks like the description of what was found on or next to the bodies, right?"

"Yes," Chloe says. "It says here that the only piece of clothing found was on the girl. A small piece of fabric."

"What did it look like?" I ask, and move closer to better see.

"There's a picture."

Chloe clicks the picture and it opens. I look at the small piece of fabric. Chloe is speaking, but I can't hear her anymore. Everything is drowned out by the sound of my heartbeat pumping in my ears. The piece of fabric is burnt on the edges, but in the middle, I can see the very clear picture of a star.

Twinkle, Twinkle Little Star.

"Mary?"

Chloe is waving a hand in front of my face. "You zoned out for a little there."

"It's the PJs," I say. "It's the girl's PJs. They had stars on them. Marcia told me the girl had stars on her PJs and the boy had *Star Wars* written on his."

Chloe freezes. She stares at me. "It does say in the report that the maid who usually worked for them said the girl usually wore PJs with stars on them, and therefore, they concluded that she was in her PJs when she died. How on earth could Marcia know that?"

"Was it mentioned in the news?" I ask.

"I don't remember hearing about it," Chloe says. "I can Google it quickly."

While Chloe googles it, I lean back in my chair. I rub my forehead, thinking about Marcia. I run through everything she told me in my mind, desperately trying to find an explanation, an answer to the question of how on earth she could know these kinds of details if she wasn't there.

"I can't find anything anywhere about it," Chloe says. She looks at me as she exhales. "What do you make of it? Do you really think...?"

"No." I say and get up from my chair. "I refuse to believe it."

42

JANUARY 2016

BLAKE FEELS SO alive he almost can't stand it. His heart pounds inside of his chest as he walks across the parking lot, his gloved hand inside of the pocket of his sweater, the knife clutched in it.

It's been awhile since he killed last, and the anticipation of the kill is overwhelming. It sends waves of chills through his body, making him feel like the most powerful creature on this planet right now.

Like a predator. Sneaking up on his prey.

It's a sensation no drug could ever give him, the thrill of taking a life, of holding the power of life or death in your hand.

He walks to the window and looks inside. He knows she is in there. He watched her from his car as she came back from the store, a bag of groceries in her hands. He watched her as she found the key in her pocket, then fumbled with the lock, almost dropping the bag. It left him with such a strong sensation in his body, knowing what he had decided to do with her, knowing that she has no idea.

She's not going to know what hit her.

He hopes she'll be screaming. He likes it when they scream and try to fight him. Gives him even more pleasure when he overpowers them, when he pins them down and they can't move. The struggle for their lives is what feeds him. Their will to survive at any cost is what he thirsts for.

He knows this one will be a struggle. She's a feisty one. He always chooses the spirited ones. It would be no fun if they just gave up, now would it?

In his mind, he goes through his previous killings, tasting every one of them again. He used to do mostly hookers that he would pick up on one of his nightly drives in the car his dad had given him. His first ever kill was a Puerto Rican woman. He picked her up in Cape Canaveral. She was beat up by some guy the night before and had bruises on her face already. He didn't really plan on killing her, he just wanted to get laid. But something about her made him want to hurt her. She was like a bruised animal, pathetic and weak. It was like she was screaming for it.

They had sex in his car, and when he came, everything inside of him just exploded in this unstoppable tsunami of anger. Some psychologists would probably argue that it was his anger towards his mother for not being there when he grew up, or maybe at his father for being just as absent, at least mentally.

Blake didn't care why, he just knew he had to do this, he had to hurt her in order to feel better himself. So he did. He grabbed her around the throat and simply held her while she tried to fight him. He is still amazed when he thinks about how calm he was, despite the rage filling him. It was like the act in itself finally calmed his inner demons, all the voices, all the emotions were finally quiet, drowned out.

When she wasn't breathing anymore, he dumped her in a garbage bin behind a restaurant. No one ever found the body. At least, he didn't think they did. He never heard anything. And he no longer cared. He knew now how to shut up the rage when it showed its ugly face, when it overwhelmed him with that itchy feeling.

But the thing is, it isn't working as well as it used to. He used to be able to wait for months, even a year in the beginning, between kills. But not lately. He needs to do it more and more often to get the calmness back.

Blake swings the door open and walks in. No one in sight. There is light coming from the bathroom. She has to be in there. Excitedly, he shuts the door quietly behind him and hurries towards the bathroom.

He hears her flush and can hear her humming. Then the water is turned on as she washes her hands.

Nice and clean.

He closes his eyes as he follows the sound of her every move. The water being turned off again, then the silence as she wipes her hands on the towel. She mumbles something at her own reflection, then turns and as she opens the door, he opens his eyes and stares at her with a wide smile.

For a quick moment, she looks startled, her eyes wide and open. When she sees the knife in his gloved hand, she gasps and runs for the door. He lets her get ahead, just for the fun of it, then storms after her, and just as her hands land on the door handle, he grabs her by her ponytail and yanks her backwards.

She shrieks and Blake clamps a hand tightly against her mouth and starts to pull her backwards. He throws her on the floor and she tries to kick him, but it hardly hurts. She is not a match for him at all. He slaps her across her face to let her know how strong he is. She screams. He closes his eyes for just a second and tastes her screams, her fear, her anxiety and terror. He feels like the Hulk, who grows bigger and stronger, then looks down at her and slaps her again.

He pins her to the ground, then places a hand on her mouth again. He doesn't want to alarm the neighbors. He doesn't want the police to arrive too early. Not until he's had his way with her, not until he has managed to shut up the unease inside of him.

"Please, don't," she begs behind his hand.

It only makes him smile even wider. The begging is the best part. He tries to imagine what it must be like being her at this moment. What is she thinking?

Will he stop if I beg? If only I can make him feel sorry for me? What if I cry? Will he know that what he is doing is wrong then?

It always amuses Blake that they try to beg. Do they really think he is someone they can reason with? That he is capable of feeling pity? Don't they know he has chosen them? That he has planned this and is determined to finish it? That if he doesn't finish it, he will explode? That there is no way back? No matter how much they plead and beg. There is no way out but death for them.

It's just the way it is.

"Don't do this," she tries again.

Blake laughs, and then slams a fist into the girl's face. It makes her shut up. But only for a few seconds. Then she starts to cry, mostly deep groans and sobs.

That's it, baby girl. Realize it is over. Let it sink in, then slowly give up the fight. I like to look into your eyes as you do.

It is his favorite moment of it all. When they finally give in, finally realize that no matter how much they fight, no matter how much they cry and plead for his mercy, there is no way out, there is nothing left for them but death.

"Why?" she asks in a daze.

He strokes her head gently with his glove, then leans over and whispers in her ear: "Because I can."

"Don't...don't..."

"Sh. There is nothing you can do. The sooner you realize it, the faster it will go," he says.

And that's when he sees it. The girl opens her eyes wide, but there is no more fight in them.

That's it. Let it go.

Blake then lifts the knife in the air above his head and the color drains from her face as he lets it sink into her body.

43

JANUARY 2016

MARCIA IS RUNNING up along the beach. She is panting heavily. It's hard to run in the sand. But she doesn't dare to go up on the street. She feels so confused. She can't get her thoughts straight. A thousand pictures are running through her mind, and she can't get them to go away, nor get the voices to shut up so she can think.

I need a drink.

Marcia stops and throws herself in the sand. Behind her, a row of big mansions are staring at her. She wonders if there are people in there, if they'll call the police if they see her. She also wonders if they have any alcohol.

Marcia closes her eyes.

"What am I even doing all the way out here?" she asks out loud. "How did I get here?"

She tries to remember, but she can't. All she knows is that she is in danger, that she can't trust anyone. She turns her head and looks at the houses again. She feels like she knows them, like she has been here before in this exact spot. She doesn't know why. Maybe they just look familiar, especially the big blue one.

Was it in a dream? It doesn't feel real.

Marcia shakes her head and turns away. She stares at the ocean. Nothing seems to make any sense anymore. She is sick and tired of remembering things, remembering her life in small bits and pieces.

Where do all these images come from? The ones of the children in their

PJs and their parents, especially the one of the mother haunts her. The wound in her stomach, the blood on her shirt, the eyes staring at the ceiling. Marcia can't remember ever seeing anything like this. And then she remembers. Like a lightning strike, she sees him. In a ball of fire, he is thrown through the living room.

Mark!

"No!"

Marcia is panting and gasping for her breath. "Oh, my God," she whispers, clasping her mouth. "I shot him. I shot Mark!"

Marcia feels dizzy and has to lay her head down in the sand. She can't believe it. She can't believe it is true.

Did I shoot him? Did I shoot my own son?

She can't remember what happened afterwards. She just remembers firing the gun at him. She remembers thinking he was bad; she remembers the fear inside of her. Then what did she do? Did she call the police? Did she lean down and listen to his heart? Did she check his pulse?

No, you didn't. You ran, you coward. You ran away like the fugitive you are.

"I had to go," she says out loud, trying to get the voices to quiet down. "I had to get away before they got to me. I was so scared. Argh!"

Marcia gets up to her feet and yells at the voices. Then she falls to her knees, crying, sobbing.

What have I done?

You killed him. Just like you killed the others.

"No!"

Marcia bends over, crying even harder. She lies down in the sand and closes her eyes, trying to make it all go away. She wants to disappear, but doesn't know how to. Could she run? Just run? But where to?

She hides her face in her hands for a few minutes, then suddenly lifts her head up again. Now with a different look in her eyes, she raises her body to her feet and stares at the blue house, suddenly remembering it.

44

JANUARY 2016

I DRIVE to Holmes Regional in Melbourne. On my way there, I call Joey to ask him to be home when Salter gets back from school. He doesn't answer the first time, so I try again. I haven't spoken to him at all today, and have no idea where he spent the night. I fear that he went back to be with her. As I redial, I feel a knot in my stomach, thinking that I am the one who pushed him back to her.

I hope that I am wrong.

"Hello?"

Finally, he picks up.

"Mary?" he says.

"Yes, it's me."

"I am glad you call..."

"I am not calling to chat. I am going to Melbourne and I just need to make sure you are home when Salter gets there in half an hour."

There is nothing but silence on the other end. For a second, I wonder if he has hung up or if we have lost the connection somehow.

"Hello?" I say.

"Is that really why you called?" he asks.

"Yes. Can I count on you?"

"So, you don't want to talk about what happened?" he continues.

I exhale and take a turn. Some idiot almost crashes into me, and I honk the horn slightly more aggressively than needed. "No. I have a lot on my plate right now. I need time."

"I thought you had taken your time. I thought you had made your decision. Wasn't that why you decided to stay here instead of going back to New York?"

"That was before Jackie. Listen, I really don't..."

"Jackie was before you came back, Mary. Don't you get it? I only saw her when I thought you didn't want me back."

I exhale. I pass the sign telling me I am entering the hospital area, and I drive into the parking lot. I stop the car and close my eyes as I put it in park. I feel so lost. I want to be with Joey, I really do. I want it for myself and for Salter. But I don't want to if it means I have to worry constantly about who he is with, if he is cheating on me again. I can't. I simply can't live like that.

"I don't," I say. "Not anymore."

"You don't what?"

"I don't want you back. Not anymore. Not like this. I can't." I touch the bridge of my nose and lean forward, taking off my seatbelt. I feel like crying. It hurts so badly inside of me I want to scream.

"But...but...Mary...it's me. It's us. It has always been us."

I can't hold the tears back anymore. I wipe them off and try to keep my cool. "I know, Joey, but I can't do this. I can't keep doing this anymore. It's just too hard. I love you, believe me, I do. And I love the idea of us together, especially for Salter's sake, but I can't. I can't take it anymore."

I can tell he is crying on the other end. This was not where or how I wanted to have this talk. But, what's done is done. I cry while holding the phone close to my ear. I feel so miserable, so devastated and destroyed.

"Mary...I...please," he is still crying on the other end. His voice is breaking; his sobs are loud. He is not even trying to hide it anymore. "Please, give me one more chance. I know I can do better. I know I can."

"Maybe you can, but I know I can't. Even if you never cheat on me again, I'll still never be able to trust you again. I am sorry."

To spare myself any more misery, I hang up. My body is shaking as I put the phone away. I sit for a few seconds and stare at the parking lot, biting my lip while tears rush across my cheeks.

45

JANUARY 2016

I HIDE my face in my hands as I finish crying, then wipe my eyes. I look at myself in the mirror and realize I look terrible. A full night of no sleep and now all the crying has messed up my face. I find my mascara and eyeliner and try to fix myself up a little, then decide there is nothing more I can do and leave the car.

Putting the conversation behind me, I walk to the hospital's entrance. I find Mark on the fifth floor. He is not alone in his room. Harry is standing next to his bed. He is talking with him, and they stop as I walk in.

"Hi," I say.

As I walk closer, I realize someone else is there. It's Jess, Marcia's sponsor. She is sitting in a chair, her back turned to me.

Mark smiles when he sees me. He doesn't look too good. Not just because of the wound in his shoulder. He is pale, his eyes are like deep black holes, and he is so skinny. I haven't seen him in weeks. He must have lost ten pounds since I last saw him. His hair looks strange.

"Mary!" Harry says and walks to me. He pulls me into his warm embrace. I am quite startled by this, but manage to hug him back awkwardly. I walk to Mark and grab his hand.

"How are you?"

"All right," he says. "The bullet only grazed me."

"He was very lucky," Harry says.

"I am so sorry for this," I say, pressing tears back. Seeing him like this breaks my heart.

"Don't be," Mark says. "You didn't do it."

"Well, I can't help feeling responsible. I should have known it was bad. I should have reacted earlier when realizing how bad her drinking had become," I say.

I feel Harry's hand on my shoulder. "You can't blame yourself."

"If anyone is to blame, it should be us," a voice says from the door. I turn and see Alex, Danny, Sandra, and Chloe as they walk inside holding balloons and flowers. I smile and shed a few tears that I wipe away.

"We knew way before you came back here that she wasn't doing well," Danny says and walks to the bedside. "Yet we didn't do anything."

"I guess we have all been too busy with our own lives and messes to realize how bad it really was," Sandra says, and walks up to him as well.

I am stunned to see her outside her house, in a place as public as a hospital, and she doesn't seem to be embarrassed at all by people seeing her. It's the first time since it happened that I have seen such strength and determination in her. It warms my heart.

"I could have done more as well," Jess says, and gets up from the chair. She walks around, introducing herself to everyone and shaking their hands.

"Me too," Harry says, and does the same.

"So, now we have all established that we didn't do enough," Chloe says. "How about we now figure out what to do about it? How to help Mark and his siblings and how to help Marcia."

"I met with her," I blurt out.

The surprise on my friend's faces is obvious. They're all speaking at the same time, so I have no idea who is saying what.

I continue. "She texted me this morning and had me come to our old surf spot in Sebastian."

"The Spanish House?" Alex says.

"Yes. I went there and met with her, thinking I could get her to turn herself in. Maybe talk sense in to her."

"Was she drunk?" Danny asks.

"No. At least I don't think so. She says she hasn't had a drink since Saturday night when I picked her up and took her home. Strangely enough, I believe her. She didn't smell like alcohol like she usually does; her speech wasn't slurred, and her eyes weren't glassy or red."

"She could have taken pills," Jess says.

"She seemed like she wasn't intoxicated or under the influence of anything, but still she was not the Marcia I know."

"What do you mean?" Jess says.

"It was like she...I don't know. Like something else was wrong... Like..."

"Like she was someone else," Mark says.

"You know what I'm talking about?"

Mark nods with a deep sigh.

"I think something is very wrong with her," I say. "Beyond the drinking. I think she is very sick."

46

JANUARY 2016

MARK IS EXHAUSTED, but feels comforted that his mother's friends are all here with him in the hospital. More than anything, he worries about his mother now.

"What do you mean sick?" Danny asks.

"I think she's suffering from a mental illness or something," Mary says. "She kept rambling about how everyone was in on a plot to get her or something. That's why she didn't want to turn herself in. She had no idea what had happened; she didn't even know that she had shot Mark."

"When did this start?" Jess asks, addressed to Mark.

He looks at her while his heart is pounding in his chest. For so long he has managed to keep his mother's condition a secret. He even thought he could get away with just telling everyone that his mother mistook him for being an intruder when she shot him. He is arguing within himself, while everyone in the room is looking at him. Can he confide in them? He knows they're all his mother's friends, that they're only trying to help. But what will happen to her if he tells everything? Will they lock her away for good? Will he have to live with his father, his abusive and violent father? He can't keep an eye on his siblings every hour of the day. He can't protect them if they send them all back there.

"Mark?" Jess asks and moves closer.

He looks her in the eyes. He knows her well. Back several months ago, when his mother had the DUI and was forced to go to the meetings, she was there for her. Jess took good care of his mother and things had gotten better for a little while. A lot better. He knew Jess played a big part in that. His mother had trusted her. So maybe he could too?

"I first knew something was wrong three years ago when she started to sound different."

"Three years ago?" Mary exclaims. Mark sees tears in her eyes. "You've been dealing with this for three years?"

"Yes. I don't know precisely when it started, but she was just different all of a sudden. She didn't drink that much back then. Not like she does now. But she never sounded happy. She didn't get excited about anything like she used to, and then there was this story about some people from her work. She worked at the fitness center on 520, the HealthPlex, in reception, and one day she told me that some of her colleagues were jealous of her and that she was certain they were planning something behind her back. Then later, she told me one day that she wasn't feeling well and that she believed that one of the scheming co-workers had stuck her with a needle with some drug to take her out of the competition for a top job. She kept complaining about feeling strange and said that she couldn't concentrate, and said it was all due to the drug. She was obsessing about it at home, constantly blaming her co-workers. I knew something was wrong, but I was eleven. What could I do? I had no idea what it could be. Later, she quit her job because she was afraid and she told me she didn't like to work on computers because the computers were bugged and they were trying to steal her many ideas. She believed she was going to invent something big and become a millionaire. All she needed was some peace and quiet to work on her ideas, and she couldn't get that when working all day."

"I bet she was so convincing you believed she would become a millionaire, right?" Jess says.

"We all did. She asked us to write lists of all the stuff we wanted to buy when we got all this money and places we would like to live. We were going to buy fifteen houses so we could live all over the world. She wanted so badly to take us to Spain. We started dreaming about all of it and couldn't wait."

"But it never happened. Instead, she got even worse, right?" Jess says taking his hand in hers. Mark feels like crying, thinking back on this, but he holds it back.

"Some days, I would come home from school and she would be sitting in the living room staring into thin air, completely zoned out for hours in a row. She would hardly blink or even change her expression. Then, after two hours like that, she would suddenly burst into laughter for no reason at all. Sometimes she would sit and stare at her hands for hours, when I would ask what was wrong with her hands, she would say they were different than they used to be. She would go from one job to another, but lose them as fast as she got them. One time when she worked at a restaurant, they called the house and told me she suddenly walked out of there and never came back. We didn't see her for days. When she finally came back, she had no idea she had been gone."

"Did she hear voices? Did she ever talk about that?" Jess asks.

"She did say that she talked to God sometimes and he told her the lottery numbers and that he was going to make us very rich. She would go into her bedroom and I could hear her talking to someone in there, even though she was alone. Sometimes she spoke in a language I didn't understand. She would scream that we were all going to die, that we couldn't drink the water because there was bacteria in it that was going to eat us up from the inside. She would tell me the walls had bugs in them. She told us we all looked different, my eyebrows were pointed upward and my ears had grown. She said things were moving when they were not. She stayed away more and more, and would come back thinking no time had passed, pretending like she hadn't been away, and then if I said something, I could tell she really had no idea. I started grocery shopping and making sure the little ones took showers. We would eat cereal mostly for all our meals, and then one day she would come home with her hands full of groceries and start to cook or take us out to eat because we had something to celebrate, but not be able to pay for it. The restaurants usually took pity on us and didn't call the police, but asked us to never come again. At the house, we never knew who would come in the door. Sweet and fun Mommy or weird Mommy or angry Mommy."

"And all this time, you had to protect your siblings and take care of them, huh?" Jess says and strokes Mark gently.

"I was always afraid. Some weeks ago, she started telling me she believed the government was controlling me. That I was part of a plot against her and that freaked me out. She would yell at me or wait behind the door and then attack me, and try to beat me when I entered the house. Sometimes I would wake up and she would be by my bed in the middle of the night, staring at me, holding a baseball bat in her hand. I became afraid to come home, and I figured me being there only made things worse. So I stayed away sometimes even at night."

While speaking, Mark had completely forgotten that the room was full of people, his mother's friends. He couldn't believe he told them everything just like that, but once he opened up, it felt like such a relief to finally tell, to finally talk to someone about this. Now he can feel the tears well up in his eyes and he can no longer hold them back. He lets them go and starts to cry.

"I am so sorry," he says. "I have failed. I should have done more. I could have helped her."

"No," Jess says. "Listen to me. Your mother is very ill. I have to say, I had no idea. She hides it well. But it sounds like she might be suffering from Schizophrenia. That is very serious. She might be out there doing stuff that she has no idea of. She might be a danger to others and herself. We need to find her. We need to find her fast."

47

JANUARY 2016

MONDAY IS ALWAYS a busy day for Kelly. She has to get up at six-thirty, make breakfast for all three of them, get Lindsey ready for school, make her lunch and drive her to school. Then she goes to Publix and gets everything for the coming week, planning every meal in detail, making sure it's organic and non-gluten. Today, she even has to go to the dry-cleaners and pick up Andrew's suit for his trip to Virginia. Then she goes back home, unpacks all the groceries, and has a quick cup of coffee before the cleaners arrive. Then she goes to the gym for an hour and a half, and grabs a sandwich when she returns to her newly cleaned house. After lunch, she does the laundry and calls the dentist to make an appointment for Lindsey, the half-yearly check-up that she always has in January. She drives to the library and picks up some books for her daughter to read before she goes back to the school and sits in the pick-up line.

The feeling of being observed seems to be gone today. Come to think of it, she hasn't seen the truck at all today. Maybe it did help that they talked to the police on Sunday. Maybe whoever has been watching her saw them go to the police station yesterday and got scared? Maybe.

"Hi sweetie, how was your day?" she asks Lindsey as she gets into the SUV and they drive off.

"Meh," the girl answers.

"Not good, huh?"

"Nicole is having a birthday party sleepover and I am not invited. She says her mom doesn't like me."

"I am sorry," Kelly says. She feels anger rise inside of her. She knows Nicole's mom well. Who does she think she is?

Kelly gets a flashback to her own childhood and all the times she wasn't invited to parties or kept out of the fun by mean girls in school. Being a teenager wasn't a fun time for her. She hates that her daughter soon has to go through that as well. It makes her want to homeschool her.

"Can we go get some ice cream?" Lindsey asks.

Kelly looks at the clock. There's a guy coming to look at the AC unit at four. It hasn't been working properly lately. She really doesn't have time for ice cream, but she can tell her daughter is really sad about the birthday-thing, and she wants to cheer her up a little.

"If we make it fast," she says.

"Yes!" her daughter exclaims.

Kelly chuckles and takes a turn towards their favorite ice cream place in Melbourne Beach, *Sundaes at the Beach*. She is in a good mood today. No brown truck and no weird people in hoodies staring at her or accidentally bumping into her makes her relieved beyond compare. She hasn't even received one phone call hang-up all day. She feels certain it is over. The small trip to the police station fixed it.

The sergeant there hadn't been much help. He basically told them he couldn't do much about it unless a crime had been committed, but he could tell his officers to drive past their house during the day, if that helped.

"That'll scare them away," Andrew told her afterwards, "Seeing a police car on the street. Don't worry. They're probably just waiting for us to go away so they can rob the house. But we're not going anywhere, and once they see the police car, they'll get lost."

Kelly didn't believe him when he told her, but now she has to admit, she was wrong. She is glad she was.

"I want a banana split!" Lindsey says, as they enter the shop.

The place is famous for its banana splits, so Kelly agrees to let her have one and she even orders one for herself. It's been many years since she last let herself indulge in such a feast, but today she feels like celebrating.

Bellies full of ice cream, whipped cream, chocolate, and bananas, they drive back to the house and park in the driveway. They barely make it inside before the AC guy arrives. Kelly calls Andrew to let him know the guy is here, and then tells him about her day.

"Not once did I see the truck, Andy. I am certain it's over."

"That's a relief," he says. "Now we can go back to living our lives normally again."

"I got your suit from the dry cleaners," she says, while Lindsey starts her homework.

"Perfect. I'll only be gone three days. You'll be fine while I'm gone, right?"

Kelly looks at her daughter, who looks up and smiles. "I think we will. I really do think we will."

"Great. Then I won't feel bad for going. You know I have to go. It's an important trip for the company."

"I know. We'll be just fine. Don't worry."

48

JANUARY 2016

I AM DEVASTATED. Completely torn apart. How could Mark have been going through all of this alone? How could he have lived like this for three years and no one knew?

Poor kid.

I can tell everyone is thinking the same as we say goodbye to Mark in the hospital and leave. No one talks in the elevator; we're all too torn up by guilt, and we can't help being a little angry with Marcia, even though we all know she can't help it.

Why didn't she ask for our help?

We have decided to all do what we can to find Marcia and get her back, so she can get help. Chloe and I have decided to go back to Sebastian, where I saw her last, and start looking for her in that area. I have no idea how she got down there in the first place. With her DUI, I didn't expect her to be driving a car, but again, with her, I really don't know what to expect anymore.

Jess decides to go with us and we all drive in my car. Meanwhile, Danny has to go back to the fire station, while Alex and Sandra told us they'll be looking for her in the Cocoa Beach area, in case she comes back. I look at the two walking close together, so close it's hard to tell if they're holding hands or not. I decide it's not my problem anymore. Angry as I am with them, especially now with what I am going through, I realize it's not my issue. If they want to make a mess, then they're on their own. I warned them; there really isn't more I can do.

"If she is, in fact, Schizophrenic, there really is no saying what she might do," Jess says as we hit A1A. "She could very well be suicidal."

"Do you think she might also be capable of killing someone?" I ask.

Chloe is sitting in the passenger seat. She looks at me. Our eyes meet. I can tell she doesn't want me to tell Jess what Marcia told me, but I feel like I have to.

"Anything is possible, really," she answers. "I mean, she shot at Mark, didn't she? Why?"

I shrug. "It was just something Marcia told me when I was alone with her earlier on the beach."

"You think she might have killed someone?" Jess asks, startled. "That is very serious."

"No. I don't think she did it, but...how do I explain this? She had these images, these visions that kept haunting her, she said. It might just be in her imagination. It didn't seem real at all."

"What kind of images?"

Chloe is signaling me to stop talking, but it's too late. Jess wants to know. I feel like it's a good idea to tell her, since Marcia told me she is a psychologist, so she should know about these things.

"I don't know. Some kids and their parents lying on the floor, the mother bleeding and the children, she believed, were dead. She kept asking me if I believed she had killed them. That's why I was wondering. Personally, I don't believe she is capable of killing anyone. Not Marcia."

"She did try to shoot her own son," Jess says.

"She thought he was an intruder," I say.

Chloe is being very quiet. I can sense that she doesn't like where this conversation is heading.

"According to what Mark told me, she knew it was him," Jess says. "She said to him that she believed he was working with the government in some conspiracy against her. But she was aware it was him when she pulled that trigger."

I can't say anything more to defend her. I haven't heard Mark's version of it, but I know in my heart that it is probably true, what Jess is saying. It just hurts so badly to know that my old childhood friend has lost it like this. The worst part is, I am starting to fear the worst. I am beginning to ask myself the question: Was Marcia there on the day the Elingston family was attacked in their own home and later killed? And if she was, then was she the one who brutally murdered that poor family? Could she commit such a horrendous act?

49

AUGUST 2006

"I DON'T TRUST HER."

Daniel looks at his mother. She is better now and sitting by the fireplace of her house. She coughs between sentences, but has regained the color in her cheeks and the feistiness in her voice.

"She told me the other day that Peter doesn't like pop music, that he doesn't like to listen to it before bedtime. According to her, Peter told her so," she says. "Peter loves music. Especially Kelly Clarkson. It's not fine art, it's not classy, but it's what he enjoys listening to. And you know it, Daniel. Now she says he likes classical music instead."

Daniel doesn't speak. He looks at the wooden floors. He doesn't want to say it, but he knows she is right. Peter loves Kelly Clarkson and listens to her all the time. She's his favorite singer, and he even has his own little dance that he does, swinging his head from side to side when they put her on.

"No woman should tell me what my boy likes and what he doesn't like," their mother continues with an angry snort. "I cared for Daniel for twenty-five years. I already know what he likes."

Daniel can't blame her for being upset. His other siblings that are present in the living room are troubled as well.

"She told me he likes brandy and champagne," his older sister says. "Our brother never liked anything with alcohol in it. Remember when we let him taste wine? He spat it right out."

"Maybe his taste has changed," Daniel says. He is trying to defend

Kristin, but he can see why they're upset. He has noticed it too. Kristin has been moving in on all areas of Peter's life. "It happens when you grow older. I didn't used to like wine either, but now I do."

"But she is changing everything," Daniel's older brother says. "Even the way Peter dresses. She told mother that what she bought for him was not what he liked to wear, then went out and bought all these suits for him, even shirts and ties. Why does Peter need to wear a tie?"

"I don't know," Daniel says with a deep exhale. He is tired of defending Kristin, but he feels like he has to. It was all his idea. He contacted her, he got her to care for Peter, and he was thrilled when she did. But now, he isn't so sure anymore. What he believed was an opening into Peter's world was starting to look more and more like a woman taking over his life. It was nothing like what Daniel had dreamt it would be.

"The reason I called you all to come today," their mother says. "Is that we need to stop this woman."

"What?" Daniel says. "But...but what about all the progress she has made with him? He goes to college now. He'll get a degree."

"To what use, Daniel? For what does he need this degree, exactly?" His brother asks. "It's not like someone is going to hire him. It's not like he can suddenly take care of himself. It's great if he enjoys it, but I'm not so sure he understands anything."

"That's not true. I've seen him in his classes. You should read the papers he writes," Daniel continues.

"That he writes? Are you even listening to yourself?" his brother says. "Peter has CP. He can't control his body. How is he supposed to write a paper?"

"Daniel. We no longer believe that he is writing them," his sister takes over.

"What?"

"We believe she might be assisting him a little too much," she continues, glancing at the other siblings, looking for backup. They're all nodding.

Daniel can't believe them. Yes, he knows it has all gone a little too far, and maybe the woman is taking over a little too much of Peter's life, but he still believes that Peter is communicating, that what he writes on that keyboard comes from him.

"The latest development is that she has told me Peter wants to move out. Apparently, he wants to move into an apartment on his own," their mother says. "There is no way he can do that. I refuse to let it happen."

50

JANUARY 2016

WE SEARCH the area around the Spanish House all afternoon, but with no luck. Marcia is nowhere to be found. Not on the beach, not in the park across the street, not in the inlet or around the pier. We talk to all the surfers and fishermen that we meet, but no one has seen her.

By nightfall, we are ready to give up.

"She could be anywhere," Chloe says, as we walk back towards the car. "There is no way we can find her once it gets dark."

The sun is setting over the land on the horizon and paints the sky pink. It is gorgeous. I stare at it for a little while, wondering if Marcia is all right. I keep seeing her face and those frightened eyes that I had seen earlier. I am afraid for her. Afraid of what she might do in her state of desperation. I know she is carrying a gun. I worry a police patrol will find her. That will never end well. She'll refuse to even talk to them, and then pull the gun. I just know she will.

"We can't give up," I say. "The police are looking for her for shooting Mark. If they find her before we do, there is no saying what will happen to her. I don't think she'll survive it."

Jess puts a hand on my shoulder. "Not everything in this world is your responsibility, Mary. Yes, Marcia is sick and a possible danger to both herself and others, but you can't help her if she doesn't want you to."

I look at her and think that it's a load of crap, probably the kind that psychologists tell themselves all the time, but this is not my patient we're talking about. This is my friend. I don't say anything, though. I am exhausted. And starving.

We get back in the car and drive home in silence. I can't believe we couldn't find Marcia. How hard can it be to find one person? I keep wondering where she could have gone to after she left me on the beach. She ran through the bushes, but where to? Where could she go? The sky is dark out now, and I have heard on the radio that a front is pushing through tonight. It is expected to cause heavy thunderstorms. The National Weather Service has issued a severe thunderstorm warning for our county from tonight until the morning, and there's a tornado watch. It's not as bad as a tornado warning, but still. It's not a night to be outdoors.

Will Marcia be able to find shelter?

I drop off Jess at the parking lot in front of her condominium in Cocoa Beach, and thank her for her help. "Anytime," she says with a smile and closes the door.

"You wanna grab a bite to eat?" I ask Chloe as we drive off.

"I can't. Gotta take care of my mom. I've been away almost all day. Sorry."

"That's okay," I say, and drive up in front of her old house on 7th Street. "By the way, did you get anything out of that tip from Arizona?" I ask, as she is about to leave the car. She nods. "It started to sound plausible. I checked with the newspapers and the police department. There's a couple up there that robbed a small liquor store recently, and they match the description. Could be them."

"Let me know if you find out more," I say with a yawn. I am so tired I can hardly see anything.

"Sure thing."

She slams the door to the car shut, and I drive off towards Joey's house. As I approach it, I am filled with an overwhelming sadness. I park outside in the driveway as it starts to rain. There is light coming from inside the house and I can see Joey in there walking into the kitchen. I am guessing he and Salter are watching a movie. I hope they have brought my dad into the living room with them. He needs the company. I sigh as I spot Salter and my dad in the living room. They seem engaged in some deep talk. Now they're laughing. They seem happy. Joey is joining them, holding a bowl of popcorn. I feel my eyes water. This is my family and I don't want to go in. I don't want to have to face Joey. I don't want to argue and ruin the atmosphere. They seem to be doing so well without me.

Instead, I take off.

51

JANUARY 2016

KNOWING I won't be able to rest or even stay still till I am sure I have been everywhere, I decide to drive around for a little, checking Marcia's usual places in Cocoa Beach. I go to the Sportsbar, the Beach Shack, and Coconuts on the Beach, even Sandbar. I check all the local places she might be, but no one has seen her for days. I walk the beach with my flashlight and look through the dunes. I talk to every drunk and homeless person I can find, but no one has seen her since Saturday.

Frustrated, I drive back. When I pass Marcia's place, I hit the brakes. The Seaview Suites is a row of small townhouses by 8th Street, across the street from the beach. It's a place where my parents never wanted me to go as a child. The rent is the cheapest on the beach, and therefore it attracts a lot of scum. There is almost always loud music coming from one of the houses and the sound of people partying.

There's light coming from Marcia's windows.

I park in front of her door and walk up. Someone is fighting loudly behind an open window somewhere. A dog is barking aggressively. I knock.

Harry smiles when he opens the door. "Mary?"

"She's not come home by any chance, has she?" I ask, thinking it's a long shot, but if she is as sick as I suspect her to be, she might as well be here as anywhere else.

He shakes his head. "I am sorry, no."

"I didn't think so. Just had to check," I say, and start to walk away.

"Wait. Don't you want to come in?"

"No. No, I couldn't."

"Please?" he asks. His eyes are pleading with me. "It's way too quiet in here without the kids."

I chuckle. "Don't tell me you miss them?"

He shrugs. "Guess I got used to the craziness around here, huh?" He looks at me. Our eyes lock. He is so handsome it almost hurts. I have to admit, I am tempted. I really want to go in. I want to be in his company.

"I just made a batch of chili. Do you want some? I have more than enough. I've gotten used to cooking for a lot of people, so I think I made way too much. You look like you could use a meal."

Really? Have you seen the extra chin I am growing?

I laugh. He is sweet. "Well, I am starving, and I have to say it smells heavenly."

He smiles again. "Come on in, then."

He rushes to the kitchen and finds a bowl for me. I sit at the table and let him serve me. I can sense that he is trying his best to make it good for me and it makes me laugh. I look at the huge pot of chili he has made.

"That is a lot of food," I say, as he pours some in my bowl.

"I know. I don't know what I would have done if you hadn't come along. I really don't like eating alone. Guess coming from a big family damaged me somehow."

"You come from a big family?" I ask, and taste the food. The chili is amazing. I feel the hunger now biting at me.

"Yes. Lots of brothers and sisters."

"Sounds nice," I say, and think about my own family. I shudder when thinking about my younger brother and who he turned out to be.

Talk about a dysfunctional family.

"And you?" Harry asks.

"I, well, it's a long story. I only have one brother, but I don't know him very well. He's a lot younger than me. As it turns out, I don't know him at all. I only really have my dad left, and he is paralyzed. That's a long story too. But back to you. Did you grow up around here?"

"Palm Beach Gardens."

"Ah, the rich area."

"It has its poor side too," he says.

"Of course. Is that where you're from? You don't look like the poor boy from the wrong side of the tracks."

"Guilty as charged. I guess you could say I was one of the rich kids. Seconds?"

I nod eagerly. I look around the room while he serves me another portion. I have never seen Marcia's house so neat, so tidy. Not that I have been there much since she moved in.

"So, what is a guy like you doing in a place like this?" I ask.

He shrugs. "Trying something new."

"Yeah, but come on. Why rent a room in this cheap place if you're rich? Why move to Cocoa Beach? Why is a guy like you not married with a bunch of children with your gorgeous athletic wife?"

He stares at me intensely. It makes me uncomfortable, but also warm inside. "Don't you just like to stick your nose in everything, huh?"

"Sorry."

His face eases up. "No, it's okay. I can't blame you for wondering; I just don't like to talk much about myself."

"Lots of baggage, huh?" I ask.

"You could say that."

52

JANUARY 2016

"SO, what are your plans for your stay here in Cocoa Beach? How long are you planning on staying?" I ask, after a couple of minutes of silence. I am still eating. I can't stop. It's just that good.

"I don't really know yet," Harry says. He stopped eating long ago, and now it's just me. He is leaning in over the table, looking at me with a wide smile. "You really like it, don't you?"

I finish chewing and swallow. "I do," I say. I get embarrassed. I have eaten three portions now, and still I could eat more. "I am sorry."

"No. No. By all means. I like to watch you eat. It's so refreshing. So many women are scared of eating. I like it when they're alive, you know? When they don't hold back. I mean, if they're willing to indulge in a wonderful meal, what else would they be willing to indulge in, right? Women who don't hold back are often the most passionate."

I blush. Seriously blush at his words. "Then you won't mind if I take a little more?"

"Not at all," he says.

I scoop up another portion and eat it while he stares at me. I can't help laughing.

"What's so funny?"

"You are. You're just staring at me. It's kind of creepy," I say.

"I can't help myself. I enjoy watching you."

I finish my plate and push it to the center of the table. It's a habit I have always had. I don't know where it comes from. I like sitting here with

Harry. He makes me feel good about myself. Joey is always on my case, teasing me about how much I eat. Here's a man who actually enjoys it. But, at the same time, I can't quite figure this guy out. Everything about him is a little strange. Why isn't he married? Why is he living here with Marcia? I haven't even been able to get out of him what he does for a living. It annoys me that he keeps avoiding my questions, but at the same time, I like him to stay a little mysterious. It's kind of sexy. It's been a long time since I have felt like this.

With Joey, it's different. We have known each other all of our lives, so there was never any mystery. There was no excitement or tickling sensation in my stomach, because—well, it was Joey. I loved him. I still love him, but I am starting to wonder if there needs to be more in a relationship, in a marriage? Were we just good friends who were married?

"You have to excuse me," Harry says, and leaves the table. He walks up the stairs to the restroom. I hear him lock the door. I sit at the table for a little while, but it's hard for me to stay still. I want to find out more about this guy so badly. Leaned up against the wall, I see a briefcase. I am guessing it's his and walk to it. I open it and look at the content. It's all news clippings. Pictures and articles. I pick it up and look at it.

What is this? It's all about that woman who was killed, the one they pulled out of the river!

So, Marcia was right when she told me he had pictures of her in his room? She told me she had seen them.

I pick up one of the photographs. I can see it's the same woman from the pictures in the newspaper, but in this picture, she is younger. Way younger. It looks like a school picture.

Why does he have this?

I look at one of the articles and notice that he has highlighted some of the names of witnesses that the police have talked to in the case. Why has he highlighted their names? The name of the woman was Shannon Fergu-son. She was a third-grade teacher at Roosevelt Elementary School. I had no idea that she was one of the teachers at Salter's school.

I hear the door open, and hurry up and close the briefcase before Harry gets down the stairs. "So, do you think you'll have room for dessert?" he asks, smiling. My eyes glance quickly at the briefcase, while I wonder if I placed it the right way so he won't see I have opened it. Harry notices my glance and looks at the briefcase as well, then back at me.

"I have ice cream."

53

JANUARY 2016

I EAT the ice cream silently, wondering who this guy really is sitting across from me. Why is he so into the murder of this woman?

"You're so quiet all of a sudden?" he asks.

"Just enjoying the ice cream," I say. "And I'm really tired now. Been quite a long day."

Harry sighs and leans back in his chair. "I know what you mean. I'm beat too. What a night and day. I worry so much about Marcia. And the kids. They didn't seem very excited by seeing their dad today. I got the feeling it's not the best for them to live with him. Maybe you know more about that than me?"

I look into Harry's eyes. Scrutinizing them. I sense such an affection for the children in him. Children he hasn't known for very long. I have no idea how to read this guy. Is it real? Is he just acting?

"I never met Carl, but I know he used to beat them. That's why she moved away and took the kids with her. That's what she told me. But, then again, I don't know any more what is real and what she has been making up. I keep wondering if I know her at all. It's a little scary. I kind of went through the same thing with my younger brother. You think you know someone and then...well..." I shrug and finish my ice cream. "I don't know if you know what I mean."

Harry grabs my hand across the table. The gesture startles me. His hands are big and warm. Mine almost disappears inside of his.

"I know exactly what you mean."

Looking into his eyes, I get the feeling he does understand. His thumb is rubbing my hand. I begin to feel like I am cheating on Joey, even though we haven't done anything.

You're done with Joey, remember? It's okay. If he can do it, then you can too.

I pull my hand out of his grip. "I should go."

He looks disappointed. Then he smiles. "Of course. It's getting late."

"My son is waiting for me."

I get up and walk to the door. I hear him behind me, and seconds later, I feel his hand on my shoulder. It's heavy and warm. I turn and look directly into his face. He grabs me and pulls me close. His breath is on my face. Our lips are close.

"Why do I get the feeling you want this just as much as I do?" he whispers.

I close my eyes and enjoy his closeness. "Because I do."

"I thought you were taken. Marcia told me..."

"Shut up," I say, and place my lips on his.

He grabs my face between his hands while we kiss. I am so close to him I can feel his heartbeat. I look into his eyes as our lips depart from one another. He is moaning. "I want this too," he whispers. "I have wanted it since the first day I saw you. You're so beautiful, Mary."

Beautiful? Me?

He looks into my eyes. He is still holding my face between his hands, lifting it slightly to better study me. His eyes are staring into mine, devouring me.

"Your eyes are so...so deep and full of life," he says.

I look down and pull his hands away. "I...I hardly know you," I say.

He is shaking his head. "No. It doesn't matter, Mary."

I take a step backwards. I shake my head. "I should go."

"Please, don't go. Please stay."

I stare at his beautiful face. I can't believe I am about to walk away from this, but it's too early for me. I am not ready. I reach the door and I can feel the handle behind my back. I stare at him, then storm towards him again and kiss him one last time before I run out of the house.

54

JANUARY 2016

WHEN MARCIA WAKES UP, it's cold. She can hear loud noises. It sounds like thunder. It's raining heavily. She can hear it and starts to wonder where she is. She sits up in the complete darkness. She's lying on the floor, but it doesn't feel like she is inside. The wind is howling and blowing through something, it sounds like a door. Lightning strikes outside and lights up everything. She sees two cars next to her.

She is in a garage.

But whose garage is it and how did I get here?

Marcia tries to remember what happened the day before. All she can recall is going to Beef O' Brady's with the kids.

"Kids eat free on Tuesdays," she mumbles to herself, as she finds her way to the window and looks outside.

She must have found shelter here last night from the storm, but how did she get in? She doesn't remember. She looks outside at the storm raging. Puddles of water have gathered in the driveway as more is pouring down. She has got to get out of there, but this is not the time to be outside. Not with all those lightning strikes. It's too dangerous. She knows she has to wait it out. But how long will this storm last? She can't risk getting caught in here. People like these, rich people like this, own guns. They protect themselves. Marcia reaches down in the side of her pants and pulls out a gun. She doesn't remember where she got it, and startled, she drops it to the ground.

Marcia feels great unease spread as she tries to remember where she is and how she got there. But there is nothing but a big black gap in her mind. No matter how hard she tries, she simply can't put the puzzle pieces together.

She wonders where her bike is, since she usually never goes anywhere without it. Not since they took her driver's license.

When was that again? Last month?

Marcia shakes her head and sits back on the ground. Lightning strikes often outside now and keeps lighting up the room. She picks up the gun and feels how heavy it is in her hand. She knows how to shoot it. She remembers how her father taught her as a child. He would take her to the woods and help her shoot cans. The memory makes her smile. She loved her father. He was the best thing about her childhood. Until the day he vanished when Marcia was eleven. Her mom told her he was hit by a car, but later in life, she learned that he had jumped out of the top of a building, convinced he could fly like a bird. She had so many fond memories of him. Some days, they would dress up like ladies and skip to the grocery store, singing the song from *The Sound of Music*, "My Favorite Things," wearing wigs and hats, and then on other days he would sit in the corner of the living room in the darkness and stare at the wall for hours, mumbling. Marcia used to think it was her fault when he had those days. That she wasn't good enough. She still wondered if it was her fault that he jumped off that building. Maybe there was something she could have done differently.

Marcia puts the gun back in her pants, then looks around as the next lightning strikes outside and lights up the driveway. There is something awfully familiar about this driveway and the house. Has she been here before? Does she know who lives here? It doesn't look like the house of any of her friends. It's way too expensive, and the neighborhood is too nice. The cars are on the luxurious side as well. None of her friends live like this. Not even Sandra, who is the richest person she knows. Sandra is more the type that saves all her money. She doesn't spend it on big houses and cars. That's not her style.

Marcia sighs, while wondering where the heck she is and how to get back to her kids.

They must be worried. Poor babies. Maybe I can take a taxi back once the storm has passed?

She realizes she has no money as she goes through her wallet. She needs money to get home.

Maybe these people have some lying around the house? They'll probably not even notice it if it's gone.

55

JANUARY 2016

I WAKE UP WITH A START. I look to my side and see Salter in the bed next to me. He looks like an angel. Joey is sleeping on the couch in the living room for now. When I got back the night before, Salter was already in bed, and it was very awkward between Joey and me. I spoke as little as possible with him, basically just told him we hadn't found Marcia and that we would be looking again tomorrow, then went to the bedroom and climbed into bed, hoping that Joey would know that I didn't want him in the bedroom. I couldn't fall asleep lying all alone, so I ended up carrying Salter into my bed with me.

Outside the window, the storm is raging. I look at it while thinking about Marcia. I so hope she has managed to find shelter somewhere.

"Where are you, Marcia?" I mumble, while looking out at the storm. It's like Niagara Falls out there. I wonder if the roof of Joey's small house will hold through it. Then I wonder about the construction site where they're building my dad's house. I hope it'll make it through the storm as well.

I look at the clock. It's only five in the morning. I still have an hour and a half before I have to get up and get Salter to school. But I can't sleep anymore. I am too worried about Marcia being out there all alone.

Then I realize something.

I have a fan base. I have followers that read what I write. They helped me with my brother. Maybe they can help me with Marcia as well?

I jump out of bed and walk to the computer and turn it on. Then I start writing. I write a post about Marcia, about how much I love her, but also about how we believe she is very sick and in need of help. I tell them that she was last seen in Sebastian Inlet on the beach, but we have no idea how she got there, or where she could be now. Then I find a picture on my phone of Marcia that I attach to the post and press send.

I know it won't go viral, and I have no idea how many of my followers are from this area, but it's worth a shot.

As soon as it is done, I go back to bed, and close my eyes for what feels like just one second before the alarm goes off. Snowflake jumps up on the bed and starts to lick Salter on the face like he always does in the morning.

"Hey. Good morning," Salter says with sleep in his eyes, then pets the dog while laughing, because it tickles when the dog licks him.

I wonder when I should tell him that we won't be living with his dad once Grandpa's house is done. How do you tell your child that his parents messed up again? Even if I blame mostly Joey, I can't help feeling guilty myself.

While Salter gets dressed, I walk into the living room. Outside our door, Bonnie and Clyde are waiting, since I told them to stay with Joey for the night. I have a hard time coping with the pig's smell at night. They attack Snowflake and me as soon as I open the door. Well, mostly Snowflake, since he is by far their favorite. The animals run around sniffing each other like they haven't seen each other in months. Even Bonnie imitates the dogs and sniffs Snowflake's behind. It's quite the sight.

Joey is still asleep on the couch, so I take all the animals into the yard so they can do their business, then walk to the kitchen and make breakfast for my son. Joey wakes up and looks at me from the couch.

"You have no idea how much it kills my back to sleep on this thing," he says grumpily.

I shrug, but don't answer. I want to say a lot of things like *you should have thought about that before you slept with someone else, again,* or *that's what you get for cheating on me—again!*

But I don't. I don't want to fight anymore. And I especially don't want to fight in front of Salter.

"I have running club today," Salter says, as he shovels in his cereal. "Someone has to pick me up at four."

"We will," I say, without looking at Joey. I try to avoid him as much as possible, even though it is hard. I hand Salter his lunchbox. "Don't worry."

"What's wrong?" he asks, scrutinizing me.

"What do you mean?"

"Have you and Dad been fighting? Why is he sleeping on the couch again?" he asks. I hear great worry in his little voice.

I sigh. This is not the time to tell him, but I still don't feel comfortable lying to my son.

"We had a fight," I say. "Let's talk about it later today, all right? You'll be late for your bus."

"Tell me, Mom."

"It's a long story, Salter. We need to talk about it when we have more time to sit down and talk it over."

Salter's face goes pale. "That bad, huh?"

"I'm sorry, sweetie," I say.

"I knew you would blow it," he says, and looks at me disappointedly. I can hardly breathe. Seeing him like this hurts too much.

"Why can't you two just figure it out?"

"I...I..." I glance at Joey, who doesn't look back at me. I can't get myself to tell Salter what really happened. Not now. Not like this. I don't want him to resent his father, the most important male figure in his life. I look at the clock on the microwave. "Salter, you're late. You'll miss your bus."

Salter bites his lip. I want to pull him close and hug him, tell him everything is going to be fine, but I can't. I can't give him what he so desperately wants.

"Can I get a kiss?" I ask.

"I'm going to be late for the bus," he says, and leaves me hanging there while storming out the door.

"He's too old for that stuff," Joey says, and walks into the kitchen.

"Maybe," I say. "But I have to try."

"Why? You're babying him. All the other kids are going to laugh at him," Joey says angrily.

"Because his mother tries to kiss him? I think he'll survive."

Joey scoffs loudly. "You're smothering him. I'm sick of it. The boy needs to grow up and be a man."

He pours himself a cup of coffee.

"Yeah, because you're such a great role model," I say sarcastically.

He looks at me indignantly. "Why is it you get to make all the decisions, huh? You run all of our lives. You decide what he wears, what school he goes to, what he eats, and what activities he goes to. Heck, you even decide if we are to be a family or not. When is it my turn? When do I get to make decisions around here?"

I grab my cup and pour some coffee in it. I look at him. "When you start acting like a real man."

With that, I leave him and go back to the bedroom and my laptop. I feel like crying as I sit down, but I don't. I am too upset, too angry with him and his behavior. I open the lid of the laptop and check my emails. I have received one new one since this morning. I immediately forget all about Joey when I read it.

56

AUGUST 2006

DANIEL IS NERVOUS. He is looking at his siblings and his mother, who seems to be getting weaker and weaker every day that passes. They are waiting outside Kristin Martin's office. She is the one who called them up and asked them to come.

"This better not be about that moving out business again," their mother says. "I told her I am not going to allow it to happen."

"Maybe it's good news," Daniel says. "Maybe Peter learned something new and she wants to show us."

Daniel is afraid the whole family is starting to resent him for bringing Kristin into Peter's life. He's scared they'll take it all away and make Peter nothing but a vegetable again. So far, Daniel hasn't agreed to let Peter stop seeing Kristin, no matter how much his siblings and mother tell him they think it should stop. He is fighting for his brother. He still believes in this treatment. He still believes his brother speaks to them, even though it is with Kristin's help. He refuses to believe otherwise.

The door to the office opens and Kristin appears in the doorway. She looks stunning, Daniel thinks. Riveting even. Daniel refuses to believe she is as manipulative as his family does.

"Come on in," she says with a wide smile.

They get up and walk inside. Daniel helps his old mother, who struggles to walk these days. Inside the office, Peter is waiting for them. He is sitting in his wheelchair, his head bent to his chest, his hands knotted in fists. He groans when he sees all of them, making the chirping noises they have come to know as excitement.

"Sit down," Kristin says, and closes the door behind her.

Daniel sits next to his mother on the leather couch. His older sister is next to him; the other siblings find chairs to sit in. Their oldest brother decides to stand. Kristin walks up to Peter and sits next to him. She looks at all of them. Daniel can sense that she is nervous. It makes him uncomfortable.

"First of all, Peter and I would like to thank you all for taking the time to come in today. I know you all have busy lives and families to take care of."

"Why are we here?" their mother says.

"I am getting to that," Kristin says. "As you all know, Peter and I have been working together for almost a year now, and it has been quite fruitful. Within a short time of my treatment beginning, he was suddenly able to communicate with the outside world for the first time in twenty-five years. It is quite an accomplishment for someone like Peter. I realized quickly that he was a very smart young man, and he has a lot to tell the world. As you know, he has been taking classes at the university with me, and enjoyed it immensely. He has grown and become a man. It is time we start treating him like it."

"If this is about him moving into his own place again, then you can forget it," their oldest brother says. "There is no way he can handle that."

"I realize that it has been hard for you all to accept the fact that Peter now has wants and wishes for his own life, but be that as it may, we have chosen to respect your concerns. Together, we have found a solution we believe will be good for all parties," Kristin says.

"And what is that?" their sister asks.

Kristin clears her throat. "That he moves in with me."

"What?" their oldest brother yells.

"Never!" their mother says.

Daniel doesn't speak. He simply stares at Peter, who doesn't move a muscle. He doesn't even look at them while they're talking. He is biting his fingers, and Daniel knows it's going to leave sores that will need treatment.

"Now, now, hear me out!" Kristin says, and manages to calm them all down. "Before you rip my head off, I have something else to tell you." She glances at Peter, then reaches out to grab his hand in hers. It seems to Daniel that she is forcing it, holding on to it really tight so it will stay still. She looks back at them and looks their mother directly in the eyes when she says the words that are going to change everything.

"The thing is...we're in love."

57

JANUARY 2016

"I NEED YOUR HELP."

Harry looks at me with that mischievous smile of his. He is standing in the doorway of Marcia's house. He is wearing only shorts. No shirt. I try not to stare at the six-pack he has going on there. The storm has passed and it has stopped raining.

"I called Sandra, but she has a doctor's appointment today; Chloe has been up all night and needs to sleep; the boys are all at work, so that just leaves me with you. I don't want to go alone," I say, trying desperately to hide the fact that I really wanted to spend time with him.

"All right, then," he says and steps aside. "Come on in. I'll get dressed."

If you have to.

"Okay. I'll just wait here."

I sit on Marcia's couch, while Harry walks upstairs. As he is almost up, I turn and look at his behind. I know I am bad, but I can't help myself. He is really something. I am beginning to think I should just get it over with and sleep with him. But I don't know if the only reason I want to is because I want to hurt Joey back. That would make me a terrible person, I think. Maybe. Maybe I totally deserve it after what Joey has put me through. I don't know. Who decides these types of things? Who gets to say if someone is being a bitch or if it's completely okay since he did the same to you?

"Ready?" Harry is standing next to me. He has put on a T-shirt. It's Hugo Boss. Nice and tight over the six-pack.

He sees that I am looking at him and I blush when I realize it. I get up and stand next to him. He is a lot taller than me. I like that. Joey is small. We're about the same size. Makes me feel big when I am with him. Maybe it's about time I was with a taller man. Someone who'll make me feel small and delicate. Well, at least smaller.

"You know what?" I ask.

He chuckles. "Can't say that I do."

"I need to ask you something before we leave."

"Yes?"

"I know this is going to sound awful, but I need to know why you have pictures and articles of that woman they found in the river? Why are you so interested in her? You even have an older picture of her from when she was much younger, and I haven't seen that in the news or anywhere else?"

I just blurt it out. No use wrapping things up. I know he'll have to put two and two together and realize I have been going through his briefcase. That might make him angry with me or even make him resent me, but I can't hold it back anymore. I need to know what is going on before I can trust him.

He looks at me for a long time without saying anything. It makes me very uncomfortable. His eyes are on me, scrutinizing me. "You mean Shannon Ferguson?" he finally asks.

I swallow hard, wondering if I have made a mistake. No. I believe in honesty before anything else.

"Yes."

"How do you even know this?" he asks. I can tell by the tone of his voice that he is annoyed with me.

"Okay. I went through your briefcase, all right? You were in the bathroom last night, and I couldn't help myself."

"Ah, 'cause I thought maybe Marcia had told you, since I know she saw the clippings when she walked into my room one day."

Yeah, that would have made me look a lot better. Think, Mary, think!

"Well, she did. That's why I wanted to see for myself," I say, trying to save my dignity.

Harry looks away. I can tell he is angry. He sits down on the couch and exhales.

I blew it, didn't I? I totally blew it.

"Well, I can't blame you for not trusting me," he says. "But still. I thought we had something. I mean, last night was..."

"I know. I felt it too," I say. "I am sorry. But you are a stranger and I... well you could say I have trust issues."

Harry looks at me, then chuckles lightly. "All right. I'll let this one pass. Because I enjoy your company so much. But next time, just ask me, okay?"

"You kind of said you didn't want to talk about yourself," I say, "But let's not get stuck in the details. What's done is done."

"Okay," he says.

We look at each other in silence for what feels like forever. Then he gesticulates with his arms. "What are we waiting for?"

"You still haven't answered my question."

"Ah, that. Right. Well, if you must know," Harry exhales deeply and touches the bridge of his nose, "Shannon was my sister."

"Your sister? Oh, my God. I am so sorry," I say, and sit down next to him. "That explains everything. The old picture, the newspaper clippings."

"I came here to try and find out what happened to her. I didn't want anyone to know who I was, so I rented a room and tried to stay hidden. I've been trying to talk to all of her friends and colleagues up here, along with anyone who saw her in the last twenty-four hours before she was killed. I've asked them about her; since I lost contact with her many years ago, I didn't know much about her. But, so far, it hasn't led to anything. Her husband is the one who saw her last; they had a fight on the night she died. So far, he is the police's main suspect, but I know my brother-in-law, and he is no killer. I am trying to help him as well."

I look at Harry, feeling all of a sudden more attracted to him than ever. "I...I am sorry," I say. "I had no idea."

"How could you? I was trying to hide it." Harry starts to laugh all of a sudden. I look at him for an answer.

"What's so funny?"

"I bet you thought I killed her, right?"

"The thought crossed my mind," I say, feeling foolish.

"It never occurred to me that people would mistake me for the actual killer, but of course, it would look that way," he says. "That is so funny."

He sighs and looks at me. "Shall we go then?"

I get up from the couch, feeling all of a sudden relieved and happy. Now I don't feel bad for liking this guy.

"So, is Harry Hanson even your real name?" I ask, as we walk outside of Marcia's house.

"As a matter of fact, it isn't."

"It did sound like a cartoon character."

"So, I guess I'm not the secret spy I desperately wanted to be," he says with a smile. "My real name is Steven."

I grab his hand and shake it. "Nice to meet you, Steven."

We get into the car and I start the engine with a roar.

"So, where are we going?" Steven asks.

"Melbourne Beach." I am backing out of the driveway as I speak. "Long story short, I received an email this morning from a guy who gave Marcia a lift yesterday from Sebastian to Melbourne Beach."

58

JANUARY 2016

WHEN KELLY WAKES up in her bed, she feels rested for the first time in weeks. She opens her eyes as the alarm clock goes off, and then looks at Andrew, who opens his eyes as well. Today, he is leaving for his business trip, so they can't be late.

While he is getting ready, Kelly walks into Lindsey's room and wakes her up. Her dog, Max, is sleeping on the bed as she enters the room. Kelly sits on the edge of the bed and kisses her daughter's forehead.

"Rise and shine," she says cheerfully. Kelly feels good today. She is relaxed and not the least bit worried that her husband is leaving for three days. For the first time in a long time, she is not worried at all.

"Is it morning already?" Lindsey says, and rubs her eyes excessively. The light is bright in her eyes. Lindsey isn't much of a morning person.

"I'm making breakfast now," Kelly says. "Come down when you're ready."

"Can I have pancakes?"

"Not today, sweetie. It's a school day. There's no time."

Lindsey makes an annoyed sigh. "Aw, I thought it was Saturday."

Kelly chuckles and leaves her, knowing she will probably have to go up there again in five minutes to make sure she gets out of bed. But Kelly doesn't mind. Not today. Not now that everything seems to be so good.

Kelly turns on the radio in the kitchen and hums along to the music while pouring cereal into Lindsey's favorite bowl. She makes coffee for herself and her husband, and soon, Andrew comes trotting down the stairs.

"I'm late. I'm late," he says.

She hands him a cup of coffee. "Not too late to have some breakfast."

"You're right," he says and sits down. He looks at his watch. "I have five minutes if I don't run into traffic on the way to the airport."

Kelly serves him some of his fitness cereal that he has been eating lately. He wanted to lose weight, he told her, and he is beginning to look quite fit. Kelly worries about his desire to look good. Is it for her or for someone else?

Don't go there, Kelly. Don't start it.

She reassures herself that it's perfectly normal for a man his age to want to look good. And besides, it is for her benefit as well. She wants him to look good too. She likes to show him off when they go to charity dinners and auctions.

Kelly walks up the stairs to see how Lindsey is doing and finds her fast asleep on top of the covers. It looks like she got up and out, and then fell asleep again. It looks funny, and Kelly can't help laughing a little.

"Lindsey," she says and strokes her hair. "You have to get up, sweetie."

The girl opens her eyes. Kelly smiles. "Let me help you get dressed."

A few minutes later, they're all sitting in the kitchen. Andrew is typing aggressively on the phone, probably answering emails, Kelly thinks to herself. She pours coffee into his Tervis cup for him to take on the road.

"I don't want to go to school today," Lindsey complains when she sits down at the table.

"I know, but you have to," Kelly says, and serves her the bowl of cereal. "Don't you have music today? You love music."

"No. It's Art today. And you know how much I hate art."

"I'm sure the teacher will come up with something fun," Andrew says, and finishes his cup of coffee.

"You ready?" Kelly asks.

"I think so. I just need to run to the bathroom real quick."

Kelly nods. He always has to go right before he leaves. It's the thing that annoys her the most, because it's what makes them always run late. Andrew disappears into the toilet, and Kelly returns to finish packing Lindsey's lunchbox. She puts it in her backpack, then looks at her daughter, who has dropped her spoon and is staring at something with her eyes and mouth wide open.

Kelly turns her head to look at what it is and sees her husband standing in the middle of the living room, a gun to his head.

59

JANUARY 2016

I AM ENJOYING Steven's company. Steven. I like this new name for him. Suits him a lot better than Harry. He truly looks like a Steven.

"So, how much do you know?" he asks, as we cross the city sign to Melbourne Beach. "Do you know where she was dropped off?"

I shake my head. "The driver wrote in the email that he picked her up on A1A, where she was hitchhiking. She told him she was going to Cocoa Beach. He was going to Cape Canaveral, so he said he could drop her off on the way, and she got in. But then, as they drove along, she suddenly freaked out. She started to scream for him to stop and said that she was armed in case he tried anything. He stopped the car at a park by the beach in Melbourne Beach, where she opened the door and jumped out. He watched her run towards the beach, cross over, and disappear down the stairs. He was in a hurry, so he took off."

"That's odd," Steven says.

"Seems like everything with Marcia is quite strange these days," I say.

I go silent for a little while and think about my meeting with her the day before. I still can't get that look in her eyes out of my mind. It wasn't Marcia. It was like it was someone else, someone completely different. It scared me senseless, and still does when I think about it. I have no idea what she is capable of. What she might do when she is in that state of mind. I can't stop thinking about those things she told me and how it all fits with the police files from the Elingston murders in 2010.

"What's the name of it?"

"Sorry, name of what?"

"The park?"

"Ah. It's Spessard Holland. The south end. It's actually right here."

I turn into the parking lot and stop the car. I grab my phone, and for just a second, I look at the display, wishing Joey had called. But he hasn't. It makes me sad. I miss him, even though I am still so angry with him.

Will I ever be able to let him go?

"So, what's the plan here?" Steven asks. He looks out at the heavy clouds above us. The front that is supposed to pass us isn't over yet. They've promised more thunderstorms all day today. The beach probably isn't the safest place to be. I open my weather app and look at the radar.

"All the storms are still way inland," I say. "It'll be at least an hour before the next one comes out here. So I say we search the beach area now. She could have found shelter from the storms under the boardwalk. She might still be there."

"Let's do this, then," Steven says, and opens his door.

We both get out of the car. I have this nervous uneasy feeling inside of me as we walk across the boardwalk and onto the beach. I push it away, thinking it's just because I am worried about Marcia. The dark—almost black clouds on the horizon look threatening. I always thought it would be easy to shoot an end-of-the world apocalypse movie here in Florida on a day with thunderstorms. It looks like it is the end of everything. Like, in that movie, my favorite from my childhood, *The Neverending Story*. When *The Nothing* arrives to destroy them all.

"Marcia?" I call.

Steven crawls in under the boardwalk. I keep walking along it. It has been raining and blowing like crazy, so there are no footprints in the sand. I stare at the deserted beach. The wind is coming from the south and is nice and warm on my skin.

"She's not under here or the other boardwalk on the north end. It doesn't look like anyone has been sleeping under there."

"Where is she then?" I look at Steven, feeling desperate and lost.

He shrugs. "I don't know. Maybe the restrooms or somewhere else in the park?"

"I think they lock the restrooms at night, and there isn't much else up there besides parking lots and bushes. But let's go check just to be sure."

60

JANUARY 2016

"WHAT ARE YOU DOING?"

Kelly's voice is shaking as she stares into the intruder's eyes. She realizes she knows those eyes. She has seen them many times before. Outside the library or Publix. Walking past her in a crowd or on the street when walking the dog.

"I know you," she says. "You helped me the other day. I had forgotten my purse when eating lunch. You came running out from the restaurant and gave it to me. I thought it was the nicest thing. Why...what...?"

"Shut up," the intruder says. The gun is unsteady in their hand. The eyes looking at Kelly are those of a madman.

"Mom?" Lindsey says.

"Sh, baby. Just stay calm and do whatever you're told to, alright?"

"We'll do anything. Just don't hurt us," Andrew says.

Kelly can hear the terror in his voice. It freaks her out.

"Everyone in the living room, now!" the intruder says. "Hurry up!"

Kelly grabs Lindsey by the hand and, trembling, they walk into the living room. Lindsey is whimpering and Kelly tries to hold her.

"Get down on your knees. All of you!" the intruder yells. There is an inconsistency to the tone of the voice.

"What do you want from us?" Andrew says, when he is on his knees, the gun pointed at the back of his head.

"What do you want from us?" the intruder repeats, mocking him.

When they're all on their knees, the intruder walks in front of them.

The intruder pulls down the hoodie on the sweater and kneels in front of Andrew. Kelly hears him gasp.

"You?"

The intruder smiles. "Yes. Me, Andrew."

"But...but I thought..."

"That you had gotten rid of me?" the intruder bursts into loud laughter.

"Who is this?" Kelly asks, feeling a stitch of anger going through her body. Is this someone Andrew has been involved with somehow? Is this some sort of revenge? To hurt his family? Is that why the intruder has been stalking them? Watching their every move? Is that why?

"Shut up, bitch," the intruder says. The gun slams into Kelly's face. Hard. Kelly gasps in pain, then tumbles to the floor. In the darkness, she can hear Lindsey scream.

It'll be okay, baby. Mommy's fine.

Kelly is out. She doesn't know how long...it might have been an hour. When she wakes up, she is still lying on the floor in the living room. Her daughter is next to her, face flat against the tiles. She is crying helplessly. Kelly blinks her eyes and returns to reality, only to realize her husband is right next to her on the other side. His face is also flat against the tiles. His eyes aren't moving. His body is limp; blood is running from a wound in his forehead. As the realization sinks in, Kelly tries to scream, but the impact of the shock is so deep she cannot get any sound across her lips.

Andrew!!

The gun is now placed to the back of Kelly's head. "Please," she finally manages to mutter through sobs of despair. "Please, don't hurt us. I'll give you anything you want. Anything."

"I need fifty-thousand dollars. Can you get me that?"

"Yes! Just don't hurt us."

"Good. And pizza. I am in the mood for a pizza."

61

AUGUST 2006

"YOU'RE WHAT?"

Daniel stares at Kristin. She is still holding Peter's hand in hers, holding onto it firmly and stroking it gently. Daniel feels like he is in a movie or a strange, surreal dream. Did she really just tell them that she and Peter were in love? Peter, who until recently had the mind of a toddler; Peter, who can't get out of his chair, who depends helplessly on the care of others; Peter, who drools and bites his fingers to blood, who can't control a muscle in his body? Peter, who is almost fifteen years younger than she is? Him? His brother?

"Excuse me?" their mother says.

She seems as baffled as the rest of them, but somehow she manages to turn it into anger. Daniel can feel it from where he is sitting. Her fragile body is twitching in fury.

"I do realize it must be hard for you all to take in, and I want you to know that I completely understand, but it doesn't take away the fact that we're in love and have been for quite some time."

"That's ridiculous," their mother says, snorting while she speaks. "Peter doesn't know what love is. He is not capable of having that kind of emotion. This has got to stop."

"I realize how strange this must sound to your ears, but it is, nevertheless, the truth," Kristin says. She lets go of Peter's hand and pulls out something from the table next to her.

"Here. This is the transcript of one of our conversations we had six months ago, when we first realized we had feelings for one another."

She hands the transcript to Daniel, who looks at it, his heart throbbing in his chest. He reads how they have talked about kissing and Peter asking Kristin if she could *ever love someone like him* and her answering *yes, I have loved you for a long time.* Then he answered that so had he, *now what do we do?*

Daniel can't stand reading this; it makes him feel sick to his stomach, and he hands the transcripts to their mother.

"This is preposterous," their mother says, holding the papers in her hand. "This doesn't prove anything. Anyone could have written this. You're manipulating him and you have been from the beginning."

Kristin looks disappointed. "I had really hoped you'd understand," she says. "We love each other. Love knows no boundaries."

"But..." Daniel starts, then stops. He has so many questions, so many things he can't comprehend. "How? How do you know it's him talking and not you? You are, after all, supporting his elbow when he writes this. How can we be sure that it comes from him and not from you, because you wished it to be so?"

Kristin stares at him. "Do you think this is my dream scenario? You think I wanted to fall in love with a man in a wheelchair? I love him for what he is inside, behind all this, and because I love him, love his wonderful sparkling personality, I love everything he is too. Even if it means he can't do a lot of things." Kristin looks at Peter again and smiles. "Yet, not everything is impossible for him. I might as well tell you right away." She clears her throat.

"I am pregnant, and it is Peter's."

Daniel stares at her, eyes wide open. He's at a loss for words. So are the others. Only their oldest brother manages to say something.

"How?! How on earth is that even possible?"

"It was Peter's greatest concern," she says. "That I wouldn't be attracted to him physically, even though I kept telling him I loved everything about him. He has CP, but that is not all he is. He is a wonderful, charming, warm intelligent person, and that is who I fell in love with. The first time we had sex was in my house one day after classes. How did it work, physically, you might wonder? Well, it wasn't easy. We lay on the bed and kissed. We took our time; Peter was overwhelmed and needed extra time. I told him we could just lie close if he wanted to. I got naked and took off his clothes..."

"Enough!"

Their mother rises to her feet. "I don't want to hear any more of..." she stops midsentence, then touches her chest. It happens so fast, Daniel hardly has a chance to react. Her face turns pale and she falls to the floor. All the siblings run to her.

"She's not breathing," Daniel's sister says. "Call 911!"

While Daniel is dialing on his phone, he watches his oldest brother approach Kristin Martin, his fist in the air in a threatening posture.

"You'll never come anywhere near this family again. You hear me? Not any of us. Not me. Not my brothers and sister, and certainly not Peter. Do you hear me?! NEVER!"

62

JANUARY 2016

WE DON'T FIND her in the restrooms or the park area either. We search the bushes and the area around the benches, but nothing. I refuse to give up and I convince Steven to go down to the beach again. I know Marcia loves the beach, and I have a feeling she will seek the beach and the ocean, even if she is sick. This is where she grew up, this is where she felt safe as a child when her father went nuts at the house. She often slept on the beach when it was really bad.

"I think we should walk a little," I say.

Steven looks at the sky. The big black darkness is getting closer. "We don't have long before that hits us," he says.

"It's long enough," I say.

"As you wish."

We start walking. I think about the kiss we shared the night before and wonder if he thinks about it too. Our hands are very close to each other when we walk, our arms rubbing against each other. I fight the urge to grab his hand in mine. I don't know if I only want him to be close to me because I am sad and wounded, if I want to hurt Joey, or if it's really because I like Steven. 'Cause I do. I really like him, but I can't stop thinking that he is not my type at all. I am usually more into the surfing lazy bad boy types. Steven is too perfect. But maybe I've changed my type? Maybe I am done with those good-for-nothing types? I know he is the type that I would like to fall in love with. I know he would treat me well. I know he would take care of me. And I would enjoy that six-pack of his.

While I think too much, as usual, he grabs my hand in his. The gesture startles me and I twitch. He looks at me, as if wanting my approval, and I smile.

"We'll find her," he says and kisses the top of my hand like a gentleman. "I am certain we will."

"I sure hope so."

We walk out of the beach park area and into a residential area, where the big beachfront mansions are lined up one after another overlooking the Atlantic. Each has its own boardwalk to the beach, and the yards are covered in sea grapes. The houses are a lot bigger than the ones you see in Cocoa Beach, even on the beach. These are three-to-four-million dollar mansions. I have heard that most of the people living here are doctors. I can't blame them. It's a little too far from a city for my taste. I like having a downtown to walk or bike to, but other than that, it's gorgeous out here. A little desolate, though.

"You think she walked all the way down here?" Steven asks.

I shrug. "She might. But, then again, she could have walked north as well."

"There's nothing here but houses."

"I know. It's a dead end," I say with an exhale and look at the sky above us. The storm is getting dangerously close now. We can hear the thunder now and see the lightning strikes in the distance.

"We need to get back to the car," Steven says, "If you don't want to be caught down here during that thing."

Disappointed as I might be that we haven't found even a trace of Marcia, I know he is right.

Being the lightning capital of the world, Florida is not a place to be outside in a thunderstorm. Every year, some tourist from up north refuses to leave the beach in time and gets struck by lightning. A guy we grew up with, Jared, was struck three times during childhood. It's one of those stories you only believe because you know him, but it's true. He survived all three times, but that is the exception to the rule. I, for one, don't want to try and see if I can do the same.

Just as we're about to turn and walk back, I spot something.

"What's that?"

"What's what?" he asks.

I walk to the boardwalk leading to one of the mansions.

"I really don't think we have time for this," he says.

"Just give me one sec."

I walk up on the boardwalk.

"That's private," he says.

"I know. I just have to..." On the boardwalk, they have a small bench where you can sit and watch the ocean. I stop and pick something up.

"Bingo." I look at Steven with a smile, just as the sky cracks above us with loud thunder. "She was here. This is her scarf. She always wears this. Even when it's ninety out. It was a present from her father before he died. She has been here. Marcia was here."

63

JANUARY 2016

KELLY'S HANDS are shaking as they press the numbers on the phone.

"Not a word, you hear me?" the intruder says, the gun pointed at Kelly's temple. "Just act normal."

"Papa's Pizza."

"Yes, hello. I would like to order a pizza," she says, her voice about to crack as her eyes, once again, glance at her husband, who is on the floor in a pool of his own blood. Lindsey is sobbing, hiding her face in her hands, while lying flat on the floor.

"Delivery or carryout? Hello? Ma'am? Are you still there?"

Kelly feels the gun being pressed harder towards her temple. She catches her breath. "Yes. I'm still here. Sorry. Delivery, please."

"Alright. What's the order?"

Kelly stares at the body of her husband. She can't take her eyes off of him. Such despair overwhelms her and she can't move. It went all right when she called the bank and asked them to bring the money. She managed to keep her cool and not lose it, but she simply doesn't have the strength to do so now. Not anymore.

What's the use anyway?

Kelly stares at the intruder, thinking there really is no use, that they'll both be killed anyway, no matter what. As soon as the intruder gets the money. The intruder certainly seems mad enough to do it.

"Ma'am? What's the order? Ma'am?"

But I'll have to sign for the money when John from the bank arrives. The intruder can't do that alone. I am still needed. I can't be killed yet.

"Ma'am? Is anything wrong, ma'am?"

"Yes," she says, her heart throbbing wildly in her chest.

"Yes, what?"

Kelly glances at her husband, then back at the intruder, who is breaking a sweat. Their eyes meet and lock.

I'll show you. I've got a few tricks up my sleeve as well. I am not down yet. I refuse to let you get away with this.

The gun in the intruder's hand is shaking heavily now. The intruder's breath comes in ragged bursts. The intruder might be playing tough, but Kelly sees right through all that. The intruder is nervous. Anxious.

You messed with the wrong woman, my friend.

"Ma'am?"

Kelly is still staring into the eyes of the intruder as she opens her mouth and finally speaks.

"Help. I am being held hostage. Me and my ..."

She doesn't get to say anymore before the phone is pulled out of her hand. The intruder shuts it off, frantically fumbling with it.

This is it. This is your chance.

Knowing she'll not get another chance, Kelly acts fast. She leaps through the air and lands on top of the intruder, pinning the intruder's body to the floor. The person beneath her screams and the gun is knocked out of their hand. It slides across the tiles. The intruder groans and whines, while Kelly throws in a punch, hitting right on the nose. The intruder screams again and Kelly is surprised at her own strength. But the intruder is stronger. The intruder grabs Kelly around the throat and manages to get a good tight grip on her. Seconds later, Kelly is gasping for air and no longer able to throw any punches. The intruder presses Kelly off. Kelly is struggling to breathe, trying to fight the intruder off her, grabbing their wrists, trying to pull away, but the intruder is a lot stronger than her, and soon she is pressed to the ground, the intruder tightening the grip on Kelly's throat. Kelly is only making gurgling sounds now. In the distance, she can hear her daughter whimpering and crying. Her vision is getting blurry, and soon there is nothing but darkness.

This is it. This is how I go. Please take good care of my daughter, God. Please take care of her.

As she drifts off and gives in to the daze, she can feel how the grip is being loosened on her throat, just before the sound of the gun going off rips through the air. After that, there is nothing but silence. Silence and darkness.

64

JANUARY 2016

"DID YOU HEAR THAT?"

Steven looks at me, his eyes wide. He turns his head and looks at the house behind us.

"Was that...?" I ask anxiously. "It wasn't thunder, was it?"

"It sounded more like a gunshot," Steven says, then pauses. "I think I know this place. This house..." Steven freezes, then looks at me. "My brother lives here."

"Your what?" I ask.

"I have only seen the place in pictures, on his Christmas cards that his wife sends out of the family. I lost connection with him many years ago. It's a long story. But I have a bad feeling about this, Mary. I have to go check."

I look at the scarf in my hand and think about Marcia. A terrifying thought hits me. What if she fired that shot? What do I do? Do I call the police?

"Let's go," I say, and pull his sleeve.

He follows me up the boardwalk leading to the house. We run as the rain starts to pour down on us. We approach the windows leading to the beach and look inside. In there, in the living room, I see Marcia. She is bent over what looks like the body of a woman on the floor. She has a gun in her hand. Not far from her lies a man in a pool of blood.

"Oh, my God," I say, and clasp my mouth.

"That's my brother!" Steven says. His voice is breaking.

"Marcia. What have you done?" I mumble under my breath. I feel devastated. I can't believe what I am seeing. It truly is heartbreaking.

Marcia moves away from the body on the floor and walks to a little girl lying on the floor further away. The girl is moving, worming around on the ground.

She is trying to get away! She's trying to get to the door. And now, Marcia is going to stop her. She's going to kill her like she killed the two others!

"Don't!!" I scream, and start hammering on the window. "Stooop, Marcia!"

The sound startles Marcia, and she turns to look at us. She doesn't seem to recognize us. She simply stares and doesn't move. Her head is tilted slightly, like she is wondering about something.

Steven is at the sliding door now and pulls it open. We storm inside and he throws himself at Marcia, knocking her to the tiles. Marcia goes down, screaming and yelling loudly.

"Help! Help!"

Steven manages to get the gun out of her hand, while I run to the daughter and grab her in my arms. She is crying helplessly, screaming in terror. I sit on the floor, pull her into my arms, and hold her tight. Her body is shivering in horror while I try to get her to calm down.

"Sh. Sh. We're here to help you."

Seconds later, I hear sirens outside. I look at Steven and our eyes meet. Marcia is still screaming underneath him, kicking him, telling him she will never give in to the government's repression; she'll never tell them anything, that aliens will come for her soon, take her back to their ship and make her pregnant, that the government wants her for her knowledge. I can't stop crying when looking at the scene and the two bodies. I realize there is no more I can do to help her.

I close my eyes as the realization sinks in. Seconds later, the house is filled with boots, loud voices, and yelling men with guns pointed at us.

65

JANUARY 2016

THE BODY IS STARTING to smell bad. Blake realizes he has to get rid of it. The last few days he has kept her in the bed, kept coming back to see her and enjoy the work of his hands. This one was special to him. It was different. She is different.

But there is a time for everything, and now it is time for him to leave her. The smell will soon be a problem, and the body will be discovered.

Blake plans to be long gone by the time it is found. He has orchestrated everything down to the smallest detail.

He lifts the body up, and puts her gently on the ground, the smell tormenting his nostrils. Blake then grabs his knife, cuts open the cheap mattress, and starts pulling out the filling.

He thinks about his sister as he prepares for his next move. Blake remembers her only vaguely from their childhood. He was only three when she left town and never looked back, so they don't have that many memories together. All he knows is that he hated her when growing up. He loathed Mary and how proud their father was of her, always bragging about her accomplishments as a journalist, her career on CNN and later at the *New York Times*.

Look at her now, Daddy dear. Oh, how the mighty have fallen.

Doing a blog. Like that is anything to be proud of. Blake knows she has a lot of followers. He is one of them, constantly keeping an eye on what she is up to, what she posts. He even comments on it using his alias, Nightrider123. But he is not impressed with what she is doing, not at all. The small piece she did on him and Olivia actually had him laughing out loud.

Like that is ever going to lead to anything.

Blake laughs again while thinking about how he has written several emails, from different accounts, using different aliases to lead them away from where he is really hiding. Using local stories of criminals robbing stores or whose description matches his and Olivia's. In that way when they check up on it, they sound plausible. The one in Arizona is his masterpiece. He just knows they'll be falling for that one. He hopes in his quiet mind that they'll all go there to look for him. It would amuse him greatly. His only regret is that he'll not be there when they find out they've been fooled. He'll be far away doing what he always does, getting himself in trouble, but never paying the price for it. It is amazing how easy it is to get away with a crime. It makes him feel invincible. It's like they can't even get close. It's too easy.

And so much fun.

Blake looks at her picture that he keeps in his pocket. A picture taken from one of the newspaper clippings that his father kept of her articles in the scrapbook. The big blue book that he had in his office and showed to his friends and colleagues, while Blake was never mentioned. Not even the time he got an A in math. His father didn't even listen when he told him. He just handed him some cash and told him to go get himself something proper to wear and to get a haircut.

"Lord knows you can afford it, boy. No need to look like a bum. Your sister always dresses nicely."

Blake destroyed the scrapbook when he was twelve, in a fit of rage, yelling at their father for his attention. He ripped it to pieces, but kept the picture.

You'll never find me, dear sis. Never. But I will find you. When you're least expecting it, I'll come for you.

66

FEBRUARY 2007

IT IS RAINING on the day the trial begins. Daniel sits with Peter in the courtroom. Peter doesn't seem to understand what is going on. At least, Daniel doesn't think he does. He is biting his hands, as he usually does when he's upset. He has been doing that excessively lately, and it worries Daniel. Peter's hands are filled with deep sores that won't heal. As long as he keeps biting them, they won't, the doctor says.

They're surrounded by their siblings, and Daniel suddenly misses his mother tremendously. He can still see the expression on her face as she fell to the ground in Kristin Martin's office that day six months ago, a hand pressed against her chest. She was dead when the ambulance arrived. Everyone in the family blames Kristin Martin for her death. Now, they want her put away.

"She completely ruined our family," their oldest brother argued when they held the first meeting about it. "She deserves to be locked up. She's a pervert and has abused all of us. Especially Peter."

The door to the courtroom is opened and Kristin is brought in, accompanied by two officers with strict looks on their faces. She has lost a lot of weight, even though she is pregnant. Her clothes are dangling on her shoulders. Her face seems longer, her cheeks are sunken in, and her eyes seem bigger than before. She is still beautiful, but not in the way she used to be. She looks like a beaten animal. The only thing thriving seems to be her growing stomach. Three months till she is due with Daniel's niece or nephew.

Daniel doesn't like to think about what will happen to the child, where it will grow up if she is convicted. No one else seems to care about it. They almost postponed the trial because of it being so close to her due date, but the family insisted on having it done before. They intend to show her no mercy for what she did.

There is no excuse. Nothing to justify her actions.

Peter groans and makes a lot of noises, and Daniel turns his head to look at him. He looks into his eyes.

Is he looking at Kristin?

One of his older brothers sees it as well and leans over to Daniel's ear. "It's only natural that he reacts to seeing her again after all she did to him."

Daniel nods. She is, after all, charged with sexual abuse of their poor defenseless brother. Living out her sick fantasies, getting pregnant with someone who has no idea what love is, who has no way of saying no.

"We were in love," Kristin says, when the trial begins and she is called to the stand. She is asked about her relationship with Peter. She turns and looks at him. "We are still in love. We're just not allowed to be, because the world doesn't acknowledge that people like Peter are capable of something as simple yet fundamental in life as to love someone."

"But the man has the mental capacity of a toddler. He has gone through many tests and they have all shown the same. How do you explain that? The man has never said a word. He can't even control his own movements. How do you know that he loves you back? He suffers from profound mental disabilities. How can you tell me he gave you consent to have sex with you?" the prosecutor asks.

"He might not be able to speak or even hold a spoon on his own, but those are motor skills. It says nothing about who he is, what he knows, or how intelligent he is," she answers.

"But the tests and assessments do, right? I mean, that is why we have the tests. To determine people's intelligence and capabilities, am I right? They're designed for that very purpose."

"That's what I used to believe, yes," Kristin says. "Until I started to work with these patients, with Peter. I realized he was smarter than we thought, and started to believe he had a private chamber in his mind, a place where all his adult thoughts were trapped behind his sickness, behind the palsy. So, it makes a lot of sense that he would fail the tests, since the tests are made for people who can answer verbally, read and write. What I found was a way for Peter to share his intelligence. I found a way to reach that chamber of his, and you will be amazed at what I discovered."

"And what, exactly, is that?"

"That Peter has a beautiful mind. A mind with a wonderful personality, who is more than capable of feeling and giving love. I fell for that mind. Not the body or the sickness. I fell in love with who he was. But the world, his family, won't accept it. They want to keep him in his prison, so the world will never hear what he has to say again. He is once again being treated like a severely impaired person and has lost all control over his life. They have taken away his freedom. They're silencing him and keeping him from becoming who he can be. Worst of all, is that he'll never be with the one he loves. If I am convicted and sent away, then he'll never get to be with his child either. Who is abusing whom here?"

As Kristin speaks she stares directly into Peter's eyes. Daniel realizes it and is truly amazed. Never in his lifetime has Peter been able to keep eye contact with anyone. Kristin smiles and tilts her head while looking at him. Her eyes water as she speaks. Much to his surprise, Daniel sees a tear leave his brother's eye as well. He watches it as it rolls across Peter's face and lands on his upper lip, where it stops.

Daniel looks at it, not knowing what to say. Meanwhile, Kristin is being grilled in the chair.

"Isn't it true that the type of treatment you used on Peter has been subject to lots of controversy?" she is asked.

"Yes," Kristin answers.

"Isn't it true that many tests made with people like Peter undergoing the same treatment and supported writing on a keyboard, have been widely criticized? Isn't it true that in one test, where the typers were asked to name objects their facilitators couldn't see or know of, that in nineteen studies of facilitated communication performed, that they found zero validation through one-hundred and eighty-three tests?"

"That was the conclusion, yes," she says, her head bent.

"So, how can you claim that it works?"

"I just know that it does. I know that he speaks to me. I'll swear on the Bible; I'll sign anything to make you believe what I say is true. I know that he loves me. I know that he wants to marry me."

A wave of shock goes through the spectators in the courtroom. The judge asks for silence. Daniel can't stop looking at his brother, as a second tear leaves the corner of his eye.

Am I making a mistake? Could it be? What if?

Daniel writes a note and passes it to the prosecutor, who reads it, then looks back at Daniel. Daniel nods.

"Your honor," the prosecutor says. "The family requests that Kristin Martin does those tests with Peter. The same tests used in the experiments where all one-hundred and eighty-three failed."

67

JANUARY 2016

THEY TAKE MY STORY. A detective writes everything I say down, and asks me a thousand questions. He has introduced himself as Deputy Brown. He's from the Brevard County Sheriff's office.

Even though it kills me, I tell him everything. I tell him I believe Marcia entered the house and killed the husband. He tells me it looks like the woman is still alive, and I watch as the paramedics take her out of the house. I tell him we entered the house because we believed Marcia was about to kill the daughter. He tells me they found the family's dog dead in the hallway when they entered.

We stay in the house for hours, going over the questions again and again. I call Joey and ask him to pick up Salter from running club at the school. While talking to the deputy, I can see Steven doing the same, while a female detective is trying to take care of the young girl. Marcia is taken away. Kicking and screaming, they have to carry her out of the house, hand-cuffed, while the gun is secured.

Then I tell the deputy the rest. I tell him I believe Marcia might have been the one who killed the Elingston family on Merritt Island six years ago, that she told me she remembered things about them, like what clothes they were wearing. I don't tell him about Chloe or the police files I have seen. There is no need to. He can connect the dots himself. Or someone else will do it for him.

"She is not well," I say. "She shot at her own son two nights ago. She thought he was part of a conspiracy against her. She is very sick, I think."

"So, what you're saying is, you believe she has done this before?" Deputy Brown says.

"Yes. I am afraid so."

"And to another part of the Elingston family?"

"Another?"

"Yes. Andrew Elingston is the name of the man who was killed here today."

"That's odd," I say. I look at Steven, who is still talking to a deputy as well. His eyes meet mine for a few seconds.

Wasn't he his brother? Does that mean...?"

"It could look like she was targeting them. Do you know if she had any grudges against the family? Any unresolved disputes?"

I shake my head. "No. I really don't."

"All right," he says. "I'll let you go for now, but we'll probably have to take you in for more questioning later."

"Okay."

The deputy leaves, and I wait for Steven to finish up as well. Seconds later, he approaches me and we're asked to leave the house. The team from forensics is coming. I take one last glance at the man lying on the floor, in the pool of blood. Someone covers the body with a white blanket.

Steven stares at his brother. I grab his hand in mine.

"I'm sorry," I say.

Steven's body is shaking. "I can't believe it."

We continue outside, and then we stop. Steven bends forward. He is gasping for breath. I put my arms around him and pull him closer. I try to comfort him, while he cries in my arms.

"I can't believe he is gone too," he mumbles and pulls away. He looks at me with terror. He clasps his face with both hands and bends forward again like he is trying to catch his breath after a long run.

"I can't believe it," he says again.

I help him get to the car, and we drive off. He cries most of the way, while I try to keep myself together enough to be the strong one. But seeing a man like Steven lose it like this makes it hard not to get emotionally carried away also. I struggle to hold back the tears.

I keep wondering about Marcia and why she would target Steven's family. Could they have done something to her years ago that I didn't know about? And what are the odds that Steven would move in with her, renting a room from the woman he was looking for? 'Cause she killed Shannon Ferguson as well, didn't she?

I can only assume so. The gruesomeness of her actions leaves me speechless. I can't believe that twice someone I love dearly has tricked me. It makes me seriously doubt my own judgment of character. Am I really that stupid? That easily manipulated?

I look at Steven. How about him? Can I really trust him?

"You knew it was Marcia, didn't you?" I ask, as we get closer to Cocoa Beach. "You knew she had killed your sister, right?"

He doesn't look at me.

"How did you know?" I ask.

"I didn't. But I knew the police had been looking at her when investigating my sister's murder. They had her in for questioning."

"What were their grounds for questioning Marcia?" I ask.

"Apparently, she told someone that she believed she had done it. That someone went to the police to report it. They questioned her and, according to the detective taking care of my sister's case, Marcia admitted that she believed she might have done it, but then withdrew the confession a few hours later, telling them she never admitted to anything. They said they still looked into her, but that they didn't have enough evidence to build a case against her."

"So, you stalked her?" I ask.

"You might call it that. I found out who she was and started to keep an eye on her. When I realized she was renting out a room, I thought it would be the perfect possibility for me to get really close to her and maybe find evidence."

"But you liked her, didn't you?"

He scoffs. "I did. Mostly, I felt bad for the children. I realized there was a person behind the coldblooded killer that I took her for. Now I think I understand better. She's sick. She's not herself. But she still killed my siblings. I don't know if I can forgive her for that, no matter how sick you tell me she is."

I exhale and drive up in front of Marcia's townhouse. We sit in the driveway in silence for a few minutes.

"I don't think I can live here anymore," he says. "I'll grab my things and go back tonight."

"I can't blame you," I say. "So, where is home to you?"

"Winter Park," he says.

I smile. It's not that far away. About an hour's drive. Maybe I could see him again. I don't know if he wants to, though. Maybe I am connected to too many bad memories. I can't blame him if he wants to just forget everything about me.

"Can I see you again?" he asks. "I know it's odd. I know I should be thinking about getting as far away as possible and putting all this behind me, but there is something about you that makes me feel peaceful. At ease. You make me happy. I hate to turn my back on that."

I smile, lean over, and kiss him. "You have my number," I whisper.

PART III

THE BOY CARRIES THE ANSWER

68

FEBRUARY 2016

"CLOSE YOUR EYES."

I roll my dad in his wheelchair down 7th Street towards the beach. I have found a chair for him that fits his needs, and even supports his head when he gets tired of holding it himself. It has extra big wheels, so it can go through sand. It cost a fortune, but is so worth it. The past few weeks, I have been walking with him on the beach every morning, letting him finally get outside. It has changed everything for him to feel the ocean breeze on his face again.

Today is a special day. Today we're not going to the beach.

"Keep them closed, Dad. No peeking."

"I'm not," he argues.

"Good."

I push him towards the driveway of my childhood home and into the lot. The tiles are brand new and make it look stunning.

"Now you can open them," I say, and stop.

I watch his face as he sees the house for the first time. He is visibly moved.

"It's done," I say. "The workers finished yesterday, and today we can move in."

"Wow," he mutters. "It's even better than the old house."

"It has a lot of new features," I say. "To make it easier for you to get around. It has everything. A lift on the stairs to elevate you in your chair to the second floor. A lift in the bedroom to help you get into bed. Everything you'll need to make this your home again. And mine."

"So, you're coming with me?" he asks.

"Of course I am. Someone has to make sure you don't get yourself into trouble, right? Salter and I will be there."

"And Snowflake?"

"Snowflake too."

"Good. I've really grown to like that dog. He keeps me company when I feel alone."

"That's what he does," I say. "Do you want to see the inside?"

"Sure. But tell me first. What about Joey?"

"Joey has his own place. You know we haven't been doing very well lately. Besides, I am seeing someone else now."

"I don't care much for that Steven guy," my dad says. "Forgive Joey and have him...move in with us. It's best for...Salter and...for the dog. Snowflake will be miserable...without Bonnie and Clyde. Mostly...Bonnie, I believe."

"We'll visit," I say, closing the discussion.

I take my dad through the house and show him how everything works. He is truly impressed and very moved. But something is off. He is not as happy as I had expected him to be.

I roll him outside in the backyard leading to the ocean. I stop his chair on the big wooden porch and he closes his eyes and breathes in the air.

"Now you can get the air you love so much every day," I say. "Isn't it wonderful? Aren't you pleased?"

He opens his eyes and looks at me. I detect a deep sadness in them, and I wonder if all this reminds him too much about his former life with Laura here or about the fire that left him paralyzed.

"It is all very, very nice...and perfect," he says.

"But...?"

"But I...really like living...at Joey's. I like...the life with all the animals... and having my family...close to me. I am afraid...I'll be lonely here...in this big house."

"You're kidding me, right?"

"I'm sorry," he says and looks away. "I am being...ungrateful."

I sigh. "No. No of course not, but living at Joey's house was temporary. You knew that. It's too small for all of us. We have kind of overstayed our welcome there. It's time we all move on."

He nods. "I know. I know. It's just...well I liked living...this close. We'll be fine here...too. I am sure...we will."

He sends me a reassuring smile, but I am not convinced.

69

FEBRUARY 2016

MARK LOOKS at the ceiling in his room. He thinks about the many nights he has lain here worrying about his mother, wondering where she is and when she'll come home. The house is quiet. It's odd, when it has been so filled with noise for so long. Even at night there would be noises coming from all his siblings, snoring or talking in their sleep. It was never quiet.

Not like it is now. Right now, it's eerily quiet.

All three of his siblings are at their father's in Orlando. They live there now. They wanted him to move there as well, when he was allowed to leave the hospital. A nice social worker told him that it was best for all of them if he lived with his father, since his mother was in prison, charged with murder. She also told him there would be a trial and that he might be asked to testify against her, if he would agree to that?

No, he wouldn't, he told her. But she said a court might tell him he had to. Unless they believed he would suffer emotional trauma for doing so. It was up to the court to decide.

His dad came to pick him up and drove him to Orlando, where his siblings greeted him. It was when looking into their eyes he knew he had to leave again as soon as possible. Especially Tim, the youngest, had changed a lot already. In their room, later at night, he showed him his back, and Rose and Tammy both told him how their father had beat them as well. Mark could feel the anger rise in him as they told him everything, and at night, he decided to leave. Not that he felt good about his decision, no he didn't. He hated having to leave them there with that monster, but if he stayed, he knew his dad would eventually break him as he had done to the others, and then he would be of no help to his siblings. It was his job to protect them, and he would do a better job if he were on the outside of it.

He just hasn't figured out how, yet.

Mark hitched back to Cocoa Beach. Hoping to find Harry in the house and ask for his help. He was disappointed—yet not surprised—to find it empty. He moved in and started going from door to door asking for work. He could do anything, he told them. Yard work, repairing garage doors, tree trimming, plucking mangoes, anything they needed. So far, it has kept him fed.

Twice the lady from DCF has been at the door to the house and knocked, flanked by officers from Cocoa Beach Police, probably looking for him, but he has managed to hide when they came inside. No one knows the house like Mark. He has his hiding spots in the small attic where they would never think of looking for him.

Today, Mark is planning to go down to the beach and ask tourists if they want a surf lesson. It's been the easiest way to make a little extra lately. Using his mother's surfboard, he gets thirty dollars an hour for pushing in the little children and teaching them to get up on the board. It's, by far, his favorite way of making a living.

Every now and then, he runs into some of his friends from school, but he doesn't tell them where he is living. He just tells them that he moved to another school. Sometimes, he can tell in their eyes that they know his story, that they have heard about his murderous crazy mother, who killed all those people and shot him as well. He loathes those pitiful looks.

They have shut off the water and electricity to the house, but Mark manages without. He goes in the ocean every morning and showers at the beach. There's even a restroom he can use when he needs to do more than pee. Electricity, he doesn't need much of yet. He eats mostly bread or dry cereal straight out of the box. It isn't very hot out yet, so he doesn't need AC either, but he knows it won't be long before he will.

He often wonders how long he can stay where he is and hopes desperately to soon be able to find a way out. He keeps thinking about his mother. He hasn't been able to go visit her in prison. He doesn't dare to. He knows she is waiting for her trial, that they're certain she killed a lot of people. He doesn't believe them. Yes, she shot at him that night when he came home, but that was in self-defense.

Mark can't stop thinking about her and how bad she must be feeling, trapped in an awful place like that. She is so fragile. Being in there is bound to kill her.

You have to do something, Mark. And you know what it is. You have to do it. Even though it is painful. There is no way back now.

70

FEBRUARY 2007

KRISTIN MARTIN'S hand is shaking as she grabs onto Peter's elbow. She has done it a thousand times before, but this time, the outcome is going to determine the course of the rest of her life.

Daniel can see on her face that she is afraid. Everyone in the courtroom is watching her, holding their breaths, as Daniel steps forward. He approaches Peter in the wheelchair and his eyes meet Kristin's shortly before he stops and looks at his brother. The plan is for him to ask a series of questions about a subject that Kristin has no knowledge of, something only Peter will know the answer to, if he is, in fact, as smart as Kristin claims him to be. The answer will hopefully help the jury determine if he is able to communicate, if he was able to give his consent to having sex with Kristin or not.

Daniel takes in a deep breath. He looks at her as he collects himself. He doesn't really know if he wants her to succeed or not. He is unsure what he hopes will come out of this. Does he want her to go to jail? Maybe. He has been lying awake so many nights cursing her for what she did, how she tricked all of them, especially him, how she manipulated him into believing what he so desperately wanted to believe. But seeing what he saw in Peter's eyes the day before in court when he looked at Kristin, he is torn. What if? What if she is right? Would he be willing to send his brother's only love, his only voice to the world to jail? Does he have the heart to doom their baby to a life without parents?

No one will take the child. You know they won't. Heck, you've already decided not to. Jill will kill you if you do. The rest of the family will disown you.

Daniel blinks. He is the one who suggested this test. Now, he must perform it. He is unsure of why he suggested it. Was it because he thought it would save her or condemn her?

It's out of your hands, Daniel. She has to prove herself.

"Alright," the prosecutor says. "Daniel. You can ask your first question."

"Okay," Daniel says, and clears his throat. He looks at his piece of paper, at the questions that he and his siblings have made together. He is struggling to keep the paper still.

"So, tell me, Peter. When we were younger, we had a dog, a golden retriever. What was his name?"

Daniel bites his lip while waiting for the reply. He avoids looking directly at Kristin as she assists Peter when he starts to type. Instead, he focuses on Peter's fingers while he types his answers slowly, one letter at a time. The answer is read out loud by someone the court has appointed. Daniel is holding his breath.

"Charlie," the woman yells. "It says Charlie."

Daniel lets out a breath of relief. "The answer is correct," he says.

"You may ask your next question now," the prosecutor says.

Daniel looks down at his paper again, then back up at Peter, whose eyes are on the ground. All this commotion is a lot for him to take.

"So, Peter, tell me, how old was Charlie when he died?"

They wait a shorter time for the answer this time.

"Five," the lady yells.

Another correct answer.

"Tell me, who is Jimmy?"

The answer comes even quicker this time.

"My favorite uncle."

Yet another correct answer.

"Who is Sigetty?"

There's a long pause before Peter writes his answer. It is read out loud. The court-lady's voice is shrill.

"My nephew."

Daniel looks at Kristin and freezes.

"Is the answer correct, Daniel?" The prosecutor asks.

Daniel shakes his head. "No."

"Let the court know that the answer is wrong," the prosecutor says. "Sigetty is another name for Peter's uncle; it's his middle name."

Maybe Peter didn't know? Daniel asks himself and gets himself ready for the next question.

"What is the frog?"

The answer arrives quickly and is read out loud.

"Our old car."

Daniel finally dares to look at Kristin. There is no way she could have known that. It is the name they gave the car when they were children because it was green like a frog. The fact that the answer is correct fills him with joy. Daniel realizes he wants Kristin to succeed. He wants them to be in love. He wants her to be right when she says she didn't do anything to Peter that he didn't agree to himself. But he is afraid that he is the only one in his family thinking this way.

"The answer is correct," he says.

The sound of surprise goes through the rows of spectators that have grown day by day as the trial has been going on. Most are journalists covering the bizarre case, but a lot of activists are occupying the seats as well, yelling every now and then for Kristin Martin to hang in there.

"Alright. Last question," the prosecutor says.

Daniel's palms are sweating and he wipes them on his trousers. The next question is the hardest one to answer. This next one, she has no way of knowing.

"I showed Peter something in the waiting room this morning before we came in here. What was it?"

The silence is devastating. Daniel looks at Kristin; their eyes meet, and he can tell she is scared. Even more than earlier.

Please be the correct answer. Please be correct for all of us. For Peter's sake. Please be correct.

The answer comes slowly, a lot slower than the others. It seems as if Peter is struggling to find the keys to press. Daniel wonders if he is too tired, if it's all a little too much for him.

The answer finally arrives and is read out loud.

"An old photo of our grandfather."

The judge looks at Daniel. "Is that correct?"

Daniel drops the paper to the ground. No one was in the waiting room with them when he showed the picture. There is no way Kristin Martin could have fabricated that.

"Yes. Yes, Your Honor. It's correct."

71

FEBRUARY 2016

I INVITE the entire crew over for a barbecue as soon as we're settled in the house. They all arrive late in the afternoon, and we hang out on the porch, eating burgers and drinking beer. It's a nice warm night out, and we decide to have a bonfire and make S'mores for the kids.

Sandra is there with Ryan, and I observe her and am not surprised to notice how she constantly looks at Alex. He glances at her constantly as well, even though he sits with his wife, Maria. Their daughter Ava hangs out with Salter down by the beach. They seem to have become quite good friends. I feel like we're walking on a volcano about to erupt with this. I am afraid what it might do to the group once their affair is found out. I am still angry with them for acting like this, for their betrayal, but what can I do? I have told them how I feel about it, still they do it anyway. I tell myself they're grown-ups and make their own choices. Even if I don't believe they're being very mature about their decisions.

It has seemed to help Sandra get back some of her confidence, though. She seems happier and stronger, even though Ryan doesn't pay any attention to her at all. He is deeply engaged in talking to Chloe. He is visibly flirting with her, and it makes me feel sick. Chloe seems to mostly think of him as very annoying. She has to be the pickiest person I have met when it comes to guys. Come to think of it, she hasn't had many boyfriends over the years. I know she was into my brother for a little while, until he showed his true colors, but that is all I have heard of. I wonder if she is ever lonely or sad with the way her life has turned out. She never shows me if she is.

"So, is Joey coming later?" Danny asks me. He is wearing a T-shirt that says *Cocoa Beach Fire Department*. I don't know anyone who is as proud of his job as Danny. It's kind of sweet.

"I don't know," I say. "I invited him, but I don't think he really wants to hang out with me lately."

"What happened with you two anyway? I thought you had figured things out? It seemed like you were doing good again."

I sip my beer and look at him. "It didn't work out. You know how it is. Sometimes it lasts, sometimes it hurts instead."

"That sounds like an Adele song," he says.

"I think it actually is a line from one of her songs," I say, laughing.

He shrugs. "I guess we just have to accept the fact that you're not getting back together, then. I am sad for you two, though. It's hard to understand. You always were so perfect together."

"Apparently, not perfect enough."

Danny nods and drinks his beer.

"What about you?" I ask. "Are you soon ready to move on?"

"I guess. It's been four months since she died. Maybe I should get back out there? I just really don't want to get onto that train, you know, going on internet-dates and all that. It has all changed so much since we were young. I don't think I can be a part of that. I tried that Tinder-thing but...it's just not me. It makes me feel so old."

"Maybe there is another way," I say.

"I heard you were seeing someone? That guy that lived at Marcia's house?"

"Yeah. We've been on a couple of dates. We've been down to Heidi's Jazz house a couple of nights and heard some great music. It's kind of become our favorite place to go together. But it's still very new."

"But, you like this guy?"

I sip the beer and nod. "Yeah. I think I do. It's just hard with Salter and Joey and everything. It's kind of hard for me to let go of the feeling that we're not going to be the happy family that I always believed in."

I look at my dad, who is sitting on the other side of Sandra. They're both laughing. I smile, thinking how great it is for my dad to be able to be with people again, to get out of his room. His physical therapy is going well, his trainer says, and he has now regained some movement in several of his fingers. That is great news, since the trainer says that if he can get some parts of his body back, then there might be a chance he can get others as well. It gives us hope.

"I miss Marcia," Danny says, and puts his feet up on the chair next to him. "You can say a lot of things about Marcia, but she sure knew how to get a party going." He chuckles lightly, then his eyes turn sad.

I know how he feels. I miss her too. Now that we're all gathered—well almost all of us—she is kind of missing. Her loud laughter, her inappropriate remarks, her getting too drunk after a few hours, her dancing and telling us we're getting old and boring. I even miss her loud music that she always somehow puts on when we reach a certain point in the evening.

"How is she, by the way?" he asks.

"I don't know."

"Have you visited her?"

I am ashamed to say I haven't. I shake my head.

"You?"

"Nope. I don't think any of us have. I feel awful. What kind of friends are we anyway?"

"I don't know," I say. "It's not that easy. I wouldn't know what to say to her. I mean, she killed a lot of people. I saw the look in her eyes when she was walking towards that girl, a young girl about Salter's age. I can't...I don't know if I can forgive and forget that easy. Especially now that I'm with Steven. I know she is sick and all, but what do you say to her? I will never be able to understand."

"Maybe we don't have to forgive and forget," Danny says. "Maybe we should just show her compassion. Show her we still love her."

I nod. He is right. Not a day goes by without me thinking about her almost every hour of the day. I feel awful that she is sitting in that prison waiting for her trial to start. I just hope she gets the help she needs. "I think you're right," I say. "Maybe you and I should go visit her someday soon?"

"I think I would like that."

"Is this supposed to be a party?!"

I turn and look at Joey, who is stepping onto the porch. I feel a pinch in my heart. I am so glad to see him. I really wanted him to come. I smile, but in the next second my smile completely freezes, when someone else steps onto the porch as well, holding Joey's hand.

"I want you to meet someone," he says. "Everyone, this is Jackie. Jackie, this is the Crew."

72

FEBRUARY 2016

DANNY GETS UP IMMEDIATELY and walks to Joey.

"Come on, man," he says. "You bring her to your ex's party?" he asks. "Not cool, Joey. Not cool."

Joey stares me down, his tongue rolling inside of his cheek. "What are you talking about? She's my girlfriend. I can't bring my girlfriend to a party now?"

"Come on, man," Danny says. "You two barely just split up. Your son is here too. Do you really want him to see this?"

"Well, she's seeing someone; why can't I?"

"She didn't bring him here, today, did she?" Danny asks.

Joey shrugs. "So what?"

Danny sighs. "You're drunk, Joey. Go home."

"No way! I'm here to be with my friends and hang out with my girl-friend; now, if you'll excuse me, I want to go mingle. Come, Jackie."

Joey walks and his shoulder pushes Danny's as he passes him. My stomach is in a knot. I walk over to Danny.

"Idiot," he mumbles.

"It's okay," I say. "But, hey. Thanks for standing up for me like that. That was very gentlemanly."

"I can't believe he would bring a date," he says.

"I can't believe he would bring *her*," I say.

"What do you mean?" Danny asks, and looks into my eyes.

"It's nothing." I shake my head and try to avoid looking at him. I don't want to tell them the story. Joey is their friend too, and I don't want to sew bad blood. It's the same with Salter. I haven't told him what happened, since I don't want him to hate his father. Instead, he hates me for leaving his dad, but I'd rather have that. His father is important for him. He's the role model.

"I know that look. It's not nothing. I know he cheated on you in New York...oh no, he cheated on you with her, down here? Ah, that makes so much sense. That's why you broke up again."

"I really can't hide anything from you, huh?"

"You shouldn't have to," Danny says. "That's what friends are for, right? If you can't tell me stuff like this, then where are we?"

Wow. I knew Danny was a good friend, but I had no idea he would back me up like this.

"Thanks," I say, and finish my beer. I glance at Joey, who is talking very loud and entertaining the others with how fast he can drink a beer. He suddenly seems like he is a teenager again.

"You want to see, huh? I bet Jackie would like to see it, wouldn't you, Jackie?" he says and grabs a new beer. "Now, time me."

He places the beer to his lips and starts to drink. I've had enough. I walk to my dad and look at him. "You ready for bed?"

"Yes," he says with a deep groan. It has become easier for him to speak. He doesn't have to stop as much to catch his breath or to focus on the words as he did earlier, but it still tires him. "It was very nice...talking to you, Sandra, but now...I'll leave. The night belongs to the young.Goodnight, my...dear."

"Goodnight Mr. Mills," Sandra says with a chuckle.

I help my dad get back to his room and into bed. I cover him up and brush his teeth, then kiss his forehead. "Thank you...for a wonderful evening," he says. "Don't let Joey get to you. He just...misses you."

"I won't, Dad. It only makes me realize it really is time to move on."

FEBRUARY 2016

"WE'LL NEED you to testify against her."

It's Monday and Detective Brown has asked me to come in to the Sherriff's office in Rockledge. I have been there several times since the incident in Melbourne. It hasn't stopped being painful yet.

"You're kidding me, right?" I say. "You have everything I told you in your files; can't you just use that?"

He shakes his head. "The thing is, we can't get a valid testimony from Marcia Little. She says one thing one day then something completely different on another. One day she tells us she is guilty, then she withdraws it the next. I need your statement."

"How about the woman?" I asked.

"She hasn't woken up yet," he says.

I suck in my breath. "Still?"

He shakes his head. "They don't know if she ever will. Her brain was deprived of oxygen for a very long time."

"So she was strangled and not shot?"

"We believe there was a fight between the two of them. Then Marcia Little tried to strangle her."

"What about the girl?" I ask, thinking it's odd that they would fight when Marcia had a gun and could easily have shot her. She had the gun in her hand when I saw her through the window. Why would she try to strangle the woman?

He shakes his head again. I can tell he is troubled by this case as well.

"She hasn't spoken to anyone since it happened. She is in such deep shock that she refuses to speak. We've tried everything. Every time we approach her with our questions, she breaks down in a severe asthma attack and needs medical attention. Her child psychologist tells us it might take a very long time before she'll be able to talk again. So far, she stays in the hospital as close to her mother as possible. They can't get her to leave her mother's bedside."

"I can't say I blame her," I say.

"But now, you might also be able to understand that, so far, all we have are yours and Steven Elingston's testimonies. You both saw Marcia there."

I stare into the eyes of Detective Brown. I don't know what to say to him. I really, really don't want to have to testify against my friend. At the same time, I want justice to be served for Steven and his family, especially the poor kid sitting in the hospital right now by her mother's bedside. It breaks my heart.

"We know her attorney will plead for insanity, so with your testimony, she will be committed to a psychiatric facility for an indeterminate period."

"So, you'll basically lock her away in a mental institution for the rest of her life," I say, swallowing hard.

"She did kill a lot of people, Mary."

I rub my forehead. I feel awful. This entire thing makes me feel like the worst person on the planet. But what are my choices? Either I say no to testifying and Steven gets no closure and he'll hate my guts, or I say yes and I am the reason my friend will be locked up for life. I know it's the right thing to say yes, but I don't feel good doing it.

"Alright," I say. "I'll testify."

"Perfect. We'll be in touch with the details." He gets up and reaches out his hand. "Thank you."

I shake my head and press back my tears. "Please don't thank me."

74

FEBRUARY 2007

ON THE MORNING of the verdict, they all hold their breaths in the courtroom as they wait for the jury to decide. Daniel can't stop looking at Kristin, while she is sitting at the table with her attorney waiting for her fate to be decided. Peter is still there as well, sitting in his wheelchair next to Daniel, seemingly indifferent to what is going on around him.

Suddenly, the red light flickers in the courtroom, signaling a verdict has been reached. Daniel looks at Kristin, who lifts her head and looks at the light as well. He wonders what is going on inside of her right now. He can't imagine how scared she must be.

Daniel sees her as she glances into the crowd and finds her mother's eyes; Kristen's mother is holding hands with Kristin's father. They have been present for all the days of the trial, supporting their daughter through it all.

During the past many weeks, they heard testimonies from expert after expert witnessing about the keyboard treatment and whether it worked or not. They heard as many opinions as there were experts. It painted the clear picture that there still is a lot of controversy about the type of treatment, the judge concluded.

The jury enters the room, one after another in a long line. Daniel looks at their faces, wondering if he can somehow read their verdict from their facial expressions. But he can't. They wear the same emotionless expression they have throughout the entire trial.

"Has the jury reached a verdict?" the judge asks.

"We have, Your Honor."

Daniel's heart is pounding loudly in his chest as they read it out loud. He can barely hear the words as they fall. The room starts to spin; his beating heart drowns the voices out.

Guilty? Did they say guilty? It can't be!

A roar of chaos goes through the courtroom. Voices, some are clapping others disagreeing. Daniel stares at Kristin, who collapses onto the defense table in loud convulsive sobs.

Daniel feels the panic spread in his body as another loud roar fills the air. Daniel turns to look at Peter, who yells at the top of his lungs. The sounds are strange and make no sense; his arms are in severe spasms, hitting his face again and again, causing his nose to start bleeding.

Daniel and his siblings jump to help Peter and hold down his hands. "We have to get him out of here," his older brother Jack says. "Before he hurts himself."

Andrew jumps for help as well, and together, they get their younger brother out of the courtroom.

"What the heck happened in there?" Daniel asks, when they get outside. Peter is still groaning loudly and they have to strap his hands down when they put him in the minivan.

"What do you mean?" Andrew asks, and shuts the door on the screaming Peter. "We won."

"Won? But...but the test. She passed the test. She got all the questions right," he says. "Peter knew about the photo. Only he could have known."

"That might be," Jack says, as Shannon joins them outside. She lights up a cigarette. The only one in the family that smokes.

"I'd say she was lucky," he continues. "She guessed it somehow."

"Plus there was the one question she didn't answer," Shannon says, blowing out smoke. As usual, Daniel's older brother by seven years, Steven, keeps his distance. He hasn't talked much to them during the trial.

"But that was one Peter could easily not have known. The rest she passed," Daniel continues. "The rest were correct. Even the one with the photo. How can they say she is guilty?"

Jack places a hand on Daniel's shoulder.

"There is nothing we can do, Daniel. The jury has spoken. She got what she deserved. This is what we wanted, remember? Now, let it go."

"What about the baby? What's going to happen to the baby?" Daniel asks, while Jack and Andrew get in the car. Andrew stops halfway and looks at him.

"You take it, if you're so eager to save it."

75

FEBRUARY 2016

STEVEN and I go to Heidi's Friday night and listen to some jazz singer from upstate. She is wonderful and I buy her CD afterwards, even though I don't have a CD player. I just feel so bad for her, since she is so talented, and I know they don't make any money in that business.

We walk home along A1A, holding hands, enjoying the nice evening air. I like February in Florida. Well, I guess I love every month here, since the weather is always so nice.

"That was a great performance tonight," Steven says. "I'm beginning to see why you love this place so much."

"It is my favorite," I say. "What's not to like? The food is great, the music awesome, and the company enjoyable."

Steven chuckles. "So, how's Dad doing?"

Steven has met my father twice and knows all about his story, but so far, my dad hasn't been very welcoming to him. He seems to still be quite hung up on Joey and wants us to figure out our differences. I try to explain to him that it is definitely over, now that he showed up with that bimbo to my house. He kind of put the nails in that coffin himself. But my dad won't accept it. I tell Steven he'll come around in time.

"Better," I say. "He's regained the use of four fingers in total now, so that gives us some hope."

"That's amazing."

"I know."

We walk in silence the rest of the way and stop in front of my dad's new house. We've reached that awkward point we always do when we have to either say goodbye or move to the next level. I know I want to, but I don't know if it's too early still. Will I ever be ready? Will he grow tired of me before I do get ready?

"So...this is me," I say. I feel bad for not inviting him inside, since he has to go all the way back to Winter Park.

"I know it's you," he says, as he leans over and kisses me. He looks me in the eyes when our lips part. He has gorgeous eyes. Just him looking at me makes my heart race. I realize I really want to be with him. I really want to go all the way with him.

"So..." he says.

"Do you want to come in?" I ask. "Salter is at his dad's."

"I thought you'd never ask."

I laugh and kiss him back. His lips are tender. I like that about him. There really isn't anything I don't like about him.

"Then come."

He follows me towards the front door, and I look for my keys, when suddenly I see something. A figure in the darkness, moving. My first thought is that it's an animal, but as it approaches, I realize it's not. It's human. It's a young boy.

It's Mark.

I walk towards him. "Mark? What are you doing here?"

He looks awful. He has always been on the skinny side, but this is ridiculous. "Who is it, Mary?" Steven asks.

"It's...it's Mark." I say, fearing his anger, knowing how much he hates Marcia right now. Mark doesn't seem to notice Steven. He is staring only at me.

"Mary," he says. "I need your help."

76

FEBRUARY 2016

"WHAT'S GOING ON, MARK?"

I put a cup of hot chocolate on the table in front of him. I spray some whipped cream in both his cup and mine.

Mark smiles with caution as he looks at the cup. This was what he wanted when I asked him what I could make for him. I was thinking more in terms of a meal or something, but if this is what he needs right now, than that is what he is getting.

"Don't think I've had hot chocolate since I was a kid," he says, with longing in his voice.

"You're still a kid," I say.

"Been awhile since I felt like one."

I sit next to him and sip my hot chocolate. I am glad that Steven decided to go back to Winter Park when I told him I had to help the boy. He seemed a little annoyed, but he'll have to live with it, I think. Right now, Mark is more important.

I exhale and look at the boy. "I know. Things must have been really bad for you, huh?"

He shrugs and looks away. "I'm fine."

"So, tell me, why aren't you at your dad's in Orlando like the rest of your brothers and your sister?"

"I ran away," he says.

"I kind of figured that part out. But why? Is it that bad there?"

Mark looks into my eyes. He reminds me of a scared bird. He doesn't answer my question. He doesn't have to. I put my hand on top of his and we drink our chocolate in silence for a little while. I know he is eager to talk to me, but it seems like he needs a little more time to get the words right. I wait patiently, even though it's getting late.

"I have to get her out of there," he says.

"Who are we talking about now? Your sister?"

He shakes his head. "Mom."

I take in a deep breath, thinking about Marcia. I know how he must feel. At least I think I do. "There really isn't much we can do," I say.

Mark slams his fist on the table. I jump.

"Yes, there is."

"What do you mean? I saw her, Mark. She was there. She shot that poor man. She told me she killed those people back six years ago. She told me she remembered what they wore, what they looked like when they were killed. I am sorry, Mark, but she is ill, and if she is convicted, then hopefully she'll get help."

"No. They'll just lock her away for life. I know how these things work," he says intensely. "She'll never get out of there again."

"But, sweetie. Maybe that's for the best. That way, she won't hurt anyone else. Out here, she is a danger to people. I know it must be hard to understand and difficult to accept that your own mother..."

He slams his fist onto the table once again. "No!"

I lean over and place my hand on his shoulder. "Mark..."

He pulls away from me and stands to his feet. He points at me and looks into my eyes while he speaks. "My mother is no killer. She might have shot at me, but that was in self-defense. She is not a ruthless killer. I know she isn't."

I stare at the young man in front of me. He suddenly seems so adult, so grown; I can no longer see him as just a child.

"You know something, don't you?" I ask.

He freezes, and then sits in his chair again. He looks down, then up at me before he finally nods.

I lean back, and then drink another sip of the chocolate, thinking I need to listen to what he has to say. I can tell by the look in his eyes that he is not just making this up. This is serious and it is eating at him.

"Tell me everything," I say. "You can trust me. You know that, right?"

It takes a while before he answers.

"I know my mom trusted you. So, I guess I can as well."

77

FEBRUARY 2016

"I HAVE NEVER TOLD this to anyone."

I find some Oreos and marshmallows to go with the hot chocolate, while Mark finds the strength to tell me what he knows. I can tell it is very difficult for him.

"I won't tell anyone either unless I have your permission," I say. "That's my promise to you. Cross my heart."

Mark nods. His eyes hit the edge of the table. I am bracing myself for what is about to come.

"I saw something," he says and looks at me again.

"What did you see?"

"On the night the woman was murdered, that teacher."

"Shannon Ferguson?"

"Yes. I saw her. Down by the river."

"You saw her?"

"Yes. I was actually looking for my sister."

"Rose?"

He nods. "I had realized she had started sneaking out at night, so I wanted to follow her and see what she was up to. I spotted her walking down Minutemen Causeway wearing a miniskirt, and I followed her on my bike. I wanted to stop her and tell her to go back, tell her it was a school night and no twelve-year-old should be out on a school night. But before I could get to her, a car stopped and she was picked up. Terrified, I followed them to the other side of the river bank, where the car stopped."

Mark stops and looks down. He shakes his head.

I grab the pack of Oreos and eat three in a row. "What did you see, Mark? Tell me."

"I saw her get dropped from the bridge. It was a full moon, so it was easy to see. I spotted the truck stop on top of the bridge, then someone got out, pulled out the body, and let it fall from the bridge I still remember the plump sound when it landed in the water."

"And you're certain it was Shannon Ferguson's body?" I ask.

"Yes. I was close to the bridge and it soon drifted towards me. I could see her face in the water. I know her."

"How do you know her, Mark?"

He looks me in the eyes. "She used to be my teacher in third grade. Her hair was shorter now, but she still looks the same."

I grab yet another Oreo, while digesting this news. "Oh, my God, Mark. Did you see who dropped her off the bridge then?"

He nods. "Yes. I didn't see the face, but it wasn't my mother. I would recognize my mother anywhere. Besides, this person drove away in a car, a dark pick-up truck. My mom doesn't even have a car. She has no license, remember?"

"She could have stolen one," I argue. "But you're certain it wasn't her?"

He nods again. "This person was tall. My mom isn't tall."

"But it was a woman?"

"I couldn't tell."

"Did you call the police?"

Mark looks into my eyes, then down at the table.

"I'm guessing you didn't," I say.

"How could I?" Mark is crying now. "My sister...Rose was in that awful car...with that awful man who was...doing things to her...and I was just standing there. If I told the police, they would take her away from me. They would ask me what I was doing there and they would know that she was selling herself to men like that. Her life would be ruined. They would know...they would know that things weren't the way they're supposed to be with my mother, with us."

"But this information might have helped your mother?" I say. "I mean, when she was arrested? She is being charged with the murder of Shannon Ferguson."

"I know she would rather go to jail herself than have her daughter taken away. Besides, who would ever believe me? She's my mom. I am supposed to try and protect her."

The kid was right. As an eyewitness, he wouldn't stand in court. But it gave me a new perspective on things. This news forced me to re-think everything I thought I knew about Marcia's case.

78

FEBRUARY 2016

I MAKE the bed in the guestroom and let Mark sleep there while I pace up and down the kitchen floor. I feel awful, confused, estranged even. What the heck is going on here? If Marcia didn't dump the body of Shannon Ferguson, then who did? And did that person also kill her? Could Mark have seen wrong? Wouldn't he be able to recognize his own mother? You'd think so.

Could he be lying?

While eating Oreos straight from the box, I sit by the computer and start researching whatever has been written about the case in the media. Scrolling through one story after another, I soon learn everything about this Shannon Ferguson that is known to the public. Nowhere does it say if she was thrown from a bridge or not. Only that she was found by someone fishing at the river one morning, a tourist hoping to catch some early fish before the sun came up. He had seen her floating towards him and wondered at first if it was a manatee.

How does Mark know the body was dumped from the bridge? Could he be speculating? Making things up? But why would he? To protect his mother? Wouldn't he have gone to the police with his information then? And why add the story about his sister to it? It didn't sound like something a fourteen-year-old would come up with.

What if he is right? What if Marcia didn't do it?

I shake my head slowly and walk to the kitchen to find a bag of chips that I bring back to the computer. I wonder if I should call Steven and tell him this. I feel like I need to share this with someone, but I am not sure Steven will take this well. He is so convinced Marcia killed her and his other siblings. But no one ever managed to answer the question why? Why would she target his family and kill them like this? They haven't even managed to establish any connection between them; they have no idea how she even knows them.

Who is that person on the bridge?

I keep imagining the figure standing up there, looking down, as the body plunges into the water beneath. It was a tall person, Mark said. It's not much to go on.

I stare at the screen, where a picture of a younger Shannon Ferguson, taken from when she was hired at Roosevelt Elementary School, fills the screen. The article speculates about who would hold a grudge against a very loved teacher in our local community. It also tells that she was stabbed thirteen times in her chest before she was dumped in the water. Forensics reports show she was still alive. Water in her lungs proves she was still breathing, and the cause of death was, therefore, drowning.

A chill goes through my body and I lean back with a sigh when my phone suddenly rings. I look at the display and realize it can only be the only other person awake at this hour around here.

Chloe.

"There is something we need to talk about," she says.

I chuckle, noticing that she brings no excuses for the late call. She never does. To her, this is the normal time to be awake.

"Sure. I'm up anyway," I say.

"I'm coming over."

Less than a minute later, she is in the kitchen of my dad's house. I make some coffee for the both of us. It's almost three o'clock anyway, and I have realized I'm not going to get any sleep tonight anyway, so I might as well stay up.

"So, what's up?" I ask, and serve her the coffee.

She has a very serious look in her eyes as she speaks. "Something is wrong. Something is very wrong."

"Okay? What are we talking about here?"

"Marcia. I took another look at her case. I simply can't believe she would do such terrible acts. I went through her case file and found this." Chloe puts a piece of paper in front of me.

"It's from the forensics report," she says. "Ballistics. From the Elingston house. The second one. Look at the results."

I look down at the paper, then back up at Chloe.

"They don't match," she says. "The bullet that killed Andrew Elingston didn't belong to the gun they found in the house. It didn't belong to Marcia's gun."

79

APRIL 2007

"HE'S IN HERE."

The nurse walking ahead of Daniel stops in front of a closed door and turns to look at him. "I have to admit, he has not been the easiest among our patients. He has caused us quite a lot of trouble."

"Peter? He's the easiest in the world," Daniel says, startled. "He's the gentlest human being on this planet."

The nurse snorts. "Well, we haven't seen much of that since he got here."

Daniel can't believe what he is hearing. It was Shannon who called the day before and told him that they had called—again—from the home where Peter lived since their mother died and since the trial ended, and told her that Peter was causing trouble there, asking them to come and visit him.

Daniel has been there a couple of times before, but work and family have been taking up a lot of time lately, and the visits have been further apart than when he lived at the house.

Maybe it is just a bad excuse for not coming because Daniel can't stand the place, can't stand to see his brother in a place like this.

But his siblings all think it is a great idea. They found the most expensive home with the best care, they say.

"He's going to love it there," Jack argued when Daniel objected and asked if there really wasn't any of them who could take Peter in. "There's going to be a lot of other people who are just like him. He's going to have a blast."

A blast is very far from what Daniel is looking at now that the nurse is opening the door to the room with the words:

"We had to strap him down."

Daniel stares at his brother lying motionless, arms and legs strapped to the bed. He has to calm himself down to not say something he might regret later on.

"Strap him down? But...why?"

"He was hurting himself and everyone else trying to help him. He smacked one of the nurses in the face and gave her a bruise. We really can't have that. It was for the good of everybody."

Daniel takes a couple of angry steps towards his brother. His wrists are bruised from trying to get loose. He is lying completely still now. Doesn't even react when Daniel approaches him. Usually, he chirps when he sees Daniel. Chirps with excitement. But not today. He is not even screaming like he usually does when he is upset or angry.

Daniel waves a hand in front of his face, but his eyes don't even blink. Daniel is shocked by this lethargy from his usually so lively brother.

"What happened to him?"

"We had to give him something to calm him down," the nurse says.

"Drugs? You gave my brother drugs?"

"He was hurting himself. And constantly gnawing at his hands. Look at them. Those sores won't heal if he continues to chew them."

"He only chews them when he is upset."

"That might be, but he has been doing it excessively since he got here. We had to do something. The wild movements with his arms are so uncontrolled we never know when he'll hit someone."

"But that's his disease, for crying out loud," Daniel says. "He can't control his muscles and movements."

The nurse sighs. "I know. But what do you want us to do? We have to wash him. We have to feed him. We can't do that if he is constantly moving. The doctor recommended it."

"I would like to be alone with him, if I may," Daniel says, struggling hard to keep his cool.

"Very well. I have places to be too," the nurse says and leaves the room.

Daniel sits next to the bed. He reaches out and grabs Peter's hand in his, something he can usually never do, since he rarely stays still. Daniel tries to get eye contact with his brother, but Peter's eyes stare eerily into the ceiling; they don't move, they hardly blink.

It's like he's not even alive anymore.

Daniel strokes his brother's hand several times, while tears leave his eyes, thinking about how alive Peter used to be when he was at the university or when debating with his classmates after class. How vibrant he used to be when working with Kristin and discovering new things with her. Daniel tries not to, but he feels so guilty for having deprived his brother of that world. No matter if she manipulated his words, it was still better than this. Wasn't it?

Now Kristin was in jail, and so was Peter.

"I am sorry, brother. You have no idea how sorry I am," he whispers.

80

FEBRUARY 2016

"THEY NEVER TOLD YOU THIS, did they?"

Chloe leans back in her chair and looks at me, her arms crossed over her chest. "The police never told you that the bullets didn't match the gun."

I shake my head pensively. "No."

"They conveniently left that out," Chloe says.

"What do you mean?" I swallow another Oreo and wonder if I'll get sick if I eat any more. Probably. They do a great job of keeping me awake, though.

"They didn't tell you because then maybe you wouldn't agree to be a witness for them. But that is also why they so desperately need you. Without yours and Steven's testimony, they have nothing. If they can't match the murder weapon with her, they don't have much to go on."

"More like *nothing* to go on," I say.

This puts me in a very difficult position for sure. I don't want to be the one to put the last nail in Marcia's coffin. I don't want to be the sole reason she is locked away for life. Especially not now that there is doubt about her guilt. I, for one, am not convinced anymore.

"There is something else," I say. I look at the door to the guestroom, where Mark is sleeping. At least I hope he is. He looked like he needed it badly.

"What's that?"

"Mark came here tonight. He's sleeping in the guest bedroom. He told me something that shook me deeply."

"Really?" Chloe sips her coffee and grabs some chips from the bag. I know she is used to eating at night as well. Well, to be frank, she does everything at night. She never eats much if she's awake during the day. Me, I eat both night and day if I can get away with it.

"I promised I would only tell if he agreed to it, but I think he knows he can trust you as well. He saw the body be dumped."

"What body?" Chloe asks.

"Shannon Ferguson. The teacher. He saw someone dump her from the bridge. He says it wasn't his mother, that this was someone taller."

"Why hasn't he said anything?"

"That's the thing. I can't tell you that because it'll break his heart; just trust me that he has thought about it every minute since, but he couldn't."

"Why? It could have helped his mother? At least in the case of Shannon Ferguson. I don't understand this."

I sigh. I can't betray Mark's trust and tell her everything. "He is afraid to get someone else in trouble, okay? Ask him yourself when he wakes up. I just can't tell you unless he agrees to. He trusts me."

"Okay. So you're telling me he saw someone else dump the body, not his mother? Am I getting that right?"

"Yes."

"So that is two deep inconsistencies in the case against Marcia," Chloe says. "We have to do something. We can't let them put her away with such light evidence."

"I couldn't agree more," I say. "But what? What do we do?"

Chloe looks pensive. She is biting the inside of her cheek.

"We could go to the detective with everything we know. Maybe they'll look into it," I say.

"You know as well as I do, they won't," Chloe says. "They have their killer. They believe she is guilty. Heck, she has even admitted to being guilty."

"But also pulled it back again," I say. "They can never use her testimony in court. She has no idea what she is saying."

"I know that and so do you, but they don't. I mean, who's to say when Marcia is clear minded and when she isn't. When she's confessing or when she's pulling it all back again? The bottom line is, they'll do anything to prove her guilt. They won't listen to loose allegations like these. So what if the gun wasn't a match? Maybe she had another one that she used and disposed of somehow?"

"Maybe she didn't act alone?" I say.

"What do you mean?"

"Maybe there was someone else in the house? The one who had the right gun, the same person who dumped the body from the bridge?"

Chloe looks pensive.

"But where does that leave Marcia? As an accomplice?" I continue.

"Maybe. Or just in the wrong place at the wrong time."

I exhale with a deep breath. "How do we find out?"

Chloe stands to her feet.

"I may have an idea."

81

FEBRUARY 2016

SHE IS SLEEPING when we enter the room at the hospital. No one notices us as we walk through the hallways. Everything is in night mode. There are no guards outside the door either. I wonder why. They were, after all, victims of an attempted murder. But, apparently, that didn't give you any extra protection. Probably because they believed they had their killer.

We walk slowly towards her. I remember her name is Lindsey from the police files. She is sitting in a chair next to her mother's bed, her head lying on top of her mother's stomach, her eyes closed. She is snoring lightly.

I put a hand on her shoulder while Chloe makes sure to close the door silently behind us. The girl gasps and looks up at me. Her eyes are still in the daze that is sleep and blinking as she looks at me. She gets agitated and starts wheezing.

"Don't be scared," I say. "I'm not here to hurt you."

She doesn't look like she believes me. The wheezing is getting worse. I can't blame her for being afraid. She doesn't say anything. I know she hasn't spoken at all since the attack in her home. I don't expect her to now, especially not to me, a complete stranger, who is trying to prove the innocence of the woman everyone believes killed her father and left her mother in a coma.

"I'm Mary. This is Chloe. We're just here to talk to you a little bit," I say. I smile and look at Chloe, who smiles as well. Her smile is far from comforting. I know I have to be quick before anyone finds us here.

"We're here to talk to you about the woman in your house, the one who was arrested in your house. I know it must be hard for you to talk about, and we won't ask you to. Just help us a little, okay?"

Lindsey stares at me. Her eyes are frightened. Again, I can't blame her. But then the unforeseen happens. The wheezing calms down and Lindsey nods. She doesn't speak, but just nods, agrees to us being there, while catching her breath. We find her inhalator on the end table by her mother's bed, and she takes a few deep breaths till the wheezing stops completely.

I grab my phone and find a photo of Marcia in it. I zoom it with my fingers so she can see her face up close. "This is her, right? She was in your house, right?"

Lindsey stares at it for quite a while, then up at me. I expect her to start wheezing again, but she doesn't. Instead she nods. Then she lifts her finger and points at me.

"Yes, yes I was there too. I didn't think you'd remember me. I came in just before the police arrived."

I am glad she remembers me and understand that is why she trusts me. I wonder if she trusts me enough. "I realize this must be very difficult for you, Lindsey. But we need to know what happened. We fear the police are about to make a mistake, one that will cost our friend to be locked up for life."

I show her the picture again. She smiles when she sees it and a warm feeling overwhelms me.

"Did this woman shoot your father?" I ask. "Was it her?"

Lindsey's wrinkles her forehead. Her eyes are torn in confusion. Determined, she shakes her head.

I look at Chloe behind me. "I knew it," she says. "I bet they never asked you."

I look at Lindsey again. "Then, who did shoot your dad?" I say, knowing very well she can't answer me.

Once again, Lindsey stares at me, then points at the phone in my hand. She opens her mouth and says the words I know will never leave me again.

"S-s-save."

She is struggling to get the word across her lips, and she speaks while pointing at Marcia. She starts to wheeze again and grabs her inhalator.

"Save? Marcia...Marcia saved you?" I say with cheer in my voice. She nods eagerly, while breathing through her inhalator.

"Marcia didn't hurt anyone, she tried to save you!"

Lindsey nods with big eyes.

Chloe grabs my arm. "Ballistics," she says. "Ballistics showed that

Marcia's gun had been fired. She had residue on her hands. It just didn't match the bullet that killed the father."

"She fired to stop the intruder, who had probably already killed Andrew Elingston. The question is if the intruder was hurt."

"Not enough for her to not be able to escape," Chloe says.

I look at the little girl in front of me. I get so emotional looking into her eyes. I can't believe this much bad can happen to one little girl. It's devastating. I lean over and kiss her forehead. She grabs me around the waist and holds me tight. It's the best hug I've had in many years.

82

FEBRUARY 2016

MARK IS awake when we get back to my dad's house. So is my father. While Chloe goes home to sleep and take care of her mother, I throw together some pancakes and serve them for my father and Mark. I miss Salter when I watch Mark eat. Salter is spending the entire weekend with his father. I realize I haven't thought about Steven once since last night.

While the others eat, I call him up.

"So, what was so urgent last night?" he asks.

I sigh. I don't feel like I can tell him everything, but I want to talk to him about it anyway.

"It's...we believe Marcia might be innocent," I say.

"What?" His tone is angry. Rightfully so. He doesn't know the entire story. I can't tell him what Mark has told me or what Lindsey told me. At least not yet, so I go with the evidence.

"Ballistics show that it wasn't her gun that killed your brother, Andrew. It was another gun."

"So what? She could have used two guns or something. Maybe ballistics is wrong. I know she did it, Mary. I saw her, she went for my niece with that gun. She would have shot her if we hadn't interfered. You know I am right. You saw it yourself."

I sigh. I don't expect him to understand. But I want him to trust me on this. "What if she was trying to save them instead?" I ask. "What if her gun was fired, but at the intruder instead?"

"What the heck? Are you kidding me?"

"I'm very serious, Steven. The evidence doesn't add up. I am telling you. Marcia could be innocent."

"But she's not. I know she isn't," he says. "She did it. She hasn't even tried to defend herself. If she saved them instead of killing them, then why doesn't she tell that to the police?"

"I don't know," I say. "She is sick. Maybe she doesn't remember."

"She has admitted her guilt."

"But also pulled it back."

"That doesn't make her innocent."

"Doesn't make her guilty either."

"But she is...she is guilty, Mary, and she'll be locked away. I promise you she will. I won't sit here and watch while she gets away with killing most of my family. I simply refuse to. Leave it alone, Mary. This is my battle to fight. We're finally about to get closure. Do you have any idea what it is like to not know what happened to your family? No, you don't. Because it was my family."

"I understand why you are upset but..."

"No buts. You leave this alone; you hear me?"

"Hey. Marcia is my friend," I say a lot harsher than intended. He's got me angry now. "I am not about to stand here and watch as they convict her when she is innocent. She has a life too; she has children too."

"Then I guess we don't have anything more to say to each other," he says.

Really? Wow!

"I guess not."

I hang up and realize I have burnt the last pancake beyond recognition. Mark looks at me from the table.

"Was that Harry?" he asks.

I nod and remove the burnt pancake.

"His real name is Steven," my dad says. "Apparently...he lied about it."

"Steven?" Mark asks.

"Yes," my dad says. "Doesn't sound like...he's going to come around here...again."

"That's too bad. I liked Harry, or Steven," Mark says.

I grab a pancake from the stack for myself.

"So did I."

83

FEBRUARY 2016

I MANAGE to get half an hour of sleep before the doorbell wakes me up. Outside is Danny. He is wearing another T-shirt with his department's logo on it, and it makes me chuckle. I try to hide it to not hurt him. He looks very muscular in this one.

"Are you ready?" he asks.

"For what?" I say sleepily.

"Remember?"

"No."

"We are going to see Marcia!" he says. "Don't tell me you've made other plans. I pulled some strings, you know how us guys in uniform like to help one another..."

"No, but I do love the way you always manage to remind me."

He looks at me, then shakes his head. "Anyway, I got us on the list for visiting her today. Normally, you have to apply first and all that, but..."

I smile. "You know someone who fixed that, am I right?"

"Sure did."

"That's perfect," I say, and lean over and kiss his cheek. "You have no idea how perfect it is."

Danny touches his cheek while I storm back in the house to get myself ready. I throw on a dress and brush my hair. I stop as I pass Mark on my way out. "Have you even seen her?" I ask. "Have you visited her?"

He shakes his head. "I can't. DCF is looking for me. They want me to go back to my dad's."

I nod. "Maybe we should wait a little before we take you, then," I say. "I'll make sure to give her a kiss from you. You're welcome to stay here in this house until we find a more suitable situation for you, all right? Be here when I get back."

He smiles. "Are you kidding me? You have an Xbox. I am never leaving this house again."

"That's Salter's. Be careful, it's a time consumer. Don't spend all day playing, okay?"

"No, ma'am."

I laugh and run for the door. Danny is standing in the doorway, waiting for me. "Shall we?" I say, and walk past him.

I tell him everything on the drive there. Except the part about Rose. I leave that out for Mark's sake. But Danny needs to know the details as well. He needs to know I believe Marcia could be innocent.

"I never believed she was guilty," he says. "Just couldn't get it to fit in."

"I know. You're a better man than I," I say.

"I sure hope so," he says with a laugh. "Since you're a woman and all..."

"You know what I mean. I feel so guilty for having believed she did it, for agreeing to testify against her."

"It's different for you," he says. "You were there. You saw her in that house, bent over the lifeless body of that woman."

"But you can't tell your little police-friends or anyone else in uniform," I say. "I don't trust them."

Danny looks at me like I am crazy, then shakes his head. "Nah, who am I kidding. I know you're right. This is a high-profile case and solving it is important. They won't back down now. Not when they feel like they're this close. I do know the guys at the Sherriff's office that well."

I sigh, content that Danny understands, as he drives up in front of the maximum security prison in the middle of nowhere on the road to Orlando. I remember it from just four months ago when I visited my brother in here. I swore I was never coming back to this place.

Guess that didn't work out very well for me.

84

FEBRUARY 2016

THEY BRING MARCIA IN. My heart drops as I see her on the other side of the glass. She looks confused, her eyes clouded. I feel the walls closing in on me, thinking about her being in here, thinking about how I was part of putting her here. How I believed she had done those awful things.

"Hey, Mary. And Danny. What a surprise," she says, sounding almost normal. But then she adds, while looking at me, "I thought you were in New York?"

I smile, but not because I am happy. Mostly because I feel so terrible for her. She needs help, not to be in jail. Being in here can't be helping her. It can't be good.

"How are you, Marcia?" Danny asks.

"I'm great, Danny. Thanks." Her voice is shrill. She leans over and whispers with great emphasis. "They're trying to kill me."

I chuckle, although I am not amused. I try to lock eyes with her. "Marcia. We need to talk to you. We need your help."

She looks at Danny, then back at me. "Of course. Anything for the crew. Just keep your voices down. You don't want *them* to hear."

"Of course not," I say, playing along. "We need you to remember something for us. Do you think you can do that?"

"Sure," she says, like it is the easiest thing in the world for her. I brace myself because I know her memories are all over the place.

"All right. So, we are trying to help you. Remember that, okay?"

She nods. "Okay."

"We don't believe you killed all those people."

She tilts her head slightly. "Oh. I hate to disappoint you, but I do believe I did. It was my lawyer...what's his name again? ...Anyway, he told me to pull back my confession, but I did it. I am pretty sure I did."

I lean over and look into her eyes. "Why? Why are you so certain?"

Marcia is surprised by the question. "Because I remember it. I still hear them scream sometimes."

"What are they screaming, Marcia? What exactly are they screaming?" I ask.

"Well they're screaming: *You did it, Marcia. You killed us!* Most of the time. Other times, they're just screaming for help."

"When they scream, are there many different voices?"

Marcia looks at me, then at Danny. "I don't understand."

"Are the voices those of children? Of men or just a woman?"

"Usually a woman, why?"

"Tell me something, Marcia, what happened to Shannon Ferguson?" I ask.

"I killed her, why?"

"How did you kill her?"

"I stabbed her and dumped her in the river, why?"

"How many times did you stab her?"

"Thirteen times," she says. The answer comes swiftly. The tone is the same as if I had asked her how many children she had. There is no emotion, no regret, and no sadness of having to relive this once again.

"And then what did you do with the body?"

"I dumped it in the river, I just told you."

"How did you transport it?" I ask.

Marcia stops. She leans back in her chair. "I...I don't really remember. I guess I must have stolen a car and taken it there. It's really very blurry."

"Try and remember. For me, Marcia. How did you dump the body?"

She shrugs. "I don't know. I just threw it in the water. I can't remember, Mary."

"Then how are you so certain you even killed her?"

Marcia sits up straight with an exhale. "Because I remember what she looked like. Not alive. When she was dead. I remember the blood. I remember the yellow shirt she was wearing. I remember the flowers of blood that had spread on it. When they showed me the pictures of the body, I recognized her. I remembered her from when she was on the couch, the one with the flowers, where she was stabbed, where I stabbed her."

"Do you remember doing it?" I ask. "Do you remember taking the knife and stabbing it into her?"

"Mary, maybe we should..." Danny tries to stop me, but I signal that he needs to back down.

Marcia looks even more confused. Her eyes are flickering.

"Do you recall what it felt like?"

Marcia shakes her head. "No."

"Where did you do it?"

"At her house."

"Did you knock her out first, or did you stab her first?"

"I don't remember."

"So, you're telling me all you remember is standing in front of a dead body, the body of Shannon Ferguson, who was lying on a couch in her house? You don't remember stabbing her; you don't remember dumping her."

Marcia is shaking her head violently now.

"Mary, I don't think this is good for her," Danny says.

"I know. I just need to get answers while she is still there mentally," I tell him, and look back at Marcia. "Tell me about what happened at the Elingston house," I say.

She nods. "I entered the house and shot the husband, then tried to strangle the woman..." Marcia looks into my eyes. I detect deep confusion in them now. "It was thundering outside. I was in the garage...I was sleeping...When I heard something...No, that wasn't then...that was something else, maybe a dream, I don't..." Her eyes go blank and she looks away. "I don't remember. The police tell me I black out when I do the bad things. When I kill. That's why I don't remember doing it. My mind isn't right, they say."

"Marcia I need you to help me, so I can help you," I say. "I know it's in there somewhere in your mind. There was someone else with you in the house that day when Andrew Elingston was killed wasn't there?"

"No. The police say I was there alone, that I acted alone."

"It doesn't matter what the police say," I say. "I am interested in what you say. What you remember."

Marcia looks like she is scrutinizing her brain. She looks at me, and then tilts her head again. "Mary? Why aren't you in New York?"

I sigh and give up. I look at Danny. "I don't think we're getting any more out of her."

"It was great to see you again, Marcia," Danny says.

"I'll get you out of here," I say, just before I get to my feet, heartbroken, crushed. "Trust me."

Her face lights up. "Great! Then maybe we can go to Beef O' Brady's. Kids eat free on Tuesdays."

85

NOVEMBER 2010

DANIEL DOESN'T LIKE daytime TV. Yet he still watches it excessively every day while waiting for the phone to ring and someone to offer him a new job. Well, maybe it isn't entirely true that he doesn't like it. He does enjoy some parts of it, like the parts when other people tell their stories and make him feel better about his own. When Jerry Springer has them jump each other in desperation to blame someone else for their lives going wrong, Daniel feels a little better about himself. Not because his life is any better than theirs are, 'cause it really isn't. No, he feels relieved because at least he knows who to blame. Himself. No one else can take credit for screwing up his life, like he can himself.

Daniel has lost everything. His job, his wife, his family. He has moved away, as far away from Florida as he could, and now he is sitting in a small condo in Upstate New York, in a small snowy town called Accord, numbering around five hundred citizens, wondering if life will ever be good again.

He can't blame Jill for leaving. Daniel started drinking and didn't care for his family in the way he was supposed to. To be frank, he hadn't for many years before then. Taking care of his brother Peter and the work with Kristin took too much of his time. He missed out on everything. He neglected them. The guilt following what happened to Peter after the trial ate him alive, and that was when he started to drink for real. Then everything else slid out of his hands. Soon he was fired, and his wife told him she'd had enough.

Coming from a wealthy family, Daniel has enough money to last him a lifetime, and for his family as well. So, he gave them a huge sum and told them not to miss him because he wasn't worth it, then left without telling them where he went.

Daniel looks at Jerry Springer as he watches the two young women fight on the stage. He is smiling and shaking his head. Daniel knows very well why Jerry is smiling. The fighting is what keeps people tuning in to his show.

A true moneymaker.

Daniel sighs and gets up from his chair. He walks to the kitchen to get another beer. He can't remember when he last ate. Maybe it doesn't matter. Daniel has played with the thought of drinking himself to death. No one would miss him. His body could rot away in the apartment until it started to smell and some neighbor called the cops. They'd find him between beer and vodka bottles. Maybe so many the door would be blocked. The place would smell so bad they'd have to wear masks to not throw up.

Except that just isn't quite Daniel's style.

The women in the TV are screaming and pulling each other's hair over some guy who watches with a sly smile, like he thinks he's the king of the world to have two women fighting over him.

Daniel watches it from the kitchen while he opens the refrigerator. The big muscular guys are now splitting them apart and the fighting part is over. As the show goes to commercials, Daniel bends down and pulls out a beer. When he looks back at the TV, it's been turned off.

What the ...?

Daniel looks around to locate the remote. He spots it on the kitchen counter.

Did I put it there?

No. Daniel always puts the remote in the same spot. He likes things to have their place and always keep them there. Thinking he's probably more drunk than he thought, Daniel grabs it and turns the TV back on. With the beer to his lips, he walks back to the recliner, sits down, and puts his feet up. He sighs, satisfied, and drinks some more of the beer, hoping he'll pass out soon and sleep the rest of the day.

No need to be awake anyway.

His eyes stare at the screen as the show returns and the two women once again plunge at each other. Daniel chuckles.

"Every freaking day it's the same. Every freaking day."

It's in the reflection of the TV screen that he realizes he is no longer alone in the apartment. Someone is standing behind his chair.

"What the...?"

He jumps out of his seat and faces the person.

"What are you doing here?"

The voice answering is calm and collected. Not at all as filled with anger or revenge as he has expected. Nothing like those people on TV. It's not remorseful either.

"You know why I am here."

86

FEBRUARY 2016

I HARDLY SPEAK a word on our way back. Danny is very quiet as well. It's not until we reach the bridge leading to the barrier island that Danny finally says something.

"So, what did you make of all that she said?"

I shrug. "All I know is that I don't believe she killed any of them. She doesn't remember anything about it. Don't you think you'd remember at least a little bit?"

He shrugs as well. "I don't know. If she's as sick as we believe, then I'm not sure we can believe anything she says. She could have blocked it out somehow. If she is really mentally ill, then I believe the brain can do that."

"True. I do suspect that she suffers from Schizophrenia. But what she does remember strikes me as odd."

"I'll give you that much," he says, and drives up in front of my dad's house. We hug goodbye and I walk inside. I yell to my dad that I am home, then grab my phone. I walk outside and sit in the sun, while wondering if I should do it or not, debating, arguing back and forth, then decide to do it anyway.

"Hello?"

"It's Mary. Now before you get mad at me again, I am not calling to say anything about what happened yesterday. I understand why you're mad at me. I am calling because I have a question for you."

Steven exhales. "All right. What is it?"

"I know it's going to sound strange, but bear with me."

"Depends on the question," he says.

"Did your sister have a couch with flowered-fabric on it in her house?"

"What?"

"I know it's odd, just answer me, please."

"Well then, the answer is no," he says. "She had two beige couches, leather, as far as I remember."

"Ah, okay," I say. "That is all. Thank you."

"That's it?" he asks. He sounds so disappointed.

I pause. "That depends," I say.

"Depends on what?"

"On you. If you're still angry with me."

Steven chuckles lightly. "I am sorry. I didn't mean to be so angry with you. Of course you're trying to protect your friend. It was wrong of me."

I smile and spot Mark as he walks up from the beach with a board under his arm. He is wearing board shorts and he is wet. He places the surfboard on the grass and showers. I am glad to see that he is not just cooped up inside. He is so skinny it hurts looking at him, and I decide I will make him a big lunch today, once I hang up with Steven.

"Apology accepted," I say.

"Great. So I get a chance to see you again?"

"Yes."

"I am glad. Maybe next weekend? We could go to Heidi's. I'll call you, okay?"

"Sounds good."

I hang up and look at Mark, who now approaches me. "Was it any good?" I ask, referring to the waves. They look small.

"A lot more fun than expected," he says. He stops in front of me. "So. How'd it go? How was she?"

"I'll be honest with you. She didn't make much sense. She seems okay, given the circumstances, though," I add, to not give him more to worry about. "Tell me one thing, did you go to Beef O' Brady's a lot?"

He grabs a towel from behind a chair and starts to dry himself. "Yeah," he says. "We went there every Tuesday. At least, we used to until she got worse. It sort of became this tradition because, you know...kids eat free. That way mom could take us out without spending a lot of money."

It makes sense. Marcia never had much to spend, and with four kids, it was probably always tight for her. It also explains why she always mentioned it when I talked to her. It was a big thing in her life to be able to take the kids out every Tuesday. It was the one thing she could hold on to, the one thing...*wait, how did she manage to remember it every Tuesday?*

"Say, Mark. Did anyone else eat with you on Tuesdays?"

"Yeah, sure. Mom's sponsor was there too."

"Jess?"

"Yes. She's the one who always knew how to find mom and make sure she came home. She would drive us all there in her truck. She would also take us home."

"Did she spend a lot of time with your mom?"

Mark shrugs. "I think so. She helped her a lot."

"Was she with you the last time you went to the restaurant?"

"Sure."

"When was that?"

"I don't know. In January some time. Five-six weeks ago. Why the sudden interest in her?"

I shake my head. "No reason. Just got me thinking. That's all."

87

FEBRUARY 2016

WHEN MARK IS inside the house, I pick up my phone again. I call Chloe.

"Just the person I wanted to talk to," she says. "I have something important I need to talk to you about."

"Me too," I say. "Back in the beginning of the investigation of the murder of Shannon Ferguson, the police looked at Marcia because someone had told them that Marcia herself believed she had done it. I need you to tell me who the person was. I need a name."

"I can tell you right away," she says. "I have the files right here. I printed all of them out, just in case they somehow managed to lock me out of their system."

I can hear her flip the pages. My heart is beating fast now. An idea is shaping in my mind, but it's still vague. I can't see the details yet.

"Here it is. Yes. Someone came to the station and told the police that Marcia Little had told her she believed she might have killed Shannon Ferguson."

"And the name?"

"It says here her name is Kristin Martin."

"That's odd," I say. "I was certain it would be Jess, Marcia's sponsor. Well, thanks anyway."

"Wait, I have something..."

"Not now, Chloe. Later, okay?"

I hang up, frustrated. No, that's putting it too mildly. I am aggravated. I am good old-fashioned pissed. I was so sure of my theory, whatever it was. I didn't have the details, but somehow I believed Jess had framed Marcia.

Something is off about her and her relationship with Marcia. She told me she hadn't seen Marcia in three months when we arrived at that AA meeting. Why did she say that if she had seen her only a few weeks ago? Why did Mark say that she always knew where to find Marcia when no one else could?

There could easily be a very ordinary explanation for all these questions, but I have this feeling, this itch, that there isn't. I sit down in front of my computer with another deep sigh, wondering how the heck I am supposed to solve this. How I am to prove Marcia's innocence? I will never be able to live with myself if she is convicted of this.

Not knowing what else to do, I decide we need food to think. In the kitchen, I start lunch, and soon Mark comes out and helps me. I am making a big portion of spaghetti and meatballs. I have a feeling Mark will like it because it has always been Marcia's favorite dish. So much about him reminds me of her when she was that age.

"Smells divine," he says.

He sets the table, and I get my dad out of bed, using the lift and help him get into the wheelchair. I bring him to the table, where he smiles when he sees Mark. He seems to enjoy having the boy here.

I feed him a spoonful of spaghetti and meatballs. "Oh, this is good," he says.

Mark digs in as well.

"So, tell me, Mark, what else do you know about Jess?" I ask. I am not ready to let go of this angle just yet.

"Not much," he says.

"Do you know her last name?"

"No."

"Do you know if she has any family? Any kids?"

"I don't think so."

"Did your mom spend a lot of time at her place?"

He shrugs. "Maybe. I never knew where she was."

We finish the meal, and I clean up, while my dad is enjoying the sun on the porch. I look at my laptop from the kitchen and an urge overwhelms me. I walk to it and sit down. I Google Jess and try to guess her last name. Then I try to search for Jess and Cocoa Beach, but only a lot of useless stuff comes up. I try something else. There is something about that name, Kristin

Martin, that rings a bell. I've heard about her somewhere before. I Google her name and...

Bingo!

I lean back with a deep sigh, as I open the first picture that Google found.

"Well, hello there...*Jess.*"

88

FEBRUARY 2016

"SHE FELL IN LOVE WITH HIM."

I am almost yelling in the phone.

"Who fell in love with who?" Chloe asks.

"Kristin Martin. She was a therapist or a professor of some sort. I knew I had heard that name before. She was that lady who fell in love with a disabled man, and was sent to jail for three years and nine months because she couldn't prove that the guy had given his consent to have sex with her."

"Ah. Now I remember. That was a long time ago, right?"

"She was convicted nine years ago."

"So, she's out now?"

"Exactly. And, get this. The disabled man was the youngest in the Elingston clan. And she is also Marcia's sponsor," I say. "Calls herself Jess. The two of them have been spending a lot of time together, I believe."

"Ah."

"I need you to find her address. It must be in the police file somewhere," I say. "I dropped her off the other day outside her condominiums, the Palmas De Majorca by 3rd Street North, but I don't know which number she lives in."

"I'll check." Chloe disappears for just a second, then returns. "Here. Apartment number 329."

"Great, thanks."

"By the way, there is something I have been meaning to talk to you about...Joey asked me to..."

"Not now, Chloe. I don't want to hear about him. I'm not ready yet. Besides, I need to find this woman."

"Don't go alone!"

"I'll be fine," I say, and hang up. Thinking about what she said, I go to my dad's room and grab his gun from his safe to bring with me, just in case.

I look at Mark who is playing Xbox in the living room and wonder if I should tell him anything, but decide not to. There is no reason to alarm him further. He's been through so much.

"I'm going out for a little while," I say to both my dad and Mark, then walk to the car. I drive to the Palmas De Majorca, where I park and walk towards the condos. I want to call the police, but I don't have enough evidence to prove anything. They'll only think I'm crazy. I need to look into her eyes while I ask her about it.

My plan is to pretend I am here to talk about Marcia, and if that doesn't work, then talk about my own addiction to food and how to get out of it. How I am going to get her to talk about the Elingston family and the murders, I haven't figured out yet. But somehow, I will.

It's one of those condominiums where the stairs and hallways are all outside. They are very common in Florida, because it is always so warm out. I walk up to the third floor, find her condo, and ring the doorbell. There is no answer. I ring again, then look in the window, covering my eyes from the light with my hands. I have to stand on my tippy-toes to reach. Inside, I immediately spot something that makes me shiver.

A couch.

Not just any couch. A couch with pink flower-covered fabric.

I swallow hard and pull back. Maybe I am in over my head here. Maybe I should get the police involved instead, but how? How am I to make them believe me? The couch was in Marcia's head, not in any evidence material. Besides, why should they believe me? Because of what Mark said? Because the woman has been in jail before? Because of a stupid couch? Still doesn't prove anything.

"Can I help you?"

An elderly woman approaches me.

"I was just visiting someone."

"I live right next door. She's not here anymore," she says and points at Jess's door. "She rented the place a year ago, fully furnished and everything. Guess she knew she wouldn't stay long. A nice woman, though. She'll be missed around here."

"Do you know where she went?" I ask, feeling my heart drop with the prospect of yet another murderer getting away on my watch.

"Yes. I spoke to her this morning when she left. She told me she was going to Winter Park. A lovely place this time of year."

I stare at the old lady, while everything inside of me is screaming.

Winter Park? She's going for the last Elingston. The only one left.

Oh, my God. She's going to kill Steven!

89

NOVEMBER 2010

THE GUN IS POINTED at him as they drive. They're in his car and he is behind the wheel. It's a long drive. Eighteen hours, and they only stop for coffee and food. Daniel is exhausted, but feels kind of uplifted as well. For the first time in a long time, he is actually doing something.

"Take me to see him," Kristin said, back at the condo.

Of course that is what she wants. To see Peter after spending almost four years in prison. Daniel can't blame her, and to be honest, he is really excited to give Peter the chance to see her again. The past years have been terrible for him, and in the end, Daniel simply stopped visiting Peter because he couldn't stand it anymore. He couldn't take seeing him lying there, strapped to his bed with dead eyes like some vegetable. He couldn't stand the guilt.

Daniel fought for years to get him out of the home. He drove his siblings crazy, constantly bugging them about it, telling them they had to do something. Anything. But they refused.

"He's fine, Daniel," Jack would say, over and over again. "He's safe. He's being taken care of."

But what did they know? They never visited Peter. They didn't even care enough to listen to what Daniel told them. They were just happy to have Peter locked away somewhere, so they no longer had to care. So they could move on with their lives and put it all behind them.

Daniel even suggested that he take care of Peter himself. He told them he could take him to his home, he and his wife would care for him, maybe hire a nurse to be there all day long. Jill protested wildly, but he told her he had to do this. That he couldn't live with himself anymore. He would do anything to get Peter out of that awful place. Even if it meant losing Jill. Daniel was desperate, the guilt was eating him so badly he couldn't sleep or eat, and that was when he started drinking, like seriously drinking. But, no matter how much he begged his siblings to let him ease Peter's pain, to give him back his life, they never would agree to it. And they had to. According to the law, they all had to agree since they had joint custody over Peter after their mother died.

"He's still in there," he kept telling them, using all the same arguments he had when they were much younger. "I know he is. What if he understands everything? What if he is a normal man with normal intelligence in there behind the disease, a man who just can't communicate because his body refuses to cooperate?"

In the end, he gave up. Gave up as everything slowly slipped out of his hands. But the guilt wouldn't leave him alone. In the end, after Jill had taken the kids and left, moving far away seemed like the only reasonable thing left to do.

"You really don't have to point that thing at me," Daniel says, as they approach the home in Rockledge.

Kristin looks down at the gun, but doesn't remove it.

"I'll take you there anyway," he continues.

She smiles cautiously. He still thinks her smile is beautiful. The years in prison have been hard on her, and she looks at least fifteen years older. Her hair is cut short and it makes her look like a boy. But she still has that quality about her.

"All right," she says, and puts the gun back in her purse. "But it's right here, in case you don't behave."

Daniel parks the car and they walk up to the entrance. He can sense Kristin is nervous. She is not allowed to be anywhere near Peter. They both know that. She could go back to prison for this.

"It'll be fine," Daniel says.

She nods with a nervous sigh. "I hope so."

Daniel presents Kristin as his wife at the counter, and soon they're both shown to Peter's room. As the nurse opens the door, and they both enter, they see Peter in his bed. Kristin cups her mouth when she sees him. Daniel feels like someone punched him in the stomach.

"Oh, my God," Kristin says, addressed to the nurse. "What have you done to him?" She walks to his bed and touches his straps. Daniel feels sick to his stomach. He can't believe how small and skinny Peter has become.

It's like there is almost nothing left of him. Not a single muscle, nothing but skin on bones. He hardly recognizes his face. Peter looks more dead than alive.

"We have to keep him strapped down," the nurse explains. "It's the only way we can keep him calm, the only way he doesn't hurt himself or others, for that matter. It's for his own good, really."

She sounds just like Daniel's daughter when explaining that she only hit her younger brother because *he started it!*

"You monsters!" Kristin says.

"As I said. It's for his own good. We have tried to contact the family and tell them—well, tell *you*, that he refuses to cooperate with us, but no one seems to react to our inquiries. Don't blame this on us," the nurse snorts angrily, then leaves the room.

"What have they done?" Kristin says, after the nurse is gone. Her voice is breaking and she is fighting to breathe between the sobs. "What have *you* done?"

She walks to Peter and unleashes the straps on his arms and legs. He doesn't move. Kristin waves a hand in front of his eyes.

"He's not reacting?"

"They probably sedated him," Daniel says, condemned by the responsibility. "I think they do that."

"Sedated? But how...why...why Daniel? Why would they do such a terrible thing? How could you let this happen?"

Daniel shrugs. "I...I've tried everything."

Kristin helps Peter to sit up by putting pillows underneath him. She sits in front of him and looks into his eyes. His head keeps turning away from her.

"He's completely lethargic," she says, startled. "Peter never used to be like this. He was in constant movement, never would settle down, weren't you, Peter?" She strokes his cheek gently while she speaks. "Dear gentle sweet Peter. You were so full of life. What have they done to you? They took everything from you. They took your beautiful voice."

When she speaks, something seems to happen to Peter. His eyes are looking at her. Kristin is crying heavily while yelling, agitated. "Did you see that, Daniel? He looked at me. He is still in there. I know you are, baby. I know you are still there. Can you see me? It's me, Kristin. Hi."

Peter's eyes are staring at her now. Daniel's heart is thumping. Next, Peter lets out a small vague sound.

"He chirped!" Daniel says, tears in his voice. "Peter just chirped again.

Just like he used to when he was happy, like he always did when we were kids. Did you hear it, Kristin, did you?"

Kristin wipes away a tear and nods with a sniffle and a light laugh. "Yes. Yes. I heard it. I told you he's still in there." Kristin points to her bag on the floor. "Could you grab that for me?"

Daniel hands it to her. "I brought something for you, darling, she says, and pulls out a keyboard. Let's see if you can remember how to use one of these. I'll help you. Just like we used to. Do you remember that?"

Peter chirps again. Daniel is struggling to hold back tears. To see life in Peter's eyes again is like seeing sunlight after years of darkness. It's such a relief, such a deep hopeful sound.

Kristin grabs Peter's elbow and holds it in her hand. Daniel moves closer to see what Peter is typing. It takes a few minutes before his arm moves and the first letter is typed. Soon the rest arrive like pearls on a string.

"He does remember how to do it," Kristin says. "I knew he would. I knew I could get him to speak again. I'll give you your voice back, Peter. What is he writing, Daniel?"

Daniel writes down each letter, then when Peter is done, he reads it. He looks at Kristin.

"Don't look at me like that. Tell me. What does it say?"

Daniel can hardly get the words across his lips.

"Please kill me."

90

FEBRUARY 2016

I DRIVE like the wind towards Orlando and Winter Park. Meanwhile, I am on the phone trying to get ahold of Steven, but he doesn't answer.

"Pick up. Pick up!"

But of course, he doesn't. I have only been to his house once, a couple of weeks ago when we went to a concert at the Amway Center in Orlando and I picked him up. So, I know where to go.

It takes me about an hour to get there. He lives in one of those nice cookie-cutter neighborhoods where all the houses are big and expensive, but they all look the same. I park in the driveway next to a brown truck, that I am afraid might be hers.

I try and call his cell one last time, and when he doesn't pick up, I storm to the front door. Not knowing what else to do, I ring the doorbell, one hand on my father's gun inside my purse.

Seconds later, Steven comes to the door. He looks surprised. "Mary?"

"Are you alright?" I ask, thinking of how Jess or Kristin held those families hostage before killing them. Maybe she is doing the same to Steven right now, maybe she is hiding somewhere behind the door, pointing her gun at him, waiting for him to say something to me, to alert me, and then shoot him. I have to be careful right now. I have to be very careful.

"Sure? Why wouldn't I be? A little startled to see you here, but..."

"Can I come in?"

He looks confused. "You know what? Now is not a very good time. The house is a mess...and well...I wasn't expecting you."

I scrutinize his eyes to see if I can detect anything, any signal, any small sign that he is, in reality, fearing for his life. I remember the many documentaries I've seen about the killing of the Elingston family in their home, and how both the accountant and the pizza deliveryman never noticed the fear in the father's eyes when he opened the door. I don't want that to happen to me.

"I think I am coming in anyway," I say, and push my way in.

I am armed and not afraid to use it.

"Mary...don't."

But it's too late. I am already inside the hallway. My phone rings and I look at the display. It's Chloe.

"I can't talk right now," I say. "I'm at Steven's. I'll call you back."

"But..."

I hang up and silence the phone before I put it in my pocket, while looking around me. No sign of her anywhere.

"Mary...I am kind of in the middle of something."

"Moom?"

The voice breaks through the air.

The voice of a child.

I turn and look into the face of a boy, about the same age as Salter. "Who are you?" he asks.

"Phillip, your mother is in the back smoking a cigarette. I am in the middle of something here," Steven says.

The boy sighs and turns away. I stare at Steven.

What the heck is going on here?

"What is this, Steven?" I ask. "Who is the boy? And who is his mother? Are you married or something?"

Steven laughs. "Divorced. You know that."

"Is the kid your son? He looks a lot like you."

The boy carries all the answers.

Steven walks to me and grabs my shoulders. "Mary. I only want the best for you. I really like you, I do. But if you keep asking all these questions, you'll get yourself in a lot of trouble, do you understand me? I say you leave now and forget you ever met me, all right?"

That's got to be the weirdest way anyone ever broke up with someone.

"But...Steven...I'm here to warn you. I know who killed your brothers and sister. And I am afraid she's coming for you."

Steven looks at me, and stares into my eyes.

"Your hands are kind of hurting my shoulders, Steven," I say.

My phone vibrates in my pocket, and I pull it out. It's a text from Chloe. Steven's hands are still holding on to my shoulders while I read it.

STEVEN ELINGSTON WAS KILLED IN 2010. GET OUT NOW!

91

FEBRUARY 2016

I TRY TO ACT CASUAL, but Steven sees it in my eyes, sees the shift from confident, to fearful. I can't hide it. He lets go of my shoulders, then shuts the front door behind him and locks it. My hand is on the gun in my purse, but I am shaking. I have no idea what is going on.

The boy carries all the answers.

Another voice approaches. It is her. It's Kristin Martin.

"What's going on in here?"

"Mary knows," Steven—or whatever his name really is—says.

Kristin looks at me. "Ah, that's too bad. I had hoped we could keep you out of this. I really liked you, Mary." As she speaks, she lifts a gun and points it at me. I pull mine and point it at her.

Kristin laughs. "Do you even know how to shoot one of these?"

"I'm a Florida girl; you figure it out."

It's a lie; I am not the type of Florida girl whose dad taught her to shoot. But I can tell it works.

Kristin's smile stiffens. "All right, but I really don't have time for this. Would you, Daniel?"

Daniel?

Daniel walks towards me and reaches out to grab the gun, when I fire it at him and hit his arm.

"What the hell?"

"Don't be a wimp," I say. "It's only a scratch. I told you I know how to shoot one of these. As a matter of fact, I have spent a lot of time on the shooting range the past three months, since I had another run-in with a murderer. Now, you two tell me what the heck is going on here before I get really mad. Who is the boy?"

The boy carries all the answers. That's what Chloe's mother told me. I have no idea how she would know, but I am going with it.

"He's mine," Kristin says. "Phillip is mine and...Peter's. Daniel's younger brother."

"The disabled one?" I ask, suddenly remembering reading that she was pregnant at the time of the trial. "You had the child in prison?"

"Yes. Well, I was taken to the hospital, and that's when they took him away from me. I didn't get to see him for four years. I never saw him learn how to crawl or even walk. They even took away my rights to be with him when I got out."

"My brother took him in," Daniel says. "My brother Steven took him in. But when Kristin got out, he didn't want her to see him. He kept her away from her own son."

"So, you killed him?" I ask.

Kristin looks at Daniel, then chuckles. "Daniel shot him in his own home. In anger."

I look at Daniel with disgust. "Your own brother? You shot him in cold blood?"

"He only got what was coming to him. It was the only way I could get custody of Phillip and Kristin could be with him again. But that wasn't all. We wanted justice for both Phillip and Peter. Peter had been suffering in the most inhumane way at the home my siblings put him in, and when Kristin and I visited him after she was released, he was so sick, so miserable that all he wanted was to die. As a matter of fact, he asked us to kill him."

"So, you killed him?" I ask.

Kristin makes a flipping sound with her lips that's barely a raspberry. "No. I love him. We love him. No, we decided to help him. To give him what he deserved, what he should have had many years ago."

"Freedom," Daniel says. "We wanted him to be free, and not only that. We wanted him to be able to have a family, to be with his son and the woman he loves."

I nod as the pieces suddenly fit. "So, you killed the other siblings so that you'd be the only one with custody of your brother, so you could decide where he lives and who he lives with, am I right?"

"It's as simple as that," Daniel says. "We're actually on our way to go and get him now. He is being discharged at my request at three o'clock today. Then we'll get as far away from here as possible. No one will look for us, since they've already caught the killer."

"Marcia," I say. "You framed her."

"If it helps anything, then I am really sorry for her, that it had to end this way. But, yes, she was perfect for our plan," Kristin says. "After getting rid of Steven in 2010, we almost got caught. The police in Denver where he lived kept asking us questions, and we realized we had to be a lot more careful. Daniel was even arrested, but luckily they didn't have enough evidence for a trial. We knew we had to find another way to make sure we wouldn't be suspects. Being a professor in psychology, I know more than anyone how fragile people with mental illnesses are, and I got the idea to find someone to take the fall for us. We took the next six years planning this, looking for the right person in all the places that you'd expect to find someone that unstable, like AA. And along came Marcia. She was perfect. I became her sponsor, and soon realized she had no idea what was reality and what was in her head. She drank way too much and had many black holes in her memory. It was perfect. So I became close with her and she stayed the night at my place a lot of times, and that's when I started showing her the pictures."

"You kept pictures?"

"Of all of them. How else would I show Peter what I have done for him, what I have done for our love? I showed them to Marcia again and again. Starting with the ones of Jack Elingston and his family. I told her how they screamed for help, how scared they were, and then told her she had done it. I told her details about them, and soon she believed she had done it. It was..."

"Perfect, I think we have established that, thank you," I say. "I can't believe you'd exploit her like this."

"Oh, it was so easy. Steven killed Shannon Fergusson in my condo. She had been fighting with her husband and called Daniel. She was crying and asking him if he would come. Since Daniel had moved back here to Winter Park, after Steven died, the two of them had gotten close."

"That explains why you knew what kind of couch she had in her home," I say. "I was wondering about that. You told me you weren't very close with her."

"We didn't used to be," he says. "I was just getting her to trust me. The fight with her husband made it perfect. He wasn't there. He had taken off, probably to be with the woman they were fighting over, the secretary. I told her I was going to visit a friend and asked her if she wanted to come with us, get something to eat. I took her to Kristin's place. I sat her on the couch and started to explain to her what was going to happen. I told her we would kill her and the rest of our siblings, so that Peter could be freed. I showed her pictures of our poor brother, so she would understand what she had done to him. Then I showed her the knife. She didn't even try and fight me. I guess we took her by surprise. I stabbed her thirteen times. Kristin took her to the bridge and dumped her. We needed to make sure they would look for a woman."

I have a bad taste in my mouth. I feel like throwing up. How could anyone be this calculated, this coldblooded?

"Wait. How did you get Marcia to be in the house in Melbourne Beach, in Andrew Elingston's house?" I ask.

"That's the beauty of it. I had no idea she was there. I had shown her pictures of the house and of the family to prepare her to take the blame for what happened, but I had never imagined she would actually be there when I entered the house. It cost me a shot to the shoulder, but it was so worth it. I couldn't have orchestrated it better myself. When she jumped out from behind the door as I was trying to strangle the mother, I knew for the first time that we were going to get away with this. I ran out of there as fast as I could and left her there, then called for the police. She was trying to save them, but instead she incriminated herself. I knew they would never believe her, even if she were capable of telling the truth. Nothing she says makes any sense. I knew she would be sentenced to undergo psychiatric treatment, and to be frank, she is better off there than out here in the world. She is sick, Mary."

I am so mad now I want to shoot her right here, but I can't. I need her to stay alive to tell all this to the police. Instead, I lower the gun so fast she doesn't react, and I shoot her in the foot. She screams and blood gushes out onto the wooden floor.

"You're the one who is sick here," I say.

Kristin lifts her gun swiftly and angrily, while humping on one leg towards me. When the shot is fired, it drowns out everything in my mind. I lose my sense of direction and have no idea what is up or down. It feels like I am falling until all I see is darkness.

FEBRUARY 2016

"MARY? MARY? GODDAMMIT, MARY, WAKE UP!"

The voice yelling is distant, but insisting. I am floating in a sea of stars when I realize it's me it's calling for. I blink my eyes and make the darkness go away. Then I smile.

"Joey?"

"Oh, thank God, Mary. You're alright!"

"Where am I?"

Another face is above me now, looking down. "Hey, Chloe. What are you doing here?"

"I came to check on you and see what you were up to this time," she says. "Are you all right?"

"I don't know. Am I?"

"You look fine," Joey says. "No holes in your body, no blood."

"But I heard a shot. Right before I passed out," I say. "I thought I had been hit."

"Well, Joey kicked the door in, and when we entered, Kristin over there was about to shoot you, so Joey shot her and we believe you slipped and hit your head on the tiles."

I feel my head and find the bump. I look at Joey while trying to sit up. I am still very dizzy.

"You saved me?" I ask.

He nods. I can tell he feels pretty good about himself. "It was nothing. Just glad I always have a gun in my truck."

"You have a gun in your truck? That's not very safe when you drive around with a nine-year-old kid."

"Maybe it's not the time or the place to discuss this," Chloe says. "We need to have a paramedic look at your head and see if they need you to go in for observation." Chloe signals one of the uniformed men, and I realize the place is swarming with them.

"What happened to Kristin Martin and Daniel Elingston?" I ask with a groan. My head is starting to really hurt now.

"They have both been taken away. Kristin in an ambulance," Joey says. "Your beloved Steven or Daniel or Harry, or whatever he calls himself these days threw himself on the floor and surrendered as soon as Kristin hit the ground."

"I am so glad you came. I don't want to think about what would have happened if you hadn't. Thank you."

"You're welcome," Joey says.

"Why were you here anyway?"

"Chloe has tried to tell you about Steven all day, but you refused to listen," Joey says. "When you picked up the phone and told her where you were, she called me immediately afterwards. She knew he wasn't who he said he was, that the real Steven Elingston was killed in his home back in 2010."

"Ah. Okay. Wait. How did she know?"

He shrugs. "She looked into him. Researched him online. Who knows why Chloe does what she does?"

I look at him as Chloe hands me an icepack. "Tell me the truth, Joey," I say.

"Yeah tell her the truth, Joey," Chloe says with a sly grin.

Joey rolls his eyes. "All right. All right. I was jealous. I told Chloe to look into him, to find out who he was, and rightfully so, I might add. Who knows what could have happened to you? You really should pick your men better."

I chuckle, but it hurts my head, so I stop.

Chloe helps me get to my feet. I close my eyes to try and get the dizziness to go away, and when I open them again, I look into the eyes of Phillip Elingston.

Suddenly, I don't feel so great about myself any longer. What will become of him after this? There is no family left for him anymore. Everyone else is dead, or going to jail.

Well...maybe not quite *everyone*.

EPILOGUE
MARCH 2016

"THANK you for bringing Phillip to us."

Kelly Elingston looks at me. She is out of her bed for the first time since the attack in her home that killed her husband and put her in a coma. She is expected to fully recover. Phillip has been staying with Salter, my dad, and me for the past several weeks until his aunt woke up and DCF could ask her if she'd be willing to take the boy.

"I figured he needed to be with family," I say. "He is, after all, your nephew."

"It'll be so good for Lindsey to have someone to play with. She still hardly speaks, but words are starting to come out of her recently. Small steps, I guess."

"I guess."

"Thank you for everything, Mary."

"It's nothing, really. I brought someone with me who wants to see you."

I open the door and ask Marcia to come in. She has been home for two weeks now and is getting better. I have found a good doctor for her and the medication is beginning to do its job. I believe I can see improvement in her every day. Meanwhile, her sister has come down from Jacksonville and has been taking care of her. Mark has moved home, and after much negotiation on my part, Carl has finally agreed to let the rest of them come back in a few months as well, if Marcia shows continuing signs of improvement. I take it as my job to help her with that.

Marcia waves awkwardly. "Hi."

"Come here," Kelly says. "I want to give you a hug."

Cautiously, Marcia moves closer, and Kelly soon grabs her in her arms. She has tears in her eyes as she holds Marcia. "You have no idea how thankful I am to you. No idea."

Marcia doesn't speak. I can sense she is tearing up as well. Lately, she has been tormented badly about how she acted when she was sick, and for her to hear that she actually did something good for someone must be a great relief. It's just what she needs right now to get back on her feet. People who love her.

"If you ever need anything, Marcia. And I do mean anything, you let me know, all right? You saved my baby's life. And mine. There is no way I can ever pay you back." Kelly lets go of Marcia and looks into her eyes.

"You're a wonderful person, you do know that, right?"

Now I am crying too.

Kelly hugs her one last time, then lets go of her, and Marcia walks over to me. I grab her hand in mine as the nurse walks in and lets us know Kelly needs her rest. Her mom has promised to come later and take both of the children with her until Kelly gets well enough to come home. Our job is done. We say goodbye and walk to the car...Marcia looking a little taller than when we came.

And rightfully so, I think to myself.

I am just so thrilled that Kristin Martin and Daniel Elingston didn't get away with any of it. The last I heard, Kristin is going to survive Joey's shot, and they'll both face prosecution for all the murders. I am working closely with Detective Brown on the case. They expect the FBI to take over sometime soon because of the murder in Denver. I don't know what my role will be yet, how much they'll need my testimony, but I am going to give them everything they need to make sure these two will get what they deserve.

The week after the shootout in Daniel Elingston's house, I went to visit their youngest brother, Peter, at the home in Rockledge. It killed me to see him, and I told Kelly Elingston everything when I came to visit her the next day. She promised me she would look into getting him to a better place. I know she even toys with the idea of letting him move into her house and be with Phillip. It's a big decision to make and requires a lot from her, but somehow, I have a feeling that she can do it.

As for Joey and me? Well, I guess time will show what happens. I am grateful that he saved me, but I still don't feel like I can trust him with my heart. Besides, he is with Jackie now, and as painful as it is, I accept it and try to move on.

I hold the door for Marcia as she gets into my car. I barely make it into my own seat before my phone rings. It's Chloe.

"I have news."

"What?"

"Your brother."

"Really?" I say, slightly skeptical. We were so certain we had traced him to Arizona, but it turned out to be a dead end. I am so glad we didn't go there, as originally planned, and make fools of ourselves.

"And this one is for real. This one I am completely certain is him."

"Great? Why are you so sure?"

"Get this. They have found Olivia. Her body was found hidden in a mattress in a motel room in Naples."

"In Naples? That's not that far from here. Has he really been this close all the time?" I ask.

"Looks like it. And it looks like he got tired of Olivia. She was probably a chain around his leg."

"And now he is free to roam."

"Exactly," she says. "It's easier for him to be on the run when he's on his own."

"That might be," I say. "But he cannot hide. Not forever at least. Sooner or later, we'll find him."

"I'd prefer sooner rather than later."

"That makes two of us."

THE END

YOU CAN'T HIDE

MARY MILLS MYSTERY BOOK 3

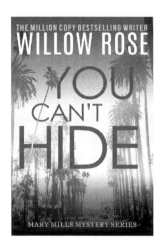

PROLOGUE
OCTOBER 2015

SHE'S NOT RUNNING, but it is close. Maria Verlinden rushes through the aisles, leaving behind the sections with towels and bathroom accessories. She hopes to be able to get through Target's dreaded toy department without Tara acting up. She doesn't have time to look at toys today. As a single mother with only one income, she can't afford to buy her toys every time they shop. Today is about getting her some new shoes, that's all. Quick in and quick out. Without spending money on anything unnecessary.

"Moom, can I get a toy?"

Maria sighs. She looks at her nine-year-old daughter as they walk past the many teddy bears staring back at them with big cute black eyes, begging Maria to buy them.

"You know Mommy can't afford it today. You need new shoes, remember? The school won't let you wear flip-flops. You have to wear sneakers."

"But, Moom, I really want a Monster High doll. Ally has one."

"Not today, honey. I am sorry..."

"But, Moom!"

Maria pulls Tara's arm a little too hard as she tries to get past the toys and into the clothing department.

"You're hurting me, Mom!"

"I'm sorry, baby. We just need to hurry. Mommy has to go to work."

Maria feels exhausted, thinking about going into the office today. Selling office supplies over the phone has to be the worst job on the planet. But she needs the money. And it sure beats working at Wal-Mart like she used to. Tara will spend the rest of the day with a neighbor who is out of work and who takes care of her when Maria has to work and they're off from school. Today is a teachers' workday so there is no school. Maria hates having to ask her neighbor for help, but what else can she do? She can't wait for Tara to be old enough to stay home alone. Maria has got to work.

"Here it is," she says and stops.

Tara is whining. She is complaining about not being able to have a toy. Maria fights the urge to yell at her. How can she be so ungrateful? She is getting new shoes, after all. Can't she be excited about that at least? Doesn't she know how much Maria has to work and save to be able to afford these shoes?

Maria has promised herself to stop yelling so much at Tara. She wants to be better about it. But the pressure of not having any money and living in a bad neighborhood at the age of almost thirty, with a nine-year-old, is getting to her. She hates her life. Worst of all, she sees no way out of it. It's not like she'll meet someone when she has a kid and as long as she lives in that awful place. She feels so stuck. She loves her daughter, but there are days she wonders how her life would have turned out had she gotten that abortion her parents told her to get, before they cut her off. But how could she? It was a baby, for crying out loud. You don't just kill a baby just because the father doesn't want it.

"This baby will destroy your life, Maria," her mother said the day she also told her to get the abortion or they would disown her. Their daughter being a single mother was apparently too much for them, too much of a disgrace. "The kid will be a bastard," they said.

Maria had no idea beforehand that her parents would react like this. But she decided to keep the child anyway, even though it would never know its father or grandparents. After all, it wasn't Tara's fault.

Maria looks at her daughter as she touches a pair of very sparkly shoes. Maria can't help smiling. Yes, Tara is annoying at times, and yes it has been hard, but she loves her; she is the love of her life. How a beautiful little girl like that could cause so much commotion was beyond her comprehension. Maria would give her the world if she could afford it.

"Can I have these, Mommy?"

Maria looks at the price. It's a little more than what she can afford. "Let's see what else there is," she says.

"Okay, Mommy, but I really like these. Ally has a pair like them."

"Good for Ally. Now, how about these over here?" Maria picks up a pair of shoes and shows them to Tara when she spots a man at the end of the aisle touching a pair of shoes but not picking them up. He spots Tara and makes a face at her. Tara laughs. "That man is funny," she says.

Maria grabs Tara's hand in hers and pulls her closer. "Do you want to try these?"

"They're ugly, Mom."

"All right. How about those over there?" Maria asks, still looking at the man who hasn't taken his eyes off of Tara. Something about him fills Maria with unease. She pulls Tara even closer. Tara looks at him again and he makes another funny face. Tara bursts into laughter. The man smiles. Maria eases up slightly. Maybe she is just being paranoid. Maria picks up another pair of shoes and shows them to Tara.

"How about these?"

"Okay. I'll try them on."

Tara grabs the shoes and sits down on the bench. She takes off her flip-flops. Maria keeps an eye on the man. He seems to be circling them, looking at shoes, but not picking any of them up. She doesn't like the way he is looking at Tara.

"Hurry up, Tara," Maria says. "I have to go to the office. They only allowed me to be an hour late today."

"I don't like these, Mommy. They're too tight on my toes."

"Then try another size," she grumbles, and pulls out a box with the same shoes in another size.

The man is still circling them, making faces at Tara whenever he gets her attention. Maria starts to wonder if there is anyone else nearby, in case he tries to steal her purse. It's very early and she hasn't seen anyone else in the store except for the cashiers at the entrance.

"Do you need help with that?" the man suddenly says to Tara.

Maria turns and sees him kneeling in front of the girl and helping her with the shoe. Maria stops breathing. She doesn't like him being this close to her daughter. But, then again, he is just being nice. Maybe he is just a lonely man. She looks at his basket; he hasn't put anything in it.

That's odd, she thinks, but then shakes the thought again. *Maybe he's just here to buy a pair of shoes just like you. You don't have anything in your basket either.*

Maria laughs at herself. The man smiles at her, then at Tara, as the shoe slides right on.

"There you are. It fits perfect. Just like *Cinderella.*"

Tara giggles. She doesn't like *Cinderella,* she is more of a *Frozen*-girl, but she is being polite. The man gets up.

"I think we have a winner, *Mom,*" he says, addressed to Maria.

"I want these," Tara says and looks proudly up at Maria.

Maria smiles, relieved. She looks at her watch. Only ten minutes till she needs to be at the office. She can't make it in time, but if they move fast then maybe she won't be too late, not so late they'll fire her. They did that last week to one of the other girls. She didn't show up and the next day they had simply given the job to someone else. They didn't even tell her, so when she finally did show up, she found someone else at her desk and had to leave. There are plenty of other girls out there who want Maria's job. They never hesitate to tell them that.

"Thank you so much," she says to the man.

"No problem, *Mom*," he says, and nods.

She knows it is silly, but for some reason she holds her purse tight to her body as she passes him. She kneels in front of her daughter and takes off the shoes that she puts back in the box.

"All right. Let's get moving," she says to Tara. Tara gets up and they start to walk. Tara turns and waves at the man as they disappear down the aisle. He makes another funny face and Tara burst into a light giggle.

As they reach the check-out and give the shoes to the cashier, Maria spots the man walking towards the exit quickly. She notices that he didn't buy anything.

At least he's gone, she thinks to herself with a light shiver when she hands the cashier the money for the shoes.

OCTOBER 2015

Tara wants to wear the shoes right after they have paid for them, and Maria lets her put them on before they leave the store. Tara laughs happily and runs circles around Maria as they walk towards the parking lot.

"Look at how fast I can run!" Tara yells.

"You are very fast," Maria says, and looks at her watch again. Just five more minutes. Her office is all the way in Melbourne. There is no way she'll make it in time. She'll be at least half an hour late. Maria sighs. She'll have to stay half an hour longer this afternoon to make up for it. Well, at least Tara is happy. She is jumping and running around giggling.

They approach the car and Maria grabs her keys and unlocks it. Tara jumps inside and Maria hurries to her door and opens it, when someone sneaks around her vehicle. It is him again. The same man that stared at them inside the store.

Maria gasps in shock.

"I'm sorry," the man says. "I didn't mean to startle you."

Maria places a hand on her chest. Her heart is beating fast. "It's okay," she says. "I am just...in a hurry."

"I was just wondering if you could help me," the man says, and moves a step closer.

Maria wonders if she should just jump inside the car and drive off. The man stares at her. Tara is yelling from inside the car.

"Come on, Mommy!"

"I really don't have any time," she says, and is about to get inside of her car.

"It'll only be one second. You see, my wife is in that car over there and she's not well. The car won't start and..."

Maria looks at the man. She feels confused, conflicted. Normally she would always help, but this time...there is something odd about this guy. She turns her head to look at the car he pointed at, but can't see anyone inside of it. Tara is yelling again.

"There's no one in the car," Maria says.

When she turns her head, the man is right in front of her. He pushes her inside the car. Maria screams.

"What are you doing?"

"Mommy?" Tara says.

The man is strong, and even though she fights him, she can't get up. "Help! Someone heeelp!"

She tries to kick him, but can't. She manages to scratch him on his arm with her nails while panic spreads inside of her. She has to get him off her. She has to get away from here, now.

"Lie still, bitch," he yells, and slaps her across the face.

Tara screams when she sees him hitting her mother. "Get out of the car, Tara," Maria yells. "Get out and run for help!"

Tara yells something, but Maria doesn't hear what it is. She just keeps screaming at the child to run for help inside Target. Maria regains more of her strength and manages to punch the attacker in the stomach, when she hears the car door open and Tara scream for help.

That's it, that's my girl.

But the attacker punches Maria in the face and she loses consciousness for a few important minutes. When she opens her eyes, Tara's screams have changed character and sound more panicked and helpless. Maria manages to look outside and sees her daughter in the arms of the man, who is carrying her over his shoulder back towards the car.

"No!"

"Oh, yes," the man says, as he throws Tara in the back of the car and slams the door shut. He approaches Maria and leans over her.

"The deal was for the both of you, *Maria.*"

OCTOBER 2015

Tara?

Maria opens her eyes. She can still taste the fumes from the white cloth that was held against her mouth until she gave up the fight. It makes her want to throw up. She is panicking. She blinks her eyes. Tara is here. Tara is right next to her on the bed. What a relief.

Tara seems to be asleep. Maybe she too is knocked out. Maria has a headache. Probably from the fumes.

We've got to get out of here.

Maria gets up from the bed. She leans over her daughter and can hear her breathing. It fills her with relief again. The girl is alive, sleeping heavily, but alive. Maria walks to the window and realizes she is in a house some-where. The view is spectacular, but she's got to be at least forty feet up. Beneath her are a tennis court and a lap-pool. She grabs the handle to the sliding door and tries to open it. It is locked and you need a key to open it.

Maria looks around the room. It is sparsely decorated with a queen bed and a dresser. Nothing on the walls. Nothing on the floors. Just white tiles. She looks at the door to the room and walks to it. She grabs the handle but —as suspected—it is locked as well.

Maria sighs and walks back to the bed. She can't see her purse anywhere, so she doesn't have her phone. Tara is breathing heavily. Maria leans over her and kisses her on the lips. She can't begin to say how happy she is that she is still alive and still here with her.

But, now what?

Where the hell are we? Are we at that awful man's place? What does he want with us?

Tara starts to slowly wake up as well. She is smacking her lips, probably thirsty. Maria realizes there is a small bathroom attached to the room and she goes in there to get some water from the tap. She finds a plastic cup and fills it. She wets Tara's lips with water. Soon Tara blinks her eyes and opens them to look at her mother.

"Mom?" she says sleepily.

Maria feels like crying, but she holds it back. "It's okay, baby. I got you some water."

Tara sits up and Maria lets her drink from the cup. When she is done, Maria drinks some as well. It tastes like chlorine, but it's better than nothing. She finishes the cup.

"Where are we, Mommy?"

"I don't know, baby."

"I wanna go home now."

"Me too. But we got to wait till the man lets us out, all right?" Maria can hear her own voice shivering as she speaks. She is terrified by what the man wants from them, but she is also determined to get out of here, alive and with her daughter in her arms. No matter what.

"What do you mean, Mommy? Has the man kidnapped us?"

"I...I don't know."

Tara is about to cry. Maria wants to cry as well, but she doesn't allow herself to. She grabs her daughter in her arms and holds her tight.

"It'll be all right, baby. Mommy will get us home; don't you worry, baby. Don't you worry."

OCTOBER 2015

There is a sound behind the door. The handle is moving, and a key is put in the lock. Maria gasps and grabs Tara. She pulls her close to her while staring at the door handle.

Who is behind that door? Is it the guy from Target? What does this person want with us? Will he kill us? Will he take Tara from me?

Maria swallows her desire to scream, as the door slowly opens. A face appears. He is big. His hair thick for his age. She has seen him before, she thinks. He reminds Maria of some actor, but she can't remember which one. The way he looks at them makes her very uncomfortable. He is wearing a suit that looks very expensive to Maria. The kind of suit her dad's clients would wear when they came to his office at the law firm.

The man places both hands on his sides and smiles. He walks towards Tara and strokes her cheek gently, with slow yet firm movements. Tara becomes stiff in her arms and Maria tries to pull her away from him.

"Look at you two," the man says. "Even prettier in real life than in the pictures. I have been looking forward to seeing you both."

"Mommy!" Tara says and throws her arms around Maria's neck.

"Where are we?" Maria says, snorting in anger. "Why are we here?"

Maria notices that the door to the room is still left open. She wonders if she can make a run for it.

The man shakes his head. "Tsk, tsk. Now don't you worry your pretty little heads with that. You're finally here, and boy how we are going to have fun together."

"I wanna go home, Mommy!" Tara says, while clinging to her mother's neck.

"Now, don't say that," the man says. "This is your new home. You will stay here with me until I get tired of you. As long as you do what I say, I will keep you alive, huh?" He touches the tip of her nose. He smiles and tilts his head. "Now, let's see what I have here." He puts a hand in his pocket and pulls out a red lollipop. He hands it to Tara. She doesn't want to take it and turns her head away while clinging tightly to her mother.

"Please, sir," Maria says. "Please, just let us go."

The man sighs. "Now, that is the only thing I can't do. See, I paid good money for the two of you and I can't get that money back if I let you go. So...well..." he shrugs and pushes the lollipop at Tara. "Here."

She shakes her head. Maria doesn't like the expression in the man's eyes when she rejects him. Anger is building and it scares her. She has seen it before in one of her earlier boyfriends.

"Take the lollipop, Tara," she says.

"But, Mooom! You always say..."

"I know what I say; just take it. Do as I tell you to."

Tara sniffles and looks at the man. He places his hand on her back and caresses it gently. Maria can't stand the way he is touching her. She feels like screaming at him, but she doesn't dare to.

Finally, Tara reaches out and grabs the lollipop.

The man sighs. "There you go. Now, that wasn't so hard, was it?"

"Say thank you," Maria says.

"Thank you," Tara sniffles.

The man reaches out and touches Tara's hair. Everything is turning inside of Maria. The man stares at Tara's hair. "You're welcome."

"Now can we go home?" Tara asks.

The man burst into a sudden laughter that makes Maria jump. "Ha!" He leans over them and says: "No, you can't. But we can play a game. Now, what would be fun to play? I know it! How about hide and go seek? Yes, that is my favorite game of all time."

"I love hide and go seek," Tara says.

The man clasps his hands. "How wonderful!" He grabs Tara by the chin. "I have a feeling you and I are going to be GREAT friends." He leans over and whispers. "Now, go...hide."

PART I

GENTLEMEN PREFER BLONDES

1

APRIL 2016

"WELCOME TO CHEATER'S."

The half-naked woman greeting Danny Schmidt in the doorway smiles. Danny nods and walks to the back of the place and finds somewhere to sit. Two girls are dancing on the podium, slithering up and down the poles. Another girl approaches him and asks him what he would like to drink. He orders a beer and hands her a tip that she puts in her bra. She winks and leaves him. Danny watches the dancers. One of them is young, barely eighteen, he thinks. Her eyes are blurry. She is very pretty and the men seem to like her. Especially one guy smoking a cigar, he claps at her every move and rains money on her. She barely notices it.

The waitress comes back. She places his beer in front of him. He gives her another tip that disappears into her bra. As she is about to leave, he grabs her wrist.

"Say, don't you have anyone younger than these two?" he asks.

She stares at him for a few seconds, scrutinizing him. "Sure." She rubs her fingertips against one another to tell him it'll cost him.

Danny smiles. "Naturally."

He hands her a hundred-dollar bill. She smiles even wider now, then leans over and whispers.

"How do you prefer them?"

The way she is standing, Danny can look down her cleavage. "Blonde and young."

"How young?"

"Fourteen-fifteen?"

She doesn't react. She is used to this kind of request. "Sure. We can get them even younger if you're willing to pay. But it's very expensive."

Danny nods. "The younger the better. He opens his jacket and shows her a bundle of money."

"All right, cowboy. Come out the back. To the VIP-section."

Danny throws a bill on the table, throws one last glance at the dancing girls, then follows the woman out behind a curtain. She tells him to sit on a couch while someone brings him a bottle of champagne. The girl opening it rubs herself against him. When it has popped she pours him a glass, then sits on his lap and rubs herself against his crotch.

"Enjoy the show, tiger," she whispers in his ear, and bites his lip before she leaves.

Danny sips the champagne while he waits. A few minutes later, the woman returns followed by three young blonde girls all dressed in sexy lingerie. By looking at their faces, he guesses them to be no more than twelve or thirteen. They're all wearing heavy make-up. The woman tells them to stand on the podium in front of Danny. They're posing for him. He rubs his chin while observing them. Music is put on and they are told to dance. They show him what they can do. He is very impressed and smiles. The woman approaches him.

"You like what you see, huh?"

"Yes."

"You want to touch? Touching costs more."

He hands her more money. She signals the girls to come closer. They swarm Danny now and he leans back on the couch. Their hands are on him, everywhere...on his chest, in his crotch. He looks into their eyes. They're all drugged, blurry. One of the girls is younger than the others, he realizes when looking into her eyes. He grabs her by the chin and looks at her face.

"You like her, huh?" the woman asks. "This is August."

"I like her," he says.

"Very good," the woman says. "She is a beauty."

"I'd like to spend the night with her."

Before the woman can say anything, Danny pulls out more money from his jacket and places it on the table. The woman doesn't say anything else.

"The back entrance is over there," she says, and grabs the two other girls and disappears.

2

APRIL 2016

"YOU FORGOT TO PACK HIM A LUNCH?"

I stare at Joey. We're standing in his townhouse. There is a mess everywhere. Clothes on the floor, cereal boxes left out on the kitchen table, dirty dishes in the sink. He looks like crap. Hasn't shaved in a week, or even showered, from what it looks like. I only stopped by to grab Salter's stuff. He's been with his dad for a few days.

I've brought Snowflake so he can say hi to his old friends. Clyde is barking at him while Snowflake sniffs Bonnie's behind. It doesn't seem like the animals have been out much, with the way they're acting up when they see us.

"Well, I didn't forget; I gave him some money to buy something."

"You know I hate it when he has to eat that food they serve in the cafeteria at the school. What is going on, Joe? You never used to be this sloppy."

He shrugs with a sigh. On the floor, I see a bra that, for obvious reasons, isn't mine. I look at it. "Is that...hers?"

Joey chuckles. "Yeah. Probably."

"So, that's it. You're partying with her and not taking anything seriously anymore?" I ask.

"What's it to you?"

"We have a kid, Joe, that's what it is to me. I don't want him to come here if you don't take care of him and if there is underwear lying all over the place." I pick up the bra, holding it between two fingers and hand it to him.

"Please, tell your girlfriend to stop throwing her undergarments everywhere. At least keep it where my son won't find it."

"You tell her yourself."

"She's here?"

"Yeah. She kind of...lives here now."

My eyes widen. "What? She moved in? Just like that?"

He shrugs again. "It was easier."

I can't believe him. I don't know what to say. I don't want to say any more. I am exhausted with this entire situation. I feel so hurt that he would move in with the woman he cheated on me with. Of course, to him it wasn't cheating, since we were separated at the time. I can't just move on. My son needs his dad and I need Joey to be a good role model for him. He isn't with the way things are right now. Joey is hardly working, he hangs out with Jackie, his girlfriend, who now apparently has moved in; they drink beers and party while I am left picking up the pieces of my son's broken heart. Salter is ten now. He is beginning to figure out what is going on and asking questions I have a hard time answering.

"So, that's it now? She is definitely a part of our lives?" I ask. "Because I sure hope you're planning on staying with her, since you chose to bring her into your son's life."

"Don't be so uptight. It's annoying," he says with a groan.

I want to shake him. I want to yell at him and tell him I need him to snap out of this, whatever it is that's going on with him. I owe the guy so much. I owe him my life. We have known each other since we were in preschool and we were married for what felt like an eternity. But now, as I am standing in front of him, I don't recognize him anymore. All my life I have known and loved this guy, but...now I feel like I don't know him at all. Why would he choose this life?

"Don't you have to work today?" I ask.

"Nope. Nothing out there for me."

"You're telling me no one needs a carpenter today or even later this week?"

He rolls his eyes at me. It makes me angry. I can't believe him. Joey has barely worked in two months. I can't help wondering if he isn't doing enough to get something, to get the jobs. Is he even out there, or does he just stay at home with her? She works at Juice 'N Java downtown, but only a few times a week. She can't be making much. I have no idea how they're getting by, how they're paying the rent.

"You know what, Mary? It really is none of your damn business," Joey growls. Clyde is barking and Snowflake runs after him. Bonnie trots after them, not really engaged in their little fight.

Joey picks up Salter's sports bag, pulls a few clothing items from the floor and throws them in, then hands it to me.

"Here. This is what you came for, right? Now you can go."

3

APRIL 2016

SHE IS ALMOST BURSTING with excitement. Paige Stover can't hide it in the car when she sees the rec center. Paige just started taking basketball lessons and loves hanging out with Coach Joe. Once a week, he gives her a private lesson, since she is very new to the game, and then the team meets every Saturday. It's expensive for her mother, Nicky, but since her parents died, Nicky inherited a good sum of money.

It feels good to finally be able to give Paige what she wants in life. After twelve years of being a poor, single mother, Nicky is finally able to give her daughter what she deserves. What all the other kids have. Paige is such a good girl, does well in school, and wants to do a lot of sports, even though she isn't among the most athletic around.

"There she is. There's my Paige-girl," Coach Joe yells when they enter the center.

Paige grabs the ball from between her mother's hands and runs towards him. They hug.

"Have you been practicing flipping your wrist like I told you to?" he asks, and shows her how to do it.

Paige repeats the gesture and he laughs putting his hands on both her arms. He hugs her again. "You sure have."

Nicky sits down and pulls out her phone, while Coach Joe starts instructing Paige. He asks her to run first to warm up, then dribble while running with the ball. Then he asks her to shoot hoops. Twenty-five shots. She misses most of them. Coach Joe laughs heartily and makes her run again, then do push-ups to build up the strength in her arms. Paige is skinny. She hasn't played many sports until recently, since they can now afford to pay for it. But she has barely any muscles.

Nicky looks at the display of her phone and goes through her emails. Her decorating business is doing well and there are several requests from new costumers. She looks at Paige and the Coach, then walks outside to make a few calls.

Nicky is very pleased to finally be able to make a living for herself. It has taken her years to get to this point, where the costumers come to her and not the other way around. It all travels by word of mouth, but it takes years to get people talking. It used to be that she had to work another job on the side. She has held many jobs as a secretary for years, but her dream has always been to have her own business. Like her father always used to say, there are two ways to live your life. Either you are busy making someone else's dream come true or you're busy making your own come true. Nicky has always known she would one day make her own dream come true. But being a single mother, after Mike left when Paige was just a baby, was hard and required that she have a steady income for many years. She couldn't just quit her job and devote herself to her business. Not until she had enough clients.

Nicky makes a couple of new appointments and plots them down in the calendar of her phone. She looks at the clock. The time is almost up. She hurries back inside, but finds the rec center empty.

"Hello?"

Nicky looks around the empty basketball court. Where can they be?

"Paige? Coach Joe?"

Nicky's heart is in her throat as she walks to the office, only to find that empty as well. "Coach Joe? Paige?" she yells again, this time slightly panicking.

They can't have left, can they? I was right outside all the time. I would have seen them. Could they have used the back entrance?

"Mom! We're right here!"

Nicky turns and sees Paige. She is standing in a doorway leading to a room Nicky hadn't noticed before. Behind her is Coach Joe, both his hands placed on Paige's shoulders. He is smiling.

"I just showed Paige a small clip from a game last weekend. We have a TV in here."

Nicky swallows hard while the worry and anxiety are pushed back. She curses her own paranoia. Of course, everything is fine.

4

SAIGON, VIETNAM, 1975

DANH NGUYEN LOOKS at his sister. She smiles and unwraps his present. He feels the excitement in every bone of his body. He has been looking forward to giving her this doll. His sister is his everything. His beautiful—three years younger—sister, Long, who makes every room brighter when she enters.

Today, she is turning eight years old. All her siblings, five brothers and four sisters, and her parents and grandparents are gathered in the house on their father's estate. Their father is a wealthy businessman, and they're fortunate enough to belong to the upper class.

"Thank you! Thank you!" Long exclaims when she sees the doll. She throws her arms around his neck. Danh holds her tight and closes his eyes.

"You're welcome," he whispers lovingly. "Only the best for *your majesty.*"

Long giggles. She loves it when Danh calls her that, when they pretend she is a princess.

"Let's eat," their mother says and claps her hands.

Her face is growing new wrinkles every day, it seems to Danh. He knows she is concerned by what is happening to their country these days. Everyone is afraid of the Communist Government and what they might do next. Danh understands some of it and sees it on his parents' faces, but he feels certain they are very safe. Their dad is a respected person in the area. He has always kept all of them safe.

Danh looks at the table with all the food and smiles again. Unlike many others, they have money enough to live well, even though they can't get the supplies they usually do, they manage to get by anyway.

"Did you hear what happened to Uong?" his grandmother suddenly says when everyone has started eating.

Danh looks up and sees his parents' reaction. Uong is the man who lives only two houses down the street. Danh hasn't heard what happened to him.

"Not now, *mẹ*," his mother says.

"I would like to hear it, *bà ngoại*," Danh says, adressing his grand-mother. He has known Lan Uoung since he was born and likes to hang out around his store. "What happened to him?"

Danh's mother shakes her head. "Not now, Danh. Today we're cele-brating."

"But..."

"*Không! No!* I said not today, Danh."

Danh can tell by the look on her face he has to let it go. He sinks into his chair and goes quiet. Still, he can't stop wondering what it is they won't talk about. Sometimes he hates being one of the young ones. His older siblings all know when to stay quiet and when to speak. Danh never does. At least he isn't the youngest anymore.

They eat in silence. Long doesn't look as happy any more and Danh makes a few funny faces at her to cheer her up. It is, after all, her birthday.

Long giggles and clasps her mouth. Danh feels better when he sees her happy. As long as she is happy, there is nothing wrong with the world.

Not until the door is kicked in.

They all hear it, but it goes so fast, Danh hardly realizes it before they have them surrounded. Ten police officers storm inside, guns pointed at them. Danh's mother starts to scream when they throw themselves at Danh's father and hold him down while putting him in handcuffs.

All Danh can think about is Long. He grabs her in his arms and covers her eyes.

"It's all part of a game, your majesty," he whispers in her ear. "They're here to celebrate your birthday and they'll just get upset if we don't play along."

The policemen order all of them to sit on the floor in the living room, while they drag their father away. Danh's mother tries to stop them, but is knocked down and beat up by an officer. The grandparents and siblings scream and cry for them to stop. Finally, they do. Bruised and beaten, their mother crawls back to her family.

Danh closes his eyes too and tries to imagine being in his favorite spot, in a canoe on the river, fishing with Long by his side. While the policemen trash the place and steal all their belongings, Danh whispers stories in Long's ears of the many times they have been fishing together, trying to get her to stop crying.

"Remember the time you fell in the water? Do you?"

"*Vâng. Yes,*" she whimpers.

"We couldn't stop laughing, remember?"

"I remember," she whispers, and he feels how she calms down in his arms, while the sound of glass shattering becomes nothing but a distant noise.

Hours later, when the sounds slowly disappear, Danh dares to open his eyes again and look around.

Everything is gone. All their belongings are either gone or destroyed. Nothing is left. A note on the wall tells them the house now belongs to the government, along with the family's other houses.

They have one day to leave.

5

APRIL 2016

MY DAD'S house is so quiet. Salter is still in school, my dad is sleeping, and so is Snowflake. I am sitting in front of the computer wondering if I can shake this morning's fight with Joey. I don't understand why he gets to me the way he does. Well, if I am being perfectly honest, then maybe I can. I am so angry with him for moving on and for acting like a teenager in love all of a sudden, not living up to his responsibilities.

After leaving him with Salter's sports bag in my hand, I had to drive to Subway and buy a sandwich for Salter and take it to the school. Call me controlling...I don't want him eating that food in the cafeteria.

The blank page is staring at me from the computer. I am trying to write an article about a democratic senator that has been travelling to spots around the globe on trips sponsored by private people, people that were known for conservative views. I am sitting on the story, since no one else has discovered this. Chloe is actually the one who gave me the information. Apparently, the guy is also known to be active in the websites and chat rooms she observes for use of child porn. She tracked him down, then broke into his computer and found all the material we needed to take him down publicly.

I, for one, can't wait.

I make myself another cup of coffee, push Joey out of my head, then start writing. Seconds later, the keyboard is glowing, and I can't stop. The material is so good and I can't wait to publish it and see this guy taken down. I know this will be a big story, one that the newspapers will have to quote us on in the morning.

Snowflake wakes up as I press publish, and someone is at the door. I get up and open it. It's Marcia. I smile happily.

"You have time for coffee?" she asks.

"Always. Come on in."

I make a new cup for myself and one for Marcia, then find some cookies in the cabinet that I bring out with it. We sit in the living room overlooking the glittering ocean. The waves aren't very good today. There is too much wind for it to be fun. Suits me well enough. I needed the time to write.

"So, how's it going?" I ask, with a cookie half eaten in my mouth.

Marcia smiles. "I'm getting the kids for the weekend," she says.

"Really? That's amazing!"

She nods. It's been a long time since I have seen that kind of light in her eyes. It makes me happy. She is doing really well on her medicine and with the help from her sister.

"Carl finally agreed to let me have them for three days in a row after my doctor called him and told him I was ready."

"I am so happy to hear that," I say, and put a hand on her shoulder. "And you're sure you can handle it, right? It's not too much? Four kids for three days can be a lot with all you're going through."

"My sister will help me," she says. "I just want to be with my babies again. I have seen them only a few hours here and there since they moved back with their dad. I miss them so much. I miss being a part of their lives, you know? I miss noticing the little differences every day as they grow older."

"I understand. I have to get used to being without Salter for several days in a row. I'm not sure I'm doing so well on that part," I say with a light laugh. "I'm not doing well with any of this, having to give up Joey and see him with that...that girl. Knowing they're together as a family with Salter when it should be me. It ain't easy, I tell you that."

"I hear you met someone?" she asks.

I grab another cookie. "You mean Tom? Yeah. We've been on a few dates. I met him through Tinder. I can't believe I tried that, but Chloe persuaded me to. He seems like a nice guy. Not a local, which is good, since we know all of them from back then. Moved here four years back from South Florida, works at the Space Center. Something with the weather stations, I am not quite sure I get it. He's tried to explain it to me several times, but I just pretend like I understand. Basically, he's the guy who tells them if the weather is good enough for a launch or not. That's how far I am." I laugh again and eat yet another cookie. Marcia follows me, which pleases me immensely, since I hate eating alone.

"Have you heard from Sandra lately?" Marcia asks.

I shake my head. "No. Not in a really long time. I have a feeling she's avoiding me. She's probably fooling around with Alex still."

Marcia stares at me and I clasp my mouth. "Whoops."

"She and Alex are fooling around?"

I make a grimace. "Yeah, well, I wasn't supposed to say anything. Me and my big mouth."

"That totally explains everything," Marcia exclaims. "I've noticed how they look at each other, but always thought it was all about them longing for each other, since they can't be together. But they're both married?"

"You're telling me. I've tried to explain that to them. I even threatened to tell their spouses, but they still continue this charade behind their backs. I can't get myself to meddle in it, though. They're grown-ups; they'll have to deal with it themselves."

"Wow," Marcia says, and leans back on the couch with her coffee between her hands.

"I know, right? To be frank, it's actually nice to have told you, because now I'm not the only one who knows."

"Speaking of betrayal, are we getting any closer to catching that brother of yours?" she asks.

I grunt. I hate talking about my brother, Blake. He is the one who poured acid on Sandra's face, making her lose her modeling career and destroying her marriage. He is a killer on the run, and I want to get him so badly.

"There's nothing new since Naples, where they found the body of Olivia Hartman," I say. "Detective Fisher has tried to work with the local police over there, but so far they haven't found any traces of him. He was long gone when they found the body inside the mattress at the motel. They're looking for him in the area, but there is no way he'd stay there after he killed her. He's not that stupid."

"Where do you think he is now?" Marcia asks.

I shrug. "Chloe is trying to track him, but he is being very clever. Doesn't use any credit cards, not any in his own name. His picture has been shown in the news over there, but they have no idea where he is. He is gone, again."

I grab another cookie, deciding if I make this my lunch, then I am allowed to have a couple more. Talking about Blake always makes me want to eat.

"So, what's the plan?" Marcia asks.

"There is no plan," I say. "We wait. We wait for him to make a mistake. Which he will sooner or later. I know that much about my dear baby brother."

6

APRIL 2016

THE WIND FEELS WARM. The strong engine of the silver Ducati lifts the bike off the road as it roars into the wind. Blake laughs out loud and speeds up. He zigzags between cars and trucks on the road. The motorcycle rockets forward. Blake yells when feeling the power beneath him.

This is the way to ride!

He stole the bike outside a restaurant in Naples right before he left town. He bought himself a helmet in Fort Meyers, a black one with a black visor. He looks badass when he wears it.

When Blake reaches a busy intersection, all the cars around him slow down. Blake doesn't. He turns the throttle, picks up even more speed, and barely avoids crashing into a stopped car as he zigzags between them across the intersection, speeding through the red light. A car hits the brakes and honks the horn aggressively. Blake doesn't give the driver the time of day. He is doing seventy-five, steering straight towards a building. The wall is approaching rapidly, but Blake doesn't brake. He aims the bike closer and closer, while the adrenalin is pumping through his veins; while imagining the collision, he sees the faces of the girls he has killed. He sees their eyes, the fear as they scream, and he feels it all over again, feels the torment, the intoxicating power.

At the last possible second, he steers the bike and spins it hard to the right. The bike tips to the side and screeches across the asphalt. Panting, he manages to get it to skid to a stop before he turns the throttle again and accelerates back onto the road, heart pounding heavily in his chest. He yells out into the air as he continues to zigzag between driving cars.

Never has he felt this free, this invincible. So many lives he has taken, so many lives destroyed, and still they haven't caught him yet; heck, they're not even close. They have no idea where he is or what will be his next move.

Freaking idiots. They'll never know. I am always gonna be one step ahead of them. Ha!

Blake zooms across the road and hits the bridge where the air shifts to the fresh salty air coming from the ocean. He takes in a deep breath. How he loathes that smell. How he hates this place.

He approaches ninety miles an hour as he crosses the bridge. The traffic is getting heavy now, as he gets closer to the island.

Freaking tourists.

The traffic is soon blocked up and Blake is going so fast he can't stop. He sees the rear end of a Toyota pick-up truck approaching fast. He can't go left or right. There is no way out.

In the last second, Blake yanks the bike across the road and is now driving against the oncoming traffic. He speeds up, the engine roaring loudly as he sees the approaching car, flickering its headlights, honking its horn. Blake is standing up on the bike now, yelling and screaming as he faces death, prepares himself for not surviving this, until the second before the car hits him...he turns and ends up in between the cars going in each direction. Knocking their side mirrors off one after the other with his fists, he drives straight through the line of cars until he can get in front of them and back onto the road.

Blake is laughing loudly at the blaring horns as he gets ahead of all of them and reaches the end of the bridge. Running another red light, he makes a turn and drives onto the island, speeding up across A1A.

As he reaches the house on the corner of 7th Street, he finally hits the brakes. The tires screech on the asphalt and the bike slips underneath him, making him turn really fast.

He is stopped.

He stares at the new house they have built that looks a lot like the old one, only bigger. In there. Behind that gate, behind those doors and walls, lives his father. His poor and helpless father, the man he has hated for his entire life, along with the sister he has always wanted dead.

7

APRIL 2016

DANNY DRIVES up to the man standing on the corner of Barton Boulevard and Huntington Lane. He rolls down the window and the guy approaches him.

"I saw your ad on Craigslist," Danny says.

"Yeah? So what?" the man asks with a sniffle.

"Personals."

The man's fingers drum on the car. He has a lit cigarette in his other hand. He smokes it and the smoke enters Danny's car.

"All right," the man says, and nods in the direction of a building. "Apartment number 245. The code is 1 1 1 for the gate."

Danny rolls up the window and drives to the gate. The complex is nice. Not among the most expensive ones around, but not cheap either. The type you'd expect retired people to live in when they come down here for the winter. It has a pool with a hot tub, a tennis court, and a small clubhouse.

No one would ever suspect what this place really hides.

Danny punches in the code and the gate opens. He drives inside and parks the car in front of the building. It's been painted in nice bright colors, in the Key West-style that many use in Florida to make it look exotic.

Danny takes in a deep breath, then walks down one of the hallways. He finds the elevator and rides to the second floor. When he gets out, his phone rings. He picks it up.

"Hey, Junior," he says, keeping his voice low.

"Dad, we're out of milk."

"I'll grab some when I come home," Danny says.

His teenage son sighs from the other end. "When will you come home? I'm really hungry."

"Maybe grab some toast instead, huh? This might take a while. How was school today?"

"Boring."

"Got any homework?"

"What do you think? I'm graduating in a month. Of course I have tons of homework."

"Then go do that, and I'm sure I'll be home to make some dinner."

"You don't sound sure. Where are you, anyway? I thought this was your day off from the fire station?"

"Yeah, well, I had some paperwork I needed to finish up. I'll be home soon. Do your homework."

Danny hangs up and looks at the display for a few seconds before he puts the phone away. He thinks about his son and the fact that he will graduate high school in just a month. He can't believe his son is growing up so fast. Life has been hard on Junior since his mom died, but at least he has his school. And then what? Junior has shown no interest in college. Will he move out? Will he get a job? Danny might be able to get him something at the fire station. He always wanted for his son to follow in his footsteps, but he has shown no interest in becoming a firefighter. Lately, it's like nothing really interests him anymore.

Danny takes in a deep breath and walks to the door with the number 245 on it. He knocks and the door is opened.

"I'm here about the ad," he says.

The woman at the door nods and he follows her inside. When the door is closed she looks at him. "Money first."

Danny nods, grabs the envelope in his pocket, and hands it to her. The woman's face lights up as she counts the many hundred dollar bills. The apartment smells bad. Like cigarettes and sex.

"She's right in here," the woman says, and walks ahead of him towards a door. She knocks on the door and a big guy opens it. "New client," the woman says.

"We're just finishing up," the big guy says. He looks at Danny. "He can watch if he likes."

Danny walks inside. Just as he enters, another man walks past Danny towards the door. They don't look at each other or exchange glances. They don't want to know who the other one is. They never want to see each other again.

The girl on the bed isn't moving. She is too drugged. Danny looks at her. "I paid extra for privacy," he grunts, and seconds later they're left alone.

8

APRIL 2016

I DRIVE Marcia to Publix and help her get groceries. It's hard for her to do even little things like shopping because she has no license after her DUI. Usually, she just goes on her bike, but she can't carry much on her bike. So her sister sometimes drives her, and every now and then I take her. Gives me time to talk to her and I enjoy that. Especially now that she is doing so much better. I realize I have missed her and who she used to be before the drinking started.

I decide to make lasagna tonight. Lasagna is Salter's favorite dish. He is supposed to stay at my house for the next week and a half, and I intend to spoil him rotten. I miss him while he is with his father. I'm not used to it yet.

"Will you come and surf with us soon, please?" I ask Marcia, as we carry out our groceries and put them in the back of my car. Marcia hasn't been surfing for a very long time.

"Yes. I was just thinking about it today. I think it would be good for me to get back out there. What does the forecast say?"

"Tomorrow is supposed to be good. Maybe once Salter is back from school around low tide? I have a date tomorrow night, and I would like to get a little exercise in before I pull on a dress again," I say with a laugh. Not because it is funny, but because I am embarrassed by how much weight I have gained lately. I don't know if it is the break-up with Joey or what, but I can't stop eating sweets. I don't even count the amount of cookies I eat in a day anymore. I don't want to know.

"A date, huh? That sounds great," Marcia says. "I should be able to go out with you two for a little while tomorrow."

"Yay," I say, and close the trunk.

I open the door to the car, and then pause. "Is that Danny?"

"Where?"

"Over there getting into his car," I say and point.

"Looks like him, but who's the girl?" Marcia asks, wrinkling her nose. "She looks a little young."

I stare at the young girl in the very short skirt. She doesn't seem to be able to walk on her own without Danny supporting her.

"Could it be one of Junior's friends?" I ask.

"If Junior had friends in a brothel," Marcia says. "That girl is doped. She looks like a junkie and a prostitute. What is he doing with her?"

I shrug. I don't like this feeling. I know Danny has had a hard time since his wife was killed last fall. I know he is lonely, but still. It is hard to tell the girl's age with the clothing and the heavy make-up, but she doesn't look a day over eighteen—if that.

Marcia waves. "Hey, Danny!"

He sees her and nods while helping the girl inside of his car. He doesn't seem to be his usual happy self, and he doesn't come over to talk to us. Instead, he nods again, gets into his seat, and drives off.

So unlike Danny.

"What was that about?" Marcia asks.

I shrug again and get in behind the wheel. "Maybe he was in a hurry."

"Danny is usually so friendly."

"I know. Maybe he didn't like us seeing him with her."

"You think he was embarrassed?"

"Yeah. Something like that. Wouldn't you be?"

I back out of the parking spot.

"Yeah," Marcia says. "I knew he was lonely, but not that he was *that* desperate. You think he likes young girls like that?"

"I don't know what he likes, but I can tell you that it worries me. Last week, I saw him come out of Cheaters in Cape Canaveral with another girl. Much like this one, only I'm pretty sure she was even younger."

"Oh, my."

"I know."

9

APRIL 2016

THE YOUNG GIRL in the picture is smiling. Her front teeth are too big for her face, but she is still pretty. Her eyes are sparkling as she holds her surfboard up for the camera. Boxer clicks the picture and looks at it more closely. He watches her features. She has brown eyes. Long dark hair. Just like what the client is asking for. But is she the one?

He is not sure.

He closes the picture again, and then continues looking through the timeline on the mother's Facebook page. The mom is stunning. He wonders if her breasts are real or not. They look almost too perfect in that light summer dress she is wearing in the next picture. Not that it usually matters to his client.

Boxer closes Facebook and moves on to the mother's Instagram. She has a lot more pictures here, and he can go through everything she has posted over the past year or so. Lots of pictures of her and her daughter. Of them at Disney World, of them at Brevard Zoo, of them eating ice cream. The mother is very into the environment and posts a lot about the dead fish in Banana River and how to save the lagoon. On Facebook, he has seen that she plans on being at the rally next weekend.

Maybe he will be there too.

A message pops up in the chat room and he turns to the needs of his client.

>What do you have for me?<

>I think I have your match. Sending pictures now.<

Boxer downloads the woman's photos to his own computer, and then uploads them in the secure chat room. He sits back in his chair and drinks from his coffee while waiting for the client's answer.

>Are the breasts real?<

>I don't know. Does it matter?<

>Not really. But do you have others?<

>I do. Give me a sec.<

Boxer grumbles as he goes back to Facebook and finds another mother and daughter that he thought of as a match. He really thought his client would like the first ones better. He downloads a few more pictures, then posts them in the chat room. This woman has smaller breasts, but a bigger behind. She is a good match, but she has recently gotten a boyfriend, and Boxer doesn't like that. Usually he only goes after the single mothers, since they're easier. They're alone more often and it takes longer before anyone discovers that they are gone.

Single moms, especially those that struggle financially, are the easiest targets. They're flakier and move around often, either for jobs or because they met someone.

>I like the first one better,< the client finally answers.

Boxer smiles widely as he looks at the pictures again. >Good choice, sir. That's a nice pair. Both of them are truly beautiful. Ready and ripe.<

>Then let's harvest. ASAP.<

Boxer smiles. He closes the chat and stares at the young girl with her surfboard. He touches the bridge of her nose with his pointer and lets it run across her young face. A beauty like her is going to make him a lot of money.

10

APRIL 2016

"I AM SO sorry for springing this on you at the last minute."

I move aside and let Chloe come in. "It's no problem, Mary," she says, and puts her laptop on the kitchen table.

Salter is on the couch with his iPad. He doesn't even look up. I know he can hear us, but he just doesn't want to. He has been in a bad mood all afternoon since I told him Chloe was going to look after him tonight.

"So your date changed his plans, huh?" Chloe asks.

"Yes," I say with a sigh. "We were supposed to go out tomorrow night, but he had to change it, so I said yes to today; otherwise, we couldn't see each other till next week. I hope it's not a big problem."

Chloe shakes her head. "It's not. Not for me at least." She throws a glance at Salter, who still doesn't pay any attention to us.

"I know. Salter is pissed. He's been at his dad's for a week and we were supposed to hang out together. But what can I do? I really want to see this guy. I think I like him."

"Salter will be fine. You'll have plenty of time together the rest of the week. It smells divine in here," Chloe says.

"I made a lasagna for you three to share."

Chloe's face is lit up. "Yum. I love your lasagna."

"I hope you didn't have other plans for tonight," I say, as I storm around, setting the table for them, wearing my dress that is a little too tight. Well, maybe not just a little.

"Me?" Chloe says. "Only work. I brought the laptop, so I can do it from here when Salter is asleep. And I brought Twister to play with Salter."

"That's awesome," I say, and take out the sizzling lasagna from the oven. "Salter loves Twister, don't you Salter?"

"Nah. Not really," he grumbles from the couch.

"Don't mind him," Chloe says. "We'll have a great night, the three of us. Don't you worry."

"Yeah, that reminds me. My dad is in his room watching TV. He's already in his chair, so if you could just roll him out here. I usually give him a fork to hold; now that he has regained sensitivity in eight of his fingers, he is actually able to hold it, and he can move the lower part of his right arm. He usually misses his mouth, so you'll have to help him out, and he spills a lot...I mean like *a lot*, but it's important for him to do it, in order to get better. I can clean up later when I get back. You don't have to think about it...and...there was something else, but now I can't remember what it was..."

Chloe places her hand on my shoulder. "We'll figure it out, Mary. Don't worry. We're going to be fine."

I sigh. "You're right. I'm obsessing. My dad can tell you what he needs. Guess I am just a little nervous about this date."

I take in another deep breath and straighten my back. "How do I look?"

She stares at me like she needs to find the right words. It's not a good sign.

"That bad, huh?" I ask.

"No. I mean. Yes. I'm sorry, Mary, but that dress is way too tight."

I chuckle. "Thanks for being honest, at least."

"Let's go upstairs and find another one," she says.

I follow her to my bedroom, where she disappears into my walk-in closet. I sit on the bed.

"We saw Danny today," I say.

"So?"

"It was so strange. Marcia and I were at Publix. We saw Danny in the parking lot. We waved, he didn't wave back, only nodded like he didn't want to talk to us. And he was with a young girl."

"So?" Chloe repeats.

"So...it's not the first time. Last week, I saw him coming out of Cheaters with another young girl on his arm."

Chloe pokes her head out of the closet. "Ah, come on."

"I'm serious, Chloe. I worry."

She disappears back inside. "You always worry."

"Well I'm worrying a lot, then," I say.

"You always worry a lot. It'll make you sick someday. I'm sure there's a perfectly good explanation for it."

"Yeah, that he likes young girls."

Chloe comes out. She looks angrily at me and points a finger at me. "No. Not Danny. Not him." She throws a dress at me. "Here, try this."

I pick it up. "Why not? Maybe he's always done this. We knew things were bad with Jean even before she was killed. Maybe this is what he was into. I just don't know what to do about it."

I put on the dress. When I look up, Chloe is right next to me.

"Let it go."

I shake my head. I can't believe her reaction to this. "I'm not going to let it go. It's illegal. And so...so wrong."

She helps me zip up in the back. The dress tightens on my body. I suck in everything I can.

"It's none of our business."

"Of course it is; how can you even say that? I love Danny, but I am not going to stand by and watch if he...if he hurts..."

Chloe turns me around and we're face to face. "Stop! Danny would never hurt anyone. You know that!"

"That's what I thought, but..."

"I don't want to hear any more about it, Mary. You do this all the time. You get this idea in your head and then you obsess about it till it drives all of us nuts. Danny is a sweet guy. He's our friend."

"Sorry. I just..."

"No. Not one single word more about this."

"All right. Geez."

"Now look at yourself and tell me you don't think this is better."

I look at myself in the mirror. The long blue dress looks really nice on me.

"See?" Chloe says. "You better listen to me."

I nod, bend forward, and kiss my friend on the forehead. "All right," I say. "I'll listen to you from now on. I'll let it go."

"Good. Now go have fun on your date."

"Yes, ma'am."

11

APRIL 1975

THE LARGE EXPLOSION makes the windows shake in the small one-room house in Saigon, where Danh and his eight siblings have lived with their mother since their homes were taken by the soldiers and their father sent to prison.

Danh is sitting on the floor with his younger sister when they hear it. Long whimpers and looks up at her big brother. Danh glares at his mother. Her face is worried.

Another explosion sends shocks through the children. They all look to their mother, who looks as scared as they are.

"What is it?" Long asks.

"Probably just thunder," Danh says. "Nothing to worry about."

Danh gets up and walks outside with his brothers. In the distance, they see smoke. Lots of smoke. Then another loud explosion. Screams in the air and lots of people in the streets. A neighbor comes running past them. Danh's older brother, Bao, stops him.

"What's going on?"

"The Vietcong's coming. They're making their way to the capitol building. We're getting out of here while we still can."

Bao looks at Danh, then at their other brothers. "What's going on?" Danh asks, confused and bewildered. He doesn't understand what is going on, but he knows it is bad. Just like on Long's birthday two months ago.

"They're coming," Bao says. "They're taking over."

With his heart in his throat, Danh walks back inside with his brothers, where their mother and sister are waiting.

"What is it, son?" their mother asks, seeing the concern on their faces.

"It is what we feared," Bao says.

Being the oldest, he has been the man of the house ever since they took their father. The responsibility has weighed on him and he looks a lot older than he really is, Danh thinks.

Their mother nods. Danh doesn't like the look on her face. It scares him.

"Get your bikes," she says. "Ride out of town and don't come back till things have calmed down. You hear me?"

"No!" Danh yells. "We're not leaving you here!"

"You must," his mother tells him. "They will make soldiers of you and rape your sister. Take her and get yourself as far away as possible, do you hear me?"

"But...but..."

Danh's mother grabs a crying Long in her arms and hands her to Danh. "You take care of your sister. You protect her, you hear me? You protect her with your life."

Danh is crying heavily now. He sniffles and nods. "Why can't you come with us?"

"I have to stay behind in case your father comes back. Besides, I'll slow you all down."

Danh looks at his mother's leg that is still bad since the beating she received when they arrested their father.

"Come on, Danh," Bao yells, standing in the doorway. "We have to hurry. They're getting closer."

Danh takes one last glance at his mother, and receives a worried look back. "Go," she whispers. "I'll be fine. I'll see you soon."

Crying, he carries his sister out the door, where Bao is waiting impatiently on his moped.

"Hurry up, Danh. Jump on the back."

12

APRIL 2016

TOM MEETS me in front of Heidi's Jazz club. I feel weird meeting someone else here, since it used to be mine and Steven's favorite place to go. But even though things went bad with him, I don't think it is fair to blame it on the Jazz club.

He whistles as he sees me walking towards him. "Wow. Look at you."

It's our third date, and I am glad the dress is classy and long and doesn't signal that I want to get laid. 'Cause I really do. Well, a part of me does. It has been forever. At least that's what it feels like. The other part of me just wants to call Joey. I can't get used to not being with him.

Tom holds the door for me as we walk inside. It is a Monday night, so I don't expect there to be a whole lot of people. That is actually another reason for us coming here. It is spring break in Cocoa Beach, and that means lots of people everywhere. I want to have Tom to myself.

Tom is not the most handsome guy I have met. Not like Steven or even like Joey. As a matter of fact, he is a little chubby, but that suits me well. I am tired of being the only chubby one in my relationships. Tom enjoys good food just as much as I do. That counts for a lot in my book.

"I got your table ready for you, Miss Mills," the lady greeting us says. We follow her to the small table close to the stage and sit down. It is dark inside, the kind of darkness that gives it a big city nightclub atmosphere. I like that about this place. The waiter approaches us and hands us menus and small flashlights to be able to see.

"Sorry that I had to change our plans in a hurry," Tom says and corrects his shirt. He is wearing a suit for our date. I love that. Joey never wore a suit for me. Not even a tie. Doesn't like the way it feels, he would say. He felt like he was being strangled. I have to say, I enjoy that Tom dresses up for me. Makes me feel like I matter to him.

"I would like a glass of Chardonnay to begin with," I say.

"I'll have an Oktoberfest-bier," Tom says, referring to the Austrian beer. The owner of the place, Heidi, is Austrian.

"And we'll have red wine with the dinner, right?" he asks.

"Yes. Red wine with the lamb," I say. That is another reason for me to choose this place. For Easter, they have the greatest lamb for the whole month of April. It is divine.

"So, why did you have to change your plans?" I ask when the waiter is gone. On the stage, the house band is setting up.

"I have a basketball tournament that I completely forgot about."

"You play basketball?" I say in surprise, thinking about his short, out of shape body.

"What? I don't look like I could play basketball?" he asks with a grin.

"I'm just surprised," I say.

"I coach basketball. Never was able to make it big myself, so now I am a coach, all right?"

"That makes more sense," I say, and sip my white wine, trying to look delicate and elegant. "Where?"

"At the rec center."

My face lights up thinking about him coaching little kids. "Aw."

"I knew that would hit a home run," he says, grinning even more. "Always works."

I chuckle as the waiter arrives with our food. The band opens by playing "Fly Me to the Moon." I secretly watch Tom as he sings along, not hitting a single note, and I notice that so far there is nothing I don't like about this guy.

13

APRIL 2016

NICKY COMES home from visiting a new client just before six o'clock. She pays the neighbor's son ten dollars and thanks him for picking up Paige and looking after her this afternoon while Nicky was in Melbourne looking at fabrics for a woman's couch.

How one woman can take so long making one little decision is beyond Nicky's comprehension. She had her go through all of her books. Nicky now worries about the rest of the house. If one decision takes this long, how will she ever finish that eighteen thousand square foot mansion? There will be other couches and furniture, and don't even get her started on the curtains.

"Hi, sweet pea," she yells up the stairs. "I'm home."

"Hi, mom," Paige answers from her room.

"I'll start dinner."

Paige doesn't answer. Probably busy on that computer again. Nicky shakes her head as she unpacks the groceries and starts dinner. She almost regrets buying it for her, since she spends so much time on that thing, but it just felt so good to finally be able to give her something that big and expensive, so as soon as she got the inheritance from her parents, she went to the Apple store and bought the biggest computer she could find and placed it in Paige's room. The girl hadn't been able to play Minecraft or Roblox like all the other kids, and was constantly left out when they discussed those games at school. It used to torment Nicky to know that her daughter was

falling behind in school where computers became more and more important every year.

Nicky turns on the TV and watches the local news as she peels the
potatoes. It's all about those dead fish in the lagoon again. Today, thousands
of dead fish have been seen in the Banana River and in people's canals.

Nicky stops peeling and turns up the volume. The condition of the
lagoon concerns her greatly. She wants to leave a world for her daughter to
grow up in. The reporter talks about the rally, arranged by a local celebrity,
that is planned for this Saturday, while showing more dead fish and then
interviewing concerned tourists who have come here for spring break to
fish.

"It's really disgusting what is going on here," a tourist from Canada
says. "I used to come here and there would be fish jumping into my boat
and the water would be crystal clear. This is bad. This is really bad."

Nicky feels a pinch of anger in her stomach as she returns to her potatoes. Meanwhile, the experts on TV argue whether the fish deaths are due
to fertilizer from people's yards, leaking septic tanks, or overpopulation of
manatees.

Nicky hurries up and puts all the potatoes in a pan with carrots and
other vegetables before she throws a Mahi Mahi fillet on top and puts it all
in the oven, thinking it is going to be terrible to not be able to eat local fish
anymore.

She runs upstairs, knocks on the door, and enters her daughter's room.
Just as expected—Paige is on the computer.

"Have you been on that thing all day?" Nicky asks.

"No. I had basketball as well."

"That's right," Nicky says. "Did you do well?"

"Yes. Coach says I can play in the tournament. We have a game on
Saturday at two."

Nicky smiles. She is so glad that Paige enjoys doing sports. There really
is no need to worry about her use of computers, is there?

"I'll have to make sure to be there for that, then," Nicky says. "Maybe
we can go together to the rally for the lagoon in the morning, then head
over to the game. How does that sound?"

Paige doesn't even look at her. She is all into her game and tapping
away on her keyboard.

"Sure, Mom. Whatever."

14

APRIL 2016

I TAKE Salter out surfing the next day after school. I feel bad for disappointing him the night before. He seems like he is still angry with me as we paddle out. I have texted Marcia to let her know that we're going out, but I secretly hope that she won't come, since I feel like my son needs to be alone with his mother.

"So, how was your day today?" I ask, when we're on the outside and wait on the next set of waves.

Salter has hardly spoken to me at all since he got back from school, and I can't stop thinking that something else is bothering him. I can't believe he can still be this mad about last night.

He shrugs. "Okay, I guess."

"Did you do anything fun?"

"Mom. This is fourth grade. We don't have time for fun."

"Ah. I forgot. Everything is so serious these days. Are there at least any girls you like in your class?"

He rolls his eyes. "Mom. Please."

"What? You used to always tell me these things."

"Well, I won't now."

"I'm not going to stop asking. I want to know everything about you, just so you know."

He rolls his eyes at me and I splash water at him. He smiles slightly. A set of waves is rolling towards us. We both start paddling for the same wave.

Salter catches it. I don't. He laughs at me as he rides past me. He does a nice turn on the lip and my heart is filled with pride.

"You know, there was actually room enough for the both of us on that wave," he says, teasing me as he comes back out.

"Very funny," I say.

"I can't believe you couldn't catch that one," he continues.

"Well, I am a little out of shape, all right. Let's leave it at that before someone gets hurt."

"A little?" he says with a grin.

"Hey!"

"Sorry," he says, laughing.

Another set of waves comes towards us. "Watch me catch this one," I say, and start to paddle.

Salter follows me. We give it all we have and share a party wave. I ride it longer than him and come back out, laughing.

"Now who's the cool one around here?"

"Certainly not you when you talk like that," he says.

"What? No street cred for that one?"

"Okay. I'll grant you a little cred. That was pretty cool."

"Thank you."

Salter goes quiet all of a sudden. He looks down in the water and his smile disappears.

"What's going on?" I ask.

He looks up. "What do you mean?"

"Come on. I'm your mother. I can tell when my son is troubled. Spit it out or I won't stop asking about it."

"It's nothing, Mom, really."

"Don't do that to me. That look on your face tells me it is a lot more than nothing. Spit. It. Out."

He looks me in the eyes. My heart starts pounding. This is serious. I know my boy. This is not a little thing.

"Promise you won't get mad," he says.

"All right. Kind of depends on what you've done."

"It's not like that. I just don't want to see you mad or sad."

"Okay. You're starting to scare me a little here, Salter."

He bites his lips while looking into my eyes. A set of waves rolls towards us, but we let it pass.

"I was thinking...that maybe I could go and live with dad for a little while?"

No!

I stare at him. My sweet baby boy. My accomplishment when every-thing else went wrong, the only one I knew I could trust and would always have by my side. He wants to leave me? He wants to go...live with his dad?

Please tell me you're kidding. Please say it is a joke. A cruel one, but just that. Just you pulling a prank on me.

"I'm serious, Mom. I really want to. I miss him. You had me for all that time in New York, and now I feel like it's his turn. He's my dad."

Joey put him up to this. It must be him. Damn you, Joey.

I swallow hard and don't even notice the next set of waves passing us. I can tell Salter is concerned; he is worried how I will react to this. He is afraid I might be sad or angry. I am angry and sad. Very much indeed. But I can't show him that.

"Well, if that's what you want, then I guess..."

I stop. I know it is what I am supposed to say, but that is not how I feel. I want to tell him what he wants to hear, but at the same time I feel like I need to be honest as well.

"You know what? No, I am not okay with it. It is painful, Salter. You know how much I love you and love being with you."

"Well, it hasn't felt like it recently," he says. "Besides, he's my dad. I want to be with him more. You're not my only parent. And it's not like we won't see each other. I'll be right down the street. Besides, I'll see you every other Wednesday and stay the weekend like I do with Dad now."

"I don't know what to say to that," I say honestly. I am pressing back tears. I sincerely wish I could just say it is okay, that I could be mature and adult enough to accept this, but I really can't. I don't want to. "I don't want you to live with your dad. I want you to live here with me."

Salter's facial expression changes. His eyes are angry now.

"I just knew it! I knew you would be like this. Why can't you ever just let me do what I want and not what you want? It's my life."

Salter turns his board before I can answer and starts to paddle for a wave. I try to stop him.

"Don't you leave me out here like this, Salter," I yell at him, but he has already caught the wave and rides it to the beach.

On his way, he passes Marcia, who is just paddling out to me. She is panting as she stops next to me. I bite my lips and hold back the tears while she smiles.

"What have I missed?"

15

APRIL 2016

THE MEN ARE STANDING shoulder to shoulder. Danny counts as many as eight men, all with the same hungry look in their eyes.

They call it a beauty pageant, as they present the girls one after the other. All the girls are wearing the same red dress. The only thing that separates them is the numbers pinned to their dresses.

Danny looks around in the arrival hall of Orlando Airport. No one who passes the windows seems to care or even wonder what is going on inside the coffee shop. They're busy with their own lives and where they're going.

These girls on the podium have just arrived as well. Taken here from countries like the Philippines, Cambodia or Thailand. Brought in on fake passports. The owner of the coffee house is the one presenting the girls, praising their best features to the men, speaking about them like they were models. But they're not. They're slaves. And they're about to be bought.

The man to Danny's right lifts his hand and points at girl number 3. He is wearing an expensive suit and jewelry. The coffee shop owner applauds him for it and takes the girl to him. She doesn't look at him; she doesn't put up a fight. She knows it is useless. She is broken and probably heavily drugged.

These people know how to break a girl. She was probably brought here thinking she was going to be an actress or a model or marry some rich American guy and be able to send back money to her family.

The man leaves with his purchase. Danny watches her as they walk past him. He guesses she can't be more than fourteen. Her family back home probably thinks she made it big, that she is the one who lucked out.

Danny turns to face the other girls. Another man makes his purchase and disappears with his girl. One buys two. Danny looks for eye contact. He tries to get it from one of the girls, to meet their eyes. But they're not there; they can't focus or look straight at him. Instead, they stare blankly into the air.

Except for one girl.

The girl with the number 2 on her dress. Her eyes are different. This girl's eyes are staring directly at Danny with a piercing gaze. There is something about her that makes Danny unable to stop looking at her. A fight. A feistiness.

This girl hasn't been broken, he thinks to himself. *There is still fight left in her. A great deal of fight.*

Danny is ready to make his bid. He wants this girl. He lifts his hand high in the air.

"I vote for number 2."

The girl is still staring at him with her feisty eyes as the owner grabs her arm and pulls her towards him. She walks reluctantly towards Danny and is handed over to him, just as the coffee shop explodes in an inferno of loud voices.

"POLICE! Everyone get down!"

With his heart in his throat, Danny turns and watches, as what looks like thirty heavily armed police officers storm the coffee shop, pointing their weapons at them. Terrified, the men try to escape, but are soon thrown to the ground and arrested. The owner of the coffee shop pulls his gun and Danny turns fast, then jumps near the girl he has just purchased, and at the second the owner fires his gun, Danny forces the girl to the ground to avoid the bullet.

Next thing Danny knows, three police officers are on top of him, dragging him away from the girl. He manages to look into her brown eyes one last time before he is knocked out.

16

APRIL 2016

I CALL up Joey when I get back inside. Salter is in his room and he doesn't want to speak to me. I am so frustrated I am about to cry.

"Did you put him up to this?" I ask, almost spitting the words out.

"What?" Joey asks.

"You must have. I...I can't believe you would do this to me, Joey. After all we have been through."

"I have no idea what you're talking about," Joey says. "Is something wrong with Salter?"

"He wants to come live with you," I say. "He just told me so."

"He does?"

"Don't sound so surprised. I know you put him up to it. What is it? You want to hurt me so badly?"

"What are you talking about? I didn't put him up to anything. If he wants to come live with his dad, well then he is more than welcome."

"How can you say that? You have no idea how to take care of a kid. You don't even pack the boy a lunch!"

"I hardly think what kind of lunch you provide determines whether you're dad of the year or not. I miss him, Mary. I think it would be good for us."

I moan. I don't know how to argue against it. I just know that I can't let this happen. I simply can't. It breaks my heart.

"Yeah...well, I don't think it's such a great idea." I can hear how childish I sound, but can't stop it.

He scoffs. "Well, there's a big surprise there."

"You can't take him from me, Joey. You simply can't. I don't know what to do without him."

Joey chuckles. "You always exaggerate, Mary. It's not like I'm taking him away from you. He'll come live here for a little while, and then he'll want to come back to Mommy after a few weeks. Don't you worry. He is a momma's boy after all. I'll just have to enjoy whatever little I get of him. Get some time one-on-one. Some man-time. It'll be good for him. I promise. You'll see him every other week for five days, like we always do. It won't be that big of a difference, Mary."

"I worry that he'll never want to come home to me again," I say, grabbing a cookie with the other hand and eating it. I am not seeing Tom for a few days, while the basketball tournament lasts anyway, so there is no need to watch my weight. Especially not when I feel sorry for myself.

"Of course he'll come home. Are you kidding me? You're his mother," Joey says, comforting me.

It works a little. Or maybe it's the cookie.

"All right...I guess there really is no other way," I say. "But you've got to make sure you pack him his lunch. Every day. And don't let that little thing of yours leave out any more lingerie, or I'll take him back, you hear me? One more bra and I'm bringing him home."

"I hear you loud and clear," Joey says. I know he is grinning. I can tell by the tone of his voice.

"I'll bring him over tomorrow after school, then," I say. "At least I get to spend tonight with him."

"And next weekend," Joey says. "Plus, feel free to stop by anytime. Bring Snowflake. Bonnie and Clyde are miserable without him."

I get a warm feeling in my body that Joey is the one missing me, but I don't say anything. It is hard being away from each other after spending most of our lives together like we have. I miss him too. Not all the bad stuff, but the good parts we shared. I barely get to indulge in the memories before I am violently pulled out of them, when I hear her voice in the background.

"Who are you talking to, baby?"

She might as well have punched me in the stomach. I can't stand the fact that she is in that house and that soon she'll be there with my son as well. She'll be there with my family. My family.

Now I feel like crying again.

"I'll be right there," Joey answers her. "Listen," he says to me.

"You gotta go. Yeah. I kind of figured."

"Sorry. We have this thing, this yoga paddle board experience that we're going to on the river."

"On the river? With all those dead fish? Good luck."

"Yeah, well, it's this environmental thing too, to make awareness and take pictures of how bad it really is, then send it to the commissioners in Cocoa Beach, hoping it'll force them to react."

"But paddle boarding, Joey? Come on. You hate paddle boarding. You're a surfer, remember?" I say.

He chuckles. "I know. But Jackie loves paddle boarding, so, you know..."

Yeah, I know that you're changing yourself for her. Why? You never changed yourself for anyone else, let alone me.

"All right then. I guess I'll see you tomorrow. I'll bring Snowflake."

I can't see it, but I know Joey is smiling. "Sounds good, Mary. The animals are going to be very happy."

"I bet."

I hang up feeling a lot better. I grab another cookie and eat it while wondering how long Salter is going to last in that house with Jackie in it and how long Jackie is going to like having Salter there. Suddenly, I worry about him and if he'll feel rejected by her and then maybe by his dad because he will feel like his dad spends more time with her than his son.

He's going to come back here all heartbroken, isn't he? How did we get to this, Joey? We weren't supposed to be the ones that got divorced. We were the ones that were supposed to last, remember?

I empty the package of cookies while obsessing over the thought. When my phone rings again, I pick it up.

It's Chloe.

"Hey there. I was just about to call you about my next article; I know you want to..."

"That's not why I am calling," she interrupts me. Her voice is so serious it feels like a punch to my face.

"What's going on, Chloe? You're scaring me."

"It's Danny," she says. "I didn't know who else to turn to. You're the only one who can afford to bail him out."

I stop breathing. "Bail him out? But what...does that mean?"

"That he has been arrested, yes."

17

APRIL 2016

IT'S BEEN six months since he last did a pick-up. Not that the demand hasn't been there for more, but he has to be careful. Boxer knows it is important to lay low for a long time after he has delivered the goods. He has to make sure the police aren't on to him. In the meantime, Boxer reads the paper every day and watches the news closely. It still amazes him how easy it is.

So far, no one seems to be missing the woman and the girl he picked up in October. What are their names again? Marie and Tara. Yes. Or is it Maria? Boxer doesn't remember anymore. It's all in the past. The girl and her mother have already moved on to their new owner, as have all the others Boxer has provided. He sees himself as a sort of a farmer selling off the cattle.

Never get attached to the cow. Don't give it a name.

"Latest news on the fish kill in Banana River Lagoon, when we get back," the lady from News 1 3 says as they cut to commercial.

Boxer gets up and walks to the kitchen. It's time to start dinner. Boxer loves to cook. Today he's preparing lamb. Thyme-garlic lamb with strata, horseradish gremolata and roasted veggies.

He puts on music while he chops the veggies and sings along. This is the time of day he feels the best, when he gets to create something with his hands. It has taken him years to get this good, but luckily Boxer has a lot of time. Since he was fired two years ago from his job, time has been all he has.

A message ticks in on his iPad. It's from one of the secured chat rooms, so he knows he must answer right away. He wipes his hands on his apron and checks who it is from.

His client's name is Dr. Seuss. Needless to say, it is a cover. Boxer isn't his real name either.

<How's my package coming along?>

<Counting on this Saturday for pick-up.>

Boxer waits for Dr. Seuss's answer, but hears a sound coming from the front of his house. He turns the iPad to face the screen down, and then walks outside.

"Hello?"

On the wooden porch, he spots the body of a man. He is lying on his back, eyes closed. Boxer sighs and approaches the man.

"Get up, you drunk," he says.

The man blinks his eyes, and then looks at Boxer and smiles. "Hey, brother. Nice view you have here."

He nods in the direction of the neighbors across the street, where the woman is bringing in groceries from her mini-van. She glances cautiously towards Boxer's house. His brother waves.

"Hello, Mrs. Dawson," Boxer says.

She waves nervously. Boxer looks at his brother. "Come on. Couldn't you at least have used the back door?" He reaches out his hand and his brother grabs it. He pulls him up, even though he is heavy. Boxer is strong.

"This is a nice neighborhood," he grumbles, as he pushes his drunken brother inside. "People don't pass out drunk on porches in nice neighborhoods."

"I know, man. I'm sorry."

Boxer helps his brother get onto the couch, and then runs to the kitchen to take the lamb off the stove. It is burnt black. Boxer sighs. He was looking forward to it.

He returns to his brother, who is half asleep on the couch. He sits down next to him.

"So, how much this time?" he asks.

The brother doesn't even open his eyes to look at him. "Only three-hundred-thousand."

Boxer sighs and nods while his brother dozes off. "All right," he says, and looks at his brother while stroking his leg gently.

"All right."

18

APRIL 2016

"WHAT ARE THE CHARGES?"

Chloe hasn't even gotten in the car before I ask. It's the morning after she called and gave me the news. I haven't slept all night. Chloe didn't want to tell me over the phone. Said she wanted to wait till she could tell me face to face. I can't stop wondering what is going on. I have a bad feeling about all this and really hope I am not right.

Tell me he was speeding; tell me he stole something from a store because he couldn't afford it; tell me has too many unpaid parking tickets. Tell me something I can accept. Not what I won't, not what I fear this is about.

Chloe sighs and closes the door to the car. Danny will be put in front of a judge and hopefully the judge will allow bail so we can get him home. That's what we're going to hear.

"If I am to pay for his bail, then I at least deserve to know what this is all about," I say, and get back out on A1A.

Chloe nods. She is not looking at me. It makes me feel very uncomfortable.

"Chloe!" I say, frustrated. "Please tell me. Why was he arrested?"

"All right. All right. Take it easy. It's just...really hard to say. I spent last night avoiding Junior's many questions."

"What did you tell him?"

"Danny wanted me to say that he had to go out of town for a few days and would be back soon."

"Wow. So you lied. Well, you're not lying to me, Chloe," I say, as we drive onto the bridge leading us to Merritt Island, the island separating our Barrier Island and Cocoa Beach with the mainland.

"Danny was arrested at the airport yesterday afternoon," Chloe says.

"At the airport?"

"He was...taken in because he was trying to..." Chloe looks at me, then out the window.

"Trying to what? Geez, you're killing me here, Chloe," I say, as we reach the last bridge over the Indian River leading to the mainland. The smell was worst going over Banana River, but I can tell the fish kill is in the Indian River as well. I see many dead fish and, with the warm weather, it smells bad.

"He was trying to buy a girl."

I almost crash the car into the guardrail. "He was what?"

"Trying to purchase a girl from Indonesia. She had just arrived in the country, thinking she was going to work in the hotel business, but it was a trafficking ring that was behind getting her here. They were trying to sell her in an auction. A slave auction. The police raided it. It was a set-up. There you have it."

"And Danny was there?"

"It appears so. Please keep your eyes on the road and please slow down a little, will you?"

"Why? What...how? How old was this girl he was trying to buy?" I ask, ignoring her comments about my driving. I am a great driver and right now I am very upset.

"Fourteen," she says.

"FOURTEEN?"

"Please watch out for the truck," Chloe says with a moan.

"Oh, my God," I groan. "I knew it. I saw him with those girls. I knew something was off, Chloe, didn't I tell you?"

"Mary!!"

I hit the brakes when the truck in front of us suddenly stops. I manage to stop our car before we hit it, but Chloe apparently doesn't think that I will and starts to scream. I stare at her while we wait for a green light.

"So, you're telling me Danny, our Danny, the firefighter, the captain of Cocoa Beach Fire Department, the sweetest guy I have known since we were just children, Danny, that Danny was arrested trying to buy a fourteen year-old Indonesian girl. And now...now, on top of it, you want me to bail him out?"

Chloe looks at me, and then she nods. "Yes. That is exactly what I am saying."

19

APRIL 2016

"I SIMPLY DON'T UNDERSTAND how you talked me into this."

I stare at Chloe, sitting next to me outside the courtroom in Orlando. It is all over. The judge set the bail for one hundred-thousand dollars. I have paid it.

Chloe grabs my hand. "You're a good person. Danny had to get out of there. We couldn't just leave him. You did the right thing. Trust me."

"Well, it doesn't feel like the right thing. It feels like I have just bailed out a pedophile."

Chloe closes her eyes and breathes in deeply. "Danny is a good man, Mary. And you know it."

"What the heck was he buying a young girl for?"

Chloe bites her lip. "I think we should ask him about that when he gets out. There he is. I see him."

I look up and spot Danny walking towards us, flanked by two court officers. Chloe gets up from the bench and walks towards him. I stay seated. I don't know what else to do. All I really want is to kick Danny and yell at him for being such a pig, a disgusting pedophile. I can't get myself to hug him like Chloe is doing right now. I simply can't.

Danny lets go of Chloe and approaches me. I feel my heart pounding in my chest. I want to run away. I want to grab my purse and just start running.

"Mary!"

I can't even smile. I look up, but my eyes are avoiding his.

"Chloe told me you paid my bail. Thank you so much."

I clear my throat and press back my desire to scold him. It can wait till the car, I decide.

Oh, my God. I have to give him a ride back!

Finally, my eyes meet his and I sense my tension ease up. In them, I see the same Danny I have loved for so many years. My Danny. My friend.

My creepy friend who buys kids! What else does he do with them?

I don't want to think about it. I close my eyes and get up.

"Mary...I..."

"Not now," Chloe says, and grabs his hand. "Let's get you out of here. Let's get you as far away from this place as we can."

I stare at her, wondering what the heck she is thinking. Why isn't she about to explode with anger and frustration? She, of all people I know, should be so enraged with Danny she can't bear to look at him. Chloe! Chloe who has devoted her life to fighting child-porn online. Chloe who has created the organization Nochildporn.org. Chloe who...created software that automatically tracks...who gives the information to the authorities..."

Hey, wait a minute!

I clasp my mouth and gasp. Both of them turn to look at me as the last piece finally falls into place.

"You...you...you two have..."

Chloe approaches me, eyes wide open, hands stretched out in front of her. "Wait till the car," she says. "Wait till we get there. Then we'll talk. We'll tell you everything you need to know, but you'll have to wait. We can't do it here. Do you think you can wait that long, Mary? Do you?"

I hold my hand tight over my lips, then nod while storming into the parking lot.

20

APRIL 2016

DANNY TAKES in a deep breath as he steps outside the courtroom again. This time as a free man. All he really wants to is to forget the past twenty-four hours and move on, but that is not going to be so easy.

He's got some explaining to do. Some serious explaining.

"Tell me everything," Mary says, as the three of them are in the car.

Chloe and Mary are in the front seats, Danny in the back. He feels like a child being questioned by his parents. Well, at least Chloe knows the entire story, so basically he just has to tell everything to Mary.

"How, how long, when and why?" Mary continues. "I mean, I can sort of guess the why, but...the rest?"

Chloe and Danny exchange looks before she starts to speak. "It started about a year ago. I ran into these ads on Craigslist where they sold young girls, you know...people pay for having sex with them. Usually, I work cases farther away and hand everything to the FBI, but these small local things... in the beginning, I alerted the sheriff's office, but they don't have the resources to crack down on all of them. They don't have a special department working sex trafficking. It's everywhere. I see it all over, Mary. These girls are being hurt and abused. I can't wait till they get the resources or till the FBI thinks it is big enough for them to deal with. It happens all over. Every day that passes by, someone is raped hundreds of times, or sold into slavery. It's nasty. I can't just sit here...and neither can Danny. We got to talking one day and I let out all my frustration about not being able to do anything...knowing about all this."

Chloe looks at Danny, who nods.

"She showed me some of it," he says. "Some of the addresses were local and I got to thinking...I mean, if I could save just one girl, then it would be worth it, wouldn't it? If just one girl could get out of this slavery. I would gladly go to jail for that."

"Okay, so let me get this straight," Mary says. "How does it work? Chloe, you..."

"I do the research and Danny goes to check it out. He goes to the bars, like the dancing places, you know gentlemen's clubs and he asks to pay a bar fine, that's the code word for wanting to purchase a girl. They take him out back and he tells them what he likes."

"Usually," Danny takes over, "I go for the youngest girl there. Or the one with the most fight left in her eyes. These people break the girls before they're sold, but some of them remain fighters and you can tell by the look in their eyes. They are the ones who won't last long. They'll get killed within a few months, often beaten to death because they refuse to submit."

"And what do you do next?" Mary asks.

It is painful for Danny to talk about this and he closes his eyes as he continues. "I buy them. If I can, I buy them for the night and tell them I want to take the girl with me. It's expensive, but worth it. I take her to a local shelter in Titusville, where she'll get the help she needs."

"How do you even afford it?" Mary asks.

"I got a huge insurance settlement when Jean died. Her life insurance. I don't need that money. I don't want it, to be frank. I use it to get the girls instead."

Mary stares at Danny. It makes him uncomfortable.

"Now you might understand why I was defending him, right?" Chloe asks, looking at Mary.

She holds a hand to her chest. Danny sees tears in her eyes. He doesn't want her to get emotional. He doesn't feel like he deserves her tears.

"I can't believe I thought..." she says, her voice breaking. "Oh, my God, I feel like the worst person on the planet right now."

"It's all right," Chloe says. "How could you have known? We kept it a secret for a very long time and would have preferred it stayed that way."

Mary reaches back and puts her hand on Danny's knee while driving. She looks at him in the rearview mirror.

"I can't tell you how sorry I am," she says. "Can you forgive me? I should have given you the benefit of the doubt at least. I should have known you were a hero."

Danny sighs and puts his hand on top of hers. He doesn't feel like a hero. "The worst part is all the girls I can't save," he says. "I've seen them. I was there. I've looked into their eyes and chosen someone else to save. That's what's keeping me up at night. That's what's torturing me every day, every hour of my life."

21

APRIL 2016

YOU'RE the worst friend ever!

The feeling of guilt is killing me as I drive the three of us back towards the beach. I can't believe I was so quick to conclude this about Danny. Danny, who has always been there for me, well for everyone really. Danny who likes to take care of everyone and every problem. Of course he was just trying to save these girls.

Of course.

"I just can't believe they would hold an auction like that in the middle of the airport, where thousands of people pass by every day," I say.

"It's not the first I've been at," Danny says.

"It happens often," Chloe says. "A lot more than you think. The airports are one of the worst places, because they fly the girls in from all over the world, tell them they're going to be models or get work so they can send money home to their families, and then when they arrive some creepy guy brings them somewhere and they're sold. Lord only knows where they go from there."

"Most of them live many years in slavery," Danny says. "They're often drugged senseless and are transported from place to place, where they are used as prostitutes, or even sold again and again. I talked to a girl who had been locked inside a small apartment for three years where she was raped by different men between twenty and fifty times a day. She kept a diary with recordings of it."

"Wow, that's really brutal," I say.

"And, it's also happening here. It's not just girls being brought in from other countries. Many of them are just ordinary American girls," he continues. "One that I saved was picked up in her own driveway while her mother was still inside the house. The girl's best friend had texted her that she would stop by and say hello, and then when she went outside to talk to her, the girl arrived with two men in a car. They grabbed the girl and dragged her inside the car."

"It happens all over, Mary," Chloe says. "Everywhere. Most people just don't see it. But I do. I face it every day."

I nod pensively while thinking that I suddenly have the deepest respect for Chloe and Danny. I just wish they didn't have to put themselves in danger the way they do. I applaud what they do, I really do, but I fear for them. Especially for Danny. He has a son who needs his father.

"But, Danny kind of got himself in some trouble last time," Chloe says. "Not at the airport, but before then."

"How so?"

"Do we have to tell her?" Danny asks.

"I think we do," Chloe says. "You're going to need a good lawyer when they find out. Mary knows one."

Danny scoffs. "Come on, Chloe, we've been over this before. They're not going to find out. I got rid of the gun. I told you."

"Still. It's registered in your name...ballistics will..."

"Hey! Hey! What's going on here?" I ask. I hate how they talk like I am not even there.

Chloe stops. She looks at me. "Danny killed someone."

"Chloe!" Danny says. "Now she is an accomplice as well."

"What? Who did you kill, Danny?"

Danny sighs. "The other day, I rescued a girl from an apartment on the mainland. I answered an ad on Craigslist. They had her in one of those gated condominiums that are usually for the snowbirds. A really nice one. I went there pretending I wanted to pay to be with her, then when I was alone with her, I told her my plan. To make a long story short, I shot the couple guarding her."

"Oh, no, Danny!" I say.

"I was just trying to stop them; I was supposed to just hurt them. Shoot them in the shoulders or legs. That's how I usually do these things. Then I call the cops anonymously and tell them there has been a shooting and they arrive and arrest them. Meanwhile, the girl and I are long gone. But the woman died from her wounds. And now Chloe fears that the police will match the bullet with my gun."

"I understand her concern," I say. "But explain this to me. Why are the people arrested if the girl isn't there?" I ask.

"Oh, we leave some child-porn on their computers and phones as well," Chloe says. "It's really the easiest task in the world."

"All right," I say. "But why do you take the girl? Why not hand her over to the police?"

Danny sighs again. "Most of these girls trust the police less than anyone. Many of them have had encounters with the police that have led to them being sent back on the streets or even sometimes back to their traffickers. I spoke to one girl who managed to escape after nine months in captivity. When she finally found a police station, they told her she was perfectly safe on the streets. They couldn't help her. They don't trust them, and frankly, I don't always either."

"Those are big words coming from you," I say and take a left turn onto A1A. Suddenly, it feels better than ever to enter my quiet little town. Still, I can't stop thinking about what Chloe just told me.

It's everywhere. Even here in this sleepy little town?

22

APRIL 2016

I MAKE us all a strong cup of coffee and make them Irish by adding a little whiskey to them. We sit in my dad's new living room and look out at the waves. My dad is awake, but wants to stay in his room and watch TV, he tells me. I don't tell him what has happened. I have promised it will stay among the three of us. I don't know what Danny will tell his son, but that is none of my business.

The ocean is raging, the strong winds blowing on-shore making it a very bad day to surf.

"Thanks," Chloe says, as I hand her the cup. Danny doesn't speak. He hardly looks at me. I can tell he is troubled.

"I can't believe you two," I say and sip my coffee. "I mean, I knew Chloe was crazy, but you, Danny? Why? Why did you agree to do this?"

Danny sips his coffee. He doesn't answer, but stares out of the big windows. I sense there is more to the story than what he has already revealed. I get the feeling he wants to keep this part to himself. I wonder if Chloe knows. I look at her to see if I can read it on her face, but I never can. She has such a poker face.

"There is something, isn't there?" I ask. "There is something else you two are not telling me."

"You know she's not going to leave it alone," Chloe says, addressed to Danny. "Once she gets an idea into her head, there is no letting go."

Danny doesn't look at her or me. He still stares at the ocean. "That's our Mary," he says.

I chuckle uncomfortably.

"That's our Mary," Chloe repeats and sips her coffee.

Danny draws in a deep sigh. I look from one to the other. It's killing me. *Why is no one saying anything? What aren't they telling me?*

I do my best to behave. I sit still on the couch and sip my coffee, while waiting for them to start talking. It lasts about half a minute.

"All right," I say, and put down my cup a little too hard on the coffee table. "Don't tell me, then. See if I care."

Chloe chuckles. "I told you she wouldn't let it go."

Danny sighs again. He turns and looks at me. "All right," he says. "Well. I guess you can say I have been trying to make up for something, making amends of sorts."

"Making up for what?" I ask.

"For me not being there."

"Being there? Where?"

He draws in a deep breath while his eyes catch those of Chloe.

"Being there for Junior?" I say, looking at them. "I don't understand... you have always been there for Junior. You're like dad of the decade for that boy...wait a minute...you have another child?"

Danny nods. "I have a daughter. I never told anyone except for Chloe."

"I've only known for about a year."

I stare at him. "But...but who...how?"

"I cheated on Jean ten years ago. With a woman I met at work. She worked at the front desk for a little while." He shakes his head. "Things were awful with me and Jean. Always have been. You know that. It doesn't matter. It was wrong and I ended it. The girl was fired because of the affair. I had her removed, which I am not proud of, I admit that. Then a year later she showed up at the station carrying a baby telling me the girl was mine. I have paid for her upbringing, sent them a check every month, but I was never there for the girl. I don't know her at all. It tortures me every day."

"So you believe saving these other girls will somehow bring you redemption?" I say.

"I know...ridiculous, right? But somehow it provides peace of mind for me. At least I can do this right, you know? Everything else I have messed up, but not this."

"Well, not until now," I say. "Now you risk losing everything."

23

APRIL 1975

BAO HONKS the horn on the moped, trying desperately to get the crowds of people blocking the road to move. Danh watches the people as they pass them, while holding onto his sister, who is still in his arms. The road is bumpy and she is crying helplessly, wanting to go back to her mother.

Danh wants to go back too, but can't forget his mother's words or the look in her eyes when she told them to get out of the town.

Now they have been driving for at least an hour and the crowds of people are only getting bigger and bigger. On their way, he sees people breaking into buildings, stealing everything that others left behind. He sees women carrying everything from children to chairs, and even some people with washing machines on the back of their motorcycles. Bao is trying to follow their two other brothers on their bikes, but soon they lose track of them. Only now and then Danh manages to spot one of their brother's bags of clothes that he has strapped to the back of his bike, but soon that disappears as well.

When it is about to get dark, they arrive at a small fishing village and finally make a stop. Bao pulls out a little money that their mother handed them as they left and buys a bag of rice and something to drink. They eat and drink without uttering a word. Long is still crying, but not as much as in the beginning. Danh tries to encourage her by making fun of the peoples' faces. The harbor is packed with people trying to get on boats and their faces are all serious and angry.

"Look at that man over there," Danh says with a chuckle. "He looks like he had lemons for breakfast, doesn't he?"

Long chuckles and wipes her nose with her hand. There is no sign of their five other brothers who left with them, but someone in the crowd has a radio. Danh listens in as the broadcaster tells them news.

"What are they saying?" Long asks.

Danh hushes her while Bao walks closer. Danh listens carefully while holding his sister's hand. It's hard to hear everything over her sobbing, but he hears enough to understand that Saigon has fallen into the hands of the Vietcong. The communists have taken over the capital.

"What are they saying, Danh?"

Bao comes closer. "Saigon has fallen," he says with a cold voice, as if he doesn't know he is talking to a child. He looks at Danh and speaks with a lower voice. "We have to get out of here. Fast. They'll come here too. Look, they're already changing the flags on those buildings over there."

"What do you mean it has fallen?" Long asks, directed at Danh. "What about mother?"

Danh presses the tears back and kneels in front of her. "Mother is fine. Don't you worry about her, your majesty," he says.

"But...but, how do you know?"

Danh smiles and touches her cheek gently. "Because they just said so. On the radio. They told us everyone in Saigon was fine. That the communists are giving them all ice cream."

Long's face lights up. "Then we should go back!"

Danh chuckles. "We will. Soon. But not yet."

"When will we go back then?" she asks, disappointed.

"Soon, Long."

"Why not now? I miss my mom. And I want to have ice cream too," she says determinedly. Long starts to pull Danh's shirt.

"We all do," Danh says, "but the thing is, Mommy told us to meet her somewhere, so I think we'd better obey, don't you?"

"She did?"

Danh sniffles. Panic is starting to erupt around them as people realize there aren't many boats left in the small harbor.

Bao grabs Danh's arm. "We have to hurry," he says.

Danh looks into Long's eyes. If only he could make them smile again. "She did. She wanted us to go on a real adventure. Are you up for a real adventure?"

"I love adventures. Will there be ice cream?" she asks.

"Once we get there, I bet there will be," he says.

"And Mommy will be there too?"

Danh bites his lip. "Who else would bring all the ice cream, huh?"

24

APRIL 2016

"I KNOW you don't like the feel of the fabric. I told you I'd have them pick the couches up again, and I have already ordered the new ones."

Nicky sighs and wipes her forehead. It is hot sitting by the community pool wearing her work clothes. Her Melbourne client is yapping on the other end about her couches, while Paige is in the water with her swim trainer, Coach Burnett. He shows her something, a new technique to help her backstroke, and she repeats it. He holds her by supporting her back to have her body float more on the surface.

"Yes, Paige. That's it," he yells, his hand still resting underneath her back. "Now, try it again."

"Yes, tomorrow. I'll make sure it's all taken care of," Nicky repeats. She sighs while the woman continues on the phone.

Why can't she let it go already?

Now she is asking her why it can't be fixed right now. Why Nicky can't just come down and take care of it.

"I don't want these couches in my house."

"Because right now I am at my daughter's swimming lessons. I have just spoken to the company and there is nothing they can do until tomorrow. They will get the right couches with the right fabric," she says. "But it will take a few days to have them shipped from up north."

Paige looks up at her from the water and waves. Nicky smiles and waves back. She wonders for a second if it is all worth it. Her dream of having her own company doesn't really seem to be as glamorous as it used to be. Dealing with these rich ladies is harder than she had expected. It is taking all of her time. And now it's going to cost her as well. She'll have to pay for the transport and shipping of those couches herself that she wrongfully ordered, the company told her. Not that she was the one who made the mistake. The lady asked for these couches, but now she's saying she didn't, that the fabric is wrong, even though they went over what type of fabric she wanted a million times. The lady says she is not going to pay for the shipping, since she wasn't the one who made the mistake, so now Nicky has to.

At least Paige is happy. Isn't she?

Nicky can't help but wonder if everything wasn't better before they got the inheritance, when they had nothing and she worked as a secretary with a low but steady income. Not to mention steady work hours. It seems like she works every waking hour of the day now. She likes it, she likes the part where she gets to be creative and come up with great ways of decorating people's beautiful houses, houses she could only dream of ever living in. That part she really enjoys, that's her dream. It's the people that bother her. The women. Spoiled women who never had to struggle for anything, who never had a dream, who don't understand that Nicky also wants to be with her kid as much as possible, even though she is building her business.

Maybe she simply started too early. Maybe if she had waited till Paige was older and maybe moved away. Of course, that would have been smarter. It's easy to be wise in hindsight, isn't it? It's not like she can stop now. She put down the money, she started it all up, and now she is actually successful, so much that she might even soon be able to move out of the crappy neighborhood she lives in. It is all clearing up for her. She just needs to be patient.

Paige has started to complain about her mother not being home as much as she used to, but that's the way things are right now. She will just have to learn to live with it. And Nicky will have to learn to live with the constant nagging feeling of guilt. *It will clear up, it'll get better.* One day, Paige will understand, and then she'll be proud of her mother, who made it on her own, who beat the odds.

You're setting a good example for your daughter. You're showing her that anything is possible, that women can do things too. It might not feel like it, but you're being a good mother.

"Did you see me, Mommy?" Paige yells, as she runs towards Nicky. "I beat my latest record in the hundred meter backstroke!"

"Careful, sweetie. Don't run on the wet floors," Nicky says, and gets up from the chair. She grabs Paige's towel from the bag and hands it to her. Nicky is sweating heavily in her skirt and shirt.

"Did you see it, Mom? Did you?"

Nicky smiles awkwardly. "Sure. I was right here."

Paige's smile freezes. "You didn't, did you? You were on the phone again, weren't you?"

"Listen, Paige," Nicky says. "I am so sorry. But I had an important client. I had to take care of it."

Paige gives her the look, that awful look of disappointment and...yup... the feeling is back. The nagging feeling of guilt.

"Okay."

Coach Burnett comes up and gives Paige a hug. "That was awesome today, kiddo," he says. "I am so proud of you."

Paige's smile lights up again. She looks at him in a way she never looks at Nicky anymore.

"I couldn't believe how fast I went. I just kept going and going."

"It was really great, Paige," he says, and high-fives her with a laugh. "You keep that up and you're going to beat my old record soon."

She grabs him around the waist and holds him tight again. "Thank you. Thank you. You're the best coach in the world. I love you, Coach Burnett."

"Well, I love you too, Paige," he says and puts his hands on her shoulders. "Next time we'll go for a new record in front crawl all right?"

"You betcha'."

She smiles from ear to ear as Nicky's phone rings again. "I am sorry," she says and steps aside. "I have to take this call."

"No worries," Coach Burnett says, while Paige looks like she finds it to be a bigger problem.

"It'll only take a sec, honey," Nicky says to her.

Nicky walks away for a few seconds while speaking to the woman once again. Meanwhile, she observes Paige and Coach Burnett as they chat and laugh together. Nicky is so pleased that Paige gets along so well with her coach. They have known each other since she was in Kindergarten and started swimming. He practically watched her grow up, as she joined the local swim team when she was only five years old. Since Paige doesn't have a father, her swim coach is one of the few male role models she has in her life, and it makes Nicky feel good that Coach Burnett is one of them. Nicky has made many bad choices in her life, but raising her child in the safe and protected environment of Cocoa Beach is not one of them.

25

APRIL 2016

WHEN CHLOE and Danny finally leave, I cook for me and my dad. My famous salmon dish. I put it in the oven, and then walk Snowflake on the beach, even though it is illegal.

I am thinking about the things Chloe and Danny revealed to me earlier in the day. It's a lot to take in at once, and even knowing the two of them as well as I do, I have to say, I am surprised. I knew Chloe did a lot, but I thought it was just from behind the computer. Danny, I understand better. He has always been a fixer, one who wanted to find a solution to problems and do something, instead of just talking about it. But, still. Risking his career, his beloved job as captain of the fire station like this? I would never have thought he would go that far.

And then he tells me he has a daughter? A daughter he has never met, never been a part of her life. That part surprises me most of all, I think. Danny has always been such a devoted and loving father to Junior, and it was all for him that he stayed with that wife of his.

Snowflake and I stay on the beach till the sun has set over the mainland and then we walk back up to the house. I think about Salter and wonder if he has done his homework. It is so strange to not have him to take care of at the house anymore. Now it's just my dad and me.

I grab the dish out of the oven and put plates on the table, then go and get my dad. I roll him into the kitchen and hand him the fork. He smiles when he sees what is on his plate. Dinner is his favorite part of the day. He has changed a lot since he was hurt in the fire. It used to be all about his work and career or about him and his new wife Laura. Now it's all about the little things in life. Eating, being with family, or the joy of simply being able to hold a fork between his fingers.

"You made my favorite," he says.

"Food is your favorite," I say, and help him get some fish on the fork. He can now lift it and reach his mouth on his own. I feel like I am seeing improvement every day now. It's truly amazing. I am very grateful to Jack, his physical therapist, who seems to do wonders with him.

The fork hits his mouth, and a little salmon falls off and lands on his chest, but most of it ends up in his mouth, and he chews with his eyes closed. "Ah. This is heavenly, Mary."

I chuckle lightly and eat some myself. I glance at Salter's empty chair while chewing. I wonder what he is eating, if he took a shower, and if he has enough clean underwear.

I feel something on my arm and realize my dad is poking his fork at me.

"He's fine," he says. "He'll be back before you know it."

"I'm not so sure," I say, and stuff my mouth with salmon and potatoes, trying hard to make the feeling go away. "I'm scared he'll like it more at his dad's than here. I don't want to be alone, Dad."

"Bah. You won't be alone," he says.

I reach out and touch his hand. "I know. I have you and Snowflake, but he's my son, Dad. I love him. I want to be with him every day. I want to talk to him when he comes home from school; I want to know every little thing that is going on with him. I don't want to just see him every other week from Wednesday till Sunday. I want to be a part of his life. A big part. He's going to grow up without me. I'll be nothing but a vague memory. I'm losing him, Dad."

"No! You listen to me, Mary. You won't lose him. Never. It's just a phase. A boy needs his mother too. But he needs both of you. And right now you have to accept that he needs his dad. A boy needs his father."

I sniffle and hold my dad's hand. I know he is right, but I don't feel like admitting it. Instead, I wipe my eyes and look at my father. I can't believe how many years I lost out on of having him in my life. It took almost losing him to understand how important he was to me.

"Just like a girl needs her dad as well," I say.

"Yes. Just like a girl needs her father."

26

APRIL 2016

MY FATHER'S words linger with me all night as I toss and turn, wondering if Salter got to bed on time, if he will get up in the morning and not miss the bus, if he will be all right without his mother. I gave him a call after dinner to say goodnight, but he didn't have time to talk for very long. He, Joey, and Jackie were watching a movie. *Inside Out*. My favorite movie to watch with Salter. Apparently, Jackie had never seen it.

The next morning, I try to sleep in, but can't. I get up, walk Snowflake, and then make breakfast for my dad and me. I can't stop thinking about what my dad said, and I call Chloe to help me with a plan that has started to shape in my mind. Early in the afternoon, I drive to Danny's house and ring the doorbell.

"Mary?"

"A girl needs her dad too," I say.

"What?"

"A girl needs her dad just as much as a boy does."

"Eh...okay...are you all right, Mary?"

"Not really. I miss Salter like crazy since he moved to his dad's place, and that got me to thinking. It's never too late, Danny."

He sighs. I can tell he is confused. "I don't know what you're talking about, Mary. And, frankly, I'm not feeling so good. I'm afraid I might get suspended from the station when they find out about my arrest."

I throw out my arms. "What better time to make amends?"

"What?"

I grab his hand in mine. He looks at me, perplexed.

"Come with me."

He follows me to the car. "Where are we going?"

"You tell me," I say, and jump in the car.

He gets in the passenger seat. "What do you mean?"

I start the engine. "You're the one who knows the address, even though you've never been there."

"What?"

"Yes, Danny. You told me you sent her a check every month. You must know the address."

Now he is getting it. "No, Mary. I can't go."

"Why not? School is out in half an hour and then she'll be home. We can go there, ring the doorbell, and see her."

Danny sighs. "I can't do that!"

"Why not? It's killing you that you haven't been there for her; now I'm telling you that you can be there. At least show her you care."

"Don't you understand? I can't just show up out of the blue. I haven't been there before. I can't just come barging into their lives like that. It's not fair to her mother. Besides, I don't think they even want me in their lives. It's too late, Mary. Now, let it go, will you, please?"

"How can you say that? It's never too late. This girl needs a father in her life just as much as anyone else. And you can give her that. It's never too late. It might be hard; it might be really hard for the both of you, but it is never too late. Ever. The girl deserves a father."

I fall back in my seat with a sigh. Exhausted from speaking. I feel so frustrated and I want to shake Danny.

"All right," he says.

My eyes grow big. "Really?"

He nods. "I mean, what's the worst that can happen? She can tell me she never wants to see me, but at least I will have tried, right?"

"That's more like it. That's the Danny I know."

Danny scoffs, then laughs.

"What?" I ask.

"It's sweet."

"What is?"

"You. How you always think you can save the world."

"Guess I'm not very good at it, huh?"

He puts a hand on my shoulder. "I think you're doing an excellent job. But it's an impossible mission, you do realize that, right? To save everyone?"

I look at him and smile. I turn the wheel. "That may be, but that never stopped me before."

27

APRIL 2016

<SO WHAT did you do today?>

Boxer looks over at his brother sleeping on the couch. He was drunk again when Boxer came home last night, even though he had promised to stay off the booze. Boxer sighs. He doesn't know what to do about him, how to help him. For years, it has been like this...nothing changes despite all the promises.

But he can't turn his back on him. He simply can't. It's not an option. His brother can't help himself. He's sick.

His brother stretches and opens his eyes. He looks at Boxer.

"Hey there," he says.

At the same time, the girl answers in the chat in Minecraft. Boxer pretends that he is a thirteen year-old boy in the game. Finding them is the easy part. It's getting them to talk to you that is hard. Actually, it's not that difficult. It's all about knowing what young girls like, how they talk, what they want. That and then listening to them, to what they have to say. Unlike their parents, Boxer takes the time to really listen. He keeps a list of their usernames and if they have given him their real names and the different aliases they use on the different social media. Lately, they're all on this new app called Musical.ly, where they make videos of themselves. Boxer loves this new thing, since he can really get a good look at the girls when they pretend to be singers and dancers in the videos, acting like grown women. If he thinks a girl might be interesting, he sends the videos to his client.

<I had school,> she answers.

<Me too. Most boring day ever,> he writes back.

<Same here.>

<So what are you doing now?>

"Hey, brother, can I grab one of these?"

Boxer looks up from the screen and spots his brother standing with a bottle of whiskey in his hand. It is fifty years old. Boxer is a collector of fine spirits and has them displayed in the living room. The bottle in his brother's hand cost him a thousand dollars.

"I'm heading over to a friend's house for dinner and I don't want to come empty-handed," the brother says.

Boxer feels the tension in his entire body as he stares at his brother and the bottle in his hand. He knows his brother isn't going to any dinner at a friend's house. He is more likely going to one of those illegal casinos in the back of some club, where he'll lose more money because he is so drunk from drinking the whiskey on his way there. Boxer knows this will happen; he knows his brother will come to him again and again asking for more money, and Boxer will give it to him. He will welcome him inside and sober him up before it starts all over again.

He knows this will happen because it has been going on for years.

You should just say no. Tell him he can't take that bottle...that he needs to clean himself up, to get a job and stay off the booze and gambling. By giving in, you're enabling him. It's not what is best for him.

"So, can I?"

Boxer sighs as his gaze meets his brother's and he is reminded of how they looked at him back then. Back when everything changed.

"Sure. Have fun."

His brother smiles. "Thanks bro. Cheers."

Boxer doesn't say anything. He feels like screaming, but is holding it back. His eyes return to the screen.

<Homework,> the girl has answered. <But I am looking forward to this weekend.>

<Because of the basketball tournament?>

<Yes. We're playing a game Saturday. I have to go to this stupid rally first with my mom, to protest against the fish-kill, but after that I am going to play with my team>

<Maybe I'll come and watch,> he writes.

<Really? But I thought you were all the way in Daytona?>

<Maybe I'll come down to see you.>

<That would be awesome. I would really like to see you IRL.>

<Me too.>

28

APRIL 2016

"I'VE CHANGED MY MIND."

Danny turns and looks at me. I ignore him. We're sitting in the car and I have just parked it in front of a very small house on Barlow Avenue. We're still in Cocoa Beach, but on the border to Cape Canaveral. The kids around here go to Capeview Elementary and I don't know many here. I do know it is an area my parents always told me to stay away from, where lots of surf bums and drug addicts live because it is cheap. It seems that nothing much has changed.

The houses are more like small beach-shacks. This one is one of the nicer ones, though. With a small porch out front and a rocking chair. A child's bike is leaning against the porch. Everything looks neat compared to the neighboring houses.

I open my door and get out. I walk to Danny's side and open his. "Come on."

He gets out with a deep sigh. "All right. Let's do this."

I am right behind Danny when he rings the doorbell. My heart is throbbing in my chest, I am hoping and praying that this will go well. If Danny doesn't somehow connect with his daughter now, then he might regret it for the rest of his life. But I also know he is right to be nervous, because there is no telling how she will react to seeing him, or how her mother will react to him showing up like this.

Right now, I just hope they're home.

There's a sound behind the door and it opens. A woman appears behind the screen door.

"Yes?"

"Maria?" Danny asks. He sounds surprised.

"Who wants to know?" the woman asks.

"It's me," Danny says. His voice is shaking. It sounds strange as he speaks his name. "Danny."

"What do you want, Danny?"

He shakes his head. "You're not Maria," he says.

She coughs. "No, I'm her mother, what's it to you?"

"I'm sorry," Danny says. "You just look so much alike."

"Well I was young when I had her; what do you want?"

"Is Maria around?" he asks.

"Nope. She moved about six months ago."

"Moved? But..." Danny looks at me for answers, then back at the woman behind the screen door.

"Listen. I don't have all day," the woman says.

"Wait. This is important," he says. "You have to listen to me. I have to talk to her. I am...I am Tara's dad."

The expression on the woman's face changes drastically. "Well then, we certainly have nothing to talk about."

She is about to close the door, but Danny is fast. He opens the screen door and puts a foot in before she can close it.

"I've got to know where they moved to," he says.

"I've got a gun in here," she says angrily.

"I'm not going to hurt you. I just need you to give me her new address," Danny says.

"I don't have it," the woman says.

"What do you mean you don't have it?" Danny is getting angry now. He pushes the door open and walks inside. The woman backs up into her living room. I follow, and soon we're all in her house.

"You tell me where she and my daughter are right now," Danny says, pointing a finger at her.

"I told you. I don't know," the woman whimpers. "I came here because...well, her father died last Christmas. I hadn't seen her in ten years, not since...the pregnancy. Her father...he was so mad that he never wanted to see her or let me see her again. So when he died, I decided I would go see her, see my granddaughter. I had the address from all the letters she sent me, the ones with pictures of Tara in them, but all I found was this empty house. None of the neighbors knew where she was. I decided to wait for her here, but she never came back."

"Wait. You have been living here since December and she hasn't come back in all that time?" I ask.

The woman nods. "I have no idea where she can be. The neighbor gave me her cell number, but it doesn't seem to work. I don't know where she is. That is the honest truth."

"Did you file a missing persons report?" I ask.

She shakes her head.

"Why not?" asks Danny.

The woman shrugs. "For all I know, she might have run off with some man. Maria is flaky that way."

"Yet you stayed in the house. Why?" I ask.

"In case she comes back," she says.

"I don't believe you," Danny says. "Wait. I have been paying child support all this time. Six months, you say? She's been gone for six months? Yet my checks have been cashed. You cashed them, didn't you? You're living here on my money, on the money that was meant to support my child?"

"I couldn't just leave it there in the mailbox, now could I?"

"And because you look like your daughter, you could cash the checks, am I right? Danny asks. "I bet you even used some of her ID."

The mother looks away.

"Didn't you?" Danny asks angrily.

The mother jumps. She's scared of Danny. "I used her passport. I found it in the drawer in her bedroom."

"Wait a minute. Something is wrong here," I say. "Why would she leave without her passport? Didn't you ever stop to wonder about that?"

The woman shrugs. The place smells heavily of smoke and old wet cigarettes. Danny is mad now. He walks to the woman and grabs her by the collar. He is shaking her back and forth.

"Stop, Danny," I yell.

"How the hell can anyone be this stupid!" he yells to her face. "How can anyone act this selfish!"

I feel like things are getting a little out of control now. I don't know how far Danny will go. He did, after all, just kill someone recently. Trying to save someone else, a young girl, yes, but still. I am scared that he has snapped, that he might hurt this woman and I can't do anything about it.

"Danny!" I say.

He finally looks at me.

"Put her down."

Realizing what he is up to, he finally lets go of her. She sinks into the couch.

"I am sorry about that," I say. I look into her eyes. She is visibly scared of Danny, which could work to our advantage. "Now, do you mind if we take a look around the house?"

The woman opens her mouth as if to speak, but then realizes that we could report her to the police for fraud, and stops herself.

"Go ahead," she says.

29

APRIL 1975

THEY PAY their last money to a man who claims he can get them onboard one of the fishing boats. Hundreds of others, maybe even thousands have the same idea, so they have to act fast.

Bao is running across the harbor towards the ships, Danh and Long try to keep up with him. Bao has the note that shows they have paid. If they lose sight of him, they might not make it on the boat.

Danh keeps an eye on Bao's red shirt in the crowd, while carrying Long on his shoulders and holding the one pack of rice they have left. He fastens his eyes on the red shirt, but soon loses it, before it reappears. This happens a few times before the red shirt and Bao are suddenly completely gone.

"Where did he go?" Danh asks and slows down. There are so many people, so many shirts, and soon he spots a red one and starts to follow it, but seconds later he realizes it doesn't belong to Bao.

Danh is close to panicking now. He tries his best to not let his sister see his panic and keeps going towards the boats, in the direction he thinks and expects Bao might have gone. Meanwhile, his eyes are searching frantically for Bao's red shirt in the crowd.

"I can't wait to see Mommy," Long exclaims from his shoulders. "I bet she missed us."

"I can't wait either," Danh says to comfort her.

He refuses to think about what it will be like once they get to wherever the boats will take them. Or how he will explain to Long why their mother isn't there. He doesn't want to think about when they will see her again, if they ever will.

There is no time to think about those things. Right now, it's all about getting out of there, fast. The explosions and sounds of gunfire are coming closer by the minute, and it won't be long before the entire area is surrounded and there will be no way out for them anymore.

But where are we going? Will there be anything for us there?

Danh has no idea. All he knows is, he promised his mother he would take Long away and he promised his brother he would follow him to the boats. Where the rest of their brothers are, there is no time to worry about either.

"Bao!" he hears Long exclaim. He looks up and sees that she is pointing. "Bao!" she repeats.

"Where?" Danh stands on his tippy toes to better see, and there, in the middle of a big crowd, fighting to get onboard an old fishing boat, he spots him; he sees the red shirt and soon recognizes his face.

"Bao!" he yells, but the sound of his voice is drowned by another explosion, this time closer to them.

He sets off to run towards Bao, when he suddenly feels hands on his body and he and Long are both lifted into the air.

"Long!" he yells, and tries desperately to see where she has been taken, but seconds later, he loses her as well, as he is shoved towards the bottom of a small boat, underneath a grating used to hold luggage and cargo. He lands on top of another body and there are arms and legs everywhere, kicking and hitting him before he can finally fight his way up and breathe again. He is fighting his growing panic and can't stop looking for his family members when another child is shoved next to him. It is dark in the boat, but her laughter gives her away.

"Danh!" she says happily.

"Your majesty!" He grabs her and holds her tight in his arms. He takes in a deep breath as he feels the boat rock. His heart starts to race as he calls out Bao's name, but receives no answer. With all the noise from the many people shoved together at the bottom of the boat, Danh realizes it is no use to yell. He'll have to wait till they arrive at their destination to start looking for his brother.

Wherever that might be.

30

APRIL 2016

THE WAVES ARE CRASHING LOUDLY on the beach when we return. I have called Chloe and asked her to come over. I make coffee for all of us and we sit on the porch while telling Chloe what has happened.

"So, you're telling me this mother never reported her daughter and grandchild missing, even though she's been gone for six months?" she asks.

I roll my dad out to sit with us and serve him some coffee and cookies. He enjoys sitting on the porch so much it makes me feel like I should be out here more, enjoy it more. All I can think about right now is Salter and whether he had a good day at school or not. I look at my phone, but he hasn't called. I guess he isn't missing me as much as I am him.

"I know. I am so angry right now," Danny says.

"And you're telling me she left everything behind?"

"Well, her car is gone, we didn't find her phone or credit cards or a wallet, but other than that, it seemed like everything was there. Her passport, lots of clothes, and even her daughter's iPad."

"She would definitely take that if she was planning on going somewhere with her kid in the back seat, right?" Chloe asks.

"Sure thing," I say. "The mother said she believes they left town either on the night of October 22nd or during the day on Friday, October 23rd. The 22nd at night was the last time one of the neighbors saw her. She was supposed to take care of Tara the next day. Maria came to her house on the 22nd and asked her if she could look after Tara the next day, on the 23rd, when Maria had to go to work. Apparently, it was a day off from school, a teacher's workday, so she had nowhere for Tara to go and the neighbor was out of work, and she had watched her before. She told the neighbor that she was going to Target with Tara in the morning to get her new shoes, and then she would drop Tara off at the neighbor's afterwards, but Maria never showed up. The neighbor waited till noon, then took off. When she came home in the evening, Maria's car still wasn't there. She hasn't seen her since."

"She didn't go to the police?" Chloe asks.

"Not the type that would," Danny says.

"I see," Chloe says and sips her coffee.

"I called her office on our way back," I say, "and she never showed up for work that day either and she never has since."

"Could the mother be right?" Chloe asks. "Could she have run away with some guy?"

Danny shrugs. "I don't know her very well, but I do know the mother is right, Maria is flaky. I mean, if he had enough money and promised to take her away from here, I bet she would."

"But leave her passport behind? And all her belongings, along with her daughter's iPad?" I say. "Kids today are very attached to their iPads; let there be no doubt about that."

"So, what are we looking at here?" Chloe asks. "Do we think something bad happened to her? To them?"

I sigh and look at Danny. He looks worried, conflicted even. I can sense how the guilt is tearing at him. I can understand why.

"All I know is, I want to find my daughter," he says. "I need to know what happened to her. If it hadn't been for Maria's mother cashing my checks, I would have noticed something was wrong a long time ago. Now six months have passed and I have no idea where to start looking for her."

I reach into my bag and pull out Tara's iPad that Maria's mother agreed to let us take when we went through their stuff. Reluctantly, of course, and only after a few threats to report her to the police.

I place it on the table in front of Chloe. "How about we start here?"

PART II

READY OR NOT

31

APRIL 2016

NICKY RUSHES THROUGH CVS, throwing remedies for lice treatment into her basket. There are so many to choose from, she doesn't have time to read the labels. She simply grabs everything and walks to the counter. There's a woman in line before her who seems to have a thousand things she needs to buy. The woman asks the cashier for something and the cashier disappears.

Nicky grumbles and looks at her phone. Five unanswered calls from her Melbourne-based client with the couch issues. Now she is calling again. Nicky can't pick it up. Not here. She can't tell her when she can make it back to the house to look at the fabric. Right now she has to go get her daughter from school, where she is waiting in the clinic because they found lice in her hair during a random check.

Why today of all days!

Today was supposed to be the day she devoted completely to her Melbourne client and her fabric issue. She really wants to get this couch issue out of the way. Getting the old ones removed cost her two hundred dollars that she can't afford to lose. She wants to move on to the carpets upstairs, since she knows she can make a lot of money on that once they get to it.

But now she has to spend the day washing and combing through Paige's hair, while washing every sheet, cover, and pillowcase in the house.

Argh!

When it is finally her turn, Nicky throws all her remedies on the counter and the woman picks them up. She moves very slowly and it annoys Nicky. After every item, she stops and checks her phone.

Come on. I'm in a hurry here.

"That'll be one hundred twenty-six dollars and forty-five cents," she says, and looks lazily at Nicky. Nicky doesn't have time to complain about the price. She swipes her card through, picks up her things, and rushes groaning out of the store.

She drives to the school and finds Paige with the nurse.

"Mom, I have lice," she says, her voice breaking.

Nicky tries to smile, while her heart is pounding with stress and adrenaline. "I know, sweetie. I got the treatment at CVS, so we'll get rid of those little bastards. Don't you worry."

They drive to the house and Nicky starts treating Paige's hair. She goes through it with the comb while Paige screams and squeals. She finds four live lice and hundreds of nits. It doesn't matter how much she combs it, new ones just keep showing up again and again.

Meanwhile, her phone is on the counter next to them, lighting up every time the woman from Melbourne calls. She puts in the shampoo that has to stay for ten minutes, and finally Nicky calls the lady back, while Paige is allowed to go on the computer until she has to wash the shampoo out. Nicky knows she'll have to comb her hair again afterwards to get the last— hopefully—dead ones out.

"Hello, Mrs. Robbins, yes I am aware I promised you I'd be there today, but you see...No, no, I know. I had another engagement, an emergency this morning, so I had to...I know...yes, yes of course, I'll be there later this afternoon. Yes. No. This time I will be there. Of course. I understand you're upset. I will be there. You have my word on this. Okay. Goodbye."

Nicky draws in a deep sigh and sits down to close her eyes just for a second. That was a close one. She almost lost her client. She's got to get better at this, as soon as she gets past this little thing.

"All right, Paige. Let's wash that hair," she yells up the stairs towards her daughter's room.

Paige doesn't answer.

With an annoyed moan, Nicky walks up the stairs while calling her name. She enters her room to find it empty. The computer is still on, Minecraft is on the screen, but there's no sign of Paige.

"Paige? Sweetie?"

She sees light coming out from her closet and opens the door. In there on the floor sits Paige, her hair still wet from the shampoo, her iPad in her lap. She has taken her shirt off and is wearing only her training bra.

"What are you doing?" Nicky asks.

Paige looks at her and blushes. She turns her iPad to face downwards. "Nothing, Mommy. Just playing."

"Why did you take your shirt off?"

"I was hot. Can't we wash that stuff out of my hair now? It feels really gross."

Nicky grabs the iPad and looks at the screen where Skype is open, but no one is there. Nicky shakes her head. She doesn't have time for this.

"Well, come on then. We need to get you showered and then Mr. Lee will be here to look after you till I get back from my client."

"Oh, no, Mommy. You know I hate math."

"I do and that's why you need a tutor, now come on, I'm in a hurry here."

32

APRIL 2016

HE GOT her to take off her shirt for him. Boxer can't believe his luck. Calling her on Skype and telling her his camera didn't work was genius. He has never tried doing this before, but it won't be the last time.

Brilliant. Absolutely brilliant, he thinks to himself, as he goes through the pictures he took of her while talking to her, asking her gently and nicely if he could see her without a shirt. He didn't think the girl would go for it, but she did. Especially after he told her how beautiful she was and that he really liked her.

The pictures don't do anything for him. Boxer isn't into that stuff, but his client is. He hopes Dr. Seuss will be especially excited to see these.

Boxer downloads the pictures to his computer, and then sends them. He gets up from his chair, feeling triumphant. If all goes well, he'll be able to make a load of money on this beauty. And her mother. Cause that's what his client likes, the girl and her mother. What Dr. Seuss does with them after he delivers them to him is none of Boxer's business. As long as he gets his money.

Does he sometimes feel bad? Does he have nightmares about the girls he takes? Yes, of course he does. He would be a monster if he didn't.

Boxer walks to the hallway and puts on his shoes and jacket. He is wearing a tie today. She loves it when he wears a tie.

While thinking about his brother, he walks to his car and drives out of town. His brother never came home last night, and Boxer is worried what kind of trouble he has gotten himself into this time.

Boxer parks the car in front of the hospice in Titusville and greets the lady behind the front desk. She recognizes him and waves.

"She's in her room," she yells after him.

"Got it," he yells back and storms to the door. He corrects his tie and hopes he doesn't have too many sweat marks on his white shirt, before he knocks.

"Come in," the thin small voice behind the door says.

Boxer pokes his head in. "It's me."

She gesticulates with her arms. "Oh, my sweet boy. Come closer so I can take a good look at you."

Boxer walks up to her wheelchair and grabs her hand. "How are you, Mom?" he asks.

"You know how I am," she says.

"I do. But is there any news? How's your blood pressure?"

"Son. I am dying from cancer and you worry about my blood pressure?"

"No. I mean...yes, I do. Last time I was here the doctor said it was too high, remember?"

"You know what I like, son? I like to sit here and watch those cars drive by. At a certain point, you get to recognize some of them. Every day they go in the morning and then come back in the afternoon. Every day. Back and forth. Always in a rush."

"That's nice, Mom. That's very nice."

"How's the job coming? They make you manager yet?" she asks.

"The job's great, Mom. It's really great."

"Good, my boy. You make me proud."

They sit quietly and look out the window for a few minutes, when the door is opened and the manager of the hospice pokes his head in.

"Could I have a little chat with you?"

They walk outside. The manager clears his throat. "Sir, I hate to bother you with this, but we haven't received your payment for the last two months."

Boxer pretends to be surprised. "Really? Well, my bank was supposed to have sent the checks automatically," he lies. "I'll have to check with them. I'll have the money for you shortly. Don't worry."

The manager eases up. He smiles and rubs his hands. "Oh, good. It's always a delicate matter when someone...I mean we wouldn't like to have to..."

"Oh, I understand. Of course you need your payment. I'll have it to you as soon as possible."

33

APRIL 2016

I CALL Salter when the two others have left. I have been waiting for him to call me, but since he hasn't done it, I finally break down and call him. I can't believe how long he can go without talking to me. As I wait for him to pick up, I debate with myself whether to tell him how angry or maybe disappointed I am or to pretend I haven't noticed that he didn't call me.

Oh, my God! When did it become this complicated?

"Hi, Mom," he says when he finally picks up.

"Well, hello there. Good to know that you're still alive," I say, trying to sound like I am joking.

"You sound mad. Are you mad?"

Kids. They see straight through you.

"No. No. Not at all. Just been missing you, that's all. How was school today?" I ask, trying hard to sound casual, as if I haven't been obsessing about him every second of this entire day.

"Oh, I didn't go to school today," he says.

"What?" Okay, now I am sounding angry. But rightfully so. I try to calm myself down. Maybe there is an explanation. "Are you sick?"

"No. No. But Dad and Jackie took me standup paddling instead."

Stand up paddling?

"What?"

"Calm down, Mom. It was just one day. It's not that big of a deal."

"Wasn't it today you had the FSA test?" I ask.

"Crap. You're right. I forgot about that."

"You forgot?"

"Yes, I forgot, all right? Sometimes people forget. They can't all be perfect and remember everything like you."

"That is the lamest argument I have ever heard," I say. "Pass me to your dad, please."

"No."

"What do you mean no?"

"No. You're just going to yell at him and blame it on Jackie, and then he's going to be all sad afterwards. He's trying his best here. He's never taken me out paddle boarding before, and I really enjoyed it."

I want to scream, but I can't. I am in too much shock. When did my son become this teenager?

"I need to speak to your dad, please. Put him on," I say.

"No. You can call his own phone," Salter says.

"Salter!"

"I'm leaving now. Goodbye," he says, then hangs up.

I stare at my phone. *What the heck was that?*

"Pick your battles, my dear."

I turn my head and look at my dad, who is sitting in his wheelchair watching TV in the living room.

"What?"

He looks at me. "You've got to pick your battles," he repeats. "Is it really worth getting so upset about? Is it worth starting a fight with Joey about?"

I gnarl. "Why are you always on Joey's side, not mine?" I ask.

"Just trying to give you a piece of advice I wish someone would have given me before I had children. You can fight and argue over the smallest of things if you want, but that's just going to make your life miserable. Think about it. This thing you're arguing about, will it matter a year from now?"

I put the phone down and get up from my chair. I don't want to hear anymore and I have to start dinner.

"It will if he doesn't pass the FSA," I say. "Then he won't get into fifth grade next year, so yes, it does matter. I'd say it matters a lot."

34

APRIL 2016

TOM CALLS me Friday morning and we chat for an hour on the phone. I feel like a teenager, lying on my bed talking to him, flirting over the phone, but it is nice. He is nice. "So, when will I see you again?" I ask.

"We have one last game tomorrow afternoon, with the junior girls team, then it's all over," he says. "Maybe we should go out to dinner tomorrow night?"

"Yes," I say, feeling my heart throb. I am already looking forward to seeing him again.

"So, what are you up to this weekend?" he asks.

"I'll go to the rally tomorrow morning. Got to support our locals when they fight for the environment, right?"

"I know. It's terrible with all those dead fish. I can't believe they can't even figure out why this is happening."

"That's what gets me infuriated as well," I say. "I'm thinking about writing a piece about it for my blog. Maybe take some pictures at the rally."

"Sounds like a great idea," he says. "You are very powerful with that blog of yours. Maybe if the outside world hears about it, the politicians will finally step up and do something. This is sure to kill the tourism."

It is time for Tom to go and we hang up. I catch myself smiling as I get out of bed. I look at the clock. It is almost ten. I can't remember the last time I stayed in bed this long. I realize my dad hasn't gotten his breakfast yet and get dressed real quick.

"I am so sorry, Dad," I say, as I enter his room. He is not mad; he is smiling, as always.

"That's okay, sweetie. I watched the most beautiful sunrise from my window and now I am watching TV," he says, and lifts the remote with his fingers. It won't be long before he'll regain all the strength and mobility in his hands again, his physical therapist told me the day before, just before he left. I am thrilled to see the progress he is making.

"Tell you what? How about I make you some pancakes?" I say, to make up for my guilt. Plus, I am starving myself and really in the mood for pancakes.

"Sounds great, honey," he says.

I whip together some batter and start to make the pancakes. My heart is hurting when my train of thoughts stops at Salter. I can't believe he is being so defiant towards me. Am I losing him?

I don't like the thought and replace it with something else. I try to imagine being Danny right now and feel bad for him. He still doesn't know if he'll be charged with anything, and if he is, he'll lose his job. On top of it all, his daughter and her mother are missing. Where could they be? I wonder how people can just disappear like that. Being gone for six months and no one does anything? What about her friends?

I think about myself and know in my heart that people would start wondering after a few days if they hadn't heard from me. That's how tight our little crew and community are. Then I think about Sandra and the fact that I haven't spoken to her in almost a week. It is strange, since I had just gotten used to having her in my life again, but it seems like she is avoiding me. Or maybe I am avoiding her. I really don't feel like having to deal with her and Alex and their affair and betrayal of their spouses. I can't take it. Not after all I am going through with Joey.

I finish making a stack of pancakes when someone knocks at the door.

"Come in," I yell, while Snowflake is all over me because he can smell the pancakes. I let him out in the yard to do his business, while Chloe walks through the front door.

"Good morning," she says. "Do I smell pancakes?"

35

APRIL 2016

I SET an extra plate on the patio table on the porch, get my dad out of bed and into his chair, then roll him outside. It's one of those gorgeous spring mornings with no wind and the ocean is glassy. It's already eighty-three degrees and the sun is shining directly at us, so I put up the umbrella.

"So, I took a look at the girl's iPad," Chloe says after her first pancake.

"And?" I ask, not getting my hopes up. It was a long shot; I know that very well. I really don't know what I expected to find on her iPad. Maybe a new address or a message to one of her friends telling them she'd be moving, or just anything to indicate they didn't just vanish, that it was somehow planned.

Chloe grabs another pancake, pours syrup on it, and takes a bite. She chews and swallows before she answers. "And I didn't find anything about them moving or her talking about having to move or anything like that."

I sigh and chew my pancake with Nutella. "I had a feeling you wouldn't."

"But I did find something else," she says. "I went through all of her history and Tara was quite active both on Twitter and Instagram. And she played Minecraft a lot."

I shrug. "So do most kids her age."

"Sure. But there's something else. She chatted with this guy, he calls himself Boxer, and he seems to be talking to her on all the platforms. He would comment on her pictures on Instagram, they were Skype friends and chatted in there, and in Minecraft and Twitter as well. She had a Facebook account, but never used it much. But it is strange how this guy seemed to appear everywhere, so I went to check on her chat history in Minecraft. The two of them started chatting two months ago, and after that it was every day."

I shrug again. "So what? They were friends. Salter has a bunch of friends he only knows from social media or Minecraft. They play together and call each other on Skype or they use the chat to communicate and find each other in the different worlds."

"I know, I know," she says and takes another bite.

I watch my dad as he is struggling to reach his mouth with the fork. His hand is shaking, his fingers white with effort. I fight my urge to help him, since he has told me he wants to do it himself. It's the only way he'll get better at it. I know he is right. But it is so very painful to watch every time he misses; the disappointment on his face is crushing me.

"Have they been talking about anything creepy?" I ask. "Like is he a pedophile, is that why you wonder about him?"

"Not that I know of," she says. "I mean, he does tell her he likes her, but it all seems very innocent. But what strikes me is the fact that he is the last person she wrote to. On October 23rd, in the early morning he wrote to her: *We don't have school today. Do you want to meet me in Roblox?*" Chloe looks at me. "Roblox is another game very similar to Minecraft..."

"I know what Roblox is," I say. "I have a ten-year-old, remember?"

"Right. Well, he asks her this, and then she writes: *I can't. Going to Target with my mom to buy new shoes. Maybe later?*"

Chloe looks at me from above the iPad again.

"Is that it?" I ask.

She puts the iPad down on the table. "Yes."

"That's really not telling us much, is it?" I say.

Chloe sighs and leans back in her chair. I realize how much my dad's new patio furniture has already rusted. Especially the legs. Good thing Chloe isn't very big, or I would fear it might break. It's amazing how fast things rust when you live on the ocean. All that salt in the air just eats right through it.

"I don't know," she says, resigned. "I just had an odd feeling about this guy, that's all. It might be nothing. I guess I was just reaching for something. I feel so bad for Danny."

"Yeah, me too," I say, and reach for my third pancake. "I wish there was more we could do."

36

APRIL 2016

THE SUN HITS him in the face and he blinks his eyes. Blake looks at his watch. The sun is right outside of his window at the Hilton where he rented a room. The hotel is right on the beach and Blake asked specifically for a room with a view, yet there is no balcony even though it overlooks the beach. Blake finds that to be very odd. He wants to sit out there at night looking over the ocean, a beer in his hand like he used to when he still lived with his father.

There is a knock on the door and Blake gets up to open it. Room service brings in his breakfast, and he digs in while thinking about his next move. He has been in Cocoa Beach for almost a week now and kept a close eye on his father's house and especially on his sister. It still amazes him how close he can get to her without her knowing it. Twice he has been right behind her when she goes into Publix to buy her groceries and he walked just a few steps behind her all through the store. Of course, she probably wouldn't recognize him even if she stared directly at him, now that he has shaved off his hair and grown a beard. But still it strikes him how very inattentive she is to her surroundings, how easy she makes it for him to get really close... and how easy it is going to be to hurt her.

Finishing his croissants and fresh fruit, Blake wipes his hands on the napkin, grabs his coffee cup, and walks to his new laptop that he just bought at the Apple store, using Olivia's debit card, of course...the secret one that she created in her aunt's name while she was still alive.

Blake touches his face and his beard. It feels strange. He hasn't quite gotten used to the feel yet. The same goes for his reflection. He can hardly recognize himself anymore.

The computer starts up and Blake starts working the keyboard. He has been planning this for quite some time and working on perfecting it. He knows Mary is completely clueless when it comes to computers, but she has Chloe. Oh, yes. Chloe, who fell for Blake once.

It has taken him all these days to create the perfect weapon against his dear sister, but now he is ready to fire it. The only regret he has is that he won't be there to see her face when it explodes.

You won't know what hit you, dear sissy. But it ain't over yet. This is just the beginning.

Blake sips his coffee while focusing intently on the computer screen. The coffee is too bitter. He walks to the remains of the breakfast table and grabs the sugar bowl, then pours a couple of teaspoons of sugar in his coffee, while watching his program unfold on the screen. Nothing but numbers to most people, but to Blake it is more beautiful than the sunrise. He drinks more coffee. It tastes better now. The numbers run over the screen and Blake feels a chill of joy in his stomach.

Almost there. Almost there.

He presses a few keys, writes some numbers and a code. The computer thinks for a few seconds, then more numbers appear before the final stage arrives. Blake looks at the screen, and then down at the return key, knowing all he now needs to do is press it and all hell will break loose.

Blake takes in the moment; he closes his eyes and pictures his sister's face. He looks at the screen again. It's a thing of beauty, isn't it?

Then he leans over the keyboard, places his finger on the return key, and presses it.

37

APRIL 2016

PAIGE HAS to stay home from school because of the lice, and Nicky has no idea what to do with her while she attends to Mrs. Robbins in Melbourne. She can't really bring her. It would be torture for everyone, and if Mrs. Robbins were to ask why Paige wasn't in school today, Nicky would have to tell her the reason, and then she would definitely be fired for bringing lice into her house. Even though they had gone through all the treatment and there were no lice in Paige's or Nicky's hair this morning when she combed through them both. There is still the risk of re-infestation.

If you miss just one of those little bastards, you'll have to do it all over again.

Nicky has thought of another solution for Paige today. One she won't be too happy about. She has called Mr. Lee and asked him to come and teach Paige some math for a few hours.

She knows she'll be very unpopular, so she hasn't told Paige. Paige is in her room, playing on her computer when Mr. Lee arrives.

Nicky opens the door and Mr. Lee bows politely. "Good morning, Mrs. Stover," he says with that cute accent. "How are you today?"

"I'm great. Thank you so much for coming on such short notice," she says, and lets him inside of her house.

Nicky likes Mr. Lee a lot. He is probably the first man she has felt attracted to since she became a mother. It is strange, since she never used to like Asian people, but Mr. Lee is different. He is tall and muscular underneath the tight white shirt. And he has that handsome smile. He has told her he works as a math teacher at a private school in Viera.

"So you had no classes today?" she asks as they walk into the kitchen.

"No. Not today."

"Guess I was really lucky then, huh?"

"Yes," he says with a wide smile. "Very lucky."

His smile warms her and she blushes. Nicky looks away, feeling silly. "There is coffee in the pot; I have made some snacks for later, some fruit and crackers, and there is lunch in the refrigerator. I hope to be back by one," she says. "Will that be okay?"

He smiles and nods. "Yes. It's just fine." Mr. Lee then grabs her arm. She feels a warmth go through her body at his touch. "Don't worry. Don't stress," he says. "It's no problem at all."

Nicky sighs happily. "You have no idea how glad I am to hear that."

"Now, go. Do your job, make your clients happy. Paige is in good hands."

"I know she is," Nicky says and grabs her purse in her hand. She picks up her phone from the charger, then yells up the stairs:

"Paige. I'm leaving. Mr. Lee is here to do math with you."

"Aw!" Paige groans from her room. She appears at the top of the stairs. "Do I have to?"

"Yes," Nicky says and throws her a kiss.

"But I was doing something on the computer," she continues.

"Don't start arguing," Nicky says. "I don't have time for this."

"You never have time. For anything anymore!" Paige yells.

"Don't give me that," Nicky says, feeling the pinch of guilt in her stomach. "You do what Mr. Lee tells you to, do you hear me?"

But Paige has already stormed into her bedroom and shut the door.

"I'll take care of her," he says. "Just go. We'll be fine."

Nicky draws in a deep breath. She looks into the eyes of Mr. Lee. He makes her feel safe. She knows Paige will be fine with him, even though she has to do math. He is good with her and makes her laugh.

"Thank you," she says as the phone starts to ring in her purse. She picks it up. "I'm sorry," she says. "It's my client. I have to go. Call me if there is anything." Nicky runs with the phone to her ear.

"Yes, Mrs. Robbins, no, I am on my way. Just caught in heavy traffic, that's all. Be there in a few minutes..."

Nicky runs to the door. The last thing she sees before she closes it is Mr. Lee walking up the stairs towards Paige's bedroom.

38

APRIL 2016

"SO, I was planning on writing a piece about the fish-kill in the lagoon," I say.

We're done eating breakfast and Chloe is helping me clean up the kitchen. I have a tendency to make quite a mess when I cook.

"For the blog," I continue.

She nods while putting a cup in the dishwasher. "That sounds like a good idea. And an important case. Very local, though. You need to really have a good angle on it to make it interesting for your readers."

"I know. I think I'll go to the rally tomorrow, take some pictures for the post, and talk to some people. Get some info from the locals. I want to figure out who is to blame for all this."

Chloe scoffs. "Don't we all?"

"I know. I feel like something is off here, you know what I mean? There are so many theories out about it being because of people using too much fertilizer in their yards or pesticides, and then others believe it's caused by the septic tanks leaking, some even blame it on the manatees. But, I'm asking, why now? These things have always happened around here; why are the fish being killed now? The other day I saw a picture from one of the canals where you couldn't see the water for all the dead fish on the surface. It looked so creepy. We've never had this kind of fish-kill before. There must be something that has changed within the past few months."

"I heard people say it might be pollution from that power plant up north. Take a look at that and you might find some answers," Chloe says.

"But I do agree. It does feel like someone is covering something up in this case. Something is off. If you can find out who, where, and what, then you have your story."

I throw out the remains of my fifth pancake and feel sick to my stomach. I ate way too much again. I decide I just won't have lunch today. That should even things out.

"I'll try that," I say.

"By the way, I've made some design changes to your blog," Chloe says and walks to my computer. She taps on the keyboard while I continue to clean up. I wipe off the stove and put the last dish in the dishwasher.

"Our blog, Chloe. You're as much a part of it as I am, if not more. I don't think I pay you enough," I say. "I mean, without you there would be no blog and no income from all those advertisers."

I turn and look at Chloe when she doesn't try and argue with me, which she always does when I try to give her money for her work. She is staring at the screen, eyes wide open, and her face pale.

"What's going on?" I ask and throw my dishtowel on the counter. The look on her face is scaring me.

"Chloe?"

"Something is very wrong," she says and taps on the keyboard again.

I walk up behind her and look over her shoulder. Then I gasp. "What on earth is this?"

She shakes her head. "I don't know. I think we've been hacked. Someone has placed a bomb in here sending out all kinds of messages to your followers. Completely spamming them. This is bad, Mary. People are going to be so pissed. We've already lost five thousand fans. If this goes on, we'll end up losing every one of them."

"What kind of messages?"

"Like this one," she says and points at the screen.

"What the heck? I never said that! And that picture of me? Where did that come from?"

Chloe shrugs. "I don't know. What are you doing in this picture anyway?"

"I was stuck in the toilet. Hey, don't judge me; I was like ten years old. How did this get on here?"

"Who has access to these photos?" Chloe asks. "Do you have them on Facebook? Instagram?"

"No. I don't have any of my childhood pictures online. Most of them were lost in the fire. I don't think my dad has any left...wait a minute," I say.

"There is someone who could have had access to them before the house burnt down."

Chloe nods. "Blake."

"Yes, Blake."

"Looks like he wants a war," Chloe says, while tapping on her computer.

"How has he done this?" I ask. "I didn't know he could do anything remotely like this on a computer."

"Well...I taught him," she says. "Now, if I could only...I need to stop this before..."

"You did what?"

"I taught him everything, all right? Remember I had a thing for your brother a while back? Well, it is very clear to me now that he used me. I taught him how to hack and how to destroy webpages like this. I was using it to destroy child-porn sites. He wanted to know more; he was interested in what I did. I thought he was interested in me...but now he is using what I taught him to get to you."

"But that means you can also stop it, right?" I ask hopefully, while Chloe's fingers dance crazily across the keyboard.

"I don't know yet," she says. "This bug he has created is pretty advanced. I can't seem to get back into the page."

"But you can stop it, right?"

Chloe doesn't answer. I stare at the screen while she works her magic. I have never seen her like this, so frantic. Meanwhile, the number of followers drops drastically by the minute. I feel so helpless. It frustrates me that I know so little about computers and the world of hacking.

"Oh, no!" Chloe exclaims.

"What? What's happening?"

"He knew I would try this, so when I did, I activated another bug."

"What bug? I don't understand anything that is going on, Chloe."

"Neither do I," she says and looks up at me.

Meanwhile, my blog is crashing on the screen, in an inferno of old pictures of me flashing on the screen one after the other, numbers and letters flying around until the screen suddenly goes black and one message remains, blinking:

READY OR NOT, HERE I COME!

39

APRIL 1975

PEOPLE on the boat are cheering as it pulls away from the shore. On the outside, some people are still trying to jump on the boat, most of them without success.

Danh holds his sister tightly in his arms. He doesn't know whether to cry or join the cheering crowd, so he chooses to do neither. He can only hope one of his brothers is on the boat with them or will be waiting for them wherever they are going to end up.

Soon after, the cheering subsides and everything in the bottom of the boat goes quiet. They have entered the big ocean.

Now what?

In the ocean, the small fishing boat hits rough seas. It feels like the boat is being thrown high into the air only to slam back onto the waves. Soon people are screaming instead of cheering. And some of them start to get sick. One after another starts to puke. Being on the bottom, a lot of it comes down on Danh. He lies on top of Long, covering her so it won't hit her as well. She is scared and whining, so he starts to sing for her, the songs their mother used to sing. It calms her down and soon she falls asleep.

By some miracle, or pure exhaustion, Danh manages to fall asleep as well. When he wakes up, it is light outside. The seas have calmed down. Many people are still asleep. That's when he sees it. Up on the deck. The red shirt.

"Bao!" he yells.

The red shirt turns around and looks towards him. Danh waves.

"Bao!"

Bao walks closer, then reaches down his hand and grabs Danh's. He pulls him up and they both help grab Long. They carry her up, away from the crowd of sleeping or sick people. Danh's heart is beating so fast. He is so happy to see his older brother he is almost about to cry.

"We're actually allowed up here on the deck," Bao says. "We're among the few who have paid for this ride."

Danh looks down at the many people at the bottom of the boat. There has got to be at least a hundred and fifty people. It seems like a lot of people for such a small boat.

"They disguised it as a cargo ship," Bao said. "Clever, huh? They hope no one will stop and check for refugees. They're carrying colas." Bao points at the many bottles.

Danh doesn't look at them. He keeps staring at his brother, wondering about the word, refugees. Was that what they were now?

He struggles with this term and wonders if that means they'll never go back again. But what about their parents? What about their many brothers? Will they ever see them again?

Long moans in her sleep and Danh hopes she won't wake up yet. He doesn't have the answers she will be seeking and he doesn't know how long he can keep lying to her, pretending everything will be all right, when he doesn't know. When he is terrified they won't.

Bao grabs a cola and throws it at Danh. "Here. The captain says we can drink these to stay hydrated. He has rice too."

Bao puts his arm around Danh's shoulder and pulls him closer. "We'll be all right, brother," he says. "Don't you worry."

Danh eases up and smiles. For a few seconds, he believes his brother is right. Until he looks down at the crowd of people on the bottom and then back at the sodas, and realizes there is far from enough for everyone.

40

APRIL 2016

"I DID IT. I'm back in!"

I literally have no nails left when the words I have been longing to hear for hours finally fall.

I get up and walk to Chloe. The table is filled with empty chocolate wrappings from me binging in anxiety. "Really? Are you sure?"

"Yes. I have taken control back of our site. It's over."

I take in a deep breath of relief, pull up a chair, and sit right next to her. "How bad is it? What's the damage?"

"We've lost a million followers so far. There might be more along the way. We still have almost four million, so it's a sustainable loss."

"Phew."

"Now all we have to do is clean up. I think I might have to make an entire new design. It may take a few days to get it completely up and running, but I think I can manage," she says.

"I have no idea what I would do without you," I say, and pour the both of us some more coffee. It is late in the afternoon and I am exhausted from this emotional rollercoaster.

Chloe sips the coffee, before she looks at me. "Maybe we should spice it up a little?" she asks.

I walk to the cabinet and grab the whiskey. I pour some in both of our cups.

"Just what the doctor ordered," she says.

I close my eyes and take a big sip. The alcohol soon makes me calmer. I am so angry with my brother I can hardly contain it. I push my anger back by eating another candy bar, just as I hear a knock, and seconds later the front door is opened. Danny walks in. He looks tired. Like he hasn't slept at all.

"She's not the only one," he says, his bloodshot eyes staring at us, looking almost manic.

"What do you mean?" Chloe looks up. Danny slams the door behind him. I just hope he doesn't wake my dad, who had to take a nap.

Snowflake attacks him, wagging his tail and whining for him to pet him. Danny greets him with a short pat on the head, then walks to us.

"I mean she is not the only one," he continues. He lifts a stack of papers in his hand. "Look at all this. I have been up all night searching the news, scanning the local newspapers for other missing persons, and look at what I found."

He throws the stack on the desk next to Chloe. "Four cases within the last two years. Four cases of missing single mothers and their child. And there seems to be a pattern to it. If you look at the dates, there are exactly six months between the disappearances. Exactly."

Danny spreads out the papers and shows us the dates. "These two, Kim and Casey Taylor, a mother and a daughter, just like the rest of them, disappeared exactly a year ago. Last seen at the mall on a surveillance camera. Kim's mother filed a missing persons report a week later, when her daughter and granddaughter still hadn't shown up, and these pictures appeared. According to the newspapers, it is believed Kim Taylor ran away with this man that she is talking to in the surveillance video, the one you can only see the back of. They closed the case, stating she had met a man and left town with him. But Kim's mother didn't believe any of that, so she has started a Facebook group to help find her daughter and grandchild. I spoke to her earlier and she told me it is odd that Kim would leave everything behind in her apartment and not even take her clothes if she had left, or made sure the cat was taken care of. She has told this to the police, but they say they believe Kim is on drugs and this is typical addict behavior. If someone comes along, offering them drugs or a better life, they leave. Next, there is this case, exactly six months earlier, to the date, Jenny and Stacey Brown disappeared. They are last seen by a neighbor in Publix, where she greeted them on their way out. Since then, no one knows what happened to them. Again, they live in a bad neighborhood; the police believe drugs were involved. The mother owed a lot of money and was known by the police for petty theft, shoplifting and so on. They believe she left town to start over somewhere else. Jenny's sister, who filed the missing persons report, accepted that explanation and stopped looking for her. Exactly six months earlier, in April 2014, two years ago, Joan and Nicola Williams disappeared. The newspapers haven't written much about it, but they did send out an Amber Alert for the daughter when the father asked the police for help, but they were never found. The story reports nothing about their home or whether they took everything or not. But it fits with the pattern. The same with Maria and Tara Verlinden. Their disappearance came exactly six months after Kim and Casey Taylor's. No one seems to care because that stupid mother of hers doesn't care. There you have it. All four cases are from Brevard County."

I grab the printed out articles that he has found and look at them one after the other. There are a lot of similarities in the cases, I can give him that, but there are still a lot of unanswered questions. It could all be coincidence. But the fact about the dates being so accurate intrigues me. I can't just ignore it.

"Six months, you say?" I look at my phone to check the date. "If you're right in your theory, then that would mean that a mother and a daughter will disappear again tomorrow?"

41

APRIL 2016

A THUNDERSTORM HITS Cocoa Beach that afternoon, just as I park the car behind the building housing city hall and the police department. I don't have an umbrella or a jacket to cover me, so I decide to make a run for it. When I go through the glass doors to the police department, I am soaking wet, and water is dripping from my hair and clothes onto the tiles. I leave a puddle as I walk across them to the front desk.

"I'm here to see Detective Chris Fisher," I say to the woman behind the counter. She seems to be pretending I don't exist and stares into her computer screen, her glasses on the tip of her nose, her red hair in a ponytail.

"Is he expecting you?" she asks, still without looking at me. I try not to let it irritate me.

"No. But it's important. He knows who I am," I say. "Just tell him Mary Mills is here and that I have some very important information for him. It's a matter of life and death." I try to sound dramatic to provoke any reaction from this lady who doesn't seem to care about anything. It doesn't work.

"Have a seat," she says, finally looking at me above her glasses.

I sit down in an uncomfortable chair. I can't sit still. This morning has been an emotional rollercoaster to put it mildly, and I can't calm down. I check my phone excessively to see if Salter has called, but he still hasn't. I worry about him. He ought to be back from school now. I hope he at least went to school today and not paddle boarding again.

I grumble and curse Joey when the door opens and Chris Fisher pokes his very round head out.

"Ah, Mary," he says, sounding like he is everything but happy to see me. He steps out and walks towards me with his usual smirk. I can never tell if he is hitting on me or being a jerk.

"To what do I owe the honor?"

I have known Chris Fisher since he was just a kid. He hasn't changed much since he was that annoying teenager who was always peeking at us older girls. He is still annoying. He is also the guy that is handling my brother's case, and so far he hasn't done much of a job finding him.

"I have several things I need to talk to you about," I say. "We should go somewhere where we can sit down, somewhere more private."

"Want to be alone with the Fisher-man, do we?" he teases me.

I don't react to his comment. Instead, I get up from my chair. He senses his joke fell flat and looks disappointed.

"I was going to Juice 'N Java for a coffee and a muffin anyway," he continues, and points towards the café across the street.

I sigh. Not very private, but if that is all I can get, I'll take it. "All right. I could go for some coffee myself."

He holds the door for me with a grin and I walk out. "So, what's up?" he says when we're in the street.

"Two things," I say. "First of all, there's my brother."

"Go on, I'm listening."

"He orchestrated an attack on my blog. He hacked in and planted something, I have no idea what it was, you'll have to ask Chloe about that, but it destroyed everything and sent out all these fake messages to my followers. He left me a creepy message stating *Ready or not, here I come.*"

Chris nods along as we walk towards the café across the street. We stop at the intersection at Minutemen Causeway.

"All right, so he is now harassing you. That's new. Seems to me like he is being reckless. He probably thinks there is no way we can catch him. That he is invincible. That's actually a good sign. Makes it easier for him to make a mistake, and then we'll find him. I want to say that I'll have my IT department take a look at it, but I don't think they can do anything that Chloe can't do. Plus, they're swamped most of the time, so it might take months before they have the time to take a look at it, and my guess is that doesn't help us much in catching Blake."

"So what you're pretty much saying is you won't do anything," I say. "That's about what I expected."

"Hey, don't be sassy. I am working on finding him. Don't you worry," Chris says while the light turns green and we cross the street. "It's just...well, I have other cases too. And as far as we know, Blake is out of the county now so..."

"I know," I say. "He's under someone else's jurisdiction."

"Until he shows up here, there really isn't much I can do."

We walk past Heidi's and enter the Juice 'N Java. Again, Chris holds the door for me and I walk in first. The place is packed as always. Lots of soldiers from the Air Force base come here for lunch or afternoon coffee, along with mostly locals. I especially like it because you don't see many tourists here. This is our place.

I order a Mint Madness iced coffee and a big chocolate muffin. We sit on the couches by the window. The place always reminds me of the coffee shop in Friends. The old-fashioned furniture, couches and soft chairs, the art on the walls is beachy, made by local artists, and under the ceiling hangs old beautiful surfboards. Sometimes they have live music playing, small bands or local performers. I have been here once for open mic night as well and enjoyed it a lot. The place has a good vibe to it. It's a great place for me to go when I once in a while miss New York, which, to my surprise, actually isn't very often. I don't miss the life I had back then.

"So, what was the other thing?" Chris asks when we're sitting down. I'm on the couch while he grabs an armchair.

I remove the magazines from the coffee table and place the articles Danny printed out in front of Chris. "I know you won't have time to read through them, but I can give you a quick summary."

"Please do," he says and stares at the stack of printed articles like he doesn't want to even touch it.

"Single mothers disappearing," I say. "And their children."

Chris looks at me, tired. "What?"

"Four cases the past two years. There might be more in the years before, I don't know, but this is what we've found so far. And, get this. There are exactly six months between every disappearance. Look here, I wrote down the dates. April 23rd 2014, October 23rd 2014, April 23rd 2015, October 23rd 2015. Look at them," I say, and point my finger aggressively at the piece of paper where I wrote down the dates. I take in a deep breath and bite into my muffin. It's nice and mushy. I realize I haven't had a real meal all day since breakfast. It's all been candy bars and cookies.

Chris just stares at the papers, then up at me. I can tell he really doesn't want to have to read it. He sighs and drinks his Loco Cocoa Latte. He even looks at his watch, as if to tell me he doesn't have time for this.

"It fits, Chris," I say. "The dates do."

He finally grabs the articles and flips through them so fast there is no way he could read anything.

"So, what you're saying is, these mothers..."

"They're all single mothers," I interrupt. "That's a pattern."

"All right, these *single* mothers. You're telling me they have all disappeared with their children? Where is the crime? They could all have left town or something." He picks out an article and reads a few lines. "Like this one, for instance, it says here in the article that she was a drug addict and moved often."

"That's exactly how I reacted in the first place as well, but the dates are very strange, and some of them left all their belongings behind. Even passports and children's iPads. You don't leave your kid's iPad behind willingly," I say, matter-of-factly.

"But it says here they did take their phones and wallets," he says.

"Sure, but why leave your passport?" I argue.

"Where is the last one? You said there were four?"

"Well, the last one was never reported to the police," I say, hoping to avoid too many questions. I want him to know that Maria and Tara are missing, but I also made a promise to Danny to not tell anyone that she was his daughter. At least not until he has told Junior about her himself, which I know he is building up the courage to do, but knowing Danny it might take a while. There is nothing worse for him than to have to disappoint someone he loves.

"So, how do you know they're missing?" he asks, puzzled.

"Well, I just know. Because I know them. I wrote all the details in this document here," I say, and point at a Word document. "Their names are Maria and Tara Verlinden. I spoke to Maria's mother yesterday and she has no idea where they are. They left everything behind. I don't think they disappeared willingly."

"But she never filed a missing persons report? That sounds a little odd to me," Fisher says, drinking his coffee.

"I know it sounds odd, but she didn't because she has no relationship with her daughter, and well...she took the money that Maria received for child support, because she...you're not even listening anymore, are you?"

Chris shakes his head and leans back in his armchair. "Come on, Mary. This is far out. Besides, I can't go into this if there isn't proof of a crime being committed. You know that. I have other stuff on my plate. Lots of stuff. We have to take care of the dog problem too."

I look up at him. "What dog problem? You don't mean people walking on the beach with dogs, do you? Please tell me that is not what keeps you busy?"

He rubs his forehead, squirming in his seat. This is embarrassing for him. "It's just that...well tourists are complaining..."

"You've got to be kidding me!" I say a little too loud.

Some of the other guests in the café turn their heads and look at me. I smile and pretend everything is fine.

"It's political, Mary. There isn't much I can do about it."

"Argh!" I exclaim. "How can that be more important than missing women and their children?"

"It's not," he says, annoyed. "But again, where is the evidence that a crime has been committed?"

"How about the missing persons reports? Some of their families have filed missing persons reports."

"And the cases have been closed. It says so here, in the article about the woman who went missing in April 2014. They closed it, concluding she had left town. I have to say it all looks like coincidence here, Mary. I can't see how they are related." He throws out his arms. "I'm really sorry."

"But the dates," I say, tapping my pointer finger at the page with the dates. "Look at the dates. If this is a pattern, then another mother and her child will disappear tomorrow. How can you close your eyes to that? We have to do something at least. How else will you be able to sleep tonight?"

He sighs and rubs his hair. "Mary. You're blowing this way out of proportion. People leave town all the time. Especially single mothers. They run away from their families, they leave because they meet a guy, or they leave because of drugs. Maybe they owe money, maybe they know someone in another state who can give them a job. Drug addicts leave their belongings behind because they don't think. They just go to for their next fix; maybe they didn't plan on staying, maybe they just stay there for a longer period of time than expected because someone is providing them with the drug they need. It's not that strange. Besides, if I were to believe that someone would disappear tomorrow, a mother and a child, how would I prevent that from happening? These women come from all over the county. Do you want us to tell all single mothers to stay home tomorrow?"

I sigh. I know he is right. We have no way of knowing who or where this will happen again or if it even will. There really isn't much anyone can do. I just feel bad for Danny that we can't get the police to help him find his daughter. But he told me so. Danny said they wouldn't take this seriously. And he was right.

I collect the papers and make them a pile again. Chris grabs my hand. I look into his eyes.

"You know what?" he says. "You have been right about these kinds of things before. You have a hunch, I'll give you that. Let me take a look at these cases and see what I can come up with, all right?"

I smile and let go of the copies. "You're a good guy, Chris," I say. "Even though you hide it well."

42

APRIL 2016

IT'S PICK-UP DAY.

Saturday morning Boxer is looking at his own reflection in the mirror. He is calm. In the beginning, when he did his first pick-up, he was nervous, afraid something might go wrong. He's not anymore. So far, all of them have gone well. And he is getting better at it.

He splashes water in his face while remembering the other times. He doesn't like it much. He doesn't like the way they scream, the way they plead and beg for him to let them go. He can still hear each and every one of them when he thinks about it. So he tries not to. But when a new pick-up date arrives, it is hard to keep those memories away. He has been dreaming about it all night, especially about the girls.

Boxer walks downstairs where his brother is still sleeping on the couch. He came back the night before, drunk and with a new debt. Boxer just paid the three hundred thousand from last week and now he has to help him out with another five hundred thousand. It stresses him out, since he doesn't have that kind of money on hand, not when he has to pay for their mother's hospice as well. Hopefully he will...after today.

"Get up, bro," he says, and grabs his brother's shoulder. He shakes it. Nothing happens. His brother smells of liquor. Boxer hates that smell. He never touches alcohol. He has seen what it has done to his brother.

"Get up. I need your help today," he says.

His brother finally blinks. Boxer doesn't understand why he insists on sleeping on the couch when he has a perfectly good guest bedroom upstairs that he could crash in.

"Help? With what?"

"I have an order for a pick-up."

His brother sits up and wipes his eyes with a yawn. "All right. Give me a few minutes to get ready."

"I'll make some coffee," Boxer says, and walks into the kitchen.

"How about some of your famous pancakes?" his brother asks.

Boxer smiles. "Sure. Why not?"

He starts to whip together some batter while suppressing the growing anxiety inside that he senses when thinking about today's task. He doesn't want to feel it. He doesn't want to feel anything, but it is hard not to.

His brother puts on his pants and comes into the kitchen. He smells and Boxer makes a grimace.

"Go get a shower," he says. "There's still time."

His brother does as he is told and comes down ten minutes later, his hair wet, and smelling a lot better. He grabs the coffee pot and pours himself a cup.

"So, where are we doing this pick-up today?" he asks, while Boxer finishes making the pancakes. He serves them for his brother while grabbing some yogurt with granola and fruit for himself. Boxer doesn't like to eat unhealthy. He wants to take care of his body.

"There's a rally today," he says while they eat. "People are protesting the fish-kill in the lagoon."

"And that's where we pick them up?"

"Yes. They will be there."

"Lots of people, though. Kind of risky, don't you think?" his brother asks. His brother has helped him do most of the pick-ups and knows how it works. There was only that one time when he was on a bender that Boxer had to do it alone. Most of the money goes to pay for his gambling anyway, so it's only fair that he helps out, Boxer thinks.

"They won't even notice," Boxer says. "Trust me. I know what I'm doing."

43

APRIL 2016

"WE'RE GOING to be late, Mom!"

Paige yells at Nicky as they rush out the door with signs in their hands. Nicky's says *Save our water. There's no Planet B!* while Paige's simply says, *It's my future you're messing with.*

Nicky really likes the slogans they have come up with and feels confident that they'll be able to shake the politicians up a little today. She has been looking forward to this day all week. Mrs. Robbins is in Miami all weekend, so now she has time to spend with her daughter. Going to this rally is a great way to bond a little over something important.

They drive to downtown and park behind city hall. They're early, but the space is already almost filled up. The Intracoastal waters and a bunch of dead fish are something that can get people to rise up from their couches.

Nicky is happy to see that so many people care. They grab their signs and walk to the front of city hall, where a sizable group has gathered. Nicky sees a handful of women she knows from Paige's school and walks to them. Paige is falling a little behind. She doesn't seem too interested in this rally and it aggravates Nicky, since she wants her daughter to know the importance of taking good care of the environment. It is, after all, her future they're rallying for.

"Hi ladies," she chirps and waves at her friends.

"Hello there, stranger," her friend Belinda says and kisses her on her cheeks. "Long time no see."

"Well, you know. Been kind of busy with the company and all."

"How's it going with that?"

"It's been good. Yeah. It's been busy, real busy."

"I want you to meet someone," Belinda says and pulls Nicky's arm.

She drags her towards a chunky woman standing with a camera between her hands. "This here is Mary Mills. You know...the famous blogger. Mary, this is Nicky. Her daughter Paige is in sixth grade."

Mary reaches out her hand and shakes Nicky's. "Nice to meet you," she says, and smiles warmly.

"Mary is writing about the rally for her blog. Isn't it exciting? She has like five million followers on that thing."

"Well, I'm technically writing about the fish-kill and what caused it, but I will be writing stuff about the rally as well, and I'll post some of the pictures I take today," Mary says. She has a nice smile.

"Good, good," Belinda says. "Oh, that's excellent. Soon the entire world will know what's going on down here. That'll get them out of their chairs, don't ya' think?" she says and pokes her elbow at Nicky.

Nicky nods. "That is awesome."

"Would it be alright if I took your picture?" Mary says. "You've got an awesome sign. Is that your daughter standing behind you?"

Nicky turns to look at Paige, who stares angrily back at her. "You said there would be other kids."

"They're coming, sweetie," Nicky says. "Now come here and smile for the camera. Hold up your sign so Mary can see it. There you go."

They pose and smile and Mary Mills takes a bunch of photos, then smiles and thanks them. "If you follow me on Facebook, I'll post all the pictures there during the day today," she says. "Are you on Facebook?"

Nicky nods. "Yes. Both Paige and I are. We would love to see them."

"Is your husband here as well?" Mary asks and looks around. "I'd love to get a picture of the entire family rallying together for the future of our children."

Nicky feels heavy. She hates when people ask about Paige's father. "No. It's just the two of us," she says.

"Okay. Say no more. I'm a single mom myself. One last thing. What's your last name?"

"Stover."

Mary writes the name down on a small pad, then looks up at Nicky with a smile. "Great. Then I'll tag you so you can see them once they're up."

"Great. Thanks."

Nicky feels a tug at her shirt. "Mom, I saw some of my friends from school. Can I walk with them?"

Finally, Paige seems to be onboard. "Well, of course, honey, Nicky says. "Remember to yell as loud as you can while you walk and put your sign up in the air. Make yourself be heard!"

44

APRIL 2016

I DON'T FEEL GOOD. I try to suppress the feeling of dread that is constantly nagging at me while I take pictures and talk to people at the rally. It's not the fish-kill that's bothering me. It's not the many stories people are feeding me of how the local politicians are trying to cover up the real cause of the fish-kill, no that's not why I feel sick to my stomach.

It's the hunch.

The feeling that something bad is going to happen. The knowledge that someone might disappear today, that a single mother somewhere might vanish along with her child, and no one knows where to.

I keep looking around at the crowd, staring at the faces of all these people. Most of them are women. Some have brought their children. As a single mother myself, I am terrified. A few minutes ago, I talked to a single mother with a little girl a few years older than Salter. Could it be her? Is she next? Am I? Was it planned, what happened to them, or was it random?

I comfort myself by telling myself that it doesn't have to be right here in Cocoa Beach that the next disappearance is happening. It could be anywhere in the surrounding towns. Rockledge, Titusville, Merritt Island, Viera. Maria and Tara lived almost in Cape Canaveral.

Am I overreacting? Am I blowing this out of proportion like Chris Fisher said? I don't know. But the feeling won't go away. It is sitting in my stomach and eating at me, slowly devouring me, making me anxious for every face in this crowd, including myself.

I am just happy that Salter is with his dad. I spoke to him before I went to bed last night and he had been to school and was doing fine, he told me. I hope he wasn't lying to me.

You've got to let it go, Mary. Let it go. You can't control everything for the rest of his life.

"Any news?" Chloe asks, as she comes up next to me.

"Good morning," I say cheerfully.

I can't believe she is here. I am amazed that I managed to talk her into coming with me for this. I didn't expect her to show up. She hates crowds and she hates being outside and usually sleeps at this hour of the day. Judging from the look on her face, she isn't exactly enjoying it. In the bright sunlight she looks paler than usual. I can't see her eyes behind those dark sunglasses, but I know they're not happy.

"I got a few leads that I want to follow up on," I say. "You were right that there are a lot of rumors about the power plant."

"I'm not talking about the fish-kill," she says with a deep sigh that makes me want to spring for coffee for her. "What did Chris Fisher say? When you spoke to him yesterday?"

"He'll look into it," I say.

She turns her head and I think she is looking at me, but I can't tell because of those sunglasses.

"He said that?"

"Believe it or not, he did. It took some convincing on my part, but that's what he finally said before he left me."

"I don't see many cops here today, though," she says and looks around us. We're standing in the middle of the crowd, as it is slowly growing bigger when more people join in.

"They're probably watching us from behind the windows while drinking coffee and eating cake," I say, and look at the building behind us. "It is awfully convenient that the rally is right outside their door. But I did see one down in front of the fire station when I got here. I also heard they have blocked off the streets."

"So what's supposed to happen next?" Chloe asks, sounding highly uninterested.

"We're supposed to walk down Minutemen yelling all the slogans," I say. "I think they're waiting for one of the organizers to step up and kind of start the whole thing. You know, take the lead. I heard that Theodor G is going to be here."

"Oh, no. I can't stand that guy. So pompous."

"Well, everyone else loves him," I say, getting a little annoyed with

Chloe's attitude. She's ruining my mood. It's enough that I have this anxious feeling inside of me, I don't want to feel depressed as well.

"I loathe rallies," Chloe says. "Too many people in one place. Everyone is so close together it's yucky."

"Yeah, but at least it's for a good cause," I say, trying to lift her spirits a little. Meanwhile, I grab the camera and take some more photos. My new subject is a dad with his young son helping him hold his sign.

"Cute."

"As if this will ever help anything," Chloe says with a scoff. "These people walking around with their signs singing hymns or yelling slogans won't save the fish, if you ask me."

"Don't be so cynical. We gotta do what we can do, right?" I say. "This is all we as a community can do right now. Show the politicians that we are angry about this and that they should do something. Ah, look, News13 is here. That's good. We need all the publicity we can get."

"Where is Danny? Why is he not here?"

"He needed some time with Junior. I think he's trying to find the courage to tell him he has a sister."

"Ouch. That's gotta hurt," Chloe says. "Got any food?"

I reach into my purse and pull something out. "Candy bar?"

"Sure. I'll take it."

"Looks like someone is stepping up," I say, as a woman walks out of the crowd with a megaphone in her hand.

"Welcome, everyone," she yells. "First of all, I want to thank everyone who has come out to support this important cause today."

A vague bit of applause spreads through the crowd, then dies.

"Oh, my," Chloe complains.

"Shh," I say, while the woman with the megaphone tells us what is going to happen.

"Did she just say that we'll be walking all the way to the country club?" Chloe says. "You've got to be kidding me! In this heat?"

"I gotta say, the idea doesn't appeal to me either," I say, as the woman is replaced by a big broad-shouldered guy that I recognize as Theodor G, the football player who started a fast food chain called Pull 'N Pork, when he retired. Like Kelly Slater, he is one of the local heroes around here. We need them today.

Theodor grabs the megaphone and the crowd finally manages to applaud loudly. He talks about the river and how it has never been this bad and how he used to play in the water as a teenager and fish. When he is done, the crowd starts to walk, Theodor in the lead, chanting and singing.

I see many mothers with their children and feel a pinch in my heart, thinking about Maria and Tara. Where are they now? What has happened to them? Why doesn't anyone care?

"I'm not walking that far," Chloe says.

"Ah, come on," I say. "You know...when in Rome and all that."

"Kill me," Chloe says, before she finally trots along behind me.

45

APRIL 2016

BOXER PARKS his car and gets out. His brother is right behind him. Minutemen is blocked off; no cars can go through while the rally is going on. The crowd is starting to leave city hall now and is walking towards the main street. Boxer and his brother grab the signs Boxer has made for them and join in. Boxer nods and greets some of his neighbors.

"Hi. How are you?" he says again and again.

His brother doesn't know anyone and he stays behind Boxer. He is not very good with people. Not like Boxer is. Boxer knows how to talk to them, how to make them feel like he is one of them, that he is part of the community. Just like when he speaks to the girls online, he has a way of making them feel like they can talk to him.

Like he's a nice guy.

"How do we find them? There are hundreds of people here," his brother finally whispers in his ear.

"I showed you their Facebook pictures. Just look for them," Boxer hisses angrily, trying to stop his brother from talking about why they are really there.

"But how? There are so many people?"

"I know," Boxer says, and holds onto the gun in his pocket. "We gotta just wait for the right moment."

"As you wish," his brother says and trots along.

"Save our lagoon. Save our river home!" Boxer yells, along with the rest of the crowd. He is holding his sign up high in the air. "This is the future for our children. Save our water!"

They walk like this for about ten minutes when his brother starts to get impatient. "Where are they?" he asks.

"I don't know," Boxer hisses.

"Well, you should know. It's all your plan."

"I didn't know there would be this many people, all right?"

"So, what do we do? All these women look alike. Many of them have children. Why don't we just grab one or the other?"

"We can't. I have a particular order for this one. I've been working on it for months. We can't take any chances here. It'll ruin everything. They have to be single moms and they have to be the ones I've picked out and the client has approved of," he whispers, hoping his brother can hear him over the crowd's loud singing and yelling. "Just trust me."

"All right. All right. I just figured it would be easier if we..."

"No! Just walk."

"All right. You're in charge."

Boxer's brother finally goes silent when Boxer's phone vibrates in his pocket. He pulls it out and sees a notification from Facebook.

"What is it?" his brother asks.

Boxer is smiling. "Someone tagged Paige in a photo. I've set it up so I get all notifications about her. If she posts anything or if someone tags her in something." He touches his screen and a picture shows up of Paige and her mother standing by city hall holding their signs.

"It looks like it was taken before they started walking," Boxer says. "But at least now we know that they're here and what their signs say."

Seconds later, the phone vibrates again. Another notification from Paige. It's the same lady who posted the first picture, but this time it shows Paige with three other girls walking on their own.

"This one is newer," he says. "Look, they're right ahead of us. That building there is the school. Roosevelt Elementary. It's no more than fifty feet ahead of us."

46

APRIL 2016

I AM KEEPING myself very busy during this rally and completely forgetting how far we are walking. I take pictures of everyone and post them on Facebook right away, trying to tag everyone, but it's getting more and more difficult.

The latest picture I took was of four young girls between eleven and twelve years of age, walking with their signs and singing along. I thought it was the cutest thing, so I had to take their picture. I love it when young kids get involved.

I tag all four girls, then move on. I photograph an elderly lady who is walking steadfastly, keeping up with everyone else, and I interview her while we walk. She tells me she is ninety-six years old.

"The river has never been in this bad a shape," she says, determined. "We've had fish-kills before, but not in this amount. It's outrageous. I am here today to support my community and show my anger towards what is going on. Those politicians are sitting on their hands and doing nothing. It's outrageous."

I write her comments down. I want to use them both on Facebook and in the article I am writing for the blog.

Chloe is trying to keep up with me, but is snarling more and more the further we go.

"Are we there yet?" she keeps asking me.

I, on the other hand, am trying to make the best of it. I find that I am actually enjoying myself. And doing something like this makes me forget that nagging dread I have been feeling since last night. I am beginning to hope that I am actually wrong about this...that Chloe, Danny, and I are only seeing ghosts.

"If I'd known this was going to happen, then I would never have..."

"Chloe," I interrupt her. "You've got to stop complaining. I am grateful that you are here, but if all you're going to do is complain, then maybe it would be better if you went back home."

"I thought you needed me here."

"I thought so too, but as it turns out, I don't. I am doing it all by myself. I love you. I am all for you. I love to hang out with you, but if you don't want to be here, just go home and I'll see you later."

Chloe looks disappointed. I still can't see her eyes, but I know how they look. I know her all too well. "So you're saying you don't need me here?"

I grab her and hug her, even though I know she hates people touching her. "See you later, Chloe."

"All right. I guess I'm going back then."

I wave and follow the crowd as it passes Chloe, who is now standing still. Some guy elbowing his way through the crowd accidentally pushes her aside.

"Hey!" she yells.

"Sorry," he says and hurries on.

I chuckle. That is so typically Chloe. Never was very good with people. And people were never very good with Chloe.

I turn around and start shooting pictures of the crowd. The guy who pushed Chloe is right in front of me and I take a few pictures, but mostly of his neck. I wonder why he is in such a hurry to get up front.

I am very pleased to see that the police have blocked off Minutemen completely for cars and they are all present by the blockade. I remind myself to put that in my article. How the local enforcement is backing up our protest. Should give them some goodwill. I need to stay good friends with them.

I take a few extra photos when something happens behind me. It starts with the unmistakable sound of tires screeching. It is followed by someone screaming. The scream makes me turn to look. I face hundreds of people who have started to run towards me. It's like a stampede.

What the hell is going on?

Between the screaming and running people, I manage to spot a car. It seems to have driven through the police blockade and into the crowd.

There is blood on the front of the car.

47

APRIL 2016

BOXER DOESN'T LOOK BACK. The people surrounding him all do. They turn to see what the screams are about while he continues ahead. In front of him, not very far away, he can see the girls. Four young girls walking in a line. They too hear the screams and the commotion coming from the back of the line and turn to look. Panic erupts as the stampeding crowd from behind surpasses Boxer and chaos is everywhere. The girls are pulled apart, some of them start to run, others are crying helplessly, calling their mother's names.

Boxer's eyes remain fixated on the girl, on Paige. She is standing still, frozen, while everything and everyone around her moves frantically like recently beheaded chickens. As he approaches her, their eyes lock.

She smiles, but not for long. The seriousness on Boxer's face causes her to stop. He approaches her and grabs her by the shoulders.

"Something happened. You've got to come with me," he yells through the screams. "Something terrible happened to your mother."

Fear spreads in her eyes. "What? What happened?"

"Something terrible. She was taken away in an ambulance. Come with me. I'll take you to the hospital," he lies.

Boxer grabs Paige's hand in his and pulls her out of the crowd. "I have my car over here, it's parked behind city hall," he says. "But we must hurry."

Screams and panic continue behind them as they leave the main road and cross the parking lot. The girl is whimpering.

"Is it bad?" she asks. "Is she hurt?"

"I don't know. But I gotta tell you, kiddo, it doesn't look too good. She was in pretty bad shape when they took her away."

"Oh. How did it happen?"

"A car drove through the blockade and hit some people."

Boxer looks around to make sure no one is watching him. Not a single person sees them. They're too busy screaming and running around. The officers present are all running towards the car that apparently did hit someone. Boxer has no idea who or how it happened or who drove the car, but he is very grateful to whoever it was. It was perfect timing. It was just the type of panic he was going for.

Boxer's own plan had been to use the gun to fire a few shots outside the crowd and create chaos that way. But since the car did all the work for him, he didn't have to.

"My car is right over here," he says, and points at the white van. He looks around to see if he can see his brother anywhere, but he doesn't seem to be there. Boxer opens the back door.

"You need to ride in the back. Jump in."

Paige hesitates and looks at him, slightly skeptical.

"Come on," Boxer says. "We've got to get out of here before everyone else gets into their cars and starts driving, then we'll get stuck in traffic. You hear those sirens? Well, that's your mother being taken to the hospital. You want to be there, right?"

Paige nods while looking at him with big brown moist eyes. He can't believe how great a liar he is, how convincing his little act is.

"Well, get in then."

Paige finally jumps in and Boxer slams the door shut behind her.

One down, one to go. Now where is that no-good brother of mine?

Finally, he spots him as he comes running towards the car. Boxer growls when he realizes he's alone.

"What the hell are you doing?" he yells. "Where is the mother? You were supposed to bring her here. You were supposed to tell her that her daughter had been hurt and that she needed to come with you, where is she?"

His brother pants heavily and leans forward to catch his breath. "I'm sorry, Boxer. I really am. She..." he pauses to breathe. "She...I couldn't find her."

48

APRIL 1975

THE DAYS ARE long and the food sparse on the boat. They have no water, only sodas, so they cook their rice in it and it tastes terrible. Danh is losing weight fast and so is his brother and especially his sister. But at least they're being fed.

Far from everyone onboard is getting anything to eat or drink for days. Most of the people on the bottom of the boat haven't paid the fare and therefore don't get to get up on deck and don't get anything. They're getting sick down there and it is spreading fast. Danh sees it every day. More and more people are getting sick and they look like they're all dying.

Danh feels awful for being one to get food, but Bao tells him to just ignore them, to be happy there is food and drink for him and his family. Long soon notices it too. That people are suffering. She doesn't understand why they can't just give those people some food.

"There are children down there," she says, crying. "They're hungry. They're thirsty."

"So are we," Bao says harshly. "It's them or us. We won't survive if they drink everything we have. Don't you understand anything?"

He has never been very good at talking to Long. He wants her to toughen up, he wants her to grow up, while Danh tries to keep her a child. He loves her innocence, her naivety, and would prefer she stayed that way all of her life. He simply loves it about her. So he tries to play games with her. As always, when he wants her to think about something else, he tells her it's all part of a game. Using empty cola bottles, he plays music for her and hopes that will make her forget everything. Most of the days, they pretend to be royalty on a ship and they have to look for pirates. That forces her to look away from the sick people. They talk about dreams and about how they are going to bathe in water when they arrive at the coast.

"There will be so much food we'll all get fat," he says.

"Also ice cream?"

"Especially ice cream, your majesty. We won't eat anything else for weeks. We'll get so fat we'll have to roll everywhere," he says, putting air in his cheeks to look fat, then trying to roll around on the deck.

Long giggles.

"No one will even be able to carry us, so fat will we be," she says, laughing her light childish laughter. The sound is like medicine for Danh's tormented soul. He has lost count of the days, but knows it has been more than two weeks so far since they left the harbor. He is sick of the ocean and longs to see land again, to feel steadfast land under his feet. But, most of all, he wants to be able to drink as much water as he can. Drinking only sodas makes him want to throw up. Once he sets his feet on solid ground again, he'll never touch a soda again. Especially not a cola.

But no matter how much Danh tries to make Long forget about the starving people at the bottom of the boat, it is no use. Every day, the smell coming from down there gets worse; the sick get worse and they all wonder how many are already dead.

Without anyone noticing it, Long rations her own portion of rice for days in a row and saves up, hiding it in the pocket of her dress. After a week, when Danh isn't looking, when he is dozing off for one unforgettable second, Long grabs the rice and walks down the ladder to the bottom, where she feeds a boy and his mother.

Danh doesn't realize what is going on until someone from the deck starts to yell at her. He opens his eyes just in time to watch Bao go after her and pull her crying and screaming up on the deck.

"Don't ever go down there again! You hear me?" He has placed his face close to hers and Danh can tell he is hurting her arm. "Never again! These people are sick. The captain won't hesitate to throw you overboard if you get sick too!"

49

APRIL 2016

I CAN'T BELIEVE what is happening around me. Such a peaceful rally, suddenly turned into an inferno of screaming people running like a mad shooter was after them. To be fair, I think most of them think that is what happened, but still. The panic is overwhelming. Kids are crying and mothers rushing them away to their cars.

Meanwhile, I am running to the scene to see what happened. I approach the area that is heavily surrounded by police and paramedics.

I can see someone lying on the ground. I see blood on the car and lots of people kneeling beside the woman who was hit by the car that accidentally ran through the police blockade.

I manage to get a step closer when I realize I know who it is.

It's that woman that I photographed earlier. What was her name again? Nicky! Nicky Stover! Oh, my God!

I spot detective Fisher among the officers and elbow my way forward. He nods and approaches me.

"You can't get through, Mary," he says and stops me.

"Where is her daughter?" I ask.

"You know this woman?"

"Not very well. But I do know her name is Nicky and that she has a daughter, Paige. Who is taking care of her?"

"Right now, we're just trying to keep her alive," he says. "The car crashed straight into her."

"Oh, my God. Do you have the driver in custody?"

"Yes. She says she didn't see anything. I mean, how hard could it be to see a police blockade and three officers guarding it?"

"Drunk driver?" I ask, while my heart pounds in my chest. Where is Paige while her mother is fighting for her life? I sure hope someone is taking care of her.

"We don't know yet. She's been taken to the station. Says she mistook the gas pedal for the brake. Tourist in a rental car."

"Oh, my."

One of the paramedics yells something and Chris disappears. He comes back towards me just as I am about to leave.

"You said you knew the daughter, right?"

"Yes," I say. "Well I don't know her. I know who she is."

"The mother is asking for her. She doesn't know where she is. Could you make sure she gets to the hospital?"

I nod. "Sure thing."

Chris nods, blinks, and points his finger at me and pretends it's a gun. *He's such a cliché.*

"What's going on?" The sound of the voice coming from behind me makes me turn around with a gasp.

"Tom? What are you doing here?" I ask and hug him.

"I was down at the rec center when I heard something was going on downtown. Someone said people had been killed. What happened? What's going on? Is that Nicky Stover?"

"Yes," I say. "Someone ran into her. A tourist ran their car through the police blockade. You know her?"

"I know her daughter. She plays on my team."

I grab his collar. "Then you have to help me find her."

50

APRIL 2016

I HAVE no idea where to start. With Tom next to me, I walk back onto Minutemen Causeway, which is now slowly getting emptied of people. I see many mothers dragging their kids away, but no Paige, no little girl all alone. We search the parking lot behind city hall where most people are getting inside their cars. We ask a few people if they have seen her, and one of them tells us she believes she saw Paige down by the high school, but she is not sure. We decide to walk in that direction.

"Who was she with?" Tom asks.

"She was walking with three other girls, also sixth graders from Roosevelt last time I saw her. They were all up front. Her mother was walking further in the back with other moms. I can't believe it...I am in shock."

I feel his hand on my shoulder to calm me down. "First, we find Paige. Then we freak out, all right?"

"Gosh, I am glad you're here with me," I say. "I would have completely freaked out by now. Thanks."

He smiles. He is not the handsomest of men, but he is slowly growing on me. I am beginning to see a beauty in his eyes that I hadn't seen before.

"Do you think she might have gone with those girls when all the panic started? Or maybe with some of their parents?" he asks. "Maybe one of the other moms took her home when they heard what happened?"

"Would you do that?" I ask, knowing he has adult children.

"No. Of course not," he says. "I would take her to the hospital so she could be with her mother."

"So, what if you don't know what happened?" I ask, my eyes steadily searching, scrutinizing the area for any young girls. The few I spot are not Paige. We keep walking down Minutemen to see if maybe some are waiting down by the school or maybe they continued all the way to the country club, maybe a group of people up front didn't hear what happened and just continued the walk?

"I would still try and get a hold of the girl's mother somehow. Call her or look for her."

"Did they have cell phones when your kids were young?" I ask with a grin.

"Very funny. I'm old, ha, ha," he says.

"Sorry. It was just too tempting," I say.

We meet some people walking the opposite way and I stop a man. "Do you know if there are any more people down that way?" I ask him. "We're looking for a young girl around eleven-twelve years old."

He shrugs. "There might be. We made it almost all the way down there before we heard what happened and decided to walk back. Terrible thing."

"All right," I say. "We'll keep walking. Thank you."

"You're welcome."

We pass the elementary school, then the high school, and meet a few people walking back, dragging their signs behind them. Somehow, the fish-kill doesn't seem all that important anymore.

I think about Nicky Stover and wonder if she'll survive being hit by that car. I get a chill, wondering how Paige will react to being told what happened, when her world will crumble. I realize I might have to be the one to tell her and I am not looking forward to that.

"It's going to be fine," he says, and puts an arm around me. I like how much he is paying attention to how I feel. Being in a new relationship is great.

"I know," I say. "I just wish we would find her, you know? She needs to know what happened to her mom."

51

APRIL 2016

IT'S NOT until we reach the country club at the end of Minutemen Causeway that I realize something is very wrong. There is hardly anyone there, a few women are packing picnic tables back into a van and removing signs. When we ask them if they have seen four young girls and show them a picture of Paige, they shake their heads.

Now I am seriously worried.

"She's not here either. What do we do?" I ask, my voice shaking.

Tom is biting his lip. "Could she have gone to the rec center? She is, after all, supposed to play in the game in a couple of hours."

"But certainly she has heard about her mother by now?" I ask, while we walk back towards city hall. "Someone must have told her."

"Maybe she went with some of her friends," Tom says. "Let's not panic here. They probably walked to the rec center...all of them together."

I grab my cell phone and look at the display. My son is in fourth grade. I wonder who I know that might know the number of some of the sixth graders or their parents. I think of Marcia. Her daughter Rose is twelve. She's in sixth grade. I call her up.

"Hi Mary. What's up?" she says on the other end.

"Do you know Paige Stover?" I ask.

"Sure. She's in Rose's class, why?"

"Do you know if Paige has a cell phone? It's important."

"I'll ask Rose. What's going on, Mary? Your voice sounds so shaky it's scaring me."

"Sorry. There was an accident at the rally. Paige's mom was hit by a car. I promised her that I would find Paige and help her get to the hospital."

"Oh, my. I'll ask Rose. One sec."

Marcia disappears for a few seconds, then returns. "She just got a cell phone, according to Rose. I have the number. I'll text it to you so you don't have to write it down. Okay?"

"Perfect," I say, and hang up.

Tom looks me in the eyes and plants both his hands on my shoulders. "I'm sure Paige is fine. I'm sure she already knows what happened and is at the hospital with her mother. You're probably getting yourself all worked up over nothing."

I nod as the phone in my hand vibrates and the number appears on my screen. I press it and wait for the tone.

"Hi...this is Paige Stover..."

"It goes directly to voicemail," I say. "I'll leave a message, just in case... Hi, this is Mary Mills. If you already know this, then you don't have to listen to it, but I just want to make sure that you know that your mother has been taken to the hospital, after a car hit her at the rally. I have been looking for you and can't find you anywhere, so if you hear this message, please be kind and shoot me a text or call me back so I know that you've gotten it. Okay. Thank you."

I hang up. We walk in silence back past the high school, the elementary school, and past the place of the accident, where the police are still working the scene. The paramedics are all gone and so is the ambulance. I feel terrible when we walk past it. Detective Fisher catches up to us.

"Mary! Did you find the daughter?" he asks.

I shake my head. "I checked the parking lot behind city hall. We walked all the way to the end. No one there had seen her. I left a message on her cell phone. I take it you haven't seen her either then? I was hoping..."

"No! She isn't at the hospital either. Her mother has been asking for her excessively."

My heart drops. I can't believe this. "She's not at the hospital either? But...but where is she then? Could she have gone home with someone?" I ask.

"Or maybe she's at the rec center," Tom repeats. "She does have a game there later today."

"I think I'll send a patrol out to look for her."

"Check the rec center," I say. "Or her friends. She was walking with three other girls from her school last time she was seen."

Fisher nods and puts a phone to his ear. "Got it," he says. "We'll find her. Don't worry. She can't have gone far."

52

APRIL 2016

"HOW COULD you have messed this up?"

Boxer is yelling at his brother. They're back at the house; Paige is sedated and they put her in the dog crate in the back. She won't wake up for hours.

"I am sorry," his brother says. "I looked everywhere like you told me. I saw them, and followed them. I found the women she was walking with, and then I saw her, but then the car went through that blockade and I lost sight of her. Everything was so chaotic. Everyone was screaming and running around. I searched and searched, but then all the police came running towards us and I had to get out of there. You told me to wait for the gunshot, but there wasn't any. Only the car and then the panic. I did my best, Boxer, I really did. You must believe me."

"The order specifically was for both mother and child. Not just the girl. Her mother as well. I can't deliver her now. I can't deliver half a package. If I can't deliver, we won't get paid. I can't pay for mom's treatment or pay off your debt. Do you understand what I'm saying? This was a big deal. This was supposed to bring in a lot of money."

"I am sorry," he repeats, but it's not enough for Boxer. He doesn't tolerate failure. It's simply not acceptable.

Boxer sits down and runs a hand through his hair. He closes his eyes and thinks of something calming. It usually helps him. But he can't seem to calm his thoughts down. Behind closed eyelids all he can see are images of war. People running for their lives. Him as just a young kid in his twenties, armed with a machine gun, pointing it at a child wearing a vest packed with explosives and a detonator in her hand.

"What do I do?" he hears himself yelling to his commander in charge.

"Shoot! Damn it! Shoot her before she detonates the thing and blows us all to pieces!"

"But she's just a kid!"

"Don't trust her. Don't even trust a kid. It's her or us, soldier. They train them for this shit. Shoot her. It's an order."

And then it happens. Boxer hesitates just long enough for the kid to lift her grip on the detonator and explode herself to pieces, taking Boxer's best friend who was standing closer than Boxer, to the grave with her.

Don't even trust a kid.

Boxer is pulled out from this memory by his brother speaking. "I can't believe I messed up so bad. I am so sorry. So, what do you want to do next?"

Boxer opens his eyes and looks at his brother. His beloved brother who has saved his life more than once, before he became a wreck, before the drinking, before the gambling.

"It's okay," he says, when he suddenly notices Paige's cell phone that he has taken from her vibrating in the basket on the table, where he places all their phones when he takes them.

He walks up and sees she has a voicemail. He presses the button and listens to the message. As he hears the words meant for her, he feels the rage once again expanding inside of him so fast it feels like he is going to burst.

When the message is over, Boxer throws the phone against the wall. The screen cracks and the phone falls to the ground. He grabs all the phones in the basket and throws them in the trash can.

"What?" his brother asks. "What is it?"

"Her mother is in the hospital. That's why you couldn't find her," he says. "It turns out she was actually the one who was hit by the car. If she's in the hospital, it'll be hard for us to get to her."

"Uh-oh, so what do we do now?"

Boxer sits down heavily on the couch. "I don't know," he says. "I have to think. I have to come up with something. And quick."

53

APRIL 1975

A FEW DAYS LATER, Long loses her appetite. She simply stops eating, and no matter how hard Danh tries to stuff rice and cola into her, she refuses. Soon, she grows weak and small and is burning up.

Danh sits with her in his arms all day and all night, trying to hide her from people, and especially from the captain. Every now and then he tries to wake her up; tears rolling across his face, he asks her if she wants to play princesses and pirates again.

"If you don't wake up, the monster will take you, the sea monster will come for you and drag you away to the cave underwater where it keeps all its princesses, you know that, Long. You must wake up, your majesty. Please, wake up," Danh pleads, tears rolling rapidly from his eyes.

After two days, Bao starts to notice something is wrong. He stares at Danh, holding Long.

"Put her down," he says.

Danh shakes his head defiantly. "No."

"Yes, Danh. Put her down. People are starting to talk."

Danh looks at Long's small and fragile face. Her skin is so pale, her eyes are closed, and small droplets of sweat make her forehead shiny.

"No. I can't. She's sleeping," he says. His heart is hurting. He keeps hoping, telling himself repeatedly that she's not sick, she's just tired, so very tired and feeble from the long trip.

If only she would eat or drink something. If just I could get her to drink some cola.

Bao approaches them, he reaches down and touches her head. The look in his eyes terrifies Danh to the core.

"She's burning up," he says with a loud whisper. "She's sick, Danh. She's very sick."

He shakes his head. He doesn't want to believe it, he refuses to. Not his Long. He has seen what happens to those down in the bottom of the boat. They wither and then when they start to smell, they're thrown overboard. They have even thrown some overboard that weren't even dead yet. To stop this disease from spreading, they have to do it as prevention. No one has been sick on the deck yet. Not until now. There is no telling how they'll react.

"No. No. She's just resting," Danh says, and pulls her away from Bao.

He covers her face with part of his jacket that he wrapped her in when she first said she was freezing. At first, he couldn't stand how she was trembling, but now he misses it. The feeling of holding a lifeless body in his arms fills him with despair.

"What's going on over here?"

"Look what you did," Danh hisses. "You woke their suspicion."

A man who has been staring at them for days finally leaves and walks to the captain. Seconds later, the captain stands in front of them flanked by two men, his gold chain necklace dangling in front of Danh's face as he bends down.

"She sick?" he asks. "They tell me she has the disease."

Danh shakes his head rapidly. "No. No. She's just tired, that's all. Weak from not getting enough food and water. She can't eat the rice, she says, tastes terrible when cooked in cola."

"Let me look at her," the captain says. "Move the jacket so I can see her face."

Danh is sweating. He is shaking in fear as he pulls back the jacket and her face is visible. The captain pulls back with a startled look. He doesn't speak; he walks backwards a few more steps, turns around, and walks away.

Still shaking, Danh pulls the jacket back to cover her face. Long is still so pretty, so delicate. Bao sinks down next to him on the deck, simply whimpering in fear till the captain returns.

"You have to go," he says. "She's too great of a risk."

"NO!" Bao says and jumps up. "You can't do that. You can't do that to us."

The captain shakes his head. "People are getting scared. She'll infect us all and then we'll be dead too. You have to go. All of you. You have all been exposed to it now. We have a small boat. It has oars. You can row."

"But...but...we'll die!"

"This is a good offer," the captain says. "Everyone else around here wanted to just throw you all overboard, but I give you this boat. You take it. It's a good offer. Boat or no boat, you're going in the water."

54

APRIL 2016

I SAY GOODBYE TO TOM, who needs to be back at the basketball tournament. I go home, and feed my dad some very late lunch, still with a worried and heavy heart. I had been right in my hunch that something bad was going to happen, I just didn't know that it would be this.

After lunch, I call up Salter. I miss hearing his voice.

"Hi, Mom, what up?"

What up? Is that how we speak now?

I decide to ignore it. "I just wanted to hear your voice. How are you?"

"I'm good."

"Did you hear about what happened at the rally today?"

"Yeah, Cayden texted me. He was there with his dad. Some tourist ran into the crowd?"

"Yes. Crazy thing. A woman was hit and is in the hospital now. She has a daughter, Paige Stover, you know her?"

"I know who she is. She's in sixth grade at my school. Plays basketball."

"Yes, that's her. I feel so bad for her."

"Me too."

I hear softness in Salter's voice again. It makes me happy. He's usually such a sweet boy. I don't like when his heart hardens into a rock like it's started doing recently, especially when talking to me.

I think about Danny and the daughter he never got to know and now maybe never will, since we can't find her. I can't stop thinking about all the single moms and their daughters that have gone missing over the past few years. Where did they go? Have they simply moved?

"Was there anything else you wanted, Mom?" Salter asks. "'Cause Dad, Jackie, and I are going fishing today."

"Not in the lagoon, are you?"

He scoffs. "No, of course not. It's filled with dead fish. Dad has borrowed a boat and we're going out on the ocean. We're leaving from Cape Canaveral."

"Wow. That sounds really great, buddy. Say, you do know not to ever go with anyone you don't know, right?"

He sighs provocatively. "Mom."

"I'm just a little worried, that's all. You do know not to trust anyone you don't know, right? You know Stranger Danger and all that, right?"

"Mom. I am not a moron."

"I'm not saying you are; I just want to make sure you realize that there are people out there who steal kids."

Okay, now you're just terrifying the kid!

"I mean, there are bad guys in this world who might..."

"Mom!" Salter says harshly. "I know these things."

I can hear Joey's voice in the background, and soon Salter disappears and Joey is there.

"Stop babying him," he says. "You gotta stop it. You are so freaking controlling. Geez."

"I am not trying to baby him. I just want to make sure everything is alright," I say. "I have the right to worry about my son."

"Why wouldn't everything be all right? Huh? Because you don't trust me, that's why. Because you don't trust anyone with your child. No one can do as good a job as you, right? Well, guess what? We're doing pretty good around here without you."

Ouch!

An awkward pause follows, where I try to gather myself. "I'll stop by with some clean clothes later today," I finally say, holding back tears.

"No need to," he says. "Jackie bought him lots of new clothes; they went to the mall this morning."

"The mall? But Salter hates the mall."

"Well, not any more. He loved it with Jackie," Joey says.

He loved it with Jackie? What's going on here?

"So, what you're basically telling me is you don't need me at all, is that it?"

"Don't start that," he says. "They're bonding. Salter and Jackie are. It's a good thing. Don't make this about you."

"But it is about me. It's all about you replacing me, leaving me out of my own damn family!" I yell.

I hear a click when Joey hangs up. I groan and throw the phone down, then I pick up a pillow, place it in front of my face, and scream into it.

55

APRIL 2016

I SPEND the rest of the afternoon working on my article, but I can't really focus on it properly. I keep writing things, then deleting them. I drink loads of coffee and stuff myself with chocolate bars, and as the day passes, I even dive into the ice cream. Ben and Jerry's, Brownie Batter. That's when you know you're in trouble, that things are really bad.

I try hard not to feel sorry for myself as I get into the story, researching online all the many theories about the fish-kill, and try to find an angle that all the newspapers haven't already covered. I know my audience is different from theirs; they're spread all over the world, so they might not have heard about the fish-kill, but I still need to add something to the story that no one has heard before, and so far I don't have anything.

Just before six, the doorbell rings, and I walk over to open it. Outside is Detective Fisher. He isn't wearing his usual smirk. It frightens me.

"Chris?"

He runs a hand through his hair several times in a row. I can tell he has been doing that a lot today, since his hair is slightly greasy.

"We haven't found her," he says.

My heart drops. "You're kidding me, right?"

He looks surprised. "Why would I kid about something like that?"

I shake my head. That was a stupid thing to say. "No. Of course not. It's no joke. She wasn't at the rec center?"

"Never showed up for the game. I had a man there all afternoon to wait and see if she did show up, while we contacted everyone that knows the family. I've spoken to all the parents from the sixth grade; no one has seen her since the rally this morning, since before the accident."

"You're scaring me," I say.

"Well, you should be. We all should be. I mean...what if something happened? I can't bear to think about if..."

"Let's not get ahead of ourselves, Detective," I say. "How's the mother, how's Nicky Stover?"

He draws in a deep breath and calms down. "Better. Lots of broken bones and temporary memory loss, doctor says. Many months of recovery in front of her, but she'll live."

"That's a relief," I say.

"Yeah. But imagine if her daughter doesn't show up after this. It's almost too cruel to bear, you know what I mean?"

"I know. I'm sure you'll find her," I say, but I know I don't sound very convincing.

"We have to find her before it gets dark, so we're walking door to door now through the entire community, asking if anyone has seen her, and we're having a big search of the entire Minutemen area. We only have one dog to help us, but it's better than nothing. We're starting here at six o'clock. We're asking the public for help, asking all who can to join us look for her. So, if you can?"

"Of course," I say. "I'll be right there. Just let me feed my dad first."

"Sure. Bring flashlights and maybe that dog of yours. We need all the help we can get."

I look at Snowflake behind me. He is wagging his tail trying to get out to the detective and talk to him. But I am holding him back. He has a tendency to jump people when he gets excited.

"Of course. No problem."

"See you down there."

56

APRIL 2016

BOXER IS out of his mind with anger and frustration. He tries not to think about it as he joins a group of people outside of city hall. They have all showed up to search for Paige Stover. A policeman came to his door earlier and asked for his help. Of course, Boxer will take part in the search. They need all the eyes and hands they can get.

An officer holds a picture up of Paige and others are showing copies to people and asking them to look at them closely.

"Paige Stover was last seen at the rally this morning. She was seen here, in front of city hall, where this picture was taken with her mother, then later way down Minutemen just before the school, where she was walking with three of her girlfriends. No one has seen her since the chaos erupted. Her mother was hit by a car and we suspect she might have seen or known about it, then run off in shock. We need people to look everywhere. In all the bushes, in the dunes at the beach, under and inside boats, in the canals, anywhere she could be hiding in case she got scared or something. She might not even know about her mother being hit by the car; maybe she was just scared by the panic, who knows? We're asking you to be careful in approaching her. If she is in shock, she might be really afraid. Should you find her, get ahold of a police officer or call 911. We'll get someone out there to help you. I want to thank everyone for coming out to help us. Now, let's find Paige!"

Boxer is handed a picture of Paige and he starts to walk along with the group. He follows them towards Minutemen where the group is split. Some walk towards the beach area while others walk towards Minutemen Causeway and the schools. He greets a couple he knows from his street.

"This is awful," the woman says.

"I know. Poor girl," Boxer says. "I just hope she's all right."

"Yes. So do we. And her poor mother too. Being hit by a car and now this? Now her daughter is missing? Can you imagine?"

Boxer shakes his head in sympathy. "I really can't."

"Well, I'm just glad so many people showed up to help with the search," the woman continues. "I remember last year when Olson's little boy ran away from home. He was found hiding under a boat, apparently too frightened to bring home his report card to his dad. Poor thing. His dad is a police officer. Nice man, but a little harsh on the kid, I can imagine. What do you say, Clark?" she says, addressed to her husband, but he doesn't answer.

As they reach Minutemen, a group of them grab each other's hands and they shape a long line. Boxer looks at the lady next to him. She is holding a dog as well, a white Goldendoodle that seems to be very excited.

Boxer looks at her hand as she reaches it out to him. He has seen her on Facebook. This is the lady that took the pictures of Paige during the rally, the ones that led him straight to her when he couldn't find her.

"It's okay. I can hold both you and the dog," she says. "This is Snowflake, by the way."

Boxer smiles. "Well, hello there, Snowflake," he says. Enjoying the attention, the dog jumps him.

"Snowflake!" The woman says and pulls the dog down. "I'm sorry. He's just very excited about people. If he spots Paige Stover in the bushes, he'll run straight to her, is my theory."

"That's nice," Boxer says.

"Shall we?" the woman says and reaches out her hand again. Boxer grabs it in his. They walk through the street and comb through all of the parking lots. Some look in the bushes along the street, others under cars and in yards in front of the houses. Walking hand in hand, they comb through the entire area until they reach the school. Some are calling her name, others worrying more quietly.

"It's nice when the community comes together like this, don't you think?" the woman asks. "It's good to know that they have your back, right? I mean, you never know when you'll need other people's help, right? It feels good to know that you're not alone around here."

Boxer nods, his eyes avoiding hers. "It sure does. It sure does."

57

APRIL 2016

THIS IS AWFUL. This is so painful I can barely stand it!

I imagine the most terrible things happening to poor Paige Stover. I try not to think about it while walking with the search group around the area of the school, but it is hard not to. I can't stop thinking about Paige's mother and how terrible she must feel.

Luckily, I know Salter is with his dad on that fishing boat. They're probably coming in by now, driving home for dinner or grabbing a burger on the way back, I imagine.

I'll have to call him again to make sure he is all right when all this is over. They can get mad all they want at me; I am a mother, and I have the right to worry.

I am walking with the group, holding hands with Danny on one side, and a man I don't know on the other. I remember seeing him before, but I don't think I have ever spoken to him. He seems very shy. Shy people make me insecure, and I have a tendency to blabber like a crazy woman when I get insecure and when I am with people that don't say much. They scare me a little because you never know where you stand with them, you never know what they think or feel about anything.

By the time we have circled the entire school area, I think I have told him my entire life story. I have even made a few jokes that were completely inappropriate for this situation. I feel embarrassed by myself and bite my tongue to shut up.

But when I do, there is one thought that I can't escape, one thought that keeps popping into my mind, and I don't want to think it.

What if Paige has been kidnapped? What if her disappearance is somehow related to all the other disappearances?

It was, after all, supposed to happen today, according to the pattern.

You can't think like that.

I shake my head and focus on the task at hand. In the distance, the sun is starting to set, and for once, I wish I could stop it or slow it down a little, just for few hours so we have more time. It is heartbreaking to know that somewhere out there Paige might be sitting, all afraid and scared and out of it. What if she has to spend the night without being found? What if she is stuck somewhere and can't get up? What if she is hurt so badly she can't move?

What if she has been kidnapped?

Danny, on my left side, is very quiet as we walk towards the high school to go through the area behind it. I have a feeling I know what he is thinking about, but of course—nosy as I am—I have to ask.

"You thinking about Tara?" I ask.

I keep my voice low so no one else can hear us, except maybe the guy to my right, but I am guessing he doesn't know Danny or me and has no idea what I am talking about.

Danny nods. He doesn't seem bothered by the question. At least not visibly. "How can I not?"

"I know. I can't stop thinking about it too. All those women and children disappearing. I can't just ignore it. It can't be just a coincidence. I don't think I believe that anymore."

"I never believed that. Not since I found out about them. Something happened to Tara and Maria. Something bad. I just know it."

"Let me ask you something," I say, still keeping my voice low. "Were you in love with Maria?"

Danny looks at me shortly, then turns his head away.

"I think you were," I say, "That's why you could never visit. You couldn't bear the fact that the woman you loved and your child, the family you couldn't be with, was right there. And you couldn't be with them no matter how badly you wanted to. Why the heck didn't you just divorce Jean?"

"In retrospect, that's what I should have done," Danny says. "I see that now. I thought about it every day. But I guess I was too much of a chicken. This was the easy way out. Maria and Tara never expected anything from me. Junior and Jean did. They were the ones who would have been most heartbroken and disappointed with me if I told them."

"So, you chose your own heartbreak over your son's and wife's? Wow. Quite the sacrifice, I think."

"Or maybe I was just a chicken," he says.

"Did you tell Junior yet?"

Danny nods.

"How did he react?" I ask. I notice there is a commotion by the canals on the other side of the road where another group is searching. I look in their direction, but can't seem to figure out what is going on. People seem upset and focused on the area over there. Some are running towards them.

"Well, he's not here with us today," Danny says, "even though I asked him politely to be, and he hasn't wanted to have anything to do with me since I told him. He refuses to even talk to me, so how do you think he took it?"

"That bad, huh?"

"Worse," Danny says with a sigh. "Seems like I am just losing everyone these days. Say. What's going on over there?"

"We found something!" a voice yells.

I look at Danny. "They found something in the canal!"

Hearts pumping, we start to run towards the group that has gathered in a place where the bushes are low and the canal very visible.

Please let her be alive. Please let her be alive.

A man crawls down; everyone waits with tension and worry until he pokes his head up. He looks terrified.

"It's a body," he says. "Help me pull it out of the water."

The men all step up. I watch while the body of a young girl is pulled out of the water and put on the grass. I walk closer and look at her pale face. Danny feels her neck for a pulse, then looks up at all of us and shakes his head.

"She's dead."

A gasp runs through the crowd.

"Is it her?" someone asks. "Is it Paige?"

I turn and look at them, then shake my head. "No. That's not Paige Stover."

"This one has been in the water for a long time," Danny says, examining her arms and neck.

"There are more," the man who spotted the body suddenly says, terror in his voice. "I see an arm sticking out between the dead fish over there! Oh, my God, the river is filled with dead bodies!"

PART III

HERE I COME

58

APRIL 2016

HE TAKES off his shoes as he walks across the tiles to not make a sound. He knew his sister would forget to lock at least one of the sliding doors to the beach. She never was very careful.

Blake walks across the tiles in the living room. It's the middle of the night. He walks by the light of his flashlight. He waited outside the house till it grew dark; it felt like it took forever for Mary to get to bed. It was way past midnight before she turned her light out, the last one in the house. He then waited an hour to make sure she was completely away in dreamland.

He stops and looks at the pictures hung by the stairs. Lots of them of Salter and Mary, the stupid dog, and even of dear old daddy, taken both before and after he was paralyzed.

But none of Blake.

He walks closer to one of Mary with her surfboard. It is from back when she was a lot younger. Blake remembers the picture. He doesn't remember the day she got that board. It was shortly after their mother had been shot. He was no more than a baby. But the picture has been staring at him from his father's desk for all of his childhood. Now, looking at it again, makes the rage come right back up in him. All the times he was called to his father's office only to be yelled at or told he was useless, meanwhile resting his eyes on that exact picture of his sister who could do nothing wrong.

"Why can't you just be a little more like your sister?" He can still hear his father going at him. On and on and on again. All through his childhood. It came to a point where Blake would know the exact words that would come out of his father's mouth. He would mimic them as they flew across his lips.

"Your sister would never have done that!" or his favorite: "You could learn a lot from your sister, young man."

Blake scoffs and walks up the stairs. He stands still by the door to Mary's room and listens, then opens it slowly and walks inside. Snowflake jumps down from her bed and runs to him wagging his tail, the crazy animal. He pets it gently and hushes it when it whimpers because it is so excited to see him.

Stupid dog.

Blake feels the knife in his pocket with his hand as he walks closer to his sister. She has not gotten smaller. Her plump body is lying heavily on the bed, half covered by her sheet. It's hot tonight and their dad has always been cheap with the AC, especially at night. Blake is guessing nothing has changed on that front.

Mary is snoring lightly, lying on her back, facing him as he leans in over her. She grunts something in her sleep. Blake looks at her fat neck and wonders how much strength he'll need to strangle her.

Mary's sleep is restless and she starts to toss and turn. By her whines and grunts, he senses she is tormented, dreaming heavily.

"What are you dreaming about, dear sister?" He whispers close to her face. "Did I bother you with my little trick destroying your blog? Are you having a nightmare? Well, you ain't seen nothing yet. I'm just getting started. I'm going to make your life as miserable as you did mine."

Blake is overwhelmed by the feeling of great power he possesses in this exact moment. He fights the urge to kill her right here and now. It's been awhile since his last kill. The sensation, the longing, the desire is back. Big time. But he can't. No, not yet.

Blake walks backwards and pets Snowflake on the top of the head before he leaves the room, a chill still running down his spine.

He hurries down the stairs and finds his dad's room, then enters. The old man is heavily asleep as well. Furor wells up in him as he approaches him. All the anger, all the frustration of never being good enough, engulfs him, and he clenches one of his hands into a fist, then holds on tight to the knife with the other.

Blake's body is trembling with anger; he bites his lips as he leans over his father's lifeless body, then whispers.

"I'm coming for you, Daddy dear. I'm coming for all of you. I'll take care of you last."

59

APRIL 1975

IT'S dark in the water. The small boat is being thrown around between the waves. It feels like the waves are playing with them, Danh thinks.

Like a lion plays with its prey before devouring it. Toying with them to wear them out, before the fatal strike is set in.

Danh holds on to his sister, who seems to grow even smaller by the hour now. She doesn't make a sound and barely breathes. Bao sits by the oars and rows, using up all his strength. Danh has no idea how long it has been since they were left there and they watched the fishing boat sail away. Six-seven hours? Maybe. It is nighttime now and they have no idea what direction they're going in, where land is. So far, they have just tried to keep in the same direction as they saw the fishing boat go, but they have been tossed and turned so much by the waves, they could have been going in circles without even noticing it.

"It's no use," Bao says, and puts the oars down.

Danh wonders if he is angry with them for putting him in this situation. Danh is shivering in fear and wants badly to cry, but has no more tears. He is terrified for Long and worries that she'll die. Her fragile body seems so lifeless in his arms.

"Please, don't leave me, your majesty," he whispers in the darkness, while Bao lays down to rest. The ocean seems to calm down a little, even though they're still being thrown around and water keeps coming into the small rowboat.

Danh wonders how long they will be able to keep the water out and how long they will be able to survive without anything to drink. They haven't had much for weeks as it is, and now they're completely without anything. Danh sobs tearless cries while smoothing his hand over her head.

"Please. I promised Mother I would take care of you. I made a promise! I can't go on without you, princess. Don't leave me."

Somehow, Danh manages to doze off way into the night, and when he wakes up, his mouth is dry and nasty, and the sun is right in his face. His skin is burning. The ocean is calm now. The first thing he sees is Bao. He is still sleeping. Half of his body is sunken into water in the bottom of the boat. Danh blinks a few times, then remembers where they are, and looks down.

"Long," he says.

She is in his lap, still wrapped in his jacket. There is no color in her face, her lips are cracked, her eyes still closed. Terrified, he leans over her small body and listens. He can't hear anything. Is she dead?

Please, don't be dead!

"Your majesty?"

Finally, she draws in a small breath. Danh leans back with a sigh of relief. Long is still alive. Bao wakes up, but barely has the strength to lift his head, let alone his body. He blinks a few times and licks his lips, but it doesn't help. Danh knows how it feels.

"We're going to die out here, aren't we?" Bao asks.

Danh shakes his head, but it barely moves. "No," he whispers. "I promised Long she would get ice cream."

Bao tries to laugh, but only a strange wheezing sound comes out of his throat. He leans his head down and closes his eyes again. Danh wants to sleep as well. He is so tired, and as hope oozes out of him, so does his will to survive.

You gotta stay awake. For Long. You gotta take care of Long!

Danh forces himself to open his eyes. They soon become heavy again and close. He has no idea for how long, but when he opens them again, he sees something. At first he believes it is a part of his dream, or an illusion of some sort. It can't be real. It simply can't.

Yet, it is still there even after he blinks.

He parts his dry lips and tries to point. "Boat," he whispers, but no one can hear it. He tries to speak again, but no sound leaves his lips, and soon he can't hold his eyelids open anymore. Seconds later, the darkness swallows him completely.

60

APRIL 2016

I HAVE the worst nightmare and wake up screaming. It's still dark outside. I sit up in my bed. I feel thirsty and walk out of my room, Snowflake running right behind me, wagging his tail because he thinks it's time to get up.

On the way down the stairs, I think about Paige and how she still hasn't been found. I wonder where she is and if she is scared. I also think about the two bodies they ended up pulling out of the canal.

Who were they?

The police had quickly arrived and blocked the area off so we couldn't see much, and soon I went home, tired and depressed because we hadn't found Paige, and slightly scared because of the bodies. It took me many hours to calm down and be able to sleep, and when I finally did, I had the strangest dream about my brother Blake.

I turn on the light in the kitchen and grab a glass that I fill with water. I feel hungry and open the refrigerator. I grab the leftovers of the stew I had made for my dad and me before I went to do the search. I never got to eat much of it, but I can do that now.

I eat out of the pan and don't even bother to heat it first. It tastes great even cold. Then I move on to the more comforting stuff. I pull out a bucket of Mint chocolate ice cream from Fat Donkey, the ice-cream place off Minutemen. It's the best ice cream in the world and I save it for when I feel especially down. I do now. Because I worry about Salter, because I worry about Paige Stover, and the disappeared women and children.

As I dig into the ice cream with my spoon, I hear a sound. It sounds like it is coming from my dad's room.

That's odd?

I put the ice cream back, then close the freezer. I walk towards my dad's room with my heart in my throat, Snowflake at my heels. Unfortunately, he is not much of a guard dog. He is even more easily scared than I am. During every thunderstorm, he creeps under my bed and shakes for hours afterwards.

I grab the door handle, turn it, and walk inside. My heart is pounding. My dad is still in his bed, on his back, snoring lightly, calmly. I relax my shoulders and walk closer to him.

That's when I notice the window is open and a vase has fallen down from the small table next to it. It isn't broken, but the flowers have fallen out, and the water has run out on the floor. I wipe it up and put the flowers back in, then look out the window before I close it.

Probably just forgot to shut it earlier today.

I feel like a fool, even though I can't remember opening it. I might have done it to give him some fresh air. I am too tired to remember.

My dad is lying peacefully, until he starts to move his fingers and hands excessively. I stare at them, remembering his physical therapist telling me this would happen, that he would experience spasms at night, in the parts where he has recently regained mobility. But then I see something that makes me tear up. His foot.

His right foot is moving too!

I gasp and pull the blanket off. I can't believe what I am seeing. My father's right foot is twitching and turning in small, almost rhythmical spasms.

"Oh, my God," I exclaim, tears streaming from my eyes. "You're actually moving your foot in your sleep, Dad."

Before I leave him, I grab my cell phone and start recording it. My hands are shaking and it is hard to hold the phone still. I can't stop crying and take several videos both of his hands and his foot.

Finally, I leave him and walk back into the hallway. On the way back towards the stairs, I pass the picture wall I have made of us of the few pictures I had left after my dad's house burnt down. Luckily, I had some copies among my things; otherwise, all my childhood pictures would have been lost.

I almost walk past it when I suddenly stop and walk a few steps backwards.

Something is different.

One of the frames is empty. The picture of me with my surfboard that I got when I was seventeen, is gone.

61

APRIL 2016

I SHOW my dad the video the next morning when we're eating breakfast. He too has tears in his eyes when he sees it.

"It's moving. It's really moving!"

I sniffle with joy and cut up some more fruit for him and help him get it on his fork. "I know. I can't believe it either. But there is definitely movement going on down there."

"I can't wait to tell Jack," he says.

"He'll be here tomorrow," I say. "I'll make sure he sees it."

My dad smiles widely. I know how badly he wants to walk again. For the first time, I have a real feeling that it is reachable, that he might be able to walk at some point again, even though I also know there is still a long way to go. Seeing how slow it has been with his fingers and hands, I know we need to brace ourselves with all the patience we can muster, but the hope is there. It is definitely there.

"I had the strangest dream last night," my dad says, after a few minutes of silence. He is chewing his fruit. I know he hates the fruit, but Jack has told him he needs to watch his weight. Being heavy makes it harder on his legs, should he ever get up on them again, since he has no muscles left in them. I am completely to blame for his weight gain, since I constantly feel so bad for him that I always make the best food. It is, after all, the only thing he can really enjoy these days, so why not get the best of the best?

Well, not anymore. I am eating the fruit with him, since I could lose a few pounds myself. Even though breakfast probably isn't my biggest problem.

"Oh, what was it about?" I ask.

"Blake," he says, his face turning very serious all of a sudden. "I dreamt about Blake."

"I dreamt about him too," I say. "What a weird coincidence."

My dad looks speculative. I try to shut my hunger up by eating a banana. I am more in the mood for pancakes, but this will have to do for now. I can't be eating pancakes in front of my poor father.

"That is odd. I woke up with the strangest feeling," he continues. My dad looks at me. "I think he's here."

"Blake? Bah. Nonsense. He and Olivia went to Naples, where he killed her. He's wanted all over the state of Florida. He's probably long gone. Out of the state. He's not stupid enough to come back here."

I help my dad get a strawberry in his mouth, while I think about the missing picture in the hallway and the open window. I shake the thought. Maybe Salter took the photo. Or it fell down or something.

My dad sighs. "I guess you're right. It is just so odd. I have this feeling that...that he is very close. It was like he spoke to me last night."

"You were just dreaming, Dad," I say. "Dreams can get so vivid sometimes."

He nods and I put a piece of watermelon on his fork. He misses his mouth and it splashes on his cheek instead.

"Ugh!" he exclaims. "I hate this! I want some real food!"

I nod. "You know what? So do I." I get up, walk to the kitchen, and open the refrigerator. I pull out bacon and a carton of eggs. "How does bacon and scrambled eggs sound?"

"Like heaven," he yells from his chair.

"Heaven it shall be. It is, after all, Sunday and the good Lord knows we deserve it," I say, and crack an egg and drop it into a bowl.

62

APRIL 2016

WE FINISH our meal and I finally feel full. My dad is also satisfied and asks me to take him out on the porch. He wants to listen to the ocean and feel the breeze on his face. After eating, that is his favorite thing to do.

I place him in the shade with a hat and sunglasses on and he sighs, satisfied, while watching the beachgoers fight with umbrellas. It's very windy today and the waves are completely blown out. A woman loses her hat and starts to run after it as it rolls across the sand.

"Thank you, sweetheart," he says, and takes in a deep breath of the fresh air. "Nothing beats this air."

"I know," I say. "It's the best place on earth."

I take Snowflake for a walk on the beach, thinking the local police force has enough going on today as it is, enough to not care if someone walks their dog on the warm sand.

I walk all the way to downtown and the restaurant, Coconuts on the Beach, where all the tourists lay almost on top of each other, then turn and walk back. When I return to the house, I find Detective Fisher waiting on the porch for me. He is engaged in a chat with my dad.

"Okay," I say, throwing out my arms. "You caught me. I was walking my dog on the beach. You can take me away now. But, I tell you this one thing, it was totally worth it. Please, just spare my dog. He has done nothing wrong."

"Quite the comedian," Fisher says, addressed to my dad.

"Always has been," he says. "Part of her charm."

Fisher chuckles.

"If you're not here to bust me and my dog, then why are you here?" I ask, and let Snowflake back into the house. He runs to the water bowl and starts to drink, dragging a heavy load of sand with him inside.

"I thought we could chat," he said.

"Sure. What about?"

"Maybe we should do this inside?" he says, and nods at my dad.

"Don't mind him," I say. "I'll tell him everything after you leave anyway. He knows everything that goes on."

"I don't watch soaps," my dad says. "What I hear around here is so much better."

Fisher laughs lightly. He grabs a chair in the shade and sits down. "All right, then. But this can't leave the house, all right?"

"I can't even leave the house," my dad says.

"Anyone want some coffee?" I ask, mostly because I really need some after the night I had.

"It's too hot for coffee," my dad says.

"I can make it ice-coffee if you ask me nicely."

"Then, yes, please," Fisher says. "I would like that."

My dad nods in agreement and I walk inside to make it for all of us. I put straws in the cups and walk back out.

"Quite the view you have here," Fisher says, as I serve it to them. "I wonder how you ever get anything done around here."

I chuckle. "Who says I do? But I can't blame it on the view. Just a lot has been going on lately."

Fisher nods, pulls out a file, and places it on the table. "Yeah. That's what I wanted to talk to you about. Those bodies...that we pulled out of the canal..."

"What about them?" I ask.

"Well, you knew about them. It's two of your girls."

"What do you mean they're my girls?"

"The ones in your articles, remember? The ones you gave to me when we were drinking coffee."

I sink back in the chair. "Really? I mean, I can't say I didn't think the thought, but still. Which ones? Please tell me it isn't Tara and Maria; please say it's not them."

"It's not them."

"Phew." My heart drops. "Then who is it?"

63

APRIL 2016

"KIM AND CASEY TAYLOR!"

Boxer yells at his brother, who sits on the couch in his living room, drinking vodka straight from the bottle. Boxer should know better than to yell at him, since it only makes him sick again, but he can't stop. Not since he saw the face of the girl they pulled out of the canal when searching for Paige Stover, has he been able to stay calm. He

recognized her right away as the girl he abducted from the mall one year ago, along with her mother.

Now they've turned up dead?

"Oh, my God," he says, as he walks back and forth. "They're going to come here, aren't they? They're going to get me for this even though I didn't kill them, aren't they?" he groans.

"Maybe they won't," his brother says and lights up a cigarette.

Boxer can't stand cigarette smoke, especially not in his house, but he also knows his brother is in a fragile mental stage right now, and if smoking helps him, then he'll have to endure it. Boxer stares at his brother as he smokes, holding the cigarette between his shaking hands, eyes closed, and he wonders what he thinks about, worries that he'll get sick again.

PTSD they told them it was once they came home from Afghanistan. They both have it, but his brother is worse than him. Boxer never understood why his brother got it worse than him, since they were both there when the bomb went off, when that little kid blew herself up.

Boxer's brother shouldn't be feeling as guilty as Boxer does. He wasn't the one who was supposed to have shot the kid; he wasn't the one who could have saved another man's life. Still, he suffered more mentally afterwards. He took it harder somehow. Boxer never understood why. Yes, Boxer was tormented by it every day and still sometimes at night as well, anguished by those small brown eyes staring at him from a face so innocent and harmless. But he has learned to live with it. Taking care of his family makes him forget. It helps him to push it back and not worry about it.

Why can't his brother do the same? He has to move on at some point, doesn't he? It's all about not thinking about it. Like with the girls. Don't get attached to them, don't like them, don't worry what happens to them after the delivery. It's not your problem. You don't have to care.

Boxer walks to the back of the house and opens the door. He kneels in front of the dog crate, where Paige looks back at him. She is still sobbing, her lips vibrating.

"Please, let me go home," she whispers.

Boxer stares at her, looks deep into her eyes, and when he does, all he sees is that kid, that little girl on that dusty road, staring at him softly like her eyes were asking him to like her, reeling him in, telling him not to shoot. And that was the reason someone had to die, that was why it all went wrong, because Boxer believed those eyes, because he allowed himself to hesitate for just one second.

It'll never happen again.

"Please. I want to go home. Why are you doing this to me? Why?"

Boxer remains motionless. He is not moved by her pleas. She is not important. She's nothing but a means to an end. And it's only fair to make these little girls pay for what Boxer and his family have had to go through, since he was a kid, just like her, that brought them into this situation in the first place. A kid, just like this young one with big brown innocent eyes just like these, destroyed everything.

"What are you going to do to me?" she asks, her voice shaking in fear. But he doesn't fall for it.

I don't owe you an answer. I don't owe you anything, you little monster!

64

APRIL 1975

DANH HARDLY FEELS it when he is lifted up and taken aboard the ship. His eyes open a few times and he thinks it is just a dream, that he is floating in the air. Maybe he is dead? Maybe this is what it feels like?

He doesn't fully wake up till three days later, when someone presses a water bottle in between his lips and he feels like he is drowning.

When he opens his eyes, he realizes it is Long holding the bottle. She is smiling. She even has a sparkle in her eyes. She is still small and skinny, and he can see her collarbone sticking out above her shirt, but she's alive. She's alive and well.

How?

Bao is sitting next to him. When he hears him cough, he turns his head. "He's awake? Finally! That took you some time, brother. Even Long came around before you did."

Danh wipes his mouth and sits up straight, covering his eyes from the brightness of the burning sun above them. He grabs the bottle and drinks greedily. He drinks too fast and chokes, then coughs and spits some of it out on the deck.

"Don't spill it," Bao scolds. "They have given us water, but not so much we can just spill it."

"Sorry," Danh says. He leans his head back against the wall behind him. He is exhausted. "Where are we?"

"On another ship. A much bigger one," Bao says. "They found us drifting in the middle of the ocean and picked us up."

Danh looks around. He spots a man with a machine gun walking by. The man glances at them shortly and he smiles, showing off a couple of gold teeth before he continues his walk. He approaches another guy who looks just like him and who is also heavily armed.

"Who are these people? They're not Vietnamese," Danh asks.

"No. We don't know where they're from. We try not to ask questions. They picked us out of the ocean and had medicine for Long. Her fever is gone already. It's a true miracle."

Danh looks at his baby sister and his heart goes soft. Her eyes are back to their sweet selves, the most beautiful sight Danh could imagine seeing. Hearing her small voice is music to him, so soothing.

"Do we know where they're heading?" Danh asks Bao.

"They haven't spoken to us much," Bao says. "They just gave us water and medicine and some bread and rice to eat." Bao grabs some bread and hands it to Danh. "It's not much, but enough to keep us alive. Now eat."

Danh pulls the bread out of Bao's hand and starts to eat, stuffing his mouth with it. He hardly chews it, but he swallows big pieces before he eats more, groaning and grunting like a wild animal.

"Take it easy, Danh," Bao says. "It takes a while for your stomach to get used to food again."

But Danh doesn't care. He eats everything Bao gave him and asks for more, but Bao tells him he can't take too much at a time, it's not good for him, and besides, they need to ration the food, they don't know when or if they'll get more.

Danh understands. He is happy with what he has gotten so far and just the fact that his sister survived this and is now playing in front of him, turning in the sunlight on the deck, dancing and humming the song their mother used to sing for them, means the world to him. Nothing could make him happier.

"That's it, your majesty," he says and claps his hands. He never thought he was going to see her dance again.

It's the best moment of his life.

Danh looks at his sister as she does her dance just like she used to back home. It's not until halfway through that he realizes her little dance has gathered a crowd. A crowd of men staring at her, wearing hungry smiles and machine guns.

65

APRIL 2016

"BUT THEY MUST HAVE BEEN KILLED RECENTLY, am I right?" I ask, as I place a plate of cookies in front of Detective Fisher.

"I mean, the bodies were pretty intact, even after lying in the water. If they had been there long, they would have been in more of a state of decay and animals would have eaten from them, am I right?"

Fisher grabs a cookie. "The bodies were exceptionally intact, yes. You're right about that. We haven't received the autopsy yet, so there really isn't much I can say on that account."

"But, where have they been? They've been gone for a year," I ask, wondering about Tara and Maria, wondering if they are in the same place as Kim and Casey Taylor were before they were killed.

"I wish I could answer that," he says.

"Of course."

Fisher clears his throat. "So far, we need to wait for the autopsy to be finished, but I felt like I needed to address this with you, since you were the one who knew about these girls disappearing. What else do you know?"

"Well, actually it wasn't me," I say and sip my coffee.

"Then who was it? Chloe?"

"No. Danny."

"Danny Schmidt?"

"Yes. He was the one who found out that Tara and Maria were missing and then started to research this and found all the other single moms that had gone missing with their daughters."

Fisher nods pensively. "All right. I guess I'll have a chat with him, then."

"I think he's working today," I say.

"I'll grab ahold of him later, then," Fisher says, and gets up from his chair. "Thanks for the coffee and the delicious cookies. You make these yourself?"

"Well, yes, I do."

"She's a magician in a kitchen," my dad says from his chair in the corner, where he has been sitting with his eyes closed during my talk with the detective.

"I thought you were sleeping," I say.

My dad answers with a wide smile. I give the detective my hand.

"Let me know if you come across anything that you think might be of importance to this case," he says.

"Sure. Let me walk you out." I open the sliding door, but the detective refuses to go first, so I do. "Have you thought about a possible link between these disappearances and Paige Stover's?" I ask, as we approach the front door.

He nods. "Naturally, I have."

"It could have gone wrong for the kidnappers," I say and open the door for him. I can tell he doesn't like me doing that. Down here, men hold the doors for the ladies, not the other way around. After living in New York, I have almost forgotten my southern etiquette. It amuses me a little. "Maybe the fact that she was in an accident threw them off?"

Fisher nods, holding his file under his arm. He walks outside towards his car, then stops.

"Just one more thing," he says.

"Yes?"

Fisher takes a step back towards me. "Why was Danny Schmidt so interested in Tara and Maria Verlinden in the first place?"

I shrug and pretend I don't know. "You'll have to ask him about that."

Fisher points at me. "I think I will. I think I will." Then he waves, turns on his heel, and walks to his car.

66

APRIL 2016

WHERE IS SHE? Where is my daughter?

It's bad enough that she has been hit by a car, that both her legs are broken and several bones in the rest of her body are too, that she can hardly move and has to lie in this hospital bed that is way too soft for her back. That's all bad enough. But the fact that she has no idea where her daughter is, is devastating.

Nicky stares out her window from Cape Canaveral Hospital. The view from her room is stunning. Intracoastal waters as far as she can see. The hospital is on a peninsula and has water all around it. It's gorgeous, but there is no way Nicky can enjoy all that. All she wants is to get out of this room and look for her daughter.

Where are you, my sweetheart? Where are you?

The nurses and doctors only focus on Nicky's health and only come in to give her medicine or to have her sign papers. Sometimes a doctor comes in and tells her how she is doing. As if she cares how her body is healing? As if she cares about any of that when her daughter is out there somewhere scared, terrified with fear because her mother is not there with her. Nicky just knows she is. She can feel it.

Nicky cries in the bed. The tears soak her pillow, while all she can do is stare out at the stupid water, the same water they just fished two bodies out of yesterday. Nicky saw it on the news last night, where she also saw the story of her own daughter gone missing and saw her picture above the phone number you could call if you saw her.

Her own daughter! Paige on TV because she is missing!

The police have been to her hospital room twice since the accident and asked her a ton of questions. They wanted to know all about the child's father, if he could have taken her, if they had any unsolved disputes between them and so on. Nicky answered all of them, telling them the father wasn't in the picture at all, that he is gone and never was interested in Paige, that she hasn't seen him in twelve years, so why would he suddenly care now?

They told her it's not unusual, so now Nicky wonders if Mike is actually out there somewhere holding the hand of their daughter. She imagines the two of them on the road together, eating burgers and milkshakes, with Paige asking him to take her back to her mother.

She must be so scared, the poor thing.

Still it is more comforting for Nicky to think about Paige being with her father than in the hands of some stranger, some pedophile who wants to harm her. Of course, she has thought about that as well. Who wouldn't?

"Nicky Stover?" A voice says and pulls her out of her nightmarish reverie.

"Yes?"

"I'm detective Fisher with Cocoa Beach Police Department." He shows her his badge.

Nicky starts to cry again. "Please tell me you found her."

His eyes tell her they haven't. "I'm sorry."

Her heart drops. "I didn't think so."

"But I want you to know that we are working as hard as we can to find her. We have called in extra help from the surrounding cities, and everyone is on the lookout for your daughter."

"That's good," she says. "Tell me you won't give up."

"I can promise you I'll do everything in my power. But I need a little help, so if you could just answer some questions..."

"Sure. Anything," Nicky says. "Just bring my baby back to me."

The detective nods. "Like I said. I'll do all that I can." He reaches into his files and pulls out a picture of a man.

"Do you recognize this man?" he asks.

Nicky nods. "Well, yes. I do."

"Does he know your daughter?"

"Yes."

"Where from?"

"From basketball, from the rec center."

The detective writes it down, then nods. "I see. Good. Thank you."

"You don't suspect *he* has taken Paige, do you?" she asks, surprised.

"Right now we're looking into all the angles we can," he replies and closes the file with the picture.

He lifts his cap as he is about to leave. "Thank you for your answer. I'll be in touch."

67

APRIL 2016

MONDAY, just before noon, Danny returns to his house after his twenty-four hour shift. He turns his key in the lock and walks inside. He puts his backpack on the couch, walks to the kitchen, and grabs a glass of water.

He sighs, looking over the river, thinking about the mother and daughter that were pulled out of that same water the day before yesterday. He was so scared that it was Tara and Maria they had found. Terrified when he helped them pull the kid's body out. Until he saw the face and knew it wasn't her.

Danny drinks his glass and empties it. He hears a sound and turns to look. It sounds like the TV is on in Junior's room. He walks down the hall-way, opens the door, and finds Junior inside, still in his bed.

"Why aren't you in school?"

"What's it to you?"

That's the most Junior has spoken to him since he told him about his sister and the affair.

"Well, it's quite important actually. You have that exam today, don't you?" Danny asks, trying hard to keep his cool and not explode in a fit of rage. Junior is graduating in just a few weeks. How can he skip school at an important time like this?

"I don't know," he grumbles.

"Yes, you do know. You never miss school. Are you at least sick?"

Junior doesn't answer. He stares at the TV and pretends Danny isn't there. "Come on, Junior," Danny says. "Don't do this to yourself."

"What do you care?"

Danny sighs deeply. He walks in and sits on the edge of the bed. Junior doesn't even look at him. "Son. You must know I care. I care a lot about you. I care that you are well, that you get a good education and don't throw everything you've worked for away like this. I care a lot."

"Not enough to not cheat on Mom," he says.

"Ouch. Guess I deserved that."

"Yes, you sure did."

At least he is talking to you. At least he's opening up now. Don't ruin it by getting mad.

"All right. You're right. I have been a terrible father. I cheated on your mother and I had another child. But at least I cared enough about you to stay here. Yes, that's right. I stayed for you, Junior. Because I felt you deserved to have a father. Meanwhile, Tara grew up without one. Meanwhile, I let the woman I love..."

"The woman you what?" Junior asks and sits up straight in the bed, eyes wide, nostrils flaring.

Danny pushes back tears, thinking about Maria and how badly he wanted to be with her back then, how he dreamt about leaving everything, leaving Jean who never loved him, who treated him like dirt, and going to live with her and their daughter.

"You heard me. I loved Maria. I was in love with her. And now she's... she's...I don't know what happened to them."

Junior stares at Danny, biting his lip. "You really loved her?"

Danny nods. "Yes. But I stayed here. To be with you. To make sure you were well taken care of."

Junior shrugs. He doesn't seem as angry as he was before. "So what? Now you want a medal?"

Danny chuckles. "No. No. I don't want that. I don't even expect you to understand, at least not till you're way older, but I think you deserve to know the truth."

Junior doesn't say any more. His glare returns to the TV and he shuts Danny out again. Danny sighs, gets up from the bed, and walks to the door. "Now I need to take a nap. It's been a long shift."

"Wait..." Junior says.

Danny pauses, hand on the door, and turns around.

"Thanks."

The look in Junior's eyes warms him. "Don't thank me," Danny says. "Just promise you'll go to school tomorrow, okay?"

He walks out of the room and down the hallway. As he grabs his phone from his backpack, there is a knock on the front door. Danny opens it.

"Detective Fisher?"

68

APRIL 2016

"SO, where were you Saturday morning between eight and nine fifteen?"

Detective Chris Fisher stares at Danny across the table in the small room at the police station. Danny is not sure he understands what is going on. They haven't told him anything. All Fisher said when he came to Danny's house was that he needed him to come to the station with him. Now he's looking at Danny in a way that makes him very uncomfortable in his chair. His hands are getting sweaty. He has known Chris Fisher since they were children, and as the captain of the fire department, Danny has worked together with the Cocoa Beach Police and Fisher for many years. But never has he seen that look on his face when speaking to him.

"I was at home. Why?" Danny answers.

"You weren't at the rally like everyone else?" Fisher asks.

"No. I was at home."

"Can anyone confirm that? Were you with someone?"

"Wait. Am I being accused of something here?"

"Just answer the question, please."

Danny thinks about Junior. Saturday morning was the time when he told him about his sister and the affair. He really doesn't feel like he can tell Detective Fisher about it. Junior got so mad, he ran out of the house, and didn't come back till the afternoon. He doesn't provide much of an alibi anyway. They were only together for maybe half an hour that morning.

"My son was home, but only early in the morning. We had breakfast together, but he left in the middle of it," he says, staying as close to the truth as possible. Then he adds, "We had a fight."

Fisher nods. "You had a fight, you say. About what?"

"Is that really important? It's kind of private."

Fisher looks seriously at him, then down at his papers. He gets up from the chair and walks around. "All right. Then tell me, what did you do after your son left?"

"I..." Danny pauses, thinking about how he broke down and cried. Danny never cries. He takes in a deep breath. He can tell Fisher notices how nervous he is. "I had a cup of coffee and sat out in the back."

Fisher walks behind his chair. "All morning? That's all you did all morning?"

"No. I went on my iPad and read a couple of articles in *Florida Today's* online paper, then went on Facebook."

Fisher walks up in front of him. "Did you post anything?"

Danny shakes his head. "No."

"Did you write any emails? 'Cause that could verify the time and date."

Danny shakes his head. He remembers sitting on the back porch with his coffee and iPad, but not really looking at it. All he did was think about his life while staring at the canal. Crying about how he had wasted his life, how all the choices he had made no longer made sense, how they had ruined so much. Worrying that he might alienate and maybe lose his son now as well, and be left with nothing. But he can't explain that to the detective. They all know him as the tough guy, the firefighter, the captain of the fire department, and the man who's saved more people with heart failure than anyone in the history of the station.

They used to look at me like a hero. Now all I see is contempt in his eyes.

"What is the nature of your relationship with Paige Stover?" Fisher asks.

Danny's eyes widen. "Is that what this is about? Paige Stover?"

"Just answer the question, please. How do you know Paige Stover?"

"From the rec center," he says. "She plays basketball down there. You know I work there as a volunteer for the basketball team and have for years. Is this really about her?"

Fisher clears his throat. "Yes. She disappeared on Saturday morning. Last seen just after nine o'clock when a car drove into the crowd at the rally."

Danny feels so confused. How can he think these things about him? "But...but I don't know anything...I didn't...you think I might have done something to her, don't you?"

Fisher sits down and rubs his stubble. He opens a file, finds a piece of paper, and slides it towards Danny.

"You were arrested recently at the airport, right?"

Danny's heart drops. So this is what this is all about. "You think because I was arrested, then that means I took Paige Stover, is that it?"

Fisher gesticulates. "You were trying to purchase a child!"

Danny leans back in the chair with a deep sigh. "I think I need a lawyer."

APRIL 2016

TOM STOPS BY MONDAY AFTERNOON. We decide to go down to the beach and hang out for a few hours while my dad naps on the porch. I don't feel too comfortable letting him see me in a swimsuit, but I decide he has to take me as I am. It's not like I can do much about it. I wear a one-piece and a cover-up dress that I only take off when we go in the water. We jump in the waves and I even take him out on a surfboard. I try to push him into a couple of waves, but he nosedives every time and never gets to even stand up before he finally gives up.

"I'm sorry," I say, when we get back on land. "I forget how hard it is to learn. When you've been surfing since you were just a kid, you tend to forget."

He laughs while shaking his wet hair. He grabs a towel and wipes his face. "Don't feel bad. It was fun. We'll try again another time. Makes me even more impressed that you can do what you do. Plus, it was great to just get out in the water. I kind of needed it. Get my mind off the latest events around here."

"You mean Paige Stover?" I ask.

"Yeah. Can you believe that she would just disappear like that?" he says.

We sit down in my beach chairs. I shake my head. "It's odd," I say. "Did you know her well?"

"Not really. She was mostly with Coach Joe, who gave her private lessons, but of course I knew her a little. She was on the team."

I think about Tara and Maria and the two bodies found in the canals on the same day that Paige disappeared. I can't stop thinking that it might all be connected somehow. I just don't see how. I wonder if I should tell him what I know, but then I remember that I promised Chris Fisher to keep it between us. If word gets out, it might spoil the investigation when people start talking. And they will talk, he said. The more people who know things, the higher the probability that someone will spill the beans at some point. I can't risk ruining anything. I don't know Tom that well yet and have no idea if he can keep a secret like that or not.

"What do you think happened to her?" he asks with a sniffle, as water comes out of his nose. I hand him a towel, knowing the feeling all too well.

"I don't know," I say. "But the more time that passes without her showing up, the more anxious I get."

"I think that goes for everyone around here. I'm glad I took today off from the cape. I can't help feeling a little guilty, you know?"

"You? Why?" I ask, surprised.

He shrugs. "I don't know. Because she was supposed to come to the rec center and play in the tournament, and when she didn't, we just went on with the game. I felt awful, but kept telling myself she would turn up at some point, that she was all right. I should have been out looking for her instead. It wasn't until later I realized she still hadn't shown up."

"You did what you could do. How could you have known?" I say, thinking about how guilty I have felt myself. "I'm the one who could have done something. I was there. I saw her; I photographed her with her friends right before she went missing. I was supposed to have brought her to her mother in the hospital. I keep going over that afternoon again and again, wondering if I could have done something differently, if there was anything I saw that can help the investigation, but I can't seem to come up with what it should be. I have told the police everything I know and remember, but none of it helped."

Tom places a hand on my shoulder. I look at him. He looks very cool with his sunglasses on, but he is so pale he almost looks like he's one of the tourists. I am guessing he doesn't go outside much.

"I think maybe you shouldn't beat yourself up like that. You've done what you could do."

"I sure hope so," I say, when my phone starts to ring from the side pocket of my chair. It's an unknown number. I pick it up. Danny is on the other end.

"I need your help, Mary. I think I got myself into some deep trouble."

70

APRIL 1975

DAYS PASS and they get no more food. Only water is brought to them, and soon they start to starve again. Danh tries to ask some of the guards with the machine guns, but they only point their guns at him and yell in a language Danh doesn't understand.

A week after they were picked up, Bao starts to run a fever. Soon, he is burning up. Danh recognizes the signs from when Long was sick, and it is with terror that he watches his older brother weaken. Without food and strength, it goes fast.

Danh starts to beg and plead with the men onboard for food and medicine. He knows they must have something, like what they gave to Long, but now they don't seem to want to help them anymore.

"No more," they tell him in Vietnamese. "No more!"

Disappointed and scared, Danh returns to Long and Bao on the deck, where they lie uncovered in the burning sun. He tries to cover Bao up with his jacket, like he did with Long, but he is so hot now that he has to remove it for him again.

Long starts to cry. "What are we going to do?" she asks.

Danh shrugs with a whimper. He is scared. Usually in a situation like this, he would do anything he could to make sure Long wasn't scared, to shelter her from the gruesomeness, but not this time. This time, he is angry with her for whining, for crying. He needs her to be strong.

"Stop crying, you baby," he says and gets to his feet. He walks away. He needs to get away.

"Danh?" she says, tears springing from her eyes.

He ignores her. Afraid of what he might say to her, he walks to the other end of the deck and stares out at the water. He feels tears on his face, but wipes them away. There is no time for this now. Crying is useless.

A guy is standing next to him. A man with a machine gun. He is watching the ocean as well. Danh turns to look at him and spots a necklace around his neck that he recognizes.

"Where did you get that?" he asks.

The man smiles, showing off some very bad teeth. He grabs the necklace and pulls it out, then he laughs.

"It belongs to someone I know," Danh says. "See, it says his name on it, right here. He was the captain of the boat I was on. What did you do to him?"

As the realization sinks in, Danh walks backwards, away from the man and his gun. He hurries back to Long and Bao, sits down, and pulls his legs up underneath himself.

"What's wrong?" Long asks.

He looks at her. Usually, he wouldn't have told her anything, but this time he decides she is grown up enough to know. "I think they killed them."

"Killed who?" she asks, sounding innocent and naïve.

"Everyone on our old boat. The captain, everyone. I remember that necklace. He used to rub it between his fingers when he spoke. It's gold. He would never have let go of that willingly. They must have killed him first."

Long doesn't speak. She stares at Danh. Bao is groaning next to them. He's barely awake.

"You think they'll kill us too?" she finally asks anxiously.

Danh looks at her and wonders if he should tell her a lie, tell her it is all a game or part of a play or to look for pirates or dance like he used to, but he decides not to. He looks into her beautiful eyes, and then shakes his head.

"I think they want to do something much worse to us."

71

APRIL 2016

I GET ahold of my lawyer James Holland and make sure he takes care of Danny. As it turns out, the police don't have any evidence pointing at Danny, it's all suspicions based on the fact that he was arrested in Orlando recently trying to purchase a child, something he hasn't even been convicted for. Holland quickly makes sure Danny gets home, and the next day I go to talk to him.

"I got suspended," he says, as he opens the door.

"Oh, no, Danny. I'm so sorry."

He walks away from the door and lets me inside. "Everyone at the station knows I was in for questioning. My superior called and told me I was suspended. I asked him if he thought I was guilty, and even though he didn't say it, I could tell he believed it. It was all in his tone of voice. I'm afraid to go downtown now, since I have a feeling the rumor is all over town that I am a suspect in Paige Stover's disappearance."

Danny throws himself on the couch with a sigh. He hides his face in his hands. "I don't think I can take any more."

I sit down next to him. I put my arm around his shoulder and pull him closer to me. "We'll figure this out somehow," I say. "We'll get to the bottom of it."

"Come on, Mary."

"I'm being serious here!"

"So you're going to do what the police haven't been able to yet?" he asks skeptically.

"If I have to. I have spoken to the others and they're behind you as well. All of them. None of us are going to let you go down on this, you hear me?"

He looks up at me. I touch his cheek. "We're here for you, Danny. Come rain or shine. Like you always have been for us."

"Are you trying to make me cry?" he asks.

"Not really," I say with a chuckle. "But if you feel like crying, then be my guest."

"They called me Boxer," he suddenly says.

"Who did?"

"The police. Chris Fisher."

"Oh, that little brat. I can't believe he would arrest you. I thought we were making progress, that I was helping him with the case. Instead, he took one look at you and believed you were his guy. I could just..." I groan and pretend to be strangling Fisher between my hands.

"He always was annoying," Danny says with a light laugh.

"I know, right? But why do you think they called you that?"

"Apparently, they've found a lot of chats going between this Boxer and Paige Stover on her computer. They showed me a transcript of it and told me they believed I had written it. I had never seen any of these messages in my life, I said, but they didn't believe me. Thank God for James Holland, that he got me out of there. I told them I would cooperate the best I could, but they would have to ask me about things I knew about, not just throw accusations at me."

I get up from the couch and find my phone in my pocket. I call Chloe. "Hey. It's me. Do you remember the name of the guy that you found had chatted with Tara on her iPad? You remember? You had a hunch about him, but I didn't believe you."

"Yeah. He was called Boxer, why?"

"I thought so," I say. "I think we need to take another close look at this guy. And most importantly find out who and where he is."

72

APRIL 2016

BOXER HAS JUST HANDED over the girl to her new owner when he enters the police station. He greets Detective Fisher in the hallway and he shows him back to his desk. Fisher folds his hands on top of his stomach and leans back.

"Thanks for coming down here. We really appreciate it. You say you saw something on the day when Paige Stover disappeared?" he asks. "Something you believe is important?"

Boxer nods. "Yes. At the rally."

"So, you were at the rally?" the detective asks.

"Yes. I was there with my brother to protest against the fish-kill. It's truly awful how our river has been destroyed."

"Yes, we all believe so, but let's get to the point here. We are interested in talking to anyone who was at the rally, as you probably know from the newscasts on TV. What did you see?"

Boxer clears his throat and tries to sound sincere. "I saw Paige Stover at the rally. She was with her mother at first, then walked with some of her friends."

Detective Fisher writes on his pad. Boxer can't help feeling a thrill go through his body as he watches him. He tries to hide it.

"So you saw her at the rally," the detective repeats.

"Yes. She was walking down Minutemen Causeway with her friends."

"And where were you?"

"Me and my brother were not far behind them. And that's when I saw him."

"Who did you see?"

Boxer clears his throat again and sits up straighter in the chair. "I don't know his name, but he was also there in the afternoon when we searched for her, walking hand in hand. I should have known something was fishy."

"Wait, wait a minute. Who did you see?"

"He's the captain at the fire station. That's all I know. He's got one of those faces you don't forget, if you know what I mean, Detective."

"Are you talking about Danny Schmidt?" the detective asks. He leans back and grabs a photo from the drawer, then places it in front of Boxer.

Boxer nods. "Yes. That's him. That's exactly who I saw."

"So, you say you saw Danny Schmidt at the rally?" he asks, while writing on his pad.

"Yes. He was there. He was elbowing his way through the crowd and pushed me aside as he did. I saw him approach the girl after the panic erupted and everyone was screaming and running around. He walked up to her, grabbed her arm and talked to her, then they left together."

Detective Fisher stares at Boxer like he doesn't quite know what to say. "And you're sure it was him?"

Boxer nods. "Yes. One hundred percent. I can't have been the only one who saw them talking."

"As a matter of fact, you aren't," he says. "We have another witness that says she saw a man talk to Paige and grab her arm, but she didn't see his face."

Oh, really?

Fisher rubs his stubble and clears his throat. "Did you see anything else? Like, did they get into a car?"

Boxer shakes his head. "I don't know. I went back to look for my brother and then we drove home."

Detective Fisher gets to his feet and reaches out his hand. "Well, thank you for being such a good and concerned citizen and bringing this to our attention."

"I am just glad to be of help," he says and gets up as well. He shakes the detective's hand.

"Oh, you were a great help," detective Fisher says with a smile. "A great help."

73

APRIL 2016

I PARK the car in front of Joey's townhouse and walk up to the entrance. The light is on inside and I hear voices. I take a few deep breaths to calm myself down a little.

I have spent the entire day with Chloe and Danny, trying to figure out who this Boxer is. Well, it was mostly Chloe who did the work from what she could get out of Tara's iPad. But so far, we still have no idea who this guy is. Only that he has chatted with both girls in chatrooms of several games and social media sites. Chloe went into the police file and found all the info they had extracted so far from Paige's computer and now we hope that she can use that to track this guy down.

Meanwhile, I have no idea how she does any of it, so I have been drinking coffee and talking to Danny and Chloe's mother, Carolyn, who I always try to chat with whenever she's awake and I am visiting their house. I think it helped Danny too to take his thoughts away a little. Carolyn was in a wonderful mood for once and told us amazing stories from her youth.

When we were about to leave, she said something I still can't get out of my mind. She is an old, very sick woman, but there was something about the way she said it. Like it was urgent.

"He misses them," she said. "That's why he keeps looking for them. Over and over again."

What on earth could she be talking about?

I shake my head, then raise my hand and knock on the door. I have Snowflake with me, since he misses Bonnie and Clyde so much, well mostly Bonnie, I think. He can smell the pig on the other side of the door and goes crazy. I can barely hold him.

The door opens and Salter looks at me. "Mom? What are you doing here?"

When Snowflake sees Bonnie, he pulls so hard on the leash I let it go and he storms inside. "What happened to, 'Hi, Mom, so good to see you, Mom; I missed you, Mom?' I'm here to pick you up," I say. "Remember?"

He looks like he doesn't understand. I continue:

"It's Tuesday. You're supposed to be with me from Wednesday till Sunday evening this week."

"I...I...we didn't think that was until tomorrow?" Salter says.

"Who is it?" Joey appears in the doorway. "Mary? What are you doing here?"

I hear loud voices coming from the living room and look in to see a couple of familiar faces. Joey's parents' faces to be exact. Both of them engaged in what looks like delightful chat with Jackie.

"You're introducing her to your parents now? That's nice," I say.

"Mary..."

"No. No. It's okay. It's your life. Even though things are moving a little too fast for me, it doesn't have to affect you in any way. I'll keep my mouth shut now. Are you ready to go, sweetie?"

"But, Mo-om, Grandpa and Granny are here."

"Come on. It's my turn to have you now. I've missed you so much and I'm not leaving here without you."

"Go get your stuff, buddy," Joey says, placing a weighty hand on his shoulder.

Salter leaves, shoulders slumped.

"I'm sorry about that," Joey says. "I didn't keep an eye on what day it was. And I'm sorry about...*that*," he nods in the direction of his parents. "I just figured, since she has moved in, they might as well meet."

"Right." I feel very uncomfortable and hope Salter is hurrying up. I don't want to say anything I'll later regret.

Salter finally comes out wearing his new clothes that Jackie bought for him. He looks ridiculous. Who buys a leather jacket for a ten-year-old? A ten-year-old in Florida? And those shoes? What the heck are those? They blink every time he walks, constantly changing colors.

His teacher called me earlier to tell me he can't wear those to school anymore, since they disturb the other students. At first, I thought she was overreacting a little, but now I understand. What's worse is, I am going to have to be the one to tell him and be the bad guy...again.

74

APRIL 2016

"MOMMY?"

Paige Stover tries to open her eyes, but her eyelids feel so heavy. She blinks several times before she succeeds in waking up and looking around. Her mommy is not there. She is not in the dog crate anymore in that awful man's house. But where is she now?

"Mommy?" she repeats and sits up. She is on a bed in a small room with nothing but the bed and a dresser. There is a window, but the curtains are pulled.

Paige gets up and walks towards the window, feeling slightly dizzy. She pulls the curtains and looks out. Water as far as the eye can see. And she is up high. Not in a condominium, but like the third floor of what looks like a house. A big house. A mansion. Below her, she can see a tennis court, a basketball court, and a lap-pool. It's all surrounded by lots and lots of palm trees. The water is not the ocean, she knows that much. She can see land on the other side and a bridge far away. It must be the Intracoastal waters, or the river, as most people call it. It all looks very familiar to her.

Paige grabs the sliding door and tries to open it, but she can't. It's locked. She looks for a way to open it, but can't find it.

"You'll need a key," a voice says behind her.

She gasps and turns. The face looking back at her smiles. "Hello, Paige."

"Who are you?"

"Well, who am I? I'm your new best friend; that's who I am."

"I'm not allowed to talk to strangers," she says. "I want my mommy. Where is she?"

The man sits on the bed. He sighs. "I'll tell you something. I wanted your mom to be here too. But they tell me she couldn't make it. Not this time. Something happened to her."

Paige starts to shake. She fights her tears. "What do you mean something happened to her?"

"Well, last thing I heard was that she was run over by a car."

Paige stares at the man. She had thought it was all a lie. While lying in the crate, she had been certain that Boxer had only told her it to make her go with him. She didn't think it was the truth.

"I want to go to the hospital and see her," she says.

The man shakes his head. "Now, I can't let you do that," he says. "But we can do something else."

"What?"

"How about we play a game?"

"I don't want to play a game. I want to see my mommy!" she yells.

The man gets up from the bed, walks to her, then slaps her across the face. It burns like crazy on her cheek. But it makes her stop crying. She stares at him, baffled, her cheek red and burning.

"There'll be no crying, do you hear me? No crying, no screaming, no trying to run away. You can't get out of here. All the doors are locked and I am the only one who can open them, so you might as well not try. I'll spare you the trouble right away. So you can't run, all right? But you can do something else. Something a lot more FUN."

"W-w-what's that?" she asks, still startled by the slap. She is terrified the man might hurt her again and her voice is shaking.

He leans over and whispers in her face, spitting slightly as he speaks. "You can HIDE!"

APRIL 2016

SALTER IS HARDLY SPEAKING to me. The next morning, I send him off to school by bus. His dad lets him bike to school, but I feel more safe with him going by bus. I don't feel like he is safe on that bike, and especially these days with the disappearance of Paige Stover, I am not comfortable with him biking to school.

I explain it to him, but he just gets mad at me. Again, I am the bad guy and he is angry at me all morning.

I feel awful as I take care of my dad. He tries to cheer me up by moving his toes that he is now capable of moving back and forth. It does cheer me up a little, and I can't help smiling when Jack, his physical therapist, arrives.

"He's doing so well," Jack says. "The video you made in the middle of the night helped him believe that he can actually move his feet, that he can regain mobility in his feet and legs again. You have no idea how much hope means for a patient like your father."

"Thank you," I say, feeling slightly overwhelmed with emotion.

He smiles. "Just thought you should know."

I leave my dad in Jack's hands and grab my bike to go to Chloe's house. She's in the kitchen as I knock and walk in.

"Coffee?" she asks.

I nod and she pours me a cup. I sip it and look at her. She looks awful. Her hair is a mess, her clothes the same as yesterday. "You been up all night?"

"Yup."

"Anything new?"

She nods. I feel relieved.

"I have a lot for you to look at, come."

I follow her to the back of the house where all her computers are lined up. It's dark and cold in there. I pull out a chair and sit next to her, my cup between my hands.

"Look at this," she says and hands me a stack of papers she has printed.

I flip through them. First is a case file for the missing persons report for Paige Stover. There are interviews with all the people who have daily contact with her, like her teacher at school, her basketball coach, her swim teacher, and her math tutor. "What am I looking for?"

"Look at the last page. A statement they took yesterday," she says, turning her chair to face me.

I find the last statement and look through it. "What the heck?" I exclaim, after reading a few lines of this guy's testimony. "He says he saw Danny talking to Paige at the rally? That he grabbed her arm and they left together? That's ridiculous. Danny wasn't even at the rally!"

Chloe nods. "Exactly, but the police are all over this. Your friend Fisher is determined Danny is the guy they're looking for."

"He is not my friend," I complain. "I just tried to help him with the case. I thought he took me seriously, but he's just interested in busting Danny."

"And now they have the eye-witness to back up their theory," she says.

"Who is this guy anyway?" I ask and look at the head of the file to see his name. "Joseph Barrow?"

"According to this, he's Paige's basketball coach, Coach Joe," Chloe says. "But check this out. It gets a lot better."

Chloe puts a stack of papers in front of me. "These are all the case files from the missing mothers and their daughters. I have pulled all of the missing persons reports. I went through all of them and this is what I found." Chloe leans over and points at the first report, Kim and Casey Taylor's file. She rests her finger on a name in the heading. "Look who showed up as an eyewitness? Stating he saw them at the mall right before they disappeared?"

APRIL 1975

"I'M SCARED, DANH."

Long looks at him with her big moist eyes. Bao is sleeping, his breath uneven and weak.

"Me too," Danh says.

"You think he'll die?"

"Stop saying that. Stop! Now, go to sleep!"

Danh looks around while his sister does as she is told. Three men are watching them, big grins on their faces, machine guns over their shoulders. Danh hasn't slept in two days; he has been watching over his brother and sister night and day, especially keeping an eye on the men on the ship who look at his sister in a way that terrifies him.

He has been begging them for medicine and food for days, but all they've given them is water and very little of it. It's not enough, and Danh is on the verge of breaking down. He is so hungry he can't even feel it anymore and so thirsty he hallucinates, seeing his dear mother coming towards him. She looks angry. Is she angry with him?

I am sorry. I failed you, Mother. I miss you so much. I don't know what to do anymore. I can't save him. I can't save Bao.

"I can help you," a voice says.

Danh opens his eyes. The sun is burning his face. The silhouette of the man standing in front of him is moving closer.

"What?"

"I have medicine," he says and kneels in front of him. Danh can now see his face properly. It's the guy wearing the captain's necklace around his neck. Danh gasps.

"I have medicine for your brother," the man says.

Danh sits up straight. Is this true? "You have medicine?"

The man nods. He reaches into his pocket and pulls out something in his closed fist. He shows it to Danh. A small bottle with the word penicillin on it, curled up in the palm of his hand. Danh looks at it with a small whimper. He knows what this is. He remembers having seen it once before, when one of his brothers was very sick. The doctor came to their house carrying a bottle just like this.

So many sleepless nights, he has been hoping and praying for medicine for Bao. But they told him there was no more onboard the ship. Long got it all, they said.

Danh reaches out to grab the bottle, but the man closes his fist and pulls it back. He is grinning from ear to ear.

"No."

"No?"

"We make a deal."

"What do you want? I'll give you anything, but I don't have much. I don't have anything of value."

The man nods. "Yes, you do." As he speaks, his eyes fall on the sleeping Long next to Danh.

Terrified, Danh shakes his head. "No. No. NO."

The man rises to his feet. The medicine disappears into his pocket again. "As you wish."

He turns and walks away. Danh grabs Long and pulls her closer. He holds her in his arms till she wakes up.

"I heard what the man said," she says, when she opens her eyes.

"What do you mean? Don't talk nonsense," Danh says.

"I want to do it," she says.

"NO! Never!"

"Bao saved my life when we were on that other boat. He refused to let them throw me overboard. Both you and he chose to get into that small boat for me. I owe him, Danh. I can do this."

77

APRIL 2016

I STARE at the name on the file. "Joseph Barrow, Joseph Barrow...who are you?"

Chloe is on the computer when Danny knocks on the door and pokes his head in.

"Hello? Anyone home?"

"In the back!" Chloe yells.

"What's up?" I ask as he comes inside. He has already helped himself to a coffee in the kitchen. He looks so tired and I am guessing he hasn't slept all night.

"The police called. They want me down for more questioning."

Chloe turns her chair to look at him. "I might have an idea why," she says, and shows him the file. "This guy walked in yesterday and told them he saw you with Paige Stover on the day she disappeared. He says you and she left the rally together."

Danny almost drops his cup out of his hand. "What? But I wasn't even there. I told them I wasn't."

"I'm guessing they aren't going to believe you after this," I say.

"Who is he?"

"His name is Joseph Barrow," I say.

"Joe?" Danny asks.

"You know him?"

"Well, of course I do. He's one of the coaches at the rec center. I've known him for years. I helped him get the job; I recommended him because he didn't have anything else when he was fired from Disney two years ago. I've known him since we were in the army together. We were deployed together in Afghanistan in '04. His brother was with us too. Terrible thing. A kid with explosives blew him up. Joe had her, could have shot her, but he hesitated and the kid exploded herself and took Joe's brother. Joe was never himself again after that."

"His brother? But it states here that he was at the rally with his brother. That's what he told them," I say.

"Yeah, he would say that. Joe went kind of cuckoo after what happened. Kept talking about his brother like he was still alive. Kept claiming he was with him everywhere. It was awful. He refused to realize his brother was gone. Hard to understand why he was so attached to him, though. The brother was a heavy drinker and gambler who cheated Joe out of a lot of money, always had him pay off his debts. As far as I know, all Joe has left is his mother who is dying from cancer."

Danny hesitates. He looks like he just remembered something. "Wait a minute."

"What?" I ask.

He looks at me. "Boxer? That's the name of the guy who we believe chatted with both Paige Stover and Tara, right?"

"Right," Chloe says.

"Oh, my God. It's so obvious. Why didn't I think of it sooner?"

"What?" I ask.

"Joseph Barrow is his name."

He looks at us like it's the most obvious thing in the world. I have no idea where he is going. I look at Chloe, who doesn't seem to have a clue either.

"Joseph Barrow," he repeats. "As in Joseph Louis Barrow, as in Joe Louis." He looks at us again. "Ah, come on, get there faster!"

"I have no idea what you're talking about?" I say.

"The boxer. The famous boxer, Joe Louis. He shares his name with him. I should have seen this from the start when Chloe told us about The Boxer."

Chloe looks at me, then at Danny. Danny looks like he isn't really sure he understands this properly yet, like he is still piecing things together in his mind.

"Oh, my God, Joe has taken Paige? And Tara?" he says. "But...he was just there the other day...helping us...you remember him," he says, addressed to me, "you held his hand when we searched for her at the school."

My heart stops. Literally. The very thought makes me sick to my stomach. "That was him?"

"Yes. I can't believe it. He was right there all the time. We've got to tell someone. We've got to tell the police."

"Who is going to believe us?" I ask.

Danny sinks into a chair. "You're right. Fisher knows all of us. Even if you do it, he'll think you're just protecting me."

"How about an anonymous tip?" Chloe asks. "Tell them we heard screaming from his house. That would give them a reason to go in and find Paige, but then again...what if he's not keeping her at his house? He might have her somewhere else."

"Chloe's got a point," Danny says. "We need to somehow figure out if he has her at his house."

PART IV

COME OUT, COME OUT WHEREVER
YOU ARE

78

APRIL 2016

AS THE SCHOOL BELL RINGS, hundreds of children run out the doors. Lots of them grab their bikes, other go in the pick-up line, while the rest go to the buses.

Blake watches them as they walk in a nice line to the yellow buses and disappear inside of them. He especially watches bus C26, carrying his dear nephew Salter.

As the bus sets off from the school grounds, Blake drives after it, keeping a distance of one to two cars between them.

The road is still blocked off on parts of Minutemen where they pulled the bodies out the other day. The police tape is still in the bushes, being tossed by the wind.

The bus stops every few minutes as it drives down A1A towards the Patrick Airforce base. It turns just before the base and goes back to A1A northbound, towards Blake's childhood home. He remembers riding in that very same bus himself as a child. Even the bus driver, Mrs. T., is still the same.

Nothing ever changes in this town.

Blake especially remembers coming home after school, being greeted only by his stepmom, Laura, who would look annoyed at him and wish him long gone. She never liked either him or Mary, but most of all she loathed him, because he was there, a constant reminder of the love that her husband lost, when his mother was shot in that very house.

Blake reminded his father of her constantly. It was almost unbearable for his father. So much that he would pay him money to leave the house, pay for anything he wanted, as long as he didn't bother him or Laura.

When Blake turned sixteen, he got a Corvette, the newest one. But his dad wasn't there to give it to him. It was just parked in the driveway, his name on a card placed underneath the windshield wipers.

HAPPY BIRTHDAY was the simple message. Not even a *Love from Dad.* Blake took it for a spin that day and drove so fast up I95 that he almost crashed. As the car spun around and he missed the tree, he couldn't stop thinking that maybe this was exactly what his dad wanted. That was why he bought him the car, so he could go and kill himself on the highway.

He wasn't going to give him the pleasure.

The bus stops in front of 7th Street and three kids get out. The last one is Salter. Blake drives his rented car into a parking spot, then gets out.

"Salter!"

Salter stops and Blake runs to him while the bus sets off and disappears. Salter looks at him as he runs towards him, his arm lifted. "Salter, wait up."

"Who are you?" Salter asks, as he approaches him.

"Don't you remember me?" Blake asks, smiling widely. He is standing right in front of him now.

Salter's expression changes drastically. He takes a step back. "You're my uncle," he says, his voice shaking.

"That's right, my boy, I am."

"W-w-what do you want?"

Blake shrugs and takes a step even closer to him. Salter is visibly intimidated by his closeness.

"Just to chat. Aren't I allowed to talk to my nephew anymore?"

"You're wanted by the police," Salter says fearfully. "My mom told me you killed someone."

Blake tilts his head. "What do you think? You think I killed her?"

"I...I never said it was a her."

Blake points his finger at him, pretending it's a gun. "Smart kid, huh? Well, I'm even smarter."

In one swift move, Blake reaches out and grabs Salter around the neck. He turns him around and places a cloth over his mouth, then counts backwards from one hundred until the boy stops fighting and becomes lifeless in his arms. As he helps Salter to the car, Blake throws a glance at the house, where he knows Mary will be waiting for her son. But she's going to wait for a very long time.

That's 2-0, dear sis.

79

APRIL 2016

I LEAVE Chloe and Danny at Chloe's house. We have planned to go to this Boxer's house later today, but I have to get back to Salter first. It's early release today, so he is home earlier than usual and he needs to do his homework. He's got a big project he should have done last week, but since his dad thought it was more important to go paddle boarding and hang out with Jackie, he hasn't done it, and now I have to make sure he starts it. I have called Sandra and asked her to come over and stay with him later today so I can go with Chloe and Danny.

It felt strange asking this of her, since I haven't spoken to her in quite some time and since I am still a little angry with her for cheating on Ryan, but you do what you have to do, right? This is important and so I have to swallow my pride.

I park my bike in the driveway and look at the clock. I still have half an hour before Salter comes home on the bus. I decide to bake a cake for him... his favorite banana cake. I am sick of being the bad guy when it comes to my son and I need to win him back somehow. Starting with a cake.

Snowflake is all excited and I let him out in the backyard. Ever since we left Joey's house, it has been hard for me to keep him busy and exercised enough. When he was with Bonnie and Clyde all day it was no problem. Now he's all over the place, especially if I am not home.

I check on my dad, who has fallen asleep in his room in front of the TV, probably exhausted from this morning's physical therapy. It tends to wear him out completely, which is good. I turn off the TV and sneak out. I throw the cake together and put it in the oven, then look at the clock.

The bus should have been there by now.

I shrug and grab a magazine while I wait. I read about how to make a cheesecake with strawberries and soon the timer buzzes on the stove. I look at my watch and wonder why Salter hasn't gotten here yet.

Maybe the bus is just late.

It happens sometimes that Mrs. T. runs late. A couple of weeks ago I freaked out because she was twenty minutes late. Turns out the bus had broken down half way and they had to wait for another one to pick them up. These things happen from time to time. I decide I don't want to allow myself to get all worked up about this like the last time.

I take out the cake and place it on the counter to cool down. It smells divine and I am certain Salter is going to absolutely love it.

Where is he?

The nagging feeling won't leave me alone and I walk to the window to look out at the road. I can't see the bus or Salter anywhere.

It'll be here in a few minutes. Relax. Will you?

I stare at the road, my heart pounding in my chest. No, I can't relax even though I'm trying to. Where is my son? It's now thirty minutes since he should have been home.

I decide to walk out to the road. The bus stops almost right outside my dad's house. It usually doesn't take him more than ten seconds to run inside.

Where the hell is he?

I spot another kid that I recognize from Salter's school. He is crossing the street with his dad. They're walking towards the beach.

"Hey," I yell, and run to them. "Did you come home by bus today?"

The kid nods. He's holding a fishing pole in his hand and so is his dad.

"Was Salter on the bus?" I ask, trying to keep calm, but freaking out completely inside.

"Yes. He got off when I did. We always do."

80

APRIL 1975

DANH'S HANDS are shaking as he grabs the syringe and the small bottle from the man. He watches with tears in his eyes as he drags Long away. She is looking back, trying to comfort him, telling him it'll be okay, not to worry.

He wants to stop her, to stop the man from taking her, but he doesn't. Instead, he looks at the medicine that has been given to him, wipes away his tears, turns around, and faces Bao.

He kneels in front of him, grabs Bao's skinny body, and turns him around. He pulls down his pants, fills the syringe, and places it to his bare skin.

"I sure hope this will help you," he whispers, as he pushes the medicine into Bao's body.

Danh sinks back on the deck and cries. Exhausted, he falls into a deep sleep and doesn't wake up till the early morning hours, when the sun is rising above the horizon.

"Long?"

Bao is next to him, blinking his eyes like he's seeing the world for the first time. "Danh?"

"Bao. You're better. You're not burning up anymore."

Bao tries to smile, but is still too weak. Danh gives him some water, the last bottle they have. He helps him drink.

"You need to rest," Danh says. "Regain your strength. I'll see if I can get you some more water and maybe steal some bread from the trash can. I did that the other day and fed me and Long."

Bao puts his head back down on Danh's jacket. "Where is Long?" he asks, lying with his eyes closed.

Danh wonders about that himself. Why hasn't she come back yet? How does he explain to Bao what has happened? What they had to do? Danh feels the tears building up in his eyes again, but he manages to push them back.

"I'll go look for food and water," he says, avoiding having to answer Bao's question. Danh gets up.

Bao doesn't say any more. He's sound asleep again, but this time with a little color to his skin and a smile on his face. At least the medicine helped. Now all he needs to do is find out what happened to his precious pearl.

Heart in his throat, Danh walks around the ship, avoiding being seen by the men with guns. He hides under stairs, behind trash cans or bags, then sneaks to the living quarters downstairs.

A long row of doors meets him down there. He hears voices coming from behind the doors, people, men laughing, some arguing. He sneaks past the first open door leading to one of the rooms and peeks inside without being seen. In there he sees beds, four beds, and a table with four men sitting around playing cards, their guns hung on the back of their chairs. There's money on the table. Danh looks to see if he can spot Long anywhere, but she's not in this room.

He keeps walking till he reaches another open door. Inside lies a man. He's sleeping, snoring, his gun with him on the bed.

Where are you, my flower? My dancing princess?

His quest leads him to yet another open door and he sneaks close to it before he peeks inside. In there, on one of the beds, he finds her. At first, he lights up, but then everything inside of him freezes.

"Long?" he says, thinking at first she could be sleeping. "Your majesty?"

As he approaches her, he begins to fear the worst. He reaches her and bends over her tiny body.

"Your majesty?"

And that is when he sees it. Danh gasps and tears spring immediately to his eyes. Long's clothes are ripped and she is bruised all over her little body. Her tiny face is pale and blood is running from her mouth. Her eyes are staring, lifeless, into the ceiling. The sight makes Danh sick with sorrow. He puts his head on her chest and starts to scream.

81

APRIL 2016

"THIRTY-FOUR, THIRTY-FIVE, THIRTY-SIX…"

Paige is running down the stairs. She goes for the double front doors first, but just as the man had told her, they're locked. Yet she pulls and shakes both handles desperately and turns all the locks, thinking she can unlock it, but it doesn't work. Next, she's running towards a set of sliding doors leading to the pool area.

"Forty, forty-one, forty-two…"

Paige is crying as she pulls the handle frantically, but the door doesn't open. She sobs, then moves on to the next door, then a window, but they're all locked. She slams her hand into a window, hammering on it while screaming for help.

"Fifty-three, fifty-four, fifty-five…"

The sound of his voice feels like knives on her skin. She runs desperately to the kitchen, but there are no knives or even pans that she can use as weapons. She runs across yet another living room while the voice of the man counting cuts through the air. She spots another set of stairs and decides to run up them.

This house is big. It's enormous. If you want me to hide, then I'll hide. I'll hide so well you'll never find me.

She realizes he is right. The only thing she can do at this point is to hide and to do it well.

"Sixty-five, sixty-six, sixty-seven…"

Hurry Paige. Hurry.

Her hands are shaking, her body trembling in fear as she opens a door upstairs and runs into a bedroom. She looks under the bed, her knees in the soft carpet. She crawls on her belly across the carpet and manages to squeeze herself in under the bed.

"Sixty-nine, seventy, seventy-one..."

This isn't good enough. He'll find you right away! As soon as he steps inside the room the first thing he'll do is look under the bed.

Paige squirms out, gets back on her feet, and looks around. There's a closet. She runs to it and opens it, remembering the time she played with the neighbor's son and she hid behind hanging coats with her feet in a pair of boots at the base of the coats, making it seem that they were just stored objects. He never found her.

But there is no room for her in there. She closes it again, her heart throbbing in her chest.

Please, help me, God. Help me hide.

Paige storms out of the room and runs further down the hallway. Her feet are soundless on the thick carpet.

"Seventy-eight, seventy-nine, eighty..."

The man is counting very loud, probably to make sure she can hear him, she thinks to herself, as she finds another door and rushes inside. She is breathing heavily, desperately, frantically letting her eyes scan the room for possible hiding places. She doesn't want to think about it, but she can't help wondering what he'll do to her if he finds her.

When he finds her.

Oh, my God, he's gonna kill me, isn't he? He's going to find me and kill me.

The look in his eyes had scared her senseless. It was the look of a madman. Paige had seen it before, in that woman from across the street, in the days before she was taken away. Paige's mother had told her she had gone crazy, because she lost one of her children, that she couldn't take care of herself or her other children anymore, and now the hospital would take care of her. Paige heard the rumors about her from the other kids. They said she tried to drive into the ocean with her kids in the car. Her eyes had the exact same look in them.

Like they were lost.

"Eighty-seven, eighty-eight, eighty-nine..."

Panting, Paige looks around this room that appears to be another sort of a living room. There's a fireplace at the end of it. The floors are wooden and creak as she walks across them. Sweat is springing from her forehead.

"Ninety-seven, ninety-eight, ninety-nine..."

Oh, my God. You've got to find a place NOW!

Paige walks fast to the fireplace and the stone chimney. She pokes her head in, grabs the sides, and starts to climb.

"ONE-HUNDRED! READY OR NOT, HERE I COME!"

Paige whimpers and continues to scoot herself upwards until her fingers touch something. She gasps and looks up. A set of eyes in a dirty face look back at her. A girl about her age.

"Who are you?" Paige whispers.

The girl doesn't answer. She lifts her pointer to her lips to signal for Paige to be quiet. Paige holds on to the walls of the chimney and places her feet on both sides to make sure she won't fall down. She clings desperately to the rocks with her fingernails, as the door to the room is blasted open.

82

APRIL 2016

WHERE THE HELL is my son?

I call Joey and, of course, he doesn't answer right away. I leave a voice-mail asking him if Salter accidentally went to his house instead, forgetting he was supposed to be with me till Sunday.

I can't wait for him to answer, so I grab my bike and ride it to his town-house and knock on the door.

"Salter? Joey?"

I can hear Bonnie and Clyde on the other side of the door, but no one opens the door. I grab my phone and call Joey again. Still no answer. I gnarr and knock again, before I decide to go back to my dad's place to see if Salter has come home. Meanwhile, I keep calling Salter's phone, but it goes directly to voicemail. He is not allowed to have it turned on at school, so I figure it's still in his backpack. I leave message number eight, then hang up.

Calm down, Mary. He probably just went to a friend's house and forgot to tell you. You know how distracted he gets sometimes. Maybe Joey even made arrangements with the parents and everything, but forgot to tell you. You've got to stay calm. Can't get yourself this worked up all the time.

It doesn't help.

I am officially freaking out now. While riding my bike back to the house, I try breathing exercises; I try thinking about surfing and the ocean, which usually calms me down, but that doesn't help either.

I throw the bike in the grass by my dad's house, and then run inside. "Salter? Salter, are you here?"

"What's going on, Mary?" my dad's voice asks from his bedroom. I run in there. "I can't find Salter. He didn't come home from school."

"Have you tried calling the school?" he asks.

"Ten times at least. They say he got on the bus as planned. I even met a kid who said he was on the bus with him and that they both got off at 7th Street."

"That's odd," my dad says. "It's not like Salter to not come home."

I sigh nervously. "I know. I don't like this, Dad. I've had a bad feeling all week. I knew something bad was going to happen."

"Now, we don't know that something bad has happened yet," he says. "Let's try and stay calm for now, all right? There could be a lot of explanations for this."

I bite my nails, even though I practically have no nails left. I look at my phone again and again. Then I call Chloe up.

"What's up?" she asks.

"Salter didn't come home from school. I'm scared, Chloe."

"Well, with everything that has been going on lately, I can't blame you," she says. "But don't you think he might be at a friend's house or something?"

"I don't know," I say.

"I'll be over in a sec."

She doesn't exaggerate. I have barely hung up before she knocks, then walks in. She gives me a hug. "Are you all right? Now, don't freak out, okay? Stay calm. It's probably nothing. You hear me?"

I bite the inside of my mouth, while I nod. "Where is Danny?" I ask.

"He went to the police station for more questioning," she says.

I try really hard to not break down and cry. My stomach is turning. It's the worst feeling in the world to not know where your child is.

83

APRIL 2016

A COUPLE OF HOURS LATER, he has still not shown up, and I am getting really anxious now. I call the crew and everyone shows up, except Danny, who we are guessing is still being questioned by the police. Even Joey finally shows his face, dragging Jackie along with him.

"Where were you all day?" I yell at him as he enters. "I've called and called and you didn't answer. Our son is missing, in case you didn't know!"

There you go. Take it all out on Joey. That'll help.

I hide my face in my hands. "I'm sorry," I say. "I'm freaking out here."

"Me too," Joey says and grabs me in his arms. He hugs me for a long time and I let go and cry. Jackie is standing awkwardly behind us, not knowing what to do with herself. Joey looks me in the eyes.

"We'll find him, okay? I promise you we'll find him."

Jackie walks closer and puts a hand on my shoulder. "Yes, Mary. He'll show up eventually. It's a small town."

She's being nice. I know she is, but I can't stand it. I can't stand her in my presence. I force a smile and nod.

"The others are in the kitchen."

They follow me there. Everyone has a phone to his or her ear. Alex looks up and nods at Joey, so does Sandra, while Chloe and Marcia are both way too engaged to notice him.

"Marcia's boy Mark is out on his bike searching the area," I say, filling him in on where we're at. "He knows all the places the boys hang out around here, like the skate park, the bike trails, and so on. If Salter has taken off with some of his friends and just decided to not tell us, he'll find him. He has even enlisted some of his friends from eighth grade to help him out. These boys know the area."

Joey nods. "That's good. That's real good."

"Marcia has also asked Mark to send out texts to everyone he knows at the high school, asking for their help and seeing if they've seen anything. Alex's daughter, Ava is the same age as Salter and she knows everyone at the school. They're busy calling people and getting them involved."

Joey nods again.

"Chloe is trying to get ahold of the bus driver who drove the school bus home, Mrs. T., to see if she knows anything, like if Salter met some friends when he got off the bus or...well, you know..." I am about to tear up, thinking about Salter meeting some creepy guy who kidnaps him, but decide to push it back. There is no time to cry now. "Well, basically anything." I pause. "Meanwhile, Sandra is making sure everyone has coffee and banana cake."

Joey smiles softly. "Salter's favorite."

"Don't remind me," I say, swallowing a knot in my throat.

"What can I do?" Joey asks. I can tell he is about to tear up. I am guessing, that seeing this, seeing all these people working like this to get our son back made it all very real to him. He is probably just realizing the seriousness of it all now.

I hand him my phone. "I want you to call the police. It's been four hours now. The sun will set in less than two hours. I need them to start looking for our boy."

Joey grabs the phone with an anxious look. "We gotta do what we can now," I say. "We have to find him before nighttime. We've simply got to."

84

APRIL 1975

DANH CARRIES Long's lifeless body up on the deck. His body is threatening to crumble as he takes one step at a time towards the bright deck, bathed in sunlight. He walks outside and turns towards the place where Bao is sitting. All the while, he is thinking about Long, imagining her dancing for him again, seeing her laugh and smile for his inner eyes, pretending, playing with him like they used to.

Your majesty! Don't leave me this way!

Men on the deck watch him as he walks. He doesn't even look at them. All he can focus on right now is her, her small fragile beat-up body between his hands.

Bao rises to his feet as he spots Danh walking towards him. Danh starts to cry again when he looks at his brother and he sees the realization sink in.

"No!" Bao says as their eyes meet. "No!"

Danh nods. He stretches out his arms towards Bao, so he can better see their sister or what is left of her.

"Please, God, no. Please not Long!"

Danh can't stand anymore. He falls to his knees, Long still in his arms. He is crying and leans forward above her body. Bao falls down on his knees as well and they cry and yell in anger.

"Why her? Why her?" Bao cries out towards the sky.

They stay like that for hours on end. As darkness sinks upon the ship, they finally do what they know they have to. They say their goodbyes, each of them tell a story of their baby sister, from when she was still alive, then in unison, they lift Long over the railing and let her fall into the vast dark ocean.

They sink onto the deck in each other's arms, and cry their way through the night, tired, exhausted, and beaten.

Especially Bao seems to have lost the will to continue. In the coming days, he walks around, not talking to Danh, just shifting between crying and staring at the ocean, and Danh soon fears for him and wonders if he is thinking about ending it all, of jumping into the ocean and leaving Danh.

But that is not what is on Bao's mind.

Three days after Long's death, he finally speaks to Danh. In the middle of the night, he comes to him carrying bread and meat leftovers from the trash can.

There's a new fire in his eyes that Danh doesn't recognize as he speaks to him. "I heard we will soon be close to land," he says, while gnawing on an already half eaten chicken bone. "I overheard two men talking about it. They think we're only two days away."

Danh lights up. There is nothing he is looking more forward to than getting off this ship. He has lost track of how long they have been on the ocean and can't wait to feel the solid ground beneath his feet again. He longs to smell the grass, to see trees and mountains. He never wants to see the ocean again after this. Never. If only Long could have been here to experience it with him. If only.

"That's good news, right?" he says.

Bao bites his lips, then gnaws on the chicken bone until there is nothing left on it. "Depends on how you look at it."

"What do you mean?"

Bao turns his head and looks straight into Danh's eyes. The look in them frightens him slightly.

"It depends on if you think it's alright for these bastards to get away with killing your sister."

85

APRIL 2016

FEET ARE WALKING across the wooden floors. Heavy feet that make the floors creak eerily, while Paige is holding on to the rocks inside the chimney. One of her fingers has already slipped and several others are on their way too.

The steps are coming closer.

"Come out, come out wherever you are," he says. "You cannot hide forever, you know. This house has eleven bedrooms and twelve bathrooms, but I know every corner, and every hiding spot. I will find you. It's only a matter of time."

Paige lets out a small whimper, then closes her eyes, biting her lip so hard she can taste blood.

Did he hear me?

More steps across the wood. Paige can see his shoes now through the opening of the chimney. She holds her breath. The girl above her doesn't move at all. Paige finds it hard to hold on. Another of her fingers slips and she is now holding on with only three fingers. She closes her eyes, sweat springing from her forehead. Her hands are getting clammy and that makes them even more slippery.

"Where are you hiding, little girl?" the man says.

Paige is clinging on to the rocks, barely holding on with her fingertips when her right hand slips and she falls to the side, barely managing to grab on to the wall with the palm of her hand. Her foot is about to lose its grip and she moves it higher up, hoping and praying the man won't hear her.

She holds her breath and waits in the silence for the man to make his move, imagining him reach his arm up the chimney, grabbing her leg and pulling her out. She is shaking with fear. Her eyes are fixated on the black shoes, when suddenly they move. She watches as they turn around and start to walk away. She listens to every step as they slowly disappear. When the door is finally closed, her hand slips again and she falls to the bottom of the chimney. Coughing and panting, she rolls onto the floor. Seconds later, a pair of legs comes out after her and a small face appears. Paige is lying on the floor, catching her breath, trying hard not to panic.

The girl comes out, then sits next to her.

"I'm Tara," she says.

"I'm Paige."

"Just arrived?" she asks.

Paige nods.

"You're good at playing this. It took a long time before I found this spot. He hasn't found me up there yet."

Paige looks at Tara. She is skinny and dirty. She looks tired. "How long have you been here?"

Tara shrugs. "Who knows? I stay hidden and live off food I find in the pantry downstairs when he leaves the house or at night. He keeps Cheerios boxes there. Lots of them. I don't think he realizes any are gone."

Paige looks at her with hope. "He leaves?"

"He does. But he always comes back."

Paige looks around. Her heart is still racing in her chest. She is trembling and can't hold her hands still.

"What does he do with you if he catches you?"

The girl doesn't look at her. She stares out the window where the sun is about to set. The river is glistening and birds are flying low.

"You don't want to know," she simply says, and Paige knows not to ask again.

86

APRIL 2016

NEVER HAS WATCHING the sun set been such a nightmare for me. I stare out the window as darkness settles on the ocean and the shadows grow longer on the beach until they finally vanish.

Where are you, Salter?

Tom has arrived too and now he brings me a cup of coffee. "How're you doing?" he asks.

I exhale and look at the steaming cup between my hands. My stomach is in one big knot. "How do I feel?" I say. "Let me tell you how I feel. I want to scream. I want to yell and scream hysterically."

"Can't blame you," Tom says and sips his own cup.

I look at him. It feels good to be near him. His calmness makes me feel better. Out of the corner of my eye, I spot Joey. He is standing across the living room, his eyes resting on me and Tom. He looks a little like a boy whose toy was stolen from him. It's the first time the two of them have been in the same room together, even though I have told him I was seeing someone. Of all the circumstances in which they could have met, this is the strangest one. I can tell Joey isn't happy about having him here, but since he brought Jackie, I don't have to care.

"Here it comes," Chloe says and turns up the volume on the TV.

Every eye in the room turns to look at the screen as the picture of my son appears behind the anchor, and she, with very serious eyes, says the words 'amber-alert' and 'missing' in the same sentence. That is when I finally break down. Seeing my baby boy on the screen like that, hearing her say that the police in Cocoa Beach want everyone to be on the lookout for this kid, shatters my heart to pieces.

I feel Tom's arm around me, trying to catch me as I fall forward to my knees, crying, weeping helplessly.

"It'll be all right, Mary," Tom says. "We'll find him. We will find him."

Chloe turns off the sound, and hurries to me. She squats next to me. "Salter is a tough kid, Mary. And you're a tough mom. We will get him home, you hear me? I won't rest till we do. None of us will."

I look up and see the faces of the crew. All my friends have approached me. They're surrounding me.

"Chloe is right," Danny says. "You're always there for us."

Marcia nods, tears in her eyes. She clenches her fists and knocks on her heart. "Always, Mary. To the end of the world."

Sandra is there too. She reaches down her hand. I grab it and let her pull me to my feet. She smiles, her eyes damp. Alex is standing behind her.

"You're not alone in this," Sandra says.

We all join in a group hug, only Joey is standing outside looking at us, Jackie by his side. The TV is still on and now the woman presents a new story. I let go of my friends and walk to it, then turn the sound back up.

"What is it, Mary?" Chloe asks.

"It's a piece about the bodies they pulled out of the river the other day," I answer. "The mom and the daughter, Kim and Casey Taylor."

"What about them?" she asks.

I turn to look at her. "They say they were embalmed."

"They were what?" she asks, lifting both her eyebrows.

"Embalmed. She just said they were embalmed before they were thrown in the water. Apparently, they can't determine exactly when they were killed, since their bodies are so pumped full of formaldehyde there is almost no decomposition."

A gazillion thoughts go through my mind as I watch the piece. They show pictures from the canal where they found the bodies, then the police state that they need the public's help in this case. I watch the pictures of Kim and Casey Taylor while they were still alive. It's all churning inside my mind, mixed with images of Tara and Maria, Paige and Salter.

"The sick bastard," I mumble.

"What's that?" Chloe asks. "Who?"

"Boxer. I think it's time for us to pay him a visit."

"You can't do that," she says.

I look at her, making sure there is no doubt that I am being serious here. Very serious.

"Try and stop me."

87

APRIL 2016

HE PULLS out his suitcase and puts it on the bed. He pulls out shirts, underwear, pants, and shoes and throws them in.

"You might need to take your jacket too where you're going," his brother says, standing in the doorway, holding a bottle of gin.

"Stay out of this," Boxer snarls, but grabs the one winter coat he owns that he's never used while living in Florida, and throws it in as well.

"So, you're just going to leave me here?" His brother lifts the bottle and drinks from it, like it was water.

Boxer stares at him and sighs. "I can't stay. I have to go. They found those two bodies and I am afraid it will only be a few days before they trace them back to me. Or they'll find out that I took Paige Stover. Even though I know they have Danny Schmidt at the station, I'm afraid. It's getting too dangerous. I've saved enough money. I'll never have to work again."

Boxer grabs the suitcase and walks out the door. His brother follows him closely down the stairs.

"What about Mom?"

Boxer stops at the bottom of the stairs, closes his eyes, and takes in a deep breath. He had to bring her up, didn't he? He simply had to poke at his guilt. His dying mother. Their dying mother.

"I don't know," he says. "I guess I'll keep paying for her. They'll take care of her at the hospice."

"But who will visit her?" his brother asks. "She'll get lonely."

"That's not my problem," Boxer hisses. "How about you do it for once? How about you do something?"

He manages to calm himself down just as there is a knock on his front door. Not just a simple knock, but an aggressive, hard knock. Not with authority like the police knock, more like someone in a hurry to get in.

Boxer puts down the suitcase, walks to the window, and looks out from behind the curtain. A woman is out there. Boxer recognizes her face from the day of the rally. She was the one who took the pictures and posted them on Facebook, leading him to Paige. He remembers her name was Mary, Mary Mills or something like that. And when they later had that search party for Paige, he was holding her hand. She had sweaty fingers, he remembers.

What does she want?

"I know you're in there!" she yells. "Open the door. Open it now."

The woman is not alone. She's with another woman. She is small, red-haired, pale, and wearing glasses. They seem harmless, so he decides to open the door.

Boxer smiles. "Hello. What can I help you with?"

He looks into the eyes of Mary Mills and quickly regrets having opened the door. They're filled with what seems to him like obsessed anger and pillars of fire.

"Where is my son?" she asks, spitting as the words leave her lips.

Boxer stares at her. He shakes his head slowly in confusion. "Your son... I...I'm not sure..."

"Don't give me that," she says. "I know you have him. What have you done with him, you sick bastard?"

"I'm not sure..." Boxer looks at the other woman for help. "What is she talking about?"

Mary takes a step closer. It frightens him a little, and without thinking about it he takes a step backwards into the living room.

"You took him, didn't you?" she says. "You took him like you took Paige Stover, like you took poor Kim and Casey Taylor, along with Maria and Tara and all the others, didn't you?"

Boxer stares at her, eyes and mouth open. He doesn't know what to say, how to deal with this.

How does she know all this?

"You did, didn't you? I can see it in your eyes," she says and points at him aggressively. "I know you're the Boxer. I know it's you!"

"Uh-oh," his brother says behind him, in between sips from his bottle. "You're in trouble now, brother. You're in deep trouble."

Boxer closes his eyes. He slumps his head, then turns around and yells at his brother:

"SHUT UP! SHUT UP! You're dead, for crying out loud. Why won't you leave me ALONE?"

88

APRIL 1975

THEY DO it in the middle of the night. Bao and Danh stay awake till everyone else on the ship has fallen asleep, some so drunk they never make it to bed, but simply pass out in their chairs.

They don't talk about what they're going to do. They don't have to. Driven by their anger and lust for revenge, they grab on to the two machete knives that Bao stole the night before and hid underneath Danh's jacket, while they waited for the right time to arrive.

They are close to shore now. All day they have been able to see land on the horizon, and according to what they have heard, the captain plans on making it to the harbor the very next day.

Except he will never set his feet on solid ground again.

They start with the sleeping quarters downstairs, sneaking down one step at a time, sweat springing on their foreheads, holding their breath, stepping lightly so they won't be heard.

Danh gets the honor of taking out the first one. He chooses the man who dragged Long away on that fatal evening, the guy who gave Danh the medicine as payment for his sister.

Danh hardly feels anything when he places the machete on his throat and simply slides it through the flesh and bones without even blinking. Blood gushes out from the wound and soaks the floor. Danh takes in a few fast breaths, watching the body as it is emptied of all life.

Danh is a little disappointed. He thought it would feel better than it did, but he still isn't satisfied. He realizes he really wants them all to die.

When Bao started talking about revenge, Danh hadn't been sure that was what he wanted. He knew he wanted to see this guy dead, but the rest? Now he has no doubt in his mind.

They all have to die.

Danh grabs the necklace from around his neck and pulls it off, then leaves the room before he enters the next.

One by one, they slaughter them in their sleep, all the sailors sleeping, even one that is still awake, coming running towards them pointing his machine gun at them, but so drunk he can't find the trigger. Danh watches Bao slaughter him and the headless body falls to the ground with a plump sound.

Danh feels no sadness, no mercy for these men, as they fall by their feet one after the other. He feels completely empty, and as they finally finish off the captain, Bao yells the cry of a warrior, holding his machete high in the air, putting one foot on the body beneath him. Danh stares at him, empty inside, until the second his eyes lock with those of a man creeping up from behind holding a machine gun.

It all goes so fast, he doesn't get to warn Bao before the shots are fired. The bullets hit Bao and his chest soon explodes, his blood hitting Danh's face.

Danh leaps through the air towards the man, cuts both his hands off with the machete, and screams as the man falls backwards before he cuts his throat.

Danh then throws himself at Bao's dead body. He is crying, helplessly trying to revive him. He lies like that for a few hours, while the ship drifts in the deep ocean, being helplessly thrown back and forth by the waves.

It's not until after the sun has set that he suddenly hears voices, foreign voices that are approaching. He doesn't want to let go of his brother's body and holds on to it, even as the ship is filled with army pants with black boots and more yelling surrounds him.

I am never letting you go again, Bao. Never.

89

APRIL 2016

"LEAVE ME ALONE!"

The guy, Boxer, is standing in front of me and is yelling loudly, but he's not yelling at me. Instead, he seems to be addressing his anger at someone inside the house, someone standing behind him, but I can't see anyone, even though I stretch my neck. All I can see is a green suitcase.

I decide I am tired of waiting. I want to see for myself if my son is here or not. I walk in, push him aside, and hurry through the living room, my eyes scanning the area for anything or anyone.

"There's no one in here." Chloe is right behind me. "Who the heck is this guy talking to?"

I shrug and look back. Boxer stays put. He doesn't seem to notice us or even care that we're in his house. He is still yelling.

"You're dead. Don't you understand that? You were killed. I saw you blow up. Stop bothering me! Leave me alone."

We stop for a second and watch as Boxer grabs his head between his hands and falls to his knees, sobbing.

"Please, just leave me alone."

What's with this guy?

I decide I don't care. Meanwhile, I run into the kitchen and look in every cabinet, calling my son's name.

"Salter. Salter, if you're here, yell or knock or something!"

We go through the two bedrooms, looking under the beds, in the closets, and in the bathrooms. We even go to the attic. Chloe lifts me up so I can crawl in. I get very dirty, but I don't find Salter, nor any sign of him or Paige being here.

"There's a room in the back, downstairs," Chloe says. "I saw a door when we came in."

"Let's check it out."

We run downstairs and find the door, then open it. I turn on the light. There is nothing in the room except a big dog-crate placed in the middle of the white tile. It's extremely clean for a room supposed to house a dog.

"Where is the dog?" I ask.

Not a dog toy anywhere in sight, no dog food, no bowl of water, not even dog hair. But there is something else. Where you close the door to the crate, a lock of long black hair is trapped.

I pull it out and hold it up in the light to better study it. "This here, my friend, isn't dog hair."

Chloe looks at it. Her eyes are serious. "You're right. This is definitely not dog hair."

She pulls out her phone.

"Who are you calling?"

"I think it's about time we involve the police in this," she says. "We're in over our heads here."

While Chloe speaks to the police and convinces them to come here, we hear the front door slam shut. Our eyes meet the second before I storm back to the living room only to find it empty, the front door closed, and the suitcase gone as well. I run outside and see a white van disappearing down the street.

90

APRIL 2016

THE MANSION soon grows dark and quiet. Tara crawls inside a closet to go to sleep, and she tells Paige to find a spot where she can sleep hidden and be ready to crawl back up in the chimney should the game start all over again.

"You never know when he'll start counting again," she says.

"Does it happen at night as well?" Paige asks.

"Usually, the nights are peaceful," she says. "So are the times when the man leaves the house. But don't let him find you. You must hide at all times."

Paige creeps under a couch and tries to fall asleep, but she can't. She is too scared and misses her mom so terribly. She still doesn't know if what Coach Joe said was true, if she was really hurt or not.

Paige's back is hurting from lying curled up underneath the couch, and soon she crawls out. She walks to the window, grabs it, and tries to open it, but with no success. She stares into the darkness of the river in front of her, wondering where her mother is and if she'll ever see her again.

She thinks about Tara and how long she has been here, trapped in this house, hiding from the man, and she wonders how long she herself will have to do the same. How long before he figures out to look up the chimney? Will she just be waiting for it to happen? Is that really all she can do?

Paige's stomach is rumbling and she remembers what Tara told her about the Cheerios in the pantry. She decides it can't hurt to sneak there now. She is starving and can't sleep.

Carefully, Paige sneaks out the door and walks down the hallway, hoping she is going in the right direction. The carpet on the stairs helps her to not make a noise. She walks carefully towards the kitchen, which she remembers running through when looking for a hiding spot. She just hopes she won't get lost in this house. She doesn't want to lose Tara or the good hiding spot. She wants to make sure she is capable of finding her way back, so she memorizes details about the rooms and hallways she walks through. A painting, a vase or a sculpture.

Finally, she reaches the kitchen and spots a door she thinks must lead to the pantry. To her surprise, she is right. It's a sight for sore eyes or hungry mouths. An El Dorado of cereal boxes from ground to ceiling. Not just Cheerios, but all kinds of cereal. Any kind, really.

Paige grabs a box of Captain Crunch and opens it. It makes a lot of noise and she stops to listen if anyone could have heard her. She holds her breath until she knows there is nothing, no one in the kitchen, before she sticks her hand into the box and stuffs her mouth with the cereal till she can contain no more.

Full and exhausted, she slides to the ground, leans her head on the box, and closes her eyes.

Just one second. I just need one...

She wakes up with a start. There is cereal on the floor and she hurries to clean it up, then place the box back on the shelf. She opens the door to the pantry and pokes her head out to make sure no one is on the other side before she sneaks out and through the kitchen. As she passes through one more living room, she sees a light coming from underneath a door that is left ajar. She stops and stares at the light, when she hears a still small voice coming from the other side.

"There you go...*your majesty.*"

Curiosity makes Paige sneak closer, till she can peak inside using just one eye. The room looks like a church room...statues and smoking incense sticks placed on a sort of an altar. In the middle sits the man. Paige gasps with fear when she sees him. He is bent over something, holding it close to him while he cries. Paige gasps again when she realizes it is a woman. The woman has long black hair that he caresses and brushes. She isn't moving. Her body is stiff. Paige takes a step backwards, clasping her mouth as she slowly realizes the woman isn't alive.

91

APRIL 2016

"LET ME GET THIS STRAIGHT. You found this hair stuck on the crate?"

Chris Fisher looks at me, holding the lock of black hair that I have given him in his hand.

"Yes. I believe it belongs to Paige Stover. But I have no proof of that. All I know is it isn't dog hair. And Paige has black hair like that."

"And you believe this guy is the same one who chatted with Paige Stover and called himself the Boxer?" he asks.

"Yes." I turn and look at Chloe, who is working with the guy's computer. "I have a feeling she might be better at filling you in on that. Right now, I am only focused on finding my son."

"And the guy, the man who lives here who you believe is the Boxer, who took Paige Stover, where is he now?"

"He drove away. I told you this already; come on, Fisher. We need to move on here. My son is out there somewhere. I need to find him."

Fisher nods, but is not ready to let me go yet. Chloe interrupts him just as he is about to ask me another question.

"I think I might have found something, but..."

Chris Fisher turns around, notepad in his hand. "What is it?"

She draws in a deep sigh. "It's kind of disturbing...I'm not sure..."

Fisher walks to her and looks over her shoulder. "What have you found?"

"First of all, I can tell you that this computer definitely belongs to the

Boxer and that he has been in contact with Paige Stover for a long time, chatting with her online. His history alone reveals that he has been visiting her Instagram profile and Musical.ly profile several times a day. He has written messages to her as well, especially in Minecraft, pretending to be a thirteen-year-old boy from Daytona, whose nickname is Boxer. He has downloaded many pictures of her from her mother's Facebook profile, from Paige's Instagram, and even videos from Musical.ly."

"So, he was stalking her," I say. I look at Fisher to make sure he gets it all and understands that this means...that Danny had nothing to do with the disappearance of Paige Stover.

"There's more. There's a lot more," Chloe adds. "First of all, Paige wasn't the only girl he was watching closely like that. I found pictures of Tara and Maria Verlinden as well, and of Kim and Casey Taylor, Jenny and Stacey Brown, and I bet if I look a little more I'll find Joan and Nicola Williams as well."

"So, he was watching all of the women who disappeared with their children, the same that we gave you the names of," I say. "I told you those cases were connected. Now do you believe me?"

Chris Fisher rubs his stubble, which is about to become a real beard one of these days. I am guessing he hasn't had much time to shave lately. A shower would probably benefit him as well.

"All right," he says. "I'll buy into some of your theory here...but what I really want to know is, where the heck are they? I mean, Kim and Casey we have found, but where are the rest? What did he do with them?"

I shrug. "Could they have ended up in the river as well?"

"No," Chloe says. She is staring at the computer screen, looking paler than usual. "The girls weren't for himself."

She looks up at me. I don't understand what she is telling me. "What do you mean, they weren't for himself?"

"I mean, he sold them. Look at this."

92

APRIL 2016

SO THIS GUY was kidnapping single moms and their children, and selling them off on the Internet. I can't believe any of this. I am staring at Chloe while she speaks, completely freaked out about this revelation. How could anyone be so cold, so calculated and cynical? To sell people? To sell mothers and their kids?

It's got to be the most disgusting thing ever.

"So what we have here is nothing but a salesman. He's not even the killer?" I say. "He didn't kill Kim and Casey Taylor, he just sold them off to someone else? I mean, who does that? And who buys them?"

"It seems to be the same guy ordering them," Chloe says, still focused on the Boxer's computer. "I don't know how much you people know, but there is a part of the Internet for guys like Boxer, where criminals can buy and sell anything and never be traced."

"The Dark Web," I say.

"I thought it was the Deep Web," Fisher says.

Chloe looks at us, annoyed. "That's what the media calls it, but there is a distinct difference between those two things. I'm not going to go into too much detail, but the Deep Web is distinct from the Dark Web." The Dark Web is the encrypted network that exists between Tor servers and their clients, whereas the Deep Web is simply the content of databases and other web services that, for one reason or another, cannot be indexed by conventional search engines."

She has already lost me and I am pretty sure she has lost Fisher as well.

"Nevertheless," she continues. "I have found and decoded an encrypted chat in here between him and this guy who calls himself Dr. Seuss. Boxer sends him pictures of the girls, and Dr. Seuss chooses from the gallery."

Chloe shows us the many pictures. I recognize two of the girls from Salter's school. It makes me sick to my stomach to realize this guy has been watching our neighborhood's kids like that, trying to sell them off.

"As far as I can tell, Paige Stover was delivered to Dr. Seuss a few days ago. Her mother was supposed to be with her, but...well you know what happened to her. My guess is Paige is there right now, in the hands of this Dr. Seuss."

"So, who is this Dr. Seuss?" Fisher asks. "And how do we find him?"

Chloe sighs. "That's the problem with the Dark Web. You can't trace anyone. You can't find them. They can do anything they want in here and never be prosecuted for it. There's a lot more to it than just criminal activity, but that's for another day when we have more time."

"So..." Fisher starts, then stops himself. He looks as confused as I feel. "So, how do we find Paige Stover?"

"We don't," Chloe says and leans back in her chair.

"What?" Fisher asks, not accepting the answer.

"At least I don't. I can't do it."

"Didn't they write down a meeting point or anything?" I ask. "How does Boxer know where to drop off Paige Stover?"

"I don't know," Chloe says. "My guess is they had another way of communicating as well when planning the details, things that aren't able to incriminate them, like using a phone. It would help a lot if we could get our hands on Boxer and maybe his phone."

Fisher sighs. "I'll have every man looking for him around here. I'm sealing this house off and will have forensics out here right away. And we'll get ahold of this guy's phone records ASAP."

"What about Danny?" I say, directed at Fisher.

"What about him?"

"You're keeping him at the station. Isn't it about time you let him go?" I continue.

Fisher sighs. "I can't. At least not till I have more to go on. I'm sorry." Fisher picks up his phone and walks out.

Chloe gets up and walks to me.

"What do you want to do now?" she asks.

I shrug. "It's getting late. Maybe we should get back to the house and see if anyone has heard anything."

Chloe nods and we walk back to our car and get in. I start the engine and look out into the darkness in front of me.

"The only thing I don't get is why would he take Salter?" I say. "You didn't find any pictures of him on the computer, did you?"

She shakes her head and I drive into the street.

"It doesn't make any sense," I mumble under my breath, as we drive back and I wonder about my son. "It makes no sense at all."

93

APRIL 2016

HE RUNS the brush carefully through her black hair. Her head is resting in his lap. He likes to pretend her eyes are looking at him, but they're not. They're staring lifelessly into the ceiling.

He has bought her a new dress. A brown dress very similar to the one his mother was wearing the last time he saw her, when she stood in the doorway of their small home in Saigon forty years ago and told him to go, to take his sister, to just leave town and not come back before it had all calmed down.

He never saw her again.

Danh draws in a deep breath and puts the brush on the table next to him. He caresses the woman's pale face gently, while humming the song his mother used to sing for him when he couldn't sleep.

"Now we can be together again. Finally, dear mother, we're together again. You, me, Bao, and Long," he mumbles, while touching her lips and running a finger up the curve of her nose.

Danh's other brothers all made it out of Saigon and Vietnam. Two of them live in Japan, one in Spain, two in Sweden, and one in Germany. Danh is the only one who ended up in the U.S. He hasn't seen them since they left Vietnam. Only written them letters and they have written back. It took many years for him to find out what happened to all of them, and it wasn't until a few years ago that he knew of the fate of his mother. That she was taken by the soldiers who came to town because she refused to tell them where her sons were. In prison, she was tortured, and finally killed.

Danh never knew what happened to his dad, and still hopes he'll one day know.

He places his hands under the woman's armpits and pulls her up. He places her in the chair at the dinner table, her hands on each side of the plate like she is about to pick up the silverware. Danh then walks to the other side of the table and sits down across from her. He forces a smile.

"Now, let's eat."

Danh picks up the box of Cheerios and pours some in his bowl, then pours milk on it and starts to eat. It was all he ate on the American aircraft carrier after they picked him up while drifting around in the ocean. They told him they found him on top of his brother's body and that he refused to let go of him. They had to take the both of them onboard their carrier. Danh was introduced to cereal by the soldiers and that was his favorite food ever since. After his retirement he never ate anything else.

When they reached land, they helped him take his brother with him to the United States. They had the body embalmed in Thailand so it wouldn't decompose during the long journey. Danh was supposed to have him buried once he arrived there, but instead he kept him in the small condo that was given to him. He bought a casket for him with a lid of glass and kept him in there for years. He didn't want him to leave him, ever again.

Danh pours himself a glass of orange juice and lifts it to salute Bao, sitting next to him at the table.

"To family," he says.

No one else lifts their glass. Danh looks at them. He sighs and puts down his own glass. "I know," he says. "I know. We're not complete. Long isn't here. I am sorry. We've been playing hide and go seek."

Danh laughs out loud and leans back in his chair. "I haven't had this much fun in years," he says. Then his face freezes. He slams his fist into the table with a loud noise.

"You're right. There is a time to play and a time to eat. I will find her. She needs to be with her family."

Danh pushes his chair out from the table.

"If you'll excuse me, I'll go get her."

94

APRIL 2016

BOXER STEPS on the gas pedal as he drives through downtown. A couple crossing the road jumps for their lives as Boxer's van barely misses them.

"Freaking tourists," he grumbles.

Boxer is sweating, his hands are moist and feel slippery on the wheel.

"You'll get us both killed if you continue like this," his brother says.

Boxer turns his head and looks at him in the passenger seat. "You again? What do you care? I thought you were already dead. Remember the bomb?"

"Vividly," his brother says, as he pulls out a bottle of vodka and starts to gulp it down. "I also remember you not shooting the kid when you were told to."

"So you're saying I killed you, is that it?" Boxer growls and takes a turn so sharp the wheels screech. He almost hits the wall of the Chinese place, Yen Yen on the corner of A1A and Minutemen.

His brother shrugs and keeps drinking. "You said it; I didn't."

Boxer screams and turns the wheel to avoid a street light. "I hate you. Do you know that? I hate you! So what if I killed you? Maybe I wanted to kill you. Have you ever thought about that? With all the gambling and the drinking. It was always my mess to clean up. You always came to me and I had to fix everything. You ruined my life! Do you even realize that? You ruined everything. Mother couldn't cope with it; she couldn't take it, and so I had to. Still, she was heartbroken when you died. And she blamed it all on me. *Why couldn't you save him, Joe? Why didn't you protect him? I told you to protect him when you left. I told you to watch over him.*"

His brother laughs.

"Why the heck is that so funny?"

Boxer is screaming when he speaks. His eyes are filled with the anger and tears gathered from years of frustration. He doesn't look at the road in front of him, only at his brother. His drinking brother who destroyed everything while alive and still does even though he is dead.

"Get out of my life!" he yells, his mouth frothing in anger.

He doesn't see the man in the street until it's too late. He turns the wheel hard and misses the man, but the van spins out of control and crashes into a wall.

At first he is confused and doesn't know where he is. He has bumped his head. It hurts. There is smoke everywhere and flames erupt at the front of the van. Boxer sobs and looks at the seat next to him.

It's empty.

"Peter?"

He looks everywhere inside the car for his brother, but he's not there anymore. Boxer doesn't understand where he is, since he is always there. Always right there next to him, ready to torment him, but now it is quiet. So quiet.

The flames are getting bigger now and he knows he has to leave fast. Boxer jumps out of the van and walks backwards away from the car while flames eat it. Peter is still nowhere to be seen.

Is he really gone?

Boxer looks at the van as it is quickly devoured, then hears sirens in the distance. He throws a glance at the road ahead of him, then looks back at the car, just as the first fire truck turns the corner at the Chinese place. Next, Boxer turns on his heel and starts to run.

95

APRIL 2016

"HE'S NOT HERE."

Joey is the first to announce it to me as I storm in the front door. He can tell by the look on my face that I have been hoping that Salter has returned while Chloe and I were gone. But, of course, he hasn't. They would have called me if he had. I just somehow had hoped that maybe he had.

"I know," I say, my shoulders slumped.

"All police cars on patrol and all firefighters are looking for him," Joey says, as he grabs me by the shoulders and hugs me. "We will find him."

Sandra pours me a cup of coffee and I take a small sip. She sits down in front of me. Ever since the accident, it has been difficult for her to smile properly, and I appreciate her effort in trying to do so now, to try and comfort me.

"How are you holding up?" she asks.

I stare into her eyes. They are still gorgeous. No one can ever take that away from her. The rest is just packaging, if you ask me.

"I don't know. I feel like panicking, but what's the use?"

Sandra nods. She is holding her coffee between her hands. "Did you find anything at that guy's house?"

I nod. "Hair. We found a lock of hair that I think must belong to Paige Stover. She has that type of hair that..."

I pause and look at Sandra without really seeing her. Thoughts and images are flickering through my mind. "Wait a minute," I say and get up.

"What?" Chloe asks and approaches me, a soda in one hand, and banana cake in the other. The sight of the cake makes my stomach turn in worry, but I shake it. I can't let myself be overwhelmed with emotions. Not now. Not when my son needs me more than ever.

"The hair," I say. "All of their hair."

"What are you talking about?" Chloe asks, mouth filled with cake.

"Why haven't we seen that?" I grab my laptop and open the article about Kim and Casey Taylor. "Look at them."

"Just get to the point, will you?" Chloe asks.

"They're all Asian. All of the kidnapped women and their children have Asian features. They all have the same long black hair and eyes. Tara is only half Asian, but she still has the characteristics."

"So, what does that mean?" Chloe asks. "I mean, besides the fact that this guy who calls himself Dr. Seuss is into Asian girls? Lots of men are."

I shrug. "I don't know. But it must mean something, right?"

Chloe bites her lip. I can tell she really wants to make me happy, make me think this will lead somewhere. "Sure. We just don't know what."

I sit down again, and then open my computer. I Google Dr. Seuss, then Asian girls. Shouldn't have done that, since it mainly brings up a lot of porn sites. I go back to Dr. Seuss again. I open Wikipedia and read through his story, thinking maybe there is a reason this guy calls himself that. Maybe there is something in his story about Asian girls or maybe just something else that made this guy choose that name, like Boxer chose his because he shared name with a famous boxer.

Shared a name?

"I think I've got it," I say and stare at the screen.

Chloe approaches me. "Got what?"

I grab my phone next to me, rush into my dad's room, and grab his gun to put in my purse.

When I return, I walk past Chloe, reach for the door handle on the front door, and look at her.

"I know who Dr. Seuss is. Let's go."

96

APRIL 2016

SHE CAN HEAR him on the stairs. She and Tara are sitting in the room upstairs by the fireplace, sharing a bowl of Cheerios that Paige brought back with her, when Paige hears it.

"He's coming," she says.

Tara shakes her head. "He can't be. He never comes up here at night. He stays down there with..."

Tara grows silent. "I call them the zombies. There used to be more. Now my mom...my mom is one of them. He places them around that table and then he has dinner with them. When I came here, there was a little girl there too. And another woman. But now they're gone. Now he sits there with my mom."

"Do you think he wants to do the same to us?" Paige asks, remembering seeing the woman he was with in the library downstairs.

Tara doesn't say anything. She doesn't have to. Paige knows that's what she is afraid of.

"He did it to the other girl," she says with a low voice. "I saw her. She was already stiff and had dead eyes when I saw her the first time."

Paige swallows hard. She listens carefully, but can't hear the steps anymore. Maybe it was just all in her head. Living in constant fear of him starting to count again has made her jumpy and nervous.

Then the sound is back. She gasps and looks at Tara, who has heard it too. Her eyes are big and wide.

"You heard that?" Paige whispers.

Tara nods. "But...I haven't heard him count. He always starts the game by counting so I can hide."

"Ready or not..." they hear him say all of a sudden. The voice sounds like it is very close to the door.

Paige gasps and looks at Tara, who sits frozen.

"Here I COME!"

As the handle turns, Tara springs for the chimney. Paige is on her tail. Tara is fast. She climbs up and makes room for Paige to get in as well. Heart throbbing in her chest, Paige climbs up the rocky walls inside the chimney, her slippery hands failing to get a good grip. She is whimpering and struggling to keep quiet. She stays still to not make a sound and hears footsteps across the wooden floors, the bowl of cereal being turned over, then more steps, and suddenly a hand grabs her leg.

"Found you!"

Paige screams as she feels the fingers surround her ankle and start to pull. Paige holds on to the rocks, but her fingers slip, and soon she is pulled downwards, her face scratching against the walls of the chimney. She tries to get a new grip and to protect herself with her hands, but she can't hold onto anything, and soon her face is smashed into the bottom of the fireplace and she screams in pain.

Whimpering and crying, she is pulled across the wooden floors and into the carpeted hallway. She is screaming for him to leave her alone and trying to kick herself free, but his grip is too strong. She tries to grab ahold of doors or the rails on the stairs. Between screaming and crying, she can hear him singing. She recognizes the song from the movie she always used to watch with her mom, The Lorax. Paige has always hated this song. And hearing it coming out of this creepy man's mouth scares her more than anything.

"How ba-a-a-ad can I be?
I'm just doing what comes naturally,
How ba-a-a-ad can I be?
How bad can I possibly be?"

He keeps singing as he walks down the stairs, banging her head on every step. Paige screams in pain and pleads with him to stop, but he completely ignores her and keeps singing:

"Well there's a principle of nature, principle of nature
That almost every creature knows,
Called survival of the fittest—survival of the fittest."

At the end of the stairs, he turns and drags her towards the library. Paige sees it approaching, the door left open, and soon she is pulled inside and placed on the floor. She screams as she sees what looks mostly like two zombies sitting at a dinner table. The man lets go of her foot, and walks to the door to close it, while still singing:

"And check it; this is how it goes,

The animal that wins gotta scratch and fight and claw and bite and punch,

And the animal that doesn't, well the animal that doesn't winds up someone else's la-la-la-la-lunch—munch, munch, munch, munch, munch."

Paige tries to crawl her way towards the door, but it is slammed shut right in front of her. The man is standing above her. He grabs her by the arms and pulls her back across the floor, kicking and screaming. He leaves her there, grabs a cord, and puts it tight around her throat, still while singing:

"I'm just saying,

How ba-a-a-ad can I be?"

97

APRIL 2016

"HE MISSES THEM."

I am driving down A1A towards downtown while explaining every-thing to Chloe. "It was actually your mom who said it to me."

"My mom? I'm not quite following you here."

"She looked at me and said to me that he misses them. And it was when thinking about that that I realized how it was all connected."

"Could you please explain it to me, then? 'Cause I don't get anything right now," she says.

"Dr. Seuss. His real name was Theodor Seuss Geisel. It was while reading his wiki page that it hit me. His real name was Theodor. Theodor G."

Chloe turns her head and looks at me. "Are you insane? The football player? The founder of Pull 'N Pork? That Theodor G? The man is a hero around here."

"Yes. I know. But it totally makes sense. I remember reading about him a few years ago in an interview where he talked about his mother and how he had recently discovered what happened to her after he fled Saigon back in '75. Theodor and his siblings all fled the country, but he lost his brother and sister during a pirate attack on the boat they were fleeing on. He never knew what happened to his parents until a few years ago, when he learned his mother had been killed in prison. That's why he's kidnapping girls and their mothers, because he misses them."

"Why doesn't he kidnap fathers and brothers then?" Chloe asks.

"Most of his brothers survived and still live all around the world; his father he never knew what happened to. But his sister and mother died, and now he's finding girls and mothers who look like them."

"That's crazy. He still lost one brother," she says, rolling her eyes. "He should be missing him too."

"I don't know the details, but I think we're on to something here," I say. "It fits with the fact that it was about two years ago that the first disappearance took place. The first Asian woman and her daughter. And then there is the name. Theodor G. It's not his real name; I remember reading that he changed it many years ago to separate himself from his past."

"This is insane, Mary. Let's go back home. You're going to embarrass yourself and me in front of the whole town if you accuse him of this."

I take a sharp turn onto Minutemen, ignoring Chloe. "He might have Salter as well. Maybe he had Boxer kidnap Salter to act like the brother or something. I have this hunch and I have got to follow it."

As we drive onto Minutemen, we see a small fire being put out by a fire truck. A couple of police cars are there too. They have blocked one side of the road. We drive past it slowly.

"What happened?" I ask.

"Looks like a car crashed into the Thai-place. Not much left of it, though. Hope no one was hurt."

I hit the gas pedal once we've passed the accident and accelerate down Minutemen Causeway. "I remember reading that he lives in this huge mansion by the country club," I say. "It has eleven bedrooms. The biggest house in Cocoa Beach."

Chloe grabs her phone and starts to tap on it.

"What are you doing?" I ask, as we drive past the two schools and into the residential area.

"Checking if you're right."

"How do you do that?"

"Wait and see."

98

APRIL 2016

"BINGO."

Chloe exclaims and looks up at me, just as I park the car in front of the big gate to Theodor G's mansion.

"What?" I ask and lean over to better see.

"I think you might be on to something after all," she says. "Look who ordered a tankful of formaldehyde two years ago?"

"Theodor G?"

"Close enough. It was ordered in the name of the company behind Pull 'N Pork, but my guess is it was him, yes. There aren't that many places around here that sell that stuff; it's mostly for funeral parlors. It was pretty easy to break into their records."

"A tankful you say? That's a lot."

Chloe nods. I stare at the huge gate and the cameras. Of course the guy has a fort. I always thought it was to keep people out, not in. I can't stop thinking about Salter and whether he is in there right now, scared to death.

"Why didn't we bring any of the guys again?" Chloe asks. "Or call the police?"

"None of them would have believed me," I say. "You hardly did." I reach into my purse and pull out my dad's 9 mm. "Besides, I did bring one of the boys."

"Maybe we should call Alex or Joey first. Have them come here."

I scoff. "You think they can do a better job than I can? I've been taking lessons at the shooting range for six months now. Besides, there's no time to waste. We can't wait for them to get here."

I get out of the car and Chloe follows me. As I step outside, I hear a scream. I look at Chloe. "You hear that? It sounded like a child."

Chloe nods. "All right. What do you want to do? The place is a fort. I'm guessing he won't be opening the door if we ring the bell."

"Are you so sure about that?" I ask.

99

APRIL 2016

THE GIRL REFUSES TO DIE. Danh is holding onto the cord as tight as he can, but the girl is still kicking and screaming, and worst of all, she is still breathing, no matter how tight he squeezes her neck.

And now there is someone by the gate. Danh sees them on the camera and recognizes the woman as that blogger, the one who interviewed him at the rally about his involvement in the protest.

What does she want now?

Danh holds onto the cord and struggles to keep the girl down, while thinking they'll go away if he ignores them. But they don't. They're still ringing the intercom and the noise disturbs him mentally.

How am I supposed to kill someone with all this noise?

Finally, the girl seems to lose the fight. The kicking becomes more random, and soon it stops completely. The intercom buzzes again and Danh growls. "All right. All right! I'm coming," he yells at the monitors, where the two women are standing looking expectantly at the gate.

He lets go of the lifeless girl, then walks out of the room and closes the door behind him. The girl is ready now and he can begin the injections as soon as she is cold. That should give him enough time to get rid of these two annoying women.

Danh presses the Intercom. "Do you have any idea what time it is?"

"Yes. I am so sorry, Mr. G," the blogger says. "I know it's late, but we were out walking my dog, and suddenly it saw a small bunny, and before we could do anything it chased it onto your property through the hedge over there. Would it be alright if we came inside and looked around for him?"

Danh grunts. He is terrified of dogs. The thought of one being loose on his property makes him very uncomfortable. He won't close an eye all night just thinking about it. And even worse if it finds its way into the house. That would be awful.

"All right," he says and presses the button to open the gate. "But hurry up. And use a leash next time you walk your dog, will you?"

"Sure. Again, I am so sorry about this, Mr. G."

Danh rolls his eyes and turns away with the intention of walking back to the girl, his soon to be new Long. He thinks he finally found the right one. He has gone through several and none of them were quite right, but this one is promising.

When he turns around, he sees a figure standing in front of him in the darkness. The figure walks into the light. He is smiling.

"What the heck are you doing here?" Danh asks, appalled by his ugly face. "You're not getting any more money until you deliver the mother. You know that."

Boxer shakes his head. "No. No. No more. Now it's your turn to do something for me."

Danh rolls his eyes again. He scratches his head. This guy annoys him. "I don't have time. I have things to do."

"You hear those sirens?" Boxer asks. "That's the police looking for me. I have nowhere to go, nowhere to hide. You have to hide me and help me get out of the country when things simmer down out there. I know you have a private jet."

"Have to?" Danh says, blowing raspberries. "I don't have to do anything."

"Oh, yes, you do. Or I'll take you down with me. I've saved everything; every chat, every deal we've made is saved on my computer."

"You did what? What kind of an idiot are you?"

"I was just protecting my future," he says. "It was all going so well. I was going to leave and get out of here. I would have brought the computer with me. But then those women came to my house..." Boxer clenches both his fists.

Danh stares at the Boxer. "What women?" He grabs Boxer by the neck and pulls him to the monitor by the front door. The two women that he let onto his property are walking around, calling the dog's name.

"These women? Tell me Boxer, *dearest*, are these the same two women?"

100

APRIL 2016

"SNOWFLAKE? SNOWFLAKE?"

I am yelling while walking around the huge yard, pretending to be looking for my dog, while Chloe and I are really studying the cameras and trying to find a way into the house.

"I think I might have found something," Chloe says, keeping her voice low. "There's no camera here by this back window. It's locked, but I know a trick."

She takes off her shirt, wraps it around her wrist and hand, then slams it through the glass. I gasp in surprise.

"Chloe! Are you alright?"

"Damn, that hurt. I thought it would be so easy. They do it on TV like it's nothing."

"Chloe, your hand is bleeding!" I grab her shirt and rip off some of the fabric from the sleeve to make a bandage, then help her get the rest of the shirt back on.

"Damn, it was my favorite," she grumbles, when she sees the ripped shirt. Blood from her hand has colored it red in spots.

"I'll buy you a new one," I say, and examine the broken window. I remove the fragments of broken glass so we won't cut ourselves. "You think he heard us?"

"Probably," Chloe says, and climbs inside, careful not to touch any of the broken glass on her way.

I follow her, and soon after we're both standing in a room inside the mansion. It's very dark. Chloe finds a door and opens it carefully, making sure no one is waiting on the other side. When she finds the hallway outside empty, we sneak out. I have the gun in my hand as we find a stair- well and walk up. I keep thinking we might find my son in one of the bedrooms. I go first through the hallway, opening one door after another, gun in my hand, examining every room we reach until I find one where the light is on and I spot two bowls of cereal tipped over on the wooden floor.

"Someone was in here," I whisper and we walk inside. The cereal and milk are scattered all over the floor in front of the chimney. Black ashes from the fireplace are spilled out, which I find odd. I bend down and look up the chimney. A small whimper makes me look further up, and I spot a set of eyes staring back at me. They belong to a little girl. She looks terrified.

"Who are you?" I ask.

She doesn't answer.

"I'm Mary. I won't hurt you."

She still doesn't open her mouth.

"Please," I say. "I can get you out of here."

Finally, she gives in. Slowly, she slides down the sides. I crawl out and help her get outside. I recognize her face from the pictures and clasp my mouth.

"Tara?"

The brown eyes in the dirty face from the soot inside the chimney stare back at me. Then she nods.

I am brought to tears. I pull her close and hug her tight. "Oh, my God, Tara. You're still alive. I can't believe I found you."

I hug her again and close my eyes. As I open them again, Chloe is standing by the door, a gun to her head. Holding the gun is Dr. Seuss. Next to him is the Boxer. Dr. Seuss looks at the girl in my arms.

"Thank you," he says. "I've been looking all over for her."

"Really?" I say. "And you never thought about looking inside the chimney?"

Dr. Seuss's eyes turns to ice. "Hand her over or your friend dies."

I look into Chloe's eyes. They tell me *no. Don't do it.* "Where is my son?" I ask, trying to stall for time.

Dr. Seuss looks confused. "What?"

"My son. Salter. You took him."

"What?"

His confusion makes me angry. I draw my gun and point it at Dr. Seuss. "Where is my son? Tell me or I'll kill you. I don't care if you kill her or anyone else. I demand to know what happened to my son!"

101

APRIL 2016

IT DOESN'T WORK. Of course it doesn't. I should have known. Especially since I have failed to notice that Boxer has his hand on a baseball bat
that he now swings and hits me in the side of my head. The blow makes me
pull the trigger, but I miss Dr. Seuss and the bullet hits the wall behind him
instead, while I fall forward into the floor with the taste of blood in my
mouth.

I am not really conscious. Still, I sense that I am being lifted up and
carried down the stairs. I feel my body being moved, but I can't do anything
about it. I hear loud voices around me and a lot of yelling, but can't really
determine if it is real or just part of a dream.

Not until I finally come back ten minutes or so later. When I do, it is all
quiet around me. I open my eyes and look into the face of Paige Stover. Her
eyes are closed and she is not moving. Her throat has marks from being
strangled. I gasp and sit up. That's when I realize I have duct tape covering
my lips. I can't scream. I can't yell or even talk.

Where am I?

My arms are tied behind my back with a cord. My legs are tied together
too. My head is pounding where the bat hit me. Paige and I aren't the only
ones in the room. There's a dinner table with two people are sitting at. I
look at Paige. Is she alive? She looks very pale.

Who are the people at the table?

I manage to get up on my feet and jump with my feet very close
together towards the table. I jump small bunny jumps to get there, and as I

approach, I get a strange sensation in my stomach. Whether it is the strong smell that makes my stomach turn or the sight that meets me, I don't know. But suddenly I feel very sick.

Zombies is the word that comes to mind. Zombies sitting at a table. Dead faces, one of them with very little hair or skin left. Dried up, dead bodies, sitting there like they were waiting to be served, but the waiter never came. Crooked bony fingers on the white tablecloth. I recognize the one body as Maria Verlinden, Tara's mom, and feel even worse.

Did she see it? Did Tara see what happened to her mom? Oh, my God, I hope she didn't.

I panic and my stomach turns so bad I feel like throwing up. But I can't. The duct tape will only make me choke on my own vomit, so I hold it back. The taste in my mouth is awful. I swallow. It burns my throat. I close my eyes and turn away from this strange scene. I jump back to Paige's body and throw myself on the floor next to her. I am crying heavily now. It's all such a mess. Where is Salter if he isn't here? I miss him terribly. I remember the look on Dr. Seuss's face when I asked about him, and I wonder if he was being truthful. Did he really not know? The thought is terrifying, because now I have no idea where to look for him, but it is also little optimistic. It leaves me with the small hope that maybe he wasn't kidnapped after all. Maybe he is just really angry with me and has run away like a normal kid.

I comfort myself with the thought of it, then start to wonder where the others can be. Where is Chloe and what about Tara? Are either of them still alive? Have they taken them somewhere? Where? How am I supposed to get out of here and find my son? Will they kill me next?

How will I ever get out of this alive?

102

APRIL 2016

"WHAT ARE WE GOING TO DO?"

Boxer is freaking out. He is walking up and down Danh's living room, frantically biting his lips. Danh takes a couple of deep breaths.

"What do you mean?"

"What do I mean? What do I mean? Look around?" Boxer points at the red-haired woman tied to a chair, the young girl next to her tied up as well. Both are grunting and gnarling behind the duct tape, struggling to get loose.

Danh looks at them and shrugs. "What about them?"

Boxer groans and pulls his hair. He gesticulates wildly as he speaks. "You have another one in there, unconscious, and a dead young girl. What do you intend to do about all of them? Don't you think someone will eventually come looking for them? Oh, my God, what if they told people they were coming here? I bet the police will be here shortly."

"They won't find anything here when they come," Danh says, while opening the box of syringes.

"What do you mean? Are you planning on killing them? All of them? Hey, man, I'm no killer. I was only in it for the money. That's all. I'm not going to kill anyone."

Danh pulls out a syringe, the biggest he has, and holds it in the air. Yes, that should do the trick. The needle is brutally big, but it will go faster this way.

"I don't have time to kill them," Danh says. He walks to the kitchen, then comes back with two more syringes, which he prepares.

"So...so what is your plan?"

Danh sighs and closes his eyes. Part of him hopes this Boxer will be gone when he opens them again, but he is still there.

"I-I-I...I can't be here...when you, I can't kill...I'm no killer."

Danh tilts his head as he looks at him, the poor thing, getting himself all worked up. "Have you heard of survival of the fittest?" Danh asks, while walking to the table and picking up a syringe. He fills it from one of the big bottles he has lined up on the table in front of him.

Boxer nods his head. "Of course I have."

Danh smiles. "Good. Good. So you understand that the animal that wins gotta scratch and fight and claw and bite and punch, and the animal that doesn't...well, the animal that doesn't winds up someone else's *la-la-la-la-lunch—munch, munch, munch, munch, munch?*"

Boxer stares at Danh. He is at loss for words, it's obvious. Danh finds it amusing. But he has no time to be playing with his little friend anymore. He walks over, grabs Boxer around his shoulders, holds him down so he can't move, then places the needle on his neck and pierces it through the skin. He empties the syringe completely before he lets go of the screaming Boxer.

"What the hell are you doing?" Boxer yells, pulling away forcefully, but it's too late. He's too slow.

"You might say I am preserving you. Did you know that formaldehyde, when injected into your body, turns into formalic acid? When the fluid enters the arteries, pressure builds throughout the veins, which means the fluid is moving throughout the body. You'll notice your veins bulging some-what. That's your blood trying to get out, the fluid is pressuring it out, so to speak. When I do it to a dead body, I usually have to open the jugular drain tube periodically to allow blood to escape and relieve the pressure. But I have never tried it to someone who is still alive. I am curious as to what will happen. Now, what do you know? The big vein on your neck is already bulging. I didn't know it would go that fast." Danh approaches his neck and touches the vein, caressing it with his finger.

"What the hell have you done to me!?" Boxer yells and pulls away, holding a hand to his neck. He stumbles backwards, looking at his hand, where the veins are now bulging too, screaming in terror.

Boxer staggers backwards through the living room, zig zagging and groaning in pain. Danh leaves him; he doesn't have time for him. He'll have to find him later and throw him in the river with the others. Just like when you kill a cockroach with spray and it runs to hide, it always shows up the next day dead on the floor somewhere. So will he.

Next, Danh picks up another syringe and turns to look at the woman and young girl in front of him.

"Who wants to be next?"

103

APRIL 2016

I HEAR voices coming from the next room, followed by loud screaming. It scares me like crazy. Then I hear a sound that doesn't scare me but fills me with relief instead. The sound is coming from Paige's mouth.

She is alive. Oh, my God, she's still alive!

"Paige," I say, muffled behind the tape.

Slowly, she opens her eyes and looks at me. She gasps and is about to scream, but then hesitates.

Good girl. Don't speak. Don't say anything.

I grumble behind the tape and finally she understands. She leans over, grabs the tape, and pulls it off. It hurts worse than getting a Brazilian wax. I only tried that once and I'm never doing it again.

I fight my urge to scream, but instead I take in a few deep breaths. "Thanks," I whisper. "Could you?" I show her my hands and she unties the cord around them. I can tell she is in pain. Her neck looks terrible. She touches it.

"He tried to strangle me with a cord," she whispers, when she sees I am looking at it.

The cord left a visible mark. I don't say anything. I just nod.

"Where is he now?" she whispers.

I nod in direction of the door, then put my pointer finger to my lips to signal that she needs to be very quiet. Meanwhile, I untie my legs. I get up and help Paige get up as well. I can tell she is shaken. The man behind the door terrifies her. We have to move fast now before he finds out we're up and running.

I look around at this strange room we've been placed in, trying to find some sort of a weapon. They took my gun when they knocked me out, and my phone. There has to be something else we can use.

I scan the entire room and finally my eyes land on two machetes hanging on the wall. In the middle hangs an old gold necklace.

Bingo.

I grab a chair and climb up to grab the machetes. I give one to Paige, and keep one for myself.

"We better hurry up," I whisper. "You ready?"

She draws in a deep breath and looks down at the big machete between her hands. "You can do it," I whisper. "If any of them come at you, you swing that beast."

"Them? There is more than one?"

"Yes," I say. "You see a man, you swing it at him. You kill him if you have to. Survival of the fittest, all right?" I say, and lift my clenched fist in the air.

We bump fists before I lift the machete up in front of me and walk towards the door. Carefully, I open it and peek out. I can't see anything, but I can hear a voice. It sounds like Dr. Seuss. He is talking to someone. I signal Paige to follow me and we walk out of the room towards where I hear the voice. I wonder if we can make it through the front door without him noticing it, but realize we can't get through the gate if we do. Plus, I need to find Tara and Chloe.

Seconds later, I find them. As we walk closer, I spot Chloe sitting in the middle of the living room, tied to a chair, Dr. Seuss is in front of her, talking to her.

What's that in his hand? What the heck is he doing to my friend?

The realization hits me like a train wreck. Dr. Seuss is holding a massive syringe in his hand, and as I stand there and watch, he places it on Chloe's skin and presses it down.

104

APRIL 2016

"TOWANDA!!!!"

I don't know why I am yelling exactly that, but the quote from *Fried Green Tomatoes* is all I can come up with as I storm through the house towards Dr. Seuss, the machete held high in the air.

I want to startle him; I want him to stop what he is doing right away. And I succeed. My yelling makes him turn and look, but the syringe stays in Chloe's skin. I swing the machete and hit him right in the face. Dr. Seuss is knocked down, but to my surprise, the knife doesn't cut anything.

Dr. Seuss falls to the ground with a bruise on his head, but is quickly back on his feet.

"What?" I ask.

Dr. Seuss laughs. "Do you have any idea how old these machetes are? Forty years old. They have never been sharpened. They're dull and couldn't cut a banana."

He walks towards me, reaching out to grab the knife, but I pull it back. Dr. Seuss sighs. He pulls out his gun and places it on Tara's head. Chloe is struggling behind the tape. I look at the syringe and wonder how much of that stuff he managed to put in her before I disturbed him. It is only half full now.

"I'm getting tired of you people," Dr. Seuss says, scratching his head with the one hand that isn't holding the gun. I watch his finger on the trigger to see if it moves. My heart stops completely, thinking about Danny and how badly he wants to be in Tara's life.

If she'll live. If any of us will survive this maniac.

"Let her go," I say.

"Or what?" Dr. Seuss says. He scratches his head again, and that's when I see it. I take a step closer.

"You have lice," I say.

He shakes his head. "What?"

"Lice. Right there. All over your hair. They've even infested your eyebrows." I reach out and snap a louse from his eyebrow and show it to him. "See?"

Dr. Seuss stares at the louse between my nails, then reach up to touch his hair, a look of utter terror on his face. While he's touching his hair with both of his hands, the gun finally pointing away from Paige, I spot my moment. I lift the machete and swing it down once again, this time harder, and to my luck it cuts through his skin and leaves an open wound in his chest.

He gasps, drops the gun, and puts both of his hands to the gushing wound. I take a step backwards while blood fills his mouth and starts spurting out. He tries to speak, but no words come out, only thick red blood.

EPILOGUE
APRIL 2016

"YOU'LL NEVER BELIEVE THIS."

Chris Fisher is at my door. I smile when I see him and let him in.

"After what I've been through, try me," I say. I walk to the kitchen and pour us some coffee. Three days have passed since the insanity at the mansion. I am still exhausted and haven't slept much. Salter is still gone and I have no idea where to look for him. It makes me sick to my stomach. I am hoping that Fisher is bringing me good news, but I have learned to not get my hopes up these days.

I serve him coffee and sip my own. We sit at the kitchen table. Fisher is in Salter's spot.

"So, what is it you don't think I'll believe?" I ask.

"Well...considering with your son and all, I know you're waiting for good news about him, but this is about something else," Fisher says. "I just thought you should know this."

"Maybe it can take my mind off Salter for a few seconds. What is it?"

"We found the cause of the massive fish-kill in the river."

I look at him, surprised. "That's awesome. What caused it?"

"Well, actually, we owe it all to you. That we found it, I mean."

I shake my head in confusion. I am very tired and not sure I am hearing things right anymore. "Me? What do you mean?"

"It was formaldehyde," he says.

"Formaldehyde?"

He nods eagerly. "There was a spill. From the tank at Theodor G's mansion. Salt had eaten away at it and it was rusting badly. It was leaking and had been for quite a while. Right into our river. Killed thousands of fish."

"You're kidding me, right?" I ask.

"Nope. We solved it. Now we can clean it up and get back to normal again. A team of specialists is out there right now; they'll flush it out, they say. I don't know how these things work, but hey, they're the experts, right?"

"That is great news. So no spill from a power plant or any other polluting chemical factory, huh? I guess my story is down the drain as well."

"Well, you're the first person I'm telling this to, so maybe if you write it now, you can get some attention on that account."

I shrug. "I'll try, even though I'm not in the mood for writing much these days."

"How are you holding up?"

I shake my head with a deep sigh. "I'm still here, aren't I?"

"Sure. How's Chloe?"

I sigh thinking about her. I can't believe she was hurt like that. Why does everyone around me keep getting hurt?

"They don't know yet. She did get a lot of the formaldehyde into her bloodstream, but they still don't know how much it has destroyed. She's gotten a blood transfusion and they hope that'll save her."

Fisher puts his hand on top of mine and squeezes it. He can tell I get emotional when talking about it. I have been living at the hospital these past days, waiting for news about Chloe and taking Paige to visit her mother.

"How's Paige doing?" he asks.

Paige has been living with me and my dad to make sure she's not alone while her mother is getting better. Nicky should be discharged in a few days, they have told me.

"Getting better," I say. "The psychologists say she is doing really good actually. I have taken her to the hospital every day to be with her mom. And I think we finally got rid of those little critters of hers, using tea tree oil, so she won't spread them to anyone else. I noticed them in her hair back when we found that lock in the Boxer's house. Filled with nits. I'd recognize those critters anywhere, since we went through it with Salter last year. Such a nightmare. But I think we've got it under control now."

"Good. That's really good," he says. I can tell he is eager to move on. "Well, I'd better...it's been a busy few weeks, I'll tell you that."

"I know. Have they found any of the other missing women or children?" I ask.

Fisher gets up and puts on his cap. He shakes his head. "Nope. All we found so far was the body of the Boxer and the embalmed bodies of Maria Verlinden and Theodor G's own brother. But they were all at the house. We'll keep looking in the river, but with all the animals out there, chances are there isn't much left of them if he dropped them in there like he did with Kim and Casey Taylor. But we'll keep looking, searching all areas of the river."

I try to smile, but it doesn't come out right. Fisher sees it.

"At least Danny gets to be with his daughter," he says. I can tell he is trying to make me feel better. "And he is now officially acquitted of everything. Even the trouble he got himself into in Orlando. They decided to drop all charges. It's not all bad, you know. And you saved those two girls. Just sayin'."

I do feel happy for Danny. I can still see that look on his face when he got to meet Tara for the first time. I took him to see her at the hospital, where she was being kept for observation. Danny tried hard, but couldn't hold back his tears as soon as he saw her. Luckily, Tara took it really well. It's not easy to lose your mother and gain a father in the same week. But she was very moved to finally meet him. She threw herself in his arms and they spoke for hours afterwards. I hope he'll be able to get custody of her and that they'll all be a family with Junior too. I am beyond thrilled that everything went so well for Danny. Especially that they never found out he killed that woman. I just hope he'll leave the police work to those who are paid for it from now on.

Well...who am I to talk?

"I know. It's just so hard to...you know be happy when...when your son..." I am tearing up as I speak, thinking about my son, and I am forced to stop. I close my eyes quickly, then look at him.

"See you around, Detective. Let me know if you have any news, alright?"

He nods and walks to the door. He stops just as he is supposed to open it, his hand resting on the handle. He hesitates, then looks back at me, biting his lip, like he wants to say something, but then changes his mind.

"Have a nice day, ma'am," he says, lifts his cap, and walks out the door.

Back in the kitchen, I am left to my own emotional roller coaster. I try hard to not cry, but it still overwhelms me. It shouldn't. I mean, we got the bad guys. They're both dead. No more disappearing single mothers and children.

But we never found my own son. Why is it I can save everyone else, but never myself? I can fix everyone else's life, but never my own?

I decide I want to write the article. Maybe it'll take my mind off things for a little while. I open the lid of my laptop and find my blog, just as an email pops up on my screen.

I open the email with a small gasp when I realize it contains a picture of Salter, sitting on the back of a motorcycle, blindfolded. In front of him, in the driver's seat, taking the selfie, is my brother, Blake Mills.

The picture comes with a message:

Careful little eyes, what you see.

To be continued...
THE END

AFTERWORD

Dear Reader,

Thank you for purchasing the first three volumes of the Mary Mills Mystery Series. My inspiration for these stories was—as many times before —taken from real life stories.

BOOK 1:

My inspiration for this story was—as many times before—taken from real life stories. Many of you might have heard about the disease Munchausen Syndrome by Proxy that Mary's mother, Penelope, suffers from. If not, you can read more here:

https://en.wikipedia.org/wiki/Munchausen_syndrome_by_proxy

It's an awful condition and the stories online of people growing up with this are plenty. It is often overlooked because many people don't believe a mother could do such terrible things to her child. It's not abnormal in these cases that the victim, the child, has organs removed before the reality is discovered. You can read one of the stories that I did when researching for my book here:

http://law.justia.com/cases/california/court-of-appeal/
3d/122/69.html

or here:

http://www.cbsnews.com/news/prosecutor-lacey-spears-was-
calculating-in-sons-salt-poisoning-death/

Furthermore, I was inspired for the girl gang led by AK, alias Liz Hester, when I stumbled over this article about a French girl gang who attacked a man and had him shop for them while humiliating him. You can read more about that here:

http://www.telegraph.co.uk/news/worldnews/europe/france/ 1396136/France-in-shock-at-girl-gang-who-tortured-youth.html

Lastly, the idea of a female killer with a slit mouth asking if she is pretty is taken from an old Japanese horror story. Read about the slit-mouthed woman here:

https://en.wikipedia.org/wiki/Kuchisake-onna

BOOK 2:

This was a tough book for me to write, because Marcia's condition was so devastating. As a writer, I have to put myself in her situation and live it with her. Imagine not knowing what you're doing half of the time, not knowing if people around you want the best for you or not, or if they're right when they tell you you're sick. It is among my greatest fears to one day wake up and realize I have been locked up for life and no one believes anything I say.

I don't think that will happen, at least not as long as I keep writing.

As always, some of the stories in this book are based on true events. So is the story of Peter Elingston, the man with Cerebral Palsy and the woman who falls in love with him. You might know of it since it has been quite a big media story, but in case you don't, here's a link to some of the articles I read about the case:

http://www.slate.com/blogs/the_slatest/2015/ 09/22/anna_stubblefield_case_the_rutgers_newark_professor_is_accused_ of_citing.html

http://www.nytimes.com/2015/10/25/magazine/the-strange-case-of-anna-stubblefield.html?smtyp=cur&_r=0

BOOK 3:

I got the idea for this story from a long post I read on Facebook. A woman described how she was in Target one day and this guy followed her and her daughter and approached her afterwards in the parking lot. She got away, but called the police who told her there is a sex trafficking ring that target moms and their daughters. She wrote the post on Facebook to warn other moms.

The story turned out to be a hoax, but it had me thinking. I was terrified when reading it and so I believed it could make a book. The part about slave-auctions in the airports is true, though. Ugly as it might be. You can read about it here:

http://www.theguardian.com/uk/2006/jun/05/ukcrime.travelnews

Furthermore, I am terrified of what my kids do on the Internet every day, who they meet, what they tell them, and how they could be tricked by some old guy lying to them. It simply terrifies me that I can't control them all the time, which I can't. So I wanted to write about that too.

Then there is the story about Danh. It's based on a lot of true stories I have read. With all that is happening in the world today, especially in Europe, we have to remember that many before them have been refugees, and that they go through terrible trials to get to their destinations, and often they lose their family members on the way. Some might not even find each other again until years later. People flee because they can't stay, and it is horrible what they go through. I wanted to describe that using Danh's story, and a lot of what I wrote is taken from real stories about people fleeing Vietnam in 1975. I made up all the terrible stuff, but what I have read is also horrifying, and many people died trying to flee the communist regime.

Here's an example of one of these remarkable stories:

http://ireport.cnn.com/docs/DOC-443335

About the fish-kill. Well, it is actually going on right now in Cocoa Beach. Thousands of fish have turned up in people's canals and no one knows why. They believe it's from a type of algae, but why it is so bad right now, they still don't know. I came up with the idea of spilling the formaldehyde because it has actually happened once. And it killed a lot of fish somewhere in California. You can read about it here:

https://news.google.com/newspapers?nid=336&dat=19820326&id=GvoyAAAAIBAJ&sjid=WoMDAAAAIBAJ&pg=5537,7427887&hl=en

If you liked *this series*, then you might enjoy my newer mystery-series, the *Eva Rae Thomas Mystery Series*. It takes place in Cocoa Beach, as well, and begins with the first book ***DON'T LIE TO ME.***

Don't forget to check out my other books if you haven't already read them. Just follow the links below. And don't forget to leave reviews, if you can.

Take care,
  Willow

Tired of too many emails? Text the word: "willowrose" to 31996 to sign up to Willow's VIP text List to get a text alert with news about New Releases, Giveaways, Bargains and Free books from Willow.

ABOUT THE AUTHOR

Willow Rose is a multi-million-copy best-selling Author and an Amazon ALL-star Author of more than 80 novels. Her books are sold all over the world.

She writes Mystery, Thriller, Paranormal, Romance, Suspense, Horror, Supernatural thrillers, and Fantasy.

Willow's books are fast-paced, nail-biting page-turners with twists you won't see coming. That's why her fans call her The Queen of Plot Twists.

Several of her books have reached the Kindle top 10 of ALL books in the US, UK, and Canada. She has sold more than three million books all over the world.

Willow lives on Florida's Space Coast with her husband and two daughters. When she is not writing or reading, you will find her surfing and watch the dolphins play in the waves of the Atlantic Ocean.

Tired of too many emails? Text the word: "willowrose" to 31996 to sign up to Willow's VIP text List to get a text alert with news about New Releases, Giveaways, Bargains and Free books from Willow.

Cover design by Juan Villar Padron,
https://www.juanjpadron.com

Special thanks to my editor Janell Parque
http://janellparque.blogspot.com/

Tired of too many emails? Text the word: "willowrose" to 31996 to
sign up to Willow's VIP text List to get a text alert with news about New
Releases, Giveaways, Bargains and Free books from Willow.

Made in the USA
Columbia, SC
18 January 2023

10646921R00450